I0746169

This Book Belongs To

THE WHITE ELEPHANT OF PANSCHIN

THE WHITE ELEPHANT OF PANSCHIN

ODESSA MOON

PESCHEL PRESS ~ HERSHEY, PA.

Visit Odessa at www.odessamoon.com

Cover design by Jake Caleb / jcalebdesign.com

ISBN-13: 978-1-950347-09-4

Library of Congress Control Number: 2020902101

First printing: February 2020, version 1.0

Cast of Characters

Veronica Bradwell: Decisions other people made constrain her own desperate need to escape.

Airik Shelleen: He faces the consequences of his and his predecessor's decisions every day.

Shelby Bradwell: She wants acceptance so badly but who would ever accept someone like her?

Malcolm Cobb: He can't have what he wants, starting with being accepted as who he is without a fight.

Neza Molony: She'd dearly love to see her nieces settled but what can she do to make that happen?

Professor Lemuel Vitebskin: He adores his carefully manufactured image but not everyone else does.

Upton Shelleen: His job description doesn't include chasing girls but he pursues them anyway.

Elliot: He doesn't want his boss to learn about his secret hobby.

Carmine: He does his job and for now, that's enough.

Lulu: She'd like more than she has and maybe, just maybe, she might get it if she's ruthless enough.

Florence: She prays every day that her past does not determine her future.

Desmond Wong: He behaves like another drone in a dead-end job, secured for him by his family's connections, but he has secrets of his own.

An unnamed thug: He's just doing his job; it's nothing personal, although he really does enjoy his job. He'd also like you to call him "sweetheart" because you don't need to know his real name.

Employees of the Twelve Happiness Luxury Hotel: They're just doing their jobs too, thank you very much. They've got kids to feed. You should be happy!

Concierge of the Twelve Happiness Luxury Hotel: He wants everyone to be happy whether they like it or not.

Gaston Shelleen: He deeply resents Airik. Why was that whippersnapper elevated over him when he'd had years and years on the job?

Mrs. Helga Grisson: If she doesn't know, then it's not worth knowing.

Dean Kangjuon: He can't understand why anybody but him should matter.

Kip McGrant: He's not a good boyfriend but they haven't quite figured that out yet. He hasn't either.

Clyde Monez: He's both devious and talented, which is why he succeeded.

Reyansh Philpott: He isn't as superior as he thinks he is.

Mrs. Wangmo: A fair-weather friend.

Simon Bradwell: He wanted what he wanted and damned everyone else to ruin without a second thought.

Sajag Burgess: He plays favorites and his underlings and subordinates despise him for it.

The desk sergeant: He's got more than enough to do and doesn't need the White Elephant's problems piled on the heap he's already managing.

Jeffen: He's ambitious too, but he's got a different, less traditional ladder to climb.

Hurkle: He's a bartender now, he used to be a prize fighter, but he's always been a member of Blue Sun

Kendra Atto: She's a well-connected princess but she won't get what she demands and expects.

Peng McGrant: He'll be very disappointed in his son when he finds out what happened.

Winifred Qiao: She didn't know why she was selected by the shamans of Panschin and neither did anyone else.

Bhupathi Middleton: He's Reyansh Philpott's best friend and so models his own behavior after his idol.

The Twelve Happiness Luxury Hotel staff doctor: The stories he could tell about the guests will make your hair stand on end. He's a professional so he plans on waiting until after he retires and moves away to cash in on them.

Marmaduke Qiao: He likes clear rules, for him and for everyone else and he enforces them. Luckily, he won't live forever.

Bertram Qiao: He never thought his daughter would be so wayward.

Frankie: He's out of his depth and terrified of failing. He knows what happens to people who fail.

Inigo Schopenhour: Airik's replacement secretary but there is a question of his loyalty. It may not be to Airik.

eronica Bradwell sat back on her heels, stretching her spine and neck as she worked out the kinks. She'd been weeding for over an hour, pulling the clumps of algae and fungal threads from around the lettuces, breaking them apart and pushing them deep into the friable loam. She had worked hard to build this soil, since very little that was natural was normal in Panschin. There was enough sunshine pouring through Dome Two to grow her vegetables and so, of course, there was more than enough light for the terraformers to grow, too.

She studied the greenish-reddish blobs clinging to her blue-green fingers. She made a fist. The wetter chunks oozed through, dropping to the soil where they lay like clotted blood.

For hundreds of years, the terraforming algae, lichens, and fungus were transforming Mars into a viable planet. They made oxygen. They built up organic material in the soil so it could be used to grow food. They supported every other kind of life on what had been a dead planet made of red sand. They made life possible. They had killed her mother.

The very air was full of microscopic spores. It was why every flat surface that was bare sand or rock and got some sunlight was soon covered with a thick layer of algae. Outside the dome, the terraformers were out-competed by most plants once the soil transformed from dead sand to something capable of supporting life. It was ironic, she thought, that the domes designed to help people survive in the far, frozen north also kept the terraformers alive.

Carefully brushing stray hairs from her forehead, she knelt and resumed her weeding. If she wanted her lettuces to grow, she had to break up the jelly-like masses. Vegetable growing could be tedious work, but it earned her desperately needed hard coin.

And, if Veronica was honest and she was always honest with

herself, it pleased her to break apart the fungal masses with her own hands instead of a hand cultivator, its tines like the talons of a bird of prey. It was risky. Breaking up the fungal masses, she supposed, released still more spores into the air. If you were susceptible to fungal infections, and Mrs. Bradwell was, you could catch one of the many wasting diseases and eventually, you died from one of them. But she argued with herself, your every breath was full of them. What was a few more? And these were immature spores, not yet viable. They would rot, instead of growing.

She dug a long slot in the soil between the rows of lettuces. Perhaps if her mother had gone outside the Domes of Panschin more often, she would have been healthier. Perhaps if her father had not cheated his investment clients and been caught red-handed, her mother would have fought harder. Everything would have been different if her father, Simon Bradwell — looking at a sure conviction — had not taken the easy way out by slitting his wrists in the bath.

As she replayed the series of events in her head, Veronica could feel the energy drain from her. Or not. It was all past now; the scandal, the grief, the hurtful divorce, the lawsuits, the bankruptcy hearings, the rest of the once-proud Bradwell family cutting her and her younger sister Shelby as though they were contaminated. All done and gone and what remained was Veronica Bradwell doing her damnedest to keep herself, Shelby, and her great-aunt Neza safe, secure, housed, and fed. Dwelling on the past did not weed or water lettuces, nor did it pay the monthly lease on the White Elephant looming behind her.

It was all past. Except when the past roared back to life.

Veronica squeezed a blob of algae into the trench. Too bad terraformers weren't edible. If they were, that would be one less worry to fret over. But the edible algae from the tanks had to be paid for, as well as the vat-grown yeasts. Government-provided mil-rats were free, but they didn't often show up in Panschin, so far to the north and well away from wherever they were manufactured. When they did get shipments, they went to the families of the miners living in the tunnels. It was assumed if you lived aboveground in a dome, even in Dome Two, you could afford to buy food.

This was not true. Many of the people who lived in Dome Two, in the formerly grand mansions now decaying into tenement houses, would cheerfully have eaten free mil-rats instead of paying hard coin for algae pudding and yeast blocks. Her little family certainly would.

She covered up the trench and moved down to the last section. It was strange to live in a mansion like the White Elephant yet worry over every penny spent. What was left of this branch of the Bradwell family looked rich to outsiders, not hanging on by their fingernails. But she and Shelby were very lucky. They had a home thanks to Auntie Neza. Its tiny yard allowed Veronica to grow a surprisingly wide array of vegetables and even some fruit. What they didn't eat, Veronica sold at the back doors of local restaurants and bars or traded to other enterprising pioneers taking over the decayed mansions of Dome Two. Truthfully, Veronica sold most of what she grew as she made more money by selling her produce to the Dappled Yak bistro than she spent purchasing algae pudding, moss crackers, or yeast blocks to eat.

They *were* lucky. They had a house with a very favorable lease, they were all healthy, Shelby had a chance at a career — if only she would paint to market instead of trying to be an artiste — she knew how to grow vegetables and write magazine articles showing other people how to do it too. That was the sole benefit of her own unfinished degree from PanU. What a waste of money that had turned out to be, trying to get a degree in Martian Literature.

Veronica pushed that regret away firmly. It had been the right thing to do at the time, and she loved literature. She smiled at the colorful lettuces, every shade of delicate, newly alive green. They were pretty enough to substitute for the flowers she grew before her world fell apart. What would her professors say if they could see her write for gardening columns about growing carrots in containers? Probably tell her she was wasting her talents. What did they know? They weren't trying to make ends meet, when the ends were so far apart.

She wiped her hands, rubbing the last of the algae onto the soil, then rubbed them cleaner on her shabby coverall. Veronica stood, her feet crunching the white gravel surrounding the sunken bed. It glinted in the filtered sun. She strolled around the sunken bed, surveying her miniature world. It would soon be time to rake the gravel again, breaking up the algae and lichens trying to establish a foothold. They were unpleasantly slippery to walk on and she couldn't afford to fall and injure herself. The white gravel also reflected every bit of the yellowed sunlight flooding through the dome and made her garden grow better.

It was very quiet at this time of day, and she wished there was a bird or two to sing. It reminded her of the last time she had been able to leave the domes of Panschin and go outside. The sky had been immense, full of scudding clouds, stretching upwards to forever, pink-tinged blue that deepened to deep blue at the horizon, a subtle shift of tone that could not be duplicated in paint. The air felt alive; a whispering breeze that carried the scent of living things and the chatter of their voices. There had been insects, many kinds of birds, and other creatures as well. The sounds always changed, unlike the recordings that people played in their homes to pretend they lived outside in the fresh air.

The steppes surrounding Panschin seemed to roll on forever, but met the horizon at long last, an endless deep sea of every shade of brown and green, bowing and rustling before the wind. The hills undulated under their cloak of grass; the sides hidden from view promised strange new lands. They were sides she would never see.

Living inside Dome Two, the most spacious dome in Panschin, was nothing like being outside. The dome made sure of that. It was high but not as high as the sky, and it suffered from an irregular, yellowish haze distorting the sky beyond. It was the largest dome in Panschin, several klicks across but you always knew you were inside a manmade structure. The immensely thick, tall stone walls supporting the glassteel made sure you could never see past the dome and out into the wider world. You always knew the size of the box you were trapped in.

The glassteel of Dome Two had yellowed with age and no longer let through the sun as it had when it was new. The ventilation may have been state of the art when Dome Two had been built, but it wasn't anything like being outside. It wasn't as nice as the ventilation in Dome Five and certainly not as nice as Dome Six. Some sections of Dome Six could even be opened during the summer heat, allowing in true sun, true breezes, even birds who took up residence in the strips of green landscape scattered among the towers. Since Dome Two could not be opened, birds rarely found their way within, even the ubiquitous steppes sparrows. Those who did tended to live on the grounds of Panschin University, where the students competed to stuff them full of crumbs. The squirrels living there were even fatter.

Veronica stared up at the dome as trying to see the wide, exciting, amazing world beyond. It was sunny outside. There were few clouds blocking the warming light. Spring was a good time in the dome, before the summer sun made it hot and stuffy and after the wild temperature swings of the winter. The moons were up somewhere (they always were) but not over Panschin. They were too far north to be visible other than as dots at the horizon, dots that would never show above the walls supporting the dome. You had to be outside on a hilltop to see them racing past the edge of the world, barely above the horizon. At night the stars were invisible, obscured by the haze of the glassteel and the few lights inside Dome Two bouncing off its underside. From inside the dome, a cloudy, rainy night didn't look much different from a clear night.

You never forgot that a translucent bowl was suspended over your head.

Veronica wove her way between the sunken beds, each edged in stone, crunching across the raked gravel. The beds that weren't full of luxuriant plant growth, in one stage of maturity or another, were crammed with terraformers. The terraformers didn't need to be watered or cared for so she left them to their own devices. When she needed a new bed, and she had the water available, she spaded under the algae and planted her precious seeds, carefully counting them out.

Astonishingly, the gardening books sent to Panschin from points south assumed you would plant many seeds and later weed out the excess plants. Veronica had quickly realized this was useless information inside the domes, considering the cost of seeds and the scarcity of soil to plant them in. Her first article for *Panschin Today* discussed how to plant only what you needed. That article launched her career as a sometime magazine writer who understood the needs of Panschin gardeners.

Unfortunately, the magazines didn't want many articles on gardening. Most people in Panschin didn't have any growing space, not even a container in front of a window. You had to live aboveground to have a window and most residents lived in the tunnels.

Yes, Veronica and Shelby were fortunate. She walked around the White Elephant, enjoying the precious, tiny yard surrounding the house. Dome Two was unique among the Panschin domes. The builders wanted to emulate what was done elsewhere on Mars, closer to the equator, where people lived outside year-round. This far north, nobody lived outside year-round, not if they wanted to stay alive through the harsh, unending winter.

The richest citizens, who all naturally expected to live in Dome Two as soon as it was built, wanted gardens to surround their grand houses. They wanted green, open space to surround Panschin University, the museums, the opera house, main library, the hotels, the shopping arcade, and restaurants. Every amenity was located in Dome Two for the benefit of those residents, and it was believed nothing could be grander or better built, so it was all built to last.

However, despite their experience with building Dome One, the builders had not reckoned on the ventilation issues a larger dome would have. Nor had they grasped how stuffy even a large dome could be in the summer. The glassteel forming the dome had been a new, improved formulation that hazed over in a manner the developer claimed could never happen. The lawsuit over that issue had been wending its way through the courts for decades, and it was widely expected a ruling would take another decade at least.

Even worse, the green spaces and yards turned out to need regular watering. Water was a precious resource in Panschin but the dome developers had overlooked the fact most places with outdoor greenery also had rain watering those gardens for free. This omission spurred another lengthy lawsuit, still being fought out in the courts.

Every green space in Dome Two had to be hand-watered. If you could afford it, you tapped into the public water system and ran expensive hoses full of expensive water. If you couldn't, like Veronica Bradwell, you scrimped and saved for what you could afford. She didn't waste a drop of water, catching and reusing that precious fluid and never letting any of it go down a drain. She carried around a heavy watering can and never watered anything that didn't need it.

It only took a few moments to circle around the house, so much larger than the garden surrounding it. Veronica reached the front yard and made her way to the mailbox mounted on the low stone wall. She looked at the estates around her. Like the White Elephant, those houses were large and the gardens tiny. Unlike the White Elephant, their tiny yards were overrun with terraforming algae whereas her little domain was green and lush with actual plants. Some of those formerly grand homes had been subdivided into small apartments. Not all of Veronica's neighbors bothered to convert their little yards into money-makers, although she was not alone in her endeavors. She caught the sound of a rooster on a rooftop. Some of those neighbors were far more experienced than she was and were more willing to take attention-drawing, lease-breaking risks.

She studied the mailbox, mottled with bright lichens, feeling the familiar mix of anticipation and dread. She hoped to find an acceptance letter and a check for her latest effort on growing limon trees in containers, but she expected the envelope to contain a rejection and it did. She was afraid to find another bill and of course there was one. This one was from the *Panschin Gazette*, asking if she wanted to renew her ad.

Veronica had, in yet another attempt to earn some money, run an advertisement listing the White Elephant as a bed and breakfast. Very few people had taken advantage of her advertisement, despite the White Elephant's convenient location near the center of Dome Two. Those who deigned to stay in Dome Two, now so déclassé but still the heart of most cultural events in Panschin, were either rich enough to choose one of the formerly grand hotels or were too poor to afford even Veronica's very reasonable rates. Everyone else who trekked to Dome Two to attend the opera or visit the museums took the trams home or stayed at the finer hotels in Dome Five and Dome Six.

She tapped the letters in her hand and counted her savings. Did she have enough to make the next lease payment? As if avoiding an uncomfortable answer, she studied the house, still well-kept, even if the style was sadly outmoded. The White Elephant was a two-story building, with two wings surrounding the lofty entrance. As customary in Panschin, there were two stories below ground, with light shafts to illuminate them during daytime. Also customary, the White Elephant did not have a true roof as there was no need for a roof under a dome. It had, instead, a rooftop terrace covering the building's footprint. Instead of a simple balustrade, the White Elephant had a low wall of pink and gray tile, similar to what a roof would be, if the White Elephant had been located where houses needed roofs to keep out the rain.

The faux roof was rimmed with lacy wrought-iron in a fanciful design of leaves and flowers. The pink and gray tiles, along with the whitewashed walls, and the purely decorative gray shutters at every large window, gave the White Elephant its nickname for as long as Veronica could remember.

Necessity may be the mother of invention, but pairing unrelated thoughts comes a close second. Veronica counted the rooms. Dare she rent them to boarders? There were plenty of them in the house, although most of the furniture had been sold. There was demand for them, from people who worked in Dome Two and did not want to live farther out and hated living underground in the tunnels. But housing above ground in Dome Three, Dome Five, and Dome Six was expensive. Dome One's ventilation was so unpleasant few people chose to live there if they could live anywhere else. Dome Four was industrial and, technically, nobody was supposed to live there at all although some people did. Dome Two was déclassé, down at heels, not where the better classes lived anymore, and could be unsafe, but it had room aplenty if you didn't mind the seedy and bohemian atmosphere accompanying the ventilation and heating issues.

The problem was Auntie Neza's lease. So favorable in many ways, it was decidedly unfavorable on the subject of subletting. Renting out rooms as a bed and breakfast narrowly skirted the issue. Those tenants were temporary. If the Second National Bank of Panschin found out she was subletting, their century lease would be voided and her little family would be out on the streets. Even so, Veronica was cautious about her advertising.

She debated what to do. Her last guests, many weeks ago, had covered the cost of the bill from the *Panschin Gazette* with some left over for the lease. The reservation book was empty. Should she renew when there was no guarantee of more paying guests? Veronica sat on the low wall, moodily running her fingers over the granite. The lichens plastered the gray granite in shades of soft greens and browns, the blotches making a pattern she could not read.

At last she sighed and decided to table the plan until next month. Optimism demanded she give the fates a chance to work their magic. There was enough cash hidden in the cracked cookie jar to try again. Maybe this next ad cycle would bring in paying guests. The Biennial Mining Conference was rapidly approaching, so it could happen. That conference always brought a flood of visitors to Panschin. They all had to stay somewhere. Maybe, Veronica smiled at the soft, earthy lichens, those visitors might even attend one of the gallery shows she hosted and buy one of the ugly paintings, earning her a tiny commission. It could happen.

iding the train north to Panschin, Airik Shelleen reflected that he didn't like traveling. So many things could go wrong, both on the road and back at home. Despite being the daimyo of Shelleen, he didn't have the control people thought he did. He had learned to his cost recently that if he didn't oversee the orders he gave, things didn't necessarily get done to his satisfaction.

To add to his difficulties, not all of his family agreed with how he was running Shelleen despite knowing what the Martian Government could do to his demesne if he failed.

Increasing his irritation, he especially didn't like traveling across a quarter of Mars with an entourage watching his every move. Before his discovery, Airik could travel by himself, keeping to his own schedule. If he spotted something interesting, say an unusual rock formation, he could stop and investigate.

No more. Worse, these people kept hovering around him, getting in his way, keeping him from doing his jobs and in general, being a nuisance.

But he had to have an entourage. When he had complained to the senior aunties and uncles of Shelleen, the same ones who took him to task for every mistake, they all said the same thing.

"You're the daimyo, so get used to it! The daimyo of an important demesne like Shelleen doesn't travel by himself. Who do you think you are? One of those destitute horse lords? They sleep in the stables with their horse rather than spend the coin on a hotel room. Is that what you want? You can't be seen that way. Nobody will take you seriously and that means nobody will take Shelleen seriously."

Airik had pointedly observed that daimyos, no matter how poor, were taken seriously wherever they went. They were still daimyos and the owners of their demesne even if they didn't have hard coin stacked to the ceilings in their treasury like everyone thought a daimyo did. Nonetheless he had to agree that he didn't want to sleep with his horse in a dirty livery stable. A clean bed with clean sheets held far more appeal.

At least on the train, he had the comforts of a private, first-class compartment. His valet, his secretary, and his bodyguard got to share a compartment next to his. This was the smallest entourage he had been able to get away with. Everyone else had been sent in advance to Panschin. They still got on his nerves, telegraphing back to relay what they did and asking for instructions. At least when it got to be too much he could retreat to his compartment when he had work to do.

There was a lot of work. He and his secretary, Upton, kept busy on the entire endless train ride north, studying over briefing papers, reviewing reports, and preparing his presentations.

While Upton was organizing a fresh batch of papers, Airik studied the handsome young man. He was another bone of contention within the family, particularly from those members who disapproved of the job he was doing managing Shelleen. Airik's choice of Upton as his secretary raised eyebrows. To him, Upton was a logical choice. He was capable, efficient, and loyal to Airik and his plan to keep Shelleen intact and unscathed in his dealings with and against the Martian government. Those were the qualities Airik required in a secretary.

But there had been … hints. Nothing overt. Nobody would dare say to the daimyo's face that he's having a relationship with his secretary. The dirty minds some people had! He couldn't understand it. It grated that an efficient, good-looking young woman would have generated just as much talk, yet somehow would have been more socially acceptable as long as Airik didn't mind the innuendos about his secretary working underneath him.

Upton's major flaw as a secretary was that he chased anything in a skirt and as he was personable, he often caught them. This distracted him from his duties — another source of irritation to Airik — but confirmed the gossip that Upton Shelleen wasn't interested in his own gender. It took pressure off of Airik from one direction but added it from another.

Airik frowned out the window at the passing steppes as if they were responsible for his predicament. They were slowly greening as Spring gradually danced north. The endless seas of grass stretching to the horizons should have soothed him; a carpet of a hundred species of waving, rustling grass fluttering under the cloud-studded sky. The steppes demanded nothing, unlike the hordes of people he dealt with every day. They all wanted something from him. The steppes didn't despise him for the difficult choices he made. The steppes had no hidden agendas, nor were they eaten up with jealousy and resentment. The steppes didn't undercut his decisions. Grass cared nothing for the pettiness of human politics. The steppes didn't care about his private life since the oceans of grass reproduced with the aid of the wind and not that of matchmakers. The steppes did not gossip other than with the wind.

His family did all of those things.

It wasn't as if he didn't want a wife. He did. Marriage promoted stability within the family, formed tighter bonds between demesnes, brought potential wealth in the form of dowries, and held the promise of children. He just didn't want to marry someone who was going to cling to him like a leech, keeping him from working, and he really didn't want someone who was marrying him as a steppingstone to power. He'd been specific to his aunties about what he wanted. It should have been easy for them to arrange introductions, guided by the detailed checklist he had supplied.

In that respect, Airik considered, plumes of grass had it easy. The wind worked its will, the grass set seed, and the next generation of grass was assured with no effort on anyone's part. It was clean-cut, with no messy emotions, dubious rationales or money involved. Stones had it even easier.

He closed his eyes and rubbed the fatigue from them. It was that damned Red Mercury lode. It had catapulted Shelleen from just another agricultural demesne to the most important one above the equator. Red Mercury was vital for the terraforming process, rarely found, and mining it would bring in a huge income for decades. Shelleen would be rolling in money, but the lode also painted a huge target on Airik's back. Sometimes, he wished it had never been discovered.

He remembered his last trip to Barsoom, the capital city of Mars. The days were filled with contentious, endless meetings and the nights with endless formal balls. Which one was the worse ordeal? he thought.

On previous trips, before the discovery, Airik could count on making awkward small talk with any woman willing to talk to him. But when the music began and the couples paired off, he was left standing against the wall, fetching cups of tea for the mothers. At the first opportunity, he would leave early, go back to the hotel, and get some sleep to prepare for the next day.

Those days were gone. Now, every one of those young and not-so-young ladies had lit up on seeing him. They weren't even subtle about the credit signs dancing in their eyes. Their families were even more avaricious, looking to get their own cut of Shelleen's new-found wealth. A young, unmarried member of a backwater demesne was not very attractive to parents hoping to marry their daughter upwards. Being the young, single daimyo of that same demesne made him attractive. The newly found wealth of Shelleen made him the handsomest, sexiest prince on the entire red planet, and he didn't like it one bit.

Upton laid the stack of papers on the traveling desk and awaited instructions. Airik dismissed him with a nod and Upton left the compartment.

Before he could turn his attention to his work, another memory surfaced. Still more embarrassing was meeting his former fiancées. Melissa and Bertrille had both insinuated they could divorce their husbands and run away with him back to Shelleen. All he had to do was say the word.

Airik rarely rolled his eyes but that had done the trick. His Aunties had tried their best, and this was the best they could do. Both engagements were short, and when they broke it off, Melissa and Bertrille used almost identical words. He was a boring, stiff, dull piece of work, and they were overjoyed to shake off the dust of Shelleen and meet better men. Men who were more exciting, men who were wealthier, men who were better connected and had more status. Men who didn't live in one of the more boring, third-tier backwaters of Mars. Men who weren't him.

It was amazing how things could change; like sand turning into stone if you only applied enough time and pressure. He had become the most desirable man on Mars without having the vital personality transplant both women insisted he needed. It had been an ordeal extricating himself from their clutches while remaining polite. To add to his consternation, neither Melissa nor Bertrille seemed to care about unofficial rivals as long as he shared his newfound wealth with *her* family.

There were no negatives at all to discovering the lode, other than his life being turned upside down, the damage done to the peasants he'd forced to settle around the mine, the toxicity released by the mining that would be present for hundreds of years, and fending off rapacious government agents and last, but not least, the armies of desperate, money-crazed squatters pouring into Shelleen.

That was probably the worst issue, dealing with the squatters, all so eager to strike it rich and not caring at all about the long-term environmental damage they did to the demesne he loved with all his heart and soul.

Of course, the lode *would* be practically on the border with the government corridor and, of course, it *would* be a major government corridor with a railway and roads, and, of course, it *would* be many days travel away from the manor house and its surrounding villages through a barren wasteland. If the lode had been in the heart of Shelleen, a long, long way away from anywhere, nobody from outside would have been able to get to it easily.

But the lode's location meant that anybody with gumption could just hike the sixty odd klicks across the government corridor from the road, across land Shelleen could not control, slip across *his* border onto *his* land, and start mining Red Mercury, poisoning the squatter and the land forever.

At least the lode was on the northern edge of Shelleen. The horse lords, Kenyatta in particular, were equally opposed to squatters. They didn't want the Red Mercury poisoning the steppes grass, so they willingly worked with Shelleen to cut the deal with the Martian government. Even now, their irritatingly independent vassals patrolled the corridor, keeping an eye out for unauthorized intrusions.

He didn't ask what the horsemen did with squatters.

They kept them out and that was what mattered. Damn free-city trash, coming onto his land, trying to strip it of its wealth and poisoning it as they went. No, he did not ask questions.

Airik sighed. Time to get to work.

He turned his attention back to the papers in the traveling desk. On top of the papers on his traveling desk was the presentation on refining Red Mercury in situ. He needed to review it with Upton, but that meant calling his secretary back in the compartment, filling it with his restless energy. He was probably prowling the passageways, chatting up the attractive female attendants and unchaperoned passengers.

Airik wondered how it would feel to be so free and easy and relaxed. Upton wasn't married. He told his family to their unanimous consternation that he didn't need to buy a cow when so much milk was free.

Airik smiled grimly as he spread the papers spread over the desk. He reached a decision. If he had to marry for the good of the demesne, then so did Upton.

He pulled out a fresh sheet of paper and drafted a letter to Auntie Zilpah. It was short and to the point. Airik sealed the letter and set it aside. Upton would deliver it to the tiny post office in the observation car, but he wouldn't know the contents until it was too late. Auntie Zilpah would rise to the challenge, he was sure, even if she hadn't yet managed his own marital challenge. She had been particularly offended by Upton's remarks and would be eager to find *him* a bride. It might even spur her to greater actions on his own behalf.

It was petty, but it pleased him to do something he had some control over. He looked again at the sealed letter. He had written it hastily. Should he have reminded Zilpah about Upton's proclivities? No, if Zilpah didn't know that Upton would probably cheat on any wife she selected, then she should be replaced by someone younger and savvier. This was her job. Everyone in the family knew Upton's tendencies so she would take them into account in her search. He moved on to the next paper.

The afternoon wore on. The train ride, despite the luxuriousness of the compartment, was boring and endless. Airik considered moving to the club car, where he could commandeer tables and spread out the paperwork. But that risked being buttonholed by people, all of whom, it seemed, had get-rich-quick schemes guaranteed to work.

Somehow his bodyguard, Carmine, never kept those people far enough away. He claimed they weren't enough of a threat to break their heads open, and if he did, that would cause more trouble for Airik and for Shelleen. They were a threat as far as Airik was concerned. They bothered him and affected his concentration. At least Carmine, with his hulking presence, intimidated most of the fortune hunters. Only the boldest ones tended to linger.

Elliot, the valet, had been the easiest person to get along with on the trip. He knew his job was to keep Airik correctly outfitted at all times, and to anticipate whatever he needed — and he did it with a maximum of efficiency. When Elliot wasn't working, he wrote in his diary. What he wrote so assiduously, Airik didn't know and he didn't care as long as it wasn't some scurrilous tell-all about Shelleen.

Airik found himself actually looking forward to Panschin, and not just to get the traveling over with. He had never visited the place. It was a center for mining with many rich lodes of various minerals in the area. Panschin was a free-city, not under the control of a demesne, and that meant just about anything went.

For a northern city, so close to the pole, it was large and bustling, and all built under enormous domes and tunnels of glassteel. You could live outdoors in the summer in Panschin, and he was told some people did, but you didn't in the winter. Not even the horse lords did that this far north, and they were proud of their tolerance for dreadful weather.

There were deep tunnels snaked into the bowels of Mars and Airik was looking forward to touring them and observing the minerals and soils. They would be so different from what he was used to seeing at Shelleen in its own small mining operations. He was looking forward to adding some prize specimens to his rock collection. That was one very nice benefit about visiting Panschin.

His contacts were as interested with rocks and geology as he was and they understood his fascination with minerals. Nobody here would have their eyes glaze over when he started talking about the different varieties of bauxite, how to mine them efficiently, use them in industry, and recycle them for reuse.

That led to thoughts of Auntie Zilpah again. For the family's main matchmaker, she was doing a terrible job of finding him a wife. Was it too much to ask that a wife not be dismissive of his interests? He didn't expect a wife to be a rockhound, but the young ladies he had been meeting weren't even polite about the subject.

Well, that wasn't quite true. They were, one and all, fascinated with gemstones. That topic they would discuss endlessly, along with the varieties of gold and silver and platinum they liked their gems to be set in. Jewels did not interest Airik, once he got past their usage in manufacturing, crystalline structure, and how certain chemical impurities would alter their color and hardness, but he seemed to be the only person who felt that way. He also seemed to be the only person who was more interested in the industrial properties of gold or diamonds but again, nobody else he spoke to saw his point of view.

This handicap did not make casual conversation easier with attractive, potential wives.

Malcolm Cobb stood before the branch manager's desk at the Second National Bank of Panschin and did his best to hang onto a blank, noncommittal, blandly smiling face. He did not clench his fists, although he wanted to. He worked hard to look nonthreatening, although his size and build made it a challenge.

He succeeded, as always, due to plenty of practice. Gods below but he hated people like Desmond Wong. They would not, could not, accept that he was smarter, as well-educated, and as skilled in finances as they were. He was a scholarship boy, plucked from the mining community because of his abilities. His brains and talent were co-opted for the greater good of Panschin. Talent such as his, a scarce and valuable resource, or so he was told, was not to be wasted.

Yet here he was, this branch manager, lounging before him with his soft gentleman's hands. Wong owed his position in life solely to his good fortune in choosing the right family when born. Cobb could sense that this man, who had never held a job he had striven for, sneered at him.

Desmond Wong had been given everything he ever had even as he firmly believed it was all due to his own, herculean efforts. This fine gentleman would not have lasted a single day in the mining shafts and tunnels snaking through the deepdown below Panschin. He could have never wiggled through those narrow, stuffy, badly lit passages, searching for the ores that made the free-city the second richest on Mars.

But Desmond Wong didn't know that. He would never know. His position in life ensured the risk would never cross his mind. And in the meantime, the branch manager of the Second National Bank of Panschin looked over Malcolm Cobb, searching for a trace of grime or dust betraying his origins as a miner.

"So you work for me now. Here in Dome Two," the balding manager said. His voice exhibited a slight lisp, and Malcolm wondered if the sibilance was an affectation of the managerial class or something he was born with. So many of the other, higher status students he met at the fancy school had those lisps, but it came and went, used only when they felt like it. The lisp, like knowing the right way to hold a pair of gilded chopsticks, might be one of those tells, denoting one's admittance into the upper reaches of society. Or maybe he was being paranoid and resentful. That was an easy pit to fall into and a hard one to escape, as he knew to his cost.

"Yes, sir, I do," Malcolm answered calmly and confidently. "I'm looking forward to it. It is a privileged assignment to be here in Dome Two with a man of your stature."

He wondered if he had laid it on too thick. Dome Two had not been a high-status location in the Second National Bank of Panschin in decades, but it would not do *him* any good to point this out to his new supervisor. He had to work with the man, after all, and the manager could harm him in a multitude of unseen ways.

Mr. Wong preened complacently and Malcolm thought, nope, not too thick. What an idiot. Doesn't understand Dome Six is the place to be, or at least Dome Five. Our exalted supervisors dumped both of us here. Him because he's incompetent and me because they want to hide me.

Mr. Wong, mollified at Malcolm's understanding how lucky they both were to be assigned to the main branch office in Dome Two, as opposed to say, Dome Three, Dome One or (worst of all) Dome Four, roused himself from his expensive throne to lead Malcolm on a tour. It was, Malcolm observed, a very nice chair. It was also a chair that had been installed decades ago, when the branch was new, and it was no longer fashionable. Floral brocade was the preferred upholstery now, not blue gingham velvet. Yes, his manager was an idiot if he didn't realize he was out of date. He smiled inwardly. An idiot who could be managed while he, Malcolm, showed just how skilled he was to the people who mattered higher up.

As he expected, the branch office matched the manager's office. It was a formerly grand building, slightly down at the heels, reflecting the lowered status of everything within Dome Two. The furnishings were shabby, containing the telltale signs of poor maintenance. Terraformers had crept within, colonizing corners and backs of chairs, laying a new pattern on the carpet outside of the normal paths for foot traffic.

Mr. Wong introduced Malcolm to the staff, all of whom from tellers to loan officers to the office secretary, exhibited that air of having seen better days elsewhere. They also, all of them, already knew who he was and where he came from. Each person took a surreptitious glance at his hands, looking for dirty nails showing he had just come out from underneath.

He smiled and made small talk with his new co-workers, making sure they knew he was clever, amiable, and ready to work. Snobby idiots, the lot of them, thinking he didn't know better.

In fact, they were right. Malcolm had recently spent a few days in the deepdown, toiling alongside his father and uncle in the Steelio shafts. He needed the money, they needed the help, and he had learned long ago to never disclose when he went underneath. A thorough scrub along with reasonable care kept his hands from betraying him, as long as the observer didn't know what calluses meant.

The day ended promptly at three, and after shaking Mr. Wong's hand and thanking him, Malcolm walked into the watery sunshine penetrating the yellowed glassteel of the dome. He had already found a room in one of the many boarding houses in Dome Two. He knew better than to say so, but he had never seen so large and grand a house before, even if it was divided up into a warren of rooms. The price was right, he didn't have to share, his room was aboveground, and it was an easy walk from the branch bank.

As he strolled along the wide street, he studied his surroundings with an eye attuned to class and style. He had never been in Dome Two before, other than school trips to the Panschin Museum of Art and other similar cultural outposts too large and too expensive to relocate. The neighborhood was astonishing, large and surprisingly green. Most amazing of all, the houses had yards surrounding them. Small yards, but Dome Six, *the* place to live in Panschin, had no such thing. Even the richest, most high-caste citizens lived in towers. Grand towers, at least from what he could observe from the outside, but Dome Six did not provide gardens to go with each of the luxury apartments in the gilded towers. Every unit in a tower shared a single small greensward and a rooftop terrace no matter how many people lived there. A tenant might be wealthy enough to lease an apartment that spanned an entire floor of a building, but any private outside space was provided by a balcony.

Malcolm Cobb studied the buildings carefully as he walked by them. These had been luxurious symbols of wealth when they were built and despite the lack of upkeep, most of them were holding up surprisingly well. Most of them had been subdivided, like his boarding house, either into miniscule flats or single-occupancy rooms with negotiated privileges. It all depended on what the lease said or what the property holder thought he could get away with. As he worked his way down the wide paved streets flanked at intersections by planters spilling over with flowers, he observed the people around him. He wondered if they all lived in Dome Two. How many of them had accounts at the local branch of his bank?

He stopped to stare at a particularly grand house, one that had not been chopped up. It had an attractive garden around it and, unusual for Panschin, an ostentatious pseudo-roof edging on the rooftop terrace constructed from pink and gray tile arranged in stripes. Even more unusual, this house had been whitewashed a blinding white, the evidence of that care still showing between the blotches of terraformers. It was not thickly carpeted from top to bottom with lichens and moss like every other building in Panschin outside Dome Six tended to be. Somebody regularly worked hard to scrape the building clean of its constantly regrowing sweater.

Malcolm knew from school how the domes and tunnels allowed a semblance of normal life this far north, but it came with a price. Because life was so unnatural within the domes, the terraformers competed successfully against the planted vegetation in a way they no longer could outside. Outside, the soil was too rich, the air too pure and sweet. Inside the domes and despite their ventilation, the air was thin enough that the terraformers weren't just growing everywhere. They were still needed. This also meant wasting diseases were more prevalent in Panschin than they were closer to the equator.

As he admired the house, an idea arose in Malcolm's mind, a way of proving himself to those supervisors who wanted to bury him forever in Dome Two. Panschin's population was growing, but Panschin wouldn't be building more domes anytime soon for them. The cost was stunning. Many newcomers would refuse to live in the tunnels. That left the surface, and as he looked around him, he saw more open space here than anywhere else. Moreover, every important cultural building in Panschin was still located in Dome Two as they couldn't be moved. He ticked them off mentally one by one. It was quite a list.

He took a deep breath, filling his nose and lungs with the air of Dome Two. The ventilation was indifferent but perhaps that could be fixed. It wasn't much different from Dome Six as far as he could tell, perhaps a bit fresher due to the masses of terraformers. The dome was yellowed but perhaps that could be fixed too. Panes could be refreshed or replaced.

If those things could be done, then the housing stock in Dome Two would suddenly be recognized for what it was: drastically undervalued.

Malcolm Cobb showed his teeth at the noticeably white house rising in front of him, the raked gravel paths surrounding garden beds full of what even he realized were real plants and not terraformers. As the assistant manager of the local branch of the Second National Bank of Panschin, he was in charge of the leases on all their properties in Dome Two. The local branch was in a dying backwater, staffed by hacks and has-beens. He doubted they had reviewed the leases in decades. Were any of those leases up for renewal? Were any leaseholders in default of their sworn obligations to the bank, the government of Panschin, or the underlying authority: the Martian Government? The Martian Government owned every bit of Mars, other than what was held by the Four Hundred families on their demesnes. All that property was rented, on exceedingly long-term leases to be sure, but the lease holders didn't *own* those properties. Leases could be sold and swapped and they were, but as the sworn representative of the Martian Government, the bank was supposed to be notified of any changes.

This would be his self-chosen job here in Dome Two. He, Malcolm Cobb, would show his versatility, his ability to make money, his ruthlessness, and his skill at detecting opportunity others ignored. He'd make piles of money for the bank, get the accounts brought up to date, and maybe, just maybe, those double-damned snobs in the hierarchy would see his value.

It could happen.

Malcolm turned and began walking up the street towards where he thought his boarding house was located. He considered the quiet, drab room waiting for him. It was his, he didn't have to share, but he didn't fit in with the low-caste workers who lived there. Not anymore. He didn't fit in at the bank, either. He hadn't fitted in at school, nor had he fit in at the Panschin School of Business. He didn't fit in very well with his family down in the tunnels nor did he fit in, not anymore, in the deepdown.

If he had not been tapped so long ago because of his intellect, he would have married by now, perhaps even had a child. He would still be part of the Steelio warren, valued by the community and valued by Steelio for the work he could do. His family loved and valued him but he wasn't really part of them anymore either. He was split between too many worlds. Would he fit in here, in Dome Two? It could happen. He would make it happen. And maybe, he would come to be valued for himself, for what he had to offer.

As long as he was daydreaming, he could think about other possibilities. A trio of pretty young women walked past him. Maybe he would even meet someone who didn't see him as a meal ticket like the girls from the tunnels did, or an exciting, risk-free chance to slum like the sisters and cousins of the upper-caste students did. Those girls, they had a future full of possibilities.

Malcolm would not and could not marry a girl from the tunnels. A tunnel girl would never be accepted in his new world and neither would their children. A girl from above would be accepted — if she was of high enough caste — by the class he was trying to enter, but a girl like that would never accept him, or his family left behind in the Steelio warren. He would not, could not walk away from them and pretend he had never been raised in the deepdown under Panschin. It was part of him and that would never change.

helby Bradwell kept her happy-go-lucky smile pinned firmly in place. No, she wouldn't be able to meet with her classmates at the trendy new restaurant in Dome Six that evening. She had so much homework to do. She didn't want to get behind in her painting classes. That Professor Vitebskin! What a demanding instructor he was and she sure didn't want to have to stay late after everyone else left. This at least, to her relief, was greeted with commiseration. The good professor was a slave-driver, an iconoclastic visionary who tolerated no one else's visions if they conflicted with his own, an all-around martinet, and a hyperactive lecher. Everybody in the Art Department at PanU could agree on these points and this conversation led away from the conversation Shelby did not want to have.

This was the conversation about why she didn't have the money to do what she wanted, go where she pleased, and dress in fashionably shredded, customized coveralls as opposed to the ones actual workers bought in mining supply stores and then wore into well-mended rags before replacing them when it was that or go nude.

It was always such a struggle to fit in, Shelby thought with annoyance and not a little self-pity. It wasn't like *she* had done anything wrong. That had been her much missed, deeply resented father. How could Simon Bradwell have destroyed every chance of her and Veronica enjoying normal lives? And their mother? That was another painful subject, despite the time that had passed since mama's death. She shoved the memories back into the past.

Shelby turned away from the rest of the lingering students, not wanting to see the speculation as to her motives, while pretending to study her latest effort. At least this time she had been included in the conversation. That was something positive, unlike her current painting. It was the usual canvas smeared with dismal shades of brown and gray, with hints of mauve and taupe. The shades of brown and gray were expected and approved by Professor Vitebskin. It was the stated goal of the art department (and his voice set the agenda) that paintings should demonstrate to everyone how ugly and gritty a city Panschin was. Shelby could agree with this view, she wanted to agree with this view, if it meant being accepted somewhere and fitting in. But she wanted color too, thus the mauve and taupe. She hoped Professor Vitebskin would not notice her forbidden choices or if he did, not think they were too gaudy an addition.

No matter what she did, Shelby just couldn't achieve the look *he* was aiming for and her grade depended upon. She couldn't tell the difference between her own efforts and those of his preferred students, despite worried and repeated study. Her shades of brown were just as sludgy, her grays as muddy. Perhaps it was her lack of verve in presenting an image she couldn't bring herself to like or her difficulty in laying down gossamer layers of translucent paint, each a different shade of scummy water, when those layers begged for rich, flamboyant color.

Maybe she just didn't have the talent she thought she did, or the talent her family insisted she did. She drew all the time, sketching everything around her and Shelby thought she was at least decent with a pencil. The drawing instructor, a lowly and generally ignored adjunct professor, said she had talent. Unfortunately, Professor Vitebskin didn't share the drawing instructor's opinion. Or maybe, Professor Vitebskin said she had no talent because she never let him corner her when nobody was around.

Shelby Bradwell, desire for good grades or not, aching need to be accepted or not, wasn't going to give that lecher a chance to paw at her. If she was careful, he'd never get the chance and she would never have to make an official complaint, thereby drawing unwanted attention to herself and her struggling family. If the hoity-toity people here knew her real situation and connected her to her father, she would never be accepted at all; not even on the margin she currently occupied.

As soon as the conversation swirling around her shifted to who was dating who, Shelby carefully gathered her supplies, escaped to the privacy of the sink, and began washing her brushes. She was fastidious with their care as she could not afford to replace them. Most of them she had found, discarded as damaged by other students who didn't *have* to wash brushes carefully when they could just buy new ones. A good cleaning had brought most of them back to usable life. Veronica would be so proud of her, Shelby thought, showing a moue of distaste as she laboriously soaped and scrubbed the bristles clean. You would think her sister enjoyed the challenges of poverty.

As soon as she could, Shelby discreetly slipped out of the studio and down the maze of hallways leading to the green quad of PanU. She might be able to catch Lulu and Florence on their way out and they could walk home together. It was a long walk but the company made it go faster. The metro in the transtube would have been faster, but that took coin none of them could spare.

As Shelby worked her way through the chattering mob, she spotted a girl she remembered from the old days when the Bradwells lived in Dome Six, before everything happened, and she had been exiled to Auntie Neza and Dome Two. So that girl was here at PanU. Gleesh. Another person from the past and definitely one to avoid.

Shelby sighed to herself. Of course that girl was here at PanU. A girl like her wouldn't be going to Panschin Community College like Lulu and Florence as that would be beneath her. That girl wasn't ambitious enough to go to the Panschin School of Business. Moreover, that girl, unless she'd had a brain transplant, was nowhere near smart enough to go the Mining and Engineering College of Panschin. PanU was the logical choice and Shelby should have anticipated it. That girl had delighted in the Bradwell's troubles and if she saw Shelby, she would be sure to spread around the old stories about Simon Bradwell causing new pain. Shelby carefully veered down another hallway, stopping to read posters about an upcoming dance recital so her back was to the mob of students. She took a moment to rearrange the bulletin board to move the upcoming art show poster front and center. The PanU Artists' Collective was sponsoring another gallery showing and the more students who knew about it and attended, the better. A few minutes later and the chance for discovery passed.

Once outside, moving around unobserved was easier and far more pleasant. Panschin University enjoyed a beautiful campus, with many actual strips of mowed grass lawn to lie on and stare up at the dome so far overhead, pretending it was the sky. There were even small trees dotted among the fancifully carved and decorated stone buildings, along with gaudy flower beds.

Shelby stopped and stared longingly at the marigolds. Their brilliant yellow flowers, splashed with red and orange speckles, glowed against their deep green feathery leaves. She would love to use those colors in her paintings. She smirked, thinking of Professor Vitebskin's reaction to such lurid hues. Even if she were to agree to a torrid affair with the old lecher, he would still probably fail her for using such blatant colors in a painting. Shelby sighed and turned away, looking for Florence and Lulu, emerging onto the surface from their own school's tunnels. They would appreciate the marigolds.

PanU was the finest school in Panschin – the school's paperwork said so all the time — but it wasn't the only one she could have attended. Shelby had been lucky to be accepted here although she was unclear as to how Veronica and Auntie Neza were paying for it. It must be scholarship money, she had finally decided, the one she had won with her portfolio although no one official had ever said so to her. The university officials must have not wanted to embarrass her in front of the rest of the student body. If it hadn't been for winning the scholarship, Shelby would be going to Panschin Community College like Lulu and Florence. PCC was conveniently co-located with PanU so it was easy to meet up with them at the main entrance to both campuses and they regularly did so.

As if to confirm their relative status, PanU's buildings were all aboveground while PCC was located underneath in classrooms carved out of the tunnels. The two entrances were close together: a grand, carved stone arch for PanU and a far less noticeable staircase leading down under into the catacombs of PCC. The two schools did share the library, the swimming pool, the gymnasium, and a few other, very expensive facilities. Otherwise, they were completely separate schools. It was, however, an open secret some of the untenured faculty at PanU also taught classes at PCC. It was also known some students took classes at both schools, although the PanU students didn't usually admit to doing such a thing to save face.

Florence and Lulu were waiting at the stone archway and Shelby hurried to join them. The light was still good and she would be able to finish another attempt at meeting Professor Vitebskin's requirements when she got home to her rooftop studio. Studio was a fine word for her end of the rooftop terrace atop the White Elephant. It held a battered dresser for supplies, a chair, and an easel, but it was hers. It was here she kept her most special paintings hidden, the ones she had not shown to anyone. They were carefully stacked behind the dresser, filling the empty space between it and the rooftop's enclosing wall. She only worked on those paintings when no one was around to comment or criticize her subject. She didn't know if she would ever be brave enough to bring them into the studios at PanU for evaluation under the perilous and acute gaze of Professor Vitebskin.

As the girls walked along, Shelby filled them in on the upcoming gallery show. This was the big quarterly show and would even include one of her own paintings. One benefit of living in the White Elephant with Auntie Neza and Veronica was the vast amount of empty space available. Shelby had taken full advantage and arranged with the PanU Artists' Collective to use the White Elephant's ballroom to show everyone's current work. This action had gone a long way to ensuring that Shelby Bradwell, despite her lack of acceptable talent, was accepted as one of the group.

After much discussion, Veronica and Auntie Neza had agreed to the scheme when Veronica had realized they could charge for the use of the space. The PanU Artists' Collective paid in several ways. The Collective provided free labor scrubbing off the ever-growing sweater of terraformers, periodic whitewashing of the White Elephant, a commission on any paintings sold (sadly very few), and a small fee to cover snacks. Another small fee was collected at the door from visitors attending a show. This last fee was split between the Collective and the White Elephant so they both made some money.

It worked out, even though Shelby thought Veronica came across as too much of a money-grubber and not enough of a patron of the arts. When she had said so, Veronica had fallen down laughing and said she didn't charge enough to hang ugly smears on the walls of her home and then have the nerve to ask money for them. So did Auntie Neza, Florence, and Lulu. It was another irritation in Shelby's life; living with people who didn't understand fine art.

She wondered if any of her family would ever try to understand what being accepted meant to her, seeing as how they rejected the paintings as being ugly smears of mud. Shelby chewed on a fingernail as the little group made its way down the sidewalk, passing by planters spilling over with deep purple smiling pansies. The paintings, if she was honest, were ugly smears of mud. There were so many prettier colors on Mars and prettier things to paint. It would be a pleasure to try and capture those pansies and their expressions. When people passed by the planters, the breeze from their body's movements made the pansies dance ever so slightly, as though they did pay attention to their surroundings.

Who would understand what had happened to her? It had hurt so much to go from a secure place in the world to one in which she had learned, at great cost, that if circumstances changed acceptance would disappear. All her friends at school had dropped her immediately when her father's malfeasance had come to light. Simon Bradwell's suicide and her mother's death had not brought any of those people back, not even to the funerals. And when she moved to Dome Two, nothing changed. The new school in Dome Two had been difficult. Nobody there had ever really accepted her. She had always been on the outside looking in. At least she could lose herself in drawing and painting. The very limited art classes had been the only place where Shelby felt welcome and then only when she was working. Outside those classrooms, nothing improved. She still wasn't one of the residents of Dome Two and she never would be.

Who would ever accept her fully, as she was? Shelby walked along with Florence and Lulu, envying them. They had plans for the future. They were both studying nursing, they had boyfriends, they had family of sorts, they had friends who visited when they could. She knew it was petty to feel this way. Florence and Lulu lived in the White Elephant because they paid for room and board with housekeeping and a few credits here and there. They didn't have the status the Bradwells used to have. Yet in a way, they had a far more secure place in the world than Shelby did.

They didn't have the ghost of Simon Bradwell hanging over them.

As they walked, Shelby noticed a well-dressed, big, blond man noticing her and Florence and Lulu. He strode along down the broad street like his bright future, unlike hers, was assured. He would be easy to sketch, with his high cheekbones and strong chin, but capturing his confident air, pinning him to paper for all time, would be harder.

Would her situation ever improve, Shelby wondered? Did she have a chance at the future she dreamed of, like that confident man so obviously did? It could happen, she supposed. And in the meantime, she had a home, the planted areas were alive with a thousand shades of green, the marigolds were the most vibrant yellows ever, and spring had made Dome Two pleasant again after the dreary winter. She could enjoy all those things and that would have to be enough.

The train pulled into the large, central station in Panschin far too early in the morning to suit Airik. The sun had not breeched the horizon; its first rays did nothing more than illuminate dark shapes against a darker backdrop.

The dining car moved its breakfast service hours earlier than normal to compensate for the train's pre-dawn arrival. It was disruptive to the digestion but this kept the passengers subdued, quiet, and uninterested in bothering Airik while he ate with yet another set of get-rich-quick schemes.

Airik looked out the window as the train slowed to a stop. He hoped that whatever transportation the Twelve Happiness Luxury Hotel arranged for his party would be swift, discreet, and quiet. He had made a point of requesting it so the odds were in his favor.

While waiting for the hotel's transportation to arrive (he was unsure of how businesses in Panschin handled such things), Airik stepped onto the platform and looked around at his first glimpse of the free-city. The disembarking passengers moved around him in a sleep-deprived fog. Amazingly, they ignored him despite standing in the open on the station's platform. He sought out his staff: Elliot was seeing to the baggage, Upton was eyeing an attractive passenger he had chatted up on the journey to no avail, while Carmine stood behind him looking threatening.

First impressions: The Panschin train station and the gateway to the free-city were decidedly unimpressive. The train had plunged into the klicks-long tunnel leading into Panschin's underground station while it was still dark. Airik didn't know if the frills and signs welcoming high-spending guests were located there. Now, he doubted it. The city's management had not made any effort here in the train station, where no incoming visitor could miss signs for the local attractions and sights. Why bother putting up billboards outside? It did not make for a good first impression, either for maintenance or forethought on the part of the local government.

He turned slowly, observing carefully what the free-city had chosen to do. The station was much smaller than Airik would have expected, given Panschin's importance, and very poorly lit. It was the second-largest free-city on Mars so he expected something more on the scale of the immense central station in Barsoom. That train station and central transportation hub were designed to awe and impress visitors with Barsoom's wealth, importance, good taste, and power. Every aspect of the Barsoom train station that Airik had observed on many trips there said "kneel, peasant, before your betters and marvel at how we do things in the heart of the empire."

Panschin did things differently.

The free-city's management must have decided there was no reason to spend money to impress or inform new arrivals of the wonders of Panschin. The station was built underground, rather than occupying precious space within any of the free-city's famous domes. The train depot's ceiling was dingy and overgrown with splotchy lichens, their spidery growth creeping across the many skylights, making them appear to be even smaller than they were. The many light fixtures also had their webbings of terraformers, ensuring the train station was dimmer than it should have been.

The walls were likewise blotchy, the bas-relief carvings obscured by the exuberant growth of unchecked terraformers. It was difficult to tell what dramatic Panschin founding story the original builders told with their bas-reliefs and statues. They were so shaggy with moss and bizarrely colored by lichens that any identifying details were obscured.

He had also not expected to see such an array of terraformers covering almost every flat surface. That was interesting and strange. The scientist in him was intrigued and ready to investigate further. He also noticed that, unlike the walls and ceilings, the seats in the waiting areas were not coated with lichens. That demanded a closer look.

He walked over, feeling the presence of Carmine behind him. Yes, the rows of seats divided into sections for the different classes of passengers as evidenced by their design – actual chairs, benches with backs, and plain benches, accessorized by a range of padding from thick to non-existent — were clean of terraformers. Bemused, Airik surmised this was due to the passengers' bodies wiping them clean through use. It was a reasonable assumption since little cleaning and removal of terraformers had been done anywhere else. The floors were clear but that was undoubtedly due to the constant foot traffic wearing away any hardy pioneer lichens.

He approached the first-class seating, conveniently both the closest waiting area and the one most likely to be kept up properly. If terraformers were here, they would be present everywhere in Panschin. Airik crouched down to check a chair-back. Its upholstery of green brocade leaves remained bright but as he neared the underside where only the most scrupulous janitor would clean, the fabric pattern disappeared under a layer of lichens.

Airik frowned. It had not occurred to him that Panschin, a city of domes and tunnels, would provide the best habitat on Mars for terraformers, wherever there was any light to fuel their growth. There wouldn't be much competition from other plants here, nor insects to eat them. He took a deep breath — drawing the train station's air deep into his lungs — then blew it out slowly. Then another. Then another, each time assessing what he sensed. The air was subtly different in how it felt, tasted, smelled, from the air on the train. That air had been changed repeatedly, even when the windows weren't being opened by the passengers. It was the next best thing to being outside.

This air now. He wrinkled his nose, then coughed. This air, Airik breathed in and out again, this air reminded him of being underground in a mining tunnel. It wasn't stale but it had an odd, off tang, and it was more still than on even the calmest day outside. It had plenty of oxygen as the terraformers were doing their job but it wasn't like being outside. Hmm. An interesting consideration and something he had not thought of when researching Panschin. None of the literature had mentioned it; not in the boosterism pumped out by the Chamber of Commerce and also not within the more scholarly literature from the Panschin Department of Mining.

What else did he not know about Panschin?

Airik stood and ran his hand over the nearby station wall. It, too, had a thin film of lichens, although the wall had been regularly swept down based on the skeletal patterns their remains made against its pale gray surface. Hmmm again.

He studied the skylights and light fixtures. How fast did terraformers grow? Those areas had to be swept regularly, otherwise the terraformers would completely block any light in their desperate attempt to survive. Hmm.

What would it be like to live surrounded by terraformers thicker than they were anywhere else on Mars? How did they keep the domes clean? This would be something else to observe while visiting the city.

"There they are. At last," Upton said, breaking his reverie.

Airik turned to see a large, smartly painted and gilded vehicle pull up alongside the platform where his party was standing, forcing its way between the pedestrians. So, people and vehicles shared the narrow road, although this was the only vehicle in sight. The name and logo of the Twelve Happiness Luxury Hotel were emblazoned in scarlet on the side and across the front in big, impossible-to-miss letters, contrasting strongly with the metallic, highly reflective silver body.

To his surprise, it was powered electrically, something he would not have expected as horses, even in Barsoom, were so much less expensive for an individual vehicle. This vehicle was as ostentatious as possible, demanding envious, resentful attention from anyone it passed. Who could afford to waste electricity on transportation that didn't move dozens of people at a time?

To his dismay, he found himself the center of attention again. The other passengers turned from collecting their baggage, meeting relatives, or dealing with train station employees to stare. Some recognized him and, despite their fatigue, started moving towards him with gleaming eyes, glad-handing smiles, and promises of sure things no doubt already on their lips.

To his horror, the driver stood and called loudly, "My lord Shelleen! Make way for the Daimyo of Shelleen, an honored guest of the Twelve Happiness Luxury Hotel!"

The driver's voice echoed throughout the station, ensuring everyone who hadn't twigged to the presence of a wealthy, potential sucker was now alert and paying attention.

Airik frowned harder. He could feel his face grow hot. He had specifically ordered the hotel he did not want to be singled out. Could they not follow basic instructions?

Upton, seeing his boss's mood swiftly change for the worse, said, "We better get moving. Carmine! Elliot! Get the bags."

Airik stomped over to the shouting driver. He and an assistant were both wearing silver metallic jumpsuits, tailored to be more formfitting than a coverall, lavishly trimmed at every single seam and edge with screaming lime-green piping, an overabundance of glittery scarlet buttons, and of course, the logo and name of the Twelve Happiness Luxury Hotel on both chest and back. The name was embroidered in more glittery scarlet down the sides of both sleeves and pant legs where anyone with taste would have left a simple stripe of color.

"My lord Shelleen! Welcome to the Twelve Happiness Luxury Hotel!" the driver cheerfully boomed out, his voice echoing off the ceiling and filling the space. He stood on a shelf-like projection at the front of the vehicle to be better heard and seen by anyone with the vicinity. He waved cheerfully to the staring crowd. "I am ecstatic to be your driver today, bringing you to the Twelve Happiness Luxury Hotel!"

"What is the meaning of this?" Airik demanded, glaring up at the driver looming overhead. "I specifically requested discreet transportation."

"I *am* being discreet, my lord Shelleen. Just as *you* requested. The Twelve Happiness Luxury Hotel prides itself on accommodating every conceivable need of its fortunate and pampered guests," the driver answered. He beamed down at Airik showing every one of his silvery teeth, then picked up a shiny scarlet metallic pennant to wave at the crowd of onlookers. At no time did he lower his voice one bit. His assistant waved as well, using a shiny silver metallic banner that flashed in the early light.

"For everyone else here, the Twelve Happiness Luxury Hotel will be happy to accommodate all of you as well! If you haven't already made your reservations, please consider us first! No other hotel in Panschin can take care of you like the Twelve Happiness Luxury Hotel can," the driver proclaimed to his slack-jawed audience.

"Discreet? How is this discreet?" Airik said icily.

The driver seemed to grin evilly. "This *is* discreet by Panschin standards. We don't adhere to what they do down in *Barsoom,* my lord." He pronounced Barsoom in the same tone that well-bred aristocrats reserved for "common people." "Yes sir, my lord Shelleen! I will be happy to show you how the Twelve Happiness Luxury Hotel usually welcomes its guests!" He nodded to his assistant who reached inside the vehicle's window and pushed a glowing red button.

Instantly, the silvery white vehicle began playing loud music with plenty of cymbals, drums, and piccolos, while a recorded chorus sang about the wonders of the Twelve Happiness Luxury Hotel. Hidden lights began to flash from the vehicle top around the station, illuminating the far reaches with rotating spotlights that showed off even better the train station's poor maintenance. They changed color as well, multicolored disks of lights chasing each other across the ceiling, walls, platform, and furnishings of the train station as well as the agog passengers and bystanders. Many of them actually retreated under the onslaught.

"Your point is made," Airik spat out. "Turn everything off and get us out of here."

"Yes sir, my lord Shelleen!" The driver jumped from his perch, reached inside, pressed the flashing red button and mercifully, the sound and light system stopped blaring. The returning dim light and quiet were a balm to eyes and ears.

He opened the door to the open-top passenger compartment with a flourish. "The Twelve Happiness Luxury Hotel is always ready to accommodate you!"

Airik said, very coldly, "Then is it possible for you to stop saying 'the Twelve Happiness Luxury Hotel' with every sentence?"

"No sir, my lord Shelleen! It's my job if I don't repeat the name of the finest hotel in Panschin, the Twelve Happiness Luxury Hotel, at every conceivable opportunity." The driver grinned cheerily at Airik. "I've got kids, and you don't want them to starve, do you? The Twelve Happiness Luxury Hotel keeps them fed. We *love* the Twelve Happiness Luxury Hotel and you will too." He winked at Airik.

By this time, Elliot and Carmine had gotten the luggage stowed safely in the trunk. Airik took his seat inside on the plush upholstery – no sign of terraformers here on the freshly scrubbed acid-green leather trimmed in more glittery scarlet and silver and lavishly printed with the hotel's logo – and sat back, his back rigid. He made himself unclench his fists and spread his hands out on his trousers.

"A refreshing beverage, my lord Shelleen?" the driver's assistant across from him asked, holding up a crystal glass etched with the hotel's logo in one hand and a bottle of something presumably alcoholic in the other, also adorned with the hotel logo. He shook the glass, making the ice tinkle within it. Even the cubes appeared to be imprinted with the hotel's logo although it was hard to tell without looking closer, something Airik wasn't about to do.

"No extra charge for you! The Twelve Happiness Luxury Hotel wants you to be happy!"

"No," Airik said. The prospect of drinking at sunrise was revolting.

The driver's assistant quickly grasped his passenger's mood.

"On behalf of the Twelve Happiness Luxury Hotel, my deepest apologies, my lord Shelleen. You need a *soothing* beverage after that train ride!" He pulled out a different bottle, with a much higher alcohol content, and waved it at Airik.

"No! If you want to accommodate me, as you've repeatedly shouted, get us to the hotel at once and do not speak unless I ask."

"Yes sir, my lord Shelleen! The Twelve Happiness Luxury Hotel is always happy to oblige your every desire!" Airik felt himself grinding his teeth while the assistant sat back, carefully leaving both bottles on display in case the honored guest changed his mind.

To Airik's immense relief, he was able to spend part of the ride in a fuming silence. First, he had to realize that a flick of his eye towards a sign was all that was necessary for the driver or the assistant to unwind a spiel about the wonders of Panschin and how the Twelve Happiness Luxury Hotel would ensure his VIP access to each and every attraction they passed. He had to pointedly inform them that he would provide a large tip, but only if they shut up.

Sadly, he could do nothing about the sound and light display the vehicle provided for passers-by at every intersection through the maze of transportation tubes from the train station to Dome Six and the hotel. The driver cheerfully insisted Panschin regulations required any motorized vehicle put on a display to warn other traffic of its presence since most of said traffic was unused to sharing the roadways. Airik glared over the sides and it did seem to be true: everyone else was walking, riding a bamboo bicycle, on skates or rolling boards, being hauled in a rickshaw, or, occasionally, riding high above the crowd in a palanquin. There were no other cars and more surprisingly, no animal-provided transportation of any kind. Alongside the roadways ran long, open-sided train cars at regular intervals on dedicated rails. It must be some kind of trolley system to transport people for longer distances, probably electrical in nature.

Airik was sure every person they passed turned to stare at the Twelve Happiness Luxury Hotel electric car. He resolved then and there to avoid using whatever transportation the hotel provided, despite guessing he would be charged for its mere availability whether he used it or not. Even a palanquin would be more discreet than what he was riding in. They had curtains to conceal their privileged occupant from the mob and didn't waste a precious resource that could be better spent on almost anything else more beneficial to the citizens.

He wondered if the hotel had palanquins and decided it was equally likely they were as gaudily painted as the electric car he was trapped in. He imagined they came with uniformed criers strutting outside it, shouting out the name of the hotel and the rider inside. The Twelve Happiness Luxury Hotel didn't seem to know the meaning of the words "privacy" and "quiet."

The trip took far longer than he would have thought an electric car would take to drive to Dome Six. Since the entire journey took place in a maze of indifferently lit transportation tunnels (only billboards were well-lit) Airik had no idea if the driver took a roundabout route to show off the billboard he was riding in. There was nothing he could do about the situation, except fume and wait. The maniacally grinning driver and his relentlessly cheery assistant were just doing their jobs, something they repeatedly assured him whenever he questioned some new irritation.

All of this made the built-in bar more inviting. Airik restrained himself, unwilling to put himself further into the grasp of the Twelve Happiness Luxury Hotel. His glare at Upton kept his secretary in check, although it did not stop him from gazing longingly at the well-stocked bar every time the sound system revived itself. Interestingly, the assistant ignored Carmine and Elliot as though they didn't fill the back of the vehicle. They were part of Airik's entourage, but as servants they didn't exist.

In the silence, Airik wondered what was waiting for him at the Twelve Happiness Luxury Hotel and the Biennial Mining Conference. He pushed the thought away, since there was nothing he could do about it, and focused on the walls of the tunnels. He tried to see if they revealed anything of their geologic nature, but the indifferent lighting defeated him. He patted his jacket pocket where his trusty rock-hammer and chisel waited patiently in their leather sheath for an interesting rock formation. The car came to a sudden stop. A group of young men in shabby coveralls were sauntering across the road. The driver shouted at them, and they responded with gestures unique to Panschin but whose meaning was obvious. For a moment, Airik imagined smacking the hammer onto the driver's head to make him stop. He called upon deeper reserves of restraint to squash that vision.

The men finished crossing and the driver sped up and took a turn, accompanied by a louder fanfare than usual and a spray of lights like fireworks, into a new, wider, tunnel. This one was maintained far better; its skylights clear of terraformers and its walls (where there were no billboards to conceal them) were painted white to maximize the ambient light. Any hint of the rock beneath had been banished. There were far more pedestrians of every variety, and if Airik was any judge of rude hand gestures and annoyed faces, all of them openly resented being pushed out of the roadway and off to the shoulders by the Twelve Happiness Luxury Hotel electric car. Any curses were muffled by the car's own sound system, now turned up since it had to be louder in this bigger space in order to be heard clearly. Or so the driver insisted.

The tunnel gradually leveled off and widened, and the car emerged at last into the watery, early morning sunshine of Dome Six. The car's fanfare and lights, still on to warn off foot traffic, were mercifully lost within the dome's space. Airik had never been claustrophobic, but it was a relief to get out of the tunnel.

Then he realized the journey was not over yet. The driver insisted on taking a long, circuitous trip through Dome Six as "he was allowed to drive only on designated roadways and did my lord Shelleen wish to stop at any point and see the sights recommended by the Twelve Happiness Luxury Hotel?"

"The hotel. Now."

The driver looked disappointed, as did his assistant, and then the maniacal grins reasserted themselves. "Yes sir, my lord Shelleen! The Twelve Happiness Luxury Hotel awaits you!"

Another long, slow drive down a wide street crowded with resentful, early morning traffic that did not want to make way led at last to the Twelve Happiness Luxury Hotel. Like the other buildings they had driven past, it rose five stories into the air and was crowned by a rooftop terrace. The walls of the hotel displayed more glass windows than masonry siding. The siding was luridly painted in lime green and scarlet, trimmed in shiny silver that reflected light like sunlit water.

Airik gratefully climbed out of the car and examined the building, hemmed in by other, equally lacy over-painted buildings separated by wide, paved paths. He wondered how the hotel kept the terraformers from caking the walls. There was a yellowish cast to the air, like he was in a light fog, and he realized that the glassteel dome was mottled. That couldn't be intentional, he thought.

He jumped as the driver shouted into his ear, "The Twelve Happiness Luxury Hotel has a lawn, my lord Shelleen!" The driver pointed towards a patch of grass spread out besides the paved walkway leading to the elaborate decorated, huge front doors. It was brilliant green and the size of an oversized conference table. "Because you are our honored guest, you will be allowed to step on the Twelve Happiness Luxury Hotel's lawn! Not every guest is allowed this signal privilege!"

Airik stared in disbelief at the grass patch and then at the driver. "That won't be necessary. Upton! Get us inside now."

The party made their way inside, between two rows of bowing bellmen all of whom were wearing dazzling silver uniforms and had their hands out. Airik ignored them to sort through his muddled glimpses of Dome Six. He concluded that all the vegetation he had observed on the trip through the dome had been in planters. Large ones in some cases to be sure, but still just large pots. Bright flowers, lacy shrubs with multi-colored leaves, even a few very small trees but everything had been in a pot. Up until this moment, with the hotel's lawn, he had not seen a single plant growing in soil in the ground, other than a terraformer. Everything was paved in one form or another. How strange.

Inside, the lobby was a festival of bright colors and noise. A pianist in the corner played an atonal melody Airik had never heard before. It rose above the chatter of conversation and clashed with the sounds of splashing fountains. All the upholstery was in the hotel's signature colors of acidic greens and scarlet with silver trim. Every wall was finished with silver and white stripes to better show off the paintings, most of which looked like smears of mud as seen from a distance. Chandeliers sparkled and glittered, filling the space with eye-searing light compared to the much dimmer outside.

The concierge bustled around the marble check-in desk and greeted Airik effusively. His uniform had more buttons than Airik had ever seen on a single garment, all scarlet. The buttons closest to the concierge's throat flashed on and off.

"My lord Shelleen!" the concierge proclaimed. "It is such an honor to have you stay with us at the Twelve Happiness Luxury Hotel! Your every wish is our command! We want you to be happy, *happy*, **happy**!"

"I will be happy to get into our suite," Airik replied. "I assume my staff from Shelleen is waiting for me?"

"Yes sir, my lord Shelleen! Your party has the finest suite the Twelve Happiness Luxury Hotel has to offer. We cater to every possible desire."

"Then why am I still standing here?"

"My lord Shelleen!" The concierge looked hurt, his eyes welling with tears and his lip quivering. "The Twelve Happiness Luxury Hotel provides every possible amenity, and I must ensure you know about them! For starters, do you require intimate company? We have a staff of willing young ladies, all of whom will be happy to make *you* happy. Just tell me what you prefer in a young lady and she – or they! — will ensure your happiness and comfort in your suite here at the Twelve Happiness Luxury Hotel."

Airik gawked at the concierge for a moment before finding his voice. "No. Absolutely not."

"My dear sir! We can accommodate other preferences if our delightful young ladies are not to your personal taste." The concierge winked and smirked. "We are absolutely discreet at the Twelve Happiness Luxury Hotel no matter who or what you select!"

"No!" If talking about arranging intimate company in a hotel lobby was considered discreet, he didn't want to know what they considered blatant.

"Yes sir, of course sir. And you, my lord Upton?"

Upton looked both bemused and offended. He said, "the day I can't get a girl on my own is the day I get buried. No."

"If either of you gentlemen change your mind? Let me know at once as I don't want to disappoint our staff young ladies. Here at the Twelve Happiness Luxury Hotel, your happiness is our happiness." The concierge smiled and smiled at this wonderful opportunity to provide happiness all around.

Airik said, very coldly, "Upton, why are we here? Who chose this place?"

Upton grimaced. "I did. It came highly recommended, sir, and they had the space for us and rest of the Shelleen personnel."

"Find some other hotel. Now."

The concierge radiated even more joy than the driver had back at the train station when Airik asked about the lack of discreet transportation.

"That won't be possible, my lord Shelleen! The mining conference has filled every hotel in Panschin. It's us or sleeping in the tunnels."

"Every hotel?" Airik demanded.

"Yes sir, my lord Shelleen! The Twelve Happiness Luxury Hotel was booked weeks ago along with every other hotel, all fourth-rate compared to us by the way, for the conference. There is no room at the inn anywhere in Panschin, not anymore. If you sleep in the tunnels or the park, you'll be arrested if you aren't mugged and murdered first! The jails of Panschin are renowned for their squalor and horribleness so I'm sure you would prefer to stay with us, here at the Twelve Happiness Luxury Hotel."

"Sir? Airik? Let's get up to our suite?" Upton said. "I'm sure things will improve."

"They had better," Airik replied. But observing the glinting sharp teeth and gleaming, avaricious eyes of the concierge, he doubted it.

Another army of bellmen appeared to carry the luggage up the four flights of stairs to the Shelleen suite, one bellman for each suitcase and each openly expecting to be tipped for doing his job. Airik was given the choice of walking up four flights of stairs, with eager Twelve Happiness Luxury Hotel employees surrounding him or being trapped in the gilded metal lace elevator – the only passenger elevator in Panschin the concierge breathlessly revealed. He snapped his fingers and behind him, appearing like magic, lined up four of the willing young ladies on staff lined up "in case he changed his mind about their services." Their hotel uniforms matched in color scheme, but unlike those of the male staff, their uniforms were missing sleeves, pant legs and had no working buttons available above the waist. Their smiles were as eager and their eyes as predatory as any Airik had ever seen.

"I'll take the stairs," he said flatly. To his surprise, Upton chose the stairs as well.

"If you insist," the concierge replied, looking deeply disappointed as they stood in front of the spurned elevator. "Should you change your mind about any of our willing young ladies, we do have a second grass lawn on the rooftop terrace. Very private, very exclusive for only the most special guests, and they say you can feel every blade of grass tickle you." He waggled his eyebrows at Airik, grinning more lasciviously than ever. The four young ladies, all breathing deeply, fluttered their eyelashes at Airik and licked their lips.

Airik looked them all over coolly, channeling the hard, icy contempt of the born and bred aristocrat. One by one, the willing young ladies turned off their smiles and looked away, abashed. The concierge alone did not wilt, although his maniacal smile dimmed. Airik then turned to Upton. "As soon as we are upstairs, start checking other hotels for cancellations."

"Yes, sir."

"You'll be disappointed!" the concierge recovered and sang out gleefully as Airik strode across the lobby towards the gleaming marble staircase. "Every room in Panschin was sold out weeks ago. You're part of our happy family here at the Twelve Happiness Luxury Hotel whether you like it or not. We'll *make* you happy!"

Airik did not deign to answer. "We'll see about that," he thought as he strode past the bellmen, ignoring them as though they didn't exist.

As they climbed the marble stairs, Upton reflected. He had never seen Airik behave this way before. He was civil even to the rudest fortune-hunter on the train. Then he remembered how Airik had dealt with Howard Shelleen when he had discovered his uncle's theft and how it put the demesne in jeopardy. Airik Shelleen was a socially awkward, mild-mannered member of the family whose hobby was collecting rocks, but he was chosen daimyo for reasons beyond coming up with the plan to manage the Red Mercury lode.

The four flights of stairs had been carefully designed and built so the risers and treads were ever so slightly out of sync, forcing a slow and stately pace upon the user. They were no challenge for Airik, fueled as he was by irritation and a deep desire to place a locked door between himself and the hovering, huffing and puffing concierge.

By the time they reached the huge, top-floor suite housing the Shelleen contingent, Upton was puffing too, as was Elliot. Carmine was as unfazed as Airik. He leaned close behind Upton's shoulder and whispered, "You need to exercise, sir. Bouncing the ladies in bed won't help you keep up with my lord Airik out in the field. Got a lot of tours of mining operations ahead of us."

Upton, embarrassed, could say nothing.

Airik felt a deep sense of relief as he stepped into the expansive top-floor suite of the Twelve Happiness Luxury Hotel. The Shelleen staff, sent ahead a few weeks before had commandeered its dining room. Extra tables were brought in to spread out the briefing papers, plans, programs, and extensive material on safety procedures for handling toxic ores. They had spent their time productively, interviewing leading figures in the Panschin mining industry, setting up meetings, connecting with the Four Hundred families that ran the demesnes in the Northern Mining Tier, and in general, making sure the daimyo could get to work right away.

Airik had been thinking on the way up the stairs about the Twelve Happiness staff and their overwhelming desire to accommodate every possible guest desire and charging for the privilege. While some expenditures were unavoidable, he knew the demesne's finances intimately. He can't afford to let the hotel digs its claws deep into the family treasury.

By the time he strode through the double doors, Airik knew what he wanted to say. He coolly studied the waiting team until he had their complete attention.

"I expect to get right to work. However, let me say this first." He met each person's eyes in turn. Some were family members or highly placed demesne citizens, while the rest were outside consultants, hired to augment Shelleen's tiny mining and geology department. He could fire those people if they did not meet his standards, but he was stuck with his relatives.

"I will be auditing the bills very carefully from the Twelve Happiness Luxury Hotel." He winced inwardly. That damned name was branded in his brain. "Shelleen does not have unlimited funds. If any of you have accrued expenses you do not wish to discuss publicly with me, our financial officers and the senior family, pay them in person *before* I get the bill. Get receipts to prove your case if questions arise."

The consultants didn't look concerned, nor did the few, high-caste Shelleen subjects. He may have seen a few sniggers when they realized what he was implying. They may have actually been working rather than frittering away Shelleen's coin.

Airik was disappointed, but not surprised, to see several staff members blanch. All of them, sadly, were family members. Did none of his family understand the pressures upon Shelleen?

I want to remind everyone we have the gallery showing next week," Shelby said, over a dinner of yeast blocks highlighted by generous servings of fresh radishes and salt to dip them in. "I want this to be the best one *ever*."

"It will be, dearest," Auntie Neza replied and took a bite of her own radish. She crunched through it with open enjoyment. "How did you get to keep these radishes, Veronica? I thought you were selling everything you grew to the Dappled Yak. Not that I'm complaining."

Veronica smiled and bit into her own sharp, peppery radish. "These were meant for raw eating, and the owner's mother was horrified they didn't look like magazine pictures. Too lumpy and spotty. Hurkle couldn't use them either."

"Oh, good heavens," Neza said. Florence and Lulu nodded. "Turning up your nose at fresh radishes because they were misshapen? The silliness of some people."

"Gallery showing! Hello? That's what's coming up." Shelby looked annoyed. "We need to be ready."

"We will be," Veronica said soothingly. She smiled winningly at her little sister, annoying Shelby still further.

"It's a special show. The biggest one of the year. Everyone will be there."

"They're all special shows," Lulu said. "You say this every time."

"Yep, sure do," Florence added. "Lulu and me have to study. Big test tomorrow. Thanks for the radishes, Veronica. They are a treat. The soup you made from the leaves was good, too."

Florence snagged the last radish, rolled it in salt, and crunched it slowly, savoring every bite of fresh vegetable. Dinner over, she and Lulu got up from the table and headed upstairs to the room they shared.

"I'll get the washing up done later," Lulu called out as the two girls left the kitchen and headed into the hallway. "I'll need a break from anatomy in a few hours."

"Thank you," Veronica said.

Neza added "I'll be done darning your socks soon."

Florence and Lulu had been terrific additions to the White Elephant household. Veronica felt so lucky to meet them at the local metro stop in the transtube. They were both nursing students at Panschin Community College, and they wanted to live close to school in Dome Two, but in something they could afford.

By the terms of the lease, Veronica couldn't have boarders, but she could have live-in household help. It was weird and snobbish, but an exploitable loophole. She couldn't afford to pay Florence and Lulu like they were real maids, but they in turn couldn't afford to pay a boarding house for meals and lodgings.

They worked out a deal. Florence and Lulu paid with housework – always desperately needed in a pile the size of the White Elephant, particularly since it was located in Dome Two — and threw a few coins to Veronica when they could. In exchange, Veronica provided a nice, furnished room for the girls to share, meals, fresh produce from the garden, assistance dealing with the college's bureaucracy and editing research papers. It had been the fresh produce that sealed the deal. Veronica gave them fresh tomato wedges to sample, and from the looks on their faces, the taste had been a revelation.

Since that meeting over a year ago, Florence and Lulu had become part of the family. It was a family formed by need instead of blood, but in Veronica's experience, need formed a stronger bond than blood despite what people claimed. Her own relatives demonstrated that when they turned their back on her and her sister. Up to that moment, they talked endlessly about how close the family was and how the Bradwells always stuck together through thick and thin. Veronica swallowed the lump that grew in her throat at the memory of their betrayal, and took a deep breath to ease the tightness in her back.

With Florence and Lulu gone, Veronica turned to Shelby who was scribbling furiously in her ever-present sketchbook. She tilted her head to get a better look. It was an angry doodle, a figure with devil horns and twirling a whip-like tail. The face strongly resembled an evil, sneering Veronica.

She suppressed a sigh. "Shelby, the show will be fine. We'll get the house swept down, the ballroom scrubbed, the windows washed, I'll rake all the paths again, I've got fresh veg coming along nicely for the nibble trays, and I've made arrangements for eggs."

Auntie Neza and Shelby both gasped. Shelby set her pencil down and left the sketched Veronica's feet unfinished. She had been on the verge of adding cloven hooves.

"Eggs? Really?" Neza said. "We haven't eaten eggs in over a year."

"Oh, Veronica," Shelby said. "That's wonderful. Did you get very many?"

Veronica looked smug. "Two dozen. I'll devil them and cut them into quarters to make them go further. Mrs. Grisson couldn't promise any more than that. She's got other clients, and they pay cash."

"What did you have to trade to get them?" Neza asked suspiciously. "You already compost everything her chickens would eat."

"Shelby's going to draw portraits of all her grandchildren."

"You promised my work without asking me?" Shelby asked. "How could you?"

"You want a successful show or not?" Veronica asked, her eyes narrowed. She glared at her sister. "A treat like deviled eggs might encourage people to buy those ugly paintings."

"They're not ugly. They are avant-garde."

"Okay, they're not ugly. They're hideous and no sane person will buy them, even with eggs as a bribe," Veronica retorted.

"These paintings will sell! I think we finally found our audience. Professor Vitebskin says all the right people will be here," Shelby snapped back. "That's why this show is so important."

"You think? He found an audience for paintings of mud? This is Panschin! People see nothing but dirt and terraformers every damn day! Paint landscapes and flowers and portraits of people's kids. Why don't any of you paint those things? Those paintings would sell."

"Veronica, you just don't understand. You are so bourgeois."

"Bourgeois people pay their debts. They don't have bill collectors stopping by their house on a regular basis," Veronica snarled back.

Auntie Neza rapped her cane on the floor. "Now, now girls," she said soothingly. "Let's not fight."

She winked at Veronica, then turned to Shelby. "Beauty is in the eyes of the beholder, dear girl. But I don't think you're worried about the cause of avant-garde art or Veronica volunteering you when it's for such a good reason. What is it really?"

Shelby set down her pencil and began pleating her napkin, worn from decades of use, into folds. When she was finished, she spread the napkin flat, and pleated it in the opposite direction. Recognizing this familiar nervous habit, Veronica and Neza waited for her to speak. They both knew from long experience that Shelby wouldn't talk until she felt able.

She didn't look up again until she had the napkin twisted into a spiral. "What if," Shelby began and stopped. "What if Mrs. Grisson doesn't like my drawings? I may not be able to draw good, accurate portraits of her grandchildren."

"Yes, you can," Veronica said. That self-righteous idiot Vitebskin had made Shelby doubt every bit of her artistic abilities. She envisioned dropping him down the nearest mineshaft where he could die of thirst in the dark if the broken bones from the fall didn't get him first. "You have real talent."

"You do lovely work, dear girl," Neza added. "Besides, Mrs. Grisson has seen your drawings of us. She knows you can do it."

"You showed her?" Shelby gasped, paled, and started twisting the napkin again. Neza put her arthritis-stiffened hand over Shelby's own, both to reassure her and to keep her from damaging the napkin still further.

"Yes, I did," Veronica answered patiently. "She loved them. Do you want eggs or not?"

Shelby fiddled with the napkin as she thought of how a good show for the PanU Artists' Collective — especially if actual sales for real money were involved — might help her win acceptance from the other students. Helga Grisson wouldn't judge her the way they did, the way Professor Vitebskin did. *She* didn't know anything about fine art. *She* dropped her 'h's and lived by her wits. *She* raised chickens and guinea pigs on her rooftop terrace and slaughtered them herself. *She* rented out rooms to boarders, cooked for them and washed their laundry. What did *her* opinion matter? Her hands went still and she looked up at her sister.

She set her jaw. "All right then. I'll do it. How many grandchildren does Mrs. Grisson have anyway?"

"Five or six," Veronica said. "She wasn't real clear. I think her younger daughter's got a new boyfriend with a kid of his own and this one might be a keeper."

"A blessing to be sure," Neza said. She smiled fondly at both of her grandnieces. Her life had improved immeasurably when they sought refuge in her home. They had given her warmth, love, companionship, and filled up an echoing, empty house.

Shelby's eyes lit up.

"Does this mean I can buy another sketchpad?" she asked hopefully. "I'd like to do bigger sketches and some studies, you know, but I need room to catch their character better."

Veronica smiled with relief. She glanced over at the cracked, bright yellow cookie jar and evaluated how many coins lurked within. "We might be able to manage that." She eyed her sister's face, hopeful and hungry. Impulsively, she decided to spend more than she should. "Maybe even some pencils."

"Ooh, that would be nice," Shelby said, her eyes going very wide. As Veronica hoped, her sister was distracted by the now all-important decision of which shade and hardness of charcoal pencil she needed the most.

The three women sat quietly in the early evening light, no one especially eager to leap up, despite the tasks needing to be finished before the light failed. They were occupied by their own thoughts: Shelby with her art supplies, Neza taking in the moment, and Veronica wondering how to raise more money to make the next lease payment.

The quiet was broken when the rusty gate in the low stone wall surrounding the White Elephant creaked its warning. The sound easily carried through the open windows.

"That's strange," Veronica said, suddenly alert.

She glanced over at the kitten calendar on the wall, one Shelby had salvaged from the recycling bin in the Art Department at PanU when no one was looking. This month's picture was of a fluffy black and white kitten wearing a vivid red bow around its neck to contrast with its bright green eyes. The unacceptable illustrations of adorable kittens were the reason a current calendar had been discarded long before its time. Someone — no one knew who — had smuggled it into the studio and pinned it to the wall. According to Shelby, it hadn't taken long for Professor Vitebskin to spot the calendar, stomp around the studio roaring in outrage, and toss it into the bin for a much-deserved pulping.

Nothing was written under today's date. "There's no one who's made an appointment for mending or produce. Florence or Lulu would have said something if their boyfriends were coming for a visit."

"Best to see who it is, Veronica," Neza said. A worried look crossed her face. "It might be important."

Veronica, followed by Shelby and much more slowly, Neza, rose and entered the hallway leading to the grand central atrium. It was possible, she thought, that it was someone looking for a room for the night. It was too late for a visit from a representative from the court and thankfully, her little family looked to be done with being lawsuit targets.

The guest book lay open and waiting on the polished table in the atrium before the front door. The grand front door didn't have a knocker anymore, another reminder of the family's fallen status. The creaky gate acted as an early warning.

She opened the door just as someone knocked sharply on the other side.

"Hello," Veronica said, smiling brightly at the stranger. It was a large doorway, and the large man filled it. He stayed on the doorstep and didn't try to enter.

"You the lease holder of this fine establishment?" the stranger asked. His accent held a slight hiss, not from anywhere in Panschin that Veronica was familiar with. He was neatly dressed in a basic business suit, rather than the ubiquitous coverall, but it, like his accent, was subtly wrong compared to what she was used to hearing and seeing in Panschin. He had shaved his head, another oddity in the domes of Panschin.

Her heart sank.

"Uh, yes, I am," she replied.

Truthfully, Neza held the lease but Veronica wasn't about to let her elderly great-aunt, the woman who had given her and her sister a home, be bullied by some officious stranger from the bank.

"You interested in subletting? Moving to a nicer part of town? My boss is very interested in this house."

"Excuse me?" she replied. At least he wasn't from the bank. The Second National Bank of Panschin strenuously disapproved of subletting and was likely to throw everyone out if they caught wind of such illegalities, along with bringing suit against the original leaseholder. Veronica often wondered how Mrs. Grisson got away with her own very loose interpretation of the rules. Nerves of steel, she supposed. There was also the fact Mrs. Grisson didn't labor under multiple handicaps like the Bradwell family did.

"Are you deaf? My boss wants your house."

Veronica stared up at his hard, unfriendly face and found her voice.

"I am not deaf. I heard you fine. You just surprised me, that's all. And the answer is no. This is our home, and we're not moving. Good day."

She started to close the door in his face and the stranger stopped it with his large foot. He pushed the door open, stepping over the threshold. He took a slow look around, taking in the wide, carved double staircase leading to the upper floor, the gracious atrium walls adorned with elaborate molding designed to impress visitors, and the views into spacious rooms opening off the hallway on both sides. If he was impressed, he didn't display it.

Those same eyes roamed over Veronica's body, and he clearly approved of what he saw. Veronica felt like she'd been licked by a large, cold tongue.

"This is a good house, and my boss wants it. I want you to think about where you gonna move to. You can have some time, but not much."

Veronica made herself meet his eyes. They were chips of blue ice. She drew a shaky breath and said firmly, "No. Leave right now, or I am calling the police."

The lust died in his eyes, and he stared down at her for a long, long moment. Veronica's mouth went dry and then dryer, but she glared up at him, willing him to say something and refusing to step back a single centimeter.

"I'm going. Start looking for another place to live."

He withdrew his foot and Veronica slammed the door closed, grateful for its heavy weight. She turned the lock and sagged against the door. She turned. Her sister and aunt were staring at her from the hallway door, their eyes wide. Neza was leaning on her cane, a sure sign her joints were hurting more than usual.

"What was that about?" Shelby asked. "Was he from the bank?"

"No. I don't know who he was," Veronica said, her voice raspy. She coughed, trying to clear her throat. "Whoever that was, he must have made a mistake. Got the wrong house, I suppose."

"Do you really think so?" Shelby said.

Veronica eyed her sister and her aunt for a moment. How could she reassure them? Lulu and Florence came racing down the stairs, concern on their faces. How much had they heard? They all had enough troubles without adding unfounded fears to the mix. Shelby, in particular, was liable to let her imagination run away with her. That was the problem with being artistic; it led to a taste for unwarranted drama.

"Yes, I'm positive," Veronica said, forcing herself to sound calm. She was relieved her nerves didn't show. "Why would anyone want this house? It's not that special. There are plenty more going begging in Dome Two. They're all white elephants, just like this one."

"Not like this one," Neza said dryly. "Our White Elephant is white. Those white elephants are covered with terraformers from top to bottom."

Shelby giggled suddenly. "They're blotchy elephants, every shade of gray and green and brown."

Veronica chuckled weakly. "Yes, they are. Shelby, why don't you help Neza back to the kitchen. Florence? Do you have any more of your joint salve? Lulu, got a minute? Let's talk in the atrium."

Veronica waited quietly with Lulu in the atrium as the last of the sunlight poured down the stairwell from the larger roof opening two floors above. It would soon be replaced by the dimmer, cooler, reflected light bouncing from the underside of the dome. It never got completely dark inside Dome Two the way it did on the steppes. With the dome blocking the way, there were never any stars to marvel at.

Lulu had a thoughtful expression on her face.

When she was sure Shelby, Neza, and Florence were all in the kitchen and out of earshot, Lulu said, "You're worried, aren't you."

It wasn't a question.

"Yep," Veronica said. "I hope it was a mistake and that, that, *oaf* had the wrong house. But even so, maybe somebody somewhere wants something, and we don't want to be in the way." She shuddered, thinking of his lustful eyes as he ogled her figure.

"I'll ask Trevor to walk by the White Elephant whenever he can," Lulu said. "I know Florence's boyfriend will keep an eye out when he's off work, too."

"You'll talk to Florence then?" Veronica asked. "I don't want Shelby to get upset, especially if this is nothing. Like I think it is."

Lulu rolled her eyes. "Oh yeah. You know? We're the same age, me and her and Florence, but sometimes she just seems so much like a little girl."

"Well, it's been really hard for her, since the scandal and our dad's suicide, and then mom dying," Veronica stopped explaining when she saw Lulu's disdainful expression.

"Life is hard for most of us, Veronica," the other girl said coolly. "We just have to get on with it. Like *you* do. Like Shelby should. I'll talk to Trevor as soon as I can." She stood up to leave.

"Thank you." It was easy to forget, Veronica realized again, how little Lulu talked about her childhood. She had reasons she didn't like sharing; reasons that didn't encourage sympathy for unfounded complaints or whining.

Veronica sighed at the empty room. Lulu was right. It was time to get on with it, so she headed back into the kitchen to talk to Shelby and Neza.

Neza was sitting down breathing in the scent from a cup of mint tea, while Shelby massaged each aching hand until she could comfortably lift it. Florence was putting the lid back onto her little jar of salve. She had learned to make it at nursing school using herbs from the PCC nursing department's extensive medicinal herb beds. It was one of the few aboveground sections of PCC, sharing precious surface space on the PanU campus.

"Neza will be okay," Florence said.

"As okay as I'll ever be at this age," Neza added. Her eyes flicked over to Shelby and then back to Veronica. She pushed aside the cup of tea. "You know, it feels a bit chilly. I'll go up to bed. I think you should close and lock all the downstairs windows tonight."

Shelby smiled brightly. "What a good idea. I'll help you upstairs, auntie Neza. While you darn, I've got studying to do."

Florence lingered, while Shelby helped Neza back to her feet, fetched her cane, and helped her limp to the stairs. The run to the front door had taken its toll.

As soon as she heard their footsteps on the stairs, Florence said, "You never saw this guy before?"

"Never. Did you or Lulu get a good look at him?"

"No, I think only you did. We weren't fast enough down the stairs. Did Neza or Shelby see his face?" Florence asked.

"I don't think so."

"Weird." Florence's face lit up. "Ooh. I'll ask Evan to come around more, walk around the house and the neighborhood."

"Good idea," Veronica replied. "Lulu said Trevor will do the same. That guy will figure out he got the wrong address."

Late that evening, after she checked the door and window locks on the ground floor for the third time, Veronica stopped by auntie Neza's room. She found her aunt sitting up in bed, reading by the light of a taper. It was clear she had been waiting for Veronica. The unfinished darning lay next to Neza on the dresser, waiting for the brighter morning light.

"Shelby's fine, already asleep," Veronica said, answering an anticipated question.

"Good. I've been thinking it over, and I've decided to go to the police station in the morning," Neza said.

Veronica stiffened and said, "Do you really think there might be danger?"

"Probably not." Neza closed her book. "But I like being careful. I'll tell them I saw prowlers. The desk sergeant will listen to me since I'm a long-time resident of Dome Two. They know me, and they know I don't make idle complaints so they won't dismiss me out of hand, unlike some of the neighbors."

She sniffed disparagingly and Veronica knew she referred to the household two blocks over. That family had moved in recently from Dome Five and expected twice daily walk-bys from the local beat policeman.

Veronica considered this. "Should I go as well?"

"Hmm. No, probably not. My complaint should do."

"I'll tell the neighbors," Veronica decided. "Starting with Mrs. Grisson. She knows everything that's going on, and she might have heard something."

Neza settled back into her pillow with a contented sigh. "You take good care of us, Veronica."

In the morning, Veronica walked all around her tiny domain and inspected every window, every door, every path, along with the squeaky gate in the low stone wall. Nothing was out of the ordinary. It was reassuring and proof she was right. That stranger wasn't planning on robbing them or assaulting them; he had the wrong address. Nonetheless, in days to come she kept the ground-floor windows locked despite the slowly growing heat of spring in Dome Two. Mrs. Grisson and the other neighbors knew nothing about the situation, but they all promised to keep a lookout and, thanks to Neza's complaint, the local police walked by the White Elephant more regularly as part of their routine beat.

Mrs. Grisson did, however, have other disquieting news.

The local branch of the Second National Bank of Panschin, the leaseholder for everyone on their block, had taken on a new assistant manager. This man was reported to be a go-getter who wanted to "get things done" and "improve the way we do business." Her informant (Doris, a junior teller who boarded with her) said he was reviewing all the leases the bank held, something that hadn't been done in decades once the exodus to Dome Six began. Fortunately, according to Mrs. Grisson's informant, it would take years for him to work his way through the filing cabinets and more years to read and digest all that fine print.

Days passed without incident, either from suspicious thugs or assistant bank managers, and Veronica began to relax again. She turned her attention to the opening of the Panschin Biennial Mining Conference and its possibility of guests for the White Elephant Bed and Breakfast, and the fast-approaching art show.

I t was a relief to Airik to bury himself in the briefing papers. This was work he could understand: analyzing columns of numbers, charts, graphs, reports and figuring out where the lies were. Numbers could and did lie but not the way people did. Any wishful thinking in a report on safety measures was due to the writer, not the numbers. They didn't claim to be other than what they were. Once you figured out how the numbers were slanted, you could correctly interpret or discard them.

Airik worked steadily throughout the morning and called a halt only when more than one person's stomach rumbled loudly enough to get his attention.

"Upton?"

Upton sprang to attention, hoping it was time to quit for a while. His typewriter, a valuable heirloom shipped from Olde Earthe, was state of the art but his fingers still got tired. Transcribing everything Airik said got boring fast but the job demanded careful attention to detail, no matter how mind-numbing it was.

"We'll break for lunch. Gaston?"

Gaston Shelleen looked up warily. He was the lead member of Shelleen's tiny mining department. He was decades older than Airik and three degrees of consanguinity away so he didn't know Airik, but he resented what he did know. He'd never been to Panschin before and had taken advantage of the hotel's varied and delightfully stimulating amenities (many more than twelve kinds were available), and he had spent the morning silently sweating over how he was going to discreetly pay for them.

Gaston did know Airik well enough to know the daimyo meant what he said. He vividly remembered what happened to Howard in the stone courtyard in front of the manor house before a mob of contemptuous peasants. He had no desire to reenact a similar scene. There was also the question of his wife. He cringed at the thought. She would have plenty to say when she discovered their only daughter's dowry had vanished into the maw of the Twelve Happiness Luxury Hotel along with a list of the services he had indulged in.

She would have even more to say when he explained why he had tried to obliterate thoughts and memories with fleshy sensation. Gaston wished desperately he had never come to Panschin and sneezed.

"Yes sir?" he said, after wiping his face. Gods but it galled to have to call this callow poindexter "sir."

"Can the hotel's restaurant seat all of us for lunch on short notice? The break will be good for everyone. We'll return to work afterwards."

"Yes sir, I believe so."

"Good. Let them know we'll be downstairs in half an hour."

Airik eyed Gaston coolly. He had been the leader of the Shelleen contingent until his arrival and had shown the most distress at his announcement that the hotel bills would be audited. Airik suppressed a sigh. Of everyone in the suite, Gaston should have known how important it was to mine the Red Mercury correctly. It poisoned everything it touched and safe handling was going to be stunningly expensive, using up every bit of Shelleen's spare treasury. Gaston had decades of experience in Shelleen's other mining operations but tin ore and copper were a far sight easier to manage than Red Mercury. Gaston would probably sacrifice peasants to do the dirty work and never once understand the peasants of Shelleen were its working backbone. They were a resource to be husbanded like any other and couldn't be wasted just because he couldn't control his own appetites.

"Airik?" Gaston said. "As a reminder, I've scheduled an afternoon meeting with Atto, Davis, Maerski, and Fuziwara. Their daimyos are eager to meet with you."

"Ah." Airik relaxed slightly. Gaston had done something useful. These gentlemen were sure to share some of his own interests in geology. They were, after all, the daimyos of the leading mining demesnes in this quadrant of the Northern Mining Tier. Maerski in particular was a powerhouse in extraction, refining, processing, sales, and shipping of ores. Those were all subjects he needed to learn in a hurry.

"I look forward to it."

The hotel's restaurant staff were extremely attentive; attentive to the point where Airik believed they would have not just cut his steak up into bits so he didn't have to struggle with a knife, but the hovering team of waitresses would have fed the tidbits to him, bite by bite. He also would not have believed any female member of the Twelve Happiness staff would wear a skimpier uniform than those of the willing young ladies he had met upon his arrival, but yes, the waitresses wore even less. It was distracting. Upton was not alone in not knowing where to look. Even Shelleen's early arrivals were still blushing at their presence.

The food was odd. Strangely spiced, heavily sauced, distractingly textured, largely unfamiliar, and not the plain, identifiable dishes he preferred. Airik had learned during his travels he liked knowing what he was eating and here, it was hard to tell. He ate it anyway.

That was the only good part of the meal.

The cheery waitresses bustled around him continuously: refilling glasses of water (triple-filtered for your happiness!) after a single sip, swapping in fresh napkins as soon as he touched one, providing warm wet towels to continuously clean his hands, replacing silverware whether it needed it or not, refilling muffin baskets as soon as one was taken, and at every opportunity, bending over the table to display their tip-generating assets. It was distracting and irritating especially as Airik noticed he was the only person at the table who seemed to want to eat quickly and get back to work.

The waitresses, despite their continual presence and the reinforcement of the maître-de who also couldn't manage to find something else to do, did little to keep away eager supplicants. As on the train, glad-handing entrepreneurs kept coming up to bother Airik with guaranteed plans for success. Many more pests would have interrupted lunch, but Carmine's hulking presence deterred the weaker specimens. No one else in the Shelleen contingent was bothered; just Airik. He was the one who counted. At least the concierge didn't come out of his lair to pester him further about "special services".

It was a relief to flee up the four flights of poorly designed marble stairs back to the suite and prepare for the arrival of the Mining Tier daimyos who ruled the territories surrounding Panschin.

Those gentlemen filed in right on time, each accompanied by

several staffers. Family most likely, Airik surmised since why would you hire outsiders when you had otherwise unemployed relatives to do the work? Atto, Davis, Maerski and Fuziwara were all older men, on par with Gaston Shelleen. Their staffs were younger, and interestingly, more than one staffer in each group was young and pretty and female. The four daimyos, despite not resembling each other, were wearing identical expressions (when they weren't scowling at each other). Apparently, none of the daimyos had anticipated their peers would have similar goals for the meeting.

Their shared expression was one Airik had come to recognize. It said "I want you to meet your future wife, the next daimyah of Shelleen." At least it was a change from the one he'd seen during lunch: "I've got a sure-fire plan to make us both rich." These men were already wealthy but they had daughters of their families to marry off and marrying up was always better than marrying down. There was no prize like an unmarried powerful daimyo: significant family connections, wealth-generating business deals, and highly placed grandchildren were inspiring spurs to action.

The four daimyos mingled, eyeing each other and jostling for position. Each presented their candidate to be the new daimyah of Shelleen. Airik didn't bother trying to catch their names. The women were all the same: young, talented, well-educated, intelligent, attractive, presumably fertile, and supremely well connected. The ideal traits for his wife in fact, as Auntie Zilpah had told him, but they all shared another trait: They viewed him from behind a screen of family obligations with credit signs dancing in their eyes. To Airik, they seemed to be jackals circling their prey.

Airik tried to learn how these daimyos managed extracting resources from their lands without destroying them. He also wanted to know their plans for the future when the ores were gone. But their answers were frustratingly vague. They talked about having men who handled the details, like they were above knowing the sordid day-to-day needs of their businesses. Since these daimyos were acknowledged experts, their vagueness came across as patronizing. It was an agonizing hour of small talk with people who had no genuine interest in what *he* needed to know, until Upton rescued him by pointing out that it was time for the next appointment.

That meeting was with the owner of Steelio, a small mining concern in Panschin. Steelio specialized in copper, something Shelleen had an abundance of. He was prepared to make small talk, but once Airik made it clear what he wanted, he eagerly fell into a detailed conversation about cooperative ventures that would enrich both himself and Shelleen. He also had an attractive, unmarried niece, Olwyn, whom he brought along. She didn't seem interested in snagging a wealthy daimyo, although her uncle did.

The rest of the day continued in the same vein, culminating in a gala dinner and dance hosted by the Twelve Happiness Luxury Hotel for the attendees of the Biennial Mining Conference. The attendees who hadn't met Airik during the day lined up to shake his hand, whisper get-rich-quick schemes in his ear, and introduce him to suitable young ladies from their households. These meetings were not enhanced by having to shout over the atonal music from by the orchestra nor enduring the heat produced by cramming too many overdressed people into a gaudy, mirrored ballroom. The other guests had even less interest in rock collecting than they did in safety procedures.

It was a relief to escape afterwards to the suite. At that point, Airik discovered opening the windows did not let in fresh, quiet night air. Instead, he was blasted back by the noise and bright lights of the nightclub scene surrounding the hotel grounds. There was a storefront or sidewalk bar everywhere in the surrounding streets. As the crowd's merriment rose, it was accessorized by party horns in a variety of inharmonious pitches. The cacophony gained in intensity as it echoed and reverberated between the buildings and off the dome.

Cursing, Airik closed the windows, leaving the room as stuffy as being in a tunnel.

In the morning, after a repeatedly interrupted breakfast, Airik spoke to the concierge about the lack of ventilation. He reacted with shocked surprise.

"My lord Shelleen, the Twelve Happiness Luxury Hotel has a state-of-the-art ventilation system, even finer than that of Dome Six," the concierge said. He palmed his chest and breathed in to emphasize the sweetness of the air. "We here at the Twelve Happiness want you to be *happy*. I can assure you the air you breathe is as fresh as all outdoors, filtered three times for your benefit. Why, you couldn't get fresher air out on the steppes!"

This was patently untrue but there was no arguing with the

concierge of the Twelve Happiness Luxury Hotel.

The day continued in the same manner, broken by a lunch Airik insisted upon being served in the suite rather than deal with the restaurant. That led to a parade of underdressed staff cooing over him and filling the suite with the odors of strange, off-putting spices, an odor that did not dissipate even when every window in the suite was opened to the noisy dome surrounding them.

Two more days passed, each more irritating than the last. Airik couldn't sleep, couldn't eat in peace, couldn't eat in the suite without making it smell even worse, couldn't focus on work, and every meeting wherever it was held devolved quickly into a plea to meet my daughter, niece, younger sister, granddaughter, or cousin. It was maddening. To add to his consternation, it turned out the winking and smirking concierge — who did not miss any opportunity to ask Airik about his intimate preferences — was right. There were no cancellations anywhere within Panschin that Upton could find. There was no place Airik could escape to, where he could think and work and figure out how to dig out the Red Mercury without poisoning his workers along with his land.

On the morning of the fifth day, Airik sat at a corner table in the hotel's restaurant hidden behind *The Panschin Gazette*. It was a poor screen but the best he could come up with. At least he could keep his back to the wall so he won't be surprised. Next to him, Carmine crunched his toast and slurped his coffee, and gave the evil eye to anyone unfamiliar who tried to approach the table.

The newspaper was crammed with stories about the Biennial Mining Conference, along with lurid stories about violent crime in the tunnels, lubricious scandals among local celebrities, and corruption running rampant within the government offices. The front-page story managed, via impressive feats of speculation, to involve all four subjects at once. He took his time reading the news. It distracted from the questionable breakfast he was eating and the grumbling from the Shelleen staff over his lack of focus. Rather than face the day that promised to be more of the same, he read every article. He even skimmed those in the baffling sports section; apparently, lizard racing was as popular here as was something called footie.

Only the classified ads remained. He looked at Carmine. The toast was gone, and he was about to pour another cup when he sensed Airik looking at him. Carmine cocked an eyebrow, asking *you ready to go?*

It was a measure of Airik's frustration that he was willing to postpone another frustrating day at work. He shook his head and leafed through the ads.

He caught sight of a tiny drawing of an elephant at the very bottom of the newspaper, tucked in with a number of other tiny rectangles crammed with too much type and not enough white space. The elephant — quite well drawn, too — adorned a small, mostly empty ad space:

The White Elephant Bed and Breakfast
Close to main transtube lines
Hidden Hideaway
Clean, Quiet, Private, Secluded
626 Oleander Lane, Dome Two
Reasonable rates; inquire within for vacancies

He stared at the ad. The words reverberated in his head like the nightly serenade of party horns: clean, quiet, private, secluded. Dome Two, the second-oldest dome in Panschin and, by far, the largest. Upton said he had checked repeatedly and every hotel in Dome Two was filled, along with Domes Six, Five, Three, and One, but he had not mentioned this place. This was a chance for escape. But the work; how would he manage that? He couldn't move the entire Shelleen party. This bed and breakfast didn't sound that large.

Then it struck him. It was a bed and breakfast, not a hotel. He could sleep there and eat breakfast and then return to the Twelve Happiness for meetings or, really, go anywhere in Panschin for meetings and tours. The city was compact for its population and boasted of its public transportation system. He would still be available to his own staff on a regular basis while not being available to anyone else.

How to do it?

"Sir? Airik?" Upton said.

"Not now," Airik replied.

Upton frowned. Airik was becoming increasingly unlike his normal coolly reserved and well-mannered self. Airik often had trouble understanding other people's motives so he hid behind a veneer of polite formality. Standard empty pleasantries gave him time to think over what had been said and left unsaid.

Upton glanced at the huge twelve-sided restaurant clock. It bore four pairs of red hands, representing the times for Panschin, Barsoom, Easternmost, and Westernmost. They weren't identified; you just had to know. He wondered again why the hotel refused to install separate clocks for important time zones like every other place he had ever been did. It was maddening. He tried again.

"Sir, we've got to get to our next meeting with Jandinaire. We'll be touring their lead and radium refining facility in Dome Four. They have the latest safety equipment installed and agreed to let you see it."

Airik put the newspaper down and gave Upton a long, cool look.

"They can wait a few minutes. I need to go back to the suite and speak with Elliot."

"Uh, we'll be late."

Airik, the secretary knew, hated being late. He didn't like his own time being wasted by having to wait and he made a point of not wasting other people's time.

"Upton. It will not kill them to wait."

Airik carefully folded the newspaper and laid it on the table besides his twelve-sided plate emblazoned with the hotel's logo. A waitress swooped in to snatch it for replacement with a fresh one and he put his hand over it, protecting it from her taloned hands. Each terrifyingly long, scarlet fingernail was adorned with a glowing decal of the Twelve Happiness logo. She backed away.

"Besides," Airik added, "this will give Jandinaire more time to get their own business requests prepped and ready. You know they'll ask for a joint deal and insist I meet every member of the family who is even remotely eligible along with those who are not."

"Yes, sir." Good heavens, Upton thought. The hotel was really getting to Airik.

Back in the suite, Airik spoke to Elliot and Carmine behind closed doors. Gaston, along with the other members of the Shelleen delegation, noticed and commented freely on the fact that Upton was not included, whereas a valet and a bodyguard were. It was embarrassing he could not answer any of their pointed questions, almost as embarrassing as not being included. Airik had always kept Upton involved in his business dealings in the past.

It seemed to Upton like an eternity but was only about half an hour when Airik emerged.

"Upton," Airik said. "I'm rearranging my appearances this afternoon. Gaston?"

Gaston tried to school the surprise from his face. Airik never deviated from a schedule unless it was an emergency. He couldn't think what had happened that he didn't already know about. "Yes sir?"

"You'll take those meetings. I'll brief you on my expectations on our way to the Jandinaire facility."

"Rearrange everything?" Upton asked. He had managed to stop gawping at Airik. "The main panel discussion that you specifically requested to attend is…" His voice trailed off on seeing Airik's icy expression.

"Yes. Everything. You'll be accompanying me this afternoon along with Elliot and Carmine. No one else. Why are we standing around? Jandinaire is waiting for us. Gaston, lead the way."

Airik strode to the double doorways, trailed by the Shelleen delegates. He ignored the whispers and waited impatiently while Gaston remembered what he was supposed to do.

The trip from the Twelve Happiness Luxury Hotel in Dome Six to the Jandinaire facility in Dome Four, at Airik's insistence, took place on the Panschin metro. He flatly refused to use any of the Twelve Happiness vehicles, preferring, as he told the concierge in the middle of the lobby in a clear carrying voice to be better heard by the other guests, to mingle with the commoners of Panschin rather than be harassed continually by overeager, grasping toadies. The concierge, desperate to regain control of a valued and very lucrative guest, begged, pleaded, and wept on his knees, but Airik remained firm. He unbent only enough to get directions to the nearest transtube station after he was told that Gaston, along with the rest of the Shelleen delegation, did not know how to get there despite the time they had spent in Panschin. That lapse earned them a long, icy glare of disapproval.

The metro station was, like the train station at the entrance to Panschin, caked with terraformers wherever indifferent housekeeping and foot traffic permitted them to grow. It was also, other than the noise and odors of the mob of people present, anonymous. No one paid any attention to Airik or the Shelleen delegation, other than grumbling about how many seats they took up on the metro car.

The journey to Dome Four was far swifter than the trip from the train station to Dome Six, making Airik wonder again about the route the electric vehicle had taken. It also made him wonder how much the hotel was charging his delegation for transportation which they could have arranged themselves for far less money.

The group emerged from the transtube station into the thick, dusty air inside Dome Four. A smiling delegation of the Jandinaire family waited for them and led them down the crowded sidewalks that snaked between buildings, warehouses, processing plants, and holding tanks. The sidewalks were regularly interrupted by pipes leading from one tank to another, with more pipes overhead. Terraformers carpeted every surface that received any sunlight at all, other than the walkways where foot traffic wore it away. No effort had been made to remove any of them. The dome overhead was low and mottled with shades of yellow and tan, obscuring the location of the sun. It made sure no one forgot they were under an immense, overturned bowl.

When Airik asked about the ubiquitous mats of algae and lichens, Nathan Jandinaire said, "We need them here in Dome Four. They clean the air, oxygenate it, and make it possible to breathe. Terraformers are a lot cheaper than installing scrubbing equipment. Better at it, too." He happily patted the tank wall they were standing beside. His fingers sank into the thick, spongy layer. When he removed his hand, it came away dripping little chunks while an imprint of his hand remained.

Airik peered closely at the thick mat of dull green algae, interwoven with fibrous red threads. They were speckled liberally with spores ready to burst open and spread themselves out still further, colonizing every surface they touched. He thought about the air he was breathing. He thought about observing every member of the Shelleen delegation never going anywhere without a stash of handkerchiefs at the ready. As he did, Upton sneezed again, along with Gaston and two other staffers, one of them from Jandinaire.

"This is healthier for your workers and yourselves?"

"It works quite well," the Jandinaire representative answered cheerfully. "No one *lives* in Dome Four, not aboveground anyway. It might be different if there was housing here."

"But don't you lose various chemicals to the terraformers that scrubbers would catch?"

"We scrape everything down on a regular basis and process the muck to salvage those raw materials," Nathan answered. "The terraformers grow back fast, which is a good thing. A freshly scraped district in Dome Four forces our crews to wear respirators."

"I see."

The Jandinaire facility was fascinating to Airik. The meeting afterwards in the paneled conference room was much less so. He was introduced to every single unmarried woman in the family over the age of sixteen. The married female family members also attended, and they discreetly made their interest clear in any affairs he'd care to conduct at his leisure.

Airik demurred as civilly as he could and insisted on returning to the refining facility for further demonstrations. There was only some pouting from the Jandinaire family, since there was still the prospect of potentially lucrative business deals. Besides, there would be time later for flirting over the catered lunch Jandinaire served at their headquarters.

Back at the hotel, Airik checked with Elliot and everything was ready. He called together the Shelleen delegates.

"I believe I have found another place to stay. If I am successful, I will be back tomorrow morning for the conference discussion on deep shaft ventilation procedures. I will no longer stay at the hotel, returning only for meetings and discussions. If not successful, I will return within the hour. Elliot, Carmine, and Upton will accompany me. Gaston?"

"Yes, Airik?" Gaston said cautiously. This was not like Airik, normally conscientious to a fault and expecting everyone else to hold to the same lofty standards.

"You will be in charge of the Shelleen delegation here at the hotel. Act in my place this afternoon and, potentially, this evening. When I return, I expect a full report of each conference and any promises made to us or by you."

"Yes, sir," Gaston said. This had to be a trap to punish him for his extracurricular activities at the hotel. Airik must have already discovered how he had been spending his time and Shelleen's money. Either that or the ever-present fug of terraformers had eaten into Airik's brain. He had to blow his nose constantly, and he wasn't the only one.

"But Airik," Upton protested. "Everyone expects to work with you personally. You are the daimyo."

Airik wiped his hand back over his thick, sensibly short hair, an uncharacteristic gesture. He snapped, "I cannot function here at the hotel. I need a quiet place to think and to process what I'm learning. Since no one has provided this for me, I am providing it."

"Sir," Gaston, wishing he had never come to Panschin and that Upton had chosen a different, less enticing hotel, said, "I have to agree with your secretary."

Airik gave Gaston a long, slow, cold stare. Some of them, thinking of the exiled Howard Shelleen, edged away from Gaston. According to family gossip, Howard never recovered from the humiliating punishment.

"Did you listen to what I said? I cannot function here. I have to do what is best for Shelleen, not what is best for others. You may, Gaston, if you like, ask for a vote of no-confidence when we return to Shelleen. It is your right. I am sure the senior family will be happy to know how you and the rest of the department have impaired my ability to keep the demesne safe and prosperous."

"Yes sir," Gaston said, echoed by the rest of the staff. He stared at the plush carpet, patterned with multiple repetitions of the Twelve Happiness logo in clashing colors. That was a vote he would lose, ensuring his permanent loss of status within the family. Airik was the reason Shelleen had kept control of the Red Mercury lode, Airik had fought the multiple lawsuits against the Martian government and won, Airik had gotten the conclave on his side, Airik was the only member of the Shelleen family those damned horse lords would work with and the city management of Purnell wasn't much more cooperative. Worse, the Shelleen peasants were completely loyal to him, personally. If the family replaced Airik as daimyo without a compelling reason, they were likely to revolt. Everyone in Shelleen from highest to lowest knew what had happened in Dairapaska.

Airik waited for a response. When he felt he had given the Shelleen delegates enough time, he broke the silence.

"Good. I, along with Elliot, Upton, and Carmine, will be coming and going as needed. We'll be dressed like common laborers and use the servants' staircases and passageways. Carmine has already found a discreet route for us to use. Elliot has procured coveralls. Upton?"

"Yes sir?"

"We will change, get our bags — Elliot has packed what we need — and find the White Elephant. Gaston?"

"Yes sir?"

"You are in charge. I expect the very best effort from you. I will get it, or I and the family will know the reason why."

"Yes sir."

What had he done? Gaston wondered if he was being set up to share Howard's fate.

Airik was relieved at how smoothly it all went.

Elliot found drab coveralls letting them blend right in. He had packed the minimum needed to sleep elsewhere, concentrating his efforts on the paperwork and Upton's precious typewriter. The route Carmine had scouted out took them down a series of hidden, narrow stairwells within the bowels of the hotel where they were ignored by the few hotel staff who saw them. Those people were running from task to task and had little time to spend asking questions. Carmine said the hotel was so large that between staff turnover, shift changes, and everyone having to be in two places at once, anyone not causing trouble who looked like they belonged and had work to do tended to be ignored.

The little group slipped out via a tertiary backdoor opening onto a quiet alley. They walked to the same metro station and disappeared into the crowd. The transtube journey was easy, and they arrived at the metro station in Dome Two.

Aboveground, Dome Two had an immense dome, higher and wider than that of Dome Six. It was more yellowed and mottled, obscuring the sky but being so much more spacious, there was less of a feeling of being trapped under a dirty garden cloche. The air wasn't any fresher but perhaps because of the size of the dome, it didn't smell as stale.

Elliot unfolded a map and they set out down the winding streets. The party marched in silence, giving Airik another opportunity to watch and judge. Dome Two was much quieter than Dome Six, yet there were plenty of people on the paved roadways. Many of the buildings in the small business district were covered with terraformers, their presence freshening the air. More surprising were the regularly placed large planters, spilling over with marigolds and pansies. Tucked in here and there were many larger planters containing small, lacy-leafed trees. There was even a small park, with much larger expanses of lawns than the Twelve Happiness boasted of. It was greener than Airik had expected after his experiences in Dome Six and brought a pang of homesickness for the green, green lands of Shelleen.

It didn't take long to leave the small, rundown business district. The area was surrounded by something very different from what Airik had observed in Dome Six or Dome Four for that matter. Dome Six had been packed with towers, four, five, even six stories high. It made the dome feel cramped. Dome Two's housing, at least in this area, was more modest and more grand. It was strangely familiar in a warped way and then Airik realized what he was seeing. The houses were miniature manor houses, far larger than what an individual family would need, and each was surrounded by a tiny walled garden as though the house ruled its own demesne. The grand mansions of Barsoom and other free-cities, many as large as Shelleen's own manor house, had plenty of land around them. Even the peasant cottages in Shelleen's villages had just as much land around each cottage, perhaps more.

As they walked down the wide, paved streets, weaving among the pedestrians, Airik worked out the reason. It had to be the dome. Dome Two was the largest dome in Panschin — the largest on Mars — but it was still limited in room. The builders couldn't provide a large house and a large garden; there wasn't enough space. Dome Six used its space more effectively since towers allowed a higher population density.

Then why, he wondered, weren't the major hotels and convention center located in Dome Two? It had a seedy, seen-better-days air about it, but it was spacious compared to Dome Six. It made no practical sense.

eronica!" Shelby called through the open window into the kitchen. "The paths look awful! I thought you said you would rake the gravel again."

"Shelby," Veronica replied, "it is on the list." She looked up at her sister from her seat at the kitchen table. She had been examining the household's bank statement. The balance was worrisomely low. "I will get to it. Right now, though, I have to sweep out the ballroom. You remember? The huge room you didn't sweep? The one where all the paintings will go? Where the Collective tracked in all that dirt when the crates were delivered?"

"I was busy! Can't Florence or Lulu do it?"

"No, they can't. They've got studying to do."

"But they're supposed to clean in exchange for living with us," Shelby said sulkily. "I've got studying to do too."

"They already do plenty, and how do you study to draw pictures of mud? I would think herbal tinctures and the diseases they go with are a lot harder to learn."

"Girls!" Auntie Neza walked into the kitchen, thumping her cane hard on the tile floor for emphasis. "Squabbling will not get any work done."

"But Neza, we're running out of time," Shelby moaned.

"All the more reason to find your tempers," Neza replied coolly. "I will help you sweep out the ballroom."

Shelby, peering through the open window into the dim kitchen, thought of her great-aunt's crippled hands clutching a broom and shame washed over her. "No, no, no," she said. "I'll do it next. I'm sorry. I'm just so worried about the show."

"We'll be fine," Veronica said soothingly. "We've hosted plenty of shows for the PanU Artists' Collective and they've all gone well. We might even sell a painting or three. It could happen."

Shelby's face lit up. "Do you really think so?"

"Yes, absolutely," Veronica lied stoutly.

Neza said, "I agree. The show will be wonderful and we'll sell more paintings than ever. You'll see."

Shelby laughed and clapped her hands, her mood swinging back to joy from apprehension. "I'll get the ballroom walls and windows started right away. That way I'll be done when everyone gets here to sweep down the walls of the house."

As soon as her footsteps could be heard crunching down the gravel path to the front door, Veronica turned to her aunt, her eyebrows meeting her hairline.

"Do you really believe that? We'll sell more paintings than ever?"

"Not a chance." Neza snorted with wry amusement. "Those ugly things? But Shelby's sweeping down the ballroom and it needed to be done."

"True." Veronica laughed, a lilting trill of amusement. It gladdened Neza's heart to hear it.

"And maybe those lazy artists will sweep down the walls without my standing over them." Veronica chuckled again. "And set up the easels and hang the paintings."

Neza snickered. "We can dream, I suppose. That's still free. I will be glad to get all those crates of easels unpacked. Ballroom's full of them. Maybe we should offer to store them in the lower basement level so we don't have to deal with delivery again."

"No, then we'd have to get the Collective to haul the crates up and down two flights of stairs every time we hosted a showing. And we'd be responsible for their upkeep and maintenance. Let the Collective pay for warehousing someplace else," Veronica replied. "We shouldn't do it for free and that's what they'd expect."

Neza sat down at the table next to Veronica with a sigh of relief at getting off her feet. "Back to business. How much money do we have left?"

Veronica frowned at the bank statement. "Not very much. The mining conference started and I was really expecting we'd get a guest or two. You know how crowded Panschin becomes. And, well, this time nothing."

She handed the statement to Neza who looked, then looked again to see if the numbers would change. Her face fell as the columns of figures flatly refused to rearrange themselves to suit the household's needs.

"Damnation," Neza said. "I hadn't realized we were so close to the bottom."

"I know." Veronica sighed wearily and slumped down still further onto the table, until her upper body rested on the surface. "Those cardoon seeds turned out to be a waste of money. Half the seeds didn't sprout and the ones that did died. I shouldn't have run that ad in the *Panschin Gazette*. Nobody saw it. I shouldn't have bought those sketchbooks for Shelby or those new pencils."

Neza looked over the kitchen thoughtfully, with its cooking utensils hanging over the stove and the cupboards half-full of dishes. "We could sell some of the furnishings in the B&B wing. The furniture is horribly old-fashioned but it's very well made and sturdy. The drapes are still in good condition too. We could sell some more of the china as well."

She heaved herself up and limped over to the cupboards. She opened the doors on the cabinets still in use.

Veronica thoughtfully studied the shelves as Neza held the door wide. Only the lower ones still held dishes. "No, not yet," she said. "The conference isn't over. We have to have furnished rooms if someone shows up as a guest. People won't pay to sleep on the floor when they can sleep in the park for free. And they expect dishes to eat off of."

Neza smiled dryly, then carefully asked, "Any chance of a magazine article selling?" She closed the cabinet doors and shuffled back to the table, grateful to sit down again.

Veronica turned away to stare out of the window onto her constricting world. "No, another set of rejections."

She fingered her necklace, enjoying the cool feel of the gray and white beads and wished she could see the sky between the houses instead of the confining dome. She straightened up, turned back to Neza and said in a determined voice, "I've got a new crop of lettuces and some other veg coming in. I know the Dappled Yak will buy it all. We can hang on for a few more months."

"I didn't know it was that bad."

Both women turned to see Shelby standing in the doorway, her hand on the frame to support herself. Her face was pale and her eyes very wide and fearful. Her jaw trembled.

"Shelby," Veronica said, "How long have you been listening?"

"Long enough," Shelby answered hotly. "I wouldn't have asked for those sketchbooks if I knew you didn't have the money. Or those pencils. Why didn't you say something?"

After a moment of waiting, Neza answered for Veronica, who had her eyes closed and her mouth shut tight. "You needed them, dear girl."

Veronica showed no signs of wanting to talk, with her shoulders hunched over waiting for another blow, so Neza added, "you have real talent. Mrs. Grisson already told me how happy she was with your first portrait of her oldest granddaughter."

"Don't change the subject," Shelby said, stumbling towards the table. She pulled out a chair and sat down heavily. "You haven't been telling me things. Why not? Aren't I part of this family?"

She made a grab for the bank statement. Veronica slapped her hand down on the paper and pulled it away from her sister's grasp.

"Don't you trust me to know what's going on?" Shelby asked. "Do you think I'm that selfish and stupid?" She wiped away an angry tear. Neza nudged her own chair closer to Shelby to put a comforting arm around her niece. Shelby pulled away, refusing the comfort she normally sought at every opportunity.

Veronica raised her head and considered her sister carefully. She thought of what Lulu had said about Shelby acting so young. Maybe the time for shielding Shelby from the harsher realities of life was over. Shelby was old enough to know what was going on.

"All right, Shelby," she said. "You are part of the family and you should know." Veronica pushed the bank statement to Shelby. She picked it up and scanned it. She puzzled over it, running down the column of expenditures that did not match the column of deposits. The more she read, the more Shelby frowned and frowned and frowned hardest of all when she reached the bottom of the page.

She looked up, running her eyes past the cupboards of familiar dishes and stared out the window while Neza and Veronica watched her silently.

"All right then," Shelby whispered. She swallowed audibly. "I'll quit school and get a job." Her voice got stronger. "They always want waitresses and chars in Dome Six."

Veronica and Neza exchanged appalled glances. It was gratifying to realize Shelby wasn't going to dissolve into a puddle of tears and woe, but there were things she didn't know. Veronica raised her eyebrows and looked quizzically at Neza. Did she want to address the situation they had both been avoiding since the day Shelby started classes at PanU with such high hopes?

Neza refused to meet Veronica's eyes and stared at the tabletop. Its bamboo surface was polished smooth from decades of use and reflected her lined face like a mirror. Veronica watched her great-aunt's pursed lip reflection and sighed deeply again. She was going to have to say it.

"Shelby, that is so very sweet of you to offer," Veronica said carefully. "We appreciate it. Truly we do. But you can't quit PanU."

Shelby stared at her sister in puzzlement. Veronica regularly had plenty of things to say about the PanU Art Department and how it prepared its graduates for the future but almost always her statements had been negative.

"Why not?" she broke the uncomfortable silence. "I just walk away from the scholarship you got me at the end of the semester. It's coming up in a few weeks. They'll give the money to someone else."

Veronica stared harder at Neza's reflection, willing her to speak so she didn't have to.

"Well," Shelby asked again. "Why not?"

This time, Neza received Veronica's message.

"Because, dear girl," Auntie Neza answered unwillingly, "you didn't get a scholarship."

Shelby stared at her aunt. "What? But why else would they take me? They looked at my portfolio. We didn't have any money to pay PanU. I wouldn't be going there if they hadn't given me a scholarship. I thought that's what happened."

Veronica reached over and squeezed both Shelby's and Neza's hands. "That's what we tried to do, sweetie. But that bastard Vitebskin didn't like your portfolio. He refused to award you the art scholarship."

Neza said, "I knew you really wanted to go there. You have such talent, dear girl. I've never seen anyone who can draw as well as you can. So, I made a deal with the bursar's office. I got a discount for you on tuition by paying for all eight semesters at once in cash. I emptied out the last of my trust fund to do so."

Shelby's jaw fell and she started to shake. Her fingers made clutching motions so Neza pushed over a napkin for her to twist.

"There's no refund," Veronica added. "If you quit, we're out that investment in your future. You have to stick it out and get your degree."

After another long silence, broken by Shelby's gasping for air while her world rearranged itself around her, Neza said, "Your sister and I wanted to do the best we could for you."

Hearing that, Shelby stood abruptly, still clutching the napkin. "What's best for me? What's best for me? Maybe you should have asked me! You could have told me. I always thought I wasn't doing something right in the studio and now I know why! I don't belong there! I was never good enough to begin with." She wiped away angry tears.

Veronica leaped to her feet. "You *are* good enough, Shelby. That stupid, self-righteous ass of a professor is the problem. He's an idiot and he wouldn't recognize a decent painting if he was hit over the head with one. Look at what he wants everyone to paint! Ugly pictures that look like what comes out of a night soil cesspool."

Her voice got louder.

"No landscapes, no vases of flowers, no portraits, and lordy, lordy, lordy, the things he has to say about kittens are insane. He got you to parrot that stupid dross and you adore kittens! He's an idiot and he wants everyone to follow him down a mineshaft of idiocy and ugliness because he couldn't draw something recognizable if you held a knife to his throat!"

"He's a genius!" Shelby snapped back.

"He's a moron!" Veronica returned. "A lecherous, narrow-minded egotist."

"He is not."

"He *is*. If he was a genius, he'd make money from his own paintings instead of telling other people how to throw dirt at a canvas."

"You are wrong."

"Shelby," Veronica said. "I still have some contacts at PanU even though I didn't manage to graduate because of what happened to us when dad, well, did what he did. Vitebskin's got everyone in the art department fooled. He's got tenure and he knows where all the bodies are buried."

She did not add what she had heard via this source of information about Professor Vitebskin's reaction to Shelby's portfolio. He thought it bourgeois, derivative, trite, middle-brow, lifeless, and twee; statements he slashed in bold red ink across her application to ensure everyone who reviewed it knew his opinion. Veronica's source told her Professor Vitebskin could be counted on saying this kind of thing if there was even a single image of a cat in a portfolio no matter what the portfolio actually looked like or how accomplished it was.

However, Shelby adored kittens and cats. She desperately missed their cat, Madame Fluff, who had been sold when they lost everything. She had included several loving portraits of Madame Fluff in her portfolio, more than enough to send Professor Vitebskin over the edge and down the shaft into the deepdown. If only, Veronica thought again, they had known in advance what set Vitebskin off. She would have ensured Shelby only included acceptable drawings that would garner the precious scholarship.

Shelby's yelling snapped her focus back to the present.

"Well then why did you spend all of Neza's trust fund to send me to PanU?" Shelby shouted. "I could have gone to PCC and spent way less money and we'd not be in this fix right now!"

"Because I was hoping you'd meet someone decent at PanU and get your Mrs. degree!" Neza said loudly. She thumped her cane on the floor, hard. "You're still a Bradwell and you deserve a better husband than anyone you'd meet at PCC."

Shelby gaped at her aunt, for once at a loss of words. Then she turned onto her sister. Veronica had her mouth snapped tightly closed and her eyes were blazing.

"You let auntie Neza do this? Veronica, how could you? You're always supposed to be so sensible. Get my Mrs. degree? Who even does that these days? You don't go to school to catch a husband. You go to school to get an education that will get you a decent job!"

Neza thumped her cane onto the floor again, harder. She kept on thumping her cane until she got their attention. "I wanted this, Shelby," she said firmly. "You're a Bradwell and a Molony. Maybe that doesn't mean much anymore, not our branch of the family, but it used to mean a lot. It was my money and I wanted the best possible chance for you."

Shelby turned back onto her sister. "And what about you? Going along with such a …" Seeing Neza's hurt expression, Shelby stopped herself in time from adding "stupid idea."

Veronica let go of her string of beads and traced out the grain of the bamboo tabletop with a fingertip so she did not have to look at her sister.

"It was auntie Neza's money so it was her choice, but I agreed. You've got real talent and I hoped you'd learn to paint really well at PanU. PCC has a good commercial art department, I checked, but I didn't think you'd be happy drawing ladies' shoes and dresses for department store adverts. You're very creative and PanU seemed the best chance to nurture your talents. And yes, maybe you would meet someone nice there. Someone with prospects."

Shelby breathed out deeply and sat back down in her chair.

After another long, empty silence, she said, "so I'm stuck."

"I'm afraid so," Veronica replied. "You have to get that degree. It's already paid for."

"It was the best choice I could make at the time, dear girl," auntie Neza said, reaching again for Shelby's hand. This time, Shelby didn't pull away. "You're so talented and I wanted so much for you to be happy."

"We'll muddle through," Veronica added. "We always do. The show's coming up, I get half the door receipts, and if we make it a really good one, maybe we'll sell some paintings. I'll earn my commission and we'll manage another couple of months."

Shelby turned to her great-aunt with cold, angry eyes. "You want me to get my Mrs. degree. If marrying is so important, then why didn't you? And look what happened to Veronica! We all thought Dean was wonderful and look how that turned out."

Neza frowned awfully at her younger niece, then sat back in her chair with resignation. All her years showed on her face and the slump of her shoulders.

Looking at Shelby, Veronica reminded herself that she was married at her age. What a mistake marrying Dean Kangjuon had turned out to be. Handsome, charming, well-connected; he had been so much fun. She had fallen madly in love with Dean and she was sure he felt the same for her since he said so all the time.

They had lived a charmed life; playing house in the White Elephant, attending classes at PanU, exploring every nook and corner of Dome Two, and socializing with so many friends. Dean knew everybody, it seemed, and that meant parties and get-togethers several times a week.

Then he cut and ran minutes after the Bradwell troubles had begun. It kept getting harder to trust people, Veronica had often thought. People you thought you knew, when every time you did you turned out to be wrong.

Neza shook her head in regret. "I made mistakes, Shelby. I said no when perhaps I shouldn't have. It worked out, I suppose. I thought so for a long time. Then Veronica and Dean moved in and the house was full of family for the first time in years. Then your dad, well, you know." Her voice trailed off.

"Yeah," Veronica said sourly. "Dad."

Neza continued, "Shelby, your father did dreadful things and ruined lives but for me, it turned out to be the best thing in years when you and your mother moved in. I know Dean left, but I had you, Veronica, and your mom. It was a real joy to spend so much time with your mother before she passed. And every day that you've been here has been a joy for me."

She squeezed Shelby's hand. "Shelby, I had no idea how much I missed by not marrying and having a family until you moved in. I can't go back and change the past but I could give you a chance to meet someone, someone you could start a family with."

Shelby looked around the kitchen, thinking of all the times she had walked home from PanU with Lulu and Florence. She had never wanted to meet any of the young men they knew from PCC. She had always refused their offers, and she never told anyone why. She didn't get dates at PanU either. She was always afraid of someone finding out what dear old dad had done. Would someone from PCC have cared?

She thought of Kip McGrant who shared many of her classes. He always wanted to talk to her, even flirt a bit, but only when nobody else was around to see him do it. The other students at PanU weren't any better. She tried hard to be friendly, joining in whenever she could, but her efforts didn't change facts. Nothing mattered more in Panschin than money, family background, and social status and the higher up the social ladder you were, the more they mattered. And here Neza actually believed she'd meet some nice young man from a good family and marry him. As soon as any nice young man found out about her background, he'd be out the door so fast it wouldn't have slammed shut by the time he was running down the street. And if he didn't object, his family would.

She could have gotten a date or two, but the young men who had asked, well. They wanted her because they wouldn't have to pay for her company but otherwise, she'd be treated the same as any prostitute. Used, discarded, and then forgotten; certainly never taken home and introduced to the family. She thought of Kip again. He'd never once even asked her out for tea and a bun at the roach coach between classes, something everyone else did routinely with their friends.

She thought of Dean and how happy Veronica and both families had been when they married. Then dear old dad's criminal activities were discovered, the Kangjuon family insisted on the divorce, and Dean didn't fight them very hard at all. He'd even agreed with them that Veronica had to change her name back to Bradwell from Kangjuon to make sure every connection was severed. It had been like Veronica turned into a cave troll in front of his eyes. What a spineless leech. Yet he still came around to chat up Veronica even though he refused to stand up to his family on her behalf.

Her sister remained coolly civil to her former husband and wouldn't speak badly of him or his family outside the safe walls of the White Elephant. Her opinion was it was all water down the shaft and there was no point dwelling on the past. Even so, Shelby didn't think Veronica would ever forgive Dean's betrayal. It was easier to be angry at Dean than their father. Wonderful, fun, loving Simon Bradwell who had destroyed their lives and made them the pariahs of Panschin.

Who could want them after dear old dad's deceptions were revealed?

Shelby broke the long silence. "A nice boy from a good family like the Kangjuons. Remember them?" She stared daggers at her sister.

Veronica winced. Her former mother-in-law had been the instigating force behind the divorce, and Dean hadn't fought his mother on the subject. Mrs. Kangjuon had been friendly when the Bradwell family was a valued connection. Afterwards, it turned out Mrs. Kangjuon believed in a scorched soil policy when dealing with unwanted former relatives. Her behavior was the reason Veronica was relieved she and Dean had never managed to have a baby during their marriage. A child would have tied her to the Kangjuons forever. She started when Shelby began talking again.

"I can accept the idea PanU would give me more scope for my so-called talent than PCC would. But how can either of you say I would meet someone nicer at PanU than I would at PCC?"

"It is a better, more exclusive, expensive school," Neza began.

Shelby twisted in her seat and glared at her great-aunt. "Better! Look at Dean. He came from a good family and they couldn't dump Veronica fast enough when everything that dad did came out. You really believe after how dad cheated all those people, anyone from a 'good family'," Shelby made quotes in the air with her fingers, "would have anything to do with me? I never talk about the past at PanU. I'm afraid of what people would say. They'd cut me and you know it."

She thought of Kip again, always cheerful and ready to talk but nearly always only when they were alone.

Veronica said wearily, "Department store adverts, Shelby. Think of a lifetime spent drawing ladies' shoes. Or pickaxes."

Shelby whipped around to glare at Veronica. "At least a job drawing adverts would bring in money. And what, you think I couldn't do better? Eventually? I could keep working on my own art in my free time and I wouldn't have to worry about digging manky paintbrushes out of recycling bins and salvaging them! I'd have money to pay for real supplies."

"Maybe you could have," Veronica said even more tiredly. "But it's done now."

"What you're really saying is I don't have any talent. I have to depend on some man to take care of me."

Veronica leaped to her feet, re-energized. "That is not what I'm saying! Don't put words into my mouth."

Shelby stood up so fast she shook the table. "It *is*. If I had talent, I wouldn't be failing everything I do there."

"Because of him! Stop believing *him* and start believing in yourself!"

"That's *enough*!" Neza shouted. "Stop this arguing right now. It gets us nowhere. Be quiet while we think. Not another *word*."

Veronica sat down as did Shelby, more slowly. Both girls fumed as they resolutely refused to look at each other or at their great-aunt. Instead, they stared at the kitten on the calendar. Its huge, unblinking green eyes stared back at them.

"Maybe I should go over to the bursar's office again," Neza said, breaking the angry silence. She had a thoughtful, far-away look on her face as though something new, something she had never before considered, had suddenly appeared before her.

"What good would that do? You already paid. You said yourself that money is lost," Shelby said hotly. "I'm stuck with a school that thinks I'm an incompetent mushroom." She did not add "and people who think I'm a waste of space" although she thought it.

"You are not incompetent," Veronica said firmly. "Do not listen to that idiot professor. He's still pissed off about Clyde Monez and the ore-cars of money he made drawing kitten pictures along with the fact that idiot couldn't draw his own way out of a wet paper bag."

"Clyde Monez has talent and I don't!"

"Clyde Monez probably wasn't any more talented at your age than you are, even if he was plenty sneakier. But he knew something we didn't," Veronica said. "He knew Vitebskin hates cats. If we'd known that little fact, I'd have made sure your portfolio was exactly what Vitebskin liked and you'd have gotten that scholarship."

"Maybe I would have won a scholarship but you don't know I would have," Shelby retorted. "Maybe Professor Vitebskin would have still thought my drawings were crappy even without Madame Fluff's portraits."

Neza thumped her cane again, trying to seize the floor and get the debate back where she wanted it. "PanU and PCC have some ties. You know they do. They share facilities and some of the professors moonlight. I might be able to persuade the bursar at PanU to transfer enough money for Shelby to take classes at PCC in place of PanU's classes."

"Oh Neza," Shelby groaned. "And what good would that do? They won't give a refund on the difference. You said so yourself that money's gone."

"Much as it pains me right now to say this, but Shelby is right," Veronica said. "What good would it do?"

Neza lifted her cane and pointed at the kitten illustration. The red bow gleamed against the kitten's black and white fur. The long ribbon ends artfully draped over the kitten's back and curled gracefully around its paws.

"See that painting on the calendar? Shelby, you draw almost as well. Clyde Monez didn't learn to draw commercial illustrations at PanU. He did it at PCC. Why can't you draw kittens and puppies and flowers and people for illustrations? Mrs. Grisson said your drawing of her granddaughter was just like she had been turned into a paper-doll and moreover, she said all her boarders agreed."

"Hmm," said Veronica, sitting up suddenly and blinking. Her mind raced down the new trail Neza had blazed. "Hmmm."

"Almost as well?" said Shelby. "Almost as well? That means I'm not nearly as good as Clyde Monez."

Veronica glared at her sister and then at the kitten illustration. "Shut up, Shelby, and listen. We didn't know what an idiot Vitebskin was until it was much too late. We do know you're talented. If auntie Neza can get PanU to let you take classes at PCC instead, you could quietly take the commercial art classes that would teach you to do magazine illustrations and calendar art. Nobody would know. You'd be like Clyde Monez. You'd have part of the fancy degree from PanU and the useful training from PCC. It could work."

"But Neza said herself that I'm not as good as Clyde Monez! I'm not as good as *that* artist is," Shelby pouted. She pointed again towards the kitten on the wall.

Veronica snarled wordlessly at the ceiling in her frustration. Did her little sister want to give up?

Neza rolled her eyes in exasperation. She loved Shelby dearly but sometimes, it seemed Shelby liked drama for its own sake, a tendency that made her ears not work as well as they should.

"Yes, Shelby," Neza said firmly, "you're not as skilled as that artist is, right now. But you will be with time and practice. We just have to get there."

"Neza's right, Shelby," Veronica said. "We keep trying. If you give up, then Vitebskin wins. Do you really believe what that idiot has to say about you and your art? You're much better than he's willing to admit to and I hope, I hope!, deep down you know it. Look at that picture. How would you make it better?"

Shelby glowered at the kitten illustration. She'd never liked how the artist had painted the kitten's eyes. They seemed flat and lifeless. And the ribbons didn't float like they should. On the other hand, technically speaking, the artist was flawless at painting kitten fur. However, beautifully painted fur didn't make kittens look lifelike. Their eyes and expressions made an observer coo over their cuteness, not the swirls patterned into their fur. But could she draw as beautifully, as realistically, as enticingly as this artist had, despite the obvious flaws? Was she the only person who saw those flaws?

The gate hinges shrieked, startling all three women. Loud voices poured in through the open window and many, many footsteps were crunching down the gravel path to the front door.

Saved, Shelby thought. "They're here." She leaped to her feet. "We've got to get the White Elephant swept down and set up."

"So they are," her sister added. "And right on time, too."

Veronica was relieved. Sweeping down the walls of the White Elephant would be a dirty, tiresome job but it would give her time to think over Neza's idea. It would give Shelby time to think about it, too. Could Neza do it? Veronica thought about her few remaining friends at PanU. One of them might suggest who to talk to. Lulu and Florence? Hmm. Probably not. The PCC school of nursing didn't have anything to do with the commercial arts wing.

Someone pounded on the front door.

Shelby headed out towards the kitchen door. She called back "don't anybody talk about this in front of them. I've got a hard-enough time at PanU as it is."

"No worries on that score," Veronica said. "You take the ballroom with Neza and I'll handle the outside crew. I can't be having any of those idiots trampling my vegetable beds."

As soon as Shelby was out of earshot, Veronica said to their aunt, "we have to do this, get Shelby into PCC. I did *not* like what she implied about how she's treated at PanU."

Neza grimaced. "No. I'll have to ask her what's really going on as opposed to what little she's said. She might be willing to tell me the truth now."

Veronica laughed ruefully. "As opposed to her big, overbearing sister, I suppose. I'll scrub terraformers off furniture myself in Dome Six if we can get Shelby into PCC. She has a chance."

"And what about you, my dear Veronica?" Neza asked. "What about your chances?"

Veronica hugged her great-aunt tightly. "One crisis at a time, Neza. First the show, then Shelby, and then me."

Neza met Veronica's light brown eyes, the same eyes as her mother and her own. "You're a Bradwell and a Molony too, dear girl. You shouldn't be scrubbing walls or floors any more than Shelby should."

Veronica smiled ruefully at her great-aunt. "Maybe so, but our creditors don't care."

It took the rest of the afternoon to get the White Elephant's exterior swept down. It was the same old story, Veronica thought wearily. Every time she hosted a show for the PanU Artists' Collective, she had to insist that the student volunteers do a careful, thorough job, sweeping the new growth of terraformers off every flat surface and not just the street-facing walls within easy reach. Some of the crew that showed up had been here for previous shows so they should have known this was part of the rent the Collective paid for her turning her home into an art gallery. They got an immense, airy space to spread out in and she got clean, white walls to amplify what little sunshine the dome allowed through.

"No!" Veronica shouted. "Do not step into the beds. That's food growing there, not algae."

"Sorry."

"Aack!" She waved her arms madly at the offenders trying to get their attention. "Don't break the windows with the push-brooms! Gently!"

"Oopsies."

"Why are you guys standing around? Do you think these walls will sweep themselves clean of terraformers?"

"Just taking a break, Veronica."

"You just got here. You don't need a break yet."

"Hey, day-laborers should be doing this kind of work. I've got delicate hands made for fine art."

Veronica put her own, decidedly undelicate hands on her hips as she glared at the complaining student. He sneered at her insolently, making her even madder. She didn't know which was more irritating, his nerve or his laziness. Was this jerk one of the ones making Shelby miserable?

She marched towards him, suddenly furious.

"If you expect to show your painting at the show tomorrow, you will work. Otherwise, the deal's off for the whole pack of you. I will cancel the exhibit and you can tell Professor Vitebskin he can find another, empty ballroom on short notice." Veronica stepped up to the suddenly unsure student and grabbed the front of his department-store coverall with both hands, surprising him with her strength. She forced him to meet her eyes.

"Do you understand me?" she snarled right into his face.

He stared at her in shock. Veronica let go, and he straightened himself up sulkily.

"I was just making a joke," he mumbled as he turned away.

"I don't have a sense of humor. Get back to work. Hey look! There's Professor Vitebskin now." Veronica pointed towards the Professor striding down the street like he owned it. "I'm sure he'll be happy to discuss moving the show to a new ballroom."

The offending student blanched, while the other members of the Collective glared at him and muttered balefully among themselves. The ones who didn't have brooms or other cleaning tools in their hands picked them up. There was — as Veronica knew — no usable, empty ballroom to be had on short notice with the Biennial Mining Conference in full swing, and certainly not as cheaply as the White Elephant or as conveniently located to PanU.

Artists! Veronica thought with contempt. Spineless, lazy, and entitled.

"Miss Bradwell," Professor Vitebskin said as he strode up the gravel path. She noticed he didn't bother closing the gate. He gave Veronica a lingering once-over, then winked at her. "Everyone working hard, I trust?"

"Almost everyone, Professor," Veronica replied smoothly. She cast a threatening glance over the suddenly hardworking crew of students. They carefully avoided meeting her gaze, focusing intently on the task in front of them, some of them for the first time since their arrival.

"You know there's always someone who wants the rest of the Collective to do their work for them while they sit back and reap the glory," she added.

Professor Vitebskin, tall, debonair, smartly turned out in a well-fitted coverall that had been artistically shredded down the legs and sleeves and painstakingly decorated with aesthetic spatters of color-coordinated paint, spun on his heel to get a better look at his students. He watched them industriously sweeping down the walls, paying close attention to the trim around the windows. He also observed the numerous missed patches of algae, multicolored splotches standing out against the building's white walls.

"So I see. Was there shirking, Miss Bradwell?"

"Not anymore, Professor Vitebskin. You inspire your students with your presence," Veronica said, and she smiled winningly at him. It was true. The student crew was working as diligently as she'd ever seen. As they watched, the offending patches of algae and moss were swept clean, leaving the White Elephant gleaming again.

He preened complacently. "So I do. How's the ballroom coming along?"

"I don't know," Veronica said. "I've been busy out here. However, Shelby and auntie Neza are supervising inside so I have hopes it will be sparkling."

Professor Vitebskin allowed himself another long, enjoyable glance over Veronica's lush figure only partly hidden by a baggy old coverall and arched his eyebrow at her. "As sparkling as the building is outside?"

"Maybe," she replied. "You'll have to see for yourself."

Get inside, you lecher, Veronica thought. You make me feel slimy.

The memory rose unbidden of the thug who had visited a few days ago, asking after the lease on the White Elephant. He hadn't been back, and no one had seen or heard anything. She pushed the thought firmly away. No use borrowing trouble when she had plenty on her hands to deal with standing around her.

"Everything's under control here, Professor. I know auntie Neza will want to consult with you about the placement of the easels."

"Of course she will," the professor replied. "She lacks vision."

He spun back and surveyed his students. Some were perched on ladders trying to reach the sections below the pseudo-roof tiles in their efforts to impress Professor Vitebskin with their keenness. Veronica watched too, hoping no one slipped and fell to their death. She couldn't afford that calamity, despite her need for pristine, reflective walls to better grow her produce and earn some coin.

"Well, that's better," said the professor. "Miss Bradwell?"

"Yes, professor?"

He raised his voice. "I'll return after inspecting the ballroom. I expect perfection and nothing less."

"Of course, Professor Vitebskin," Veronica said. "I'll remind your students, just in case they forget in the next ten minutes."

He let his smile linger on her a few moments longer than necessary and then sauntered down the gravel path around the house. Veronica watched him go, noticing that yes, someone – not him, she was positive – had ironed his coverall after scrubbing it immaculately clean. There wasn't a single stain, smear, shredded area, or rip present other than what would enhance its fashionable appearance. She looked at her well-worn, grubby, wrinkled coverall. Every worn spot and stain were earned through hard service.

Artists with money, Veronica thought, and rolled her eyes again.

She looked up at the students supposedly scraping the sweater of terraformers from the cornices and yelled "Hey! Quit shirking! The professor's gone but I'm not!"

As Professor Vitebskin strolled around the White Elephant, he considered the problem of Veronica Bradwell and more importantly, her sister Shelby. Veronica was attractive in her own way but she had a distressing independence of mind. Oh, she was always properly respectful towards him but there was still that slight air implying she didn't mean it. She was respectful because she had to be and the second she didn't have to respect him anymore, she'd quit and be glad.

Shelby, now, there was a delectable morsel. Tall, willowy, lovely bone structure, glowingly even skin, naïve, and desperate to fit in. No real talent of course, but with that face and body, she didn't need any talent to be an acceptable bed partner. She tried so hard in his classes, struggling for his approval, and yet, she didn't let herself take that next step to attract his attention. It was as if she recognized how little artistic ability she had and coming on to him for a better grade would prove it to the world. Terrible family background however, which made her completely unacceptable as a potential candidate for Mrs. Vitebskin number four.

Professor Vitebskin thought of the soon-to-be-former Mrs. Vitebskin number three and shuddered theatrically. The divorce was going to be very expensive but what could he do? It was time to move on, get that barren witch out of his house and her nasty, sly, sneaking cat along with her. Cinnamon would be pleased as well, although losing the cat meant his precious dog lost his favorite chew toy. On the other hand, unlike the witch, Shelby Bradwell worshipped him for the genius he was. Her adoration and beauty would certainly make for an enjoyable, casual liaison. Co-eds could be so much fun, and they so rarely were willing to say anything untoward afterwards. It was too embarrassing for them to admit how silly and immature they were.

The professor stopped at the grand double front door to the White Elephant, struck by a sudden thought. Shelby would be a sweet treat but having the house for huge gallery showings was far more valuable. If he pursued her, she might say something to that irritating sister of hers or her great-aunt. The great-aunt might be too genteel to say anything but Veronica would undoubtedly make a fuss, starting with refusing to ever host an art exhibit for the Collective again. He'd have to make other, far more expensive arrangements. PanU's display facilities, while convenient, were completely inadequate to fulfill his vision.

No, Shelby Bradwell, despite her delicious and lovely neediness, was out of bounds. At least for now. Professor Vitebskin smiled complacently at his reflection in the freshly polished pink glass window set into the door. If he was patient and scattered a few crumbs of praise, Shelby might approach him on her own and then nobody could complain about his morals.

Professor Vitebskin did not bother knocking at the front door and waiting for admittance. He knew no servant would open it for him as the family was too poor to employ one and, anyways, Shelby was expecting him.

He pushed open the door and stepped into the grand, empty atrium brilliantly illuminated by light cascading through the enormous roof opening high overhead. He paused, soaking in its gloriousness. PanU's own facilities paled in comparison. The wide, polished, outdated hall table was the only piece of furniture. Its unfashionableness worked beautifully in the space, as if it had been made to precisely fit where it sat. The two curved staircases arched to the second floor and beyond to the rooftop terrace. The railing framed the opening to the dome. The staircases' elaborately carved, golden balustrades added just the right, florid touch, glinting in the yellowed sunlight the dome permitted.

He turned slowly, admiring the blank wall space and imagining on them the paintings of his most favored students. Shelby Bradwell would not be in that august group, although … perhaps ….

No, it was far too soon to toss her a crumb this large. She had several semesters to go and he had plenty of time for her. Other sweet young co-eds abounded.

No, he shook his head regretfully. An affair with any student right now might come to the attention of the witch and cost him dearly in the divorce. That barren witch, the professor thought grimly, remembered quite well how *she* had supplanted Mrs. Vitebskin number two and was always on the lookout for younger, presumably fertile rivals. It would be foolhardy to provide her lawyers with ammunition.

"So, pure and unadulterated art it is," he decided. "Who would best benefit from being showcased in this marvelous space?"

He stroked his fashionably razored short beard as he considered how the sunshine from far above would flow over the walls, illuminating the paintings in a way oil lamps never could, followed by a slow, sensuous decline into twilight and velvety gray darkness. Only then the oil lamps would be lit, their flickering light showcasing different aspects of the same paintings. Could he persuade the Bradwells to turn on their expensive electric fixtures? They would insist the Collective reimburse them for the cost and that would be an argument he might not win. More seriously, was the quality of electric light as warm and rich as what the oil lamps provided? Electric light was steady and boring, never changing and that made it dull. No, more aesthetic to not bother. And all the while, no matter what he chose, the opening overhead would continue to provide a soft, low-key glow but it would no longer flood the space with light as it did during the day. Rather, it would act as an unobtrusive focal counterpoint to whatever lighting he chose, there but not there.

The selection process was a demanding and aesthetic challenge, particularly since each painting would not be admired alone, but instead be surrounded by its fellows, competing for the eye of the viewer. Moreover, the paintings for the atrium would set the tone for the rest of the works in the ballroom. Which ones should be saved for the grand finale? What paintings could stand alone? Were there those that would only look their best when contrasted with another? What would be the best order of presentation? He envisioned combinations of works that would progress from the atrium and around the ballroom so the experience builds like a symphony to the final works, its finale surprising, yet inevitable and correct, when the viewer evaluated what had led to that exact moment in both space and time.

"Professor Vitebskin, you surprised me," Auntie Neza said, right in his ear. "I didn't hear a knock at the door."

He jumped, his trance broken, disconcerted at how quietly the stooped old lady moved on that tacky cane of hers. For some mysterious reason, she had chosen a gaudy, shiny hot-pink enamel finish rather than something more appropriately sedate. That pink, the professor thought with a grimace, was a color only suitable for a teenager's nail polish.

"Veronica told me to come on in," he replied quickly, mentally cursing himself for feeling a twinge of guilt over how he and the PanU Artists' Collective were using the Bradwell family's sole asset. The Collective should have been paying far more for this elegant space and the even more spacious, high-ceiling ballroom than with just door receipts, commissions on any sold paintings, whitewashing, and cleaning the building free of Panschin's ubiquitous carpet of terraformers. This space was worth real money.

When Shelby Bradwell had showed up in his studio, after he rejected her wretched scholarship portfolio, Professor Vitebskin inquired how she had been able to afford PanU. After an exhilarating tussle between the sheets, the bursar's secretary had been deliciously accommodating and told him everything. He investigated this social-climbing interloper and discovered the facts about the Bradwell family and what Mr. Bradwell had inflicted on his unfortunate clients.

It was all very sad.

In his opinion, Shelby Bradwell should have never been admitted by PanU. It showed a distinct lowering of standards on both the social and the artistic levels. Nonetheless, as the professor admired the ornate crown molding rather than meet the old biddy's piercing gaze, he had to admit Shelby Bradwell's home was useful. She had offered it to the PanU Artists' Collective in exchange for social acceptance and they had taken full advantage of her naivety and her family's ignorance of the value contained within the White Elephant.

"Well," Neza Molony said tartly, "I'm glad to know my niece gave you free range of our home."

"I would never presume otherwise, Miss Molony," the professor replied. What had happened, he wondered. The old biddy had always been sweet and welcoming at previous shows. This hostile manner was uncomfortably new.

He added "I was admiring the atrium. It needs the right paintings, to do it and them justice. The choice of paintings for the entry, where they will be seen first by visitors, should not be a casual or hasty decision."

"Well, I suppose that's true," Neza said, sounding only somewhat mollified.

"It is true. Now about those easel placements. Veronica implied that you needed assistance with setting them up."

"We wouldn't need assistance if those lazy students of yours did more of the work, rather than expecting an old lady like me to do the heavy lifting." She shook her garish cane at him, making it flash pink rays in the sunlight. He turned his head from the spectacle.

"I see." Professor Vitebskin frowned awfully as her words penetrated the shiny pink slashes her cane burned across his retinas. "More shirking. We'll see about *that*."

He strode towards the ballroom entrance angry at the Collective work party he had sent ahead to get the place set up. Those fools. Didn't they understand the importance of this show? He had run adverts in all the important journals, directed posters to be tacked up all over Panschin, and invited deep-pocketed collectors to see the new crop of artists. Most importantly, everyone who saw the show would acknowledge his own genius for recognizing and nurturing new, groundbreaking talent. The artists he mentored today would fill the museums and collections of tomorrow, lauded by the ages, and every one of them would know who they owed their careers to. It would be Professor Lemuel Vitebskin, with his golden eye for artistic talent, that's who.

He stopped at the ballroom entrance and watched silent and unnoticed. He felt the steam rise in him. Neza had been correct on all counts. Some of the easels lay on their sides. The rest were still waiting to be unpacked, despite the work crew being fully briefed on what to do. Shelby was struggling to open a crate, half-heartedly assisted by that feckless poseur, Kip McGrant, while everyone else was standing around gossiping. Worst of all, not a single painting had been unwrapped and placed on an easel to allow him to make the critical decisions about placement. They loitered in anonymous stacks, still encased in their shipping cocoons.

Professor Vitebskin snarled silently, coldly furious. His time was extremely valuable. It was not to be wasted setting up easels or unpacking paintings. That work was for people who were still on the bottom rung of the ladder of success. Every one of those students knew he made careers but did they care? Apparently not.

Next to him, Neza hissed, "See? Only my Shelby wants to make the show a success. She's the reason anything got done at all. Every time there's a show, the Collective sends over lazier students. Who chose those kids anyway?"

Professor Vitebskin had hand-picked the delegation currently milling about uselessly but he wasn't about to admit that to the old biddy.

He stepped into the middle of the room, clapping his hands with each step, and yelled "What is the meaning of this? I expected results, not this shirking and lazing about!"

Their faces were a delicious blend of shock and horror. Gasps echoed in the suddenly silent room. Many of them, presumably recalling that their participation in the exhibition was being graded, sprang into action. As he and Neza watched, the crates were rapidly crowbarred open, easels assembled, and paintings unpacked.

Professor Vitebskin tapped his gaspingly expensive watch (a genuine heirloom from Olde Earthe) pointedly.

"We have a show to put on, people. A show! Important patrons will attend, see your paintings, and decide if any of you are capable enough artists that they want your art hanging in their homes and businesses," he announced, spurring still greater efforts.

The professor strode around the ballroom as his students slaved, watching intently to see who was particularly diligent. Shelby, he noted with disgust, worked the hardest. She had the smallest amount of talent in the room — even less than the buffoon Kip who had abandoned her to suck up to a girl more socially important but less attractive — and was the least likely student to sell a painting or acquire a patron. Did his more talented protégées work harder and strive for the glittering reward that lay before them? They did not.

You would think, Professor Vitebskin thought with even more disgust as he passed a slacker who he had believed would excel, they didn't care about a career in the fine arts. They just wanted to pass the time while wasting their parents' money. It was depressing; spending his life trying to develop artists from this dross.

Ingratitude, that's what it was. At least none of these ungrateful little lackwits showed the sneakiness of Clyde Monez. He learned his lesson. He had made careful overtures to the instructors in the PCC commercial arts department, offering them a chance to show their own, personal efforts (pitiful though they were). In exchange, they promised to inform him if any of *his* students were subverting a calling towards high art by prostituting themselves on the altar of commerce.

Professor Vitebskin smiled grimly — alarming one student who caught his expression into rearranging a previously perfectly placed painting — thinking of his former protégé's betrayal. If he caught any of his students slumming, he'd toss them out of his studio forthwith. If they wanted to scribble infant wear for department store adverts, they needn't take up precious space at PanU. His studio and his instruction were reserved for serious artists, not commercial hacks.

Hours later, the easels had been finally arranged to Professor Vitebskin's satisfaction and most of them displayed paintings. The ballroom and the entry hall had been swept clean again, removing all traces of packing material and student effort. The exterior of the White Elephant was as white as it could be, short of a fresh coat of whitewash and that wasn't on the schedule for this exhibition. The gravel walks had been re-raked by a grumbling student, a sop the professor threw to Veronica after she pointed out she wouldn't have time to re-rake them to make them sparkle.

From halfway up the stairs in the entry hall, Professor Vitebskin addressed the gathering of students, Veronica, Shelby, and auntie Neza. He gazed down at the group anxiously awaiting his verdict.

"The display looks," he paused for effect, "acceptable."

The waiting crowd, tired and wrung out, breathed out a collective sigh of relief.

"For now."

The crowd wilted. Veronica managed to keep from groaning out loud. Neza frowned at the floor and worried over how soon she could get some more liniment for her joints from Florence. Shelby squeezed her eyes shut and wished the students would leave. More than one person had asked her if she was related to "that Simon Bradwell." The gossip was spreading at last.

When the muttering subsided, Professor Vitebskin said, "I will return tomorrow afternoon before the show to arrange the last, few paintings from our graduates. Those will be delivered tomorrow. I will, at that time, make any last-minute corrections in placement. These members of the Collective," he rattled off a list of names and the time, "must be here to assist me. I expect everyone in class tomorrow morning. No more shirking! I expect much better than this from the future artists of Panschin. Do not disappoint me."

Professor Vitebskin then descended the staircase slowly, watching his students for any signs of disgruntlement. Those malcontents would have to exhibit stellar workmanship in the future to offset their laziness today. Actions had consequences, and it was time they learned that fact. He took his leave of the Bradwells and headed out the door of the White Elephant.

He strode along the streets, whistling cheerfully all the way back to the PanU campus, secure in the knowledge of a job well done. Tomorrow, Professor Vitebskin knew, would be a superior show. He would make it happen.

Back at the White Elephant, as Professor Vitebskin closed the door, Veronica took his place on the stairs. She did not want to give anyone a chance to escape before she had her say.

"You guys the professor said to report tomorrow? I expect you to be early! Not. On. Time. *Early!* There's still plenty of work to do, and I want this place immaculate when the professor arrives." She pointed at each of the named students in turn, starting with the outside crew. "Now get out of here and close the gate behind you."

From the stairs, she watched the Collective leave the White Elephant through narrowed eyes. Shelby stood by the door, smiling and holding it open. Not one person spoke to her. Not a word of thanks, not a goodbye, not a "I'll see you tomorrow." Her sister might have been a parlor maid for all the consideration she received. Veronica's hands gripped the balustrade until her fingers hurt, watching Shelby's face reflect her pain and sadness.

Shelby knew how she was regarded by the other students in the PanU art department and now Veronica knew too.

That night, after Shelby had fallen into bed, Veronica spoke quietly to Auntie Neza. "It's settled. As soon as you can, talk to the bursar's office about PCC. Get Shelby out of that pile of tailings. No wonder she was ready to quit and scrub floors in Dome Six."

Neza fumed, "The nerve of those students. This is our home and not one word of thanks to Shelby or to us do we get. I don't see any of their families opening their home to a parade of strangers to look at ugly paintings."

"Nope," Veronica replied. "I wonder if we should host the Collective again. I do get the White Elephant swept down from top to bottom, even whitewashed, but it's such a hassle dealing with the Collective, those awful paintings, and Vitebskin lording over us all. I was sure it would help Shelby but, well …"

"I don't think it does," Neza said slowly. "Not any more. I'll make an appointment for first thing next week."

"Do that. Get some sleep. Tomorrow's going to be a long day."

Neza suddenly smiled at her great-niece. "It will be a better day, dear girl. We deserve one."

Veronica laughed, suddenly cheerful again. "Yep, a new day so why not a better one? It could happen."

Shelby grimly endured the morning's classes. She was no longer just Shelby Bradwell, poor and talentless hack. She had become, overnight, Shelby Bradwell, daughter of the notorious Simon Bradwell, problem gambler, thief, swindler, liar and embezzler, who then suicided rather than face his defrauded victims and justice in the courts of Panschin. The fact that Shelby had nothing to do with her father's investment business or his crimes didn't matter. Wherever she went on the campus — the classrooms, the hallways, the cafeteria, the studio, even the grassy quad — the whispers and finger-pointing followed her. Being ignored become an idyllic pleasure in retrospect.

The instructors were better behaved. They had the decency to wait until she left their presence to rehash lurid old stories about embezzlement and swindles.

It was with relief that Shelby left the campus for the long walk home to the White Elephant. She didn't wait for Lulu and Florence. She would see many of the students again at home, and she needed time to herself now.

Shelby fumed as she walked, ignoring for the first time ever the flamboyant pansies spilling from the planters and smiling up at her. Afterwards? Well. Maybe it was time to quit hosting the PanU Artists Collective. She'd still have to gut out the remaining semesters Neza had paid for but she wouldn't have to have those people in her home ever again.

The question Shelby chewed over as she walked along, head down, was would Veronica agree? The money from the door receipts was needed, far more desperately than she had realized. Plus, Veronica got plenty of free labor. They would have never been able to keep the White Elephant whitewashed or its exterior walls swept clean without the Collective doing those tasks. Their donated hard work allowed her sister to wring out every bit of energy from the dome-filtered sunshine. The less prepossessing vegetables she grew were food for their own table while the more attractive specimens earned coin at the Dappled Yak, coin Veronica used to pay the lease. That meant the Collective paid twice.

Whichever way Veronica chose, it would be awful. As she walked through the small downtown business district, Shelby noticed the Dappled Yak. The restaurant had a sign in their window advertising fresh, locally grown vegetables. Veronica's vegetables, although the sign didn't say so.

She stopped and sighed wistfully, staring through the plate-glass window at the small round tables filling the room. She had never eaten there, never even gone inside past the kitchen door when she helped Veronica make a delivery. Each table had a cheerful yellow gingham tablecloth, a vase with a bright red zinnia, and many of those tables had customers. The walls were covered by murals of landscapes, giving a feel of being outside. Maybe the Dappled Yak would take her on as a waitress. She could do the minimum effort required by the university, work an afternoon or evening shift waiting tables, and help keep the wolf from the door.

Then Shelby noticed people she recognized from PanU sitting around a table. They were laughing at some joke. She'd be a joke, waiting on people who would despise her still more. It hurt to think about, but the same chance of discovery lurked if she worked almost anywhere in Dome Six. At the Dappled Yak, she'd be closer to home, closer to escape.

Shelby shuddered, jerked away from the window, and plodded home, her head down. The day couldn't end soon enough, but the gallery showing meant she had hours and hours to endure before she could fall into bed and oblivion.

The laughing PanU students annoyed Malcolm Cobb, who lingered over his tea, the last of his lunch, and a slice of wintenberry pie to come. He'd taken to enjoying an early lunch at the Dappled Yak. Alone. He could afford it, it was convenient, he had to eat anyway, and it got him out of the branch office of the bank. It hadn't taken him long to realize he didn't want to eat with his new colleagues. They watched him like hawks, looking for any fault in his table manners. It got tiring to be on his guard all the time, particularly when he suspected he had to meet higher standards than they did.

The food at the Dappled Yak was very good and he was coming to recognize how fresh the salad vegetables were. They didn't have that off-taste announcing they'd been shipped in days before from the open-air steppes farms far to the south, or the metallic pong seasoning everything originating from the hydroponics facility. Nor did they come from the farms outside the dome. The waitress said the steppes were still iced over, trapped in the thrall of the endless Martian winter. But the Dappled Yak, she noted with pride, had fresh vegetables supplied by a local grower.

He thought about her statement as he sipped his tea. A local grower. Who could that be? Did that grower's lease belong to the Second National Bank of Panschin? Agriculture was one of the many things that was never supposed to happen in Dome Two; ornamental gardening was fine since it demonstrated good taste and money to spare.

He thought about the leases he had been reviewing since his arrival at the local branch office. They were stranger than what he had studied in business school. Most of them dated back to Dome Two's earliest days, when only the wealthiest people lived here. As they moved out, many of those leases had been modified extensively. But the bottom line said the lease holders could not do whatever they damn well pleased. Anything not spelled out in the lease required getting permission first from the bank.

So far, he hadn't seen any leases that permitted growing food. Did this grower ask for permission? He picked up the last radish and bit into it thoughtfully, relishing the crisp crunch and peppery taste.

How flexible could he be in a negotiation? He would have to persuade his supervisor who was already proving to be troublesome to work with. Desmond Wong didn't like change, probably because any improvements in how the branch was run would demonstrate exactly how incompetent he was in running the place. The other office hacks were much the same. They worked like wheels turning in a comfortable and familiar rut. None of them were going places. All of them held onto their jobs because of inertia and family connections. He would not get backing from within his own office, making it impossible to negotiate with headquarters in Dome Six. It would be hard enough as it was because of his own background as a scholarship boy.

It would be a shame to shut down a grower who provided vegetables like this. Whoever he was, his produce was quite likely one of the reasons the Dappled Yak stayed in business. The tiny business district depended on supplying local customers since no one came here from one of the other domes to shop or dine.

He would have to be careful, Malcolm realized. He wanted to demonstrate the value inherent within Dome Two, not damage existing businesses. It hadn't taken long to see how many of the local shops were hanging on by their fingernails. During his short time living in Dome Two, he had come to appreciate its openness, the freedom to walk around through the vast interior, and the fascinating mix of high culture and seedy bohemians. The cultural facilities were amazing and most of the time, they sat empty.

A movement at the window caught his eye. There she was again, the brown-haired, willowy beauty he saw sometimes when he was exploring Dome Two. Her hair caught the light, making a fluffy cloud framing her beautiful face. She was alone, not with her two regular girlfriends. She looked miserable.

He put down his fork and stared, his slice of wintenberry pie forgotten. He wondered again who she was.

Malcolm had seen her several times. Each time he saw her, he felt his heart wrench. She was probably a student at PanU. He often spotted her sitting cross-legged in front of a planter of flowers, drawing in a sketchpad. She wore a neat, clean coverall, like so many people in Panschin did, but she didn't look to him like a low-caste girl from the mines. The way she carried herself said upper-caste. Her profile, her slim hands, her beautifully even deep blue-green complexion; they all told him she was not the kind of girl who would ever talk to a jumped-up scholarship boy from the mines.

How could a beauty like her be miserable?

He knew what those girls were like. He'd met enough sisters and cousins of the upper-caste boys he shared classroom space with, first in various prep schools and then at the Panschin School of Business. Those charmed girls floated through their golden lives, insulated from any kind of hardship or pain. Those girls never gave him the time of day. He didn't exist for them. Except when he did and no one was there to watch a princess from a tower in Dome Six indulge in some fun, safe slumming with a bad boy she wasn't supposed to meet. Malcolm smirked at the window, remembering. He'd had plenty of fun too, but it was riskier for him, since he had more to lose. Unlike him, those girls wouldn't end up in the Dirac mines on trumped-up charges. It was risky, but worth it.

This girl though. He could feel his heart seize in his chest again as he watched her expressive, woebegone face. He smiled warmly at her, standing on the sidewalk on the other side of a sheet of glass, but she didn't see him. She never saw him. He didn't exist for her either.

He stood up. This time he would introduce himself, and not stand there tongue-tied. He, Malcolm Cobb, may have been a scholarship boy from the mines but he had real value. He was smart, he worked hard, he was ambitious, he was fit, he was attractive in a rough-hewn sort of way (a classmate's sister had told him that in bed), and not one girl he'd ever been with had a problem with his company. They came back for more.

Another expression flashed across her face as she stared inside the restaurant at another table of customers. She turned away from the window and vanished down the street, without noticing him. He was invisible, a man made of glass, and she didn't see him.

He sat, his heart aching. He saw *her*. Malcolm stared at the table lost in thought. Next time, he would introduce himself to that pensive beauty and then, perhaps, she would see him.

The chipper waitress came by, happy to flirt with a good-looking customer. He was no longer feeling flirtatious, so he paid his tab and left the Dappled Yak to stand on the street, staring down it to where he thought his Dome Two princess went. He wouldn't hesitate next time.

In the meantime, he had work to do.

He had been seeing posters tacked up all over the business district for a gallery showing of fine art presented by the PanU Artists' Collective. Normally, Malcolm wouldn't have bothered with an art show but the posters said this one was located in a house in Dome Two and not at the university. He looked up the street address. It was a property leased from the Second National Bank of Panschin. This was a chance to go inside one of the leased properties without anyone knowing who he was and getting a better feel for the needs and activities of Dome Two residents. He'd have to keep his occupation a secret. If he showed up as the assistant manager of the bank, he'd be allowed in but it was doubtful anyone would talk to him.

The show was tonight and he was fairly sure he knew which house. It was the surprisingly well-kept white house that had real plants growing in the tiny garden. In the meantime, he would dig out the lease from its tomb in the wall of filing cabinets and read it through to discover what was allowed and what was not. It would be a good distraction from his Dome Two princess, who she was, and why she was so unhappy. A vision of her face appeared before him, the very last one he saw before she turned away and darted down the street without ever seeing him. Was it fear?

eronica stretched her cramped fingers and wiggled them. She had spent a long morning prepping the trays of nibbles for the PanU Artists' Collective show. When she tired, she reminded herself this might be the last time. "For Shelby's sake," Veronica repeated as a mantra to stay motivated washing greens, scrubbing roots, and frying blocks of yeast. "I'm doing this for Shelby and not that pack of snobs."

She needed to have everything finished as once the Collective showed up, she'd have to supervise the lazy jerks or they would get nothing done. Veronica slashed a daikon into coins, wishing they would turn into money so she didn't have to put her sister through another gallery show. Or the fingers of some of those jerks, for treating her little sister as worthless.

She caught the sound of the gate creaking and checked the clock. It was too early for Mrs. Grisson to come by with the eggs and despite what she had demanded yesterday, Veronica didn't expect anyone from the Collective to show up one minute earlier than Professor Vitebskin had ordered them to.

The back door opened and Shelby stumbled inside. Her eyes were red and her normally glowing complexion was ashy.

"Shelby?" she asked. "What's wrong? You're home early." She had not seen her sister look so distraught since their mother's death.

"I'm not that early," she replied in a flat voice. "The gallery show, remember? Vitebskin let us go early so I came straight home."

Veronica paused, hoping she'd say more, before saying, "Well, that was nice of him, I suppose."

"I'm going upstairs to wash up. I'll be down to help finish setting up when the Collective arrives."

"Where are Florence and Lulu?"

"I don't know. I didn't wait for them. Do we have to talk? I'm tired. I want to wash up and get ready for the show."

Veronica gave her sister a long, long look over, noting her dried tear tracks and uneven breathing. "Sure. Maybe you should lie down for a bit too. Take your time."

Shelby turned towards the door leading to the hall, then turned back to her sister. Her jaw trembled. She leaned up against the table, letting it support her weight, then slumped into the chair.

"They found out today. Somebody, I don't know who, figured out that I'm Simon Bradwell's daughter and so are you. It was awful, Veronica. The things everyone said. Worst of all, some of the instructors? Dear old dad cheated them too. Students too. One girl," Shelby gulped back a moan. "One girl told me that her family had been ruined."

Veronica frowned at the knife in her hands and then very carefully laid it down on the countertop, keeping the honed edge well away from her and her sister.

"Not that ruined if she could afford to go to PanU."

"Who cares? Maybe she earned a scholarship, unlike me!" Shelby screamed, startling her sister. "Maybe someone in her family put themselves into bankruptcy to pay for that hellhole!" She burst into tears.

Veronica watched her sister sob for a few moments, steeled herself against reopening her own heartache, and then sat down besides Shelby. She put her arms around her sister, stroked her hair, and made soothing noises. She let Shelby cry herself empty.

Before she realized it, she was crying, too; angry tears at their father for destroying their lives and so many others because he couldn't control his own appetites, heated tears at their mother who had given up when her daughters needed her, furious tears at Dean and his family who had abandoned her without a second thought, resentful tears over the vanished relatives who could have helped and refused, embarrassed tears for the casual cruelty of strangers, painful tears for being trapped in Panschin forever.

She choked and coughed and made herself stop. She thought she had cried out those tears long ago. Shelby's tears were fresh, new, raw. She was still learning how to grow an armor shell. She needed her big sister to hold her and be strong for her.

Who was there to hold me, Veronica thought as her sister wept out grief, fury, and anguish.

She heard a chair scrape behind her. She felt a presence. Auntie

Neza sat down and did her best to hold them both.

Auntie Neza had held Veronica on many, many nights when she wept lakes of tears. Veronica swallowed the last of her tears. Shelby needed reassurance more. Her sister's hurt tears were new. Her outrage and grief were old and needed to be set aside. There was a gallery show to put on and it would be just like some sneering member of the PanU Artists' Collective to show up early, and see their anguish. She imagined them acting spiteful towards her little sister for not having a thicker skin, for not being able to take a joke, as if she shouldn't feel the pain from their knives

Veronica let her anger fuel her, filling her with energy. "Neza, can you help Shelby upstairs to wash up? Mrs. Grisson will be here soon with the eggs. We have a show to get ready for."

"That show," Shelby moaned and cried harder.

"Shelby," Veronica snapped out, "we will never host another show for those poncy sods again. This is the last one. Pull yourself together and every time one of those, those self-righteous oafs says something, remind yourself that we will never allow any of those snobs in this house again. I will scrub terraformers off toilets in Dome Six to keep them out."

But the thought of going outside her constricting, familiar, safe little world of Dome Two into the rest of Panschin tied her stomach up in knots. Shelby wasn't the only member of the Bradwell family who had to cope with nasty gossip and mean-spirited innuendo. Going to Dome Six meant possibly running into former friends and cold relatives. Unpleasant memories swamped her, bringing back a few more tears. What would they say, seeing her on her knees scrubbing moss off a wall like some low-caste housemaid? Bile rose, and she choked it back.

Veronica wrenched herself upright, then leaned over the table bracing herself on her hands, trying to control her breathing and ignoring the sting in her eyes. She shoved old memories away, focusing on the here and now.

"But the money," Shelby gasped.

"This is the last show," Veronica said, her voice rough. "We'll figure something out."

Neza nodded, not trusting her own voice.

Outside, the gate shrieked its warning.

"That'll be Mrs. Grisson with the eggs," Veronica announced to the kitten calendar so she did not have to show her own anguished face to her sister or her aunt. "Shelby, you know she'll ask questions so if you don't want to answer them, go upstairs."

"Come on, Shelby," Neza said gently. "Things will get better. You'll see."

Veronica watched her sister and her aunt walk out of the room. Would things ever get better? She forced back the fresh wave of self-pity. They had a roof over their heads, food, even some friends and helpful neighbors, she reminded herself. Things *would* get better. They had to. Time to get back to work, so she forced herself upright, returned to the counter, rinsed her face, and started peeling daikon.

Mrs. Grisson tapped at the back door and came in, bearing in triumph a basket of eggs. Despite being asked, she adamantly refused to use the front door, insisting that a door so grand wasn't for the likes of her. Veronica suspected walking around the White Elephant gave Mrs. Grisson a chance to inspect her gardening efforts as it always took far longer for Helga Grisson to walk around the house than it did anyone else.

"Hi, Veronica," Mrs. Grisson said cheerfully. "Lovely day for a show."

"It's always a lovely day in the spring inside a dome," Veronica replied.

"Well yes! Why without the dome, we'd be shivering in our boots if we hadn't froze to death already. Got to appreciate what you've got, you know."

"Yes, that's true. Thanks so much for the eggs. I know they'll be enjoyed."

"Maybe someone'll buy one of them manky pictures if they eat an egg or two. Soften 'em up, make their head go squashy and then their wallets'll ease open."

Veronica laughed; her spirits revived by Mrs. Grisson's optimism. There was a woman with nerves of steel who coped with everything life threw at her. Someday, she'd find out how Mrs. Grisson managed such a feat.

"We keep hoping the same thing. Sure you don't want to drop in and take a look-see this evening? All new paintings with plenty of nibbles and plonk to make them go down easier."

"Lordy no," Mrs. Grisson said. She wrinkled her nose. "One round of what looks like a chicken's leavings was enough. Why's Shelby going to that silly school anyways? Her picture of my little granddaughter is just like she's alive there on the paper. That school will make Shelby start drawing dirt, like those other students do, and that'd be a real shame."

"Yes, yes it would."

Rather than leaving, Mrs. Grisson fussed over the eggs in the basket for a moment, a sure sign she had more to say. Veronica returned to her vegetables and waited her out, knowing it never took long for Mrs. Grisson to come to the point. She was a busy woman and didn't believe in wasting time.

"One of my boarders, he's a maintenance man up to PanU, did you know that?"

"Uh, no, no I did not." Mrs. Grisson's phrasing implied her information was important enough to require an offer of repayment, even though she, as a good neighbor, might refuse the offer, reserving the right of repayment for later if she needed it.

"Would you like a cup of tea? And a cookie?" Mrs. Grisson would be far more appreciative of the cookies Veronica had baked for the gallery show than the visitors. They would expect it as their due.

"No thanks, Veronica. I know you got plenty to do to get ready for that show. My boarder, he told me that some sod found out about your and Shelby's dad and spread it all over the school last night and this morning."

Veronica breathed out gustily and closed her eyes in pain, reopening them to see Mrs. Grisson watching her in sympathy.

"Shelby found out today. She came home in tears." That was, Veronica discovered, surprisingly hard to admit out loud.

"I don't doubt it. My boarder, he said they were saying awful things, as though our Shelby had anything to do with your dad's crimes. You tell Shelby she's got real talent and everyone in the family loves the pictures she's drawn for us. We know how special she is, and if she needs something, just ask."

Veronica sat down heavily. "People can be cruel. I'll tell Shelby you were asking about her and how much everyone likes her drawings."

"You do that, Veronica. And if you need something, you can ask too," Mrs. Grisson said. "My door is always open to good neighbors like you and your sister and your auntie."

Veronica finished the trays of nibbles, arranged as temptingly as she knew how. She arranged the eggs, carefully deviled and quartered to make them go further, front and center. She kept most of them in reserve, planning to bring them out gradually so they didn't get devoured within seconds. Even if she disliked the cause of avant-garde art more than ever, she'd do the best job she could because she'd rather be damned than show one hint of pain to that pack of sods. She placed the trays in the cold room, then walked back to the kitchen to see what tasks she had left.

The gate shrieked another warning. The clock insisted it was too early for even the most eager-beaver members of the PanU Artists' Collective to arrive. Veronica frowned at the kitten watching her from the wall. More bad news. No, that was being silly. She trotted to the front door, pasted on a smile, and yanked it open without bothering to peer through the pink glass inset or waiting for a knock.

Four strange men stood on her doorstep.

She stared at them, at a loss for words. Were they the thug's friends?

They were a mixed group in appearance, despite wearing new, standard-issue coveralls. The man bringing up the rear was bigger than the thug who had come to the door days ago, asking about subletting the house. Were they here to make fresh threats? Now?

Then she realized they were carrying luggage.

"Uh, hello?" Veronica said.

"Is this the White Elephant?" the man carrying the smallest bag asked. His accent was odd, which meant he wasn't a local. There was a flicker of a smile, an appreciation of her presence, before it vanished. He looked around as if he was unsure of why he was standing there. She opened her mouth to speak and then he butted in.

"Do you have a room?"

Relief washed over her. All thoughts of the coming show vanished. "Yes, yes, I do. Won't you come in?"

Paying guests had arrived at last. They were saved.

It had been an easy walk from the tiny business district to the residential area on the map. As Airik's group walked along, he studied the conditions of the manor houses in miniature lining the street. As each one hove into view, he reconsidered the rightness of his decision to escape the Twelve Happiness Luxury Hotel.

The buildings here, unlike Dome Six, were in various stages of decay. Most of them were cloaked in the ubiquitous carpet of terraformers. Some buildings were furry with as thick a build-up as any he had seen in Dome Four. Most buildings had clean windows, but there were a few where even the windows were caked over. Or so he assumed, as Airik didn't believe anyone would build a residence without windows. The windows of those buildings were indicated by bumps underneath the sweater of moss, outlining their frames.

The business district, not surprisingly, had been better maintained.

Few of the houses had been swept clean recently. The garden areas behind their low, encircling walls were scientific displays of every form of algae, moss, and lichens found on Mars. In many of the gardens, the terraformers grew rampant, as they must have during the earliest days of settlement of the planet. A few showed attempts at actual gardening, ranging from straggling ornamentals to what he easily recognized as serious and dedicated food production.

How do they water these plants? Airik thought. He looked up at the dome looming overhead, blocking sun and wind and rain. How did that immense bowl stay so clean? And on both sides? With all that sunshine, the dome should be wearing a meter-thick layer of terraformers, inside and out. He would have to find out. How did Dome Six stay so clean?

Matching his pace beside Airik, Upton muttered something about his back breaking. Airik ignored Upton's mutterings, ascribing them to having to lug his typewriter in its case, rather than having a servant do so, along with his valise. He glanced behind at Elliot. He was staring around him avidly between tracing their progress on his map. He would have to question him later. His valet had a surprisingly good eye and memory for detail, almost as though he were taking mental notes. He was proving useful as a second set of loyal, reliable eyes. Carmine, bringing up the rear, said nothing but he too would make a report to Airik later on about his impressions.

"Here sir," Elliot announced. He stopped at an intersection, marked in its center with a planter spilling over with marigolds, their flame orange and sunny yellow shockingly vivid against the shaggy, muted greens and browns of the terraformers coating the planter. A sign post reared out of the planter, indicating the name of the street they were crossing. "Oleander Lane. We'll turn left and the White Elephant should be about halfway down at number 626."

"Very good," Airik said. He paused to stare, disconcerted, at the corner building. The once immense mansion was so caked in terraformers that it resembled an overgrown stump. The heavy comforter of moss showed barely a ripple as it shrouded whatever architectural features the building once had. The terraformers in this property's garden looked to be shin-deep. He thought of the Twelve Happiness Luxury Hotel. It was clean to the point of being sanitary. Nothing there was furry-plush other than carpets and towels.

He stood there, contemplating a way to turn back without losing respect, when he caught the far away sound of a bird singing over the low hum of people going about their business under a sound-trapping dome. It was the first bird he had heard since boarding the train in Purnell. A steppes sparrow, based on the staccato rise and fall of its song, unless he missed his guess. His spirits lifted. The bird was a good omen. Bird song was immensely preferable to a cacophony of party horns.

"We'll keep going," he announced.

Besides him, Upton coughed, and then coughed again. He dropped his valise suddenly.

"Airik," he pulled out a handkerchief. "This place looks terrible." He sneezed and blew his nose loudly.

"Yes, it does," Airik admitted. "It's also far quieter and the air feels fresher."

"Because we're stranded in an oxygen factory," Upton muttered. "What *are* we breathing? My lungs are bathing in spores."

Despite how much Upton loathed the Twelve Happiness Luxury Hotel, everything he had seen here was making the hotel look like heaven. It certainly had far more attractive scenery in its female staff than anyone he had seen on the streets since their departure. The girl-watching there was superb. He'd also managed to chat up some of the female guests on the wonders of Panschin. He had yet to get further than the lobby with any of them, but he had hopes. Regrettably, Airik would never accept his secretary's preferences as a reason to put up with the Twelve Happiness Luxury Hotel so Dome Two it was.

Airik led the way down Oleander Lane, looking up at the house numbers. Upton groaned and shifted the typewriter with his valise, trying to balance how quickly they pull his arms from their sockets. Could he coax Carmine into carrying another bag? No, Upton thought with dismay. The bodyguard already thought he was a lightweight. Why confirm his opinion?

Halfway down the block, Airik stopped, and the group was rewarded by the sight of a mansion in good repair, standing proudly among its furrier neighbors. Even without the street address, Airik recognized the White Elephant. This building gleamed white in the dome's watery sunshine. Its completely useless shutters – shutters! In a dome! – gleamed a cool, clean gray against the white walls. They were trimmed out in pink and a darker gray to echo the roof tiles. Even the lacy wrought-iron balustrade atop the roof tiles looked clean and sharp silhouetted against the dome. No terraformers coated and concealed this building. The low stone wall had its share of lichens, but it too, had been recently swept clean, revealing the rough granite chunks it had been constructed from.

He opened the wrought-iron gate and winced at the screech of unoiled metal. It was surprising when the building was so well maintained. Inside the gate, the gravel path sparkled white. Airik paused to let Upton catch up while he looked around with an evaluating eye. This tiny garden was filled with plant beds edged with stones. He wondered why they were sunk into the gravel, instead of heaped up as normal. Their contents varied wildly; lettuces and other greens, radishes, tied-up tomatoes that had yet to set fruit, and more vegetables at varying stages of development. Other beds were filled to bursting with terraformers running rampant. That was strange but the vegetable beds were immaculately weeded so he assumed the gardener know what he was doing.

Seeing the kitchen garden sent a pang of homesickness shooting through him for Shelleen, so far away. He shrugged it off. The needs of the demesne and what he could learn from the Conference came first.

Airik led the group up the gravel path towards the grand double front door. It was quiet enough he could hear the gravel crunching beneath their feet. He might be able to finally focus on the immense amount of material he had to learn. The Biennial Mining Conference, despite all the aggravations, had provided him an avalanche of information to digest and the promise of more to come.

He stopped on the wide front threshold, a slab of very fine pink and gray granite speckled with black and polished to a sheen. The double doors each had an insert of pink glass, matching the transom and sidelights, and concealing the house's interior. The doorway was framed with the only ornamental plants he had seen inside the stone wall; two planters spilling over with marigolds, the same kind as were in the planter at the intersection. He searched for the door knocker and found none. Only a shadow on the paint showed where a pair had been installed. He reached out to rap his knuckles on the door when it was wrenched open.

The young woman stared at him for a long moment, as though she almost recognized who she was seeing and was trying to place him.

"Uh, hello?" Her voice was pitched low, lower than he expected in a woman. She enunciated clearly and in that strange way he had come to identify with Panschin.

"Is this the White Elephant?" Airik asked. He looked around, stunned at how beautiful an entrance hall could look. He also registered a row of easels against each wall, with what appeared to be the results of target practice involving mud and mustard. He finished up by looking at her. She didn't seem to know what to do with him, so he smiled. She smiled in return and he thought, Do not let her recognize me. His face resumed its old ways and he asked, "Do you have a room?"

Veronica smiled broadly at him, and he had this impression that she was welcoming him home.

Oddly, it didn't bother him.

"Yes, yes, I do. Won't you come in?" she said fervently.

Saved, we're saved, Veronica thought, then amended, "at least for another month or two."

To the party she said, "I'm Veronica Bradwell. Welcome to the White Elephant." She led the way through the spacious atrium to the table waiting between the wings of the double staircase spiraling upwards to the second floor and then the rooftop terrace. The guestbook lay open as if in anticipation.

Veronica turned to the men. They were staring all around them, as well they might. The contrast between the beautifully designed soaring space with its impressively complex crown molding, ornate double staircase spiraling up to the rooftop opening two floors above, polished floor, gilded balustrades, and the ugly paintings of mud and dirt was dissonance made visual.

"I'll need your names please," she said, opening the guestbook to a new, blank page. That way, the new guests wouldn't see how long it had been since she had hosted anyone and wonder what was wrong with the White Elephant.

"I am Airik Jones," the leader of the group said. He nodded and with a hand introduced the men: "My cousins Upton, Elliot, and Carmine."

Veronica stopped writing. Cousins? Really? He expected her to believe that? Airik and Upton bore a faint resemblance in their noses and the tinge of red in their hair, but Elliot and Carmine didn't resemble anyone but themselves. Their coveralls were so new they were still starchy. Why would he lie? Then she thought of the lease and desperately needed money.

"Of course," she chirped. "Are you in town for the Biennial Mining Conference?"

Airik hesitated, then said, "Yes, we are."

Veronica smiled eagerly at him. She could help him, ensuring he was happy with his choice of staying at the White Elephant.

Her smile had an unexpected effect on Airik. *She knows,* he thought. *This won't work. She wants an affair, she wants money, she wants something. I'll be stuck with that damned hotel. I'll never get anything done and this entire trip to Panschin will have been wasted.*

"I believe most of the conference events are taking place in Dome Six. There are several transtube stations within walking distance. I'll mark out the best ones for you," Veronica said. "Officially, the transtube station in the business district is closer, but everyone here uses the one down the block when they have to go to Dome Six."

"Thank you, Miss Bradwell." Airik couldn't quite conceal his relief.

She hemmed for a moment, worrying Airik again.

"Ah, will you be wanting separate rooms?"

"Yes. And I will need space to spread out paperwork."

"I can do that. Will you be staying long?"

"Until the end of the conference, Miss Bradwell."

Veronica thought her heart would stop. Almost two weeks of paying guests! And four separate rooms!

"That will be," she named her price, "for each of you per night. In cash, please and in advance." *Please, please, please, let him agree and pay,* she fretted.

Airik added up the numbers mentally. He couldn't keep himself from reacting. Miss Bradwell's rates for their entire stay wouldn't cover the cost of a single night for him alone at the Twelve Happiness.

"This does include breakfast?" he asked suspiciously.

"Yes, that's why we're called a bed and breakfast," Veronica shot back and wanted to bite her tongue off. She smiled at him as apologetically as she could manage.

She doesn't have any idea who I am, Airik realized. If she did, she would have fawned all over me and then asked for ten times as much money.

"This is acceptable, Miss Bradwell."

"Veronica! Do we have guests?" a voice called out from overhead.

"Auntie Neza, yes we do. Mr. Jones? My aunt Neza Molony."

Airik took a good look at the old woman limping down the stairs, shiny pink cane in hand. There was no sign of recognition on her curious face as she looked him and his group over carefully.

"Is there anything else I should know, Miss Bradwell?"

The gate's cry was followed by crunching up the gravel at a good clip, and the front door was flung open. Two young women trotted in, both out of breath.

"Veronica, Shelby didn't wait for us. Do you know where she is?" Florence panted out.

Lulu stared at the strange men standing next to Veronica by the hall table and the open guest book at Veronica's hand. "We got guests?"

"Yes, we do. Shelby came home already. She's upstairs. Go check on her, while I deal with our guests," Veronica said. She tried to beam a message to Florence and Lulu to not ask any more questions and to her great relief, they gave the Jones men searching looks and then walked around them to climb the stairs. Auntie Neza turned and slowly made her way back upstairs as well.

"Are these other guests, Miss Bradwell?" Airik asked.

"No, they're my sister and my, uh, cousins," she answered.

He seemed to be the only member of the Jones party who was able to speak. How strange, Veronica thought, although he was not the only one with eyeballs. That Upton cousin made no bones about enjoying the view of Florence and Lulu trotting up the stairs. Fortunately, he didn't speak. The other two men, if they paid attention, were far more discreet about their roving eyes.

Airik kept his expression naturally neutral, but suspicion arose in him. He had also watched Florence and Lulu, both attractive young women, trot up the stairs along with the old woman to meet another presumably attractive young woman. And here was Miss Bradwell, also very attractive, standing in front of him with only a table to separate them. He recalled the concierge at the Twelve Happiness and his salacious "special services" with an inward shudder. Better find out exactly what kind of a hotel he was standing in.

He leaned over the table, embarrassed at having to ask this question. "I beg your pardon for asking. Do you make introductions, Miss Bradwell? Intimate ones?"

Veronica blinked. She was silent for a long, uncomfortable pause as she puzzled over his question. Then she got it, and her face flamed with embarrassment. Even though he spoke in a low tone, the room's architecture made sure everyone heard it. He might as well have stood in the street and shouted.

"Certainly not!" she snapped, rearing back in outrage. "We are a respectable household. If you insist on that sort of, of, uh, 'accommodation,' you must go elsewhere. Like Dome Six." She forced herself to keep calm. She gripped the edge of the table and added, "I also do not provide sightseeing tours, introductions to important people or celebrities, arrange for shopping expeditions, provide transportation, or anything else that a hotel offers." She stared at him, waiting tensely to see what he would say.

He showed no sign of being offended, disappointed, or titillated. "I see. If I may, what do you provide, Miss Bradwell?" Airik asked doggedly.

"A clean room for each of you, privacy, and breakfast. If you want other meals, you have to arrange for them in advance, and I'll charge you for them."

Airik couldn't figure out why he kept questioning Miss Bradwell, remaining in her presence. He should have checked in by now and been in his room reading briefing papers. "You do want to rent rooms to us, though. Is that correct?"

"Yes, yes, of course. But Mr. Jones, I want you to be comfortable and happy with us and that means you have to understand what I will and won't do," Veronica replied.

"Very good then, Miss Bradwell," Airik replied. He liked clear rules and these seemed clear enough, although the word "happy" had recently acquired unpleasant connotations of organized, mandatory cheerfulness with a psychotic edge. "We will have privacy?"

"Yes. Oh, lordy. I forgot," Veronica said and bit her lip.

Airik arched an eyebrow at her.

She gritted her teeth, hoping he wouldn't decide to leave for greener pastures someplace else when she told him what was in store for the evening.

"The White Elephant is hosting a gallery showing starting tonight for the Panschin University Artists' Collective. There will be some noise but as long as your group stays upstairs, you won't be bothered."

Mr. Jones looked puzzled. "An artists' collective?"

"Yes," Veronica said. She waved her hand around at the paintings adorning the space. "They created these paintings. My sister is a member, and we help them out by hosting showings. All of these paintings are for sale. Our opening night, that's tonight, will have lots of people, food, conversation, and maybe," – she had to pause to keep the disdain from her voice – "someone will buy a painting. There's more in the ballroom and a few more are arriving in the next two hours." She inclined her head towards the blank space right behind her. The movement shifted her ponytail of glossy, dark hair draped across her shoulder and against her neck.

Airik looked around again at the paintings on their easels. They did not improve with a more careful viewing. Nor did the sunlight streaming in from above highlight any of their attractive attributes as it did with Miss Bradwell's hair and her blue-green, beautifully even skin.

He noted this unaccustomed conclusion with surprise and wrenched his attention back to the topic at hand. "Are they all like this?"

"I'm afraid so," Veronica replied. "They are, so I am told, avant-garde art that is beyond the understanding of mere bourgeois mortals like me." She smiled suddenly at him and chuckled.

Airik felt his heart seize at the sound of her sharing what he thought might be a small joke with him. He firmly repressed the curious, unfamiliar sensation, along with his sudden, intense awareness of her glossy, dark head of hair.

"Anyways," Veronica went on, "I'll try and keep the noise of the last-minute preparations down. Oh! I know I don't provide meals other than breakfast, but we will be serving extensive nibbles this evening if you and your" — she hesitated and glanced at each of them in turn —

"cousins wish to come downstairs. Otherwise, I provide a list of restaurants in the area who would be thrilled to have your business."

Airik's expression did not change, while Upton looked interested. The other two men's expressions remained blank. She recognized that lack of facial mobility. Servants, Veronica deduced.

"Very thoughtful of you, Miss Bradwell," Airik said.

"However," Veronica said, "if you do come down, please do not show any interest in any of the paintings unless you actually want to buy one. These artists, you can't imagine what they're like, will pester you to no end if they think you have any money."

Airik allowed himself a cool smile, thinking of the money-grubbers who had pestered him. Artists couldn't possibly compete in that avaricious league. "That won't be a problem."

"As long as you don't encourage them, they'll leave you alone," she added, wanting to be perfectly clear about the peril her guests were venturing into.

"These artists understand the meaning of 'no'?" Airik asked, eyebrows slightly raised.

Veronica waved her hand at the paintings again and made a face. "They're used to rejection. I'm sure you can see why." She noticed that Mr. Jones had cool, very intelligent hazel eyes.

"Very good." Airik nodded to Upton, who approached the table. He pulled from inside his coat a wallet. She registered its weight. He glanced at the bill, unsnapped a side clasp, and pulled a handful of coins. Veronica wanted to scream and dance as he counted out the heavy silver coins, each adorned with proud Ares crushing a representation of Olde Earthe beneath his armor-shod feet.

She scooped the coins and stuffed them into her coverall's pockets. "May I ask where you're from, Mr. Jones?" she asked, keeping her voice calm. She congratulated herself for not giggling manically with each coin she picked up, earmarking them as she went for current and future needs.

Airik hesitated. "Barsoom."

Veronica caught his hesitation and thought, Sure you are, wearing brand-spanking-new coveralls like I see on the streets every day. But what do I care? Aloud she said smoothly, "How exciting. All the way from Barsoom for the mining conference. I've never been there. Panschin will be very different for you, I'm sure. Shall we go upstairs and get you settled?"

She walked around the table and picked up Airik's bag, along with another piece of luggage.

He stared at her for a moment, unmoving, so she waited for him to get the hint.

"Do you have no staff, Miss Bradwell?"

Oh lordy, Veronica thought in dismay. What is it now?

"No, I do not," she said. "Me, my sister, my aunt, and my cousins, as I said. I'll be back down to get the rest of your bags. Let's get you upstairs before the Collective shows up."

"Put my bags down, Miss Bradwell, and step away. Now."

"Please, it's all right," she said. "We offer the same bellhop service as a hotel, only in our own way. Inwardly, she prayed, Please, please, don't back out when I've finally got some money. But she did as he asked.

To her surprise, Airik stepped forward and picked up his valises.

"You may proceed, Miss Bradwell," he said.

Veronica gave him a quizzical look. Not one of her other guests had ever carried their own luggage. She shrugged mentally and smiled at him. Then, even more surprising, Mr. Jones caught his cousin Upton's eyes, flicked his own at the valise and large case at his cousin's feet, and Upton picked up his own luggage, as did the other two cousins who didn't look at all like relatives.

She noticed that they did not have to be reminded to carry their own luggage. Definitely servants.

"Thank you, Mr. Jones. Right this way."

As Airik followed Veronica up the stairs, he turned the thought over and over that Miss Bradwell had no staff to assist her. He wouldn't be bothered. He would be left in peace. He could work. He could feel himself relax with each step up the properly designed and constructed curving staircase to the second floor. He had made the correct decision.

Upstairs, Veronica turned to the right side of the landing, leading her new guests down the normally empty wing. She was deeply grateful Shelby and Florence had scrubbed the guest wing from top to bottom in anticipation of the Biennial Mining Conference. Every room sparkled and there wasn't a terraformer to be seen. She hoped that Neza or someone, knowing they actually had guests, had thought to race down and open all the windows in the guest rooms and pull back the drapes, letting the light inside to show off how spotless the rooms were.

Airik paused as soon as he entered the hallway as the ceiling caught his attention. It was studded at regular intervals by what looked like shiny, giant faceted stones, as though he was looking at the bottom of diamonds in their settings. There were four in all. They glowed, spilling light into the otherwise unlit hallway. A window at the far end provided the other illumination as did the light coming from the open ceiling from the atrium. He studied that too, having never, before coming to Panschin, seen buildings with big holes left open to the sky deliberately cut into their roofs. In his experience, skylights required glass and plenty of flashing to keep out the weather.

"What are these objects in the ceiling, Miss Bradwell?" he asked.

"Deck prisms," she replied. "Most houses in Dome Two have them and I suppose plenty of other places in Panschin do too."

She pointed towards a coordinating set of equally shiny flat disks set in the floor of the hallway, one disk in front of each pair of doors. They were the size of dinner plates, indicating the tops of their ceiling counterparts directly overhead were the same size. Each door, Airik noted, was topped with an open transom, probably to better distribute the light.

Veronica said "as you can see, we've also got deck prisms in the floor and there are some on the ground floor for sublevel number one. They let sunlight fall through from the dome into the house."

Airik stepped up to the floor disk and peered down. He couldn't see through it. He looked up to its partner in the ceiling overhead. The faceting kept him from seeing through it to the outside. This was probably, he deduced, the reason why he couldn't see down through the floor prisms to the level below. The faceting refracted and broke the light, increasing the sparkle while maintaining privacy. Fascinating. He would have to see about installing prisms in the manor house in Shelleen.

"I can step on these, Miss Bradwell?"

"You sure can, Mr. Jones."

He studied the prisms again, making the rest of his party wait patiently, then made his best guess after running down the possibilities. What a wonderful concept for maximizing free sunlight. "Are they glass?"

"They are, Mr. Jones."

"Why are they called deck prisms? I understand the prism part but not the deck."

Veronica puzzled over his question. She finally said "You know, I have no idea. Everybody calls them that."

How nice, she thought. He waited for me to answer and he's not being nasty because I don't know why they're called deck prisms. She smiled at him again. Airik Jones was surprisingly easy to smile at. The light streaming from the prism over his head caught the reddish tint in his hair, making it catch fire.

Airik stepped on the disk and then stepped off it, testing how it felt underfoot. Honesty is so refreshing, he thought. She didn't lie or make excuses. She didn't know and she said so.

Behind them both, Upton watched the interchange and wanted to groan. He was tired, his nose was running again, his arms hurt from the weight of the typewriter in its case, and if Airik thought this was the way to make conversation with a pretty young woman, he was mistaken.

Outside, the gate shrieked its warning.

"Oh, dear," Veronica said. "That must be the Collective with the last of the mud paintings. Uh, this door" – she indicated the first door on the left – "is the shared loo. We have our own so you'll have some privacy. The door opposite is for storage. After that, the next six doors are guest rooms."

She trotted down the hallway to the second door on the left, opening it for Airik to follow.

He peered inside, seeing a quiet, simple room. The bamboo floors shone in the cool light coming in from the open windows. Their heavy, deep pink brocade drapes had been fully pulled back. The walls were pale cream. The furniture consisted of a large bed, dresser, a small table, a chair, a mirror, and, surprisingly after the dreadful paintings he had seen downstairs, a fairly good rendering of a vase of flowers. A brightly colored braided rug lay next to the bed.

"Are all the rooms like this, Miss Bradwell?"

"Yes, they are." Veronica was distracted by the sound of the front door opening and people coming in and talking. She recognized Lulu's and realized she had taken charge. Good. She wouldn't take any grief from the Collective. An older student had once, during a previous show, goosed Lulu. She had whipped around and slapped him across his face as hard as she could and screamed at him to keep his damned paws to himself or she'd cut them off at the elbows. The onlookers were appalled and delighted at the free show. The student was mortified at being caught out so publicly, and according to Shelby, spent the rest of the term living it down. Lulu remained unembarrassed and uncowed and that student never again got fresh at the White Elephant. Even better, the other more forward members of the Collective also got the message. Their eyes might roam but their hands stayed at home.

Lulu also didn't tolerate laziness.

Veronica decided to relax about the situation unfolding in the atrium. She could spend time with her paying guests upstairs, knowing downstairs was in good hands.

"The rooms are all the same so you can choose as you like," she said.

Airik turned around slowly, taking in the space, then walked to the open window to look out. Down below, he saw several young men wrestling large, flat, wrapped rectangles up the walk toward the double doors.

"More paintings, Miss Bradwell?"

Veronica came to the window to stand next to him. "Yep, sure are. These paintings are from Professor Vitebskin's special students. They've graduated, but they're building their career in the fine arts so they still show with the Collective."

"I see," Airik said, wondering how you could have a career painting pictures that looked like a close-up of a badly managed excavation site. He didn't want to move away from the window, as it was very pleasant standing so close to Miss Bradwell. She smelled faintly of violets, also very pleasant.

He pushed the thought away.

"Does each room have a table similar to this one?"

"Yes, they do."

"I may need to move them around to give me enough space to spread out my reports."

A crash resounded from downstairs.

"Damn them," Veronica swore. She flushed, wanting to bite her tongue again. "Forgive me, please. Move the tables as you need to, Mr. Jones. I'll bring up the restaurant list so you and your cousins can get dinner later on." She nervously shifted her weight, caught between helping paying guests and keeping an eye on the Collective.

Airik noted her distress. "Go take care of downstairs, Miss Bradwell."

She smiled at him again, wondering why it was so easy to smile at this stranger. "Remember, if you go downstairs to see the show, you don't have to buy anything."

They heard another smaller crash followed by a woman swearing. Her invective was loud, inventive, detailed, colorful, and she did not once repeat herself.

To her surprise, the large silent man spoke. "Nice use of words."

"Lordy," Veronica said, wanting to wince at Lulu's language. "I'd better rescue Lulu before she strangles some idiot student."

She ran out the door, making sure to close it behind her, and they heard her quick footsteps echoing down the hall.

"This is quite different from the Twelve Happiness," Upton said. He didn't sound happy. Taking a good look around the room, he cataloged its faults. Where was the plush carpet his feet could sink into up to his ankles? The expensive art? The mirrors? The exquisite objects carefully arranged on each flat surface? The immense floral arrangements scenting the air? The complimentary champagne, array of pastries, and fruit tray?

Airik gave him a long, cool gaze reminding Upton, clearer than any words could, who was the daimyo and who was not.

"Yes," Airik said, "Quieter and far less intrusive in every way. Carmine, I need you and Elliot to move the tables from the other rooms so I have space to spread out reports. Elliot, take care of the baggage and as soon as Miss Bradwell sends up the list of food places, go out and place an order. Annotate the map as needed. Upton, get out the reports. I'll start with the Jandinaire specifications."

He was rewarded with a chorus of "yes, sir."

"Sir?" Carmine said.

"Yes?"

"With everyone downstairs for this artist thing, I need to take a good look around the White Elephant. See what I can see."

Airik gave his bodyguard a cool nod of approval.

"Report back with your findings."

"Yes, sir."

Veronica stopped on the stairs to see Lulu telling one of the Collective off amid the chatter, unwrapping noises, and thuds. She hoped Shelby had gotten herself together enough to help set up the last few paintings. If she didn't show up, it would be talked about. If she arrived looking hurt and wounded, it would be talked about more. The best-case scenario was for Shelby to work hard and keep her head high. Despite the gossip, no one could find fault with her behavior.

Her own behavior was a different story. It was going to be darned hard to keep control of herself, while wanting to toss the entire pack of the Collective along with their ugly canvases out onto the street. She paused halfway down the stairs to breathe slowly; her fingers clenched around the banister. She would earn half the door receipts. Despite Mr. Jones' money weighing down her pocket, she couldn't afford to throw away good coin. She would never again host a gallery showing in the White Elephant and who knew when the next guest would show up?

That led to thoughts of Mr. Jones. He had been surprisingly easy to talk to since it seemed like he genuinely wanted information. He had looked very uncomfortable asking about "intimate introductions," almost as though he was forcing himself to ask such a question because he felt he had to for some strange reason. That Upton cousin would have leered and said something racy, no doubt on that score. Not Mr. Jones. He was a gentleman.

She stopped again. Why did she feel comfortable around Mr. Jones?

Veronica bit her lip again, thinking hard. Comfortable was not an emotion to trust. She had felt comfortable around Dean Kangjuon and look how that had ended. No, emotions of any kind weren't to be trusted, especially with a man she didn't know at all. Once the mining conference was over, Mr. Jones would leave, along with his cousins who so obviously weren't cousins. And why would someone who could afford servants stay at the White Elephant?

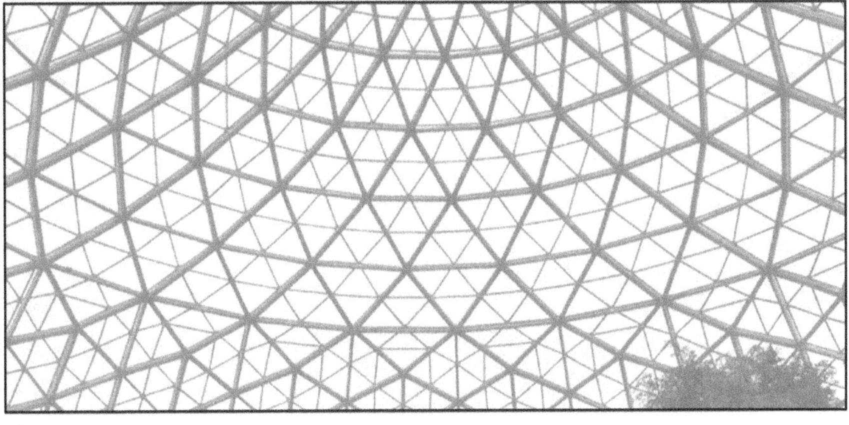

irik plunged into the Jandinaire specifications report, able, at last, to concentrate. As he expected, they glossed over certain maintenance issues he already knew about while highlighting only the successes of their patented processes. The report was very carefully written so anyone without prior knowledge would assume that Jandinaire's safety equipment would perform flawlessly and be easy to maintain, thus worth the high cost. He knew better. He had read their past reports along with analyses supplied by their competitors.

"Upton?"

His secretary looked up from unpacking and sorting the rest of the paperwork. "Yes, sir?"

"Take notes." He waited until Upton was ready, then proceeded: "The Jandinaire equipment has the following flaws so Shelleen requires subsequent modifications and price reductions if they expect a deal." Airik reiterated them in detail.

As he took dictation, Upton relaxed. The daimyo was back on track at last. It might be worth hiding in this seedy dump in run-down Dome Two.

They spent the next few hours working through the more important proposals. Elliot brought in sandwiches and drinks from a restaurant Miss Bradwell recommended called the Dappled Yak. Airik appreciated that they were simple, well-made, and quite good. Somehow, the Dappled Yak managed to avoid the metallic pong he noticed in the greens at the Twelve Happiness.

His only other interruption came about an hour after Miss Bradwell left Airik to work in peace. After moving the tables and helping unpack, Carmine left to examine the White Elephant for security issues. He reported to Airik of his findings.

"Sir? As Miss Bradwell says, there's five people living here. One old lady plus the four young ladies. The old lady gets a room to herself in the other wing, the other ladies share, two to a room. None of them look to be those kind of women, like what the hotel kept offering. If they are those kind of women, they don't bring their work home. The other three bedrooms in the other wing are empty."

"Empty of people?" Airik asked. It was very odd that a building of this size would have only five people living in it and all of them female. There were twelve bedrooms alone and that didn't include servants' quarters wherever those were hidden and then there was that ballroom. Had Miss Bradwell lied about other staff or servants? What was going on? And why did he care?

"Barebones empty, sir," Carmine replied. "Not so much as a broken chair in them. Swept clean regularly from the look of them, but nobody lives there. Upstairs there's a terrace that covers the whole house. Mostly empty, too. Got a few chairs, beat-up sofa, and a table at one end and a small painting setup at the other. Nice view of the area from up top if you don't mind all that glassteel hanging right over your head."

Carmine also discovered a carefully hidden set of paintings on the rooftop terrace, ones that strongly contrasted with the ugly canvases in the atrium. He chose not to mention them since the painter clearly didn't want them revealed and their presence did not affect Airik. He covered them back up, making sure no one knew he had found them.

"And downstairs? Miss Bradwell implied there were belowground levels to the house."

Airik knew, from his research for the trip, that much of Panschin lay beneath the domes in repurposed mining tunnels. The vast majority of the working-class population lived there, many of those miners and their families rarely coming aboveground into the domes. Even fewer ever went outside the domes.

"Haven't checked yet, sir. Downstairs aboveground is a nuthouse. All these people getting in each other's ways trying to hang more ugly pictures. Miss Bradwell's riding herd on them and not getting any place."

"I see," Airik said. He paused. "Does she require assistance?"

Upton stared at his boss's profile and exchanged surprised shrugs with Elliot, who looked equally baffled. Carmine had better control but he was also standing in front of Airik.

He said, carefully, "I don't believe so, sir. Main trouble, from what I could see from the landing, was that she wanted them to work and they won't. So her and her sister and those two cousins are doing most of the job unpacking and rearranging. The others down there, all from the Collective I guess, are mostly standing around jawing when they're not getting in the way. She said something about some professor showing up, and he wouldn't be pleased."

Airik leaned back, his eyes closed for several minutes evaluating Carmine's report, oblivious to his baffled, waiting staff. Did he want to assist Miss Bradwell? She had rented him rooms but he had no further obligations to her, and she had been clear about her obligations to him. Her expectations from him were those of any paying guest: paying promptly, behaving like a gentleman, and not making too much of a mess. He had a mountain of work waiting for him, and he did not need to add to it by taking on Miss Bradwell's problems.

More importantly, he was safely anonymous as long as he remained within those rooms. Going downstairs meant being surrounded by the … Collective was it? It was possible a student might recognize him. This professor, whoever he was, would grasp the importance of the daimyo of Shelleen. Since his arrival, Airik had seen his sketched image in every newspaper in Panschin along with grossly exaggerated stories of Shelleen's discovery of Red Mercury and its wealth, real and potential. It was better to remain where he was, focused on his business.

Still, it bothered him that Miss Bradwell needed help. Why? He had no idea why it bothered him. He shrugged off those disquieting emotions and returned to the proposal from Maerski laying before him on the table. They wanted to participate in the initial excavation of the Red Mercury Lode, exchanging their expertise for future favors to be determined by them at a later date, along with exactly how much they expected to be paid. They must think he was an ignorant yokel, Airik decided, and began dictating a letter refusing their proposition. Instead, he proposed an alliance that would benefit Shelleen while throwing them some money, albeit a much smaller amount than Maerski expected.

As he spoke and Upton wrote, the noise from downstairs kept distracting him. Perhaps later, he would visit the show and see if the paintings had miraculously improved or if the artists could explain their aesthetic choices to his satisfaction. If he stayed in the background, wearing standard issue coveralls, he could remain unnoticed. He smiled at the prospect. No one would expect a daimyo at a student art show far from his demesne. Most of those newspaper drawings didn't look much like him anyway, giving him another potential layer of protection. His decision made, he was able to concentrate fully on the report at hand.

Veronica did not race downstairs to stop Lulu from throttling some student who probably deserved it. Instead, she checked on Shelby. She expected to find her little sister sobbing or hiding, attended by auntie Neza wielding sympathetic cups of mint tea. To her surprise, her sister was not burying herself in their shared room. It was empty, as was Neza's room and Lulu and Florence's shared bedroom. She thought for a moment. Could Shelby be hiding from the Collective, those snobby sods, up on the rooftop terrace? There was the risk that some student from PanU would go up there to gape at the skyline within the dome so probably not. There were also the subbasement levels, but getting there meant going down the grand central staircase where she was sure to be spotted by someone from the Collective. But if Shelby did venture into the subbasement catacombs, she'd never be found until she wanted to be.

Veronica chewed on her lip, thinking. Would Shelby be upset enough to hide down there, in those spooky, echoing, poorly lit rooms? She rarely went belowground without a compelling reason and when she did, she hated going past the area lit by the rooftop opening. She always wanted a rushlight to light her way and once downstairs, tried to stay near the light-shafts. Shelby didn't even like going into the metro stations to use the transtubes. Which was the lesser of two evils: the subbasement levels or the PanU Artist's Collective?

From downstairs, she heard Lulu yelling, her creative swearing echoing up the atrium. Veronica groaned. Maybe Shelby was in the ballroom helping out. She headed downstairs and took over, to the great relief of the Collective. She sent Lulu to set up tables in the dining room where the snacks would go.

Unfortunately, she quickly realized Lulu had gotten more work out of them than she would. The members of the Collective had decided that her wishes could be ignored. It had to be because the students were afraid of Lulu since she, unlike Veronica, radiated menace. Lulu didn't have anything to lose by roughing up an upper-caste student as she could disappear down into the tunnels where she'd never be found and they could tell. As least, that's how it seemed to Veronica after a very frustrating half-hour. She had to resort to threatening them with Professor Vitebskin, and to her horror, wishing impatiently he would appear and take charge.

She'd never had so much trouble getting the Collective to follow orders before. As Shelby had reported, the gossip was finally spreading across PanU. No one in the Collective wanted to do anything helpful for Simon Bradwell's daughter. No wonder Shelby was hiding, but where?

Veronica took a quick pass through the ballroom, hoping to find her sister, and there she was, grimly unpacking another painting and ignoring everyone gossiping around her. She trotted over to her sister, glaring at lazy students that she passed. One of them was actually leaning up against an easel and putting it in danger of falling over.

"Shelby," Veronica whispered, when she reached her sister. "You okay?"

"Yes," her sister muttered. "This is the last time, right? For ever and ever?"

"Yep," Veronica said, looking coldly around them at the beautiful, high-ceilinged room filled with mud-smeared canvases. "Never again. I have never seen the Collective being this useless. Worthless deadweights, every last one of them."

Shelby straightened her back with a groan, picked up the painting from its display easel and turned it upside down, frowned at it, then rotated it again another quarter-turn. It did not look better to Veronica but Shelby seemed happier with its new orientation.

"They think we're the worthless deadweights. Everyone here knows the story about dear old dad, in great detail. As a result, they've decided they don't have to work for a pile of tailings like us. We should work, but they don't have to. We're not good enough to tell any of them what to do," she said bitterly. "Like we're cheating them into working."

Veronica clenched her fists as fury shot through her. "Shelby, if I didn't need the money from this show, I'd throw those damned sods out right now. I'm so sorry to put you through this."

"Don't be," her sister replied. "You have to do this, I have to do this, and afterwards, well, we don't have to do this anymore."

The sisters' eyes met and, for once, they were in perfect accord.

"I am, for the very first time, looking forward to Vitebskin's arrival," Veronica said. "He'll have a fit when he sees these clods standing around."

Shelby grinned at her sister, her face lighting up with angry joy. "He will be furious. I can't wait."

Veronica and Shelby didn't have to wait long. The gate thundered a warning, which the students ignored. Veronica smirked. She decided, on the spot, not to answer the door. Neza had told her Professor Vitebskin could be expected to waltz right in. Why alert the Collective that their master had arrived and forestall the explosion of invective they so richly deserved?

She guided Shelby to a spot where they could see the front door.

And explode he did. He opened the door himself without bothering to knock, ensuring no one was alerted. He took one look around at the lack of preparation in the atrium and ripped into the Collective members standing idly around. Veronica watched with enjoyment as Professor Vitebskin lambasted those students who had been the most disparaging to her earlier. He didn't know or care about their behavior toward the Bradwells, he was exceedingly unlikely to care how the Bradwells felt about it, but Professor Vitebskin could be counted on to care very much about the image he presented to the art world of Panschin. The Collective had let him down and nothing could matter more than that.

He stormed, fuming and furious, into the ballroom and screamed in outrage at seeing the untidy heap of still-cocooned paintings. These newly arrived paintings, stacked on top of each other in a way that threatened their integrity, were from his most favored protégés. They were talented enough to see their works grace the mansions and museums of Panschin and, maybe, travel further still, into the lofty and rarified reaches of Barsoom itself, thus burnishing his own image still more. Seeing them treated like he would, well, treat Shelby's paintings, sent him into a state verging on apoplexy.

Veronica noticed that Lulu had wandered in from the dining room. Judging from her expression, his language was vivid enough to be worth noting for future use.

Veronica had never heard such a diatribe. While wonderful and memorable to hear, this was far louder and fouler than she anticipated. She, unlike Lulu, did not take notes. She spent that blue five minutes praying her guests upstairs wouldn't overhear the good professor and wonder again what kind of bed and breakfast they were paying for. Fortunately, the professor was in the ballroom and the draperies, along with the canvases, might muffle much of the sound. Upstairs the doors were, she hoped, closed against the flood.

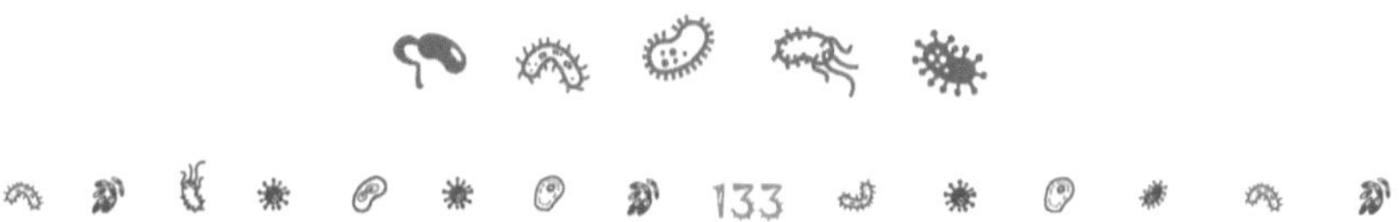

Professor Vitebskin finally wound down and he watched in stony, furious silence as his former favorite students wilted into slimy heaps of algae fresh from the tanks. He did not feel one particle of compassion for any of them. They were useless wastes of space and wasting his time and their parents' money at Panschin University. Adding to his humiliation after he finished raking his disappointing students over the coals, he realized that talentless hack, Shelby Bradwell, and her not properly respectful sister, Veronica, had witnessed every minute.

To top off his afternoon, Neza then showed up from out of some hole or other, striking her gaudy pink cane onto the floor of the ballroom with every step. She did not bother with polite greetings.

"What the hellation is wrong with you!" she screamed. "We open our home to the Collective, invite strangers onto our property, and then we're expected to do all the work? My nieces have been slaving on this show. Yesterday was bad enough, but today! I don't know where to start. Do you know one of your precious students pushed me into a wall? Because I couldn't get out of his way fast enough! And then, was he in a hurry to get to work? No," – Neza grabbed Professor Vitebskin's coverall and tried to yank him closer to her livid face – "he sat down on one of *your* precious new paintings. He could have crushed it, and he could have broken my leg."

She let go of Professor Vitebskin. Veronica, who had not known this had happened, charged up to them.

"What? Lordy, are you all right, auntie Neza? Who was it? I will shove whoever it was face-first through one of these damn paintings," Veronica said to her aunt. Then she whipped around to Professor Vitebskin.

"This is how we're to be treated? Is it?" she snarled at him.

Professor Vitebskin swiftly stepped back out of range of Veronica's much stronger hands, straightened his coverall collar and smoothed the front where Neza's hands had worked wrinkles into the crisply ironed cloth. His mind raced. Veronica could throw them out of the White Elephant and cancel the show. He couldn't locate another venue on zero notice, even the substandard one on the university's grounds. And then he'd have to move all those paintings. What would potential patrons say about his competence and abilities to manage people?

"It is not, Miss Bradwell," he replied icily. "I am appalled at the Collective's behavior. I will start by punishing the miscreant. Who was it?"

Neza pointed the student out, using her cane to be sure everyone saw at whom she was aiming. It turned out to be the same lout who had informed Veronica the previous day that he was too refined for manual labor.

Veronica said, "Oh that idiot! No surprise there. He was a problem for me yesterday." She smirked at the Professor as she threw fuel onto the fire. "He doesn't think he needs to do any work at all for the good of the Collective. He told me so himself."

Professor Vitebskin fumed. Reyansh Philpott. He had long had his eye on this particular joker, suspecting that *he* had been the one who smuggled the kitten calendar into the studio, thus defacing that sacred temple with venal, commercial hackwork. This lazy mazhor was marginally talented, relying on his connections to overcome his lack of artistic ability. He was wrong on that score and now he jeopardized a show that Professor Vitebskin was counting on to keep his name in front of everyone in the Panschin art establishment.

He grabbed his soon-to-be-former student by the front of his coverall, although with a much firmer grip than Neza had used, and started his lecture, his angry face close enough to risk biting the student's nose.

If Veronica thought Professor Vitebskin had turned the air bright blue before, she marveled at the new, more intense shade he evoked.

Lulu whispered, "Wow. I only heard language like that in the tunnel bars under Dome Four. Where did he learn those words, a fancy professor like him?"

Neza said, "That wretch didn't hurt me, Veronica. And, I have to say, I feel much better now, watching him get called on for his behavior. My goodness. Such language." She fanned herself. "I would faint if that arrogant sod didn't deserve every word."

Shelby said, "Oh. That jerk. Reyansh Philpott. He's nasty to everyone. I hope Vitebskin throws him out of the house onto his skull."

Veronica asked, "He's been nasty to you?"

Shelby's mouth tightened at the memories. "Oh yeah." Her face had gone dark with fury and her shoulders were hunched as though warding off a blow.

"Shelby, sweetie, I will make sure Vitebskin chucks that idiot face-first out onto the gravel," her sister replied. So, Reyansh Philpott had hurt two members of her family, the sod.

She didn't have to. As Veronica marched up to Vitebskin with her new demand that if he wanted to the show to go on, he had to get rid of Reyansh Philpott, the professor reached a pinnacle of rhetoric.

"You've jeopardized everything, everything I and the Collective have worked for! Get out. You have failed the semester, you've failed your degree program, and I will see to it that the University throws you out on your lazy, worthless, disrespectful ass."

Philpott looked around and around the gaping crowd in the ballroom and saw no support from anyone. His bridges burned, he shouted, "You are a sterile ass, everyone in the Collective is a pack of suck-ups, and you couldn't draw anything recognizable if your life depended on it. Your vision is just as empty as your ball-sack. You'll be hearing from my dad. He'll sue you *and* PanU!"

He stomped to the front door, leaving Professor Vitebskin purple with rage.

Shelby watched Philpott storm out of the ballroom, watched everyone else stand around mesmerized by the spectacle, watched the spluttering and incoherent professor, thought of the family's need for money, and steeled herself.

"Professor?" she called over the gasps and chatter from the Collective. This story was going to race around PanU at top speed and might even push aside the gossip about her. It was well known but never publicly admitted that none of Professor Vitebskin's three wives or his numerous liaisons had produced offspring. He also never drew anything identifiable, leaving that kind of mundane drawing instruction to one of the lesser adjunct professors.

"Don't listen to him." She glanced over at Veronica, trying to beam her a message. "We don't have much time to finish getting ready. People will be here soon."

Veronica gaped at her little mine mouse of a sister in amazement, then caught Shelby's underlying message. Not just people would be here soon but paying people and the White Elephant was due half the door receipts.

"Shelby's right!" she announced. "We've got a gallery showing to host. Professor Vitebskin, you take charge of the Collective in the ballroom and I'll get back to the atrium. Decide if you want any paintings moved around."

Professor Vitebskin recovered enough to seize the lifeline Veronica tossed him.

"Why is everyone standing around? Get back to work," he roared.

Things moved quickly after that.

Professor Vitebskin worked furiously, arranging and re-arranging the paintings to accommodate the arrival of his protégés' paintings and punish unworthy members of the Collective. In between issuing orders and thinking of new ones, he spared a moment's thought towards Shelby's own pitiful effort. He had allowed her to enter a single painting in the gallery showing, since it took place in the White Elephant.

He went and stood in front of the offending piece, studying its slashes of various shades of brown and gray and, appallingly, smears of what looked suspiciously like a lavender-tinged tan verging on mauve. Should he move it to a better position, out of the backwater it languished in? She had, after all, worked hard despite her complete lack of artistic ability.

Across the ballroom, Shelby spotted him standing in front of her painting, stroking his fashionably razored beard in the manner she knew so well. She went to find her sister.

"Veronica," Shelby hissed. "Professor Vitebskin is looking at my painting. My painting! He might move it to a better location."

Veronica, via a tremendous act of will, managed not to roll her eyes. "So?"

"So he might like it."

She decided to let her sister down gently. "I suppose that could happen."

"I really worked hard on this one."

"I know you did. You work hard on all of them."

"Veronica, you're not taking me seriously."

Veronica gritted her teeth. "Shelby. Don't get your hopes up. Okay?"

"This time is different!"

"Miss Bradwell. Shelby," Professor Vitebskin called out. He strode over to the two women, Shelby eagerly smiling at him and Veronica trying hard to look less sour over what she was afraid was coming.

"Everything is in place. I'll return within the hour to greet our first guests."

"Of course, Professor," Veronica said. "And we get half the door receipts and a commission on every sale."

"Naturally."

"Are there any other changes, Professor Vitebskin?" Shelby asked enthusiastically.

He gave her a look consigning her to a remote tunnel for her open stupidity.

"No, Shelby. I said everything was in place and I meant it. Good day, Miss Bradwell."

He spun on his heel and headed out the door.

Shelby stared at his back, then at the door closing behind him, then raced off to the ballroom to see if her painting had been moved. It had not. It was still tucked into a corner, where it was unlikely to be observed, hanging around with all the other rejects from the also-rans in the PanU Art Department. She stood rooted to the floor, seeing again how she rated against the other members of the Collective, despite how hard she tried.

"I'm sorry, sweetie," Veronica said, coming up behind her. She draped an arm around her sister. "He's a cave troll."

Shelby could feel her jaw trembling and she tasted bile. "I really thought that maybe, this time, he'd...."

"It's his show and he wants everything exactly the way he wants it," her sister said. "This is what he wants, your painting shoved into a corner where no one will notice it because it doesn't suit his precious *vision*."

Shelby stared at her painting for a long, long moment. "It doesn't matter what I do, does it."

"I don't think so."

"And I'm stuck at PanU with people who think I'm rotted scum from a contaminated algae tank."

"Maybe not. Auntie Neza got an appointment with the bursar next week. We'll get you out of there."

"All right then," Shelby said. "All right then."

Veronica saw the Collective out, closing the heavy front doors with more force than necessary. Everything was in place for paying guests to arrive. If the evening went as usual, a horde of wealthy art patrons would show up, pay their credits at the door, gawk at the paintings, gossip about each other, gossip more about the people who weren't present to defend themselves, and eat far more than a few credit's worth of food.

The evening always went better when it was well-lubricated, something they had learned after the first gallery show at the White Elephant. Fortunately, Professor Vitebskin provided plenty of alcohol, probably using his Art Department expense account courtesy of PanU. Veronica had always been careful not to ask how he paid for this luxury, so she could then legitimately claim ignorance when he was audited.

Despite the presence of free food and copious amounts of cheap wine — both resting comfortably in the cold room — she did not expect to sell any paintings. They rarely did. In her more cynical moments, Veronica wondered if the good professor arranged for the sales to take place elsewhere to pocket her fee.

Once the opening was over, she would be expected to open the White Elephant for the next two weeks to anyone willing to make an appointment to contemplate the paintings in quiet isolation. No matter how many appointments Professor Vitebskin arranged, somehow, paintings rarely sold. Yet Shelby told her that paintings did sell, according to the gossip back at the university. Maybe, Veronica thought to herself, she wasn't being cynical. She was being an astute observer of reality.

There was nothing she could do about it. What she could do was go upstairs and tell Mr. Jones what to expect over the next two weeks, and invite his party to the gallery show. It would be open soon and he could, if he wanted to, rub elbows with the art crowd of Panschin, while eating free food and drinking free wine. That might be enough to bring him down.

Why did she want Mr. Jones to come downstairs? He'd see a ballroom full of ugly art and her walking around with a tray of snacks like a tavern waitress. The idea was painful and humiliating, yet she would be glad to see him.

She angrily pushed those thoughts away. It must be the smell of paint, she decided, coupled with the frustration of dealing with the Collective. She marched upstairs to do the right thing by her guests, giving them the schedule for the evening and explain the tentative schedule for the next two weeks.

The White Elephant had its gate and doors flung wide open, inviting in anyone who wandered down the street. Auntie Neza was posted at a small table outside the doors, collecting a few credits from everyone who showed up. True to her upbringing, she smiled and made polite conversation with each arrival, including those who remembered her from better days in the past and either remarked on her new, lowered position in the world or pretended that nothing had happened to change her status. She preferred dealing with people who said something as then, there were no misunderstandings. Former friends who pretended nothing was wrong tended to suddenly go deaf when Neza asked about social get-togethers, relatives in common, and invitations lost in the mail.

Worse, those conversations made her fret over how bad it had gotten for Shelby at PanU. She had completely misjudged how her niece would be accepted. She was getting old. She sighed at the passing of time, and gave thanks that they would no longer deal with this riff-raff, professors included.

As always, many, many visitors came from the upper reaches of Panschin society, all excited at the prospect of safe slumming in the bohemian backwater that Dome Two had become. It was a chance to see and be seen, and later on brag to their more timid friends about the experience of getting off at the seedy transtube station and braving the business district and streets of Dome Two. The colorful denizens they passed could be counted on to oblige the out-of-domers with a good story if they saw a chance to earn some coin by begging, sidewalk vending, or street busking. While it was extremely rare that visitors got mugged — the denizens knew *that* would be bad for future business —they made sure the threat remained, adding piquancy to the evening.

Older visitors remembered when Dome Two had been *the* place to live. They marveled at the ruined mansions they strolled past, discussing how nobody knew how to take care of wonderful, old buildings anymore and wasn't it a shame that the great cultural institutions couldn't be moved to the more salubrious climes of Dome Six.

The business district entrepreneurs all prepared for the large influx of visitors. They had hung prominent signs advertising goods and services that could not be found in Dome One (government issue only), Dome Three (plebeian), Dome Four (industrial use only), Dome Five (boringly respectable), or Dome Six (your friends already have one or they were never brave enough to eat here). Everything about Dome Two was *unique* and if you shopped here, that uniqueness would rub off on you. To ensure that every possible visitor to the White Elephant gallery showing passed through the business district, signs within the transtube stations had been removed or defaced, forcing visitors to use the official transtube station and not the one closest to the White Elephant.

Waiting at the outskirts of the business district (thus ensuring friends and relatives with a shop got a chance at some coin) were rickshaw haulers and sedan chair men. There were always a few visitors who would balk at walking like any pedestrian on common, shared streets. They would, of course, be charged far more than the going rate within Dome Two for the short trip from the business district to the White Elephant. They would be charged even more for the return trip later on, especially if they were too drunk to notice.

Police protection was beefed up, as much as it could be, since although the *potential* risk of being robbed added spice to the evening, an actual robbery meant lawsuits and unpleasant investigations from higher up in the administrative chain. While the beat patrolmen frowned upon muggers and pickpockets, they did nothing to stop enterprising young women from negotiating their virtue with well-heeled visitors. They had bills to pay too, after all, and their signature dress and cries of "oooo eeeee!" and "care for a waltz?" added exciting local color.

All in all, a gallery showing at the White Elephant provided much-needed income for much of Dome Two and, as such, Dome Two got behind the show, promoting it to all and sundry. Veronica had been astonished when, during the promotion of the first show at the White Elephant, she saw how the local business owners took full advantage of any possible chance to extract cash from out-of-dome visitors. After the aggravation and dust from the first gallery show settled, she made it a point to pass along the news that gallery showings at the White Elephant couldn't be relied upon for a steady income. They were dependent on

Shelby's relationship with the PanU Artists' Collective and when that stopped, the shows would stop.

The response from the business community of Dome Two to her concerned inquiry was succinct: so what? We seize our opportunities when and where we can.

Veronica contemplated the local business community's struggles as she poured cheap, bubbly wine into every piece of stemmed glassware the White Elephant owned or borrowed. This would be the very last showing. She'd never have to subject her family to the Collective again. Their household would manage, somehow, just like every other household and business in Dome Two. You took your opportunities where and when you could.

She took a quick, illicit sip from a glass of wine, enjoying how the bubbles tickled her throat. She had drunk better in the past but Professor Vitebskin, knowing his audience, purchased vast quantities of hooch fermented from Panschin's tanks over skimpier amounts of top-quality wines imported from the wineries farther south. In his stated experience — based on too many faculty functions — as long as the labels remained unseen, none of the guests would recognize they were drinking cheap, down-market plonk. He was correct. She had even seen a clique of wine snobs trading guesses about the vintage, year, and origin of what was being served. Most of the wine would be swilled down and if there were unopened bottles, he would retrieve them for later use.

Catching Shelby's eye, she lifted a glass and toasted her sister for growing a spine. A puzzled look came over her sister's face before returning to setting up trays of nibbles in the ballroom. Veronica took a sip. Should she open every bottle, even if no wine was poured from them? Then she could keep the bottles for trading later on. She enjoyed another sip, a rare treat these days, and decided no. Cheating people was something Simon Bradwell did and she was nothing like her father. She would not seize "every opportunity," only the ones that didn't taint her soul.

Veronica downed the rest of the glass, borrowing fresh courage, and returned the glass to the kitchen to be washed and refilled. Most of her evening would consist of collecting empty glasses promptly so they could be washed and reused. She had borrowed as many as possible but few people living in Dome Two kept large collections of stemware anymore. It made the array on hand varied in the extreme, helping people to better identify their own wineglass. Assigning Lulu the job of washing up kept her busy and safely away from irritating and being irritated by the paying customers.

From an upstairs window, Carmine discreetly watched the goings-on out front. It made a change from quietly monitoring the activities in the atrium from the top of the stairwell. It looked like the gallery show was ready and the White Elephant had opened its doors to the art-loving public. He checked what passed for the sky, hoping to see some signs of the sun. The dome didn't seem to reflect the passage of the sun through its arc, yet the light gradually shifted and changed through the day, dimming into twilight. It was taking more time than he would have believed to understand and correlate changes in the dome's lighting with how he knew the sun and clouds behaved. He wondered if he was the only person from Shelleen to miss being outdoors.

"Sir?" he said.

Airik looked up from the report he had been annotating from Chung/Banerjee. It was filled with discrepancies and had taken three readings to decipher exactly what the seller was trying to sell and to sort the fact from fiction.

"I know Miss Bradwell hasn't been back upstairs to tell you so, but it looks like the gallery show has started. There's people coming up the walk and the old lady is taking their money at the door."

Airik thought about what he wanted to do next. Carmine waited with the stolid mien of a good servant, revealing nothing of his strong interest in his boss's personal life. His daimyo needed to marry for the good of the demesne. This Miss Bradwell had caught Airik Shelleen's interest in a way that Carmine had never before observed. True, she was not a member of the Four Hundred but then his daimyo had never fretted about status. He was interested in competence, character, and hard work. Miss Bradwell met those qualifications from what Carmine had seen since his arrival. She was also pretty, although not the knockout her sister was.

Closing the report's folder, Airik considered. He had made serious headway into the pile of documents, but there were still a few papers left. He could go on for another hour.

Spotted his boss's indecision, Upton yawned ostentatiously while cracking his knuckles over the typewriter. The paintings were hideous but a break was a break.

As if he had subconsciously sensed Upton's mood, Airik realized he was a little fatigued. He could legitimately take a break and let his mind clear. He needed to mull over what he had read. In the meantime, he could see Miss Bradwell again. Why did he want to see Miss Bradwell again?

Upton's hopes rose seeing the stress leave his boss' face. Going downstairs would let him chat up Shelby. He'd seen her from a distance when stretching his legs and peeking down the atrium stairwell at the chaos below. Veronica Bradwell was attractive enough, but her sister Shelby was a stunner and absolutely worth the favor of his time. There was also Florence, pretty and well-shaped. And then there was Lulu. She had the allure of a beautifully honed, finely crafted dagger; handsome and dangerous. Such fire, such language. She'd be an exciting challenge. Many of the co-eds he'd spotted in the Collective were also quite attractive, despite their dreary, figure-concealing coveralls. There would be art-loving visitors, many of whom needed the benefit of his company. And there'd be snacks and, hopefully, some kind of libation to make the paintings more palatable. He shuddered. That art needed alcohol. Why didn't the artists of PanU do nude figure studies? Those would make for much more acceptable viewing, no matter what their artistic merits were.

Elliot, watching the others, chose not to voice an opinion. A good valet never did, unless asked. However, his extensive diary would get a huge, new addition as soon as he was alone and unobserved. Airik's gift of a private room at the White Elephant had been unexpected, and he planned to take advantage of the privacy. This trip to Panschin was giving him plenty to write about in his unofficial and unauthorized history of the demesne of Shelleen. He had high hopes that since he did all the packing and unpacking, no one would discover his writings until he was ready to release them into the wider world. At home in Shelleen, he wrote every night in secret and when he was finished, those notebooks disappeared into their hidey-hole. The trip to Panschin had been edifying, but until Airik's escape to the White Elephant he had been unable to write any of it down.

"Carmine," Airik said. "I'll go downstairs in a half-hour or so. Stay unobtrusive."

Carmine said, "Yes, sir," while remaining impassive as ever. This was a tricky request. He was too big to blend into the background. He filled the foreground of whatever area he was in. It just happened and there wasn't much he could do about it. "I'll do my best."

"Upton?"

"Yes, sir?" Upton smiled brightly at his boss. At last, something fun to do that would last longer than a stolen minute on a break.

"Do not make a fool of yourself with any of the women, young or old, downstairs, particularly Miss Bradwell, her sister, or her cousins. Do not tell anyone who you are or who I am. I want to remain anonymous, and I will not be pleased with the person who reveals my identity."

"Yes, sir." Upton's smile dimmed.

"Elliot?"

"Yes, sir," his valet replied.

"You may come down or not as you choose. Be discreet."

"Of course, sir. May I add the coveralls will make a sufficient camouflage. It's common for the residents of Panschin to wear them and indeed, all the Collective artists wear them and so do, I fear, some of the guests I have observed walking towards the White Elephant." Elliot shuddered ever so slightly over the complete lack of style and taste exhibited by the citizens of Panschin. It was truly a backwater.

Airik allowed himself a smile. "Very good. We'll blend right in."

Upton chose not to comment. What if they didn't? What then? They'd be back at the Twelve Happiness Luxury Hotel within short order. There was no chance of keeping hordes of glad-handers, conmen, and reporters away from Airik here. He glanced over at the bed. It wasn't, he was sure, going to be anywhere near as comfortable as the bed at the hotel. No chance of pleasant company either. On the other hand, anything that kept Airik happy and fully functional was worth the risk, and he seemed to really want to go downstairs and look at ugly paintings.

That thought stopped him cold. Airik had never previously shown an interest in art, avant-garde or otherwise. Going over eye-glazing reports was his idea of fun. What was the attraction? Was it their hostess, Miss Bradwell? He looked over at Airik absorbed in yet another report. It couldn't be. Could it?

Malcolm Cobb shot his cuffs and adjusted the neckline of his suit in the cracked mirror over his dresser. He looked as good as he was going to get in his conservative, well-cut and well-fitted business suit. It was a very traditional deep blue, with every seam piped in gold, gold buttons, and a faint woven stripe of tone-on-tone diamonds. He couldn't afford the newest men's fashion of floral brocade, and he didn't like those patterned suits anyways. He certainly wasn't going to wear a coverall; he no longer needed to wear one unless he was underneath in the deepdown and anyways, his were the real, company-issued garment. They were worn, stained, and patched, a dead giveaway compared to the ones he saw being worn by people who didn't need to perform manual labor to earn their living.

He examined his hands, turning them over and over. Clean, they were clean, with immaculate nails. No one who saw his hands — as long as they didn't know what a callus was — would guess he had been underneath recently, helping his relatives dig out that seam of copper for Steelio. He was the assistant bank manager of the local branch of the Second National Bank of Panschin and unless he said differently, no one at this gallery opening would know his true background.

He wished he believed in himself more. Somehow, everyone always knew, and he turned back into just another overdressed, jumped-up scholarship boy, wanting more than a tunnel rat was supposed to have.

No, he told himself firmly. No one there would know. How could they? Unless, of course, the other guests turned out to be friends or relatives of the idiots he had gone to school with. They all would know. He frowned at the mirror, the crack in it splitting his reflection into two halves that didn't quite meet right. No. He was smart, he was hardworking, he was ambitious, and there was nothing wrong with any of those traits or with him. Panschin was a growing city, and they needed talent. The city needed him. He earned his start here in Dome Two, and he would use all those skills to prove that Dome Two was undervalued.

Dome Two needed him even more than the rest of Panschin, although no one here knew that yet. This art show was an excellent chance for an evening out, meet people who didn't know his background, and find out exactly what was happening with the leaseholder of the building, the White Elephant. What a strange name. There were elephants on Mars, but not many and they all lived at the equator in the Wild Side jungles, not in Barsoom and certainly not in Panschin. He had checked. Now that he knew what an elephant was, it was even stranger to name a building after one. Perhaps it was the size. And why white?

Elephants were gray.

He might even start finding out more about how the business district was hanging on. Not surprisingly, few of the local establishments were open to discussing their business dealings with a representative of the Martian government. They didn't trust him to look out for their best interests, not yet. He had to prove himself to them too.

He smiled at his split reflection. He liked Dome Two. It wasn't strictly one thing or the other like the other domes and tunnels; it was as mixed-up a group of people, buildings, businesses and amenities as he had seen anywhere in Panschin. This might be a place he could fit into, a place that could become home. Dome Two allowed the freedom to reinvent oneself and the room to do it in. Here, here, he might have a future.

In the meantime, he had work to do. Malcolm ran over the lease to the White Elephant, 626 Oleander Lane, one more time. It was standard legalese, without too many unusual changes added over the decades. How were they passing off this art gallery business then, since they weren't supposed to use the building for commercial purposes? He would have to be careful in his questions. The wrong one would spook the leaseholders or worse, alert his boss, Desmond Wong, who might cause him or them trouble. He would never be trusted by anyone in Dome Two if his actions got someone evicted from their home for a specious reason.

Airik paused at the top of the stairwell, looking down the atrium to the floor below. Quite a few people swirled around between the two curved staircases, circulating from the ballroom on one side to the spacious dining room on the other. Their chatter rose up into the atrium, filling it with a hum and buzz. More than a few of them were dressed in the ubiquitous coverall, something that he was coming to realize was the official Panschin uniform for most purposes. Strangely, most of the coveralls did not look like the people wearing them did any real work as opposed to what he had observed during the transtube rides or the tour of the Jandinaire facility in Dome Four. Some looked like they were made of silk instead of canvas; one woman wore what looked like velvet with hammered silver buttons. The wear spots looked decorative, as though they had been made deliberately, rather than ground-in via hard labor. He had a hard time wrapping his mind around the concept since coveralls, including the ones *he* wore in the field back home in Shelleen, were strictly utilitarian garments.

Nobody looked up as he quietly slipped down the stairs. He was invisible and would remain that way, at least until someone recognized him as the daimyo of Shelleen.

"Excuse me," someone said behind him as he reached the base of the staircase.

Airik stiffened and turned. Damnation, identified already? Would he never escape?

Miss Bradwell was smiling and holding a tray of wine glasses. "Something to drink? I promise it will make the paintings go down easier."

He unbent enough to smile back at her in his relief. "Thank you, Miss Bradwell."

He couldn't think of anything else to say. His normally active brain went blank. Worse, his standard conversation about the weather, a fallback position when he didn't know what to say, vanished into the ether. Fortunately, she did have something to say.

"Shelby's circulating with a tray of nibbles and there are more on tables in the dining room and the ballroom. Oh," Veronica smiled at him and his heart leaped.

"We also have deviled eggs!"

She beamed at him with an enthusiasm Airik had only seen once before when a third cousin presented his fiancée with a diamond necklace, welcoming her to Shelleen and the family.

"Uh, really? Eggs?"

"Yes," she gushed. "They're a real treat in Panschin." Veronica stopped and disappointment flashed across her mobile face. "Oh. You're from Barsoom. Eggs must be routine. Anyways, enjoy the evening and remember, say no. The artists are used to it so don't worry about hurting their feelings."

She scowled suddenly but not, it seemed, at him. She met his eyes, her own suspiciously bright. "They won't care about yours, I can promise you that."

Another voice intruded.

"Well, well. Veronica Bradwell waiting on tables like some chola. How the mighty have fallen."

Veronica flinched, pasted on a smile even Airik recognized as forced, and lifted her tray of mismatched stemware higher, like a shield.

"Glass of wine, Mrs. Wangmo?"

"No. I would never have come here if I knew *you* were handing out refreshments. They might be poisoned."

Veronica stiffened and said, "and yet you gave my auntie Neza coin at the door to get in. That didn't give you a clue as to who's house this was?"

Mrs. Wangmo glared at Veronica; her lip curled in disdain. "She isn't a Bradwell. You are."

Mrs. Wangmo was a formidable matron, her graying curls clamped into a currently fashionable hairstyle although not one, Veronica noticed, that was age-appropriate. Her coverall was made of yellow silk and well-adorned with an extensive collection of jeweled brooches.

"I am not my father. If you will please excuse me, other guests do need drinks," Veronica said flatly.

"One moment, Miss Bradwell," Airik said, daring to put a hand on her shoulder to keep her from fleeing. "Who is this rude … person?" He tilted his head towards the visibly swelling Mrs. Wangmo.

"Who the hell are you?" Mrs. Wangmo snarled, not giving Veronica a chance to answer the question herself.

"I'm Airik Jones. From Barsoom. I'm here for the Biennial Mining Conference." He gave her a long, icy stare consigning her to her place outside everything acceptable, dismissed her as nothing without needing to use a single syllable, then refocused on Veronica, his expression much warmer.

"Ugh. Mining. Disgusting." Mrs. Wangmo tried to give the same look to Airik, failed, then said to Veronica, "you do associate with low elements. Your mother would be heartbroken." She stalked off, but not before snagging the biggest glass of wine.

Veronica bit her lip hard, trying to control herself. It hurt. After all this time, it still hurt. But Airik Jones, her paying guest, looked concerned about her. He didn't know what was going on and he deserved an answer.

"I am so sorry you had to witness that. Please don't worry about me. Mrs. Wangmo was one of my mother's friends from before—" Veronica took a deep breath. "My father embezzled some of her money."

She waited nervously to see what he would say at such a revelation.

Airik ran over everything he had seen since his arrival at the White Elephant, the clear lack of money, and the even clearer need for it. Miss Bradwell obviously didn't have a stash of ill-gotten gains to draw on. If she had, the house would have been fully furnished, competently staffed, and she would not be hosting total strangers with a tray of mismatched wine glasses. Nor was she trying to earn money via some other, illicit manner demonstrated by her list of what she would and would not do with guests.

"But you are not your father."

"No." Her relief at Airik's statement was intense. "But not everyone can accept that." Veronica gazed to where Mrs. Wangmo disappeared into the crowd. "She was always such a snob about her wine. I wonder if she'll figure out she's drinking plonk from the tanks."

Airik lifted his glass to his eyes, observing tiny bubbles rising to the surface, the slight tinge of pink, and the fact that his glass did not match any of the others on Veronica's tray although the liquid filling them was identical. He took a considering sip, noticing a hint of something he'd never had in wine before but it wasn't bad. "It seems acceptable. What is plonk?"

Veronica smiled at him impishly. "Wine normal people drink when they aren't trying to impress anyone. It's drinkable and cheap."

She took a quick look around. "I have to go warn Shelby that Mrs. Wangmo is here. Please excuse me and make sure you get an egg before they're gobbled up. They won't last long with this crowd."

"Of course, Miss Bradwell," Airik said. He filed the name "Wangmo" away for later reference, along with "Bradwell." He would have some research projects for Elliot tomorrow. He liked knowing who he was dealing with and he already knew he did not like Mrs. Wangmo or her attitude towards the main industry in Panschin, fueling most of its wealth. Miss Bradwell, on the other hand, he did like. What had happened? What did her father do? Why had he leaped to aid his hostess? And the feel of her shoulder under his hand reminded him it had been a long, long time since his last intimacies with a woman. He pushed all those disquieting emotions away since now was not the time to examine them.

He continued to circulate, staying quietly in the background and, as he had hoped, he was treated by everyone as a nonentity. It was a relief and a pleasure to regain anonymity, although he wished he could have revealed himself to Mrs. Wangmo. She would have collapsed into a puddle at having not just a daimyo, but the Red Mercury Daimyo. But, he reminded himself with a taste of the plonk, you couldn't have it both ways. You couldn't drink fine wine and swan about oozing power while wishing people would leave you alone.

He turned his attention to the paintings. As he had suspected, they did not improve upon a closer inspection. The closer inspection of their surroundings demonstrated how beautifully designed the White Elephant had been, when it and Dome Two were new and fashionable. It made its current circumstances even stranger. Elliot's report would be welcome.

Veronica found Shelby handing round seasoned, fried blocks of yeast in the ballroom, her face set in stone. The guests she was serving were ignoring her, despite being members of the Collective and fellow students at PanU. One of them was Kip McGrant, accompanied by a fond older couple who must have been his parents. Like the others, he was pretending he didn't know the waitress.

"Shelby, got a minute?"

"Sure."

They retreated to an empty corner of the ballroom, the one where – as Veronica realized too late – Shelby's painting was exiled.

Shelby grimaced at her painting. "What is it now? This evening is awful enough already." She stared at the offending canvas rather than look at her sister. What was wrong with this one? She thought she had toned down the colors she loved enough to make it acceptable to Professor Vitebskin's exacting standards. There was only the merest hint of lavender, replacing the royal purple she had wanted to use.

Veronica sighed. "Mrs. Wangmo is here."

The painting lost all of its interest for Shelby. "That hag? That cave troll? Since when does she set foot in Dome Two?"

"I'd guess since she discovered a love of social climbing via avant-garde art appreciation," Veronica replied dryly. She looked pointedly at the display of paintings in front of her. Shelby's at least had some color other than shades of dirt. "Her other methods must not be working today. Anyways, she's already been rude to me. If she spots you, don't expect her to be any nicer."

"She wouldn't visit mama after dad, well, you know, and we moved here. She wouldn't even come to mama's funeral. Now she comes here?" Shelby said, her voice laced with hurt.

Veronica awkwardly hugged her sister, taking care not to spill the tray. "I know, sweetie. So far, I haven't seen anyone else from the old days. But if Mrs. Wangmo is here, then her coven won't be far behind."

"Damn them all," Shelby muttered. "They could have helped."

"Miss?" a visitor said. "Are you handing out these drinks or snacks? My party would like some."

Veronica whispered to her sister, "Never again. Keep reminding yourself. Never again."

She pasted on a smile for the paying guest. "Of course. Forgive me. Wine? And my sister will get you a nibble."

Malcolm Cobb watched the goings on at the White Elephant from across the street. The house was immaculate, even glowing compared to its neighbors. It was almost as pristine as a building in Dome Six would have been where it was far easier to keep a structure clean of terraformers. Whatever else the leaseholder was doing of questionable legality; he was keeping the house and grounds in tiptop condition.

That was an important consideration since it had been obvious to Malcolm since day one that not every leaseholder in Dome Two cared about the conditions of their properties. This lackadaisical attitude towards bank and thus government property extended into his own branch bank. If Desmond Wong had been doing his job properly, then every property belonging to the Second National Bank of Panschin would look more like the White Elephant and less like the house next door, almost consumed by a blanket of terraformers. Only the windows were clear, indicating someone still lived there.

Malcolm frowned at that building, its tiny yard shin-deep in more terraformers. He had never seen such a variety of murky greens and muddy browns, all running into each other until you couldn't tell where one type of terraformer ended and the next clump began. That ruined mansion, along with every other property on Oleander Lane belonged to the Second National Bank of Panschin's portfolio, yet it looked like it was inhabited by squatters. What was his boss doing? This kind of incompetence was bordering on criminal. When was the last time anyone from the office had been by to check on the properties? Heads might roll if word of this malfeasance got out.

He smiled coldly down at the lichens blanketing the wall he was standing next to, thick enough to conceal the type of stone it was constructed from. He would have to be careful in how he proceeded. He didn't want his own head to roll, sacrificed by Desmond Wong's lies in a vain effort to save his own lazy skin. That was the risk, but without risk, there was no chance for gain.

Malcolm took a moment to dust himself off, making sure he didn't retain a film of terraformers from his surroundings. He waited for a break in the foot traffic and then quietly strode across the street.

Inside the opened gate, he took a closer look around. The garden area was amazingly well-kept. Even the low, surrounding wall had been swept down, allowing its granite nature to shine forth. Only the most determined, most decorative lichens remained. The paths of white gravel had been raked not just recently, but regularly. They didn't have any blobby bits marring their appearance. Some of the garden — beds? — he wasn't sure what you called a section of a garden. A room? They were full of terraformers but those had been corralled within stone edgings and not allowed to colonize the paths. Other beds — he decided on the word — were full of plants, real plants like the flowers he had admired in planters in the business district.

The front door was wide open, flanked by an old lady at a table taking money and a pair of planters, spilling over with flowers, the only flowers in the garden belonging to the White Elephant. They looked to be made of fire; a profusion of yellows, oranges, and reds tumbling over each other against glossy green leaves.

The planters reminded him of his Dome Two brunette beauty and the time he had seen her drawing a planter full of vivid purple and yellow flowers. He had gone up to get a closer look at the planter after she left, hoping to see what had entranced her. The flowers had markings that made them look almost like smiling faces. They saw him but she had not. She never saw him. He still had no idea who she was or what had upset her so much outside the window of the Dappled Yak.

He sighed and got back to the business at hand. He marched confidently up to the front door. The posters stated a collection would be taken at the door to benefit the arts so he was ready with some coin. He wondered why anyone who could afford to paint pictures for a living needed to collect still more money from the public. There couldn't be much money in painting so only people who were already rich could afford to be artists. Why then did they need to beg for more coin? It was a puzzle and another subject that could trip him up when dealing with people who had been born knowing the answer.

"Hello," the old lady said to him. "Welcome to the White Elephant and the show. Donations here please." She smiled warmly and held up a basket so he could put in his money.

She looked friendly and approachable; a notion reinforced by the shiny, bright pink cane leaning against the table. It was not a hoity-toity color. In fact, one of his young cousins proudly wore nail polish of the same shade.

Malcolm decided to take the risk.

"Why do you need donations? I thought only people who could afford to be artists were artists. Regular people have to work for their livings," he asked pleasantly. He smiled at the old lady in case there had been a sting in his question.

Neza stared at him, at a loss for words. No one had ever asked before. It was just understood that the arts needed supporting. There was the unspoken corollary that the White Elephant needed its share since hosting a show took cash as the owner of any exhibit hall would tell you. Rent and utilities had to be paid. He was a good-looking man in a rough-hewn sort of way so it wasn't a hardship to stare at him, and, she realized, he was waiting patiently for an answer. It hadn't been a rhetorical question. He wanted to know.

"We have bills to pay just like everyone else," Neza answered smartly. "We can only get so far on barter and volunteer efforts. Would you like to purchase a ticket?"

She shook the basket again at him. This man didn't know how to behave at a show, so who was he? Nobody who actually lived in Dome Two would pay to see the paintings; the interested residents and business owners would come by later in the week when it was free and the White Elephant was empty of out-of-domers. Paying visitors fell into neat categories: members of the Collective, their friends and relatives, anyone else they could dragoon into attending, other students looking for something to do, faculty members with time on their hands, bored thrill-seekers from Dome Six, and the Panschin art community.

She was suddenly chilled by the memory of the thug who had threatened Veronica the previous week. But the fleeting, dim glimpse she had caught of him didn't resemble this man. This man was very well dressed, for starters, the most formally dressed person in the entire White Elephant. Neza did not consider velvet coveralls to be proper attire for any function. She was wearing a white blouse and long, dark skirt; discreet, easy to maintain, and appropriate for her current activity and station in life.

"Yes, I would." Malcolm dropped some coin into the basket and took his paper ticket. "What kind of art will I see? The posters said this was the PanU Artists' Collective. I'm not familiar with them."

Neza tried desperately to place him. Had she seen this man in the business district? He couldn't be from the Panschin arts community or he would know all about the Collective.

"They're the student group from PanU," Neza said. "This show is a way for them to make their debut in a more formal setting than the University, to see and be seen by art collectors."

"Oh. I didn't know that."

"Are you new to Dome Two?" Neza asked.

He smiled at her. "Pretty new. I'm Malcolm Cobb. I moved in a few weeks ago."

Neza thought her heart would stop. This was the new assistant bank manager Mrs. Grisson had warned them about. The ambitious go-getter who was going to make changes. The man who held their lease and thus the future of the Bradwell family in his hand. A lifetime of deportment came to her aid, enabling her to speak without her voice shaking.

"I'm Neza Molony. Welcome to Dome Two. Please, enjoy the show and have a glass of wine and a nibble or two." She forced a smile up at him, while considering how quickly she could abandon her post and find Veronica.

Malcolm noted the sudden change in Neza Molony's manner when he told her his name although she concealed it well beneath a veneer of good manners. He thanked her and strode in through the open door into the atrium, wondering about the expression he saw flash across her face.

It wasn't disdain. He was familiar enough with that reaction; he saw it all the time. It was …. Uneasiness? Fear? Certainly, the old woman was taken aback by his name.

He looked up, stopped dead, and stared all around the atrium of the White Elephant, every thought of his hostess at the door shoved aside. The two-story entryway was sumptuous; the heart of the kind of mansion he had daydreamed of owning someday, with twin, curved staircases soaring gracefully to the second floor and the ceiling open to the dome, where the last of the afternoon sun poured down. The balustrades were gilded, the crown and floor moldings were deep and detailed, the parquet bamboo floors gleamed, and the ugliest art he had ever seen desecrated the rich cream walls.

The painting in front of him was *dreadful*, smears of what looked like a wide variety of shit from a host of people – some of them with serious intestinal issues – slapped on the canvas. Malcolm tore his eyes away from the train wreck in front of him to the other walls and the freestanding easels scattered about. Those paintings were all as bad. He had always believed he knew what fine art was. He had visited the Panschin Museum of Fine Art and nothing on their walls looked like this. This was art? No wonder the old lady was taking donations at the door. Nobody would pay for this kind of excrement. It wasn't even useful as fertilizer.

Where were the landscapes? Vases of flowers? Cloudscapes? Portraits of famous people or beautiful women? Historic paintings showing the heroic founding of Mars or the building and settlement of Panschin? Religious paintings to instruct on morals and culture?

Inspirational paintings showing the hoped-for devastation and destruction of Olde Earthe, those rapacious, bloodsucking bastards? He didn't expect to see paintings of kittens in baskets or big-eyed puppies; he was sophisticated enough to know they were suitable only as magazine illustrations for sentimental stories. But this! This was a waste of paint.

Malcolm turned away, doing his best to hide his revulsion and knowing he was not succeeding. So, this was contemporary fine art. No wonder the city of Panschin needed to look for ambition and talent in the working classes; the upper classes had all gone soft in the head. He worked his way through the crowd of chattering onlookers towards the ballroom. He noticed the other visitors seemed more interested in swilling wine from a wide variety of stemmed glasses and talking about people who weren't present. They were ignoring the art uglifying the walls as if it didn't exist.

An attractive young woman holding a tray of mismatched stemware stopped him. She was wearing a coverall that, while clean, looked like a coverall should. That is, the wear spots appeared to have been worn in through actual labor as opposed to being purely decorative nor did she load it up with ostentatious jewelry. She smiled brightly at him.

"Glass of wine?"

"Yes, thank you," Malcolm answered, and took a glass. The waitress didn't appear to magically know he was a tunnel rat turned scholarship boy and he felt himself relax. He took the chance to look more carefully at the glass in his hand. The beverage was sparkling wine, and it tasted fine. It was the glasses that were confusing. Was this the newest fad among the upper classes, to use several dozen styles of wineglasses to show off how many patterns a household could afford? You never knew.

He drifted into the ballroom, following the crowd in a quest to discover the real art that had to be hidden there, probably to contrast more strongly with the depressing images in the atrium. It was also a chance to listen discreetly to more conversations. He recognized no one, and no one seemed to know or care who he was. His anonymity gave him the luxury to study the paintings without being bothered. He realized his error at once in thinking the paintings in the ballroom would be more beautiful or understandable. They weren't. Only one, a canvas tucked into a corner, had any color other than shades of dirt smeared upon it. It had streaks of light purple, a balm to the eye after mountains of tailings.

Neza seethed in frustration. She hoped to see Florence or Shelby trot past with a tray, or better, Veronica. She couldn't leave the table or someone was guaranteed to sneak inside without paying for the privilege of viewing avant-garde art.

Then she spotted *him* sauntering down the street. She prayed he would pass by the gate, pretend the White Elephant did not exist, and that he did not know its inhabitants.

He did not oblige. He stopped, gazed up at the house, ambled past the open gate, and strolled up the gravel path as though he still had every right to be on the property. He stopped at the table and loomed over her; a smarmy smile fixed in place.

"Neza, so nice to see you again," Dean Kangjuon drawled, his voice affected as ever. "How's my Ronnie?"

It took determination for Neza to not say "wishing she'd never married you, you spineless cave-worm." She deeply regretted that she'd urged Veronica to marry Dean; such a nice young man from such a good family. It took more effort to remind herself Veronica hadn't needed much encouragement so the debacle wasn't completely her fault. Dean was a smooth-talker, charming as all get out, and handsome enough to sell soap in an advert.

Although… Hmm. Neza gave him a more critical look over, while he preened under her eyes. He was looking puffy around the edges as though the effects of dissipation were setting in. He would normally be immaculately dressed — Dean Kangjuon wouldn't be caught dead in any garment that whiffed of manual labor — yet his shirt cuffs were starting to fray, and was that a missing button? His hairstyle desperately needed a trim to maintain its sharp lines. Interesting.

But he was a minor problem while the real problem was roaming the White Elephant looking for reasons to throw them out for lease violations.

"We're busy, Dean," Neza said. "And Veronica is very busy. Could you come back later? Say next year?"

"No, I can't. Neza, I need to see Ronnie now." He winked at her. "You know how it is."

"No, I don't."

Instead of bothering to answer, Dean stepped around the table towards the door. Neza swung her shiny pink cane out to trip him but he stopped himself in time.

She shook her jingling basket at him. "Dean, we're hosting a gallery showing for PanU. If you want inside, you have to pay like everyone else."

He glared at her, then at the basket. "Fine. How much?"

Neza tripled what she charged everyone else — the amount was right there on the discreet sign as a suggested donation — and to her surprise, Dean paid without complaining about her overcharging him. He did need to speak to her niece, his ex-wife.

She let him in, craning her neck in a vain attempt to spot someone, anyone who could be trusted to man the front door. No one obliged her. Instead, she stayed and fielded a steady trickle of talkative visitors, enriching the White Elephant's coffers while keeping her trapped and unable to alert Veronica to what lay in store for her.

Veronica was kept occupied circulating her tray of plonk, snagging empty glasses and returning to the fray with washed and refilled ones. It was amazing how much the gossiping crowd was drinking, while still being able to stand up. She mentioned in the kitchen that she hoped they wouldn't run out. Lulu, elbow deep in her tub of sudsy water, suggested collecting abandoned but partially full wineglasses, pouring the contents together and re-serving them. No one would notice. Veronica giggled with amusement about serving Mrs. Wangmo a glass containing the remains of several people's drinks but nixed Lulu's idea, despite its merits in recycling and cost-effective waste management. Instead she poured the dregs into a bucket for later use on the garden beds.

She returned to the atrium with a fresh tray, still snickering at Lulu's idea and stopped short. Airik Jones was back in front of Professor Vitebskin's most favored protégé's painting. He held an empty wineglass and she decided he needed a refill. He was a friendly face, and she needed someone who would see her as a person and not a lazy waitress of questionable background.

She refused to think deeply about why she wanted to see a man whom she knew for less than a few hours. It was good enough he hadn't cut her dead when she confessed about her dad's embezzlement. That put him one up over plenty of former friends who still refused to speak to her, despite her own innocence and all the time that had passed.

A glimpse of a familiar face caught Airik's eye, and he turned to see Veronica working through the crowd. He looked at his empty glass and decided he needed a refill. She had been correct; alcohol did help the paintings although not enough. For one, he could still see them. This time, he would be able to make conversation with her. He had thought of questions about how the atrium skylight functioned throughout the year. When that line of conversation flagged (which he expected), he could then ask about the arrangement of the paintings. There seemed to be an underlying theme, bizarre as that concept was, but he hadn't figured it out.

Unfortunately, someone else waylaid her. A strikingly handsome, well-dressed and confident man had headed straight for her, the crowd parting between them as though the stranger had choreographed it in advance.

"Ronnie!" the stranger called out, beaming with cheery good humor.

Veronica turned to see who was summoning her and her look of dismay was clear even from across the atrium. He pushed through the onlookers, none of whom parted before him. Airik had a sudden, irritated flash that if this mob knew he was the daimyo of Shelleen, they'd get out of his way. But his common sense reasserted itself, informing him that if he was recognized, then *he'd* be the one mobbed when people currently ignoring him realized their chance to sell him on idiotic business schemes and unwanted intimate family connections. He'd lose either way.

Veronica didn't bother pasting on a smile for Dean, a fact Airik also noticed and filed away since it contrasted so strongly with how amiable she had been with everyone else, even Mrs. Wangmo.

"Don't call me Ronnie, you know I hate it," she said. "Did you pay for a ticket?"

Dean briefly looked annoyed; then replaced the expression with a charming smile for someone he dearly missed.

"You are such a kidder, Ronnie," he said. "I bought my ticket from Neza. Want to see it?" He winked salaciously at her. "I can show you other things too. You always liked that."

Veronica stifled a groan. All this time and Dean still believed she'd fall at his feet with her legs spread. Those days were long gone. She stepped away from his attempted hug and used her full tray of wine to block him.

"What do you want, Dean? I'm busy so make it quick."

"Fine, if that's the way you want to be."

"I do, so get on with it."

"Ronnie, I have a terrific deal for you. It will make us both rich."

"Oh, Dean, those deals never work. If they did, my dad's terrific deals would have worked, and we'd already be rich. And we'd still be married."

She grinned at him suddenly, showing all her teeth, but her expression wasn't friendly. "I guess things did work out for the best." She did not offer him a drink from her tray.

Dean dropped his charming smile and grabbed Veronica's arm, narrowly missing knocking over a glass.

"Ronnie, you have to listen to me. It's important."

Veronica tried to pull away from him without dropping her tray. None of the glasses on this tray belonged to the White Elephant and any she broke, she would have to replace.

"Dean, you are no longer my husband so I no longer have to listen to you. Let go of me and go away," she retorted.

"Miss Bradwell, is this person bothering you?" Airik asked icily. He had shoved his way towards them, forcing the interested bystanders to part for him. He looked even colder than he had when speaking to Mrs. Wangmo.

Dean glanced at this officious stranger, dismissed him as a nonentity, turning his attention back to Veronica. He did let go of her arm, and she stepped back at once, well out of reach and much closer to Airik Jones.

"Ronnie, I need this."

"Mr. Jones, ignore this idiot please," Veronica said to him.

To her former husband she said, "Dean, whatever it is, I don't need it. And you don't need me. You told me so yourself as did your entire family."

His face darkened with anger, and he started to raise his fist. She hastily stepped back, shielding herself partially behind Airik.

"Get out or I'll call security and have you thrown out. Do you want that in front of this crowd?" Veronica said firmly, hoping he wouldn't hear the lie. Unlike her father, she didn't look upon lying as an art form, and she wasn't very good at it. She noted Dean's worried expression and added, "You know how people talk. Someone might even tell your mother you were here. What would she say?" That last wasn't a lie, more of a threat, really.

It was a shot in the dark, but judging from Dean's face it scored. His skin was turning the same color as the wine, and all his handsomeness fled.

"You are making a mistake, and you will regret it," he grated out. He noticed that Mr. Jones had moved closer to Veronica, almost as though he knew her well enough to be concerned about her wellbeing. "And who is this fool? Another new man to warm your bed?"

Veronica gasped in outrage. She stepped away from Airik and in front of him. "How dare you! Unlike you, I don't sleep around, I have never slept around, and for your information, Mr. Jones is a guest."

For his part, Airik was frozen with rage. He had not been this angry since discovering what Howard had done to endanger all of Shelleen. Sadly, he could not have Dean flogged in the public square in front of a horde of peasants and all of Dean's horrified and chastened relatives. He found his hand going directly to his rock-hammer and chisel tucked in his pocket. They couldn't be used either, any more than he could have used them on the driver of the Twelve Happiness Luxury Hotel vehicle and that person had been only doing his job. Whoever Dean was, and whoever he had been to Veronica Bradwell, he had no reason to threaten her.

"You need to …," Airik began.

"I'm going," Dean interrupted. He had paled, his eyes suddenly very wide, and he spun on his heel and walked quickly away, heading for the dining room.

Veronica tried to get her heartbeat and breathing back under control. Mr. Jones, her guest, stood there and she had to say something to him, even if she didn't have to say anything to the people standing around enjoying the free show. The tray shook in her hands, making the glasses clink and the wine fizz.

"I'm so sorry you had to see that, Mr. Jones." She chuckled weakly. "I'm always apologizing to you. Dean is another part of my past come back to haunt me. My former husband."

"Yes," Airik replied. He took the tray from her nerveless hands. "I deduced that from your conversation with him." A statement from the conversation leaped out at him because it did not match what he had observed since his arrival.

"Do you have a security staff?"

Confused, Veronica gaped at him for a moment, then chuckled again, even more weakly. "Oh, no, I don't. I lied to Dean." She flushed in embarrassment. "I, well, I didn't know what I was going to do if he ignored me, and it was the only thing I could think of that he might listen to and stop causing trouble."

She indicated the people standing around who were suddenly deeply interested in the art they had previously been oblivious to. "I certainly couldn't involve the gallery show-goers."

Airik gazed coolly around the atrium. No one in the crowd met his eyes. "I would have to agree, Miss Bradwell. I do not believe anyone here would have gotten involved on your behalf."

She knew he was correct, standing there holding the tray of stemware she had almost dropped. Veronica didn't know what to say to him next so she took refuge in the inane. "Glass of wine? I was coming to give you one."

Airik smiled at her. "And I was coming to get one."

He sounded like an idiot and wondered why he cared. More shocking, now that his adrenaline levels were going back to normal, was the realization of how strongly he had reacted to the altercation between Miss Bradwell and her ex-husband. Why did he care? And why did it matter to him that Miss Bradwell had an ex-husband? He would have to send Elliot out first thing tomorrow to start that report. Airik knew he always functioned better when he had facts and not just hearsay. He was operating blind with Miss Bradwell. She, he was coming to realize, clouded his judgment.

A couple of easels away in the atrium, hidden by the crowd, Professor Vitebskin eavesdropped on the encounter between Veronica Bradwell, some reddish-haired stranger, and her ex-husband with great enjoyment. He decided it was time to discover the identity of this nondescript man with the penetrating eyes. He was unfamiliar, yet here he was at the PanU Artists' Collective show studying the paintings intently. This stranger had taken his time, moving through the show slowly, and even seemed to have noticed the underlying theme since he had followed the progression of paintings that he, Professor Vitebskin, had taken such pains over. Very few other gallery goers had. Could he be a patron of the arts?

Moreover, he seemed to know Veronica Bradwell. He had intervened in the heated conversation between her and her ex and then taken the tray of wineglasses from her rather than see her drop it and was only now returning it. No one would take such care of a stranger.

The professor felt a thrill run through him, contemplating a sale to a hitherto unknown connoisseur of the avant-garde. If he handled the sale off the premises, Miss Bradwell would not receive a commission and he, Professor Vitebskin, could pocket that coin. He needed the money for his legal fees and that Miss Bradwell, who had never been properly respectful towards him and was even less so now for some reason, had no such needs. Poverty wasn't a good enough reason. If she needed money, she could scrub floors on her hands and knees in Dome Six, and it would serve her right. Maybe she could scrub toilets alongside the soon-to-be-former Mrs. Vitebskin number three.

It was a deeply pleasant thought, providing him a genuinely warm expression as he strode forward to her and her mysterious companion.

"Miss Bradwell," Professor Vitebskin cooed in his silkiest tone. "Please, introduce me to this gentleman."

Veronica tried to school her face but couldn't manage avoiding a flash of distaste. She'd been dodging Professor Vitebskin since the start of the show. She knew how to serve plonk, she understood the importance of hiding the labels on the wine bottles, and she did not need him micro-managing her handling the backstage needs of the show, particularly since he had not provided anyone from the Collective to assist her. This was the last show, she reminded herself. Once she had her share of the ticket receipts, she could stop being polite.

"Of course, Professor," she said, trying to sound less sour. "May I introduce my guest, Airik Jones? He's here in Panschin for the mining conference." She turned to Airik who had an odd, frozen expression on his face.

"Mr. Jones? This is Professor Lemuel Vitebskin, the head of the PanU Art Department, the driving force behind the PanU Artists' Collective, and the instigator of this gallery showing."

To Airik's intense relief, Professor Vitebskin did not shout "The Daimyo of Shelleen!" and alert everyone in the atrium to his true identity. In fact, he didn't show any sign of recognition at all.

"The mining conference, eh?" Professor Vitebskin said. He thought "how pedestrian" but managed to stop himself from saying it. This man might have money and it wouldn't do to offend him. If he was highly placed in the industry, he had money to burn and he could possibly introduce other such mining people to Professor Vitebskin and the fine arts. That kind of wealth deserved to be shared.

"So, you aren't from Panschin?" he said, looking for an opening.

He doesn't know who I am, Airik realized, feeling relief wash over him like a soothing breeze on a hot summer day. He may be a university professor but he doesn't read newspapers.

"I'm from Barsoom."

"Really?" Professor Vitebskin gushed, his face alight with joy. "Barsoom? Are you an art appreciator? If so, let me be the first to welcome you to Panschin. My students are the future of fine art, and I know that any of their efforts will grace your home in Barsoom."

Barsoom! The very beating heart of culture, art, and refinement. Professor Vitebskin wanted to jump up and down and scream with joy. Despite his efforts, he had no contacts in Barsoom and here a visitor from those exalted halls had dropped into his lap. He could guide Mr. Jones to exactly the right painting, a painting that would open doors to the museums of Barsoom, a painting that would get him, Professor Vitebskin, the hell out of Panschin and out in the wider world where he deserved to be.

He'd never had to work with another ungrateful, lazy student again. He'd never again waste time in departmental infighting over inadequate budgets. He would never again have to deal with jealous professors and untalented instructors. He would make careers in a way that he never had before. His vision would define the art world for generations to come. His name would live forever, enshrined in monographs and museum catalogs as the prophetic finder of the greatest painters on Mars. Every one of those artists would be in his debt.

He could even — he allowed himself to see the shining vista stretching before him — have his own paintings hung in Barsoom. He would not just be the discoverer of new talent; he too would be finally recognized as the virtuoso he was. No longer would he be just a talent scout; his own, hitherto undiscovered, creative genius would be acknowledged. He would be revered on every possible artistic level.

The world lay before him at his feet; supine, gloriously lascivious, and panting in her eagerness to know him better.

As Professor Vitebskin watched the glittering future unfold before him, he became aware that both Veronica and Mr. Jones were eyeing him but not with adulation.

"Are you all right, Professor?" Veronica asked. He didn't seem drunk, nor did he seem to be having a stroke. He definitely did seem to have had his mind evaporate, standing there with his mouth agape and a thousand-yard stare.

"I am perfectly fine, Miss Bradwell," Professor Vitebskin answered absently. She was no longer of any importance. He'd never again have to produce a show at the White Elephant and deal with her or anyone else in the PanU Artists' Collective, the thankless sods.

"Mr. Jones, tell me, what inspires you about our paintings," Professor Vitebskin said earnestly. "Which work of my students speaks to you."

He had to forcibly keep his hands at his sides, rather than clutching Mr. Jones to his bosom and dragging him through the White Elephant to study each painting more closely in case Mr. Jones had missed some exquisite display of technique or some particularly beautiful handling of color theory.

Airik thought for a moment, running over his mental list of the paintings. He had taken a careful look at each of them, both from a few steps away and up-close. Professor Vitebskin gazed at him in open admiration, giving him plenty of time to make this all-important decision.

Veronica considered wandering off to hand out more wine but decided to stay by her guest, protecting him as best she could from the clutches of Professor Vitebskin and the PanU Artists' Collective. The commission on a sale would be very nice and extremely useful but Mr. Jones deserved better art to hang on his walls. She included Shelby's entry in the gallery showing, despite it being painted by her sister. Shelby had done better work, even if it didn't meet Professor Vitebskin's criteria. They had examples hanging in all the upstairs bedrooms.

Like Professor Vitebskin, she waited nervously to see what Airik Jones would say.

"None of them," Airik said.

"Excuse me?" Professor Vitebskin said, suddenly chilled to the bone. He must have misheard. "I don't understand."

"They are appalling. What is the aim of these paintings?" Airik asked. "Their purpose in existing?" He waved his glass at the painting looming over them, its subject looking remarkably like what he had once observed scraped out of an improperly handled manure pit, spread onto a field, and then plowed under.

Professor Vitebskin watched his glittering dream crumple into shards of slag glass, loaded with razor sharp edges designed to draw blood in the most painful manner. The world got up, rearranged her garments, and stalked away, laughing cruelly at his presumptuousness.

"Their purpose? Their purpose? Why to illustrate the ugliness of Panschin and the extractive industries. To show solidarity with the toiling masses. To demonstrate what mining is and does," he sputtered.

"If the purpose of these paintings is to demonstrate any kind of mining techniques," Airik replied coldly, "then they have failed dismally. They are a mass of pigment thrown haphazardly upon a canvas and as such, cannot be used as any sort of guideline."

"A guideline?" Professor Vitebskin drew himself up in outrage. "That is technical drawing, competent to be sure, but completely lacking in any kind of artistic vision. It is hackwork for hire."

Airik stared at the professor in disbelief, taking in his crisply ironed charcoal gray coverall, artistically decorated with sprays and spatters of silver and gold paint and wear spots carefully added via sanding the fabric. His clothes, his grooming, and his hands said he obviously knew nothing about manual labor so there was no point in wasting words on the subject.

The professor, however, should understand something about the diverse fields of art.

"Good technical drawing," he finally said as the professor fumed, "*is* artistic. It allows information to be passed from one person to the next in a compact, complete form. A good technical artist's efforts are worth every penny, whereas these paintings are no longer worth the sum of their materials or the time expended upon them."

Veronica, who happened to fully agree with Airik Jones, took real enjoyment at seeing the wave of purple rage pass over Professor Vitebskin. He looked almost as angry as he had earlier when Reyansh Philpott had told him off. She wanted to salute her guest with a toast but her hands were full with the tray.

"You sir, are an ass with a plebeian, bourgeois mindset and no understanding whatsoever of creative vision," Professor Vitebskin spat. He grabbed a glass from Veronica's tray, slugged back some plonk, and stalked off into the ballroom where the possibility of other prey lurked.

Veronica giggled. "Well done, Mr. Jones. You'll be left in peace for sure."

"Miss Bradwell?" Airik asked. "This man is a university professor?"

"He is, Mr. Jones. Why do you ask?"

"I do not believe he understands that plebeian and bourgeois are not synonyms."

Veronica beamed at Airik Jones, warming his heart. She laughed and said, "He's fine arts and not languages. You shouldn't expect any better, really. All those paint fumes soften their heads."

"I see," said Airik and smiled at Veronica Bradwell. He had not meant to make a joke, but she had laughed as though he had. He admired the line of her throat as she laughed, noticing the pulse in the hollow of her throat and how her blue-green skin was highlighted by her string of cloudy gray beads. Yes, she definitely impaired his judgment since he would have normally focused on her beads first to decide what stone they were made from instead of how her skin would feel under his fingertips.

Upton had been circulating slowly between the atrium, the ballroom, and the dining room. Airik's insistence that he not chat up either Bradwell sister or their two cousins had cast a pall over his enjoyment of the show.

He had to remind himself that it was probably just as well. Veronica was ferrying trays of wineglasses, Shelby was running around with trays of something everyone here ate willingly that he found disgusting, and Florence was racing back and forth from some back-pantry refilling serving trays. None of them had time to chat. Lulu did have time to chat, in between stints at her washtub of dishes, but she looked at him like a bug that needed to be crushed. The cook's knife she picked up and threatened to use on the protruding portions of his body had reinforced his decision to stay out of the kitchen.

The co-eds he had such high hopes over meeting weren't much better. They all seemed to have hostile boyfriends in tow. There was also a language barrier. The PanU Artists' Collective seemed to use an unintelligible slang all of its own, making the Panschin accent harder to understand than it should have been. You would think they didn't want to talk to charming strangers.

The rest of the visitors had not been any more rewarding. More than a few of the ladies appeared unattached and eager to meet someone new and charming. Sadly, he did not wish to attach himself to any of them enough to figure out how to go somewhere else in the wilds of Dome Two and then quietly return afterwards. Women of a certain age were energetic and adventurous but they were also experienced enough to demand nice hotel rooms instead of a quick shag behind a hedge. Upton had learned conclusively that with the Biennial Mining Conference in Panschin, there were no hotel rooms to be found anywhere. Only places like the White Elephant had room at the inn, and if you didn't already know they existed, they didn't exist.

There was the upstairs of the White Elephant, with several available rooms. He thought of Airik's reaction if he found out and shuddered. Airik wanted peace and quiet and no possibility of discovery, problems, or anything, really, that would interfere with his work. If Veronica Bradwell discovered that he, Upton, was using a room for illicit purposes, she was likely to throw them all out and refuse to refund any of the room fees. And afterwards, he would have to explain himself to Airik, followed by the Shelleen delegation here in Panschin, and then the family back home. The skin on his back twitched.

He rolled his eyes at the unfairness of it all, sipped some more cheap wine, and searched for something remotely edible on the snack trays. Thank the gods there were radishes and sliced daikon along with the yeast blocks and the utterly disgusting little dumplings filled with green muck. The Twelve Happiness Luxury Hotel, noisy, annoying and overbearing as it was, could be counted on for better food. He went searching for another glass or two of wine to wash it all down and away.

Carmine circulated quietly, as Airik requested. It was easier than he thought to stay in the background, drink a lone glass of wine and eat weird but free snacks. Most of them were acceptable but he didn't think he'd ever be hungry enough to eat a second dumpling filled with green slime. The pictures were ugly but there was no help for that. He never wandered far from Airik, always keeping him in eyeshot. He kept a weather eye out for anyone from the Twelve Happiness Luxury Hotel or the various meetings. So far, it did not appear that anyone from the extraction industries had a taste for art, at least this kind of art. They were practical-minded business people, so Carmine assumed they considered this sort of art a waste of money. But you never knew, so he kept a lookout in case Airik needed to retreat back upstairs.

"Carmine," Elliot stepped to his side and asked quietly. They were watching the daimyo, Miss Bradwell, and some idiot claiming to be her husband. "Should you step in?"

"Nah. He's doing fine."

"I meant to assist Miss Bradwell."

Carmine gave him a look. "I would not be doing my lord Airik any favors, making him look bad."

Elliot thought this over. "Ah. I think I understand."

"My lord Airik has to marry for the good of the demesne. It's time and past," Carmine said. He crossed his arms across his chest, keeping a closer eye on the action than he would admit to Elliot. He was sure he wouldn't be needed, however. The ex-husband didn't carry himself like a fighter of men. A woman, now that would be different. He looked the type who'd slap a woman around and be able to fully justify his abuse afterwards. Yep, he grabbed her arm. He just proved it.

"This is true. He should. However, Airik has never carried on like Upton," Elliot said. "He does not go looking for cheap flings and tawdry affairs."

As if by a mutual signal, both men looked into the ballroom where Upton was trying to chat up a pretty co-ed, the fourth one in a row by Elliot's count and he knew, given the size of the first floor and the crowd, he had missed at least one other such encounter, probably more, given the amount of time that had elapsed since they all came downstairs.

Elliot added, "My lord Airik would be *serious* about his intentions, but Miss Bradwell is not part of the Four Hundred. Whatever you may think, she is most unsuitable."

Carmine snorted. "I didn't meet either of those two first fiancées when they visited Shelleen. That Miss Melissa and Miss Bertrille. My lord Airik didn't need a bodyguard back then. I heard about them later on though, what they had to say to him. Then I saw how they acted in

Barsoom, practically climbing on top of Airik and in front of their husbands too! Those ladies are Four Hundred. You think they're better than Miss Bradwell?"

He did not add that he'd always believed Elliot was a dyed-in-the-wool snob and nosy to boot, always asking questions, prying and spying. Of course Elliot would prefer a lady from the Four Hundred for the daimyo's wife. Status was at stake, and Miss Bradwell had none. It wouldn't matter to Elliot that Miss Bradwell had been pleasant and smiling since he'd come downstairs and made sure he knew where everything was, just like he was a real guest. Her sister and both of her cousins, although they didn't look related, had been just as nice.

Elliot pursed his lips. He had observed both Miss Melissa and Miss Bertrille during their visits to Shelleen. The Four Hundred nearly always used arranged marriages to keep the money within the families and the bloodlines well-mixed while avoiding dilution from commoners. Sadly, he had not been impressed with either of the young ladies, despite their quality backgrounds. They had been flighty and shallow, but what could you do? Shelleen had been an agricultural backwater and the family had to take the marriage arrangements they could get. Now that it no longer had to, thanks to the Red Mercury lode, the daimyo was digging in his heels and refusing the choices being presented to him.

"I will agree Miss Bradwell seems to have character. Even so, nothing will come of it," Elliot said. "The family would never approve."

"Probably not," Carmine agreed distractedly. What had the ex-husband seen that made him scarper off like a frightened rabbit? Most of the guests didn't carry themselves like they could be dangerous. He'd have to study the crowd more closely and figure out what he missed. A few candidates didn't fit in but their behavior had been exemplary. He'd have to watch them more closely.

At the doorway to the ballroom, Professor Vitebskin stood shaking with fury. He fought for calmness. Damn Airik Jones. The cheap philistine. It was probably Veronica Bradwell's fault he didn't properly appreciate avant-garde art and want to pour money into a collection of marvelous paintings. She'd probably lied about Jones being from Barsoom, too. The man was obviously a yokel from some gods-forsaken backwater way out in the provinces.

The professor moved away from the door, bracing his hand on the wall for support. That didn't make sense. The Bradwell family needed the commission it would earn on a painting sale. Even Veronica, disrespectful as she was, knew the value of a credit. Look at how hard she had bargained over the PanU Artists' Collective paying the cost of the nibbles being served. She had even insisted on being reimbursed for the cost of the vegetables she grew, vegetables that she should have willingly and graciously contributed to the greater cause of the arts. The bitch. Scrubbing toilets was too good for her. She should scrape out cesspits.

He took a deep, calming breath, then several more. He had spotted another visitor to the show, a very well-dressed stranger. This man was not part of the Panschin arts establishment, all of whom Professor Vitebskin knew on sight. The stranger had openly disliked the stunning painting hung front and center in the atrium, the finest work of Professor Vitebskin's favorite protégé. However, the stranger was still here, still looking at the paintings. There was hope that this man might become a new art fancier. More importantly, he did not seem to know Veronica Bradwell from a hole in the ground. He needed guidance to appreciate what he was seeing and the Bradwell family wouldn't interfere for bizarre reasons of their own.

Professor Vitebskin smoothed the collar of his coverall, ran his fingers through his hair to freshen its properly tousled look, and settled himself to the task of seeking out and educating this potential new collector. This rabbit would not get away.

helby trotted around and around the ballroom, dispensing nibbles from her tray and trying hard to smile pleasantly at everyone. So many of the gallery goers were familiar to her and yet they had totally forgotten they saw her daily in the art studio or on campus. She had turned into the help, another lazy waitress who didn't respond fast enough to the snap of fingers. She kept reminding herself what her sister said: "Never again."

She also kept asking herself why no one else in the Collective volunteered to help serve the guests. The students were willing to set up the display, even scrape the outside of the White Elephant clean, but run their legs off ferrying cheap wine and nibbles to the Panschin art establishment? That was different somehow; as if being seen in a service capacity was unacceptable. Based on how she was being treated, Shelby concluded that solidarity with the working class meant lording over them, not working with them.

Kip's McGrant's indifference today was especially painful. She was slowly coming to realize that Kip did like her. He liked her very much, but only when there was no one around to notice he was slumming. When no one who mattered was around, he was funny and interested in what she did and always eager to talk and joke. When people who mattered were around — those higher up on the social ladder which was everyone where Shelby was concerned — he treated her like furniture.

The sad truth, Shelby, realized, was that Kip was like every other guy she'd met since being forced to move to Dome Two. She knew she was pretty, but being pretty without a good family to back you up didn't get you anywhere other than into a hotel room renting by the hour. Kip didn't even respect her enough to introduce her to his parents as a fellow student and a member of the PanU Artists' Collective, although, she noticed, he had done that with the other Collective members.

And here auntie Neza had believed she'd meet some nice young man from a good family at PanU. That would never happen and this evening brought home how delusional her great-aunt had been. Shelby offered her tray of algae dumplings to another finger-snapping gallery goer who saw her tray, accepted her nibbles, but didn't see her. If Neza could get her into PCC's commercial arts department, she wouldn't complain about doing hack work for hire, drawing treacly illustrations of kittens or worse, pickaxes. It was still art, she'd make some hard coin, and she could draw what she wanted in her off hours.

Her tray empty again — it was amazing how these people stuffed themselves when they could claim it was for a good cause — Shelby worked her way through the crowd, invisible to everyone, to get a fresh tray from Florence. Waiting tables at the Dappled Yak had to be better than this; she'd be seen and she'd get paid. She spotted Mrs. Wangmo, who did see her, and demanded a dumpling while curling her lip in open disdain. At least, Shelby thought, she had been seen even if it had been with a sneer. It meant she existed.

Back in the ballroom, she worked her way patiently through the crowd towards the far corner where her painting was ignored with the other also-rans. Kip's sludgy effort was languishing here which wasn't surprising. Her paintings didn't meet Professor Vitebskin's standards no matter what she did. Kip didn't put in nearly as much effort at his art and she often wondered why he was in the Art Department in the first place. He didn't care about fine art the way she did. In fact, he didn't seem to care about creating like most of the other students did. It was a mystery. Watching Kip chatting up another pretty fellow-student and introducing that girl to his parents made Shelby not want to solve his mystery any more.

Malcolm had his fill of painting, but he slowly worked his way around the ballroom, pretending to take another look. It gave him a chance to explore the public areas of the White Elephant and consider what to do next. He didn't recognize the guests nor did anyone recognize him. This wasn't, he thought, the worst thing to happen. He was invisible but that was better than being openly disdained. Interestingly, like the waitress who had given him his glass of wine, anyone who did meet his gaze did not seem to automatically think "scholarship boy" or "jumped-up tunnel rat." He was a well-dressed connoisseur of the arts, but also a stranger without a known place in the social hierarchy. As of yet, no one wanted to go first. This group fit a familiar pattern; they were curious about him but not prepared to introduce themselves to a total stranger of unknown status, especially when it was so much more fun to rip apart acquaintances who weren't present to defend themselves.

There were other mysteries to occupy him as well. He could not figure out why Neza Molony, the lease-holder, was taking money with a little basket at the front door. Wasn't she the hostess? It was her house. Everything he had been taught said she should be holding court in this beautiful, grand mansion while wearing elegant, expensive clothes. She should be receiving visitors like a daimyah in the Four Hundred. Someone else — one of the students for example — should be manning the front door. The PanU Artists' Collective had found the young woman who had given him his glass of wine. Surely, they could have found other volunteers to do the scutwork.

Malcolm slowly scanned the crowd. Based on the people eating, the Collective had someone handing out nibbles although they had not gotten enough volunteers for this task either. The scattered tables with trays perched on them weren't up to the task, emptying out rapidly but not being refilled nearly as fast. It would be nice to get something to eat. He recognized the young lady ferrying trays back and forth and wondered if he would see the rest of her trio, particularly the one he most wanted to meet.

Then he saw her. His Dome Two brunette beauty. She was carrying a tray, loaded with nibbles, and running back and forth between patrons when they snapped their fingers at her, wanting service right now rather than walk to a tray on a table and serve themselves. She wore a tired, pasted-on smile, the kind he was very familiar with. He'd worn it himself many times when he had to look pleasant and helpful no matter how he seethed inside.

What was she doing here? If she was a student at PanU, like he thought she was, shouldn't she be one of the guests? She couldn't be a student at PanU, the way she was being treated. Everyone there was upper-class and higher. Scholarship boys like him didn't go to PanU. They went to the more practical schools where they got a practical education to repay the money invested in them by the taxpayers of Panschin. Yet here she was, being ordered about like some tunnel girl in a cheap café. Everything he had observed about her said she was from the upper levels of society. What was he missing?

He watched her closely but unobtrusively, giving himself time to decide what to say. It was clear she didn't have time for idle conversation. He already knew he did not want to snap his fingers for service. Whoever his Dome Two beauty was, she deserved better. He would not treat her the way the rest of the crowd was doing.

He began quietly tracking her, waiting for a chance to introduce himself and, at last, she emptied out her tray. But instead of heading back towards the dining room for a refill, she retreated to the far corner of the ballroom. He made a snap decision and followed her. This was his chance to introduce himself and maybe, this time, she would see him.

He wouldn't be invisible anymore.

Tray empty again, Shelby retreated to the ignored corner where she could snatch a few minutes of peace before returning to the fray. The way Professor Vitebskin had arranged the paintings on their easels ensured that very few people made it all the way back here. She didn't bother studying her own entry again, fretting over why it didn't make the grade when, to her eyes at least, it stood out from the other sludgy efforts relegated to the dross heap. That was a waste of time and energy she could put to better use catching her breath and calming herself enough to wait on people who despised her.

She spotted him again, threading his way between the easels. He was far and away the best-dressed visitor to the show. He wore a conservative business suit, making him stand out in a crowd of people ostentatiously wearing fashionable coveralls that had never seen real labor. Another upper-class twit, no doubt, and trying to get her alone.

She frowned, thinking hard. Based on his clothes, he was probably one of those upper-class businessmen or mine owners who squeezed every possible bit of work out of his underlings and threw away their used-up husks into the tailings. Those people never wore coveralls, even velvet ones. Yet what was he doing here at the White Elephant?

The entire point of the PanU Artists' Collective was to demonstrate, via art, how the working classes were exploited by their betters. The people who came to the shows all claimed solidarity with their exploited brethren.

That was what Professor Vitebskin proclaimed over and over, a speech backed up by the other instructors in the Art Department as well as quite a few professors from the other PanU departments. Shelby had repeated this spiel to Veronica soon after arriving at PanU and then listened to her sister's gales of laughter, laughter which ended in Veronica's own speech about paying attention to costly actions instead of cheap, empty words. Auntie Neza refused to comment, but her sniff of disdain made her point. Shelby had passed along the same lecture to Lulu and Florence. Their reaction wasn't any better than Veronica's, although Lulu used words she'd never heard before to express her opinion of the PanU faculty. Florence was more tactful. She was also kind enough to provide definitions for Lulu's vocabulary. The memory still stung, and Shelby never brought the subject up again.

Shelby thought harder, trapped in the corner with no way out other than past him, knocking over an easel, or through a window. For the first time, she was allowing herself to see the incongruity between what she was told, over and over, and how those lecturers actually behaved when in the presence of lower-status peons. She and her sister fit the bill now after what dear old dad had done to them. Lulu and Florence had a better fitting place in Panschin. They were who they were, without an up and down ore-car ride of status changes to confuse the issue.

And, she had to admit, she'd never seen anyone at the gallery shows the White Elephant hosted who came from any of the business classes, wealthy or not. Veronica had told her that while the business owners in Dome Two would stop by later on in the week, they only came to jeer and snicker and gossip. Whatever kind of art those people bought to hang on their walls must not look like what the Panschin art establishment liked. So why was this man here? He didn't fit into the crowd she knew. Perhaps she was misjudging him. He might really be here for the art. It wasn't like he knew who she was.

Still, he looked vaguely familiar, as though she'd seen him on the streets of Dome Two. Well. She'd find out soon enough and if he bought a painting, they'd earn some money.

Malcolm eyed his Dome Two princess with trepidation. She looked like she was squaring up for a fight, although she did not appear to recognize him as a former tunnel rat. He blurted out the first thing he thought of, a question that had bugged him since he'd walked into the White Elephant. Everything else he'd planned on saying to her vanished down a shaft into the deepdown.

"Miss? Could you tell me something about these paintings?" He waved a hand at the ballroom behind them, crammed with ugly canvases only partly obscured by the gallery-goers milling around them and filling the room with a low buzz of noise.

Shelby smiled thinly at the stranger. He didn't seem to be picking her up, although it was early moments. Better, this was a question she could answer, having just been thinking over it herself. She knew the lecture by heart, having heard it so many times. She launched into her subject about worker exploitation and how art spoke the things polite society preferred to ignore and how, if only the masses understood the purpose of this art, they would embrace the truth of their exploitation fully and wholeheartedly.

Shelby found herself running out of words as she realized this well-dressed, good-looking in a rough-hewn way stranger was looking at her like she was crazy.

"Anyways, that's the rationale," she finished, trying to project some confidence in a statement she no longer believed in. .

"You really think that?" the stranger asked her. He didn't appear to believe a single word she had said.

"Yeah. I mean, sure, why not," Shelby said and rolled her eyes. "It's what they tell us at university. All the time. Look, Mr. uh,"

"Malcolm Cobb."

"Mr. Cobb. I'm the only waitress, so I've got to get back to work." She curled her lip but not at him. She stared over his shoulder to the gallery-goers discussing everything but the art hanging on the walls and what it represented. "This crowd won't feed itself."

"Do you really believe that dross? Because it doesn't sound like you do," Malcolm said. Damn, damn, damn. Where was his prepared speech? Why was he arguing with her?

Shelby stared at him for a long, pensive moment, meeting his dark brown eyes.

"I don't know anymore," she admitted.

She'd never see him again so she could be honest in a way she couldn't be with her family without being teased. She certainly couldn't admit disbelief in the approved canon at PanU or in front of any member of the Collective. Doing so would make her an even bigger pariah.

He said, "whoever told you that dross might think it's true, but I can tell you real working-class people like pretty, not these tailings. The only even marginally attractive painting here is the one behind you. It's got some light purple instead of just shades of dirt. And you think this crowd cares about what goes on in the tunnels? They don't."

Shelby snorted audibly and gave him a good looking over. He was as well-dressed as her father used to be, back when Simon Bradwell was still masquerading as a respected and wealthy investment counselor and pillar of the Panschin business community.

"And how would you know? What do you do for a living, all dressed up like you've never done an honest day's work in your life."

"I'm the assistant manager of the local branch of the Second National Bank of Panschin."

All the anger she'd been tamping down for the last few days roared into life. Shelby stepped up to him to prod his broad chest with her finger and glare up at his face.

"See? This is exactly what I'm talking about. You work for a bank! How could you possibly know anything about how real people struggle? You don't know what it's like to scrape by, always worrying about how to make ends meet, which bill to pay, can you make the lease this month."

As she spoke, a warning sign started flashing in her brain. Bank. Assistant manager. But not just any bank and not just any assistant manager. The Second National Bank of Panschin, the bank that held the lease on the White Elephant.

For his part, Malcolm didn't know what to say, other than to think in amazement, she doesn't know who I am. She doesn't know where I came from, my background, growing up and mining for Steelio, where my family still lives. She doesn't know. He still didn't know her name. He also realized that all she saw was him, and that was all she saw. Unlike everyone else he knew, she saw the man standing in front of her and she only knew what he told her.

Neza finally got a break in the trickle of visitors. No one was on the street as far as she could peer down it in every direction. She grabbed her basket, heavy with coin — this had been the most successful gallery showing to date — her cane, and went in search of Veronica.

She didn't have to search far. Veronica was standing in the atrium, laughing as though Mr. Jones, standing right next to her, had said something funny. It was a joy to see her niece relax enough to enjoy herself, especially considering how aggravating the day had been. She must not have run into Dean yet.

Veronica caught sight of her aunt determinedly working her way through the crowd.

"Please excuse me, Mr. Jones. Auntie Neza, do you need a break?" she asked.

"No, no, we've got problems," Neza replied. She cast a wary look at Mr. Jones.

Veronica caught her aunt's glance and said reassuringly, "Mr. Jones already knows about Dean. We spoke and he left."

Neza was momentarily distracted. "Dean left? Not through the front door or I'd have seen him. No, he's not the problem."

"Neza, please don't be mysterious," Veronica said. "And who's at the front door?"

Her aunt jerked her head at Mr. Jones who was standing by, his face reserved as ever but with alert, intent eyes.

"We have to talk, Veronica. I only need a minute."

"Go ahead, Miss Bradwell," Mr. Jones said. "I'll give you some privacy."

As soon as Airik turned away to investigate a canvas out of earshot, Neza whispered to Veronica, "He's here!"

"Who? Dean?" Veronica was still confused.

"Not that fool. Malcolm Cobb!"

To Neza's dismay, Veronica looked blank. Then comprehension bloomed across her face.

"The one Mrs. Grisson warned us about? The assistant manager of the bank? Our lease holder?"

"Yes! He's wandering around the White Elephant right now."

"Oh, lordy," Veronica said. She looked down at her tray, the wine in the glasses fizzing as her hands trembled, shaking the glasses. "He told you? What does he look like?"

"Yes, he introduced himself to me at the front door. He's big and good-looking, and he's the best dressed man here. Conservative business suit, deep blue with gold piping and brass buttons," Neza hissed.

Veronica racked her brains over the gallery-going crowd she'd served, finally placing him. "I gave him a glass of wine," she said. "He didn't say anything to me."

"You're a waitress tonight, dear girl," Neza replied tartly. "That makes you staff. Why should a banker talk to you?"

"I better find him quick."

"I've got to get back and mind the door," Neza said. "Remember, gold piping and buttons on a deep blue suit instead of a ridiculous, tarted-up coverall like Professor Vitebskin is wearing."

Shelby wanted desperately to rewind her speech. She sounded like a fool and quite possibly had offended the man who could throw them out of their house.

"Don't throw us out," she blurted and wanted even more desperately to retract a statement which could have put ideas into Mr. Cobb's head.

He gave her another puzzled look. "I wasn't planning on throwing anyone out. We, I, don't operate that way."

"All bankers do!" Shelby flared up. "All you want is money." Shut up, shut up, SHUT UP! she screamed at herself.

"No, only bankers in melodramas do that," Malcolm said patiently. Why did everyone think such a thing? "Real bankers have to follow government regulations. There's not a lot of leeway." Damn, damn, damn. His Dome Two princess was either a beautiful twit or very naïve. Something struck him.

"Why are you so concerned anyway? Where do you live? Who are you?"

"I'm Shelby Bradwell."

Long training in never showing his emotions rushed to Malcolm's aid. Bradwell was a name he knew well. He had studied the notorious case in business college. Simon Bradwell had embezzled enough money, ruined enough lives, consorted with criminals (this hadn't been proven in court although plenty of evidence indicated such activities), and swindled enough businesses to ensure his place for generations as a case study in what to watch for. The fact that no one had discovered where a good chunk of the missing money had gone — the paper trail indicated not all of it went to illegal gambling — added still more interest. His dramatic suicide on the eve of his trial provided the finishing touch to the lurid story. Best of all, since it was all so recent, there were plenty of living witnesses eager to rehash the case, amplifying every detail in full along with plenty of speculation as to where the missing money was hidden.

Simon Bradwell had also left behind relatives.

I should have lied, Shelby thought, watching his face closely. But it doesn't look like he's heard of us, so that's something.

"Miss Bradwell," Malcolm began.

"Shelby! What is wrong with you?" Professor Vitebskin called out. "Why the hell aren't you serving our guests?" He came marching up behind Malcolm Cobb, glaring at Shelby with every step.

With Shelby firmly relegated to her place, Professor Vitebskin smiled graciously at his well-dressed, potentially lucrative connoisseur of the arts.

He said, "Please forgive Shelby for pestering you. She's one of my students. Shelby, run along. Lots of hungry gallery-goers are waiting for you so quit neglecting them. I'm Professor Vitebskin, head of the PanU Art Department and leader of the PanU Artists' Collective. And you are?"

"Malcolm Cobb," Malcolm answered. It had not escaped his notice how pale Shelby had gone, or how her lips had tightened with hurt fury. "I'm the new assistant manager at the local branch of the Second National Bank of Panschin."

Damnation, thought Professor Vitebskin. An overdressed, penniless flunky. I have to be polite, since he might have some connections somewhere. He said, "And which of our wonderful paintings do you favor? Any of them would grace your home and mark you as a patron of the arts."

"They're all horrible," Malcolm replied, "other than the one behind me with the light purple smears. It has some color and that makes it slightly less horrible."

"But still horrible?" Shelby interjected, earning her another scowl from Professor Vitebskin.

"Yes," Malcolm said, puzzled at her tone. He couldn't figure out the unspoken conversation Shelby and the professor were apparently having, shooting angry glares at each other. The professor won the struggle and Shelby looked at the floor. Her shoulders slumped, she made a move to escape.

"Would you like to tell him, Shelby, or shall I?" Professor Vitebskin asked in his most pleasant voice.

She stopped in her tracks and came back to angry, resentful life. "I'll do it, Professor. That painting is mine, Mr. Cobb. It's back in this corner with all the other rejects, tripe, and hackwork. Mine is, as Professor Vitebskin will tell you, mediocre drivel. The only reason I was allowed to enter a painting was because the White Elephant is my home, and my family hosts the exhibit."

Shelby glared at Malcolm Cobb, daring him to say anything about the quality of her painting. Her eyes were suspiciously bright and her jaw trembled. "I have to go. People want food."

"Let her go, Mr. Cobb, and I'll show you far better examples from far more talented artists than our little Shelby," Professor Vitebskin said. "I have some protégés in our show who have exquisite work that is very reasonably priced and sure to increase in value over the years."

Malcolm watched Professor Vitebskin steadily, not moving, not speaking, and waited for him to talk some more. This talent had done him favors in the past as it encouraged whoever he was with to become uncomfortable and fill the empty silence with plenty of revealing words.

He was rewarded when Professor Vitebskin said, "Shall we proceed back to the atrium? I arranged the show to provide the viewer with a progression of experiences, each building on the next and culminating in the very best the PanU Artists' Collective has to offer."

"I think," Malcolm said, "I've seen enough. I've also seen that I do not like how you treat your students, starting with Miss Bradwell. I have also noticed the Collective does not believe in staffing its own shows or Miss Bradwell would not be alone other than the young woman handing out wine and the young woman ferrying trays. Your Collective doesn't support its own show."

Professor Vitebskin forced out a smile and a lie. "Those students who were to assist fell ill and could not be here."

"And none of their fellows cared enough to step into the breach? Such brotherhood and solidarity," Malcolm scoffed. "Quite different from what Miss Bradwell was telling me about the goals of the Collective."

"You do not understand," Professor Vitebskin began.

"I think I do."

"Mr. Cobb!" a voice sang out. Malcolm looked past the fuming professor to the much more pleasant sight of the young lady with the tray of mismatched wineglasses bearing down on them.

"Yes?"

"What is it now, Miss Bradwell?" Professor Vitebskin asked wearily. Couldn't she hand out wine someplace else? The White Elephant was packed with gallery-goers all of whom needed a drink. Gods knew he did.

Malcolm paused. This was also Miss Bradwell? Now that he looked, there was a resemblance. Since Shelby Bradwell was right behind her sister, carrying a reloaded tray of nibbles, he could easily spot the similarities. The answer came to him. Simon Bradwell had two daughters and these two young women must be them. Their connection to the White Elephant eluded him, but that answer would arrive in due time.

"Another glass of wine, Mr. Cobb?" Veronica said as sweetly as she could. She did not offer a glass to Professor Vitebskin, relying on his often-demonstrated ability to take one for himself.

She spared a scowl at the professor and added, smiling cheerfully at Malcolm, "alcohol makes the paintings go down much easier." This earned her a hateful glower in return that should have set her hair on fire.

"Thank you, Miss Bradwell," Malcolm struggled to keep his face bland. Shelby offered him a nibble from her fully reloaded tray, trying hard for a placating smile that would erase her earlier insinuations about evil, money-grubbing bankers throwing innocent people out onto the streets to starve.

"Are you enjoying the show?" Veronica asked.

"I think the paintings are wastes of paint," Malcolm answered.

This statement earned him a glower from Professor Vitebskin who would have left in a huff, but his way was now blocked by that damned philistine from the sticks, Airik Jones.

"I do have some questions, Miss Bradwell," Malcolm added. "Why are you hosting this event since you don't seem to care for it?"

Veronica thought of the lease stipulations.

"I am allowed to do this," she said firmly. "I can host parties whenever I want to, as can any lease-holder."

This was not the answer he had been expecting but Malcolm Cobb was nothing if not flexible. If she wanted to debate the terms of her lease, despite not being the person who had signed, he could do that. He probably knew it better than she did.

"That is true, Miss Bradwell, but then why are you charging admission? And letting in anyone who can pay? That's not how parties are hosted."

"Because it's a cultural fund-raiser," Shelby volunteered promptly. "To raise money for the arts."

"That's right," Veronica hastened to say. "We're allowed to do that, too. Would you like a deviled egg? Shelby, bring them up."

She quietly thanked herself for her forethought in keeping a few back when she saw Mr. Cobb's expression brighten.

"Yes, thank you." He offered a warm smile at Shelby as she brought the tray to him.

Eggs were a rare and expensive treat although how could they afford them when the recent history of the White Elephant's lease indicated payment difficulties? It was always paid, but more and more often, at the last possible moment.

"Where did you get them?" he asked, genuinely curious as he picked one from the tray. Eggs were not easy to come by at this time of the year. He took a bite, savoring the rich taste.

Veronica thought quickly for a plausible, socially acceptable response that fell within the parameters of a Dome Two lease. Unfortunately, Shelby answered for her.

"Our neighbor, Mrs. Grisson gave us them from her chickens," she blurted out. "She lives right down the street."

That got Malcolm's attention. Was Mrs. Grisson his mysterious farmer who provided the vegetables he'd been eating at the Dappled Yak? Agricultural efforts were not acceptable in any of the lease covenants in Dome Two and raising livestock was even less so. He'd have to tread carefully to avoid bringing trouble onto these people.

Veronica scowled at her sister and said, "They're pets! Mrs. Grisson keeps chickens as pets."

Both Malcolm and Professor Vitebskin looked baffled. The professor stopped sidling away, now that the conversation had suddenly gotten interesting and there was a chance those wretched Bradwell sisters would be tossed out onto their ear.

"Pets?" Malcolm asked, disconcerted. He understood the concept but he had little experience with it. Cats were pets, expensive ones, too. So were little dogs. He knew he wasn't personally acquainted with anyone who actually owned a pet since the people who could afford one bragged about the subject constantly. "I thought chickens laid eggs?"

"They're useful pets," Veronica said. "Pets are allowed." Her eyes darted around, hoping for inspiration, and found it in an unlikely source. She smiled widely at the group.

"People in Barsoom keep chickens as pets," she said brightly. "Isn't that right, Mr. Jones."

She shot him a desperate plea for aid.

Airik had been standing back and unobtrusively listening, concerned over what was going to happen to Miss Bradwell. He was unwilling to examine his motives since he would then have to retreat back upstairs and go back to reading briefing papers on safety techniques. Since meeting Veronica Bradwell, they had lost much of their fascination.

"Mr. Jones is from Barsoom and in town for the Biennial Mining Conference," Veronica added.

Malcolm was, with tremendous effort, able to stop himself from gaping slack-jawed at Mr. Jones from Barsoom. It couldn't be. The daimyo of Shelleen at some ridiculous art exhibit in Dome Two? It had to be someone who resembled the man he'd been reading about in the Panschin business journals. Those line drawings were not always accurate; they were often drawn from descriptions or were drawings of drawings or blurry photographs. This man didn't look nearly the heroic leader his images in the Panschin newspapers implied, but even so, he had that faint air about him of someone who expected people to listen and obey without question.

For his part, Airik kept his face blank and counted on his normally boring appearance and standard-issue coverall to provide camouflage. It had worked so far and Mr. Cobb didn't seem to recognize him anymore than that annoying fool Vitebskin had. Having a banker not know him made Airik question the competence and acumen of the businessmen of Panschin more than he already was. He made a mental note to go over every business proposal even more carefully.

"Yes, people in Barsoom do many odd things. Some do keep chickens as pets," Airik said after a moment of thought while everyone waited, all eyes upon him.

It wasn't a complete lie. In Airik's experience, however ridiculous a behavior, you could count on someone in Barsoom doing it and telling you all about it, whether you wanted to know or not. He had also observed peasant children in Shelleen carrying around chickens and petting them. Besides, his lie was rewarded with Veronica's immense smile of relief. She beamed at him, and it felt like the sun coming out, despite the dome overhead blocking its life-giving rays. It warmed him and he wanted to see her smile like that at him again.

Professor Vitebskin, irritated beyond all measure at how total strangers kept leaping to the aid of the Bradwell sisters, said, "I have never heard of anything so absurd. Chickens are agricultural beasts. They are not pets and anyone raising them in any of the domes is cheating on the terms of their lease."

Airik frowned at Professor Vitebskin for trying to incite more trouble for Miss Bradwell. He said "chickens are not beasts. They are birds, part of the large class of poultry. You may be a university professor but you seem to have gaps in your knowledge. Large ones."

"How dare you insinuate that my education is not the finest," Professor Vitebskin sputtered.

"Your own words condemn you," Airik replied coldly.

Malcolm's mind raced. Why would the daimyo of Shelleen be hiding in Dome Two under an assumed name? Should someone know about it? What if he was wrong? He would make a fool of himself and prove that everyone who belittled him as a jumped-up tunnel rat was correct. If he was right, then he needed to discover why the daimyo of Shelleen was visiting Dome Two and what his connection was to the White Elephant. It could help him in his self-assigned task to demonstrate the value of Dome Two to his superiors in the Second National Bank of Panschin. He had to be careful, though. An angry daimyo could bring down an avalanche of trouble on him. Daimyos and the Four Hundred were supposed to have no authority in the free-cities but anyone with sense knew that wasn't true. Their reach was vast.

And there was Shelby Bradwell, anxiously holding her tray of nibbles for him to choose from. His Dome Two beauty had problems of her own, that was clear enough, and he wasn't about to make them worse. If he made them better, she might smile at him the way her sister was smiling at this Mr. Jones, supposedly from Barsoom.

"I suppose," Malcolm said carefully, "that chickens could be pets."

Veronica nodded eagerly. "Yes, absolutely." Her sister Shelby smiled at him too, also nodding in agreement.

"You are all insane," said Professor Vitebskin. "My little dog, Cinnamon, is a pet, the finest one in all of Dome Six. He's the smartest, most faithful, loyal, handsomest dog you'll ever meet. Chickens are not pets."

"Another gap in your knowledge base," Airik said coolly, earning him another smile of appreciation from Veronica, and as a bonus, a stifled giggle from her sister.

"There you are. I been looking for you." Another voice intruded, one that Veronica recognized at once from the faint, hissing accent.

Veronica gasped and tensed, a motion that caught Airik's attention at once. She turned around slowly, hoping she was wrong.

Her heart sank. It was the same oversized, aggressive-looking man with the shaved head she had spoken to the previous week, the man she had turned away from the White Elephant. As before, he wore a neat, plain business suit instead of a coverall. As before, the tailor had not cut this particular suit to minimize his bulk or designed it to make him look harmless. More importantly, the better lighting in the ballroom demonstrated that his tailor definitely wasn't from Panschin. The oddly cut suit in conjunction with the man's hissing accent said very plainly "I'm not from around here."

She wondered when he had arrived and worried more why Neza had allowed him inside the White Elephant. Then she remembered Neza hadn't gotten a clear look at him that evening. She, Veronica, was the only member of the household who had seen his face. Plus, there was the fact that even if Neza had recognized the man, she couldn't have stopped him.

His face was less friendly and reassuring than it had been then.

"I been looking around and except for all those ugly-shit pictures you got trashing up the place, I like your house," he said. "I like it a lot. My boss, he likes it too, and he wants you to know you're running out of time to think where you gonna move to."

Veronica took a deep breath and said as steadily as she could, "I told you then and I'll tell you now. This is our home, we are not moving, and I am not subleasing to you or to anyone. I want you to leave."

Malcolm went very still hearing this statement. He assessed the stranger, his prohibited demand, his aggressive stance, and how the Bradwell sisters reacted to his presence. Shelby had paled dramatically and stepped closer to the group, closer to him, and away from the stranger. Her sister Veronica's hands were trembling, enough to make the stemmed glasses of wine rattle slightly on the tray and the wine fizz. They could do very little to discourage a threatening stranger in their home.

He cast glanced around the isolated corner of the ballroom they were currently occupying. No one who might be helpful was nearby. Professor Vitebskin, who apparently did know the Bradwell sisters in some capacity, was again edging away. No help would come from that quarter, despite the professor's use of their house for his horrible paintings.

Mr. Jones was more interesting. His face had gone very cold and that faint air of expecting to be obeyed had intensified. He didn't look like a man who indulged in bar brawls, but he wasn't pretending nothing was happening either. What was his connection to the Bradwell family?

It was time to do something. Malcolm had to work at looking non-threatening; like someone who could be trusted to safely manage your money. Now, he could relax and look like someone you didn't want to meet in a dark alley or a well-lit one for that matter.

Malcolm let his teeth show, flexed his hands, and stepped toward the thug. When he was sure he had the man's attention, he announced, "I'm Malcolm Cobb. I'm the assistant manager of the Second National Bank of Panschin. We hold this lease in trust to the Martian government. We don't allow subleasing, nor do we condone harassing our tenants. If you force the leaseholder to sublet, we will throw you out, repossess the property, and we will press charges."

The stranger gave Malcolm a good looking over. He looked like he was inclined to dismiss him because of his clothes — but his stare paused on Malcolm's callused hands. He hesitated, grinned suddenly, and said, "you're just an overdressed flunky. My boss gets what he wants, and he wants this house." He leaned forward slightly, looking bigger.

Airik found himself reevaluating Malcolm Cobb. Perhaps he was not incompetent in every area. The banker felt responsible for the properties in his care. He also noticed that Veronica was more upset than she had been over her ex-husband, Dean Kangjuon. Dean threatened her and she'd been afraid, but this situation seemed worse. Airik knew he was operating without enough facts, but he didn't like what he saw.

"I agree with Mr. Cobb and Miss Bradwell," Airik stepped next to Malcolm. "This property is not available and you must leave. Now."

The thug gave him a more dismissive look than he had given the larger banker, although again, Airik noticed, his eyes darted to his hands. Airik's own hands, while immaculately clean, were not the soft hands of a gentleman. He spent far too many hours in the field, wielding a shovel or a pickaxe himself and had the calluses to prove it. He rarely had time to wait for someone else to investigate an outcropping or seam and could do the job faster himself rather than explaining what he wanted to a peasant. Even now, as the daimyo, Airik still got his hands dirty when he needed to.

"That's real nice of you two gentlemen," the stranger sneered over the word, "helping out these ladies. Getting something for it in exchange, I hope?"

He leered openly at Veronica who was appalled and then even more so when he spotted Shelby, hovering anxiously behind her sister. His eyes lit up and he ran his tongue across his lips, as he ran his eyes all over her body.

"Didn't see *you* when I was here last. I'd remember *you*. You will be *a treat*."

Shelby gasped audibly and cringed at his implied threat. Professor Vitebskin moved back, bumping against the easels and making them scrape against the floor.

"How dare you speak to my sister," Veronica said icily. "You are disgusting." She moved to better shield Shelby. She wished she could throw the loaded tray of wineglasses at him but that meant cleaning up broken glass and plonk, followed by replacing all the glassware. More importantly, it was unlikely to do any good. She would only enrage the man and make him more dangerous. She doubted he would hold still long enough to let her slash his throat with a piece of broken glass.

"That is quite enough from you," Airik announced, using every bit of bred-in-the-bone aristocratic hauteur at his command. He moved closer to the thug, even while Professor Vitebskin attempted to move further away, hampered by his arrangement of easels.

Veronica glanced his way. Mr. Jones' facial features had not rearranged themselves and yet, he looked very different; he looked and spoke like a man used to being obeyed without question.

Malcolm revised the odds of this stranger from Barsoom actually being the daimyo of Shelleen instead of a chance lookalike. This man expected results and people who didn't meet his expectations suffered for their lapses. Malcolm moved closer to the thug, noticing as he did that Mr. Jones did so too. Interesting.

Professor Vitebskin, trying hard to keep the easel from crashing to the floor and drawing attention to himself, also noticed and snarled inwardly. Airik Jones was more than another mouth-breathing yokel gawking at the big city. It was still doubtful he was from Barsoom; there were plenty of minor, impoverished free-cities on Mars buried in the provinces along with fourth-tier aristocrats from obscure, poverty-stricken demesnes.

The stranger's expression never changed. He scanned Malcolm and Airik again, re-evaluating them as possible threats. He also threw a glance at Professor Vitebskin, openly and contemptuously dismissing him out of hand as being less dangerous than Veronica Bradwell clutching her tray of shivering wineglasses.

"So your name's Bradwell," the stranger said. "I'll make sure to tell my boss. We'll be in touch, with you and your delicious sister." He winked at Shelby, raked his eyes over Veronica again, this time more slowly as if he was reassessing her, and clicked his tongue. "Soon."

He swaggered away, but stopped next to Professor Vitebskin (trying to blend into a canvas resting on an easel) to say, "You are a sodding little git, and your pictures look like shit. Your dog on the other hand is worth something. Little dogs make good eating, good as chickens."

Professor Vitebskin blanched and let go of the easel. It would have crashed, but Shelby rushed to steady it. The thug spared her another leer and swaggered out.

Veronica was stricken and didn't know what to do. She watched the thug stride into the ballroom like he already owned it, her hands shaking and rattling the wineglasses on the tray, but otherwise unable to move or speak. Airik stepped forward and took the tray from her again and the thought flashed through her mind that she wished she could hug him for being so considerate of a near total stranger's needs.

The thug had come back, she thought. He hadn't made a mistake coming to the White Elephant. The mistake was hers. She had completely misjudged his intent, dismissed him as a lost stranger albeit an unpleasant one, and pushed the unpleasant incident out of her mind. She had been concerned enough to go to the police and then stopped as though she had done enough. She hadn't seriously considered he meant every word. His boss, whoever *that* was, wanted the White Elephant, and he had every intention of getting it. She had put her family in harm's way, and she still didn't know why anyone would want their house.

She glanced at Airik Jones. She liked him and he had been considerate and helpful, but what did that mean? She knew nothing of him, including his true name since she doubted that it was Jones. Events kept proving she couldn't trust her intuition and that meant she couldn't trust him.

"Miss Bradwell—," Malcolm began.

"Wait," Airik held up his hand, interrupting him. "Miss Bradwell. This man has been here before?"

Malcolm revised his guess about Mr. Jones' true identity upwards again and waited to see what Miss Bradwell would say. She looked ill and her sister, Shelby, didn't look any better. This might be the reason she had looked so unhappy outside the Dappled Yak, giving him another reason to be helpful.

Veronica tried to speak, coughed, then croaked out, "Yes, a few days ago. I thought he was lost, had the wrong house." It was humiliating to admit how wrong she had been.

"I see," Airik said. "Mr. Cobb, I assume this sort of behavior is both unusual and unacceptable in Panschin?"

Malcolm laughed harshly. "Illegal as all hell too. What I can't understand is why he would want *this* house so badly. There are plenty of mansions in Dome Two going begging. This house is in exceptionally fine condition, but that's not enough of a reason. The houses in this dome were built to last and the builders understood terraformers would be a constant problem. But there isn't a house within Dome Two that couldn't be cleaned and restored back to its original condition."

"You know this for sure?" Airik asked.

"I realized the day I was assigned to this branch that Dome Two was severely undervalued. I did my research. But as I said, there are plenty of empty houses going begging. Discreet squatters don't get noticed."

"I see. So, there is something about this particular house that is unusually desirable." Airik thought of the PanU Artists' Collective and why it using a private residence for their exhibit rather than the university facilities.

"Professor Vitebskin, does this matter involve you?" he asked sharply.

"What? No!" Professor Vitebskin was still shaking. "That hooligan, that monster, he threatened to *eat* my precious Cinnamon."

Airik gave him a contemptuous look. The professor's main concern was a dog? Not the safety and wellbeing of the Bradwell family whom he was using for his own purposes?

Shelby, like her sister, didn't know what to say to any of this, other than agonize over what was going to happen next. The way that goon had looked at her made her feel slimy all over. She seized on a chance to focus on something else, something other than her own safety and security.

"Professor," Shelby grimaced and said, "I'm sure he didn't mean it about Cinnamon. No one would ever do such a thing."

Malcolm thought, It depended on how hungry you were. Starvation's a tremendous motivator. He noticed Airik Jones chose not to reassure Shelby on the same point. Interesting.

"I think he meant it, about eating the professor's dog," Veronica said roughly.

Professor Vitebskin clutched at his chest again at her words, crumpling his perfectly ironed coverall front into wrinkles, cracking the decorative paint spatters.

"I think," Veronica went on, "he meant everything he said last week and he meant every word tonight about taking our house. Shelby, we have to talk to Neza and figure out what to do."

"Do?" Shelby cried. "Do? How can we stop someone like that?"

"You do it with allies, Miss Bradwell," Airik said.

"And who would that be?" Veronica snapped at him, all her bitterness rushing out like an avalanche. "We're pariahs because of dear old dad." She snatched the tray back from his hands, making the glasses tremble and the wine fizz.

"Veronica," Shelby began, near tears. "Don't bring that up." She shot a pleading glance at her stricken sister, then one at the banker who held their lease. She was sure if Mr. Cobb knew who they were, he wouldn't hesitate to throw them out, and he would include auntie Neza, Florence, and Lulu because they were tainted by association.

Veronica stared at the tray in her hands and watched the bubbles fizz up to the surface, breaking with the tiniest of pops, inaudible against her pounding heart and the buzz of mindless chatter filling the ballroom. She forced herself back to calmness while Airik Jones, her guest, waited patiently for her to regain control. She was able to gaze back into his cool hazel eyes.

"Forgive me, Mr. Jones," Veronica said, the words rasping on her dry throat. "I was unpardonably rude to you and you've been nothing but helpful to me."

Airik allowed himself the smallest of smiles. She still had no idea who he was. He had observed her being courteous with all the gallery-goers, not reserving her good manners for only those people who could benefit her. Veronica Bradwell had even stayed civil to the very unpleasant Mrs. Wangmo. He liked that. She had managed her former husband, despite his provocations. She didn't fall apart into hysteria when the thug confronted her. He liked that too. Her grace under pressure compared very well to the young women who were being pushed onto him as suitable candidates for the daimyah of Shelleen. He shoved that thought away at once to focus on the problem at hand.

"Think nothing of it. I suspect today has been a difficult day as well as the culmination of many difficult days."

"Yes, it has."

"I've been thinking," Malcolm began.

He was interrupted again.

"Sir — I mean, Airik," Carmine said, slightly out of breath as he came around the easel, again blocking Professor Vitebskin's escape route.

"Saw that big guy come out of this corner. He bother you any?"

"No," Airik answered calmly. "His interest was in Miss Bradwell's house."

"The house?" asked Carmine, openly thrown by Airik's answer. "Why would someone like him care about a house?"

Malcolm took in the oversized man wearing a coverall stiff with newness, his concern over Mr. Jones from Barsoom, the trouble with his name, and thought "bodyguard." He still needed to do some research to confirm his guess, but that would have to wait. The Bradwell sisters and Neza Molony, who actually held the lease, were of much greater concern.

"A good question," Malcolm answered, before Airik Jones had a chance to say something. "I don't know why this particular house, but that hoodlum and whoever his boss is probably cannot withstand official scrutiny from the bank. Thus, the threat to Miss Bradwell to force her to sublet."

Airik revised his estimate upward of Mr. Cobb's mental acuity. "That sounds plausible."

Veronica watched in consternation as her guest and her banker discussed her situation as though she wasn't standing right in front of them. Mr. Cobb, at least, had a legitimate reason to be concerned and could be the ally Mr. Jones suggested. He, on the other hand, was just another visitor to Panschin for the mining conference and would be leaving when the conference was over, never to return. She would never see him again. That was just as well since he clouded her thinking.

"Excuse me," Veronica said firmly. "Mr. Cobb, I appreciate and need the bank's help in this matter. I have no idea why that thug wants the White Elephant. It's just a house, but it is *our* house. I will speak to the police in the morning and anything the bank can do to investigate further would be most helpful."

"Mr. Jones," she turned to Airik. "I appreciate your wanting to help. I do. But you are my guest, so my problem is not your concern." She stepped closer to him, feeling drawn to his cool hazel eyes, something that was becoming easier to do. "You're here for the conference and you need to focus on that task. Your job probably depends on it."

She smiled up at him. "Thank you for your help. We'll be fine."

Words failed Airik again, looking into Veronica's face and wanting to fall into her dark, luminous eyes. His thoughts were a jumble. She didn't need his help. She didn't want his help. She had no idea who he was, and she wasn't going to use a stranger, squeeze out what she needed, and then toss the remains aside. Unlike his family, she didn't expect him to rescue her and solve her problems. Unlike everyone else he had met since becoming the daimyo of Shelleen, she didn't *want* something from him, despite her obvious needs. It was a deeply unfamiliar situation to see someone who could use assistance, yet who didn't demand his immediate attention. A thought struck him, allowing him speech.

"Nonetheless, Miss Bradwell, I am here and will remain through the conference. If I see the need, I will step in."

Veronica thought about being alone in the house, with only her sister, her aunt, Florence and Lulu. Lulu, if she wasn't caught unawares, could defend herself but she still couldn't tackle that oversized thug singlehanded in any kind of a fair fight. The rest of them, well. Any conflict would end badly. She shuddered at the thought of her elderly aunt confronting a man twice her size and a third her age. What would Neza do; threaten him with her cane? The police couldn't permanently station a beat patrolman in front of the house. They would wait until after the crime occurred to arrive in force. Having Mr. Jones and his cousins in the house, especially Carmine, would be useful while she was sorting out the mess her life had suddenly become.

She smiled up at him, something that was becoming very easy to do. "That would be lovely. But only if there's a need. You do have your job to look out for."

Airik thought of running Shelleen's day to day affairs, the uneasy collaboration with the other demesnes in the quad, the restive city council of Purnell, the Martian government looking over his shoulder, the immense task of managing the Red Mercury lode, his peasants who were convinced he was bringing a golden age to Shelleen, and the even larger task of managing his family's expectations.

"Yes, so I do."

"Mr. Cobb," Veronica said, turning back to her other problem. "Would you stop by the police station on your way home and register a complaint? It would have more force coming from you as a representative of the bank."

"I had planned on doing so, Miss Bradwell," Malcolm answered. "I will also alert my supervisor, Mr. Wong, about the situation."

He did not make any move to leave promptly on those important errands, remaining right where he stood.

Darn it, Veronica thought. Mr. Cobb wasn't taking her hint and leaving right away for the police substation. The only good thing about being threatened in front of the bank representative was that it provided him with a much bigger problem to manage than her possible lease violations. Vegetable gardening for cash and renting out rooms as a bed and breakfast paled in comparison to someone trying to illegally occupy bank property and harass the rightful tenants.

"Carmine," Airik said, interrupting her thoughts. "Would you take a walk around the White Elephant, interior and exterior?"

"Already planning on it, uh, Airik," Carmine answered.

Definitely a bodyguard, Malcolm thought. One who'd been told to use Mr. Jones' first name to deflect attention and who'd been told to stay in the background to avoid notice.

Definitely a servant of some kind, Veronica thought. Carmine expects to say 'sir,' and he's having trouble managing a first name.

I thought they were cousins? Shelby thought. So why is he having trouble with Mr. Jones' first name?

What is wrong with these people, Professor Vitebskin thought. Don't they care about the threat to my dog? And the show! Oh Gods, what will happen to the art?

"Miss Bradwell," the Professor said firmly. "The show. We cannot possibly pull the paintings out."

All eyes swiveled to Professor Vitebskin and he glared right back at them. He knew what was important. "You know many of our patrons need time to make a carefully considered decision as to which painting to purchase for their home. However, the paintings are at risk. They might be stolen! How are you planning on protecting them?"

Veronica opened her mouth, thought better of what she wanted to say, then decided to say it anyway.

"Professor Vitebskin, the paintings will be fine. No one's going to steal anything so hideous, just like no one's going to buy any of the horrible things."

"They could be vandalized, Miss Bradwell. Vandalized," Professor Vitebskin shot back.

"How would you be able to tell?" Airik asked coolly. "Every piece here could only benefit from having more paint thrown onto the canvas at random."

Malcolm caught Shelby's eye and flashed a lightning quick smile at her and was rewarded with a quick smile of her own. She might be naïve, but even under the stress she had a sense of humor.

"I'm sure they'll be safe, Professor Vitebskin," Shelby said soothingly. "Just like Cinnamon will be safe." She smiled at the professor brightly.

"Shelby," Professor Vitebskin said. "You are naïve."

Veronica watched her sister's face fall, held the tray of wineglasses very firmly to keep from throwing them at the Professor, and said, "Professor, one more nasty word from you about my sister and I will vandalize those ugly pieces of dross myself with a kitchen knife."

"You wouldn't dare," Professor Vitebskin said.

"Professor—," Veronica was interrupted.

"Professor Vitebskin! There you are. I've been looking all over for you." An older, noticeably well-fed gentleman — luxuriously upholstered in an extreme version of the latest fashion — approached the little group in the corner.

Veronica didn't know who he was but Professor Vitebskin did. He had pasted on a blandly sour smile that went nowhere near his eyes. Interestingly, Mr. Cobb was wearing the same expression. Mr. Jones looked as reserved as ever. Shelby shrugged at her sister and mouthed, "I don't know who he is but he's better than another threat to us from some oversized goon."

"Mr. Burgess. What a pleasure. I had hoped to see you tonight," Professor Vitebskin said.

"And you are, Vitebskin, you are. I have to say, I'm getting bored with this tiresome genre of paintings you keep pushing. Don't you have something new?" Mr. Burgess said. "Something I and everyone else haven't seen a dozen times over?"

Professor Vitebskin's face tightened. "I assure you, Mr. Burgess, what you see tonight is the wave of the future."

"Not any more," Mr. Burgess responded with a dismissive wave of his hand. He wore a gemmed ring on each finger and they glinted in the light. "Say, I know you." He pointed to Airik Jones.

"I don't believe so," Airik answered calmly.

"Yes, I do! You were that rude rickshaw hauler who brought me here and overcharged me for the ride. What are you doing stinking up an art gallery?" Mr. Burgess said, his face darkening with righteous fury.

"Mr. Burgess," Veronica said sharply. "Mr. Jones is my guest from Barsoom, here for the Biennial Mining Conference. How dare you accuse a respectable businessman of behaving badly."

"It's quite true," Malcolm Cobb added. "I met Mr. Jones earlier this evening. He is not a rickshaw hauler."

"Oh. You. I didn't know you knew anything about art, Cobb," Mr. Burgess replied, curling his lip in a sneer.

"I'm learning, Mr. Burgess," Malcolm replied, managing to keep his voice perfectly civil despite the urge to break his wineglass on an easel leg and slash Burgess's throat with the razor-sharp edge. "I am taking advantage of the dome's many amenities such as a show like this one."

"So, you're enjoying your stay here in Dome Two? Excellent. You'll be stuck here for the rest of your hopefully short career if I have anything to say about it," Mr. Burgess said cheerfully. He had a nasty edge to his voice and a vindictive sparkle in his eye.

Mr. Burgess turned his attention back to his original target.

"Vitebskin, I am very disappointed in this show. I am even more disappointed in who you allowed into the show." His eyes flicked over

Airik and Malcolm. "Have you no standards, man? And what's this about you abusing young Philpott?"

Veronica got there first, while the professor goggled and franticly tried to think of something to say that wouldn't cause him trouble later on. What little patience *she* had left was fraying to its ragged ends. She snapped, "Reyansh Philpott assaulted my great aunt, refused to work for the greater good of the Collective and was rude to everyone in the White Elephant. Professor Vitebskin was responsible enough to point out the error of his ways. If you, Mr. Burgess, have a problem in my home or with my guests, you may leave it at once."

"A likely story! Young Philpott is a gentleman. And just who are you?"

"Veronica Bradwell."

A flash of emotion showed in his eyes and then Mr. Burgess's face darkened still further. "Bradwell as in that ne'er-do-well, thieving conman Simon Bradwell?"

"Yes, Mr. Burgess. That Simon Bradwell. And no matter what my father may have done, his actions do not allow you to intrude into my home or criticize my guests or the gallery show or any of the people who worked so hard on it."

A slow, evil smile crawled across Mr. Burgess's face, making itself comfortable in familiar territory. "Your home? We'll see about that. Cobb. Look into the lease at once. Make sure every and I do mean every single clause is being adhered to. To the letter."

Malcolm said, in a carefully neutral tone, "I already investigated the lease on the White Elephant when I discovered it was part of the branch's portfolio of properties. Miss Bradwell is not only in complete compliance with every clause, she maintains the property in immaculate condition, and she is a staunch supporter of the arts community. All of our tenants should do as well by the bank as Miss Bradwell."

Mr. Burgess stopped smiling. "Trying to be proactive?" The smile slunk back. "If you're lying, Cobb, and I will check, your career with the Second National is over." The smile got wider. "We may even prosecute."

Malcolm clenched his fists, concealing the motion behind his back. "Well?"

"I am not lying, Mr. Burgess. As you will discover." Malcolm reminded himself of his other, personal project. He was making slow progress but there were hints he was digging in the correct area. The knowledge strengthened him, allowing him to show Burgess a bland face instead of a snarl.

"What is your position with the Second National Bank of Panschin?" Airik asked coldly.

Mr. Burgess turned on him and harrumphed.

"And what the hell does a gouging rickshaw hauler need to know about that?"

Airik stared down Mr. Burgess in icy silence, taking in every detail in the man in front of him and as he did so, Mr. Burgess became uneasy. The hairs on the back of his neck prickled.

"Well?" he demanded, trying to take back control from this uppity nonentity and remind him of his place in the hierarchy of Panschin.

"Mr. Burgess," Veronica interrupted firmly, gripping the tray of wineglasses tightly so they didn't rattle against each other and she didn't throw the tray at him. "You claim to be a gentleman. Gentlemen are never rude to anyone, particularly those persons who are lower than them on the social hierarchy. A gentleman is supposed to set the example by his behavior and you sir, I am sorry to say, are not living up to that standard."

Mr. Burgess turned from Airik to an easier, safer target.

"And how would the likes of you know?"

"Perhaps you have forgotten what the Bradwell family once was. It's understandable," Veronica smiled smoothly. "You are getting up in years and time has such a way of flying by."

Mr. Burgess began to sputter as she continued. "I know my father did not live up to the ideal standard but he, despite his criminal activities, was never rude to anyone. Unlike you. Do leave, Mr. Burgess, or I shall have to call the police and have you removed. I know you wouldn't want the embarrassment."

Airik gave her an approving look. "My cousin," — he waved a hand towards Carmine who looked appraisingly at Mr. Burgess — "and I will help you to the front door."

For the first time, Mr. Burgess noticed the hulking man who appeared at Mr. Jones's side and decided to pay attention to the prickling on the back of his neck. It was intensifying. He still had some things to say, ensuring the fools standing in front of him understood exactly who was in charge.

"Miss Bradwell, I will investigate your handling of your lease personally. If you give me one reason, no matter how minor, to throw you out on the street, I will. Vitebskin, you disappoint me, and I'll make sure the university and the board of trustees know it. Cobb, your career is on the line. And as for you, Jones, if that is really your name, I will personally contact the rickshaw hauler's guild and complain to the Guildmaster about your unacceptable conduct."

He spun on his heel and stalked away, his stiff back radiating fury at being thwarted.

Shelby broke the silence.

"Mr. Burgess really likes algae dumplings."

All eyes turned to her.

"What?" Veronica said. This was the dreadful ending of a dreadful day, she thought it couldn't get worse, and now her sister had lost her mind. "He could stand to lose a quite a few stone, but what?"

Shelby giggled, a light happy sound with an underlying edge of hysteria bubbling away and threatening escape. The tray in her hands shook. "He's got algae down his front from where a dumpling burst when he bit into it. He must not have noticed because the smears blend in with the leaves on his floral suit. And from the amount of green drips, well, he ate a lot of dumplings."

As she giggled, unable to stop herself, Airik thought, Aha. So that *was* pond scum inside those dough balls.

Carmine thought, Good thing I only ate one.

Malcolm thought, She's observant enough to find something funny in bad circumstances.

Dimwitted, Professor Vitebskin thought, even if she can use her eyes.

"Hey, some service over here please?" one of the gallery-goers called out.

Veronica seized her chance to escape and smiled graciously at the little group. "Duty calls. Shelby, back into the fray."

Her sister was still giggling nervously, the tray of nibbles shaking precariously, and waiting on guests might preoccupy her enough to let Shelby regain her equanimity. All the while Veronica thought damn, damn, damn. That thug came back. What am I going to do? And Mr.

Cobb showing up. Why can't he go to the police station right now? Get someone here while that goon is waiting to be arrested? And Mr. Burgess.

The Bradwell sisters waded back into the crowd, leaving Airik Jones, Malcolm Cobb, and Professor Vitebskin to eye each other, while Carmine Jones hovered discreetly in the background.

Airik tipped his head at Carmine who responded promptly, listened to his low-voiced request, and then melted back into the crowd.

Malcolm watched their byplay, hoping it meant Mr. Jones was having his otherwise wasted bodyguard make a thorough inspection of the White Elephant, inside and out.

As soon as the hulking bodyguard left, Malcolm said smoothly, "have you been in Panschin long, Mr. Jones?"

"A few days," Airik replied. "The conference has been interesting. How do you know Mr. Burgess, if I may ask? I can guess Professor Vitebskin knows Mr. Burgess through university connections."

Malcolm scowled at the name as did Professor Vitebskin.

"Mr. Burgess is a vice-president at Second National in charge of various outreach programs," Malcolm said.

Airik thought this over. Malcolm Cobb was apparently low-level so it perhaps wasn't a surprise he didn't recognize the daimyo of Shelleen. Even the professor might be excused on the basis of being an artist and so not capable of reading up on current events. But for a vice-president of a large institution to not know? Not a competent man, then. Despite his high-level position, Mr. Burgess also recognized and actively disliked Malcolm Cobb, another interesting and perhaps useful fact.

"He's a pushy, pretentious tin-pot dictator," Professor Vitebskin growled to both men. "He's a buffoon who likes to throw his weight around. He's a bully who belittles people who can't fight back." The professor thought of Reyansh Philpott, and the damage control he was going have to do back at PanU over the incident and closed his eyes in pain. Philpott, that mazhor, had worked both fast and competently, skills he had never previously demonstrated in his studies.

He turned his back on Jones and Cobb and strode away, disappearing into the chattering crowd, considering whose ass he would have to kiss to make this new problem vanish.

"Takes one to know one," Malcolm said dryly.

"Yes, it does," Airik said.

"If you would excuse me, Mr. Jones. Enjoy your stay in Panschin. And I did mean everything I said."

"As did I, Mr. Cobb."

Malcolm walked into the crowd of gallery-goers, thinking hard. Shelby Bradwell, his Dome Two beauty, needed him. Something very strange was going on in Dome Two where a ruffian was trying to take over a particular house when houses went begging on every street. And how and why was the daimyo of Shelleen involved?

That last thought brought a cold gleam to his eyes. Mr. Burgess might be the man who was ruined by running afoul of a powerful, well-connected daimyo, and it couldn't happen to a more deserving sack of shit.

Airik watched Mr. Cobb work his way around the easels, an apparent goal in mind based on how he maneuvered through the obstacle course they presented. He considered the character of the banker thoughtfully, based on what he had observed. Would this low-level banker assist Miss Bradwell? Talking to the police would be easy. Standing up to the likes of Mr. Burgess who could destroy him was another matter.

He himself could put a word in the right ear about Burgess, but at what cost? The four daimyos of Panschin's quad enjoyed extensive interests and holdings within the free-city over and above their vast demesnes surrounding the free-city. But that would mean revealing his whereabouts and breaking his privacy, the only thing that was letting him get the work done he needed to do for his own demesne. Moreover, each of those daimyos — Atto, Maerski, Davis, and Fuziwara — would expect significant concessions from him in exchange. The same would be true of any of the mine owners in Panschin. They would insist on repayment.

He owed Veronica Bradwell nothing, other than the room fees he had already paid. This would require thought.

eronica led her sister through the crowd of outstretched hands and gaping mouths — were all these people bottomless pits needing to be stuffed with nibbles and plonk? – both of them dispensing treats as needed. As soon as they were out of the ballroom, as if headed to the kitchen to refill the trays, she glanced around and herded her sister into the alcove between the winding circular staircases to the second floor. Professor Vitebskin's protégé's painting loomed down over them, ignored by everyone. She hoped its off-putting presence would ensure a moment of privacy.

"Shelby," Veronica said sharply, getting right to the point. "I know this has been a terrible, terrible day, but you have to get hold of yourself. We both have to."

Shelby glared at her sister. "I am not going to get hysterical, if that's what you're implying."

"Are you sure? The way you were giggling back there? We can't afford to panic."

"I am not stupid. I am not a child. But tell me, please!" Shelby glared at her sister harder. "Exactly what can we afford to do?"

"I don't know yet. I'll think of something. We'll think of something. You, me, auntie Neza, Lulu, and Florence."

"Lulu and Florence may not want to get involved," Shelby said. She didn't want to bring up the unpleasant possibility but it had to be said. "They're not family."

Veronica scowled at the painting looming over them, a study in shades of dreck. The fading light falling through the open skylight from the dome above turned what had been an ugly painting into one that was dismal and foreboding. The flickering oil lamps made the effect still more ominous. She decided to not take it as an omen but as an example of how not to paint an attractive, saleable picture.

"They may not be blood relatives but look how our blood relatives treat us. I'll take my chances. And if Florence or Lulu decide to abandon us, we'll let them make that choice."

"But do you have any ideas?" Shelby persisted. "I don't. Nobody at university will help me. They wouldn't even talk to me tonight."

"I saw that," her sister replied with a moue of distaste. "Pathetic sods, the lot of them. But we've got some decent money thanks to Mr. Jones renting out rooms for the mining conference. And Mr. Cobb knows about the thug and he'll worry about that situation a lot more than about my renting out a room or market gardening."

"If he helps us," Shelby said, her voice much lower. "That gross Mr. Burgess didn't like him at all, even less than he liked us. I wonder why?"

"Who knows," Veronica said. "I doubt if either of them will tell us. Anyway, the evening will be over soon and we made, looking at the crowd, some money there too. I'll talk to Neza, Florence, and Lulu, and let them know what happened."

She set her tray on the floor and hugged her sister. "We'll figure out something. Maybe Mrs. Grisson will rent us rooms after Mr. Burgess or that awful goon kick us out."

Shelby made a face, thinking of Mrs. Grisson's regular tenants, thought better of it since none of them despised the Bradwells for existing, and sighed. "Would she have space?"

"Maybe. And if she doesn't, she'll know who will in Dome Two. I'll talk to Florence and Lulu. No point in worrying Neza yet. I'll tell her in the morning."

"Why is Neza worried? Oh, right. Mr. Cobb."

"And Dean showed up too," Veronica replied with a grimace.

"Dean showed up?" Shelby asked. "I never saw him."

"He wanted to get me involved in some silly get-rich-quick scheme. I wouldn't listen to him," Veronica said. "As if I would do such a thing after dear old dad cheated everyone in Panschin with similar schemes. At least Dean was easy to get rid of."

Both girls were lost in their thoughts, each wearing a similar expression of pain, grief, and anger.

Veronica sighed. "Start by rearranging the trays of nibbles in the ballroom to freshen them and then refill only as needed. I don't want to run out and if anything's left, well, that's breakfast. I'll talk to Lulu and then Florence. If you see or hear anything, tell me at once."

"Hey, I just thought of something," Shelby said with a sudden grin. "Mr. Burgess and that awful thug might have to fight it out over who gets to keep the White Elephant." She laughed at her vivid mental picture. It would make a funny cartoon; one she would enjoy sketching.

Veronica laughed too. "Mr. Burgess outweighs him so it might not be a totally unfair fight. If he fell on top of the thug, he'd smother him for certain. Anyways, keep an eye out."

"Got it," Shelby said. She picked up her empty tray tiredly, pasted on a fake smile, and headed back into the ballroom. She thought of waiting tables at the Dappled Yak. It seemed very likely she'd be working there or some similar place. At least there she'd be slipped some coin for her work. While the gallery-goers had eaten and drunk their money's worth, none of them would throw a few coins her way for waiting on them.

Already a few people were staggering towards the front door, having swilled down plenty of plonk to ease the pain of viewing the art. They faced a long, dark walk back to the business district and the transtube station. Shelby knew, from previous shows, most of the Dome Two rickshaw haulers and sedan-chair men would be conveniently stationed out on the street for just such emergencies. The darker and later it got, the more they charged and they got their fares too from nervous, drunk out-of-domers. She'd have to remember to tell Veronica one of them might have seen something while trolling the streets for passengers.

The prospect of losing her home again made her problems fitting in at PanU pale by comparison. She had gotten used to Dome Two. She would never admit to it, but Dome Two was more beautiful, green, and vibrant with life than Dome Six ever was. Dome Two had real parks and anyone could visit them without special permission. You regularly saw real birds flitting about and you heard them singing. There were real squirrels in the quad at PanU, fat ones who begged for scraps. Dome Six had nothing like that. Every animal there, other than the rats, was a coddled pet. The birds were all in cages. Parks were open only to their paying members.

She headed back towards the ballroom and hovering just inside the door, as if he'd been waiting for her, was Mr. Cobb.

He strode up to her confidently, as though she couldn't possibly not want to talk to him. And of course, Shelby knew, she had to. Where did he find the confidence he was radiating after Mr. Burgess's implied threat? Maybe, she thought with despair, he'd already decided to back the clear winner. Even so, if there was a slim chance he would take their side against Mr. Burgess, she had to seize that opportunity. The police and the bank would both be very interested in keeping out lawbreaking thugs. Lease issues were a different matter, one where the police would favor the bank and not them.

As she grew nearer, the feeling grew that she had seen him before out and around in Dome Two. Now that she was calmer, she concluded that Malcolm Cobb looked attractive, especially compared to Mr. Burgess. His suit was deep blue, conservative, well-fitted to accentuate his broad chest and shoulders, his complete lack of a vast paunch, and it did not, unlike Mr. Burgess's much more fashionable attire, remind her of the extravagantly floral drapes in PanU's cafeteria. She stifled a smirk at that thought. Mr. Burgess needed the cafeteria drapes to make his clothes because that was the only way he'd get enough fabric to wrap around himself. They also camouflaged his foul eating habits.

Shelby realized something else. As awful and lewd as that yahoo had been, threatening her and her sister over the White Elephant, the threat from Mr. Burgess was more real. He had the law on his side and Veronica had broken the lease. Either way, they'd end up on the street but if criminals invaded, the Bradwell family would have legal help and public sympathy. If the bank threw them out, they were finished. Malcolm Cobb was right to be confident; he was their only chance at defeating Mr. Burgess.

"All right then," Shelby murmured. "All right then."

As she neared, Malcolm smiled at Shelby and nodded. "Miss Bradwell." It was easy to do now he knew her name. She was even more beautiful than he had thought and the effect was not wearing off. If anything, her allure was stronger. He was almost close enough to touch her, an enticing thought he firmly squashed.

"Hello again, Mr. Cobb," Shelby replied. She lifted her empty tray. "I've got to rearrange the nibble trays in the ballroom. Did you want something?"

She winced inwardly. Gods below, but she sounded like a fool. It felt like her brain shut off when he spoke to her, allowing any piece of drivel to surface while she stared at his jawline, the breadth of his shoulders, and his strong, well-shaped hands. She was sure he wanted the same thing every other man wanted from her. With Mr. Burgess's threat to him and to them, he had even less incentive to treat her with respect.

"I thought about what you said," he said, "about the purpose of the

PanU Artists' Collective." Shelby was caught off-guard. She'd been expecting a lewd proposition she'd have to refuse as tactfully as she could manage.

"Yes, about that," she replied, trying to remember exactly what silliness she had spouted. She cringed inwardly, comparing it to the real problems bearing down on her. No wonder Lulu and everyone else had been so dismissive.

He didn't give her much time to think. "Do you want to know how real working-class people feel about art? You and the other students in the Collective? I can show all of you."

Shelby paused in the act of moving a plate of algae crisps to her tray.

"Uh, could you please explain?"

Malcolm had thought hard over how to approach his Dome Two princess the second time. He knew how he reacted to her, but not what she would think of him. Was she the kind of woman he hoped she was? Before Simon Bradwell had leaped so spectacularly down a mine shaft, dragging his family with him into ruin, Shelby would have been brought up as a princess in Dome Six. He knew — oh how well he knew — how those girls sneered at his background, his family, his friends, and how they belittled the labor that made them and the free-city of Panschin rich. To their way of thinking, he was a toy to play with. Playing with them was enjoyable, no question, but at the end of the day, what he wanted for himself was immaterial. The resentment ate at his soul.

He had already observed Shelby Bradwell could be naïve and inexperienced, hence her belief in and loyalty to the Collective's ridiculous way of thinking. They had accepted her and he knew very well what that meant. Even if it was seasoned with daily, petty humiliations, it was better than being rejected. She might get fed up with the bullying and walk away with him.

Or she could be a worse snob than them all. She had already fallen so far that falling further was completely unacceptable. She'd fight and claw her way back to social acceptance, and she wouldn't be able to do that with him. And worse, what would she think of his family?

If Shelby was who he hoped her to be, she would accept his people as human and not as dirty-handed tunnel rats who never saw the light of day. He didn't know. She would have to show him. He would have to take the risk. Would she be worth what that wanking slime Burgess could do to him?

He took the plunge.

"I can take you and anyone else who wants to come along down into the tunnels."

Shelby's eyes opened wide. She didn't like going into the White Elephant's basement levels. The transtubes were always unpleasant. This would be deeper down.

"Into the mining tunnels?" she asked hesitantly.

"No, you're not crew. Miner's housing. The Steelio warren to be precise."

Shelby nearly dropped the tray. "People *live* underneath?" She wanted to bite her tongue all over again. She knew there was housing in the tunnels; it was what Florence and Lulu had escaped from. Warrens sounded awful; too many people crammed into too little space in the dark.

"Yes, they do. Didn't you know that?"

He was looking at her like she was stupid again. No, not stupid. Like he couldn't quite believe she didn't know. Like she was naïve.

Malcolm watched her face carefully. She had paled and her breathing had quickened. The knuckles of her hands were tight from clutching her tray. He had guessed, from his observations, that every emotion she felt showed on her expressive face. It did now, proving he was correct. She was afraid.

Shelby swallowed. "I knew. I, I just don't like to think about it. All that weight of rock overhead."

"You get used to it," he said gently. "It's perfectly safe." He paused, watching her chest raise and fall with her quickened breathing. She was visibly trying not to tremble. He tore his eyes away, back to her face.

"I'll keep you safe."

She couldn't answer. He wanted to take her into the tunnels deep underground. The housing tunnels were far deeper than the basement levels, deeper than the PCC classrooms, deeper than the transtube tunnels that connected the domes. Many of the housing tunnels were repurposed mining tunnels, once the veins of ore had been stripped out leaving nothing behind of value other than echoing, ink-black, airless caverns. The tunnels formed a complex, three-dimensional maze underneath Panschin. Even miners who knew a section well could get lost forever in another section.

The weight of the dome that her sister found so oppressive never bothered Shelby. It kept out the weather and kept the city, so close to Northernmost, safe from the harsh, seemingly endless winter. But going underneath, even when the tunnel was well-lit like the transtube station, was different. She could feel the weight of millions of tons of rock weighing overhead, waiting to collapse and crush her and anyone else unfortunate enough to be caught. Cave-ins did happen sometimes. Not everyone trapped in one survived long enough to be rescued. You could suffocate while they were digging you out, lying there in agony with bones smashed into gravel and torn, bleeding limbs that sprayed your blood into the unforgiving rock.

She steadied herself, leaning against the heavily carved molding framing the wide entrance to the ballroom. Its ceiling was so high, the room so spacious, lined with windows letting in light and providing a view of the wider world. The atrium overhead opened to the dome high above, letting more light and air pour in. The White Elephant was airy and open in a way a tunnel could never be. There was color, movement, sound, and life. The tunnels below were bored through dead rock and that rock hated the life intruding into it.

Shelby knew her fears were irrational, and she had learned not to say anything. Going underground was normal in Panschin. It was part of everyday life and so pointless to fret about. But when she went underground, she couldn't stop worrying until she was safely above-ground.

Malcolm watched her carefully. If she refused, it wasn't because she despised the people who lived and toiled in the tunnels. It was because she was afraid of the deepdown. Not everyone in Panschin could live or even travel underground. There were those who got surface sickness and it looked like Shelby Bradwell might be one of them.

"Miss Bradwell," he said. "If you can't, don't worry about it."

His words did not reassure her. If she didn't go with him, what would he do to her and her sister and her aunt? Shelby knew her sister worried over the lease stipulations, gauging carefully what she thought she could get away with to keep their household afloat. Mr. Cobb was responsible for their compliance. Mr. Cobb had that awful cave troll, Burgess, pressuring him. Would he stand up to that fat, messy slob who wore a suit made of floral drapes for tenants he didn't know, especially one who rejected him without a damn good reason?

She couldn't move again. She just couldn't. Leaving Dome Six had been traumatic enough. They might not find another home inside the now familiar, safe Dome Two. Shelby had learned where everything was. She had a place, even if it wasn't always happy. She was aboveground in Dome Two. There was space and air and light and sound and color. There was room to run, room to escape and hide in, room to sit quietly and sketch brilliant flowers in the sunshine undisturbed. Dome One was awful and after that, the tunnels.

She stopped her train of thought. She was letting her fears run away with her again. She knew it. She was better than this. She forced herself upright, not relying on the wall to support her. She was not a child.

"I would like to try," Shelby said. Her voice didn't shake and she was proud of that show of strength.

Malcolm saw the determination settle on her face, and smiled. Shelby Bradwell might be the woman he hoped she was.

"What is your schedule tomorrow?" he asked.

Shelby wanted to shake all over again. Tomorrow! That gave her no time at all to steel herself but it also meant she didn't have much time to stew over her situation.

"I finish my classes by 2PM," she answered. "I'll be in the Art Department at PanU. Lots of other members of the Collective will still be there, too."

"Good. I'll be there. I'll take everyone who wants to come down with us into the Steelio warrens."

"Hey girlie! You with the tray," a voice slurred out from the ballroom. "Is there anything left to eat?"

Shelby gripped her tray firmly. Would this evening never end? She looked up and Mr. Cobb's eyes were sympathetic. He turned and gazed into the ballroom at the speaker with open contempt, then turned back to her, his expression much warmer.

"I know you have work to do, Miss Bradwell, so I won't keep you. I'm on my way to the police station next, after I take a look all around the block." Malcolm smiled at her and was rewarded with a tiny, real smile. "Don't worry about Burgess. Despite behaving like a banker in a melodrama, he's not as powerful as he thinks he is."

"Really?" A flash of hope speared through her, encouraging her that things might not be as bad as she feared. Malcolm Cobb might help them, if she was friendly enough. It would be much more pleasant to be friendly with him than it would be with either the gross Burgess or that crude goon.

"Yes. Burgess has his weaknesses. I'm looking forward to tomorrow," he said.

"Tomorrow," Shelby said and she fled into the ballroom, where, as she suspected and Malcolm Cobb must have noticed, there were still plenty of nibbles on the table trays. This drunk guest wanted them served to him instead of having to lurch across the room on very unsteady legs.

Maybe the fool drank so much the tables were moving on their own, she thought uncharitably as she provided him with algae dumplings and blocks of yeast while he tried to leer down her unaccommodating neckline. She never liked leaving the top few buttons open on her coverall and lewd fools like this one were one of her reasons. If Mr. Cobb had tried for an eyeful, he had been exceptionally discreet.

Veronica noted with relief that more gallery-goers were leaving. The house was slowly emptying. There would be food left over for tomorrow and perhaps even an opened, unfinished bottle of wine. She'd have a glass or two herself, once the house was locked up tight.

The thug had not come back. Neza had seen nothing and she admitted she hadn't particularly noticed him when he came in, other than that he didn't look like the usual guest. She thought he had not been alone, a worrisome thought.

Neither Florence nor Lulu had seen the thug or his mysterious companion. Lulu, however, had seen Dean. He had gone out through the kitchen door and into the back garden.

"He was in a tearing hurry," Lulu said. "Didn't stop to chat me up like he usually does."

"He must have avoided me altogether," Florence added. "Never saw him in that crowd."

"Odd," Veronica replied and put it out of her mind. Dean had become a petty annoyance.

She strolled around the ballroom, encouraging gallery-goers to think about going home before the rickshaw haulers and sedan-chair men called it a night and Dome Two got even darker. This had the desired effect; out-of-domers promptly left while Dome Two residents made some coin. Dome Two's nights were always considerably darker than

Dome Six's, making those residents more nervous than they should have been. Veronica also, on Shelby's suggestion, spoke to the rickshaw haulers and sedan-chair men about the threats made to her. In return, she received promises that they'd keep an eye out. Airik Jones was right, she reflected. She needed allies; as part of the community, she had them in Dome Two if she asked.

As she made another circuit to collect the last of the wine glasses — it was amazing how people hid them in odd corners rather than put them on the table set up for this purpose — Airik Jones spotted her and changed course to meet her. She thought he had already retired for the night.

"Miss Bradwell," he began.

"Mr. Jones," she said, wanting to reassure him. "My apologies. This wasn't quite the quiet haven I promised you this afternoon."

"Quite all right," he said. "Carmine checked every floor, including the basement levels, your garden, and the local streets and saw nothing out of the ordinary. I'll have him go out again, when you're ready to lock up the house."

Veronica was deeply grateful for the reprieve. She wouldn't have to venture out, by herself, in the rapidly gathering dark. Talking to the rickshaw haulers out in front of the White Elephant had made her jumpy enough, and she knew them.

"Thank you," she smiled at him, her eyes alight with relief.

"And," Airik went on, "I spoke with Upton and Elliot. Upton saw nothing, but Elliot did."

He paused to let her absorb the information.

"Something we could tell the police?"

"Possibly. Elliot is very observant, particularly in matters of dress and behavior."

Valet, Veronica interpreted. Why, if Mr. Jones can afford a valet is he staying here? Must have been a last-minute trip for the conference and every other hotel was booked. It was reassuring to finally work out the answer for their presence.

"Elliot noticed the man who threatened you because he did not fit in with the local crowd. He was accompanied by another man, who also did not blend in."

"Yes, Neza said he might have been with someone."

"Elliot believes this other man, the one we did not directly observe, was, based on clothing and behavior, the thug's boss. He does not believe these men are long-time residents of Panschin. This boss-type must have seen the incident with you, your sister, myself and Mr. Cobb. He was very unhappy, said so in no uncertain terms, and those two men left at once."

"Because that goon threatened me and my sister in front of witnesses," Veronica said slowly.

Miss Bradwell could think as well as display grace under pressure, Airik noticed with pleasure. Pressure turned some stone to rubble. Pressure also turned carbon into diamonds. She compared very well to the young ladies being foisted on him as suitable brides.

But he pushed the thought back into its corner where it refused to remain. The Shelleen family would never accept her. She had no connections, no background, and no wealth. The thought distressed him and he pushed it away, burying it still further.

"Miss Bradwell, Mr. Jones," Professor Vitebskin said as he walked, not quite as steadily, from wherever he had been lurking. He handed Veronica an empty wine glass.

Veronica didn't bother pasting on a smile. "Yes, Professor?"

"I'll send someone by tomorrow and every day there after to check on the safety of the paintings."

"Oh. How thoughtful of you," Veronica said. She restrained herself from rolling her eyes. A student, even one from the PanU Artists' Collective, should be capable of summoning the police if he found their bodies blocking the doorway into the ballroom.

"You have your priorities in order," Airik said dryly.

"Ignorant yokels from the hinterland, such as yourself, do not understand the importance of art. Fortunately, I do," Professor Vitebskin replied loftily.

He stood there, swaying slightly, obviously debating with himself on saying something further.

Veronica received his message, suppressed a groan, and got to the point. "Was there something else, Professor?"

He pursed his lips in distaste and forced out, "My thanks for hosting the show and for speaking to Burgess on my behalf."

"I may dislike avant-garde art, Professor Vitebskin, but that does not mean I can't recognize how much hard work you and the Collective did. None of you deserved what Mr. Burgess had to say."

"You don't know the half of it, Miss Bradwell," Professor Vitebskin said. "Have Shelby bring the Collective's half of the door receipts with her in the morning. I'll send someone else by to get the unopened bottles tomorrow. Good night to you both."

He plucked a half-full wine glass from Veronica's collection of salvaged stemware waiting to be emptied and washed, slugged it back, and made his erratic way to the front door. His steps were not quite straight but he managed to avoid running into the easels while accepting congratulations on the show from the other departing patrons.

Veronica watched him go, Airik standing quietly by her side, and as other gallery-goers tottered in their little groups to the door and stumbled down the front path to the waiting rickshaw haulers, she said, "never again."

"No?" Airik asked.

"No. Hosting these shows hasn't helped Shelby in the least and somehow paintings never get sold for me to earn a commission. At least I got the White Elephant scrubbed clean but that may not matter anymore either."

"Do not despair, Miss Bradwell," Airik said calmly. "You are not alone, and you do have allies."

She smiled up at him and his heart melted. "So I do."

Airik contemplated his breakfast with equanimity. He had gotten up with the morning sun or what passed for it within the dome. He had experienced his first night of actual sleep since arriving in Panschin, enjoyed sleeping near open windows with no party horns, and been awakened by the familiar sound of a distant rooster. While he sweated through his morning exercises, he reflected on how a rooster got into Dome Two and decided it must belong to Mrs. Grisson, lording over her flock of pet chickens. Afterwards, he felt much more like himself and ready to face whatever Panschin threw at him, including the odd array of food on the table before him. Elliot and Carmine were already digging in. Upton looked miserable and bleary-eyed, no doubt due, Airik thought uncharitably, to the amount of cheap wine he had ingested the previous evening.

They sat in quiet splendor in the otherwise deserted and spacious dining room. Veronica efficiently ferried dishes back and forth, and never bothered him once she made sure he and the rest of his party had what they needed. She provided him with a newspaper which did not — to his relief — feature a frontpage story about the missing daimyo of Shelleen. Gaston had covered up his disappearance. He had made the correct choice in staying and was in no hurry to get back to the Twelve Happiness Luxury Hotel and discover what negotiations and agreements Gaston might have entangled Shelleen in.

When Veronica came in with a fresh pitcher of water, Airik searched for a topic that would keep her nearby. He chose not to examine his motives, telling himself it was to ensure his stay at the White Elephant remained peaceful, with no more surprises.

"Miss Bradwell?"

"Yes, Mr. Jones?" Veronica felt better, and it showed in her face. The fears of the previous evening had receded as her natural optimism reasserted itself. She had a plan for what to do next, her little family wasn't going to be kicked out of their home that minute, she had some money, and she had allies.

Her attractive proximity made Airik's brain empty itself out of his planned conversation so he grabbed a random thought.

"Is Professor Vitebskin the only art instructor with Panschin University? I don't recall seeing any others."

"Oh no, but he's the only one who counts. There are a number of instructors in the department, even a few full professors, but none of them came by last night."

She stopped, chuckled, and added, "think of the planet Jupiter and his moons orbiting around him and how little power they have. The situation is similar."

"Jupiter is a gas giant," Airik said and wanted to kick himself for stating something so inane.

To his immense pleasure, Veronica giggled, beamed at him, and said, "Yes, the analogy works on so many levels."

She had laughed with him, as though he had made a real joke. The morning became even brighter for Airik.

Shelby stood at the doorway and snickered. "Good one, Mr. Jones. I'll have to remember that one."

Her face became suddenly more serious.

"Veronica? I'm going to be back very late, I'm not sure how late. Lulu and Florence already know," Shelby said.

"Know what?" Veronica asked.

"Uh," Shelby hemmed, not meeting her sister's eyes.

"Well?"

"Mr. Cobb is taking me and the other art students into the miners' housing this afternoon so we can get their real opinion on art. I've got to run, or I'll be late."

"What?" Veronica said sharply. "You're going off with Mr. Cobb? We don't know anything about him!"

"I'll be fine and I won't be alone. He invited everyone in the department, the entire Collective. Lulu said I'll be fine. They're waiting for me. Oh!"

Shelby ran up to Veronica and handed her some drawings. "I sketched that thug a few times last night before turning in so you've got some pictures to hand around. Bye!"

She darted out the door before Veronica, standing with her mouth open, could say anything else. She sat down hard, in one of the empty chairs. She laid Shelby's drawings on the table, ignoring them.

"Oh no." Her hand went of its own accord to the cool, cloudy beads around her neck.

"Miss Bradwell, I spoke briefly with Mr. Cobb. He did not strike me as wanting to harm your sister," Airik said. "I'm sure she will be quite safe." He watched her fingers twine through the string of irregular, cloudy beads and thought again of how soft her skin would feel under his own hands.

Veronica shook her head, trying to clear it. "Shelby talked to Lulu but not to me."

"Veronica?" Auntie Neza limped into the dining room from the kitchen. "She spoke to me as well. Shelby didn't want to upset you. She'll be part of a large group, and Lulu and Florence both insisted she would be well taken care of."

"And how do they know?" Veronica demanded.

Airik forced himself to pay attention to the old woman and not to the distracting beads around Veronica's throat or the earbobs dangling enticingly by her neck. He had yet to decide what stone they were as his thoughts kept returning to what her skin felt like instead of running down gem possibilities.

"They seemed quite sure," Neza said. "You know Lulu. If she thought it wasn't safe for Shelby, she would have had plenty to say.

They're visiting the Steelio warrens."

"Safe for Lulu and safe for Shelby are two different things," Veronica said tartly. "You could dump Lulu anywhere in Panschin, including the tunnel bars under Dome Four, and she'd be fine. Shelby, on the other hand…"

"Veronica," Neza said calmly. "You were married when you were Shelby's age. Give her a chance to spread her own wings a little bit. Lulu said the Steelio warrens were very respectable."

Airik said, "We know Mr. Cobb. We know who he works for. The branch bank will have all the details about him. If Shelby does not return, we have a starting point."

Upton, who had been nibbling at something resembling dry toast but wasn't made of any grain he'd ever eaten before, looked up at the word "we." The daimyo of Shelleen, who had more than enough to do, had, for some mysterious reason, concerned himself with the wellbeing of the Bradwell sisters. His queasy stomach lurched, distracting him, and he promptly forgot what he had heard in his effort to keep his breakfast where it belonged.

Elliot and Carmine also looked up, traded glances, and said nothing. They did, however, listen more carefully to the conversation. They both also took a discreet look at Shelby's drawings, abandoned on the table. Elliot nodded in approval to Carmine; she had captured the thug surprisingly well.

"Moreover," Airik continued, "we know where your sister is going. Steelio, while a large operation, will have people who can find out where in their housing Mr. Cobb went."

"Steelio. Why Steelio?" Veronica asked her aunt. "Did Shelby say anything?"

"No, she didn't." Neza replied. "I'd guess Mr. Cobb must have an acquaintance who works for the company who can take them down below. He's a banker. He's probably never been lower down than the transtubes."

"Are you familiar with Steelio, Miss Bradwell?" Airik asked.

"No, they're just another mining concern," Veronica answered distractedly. It was possible dear old dad had swindled Steelio, along with so many other unfortunate clients, but she couldn't quite remember why she knew the name. Then she remembered Inigo Schopenhour and Olwyn Steelio and their families' dispute. It had been a long time since she had seen either of them. But Mr. Jones wouldn't be interested in local gossip about star-crossed lovers.

What was Shelby up to? Mr. Cobb had no reason to pay attention to her beautiful little sister other than, she shuddered, the usual reason. Shelby, she feared, was too naïve to understand what she might be getting herself into, and it probably wouldn't help the situation with Mr. Burgess one bit. Malcolm Cobb worked for that cave troll. He was unlikely to be an ally, despite what he had said last night and what Mr. Jones was saying now.

Veronica fumed as she sat at the dining room table, twisting her beads in agitation, her earlier better mood gone like condensation burned off the dome. She wanted to march to the university and demand that her little sister come home at once, but knew her sister wouldn't thank her for embarrassing her in front of the other students. It would give them one more reason to despise Shelby Bradwell.

Plus, what Neza said was correct. Shelby was growing up. Veronica thought of Lulu's opinion of how she sheltered her little sister. They were both right. Shelby would be fine. Her sister had to be. She had a long list of people to speak to about both the out-of-town thug and Mr. Burgess, a process that would take hours and had to be done. Shelby would have to manage on her own.

She became aware that Mr. Jones was watching her with some concern. Why did he care? It made no sense, other than simple human kindness, a rare commodity since their father's crimes were revealed.

"I hope you are correct about my sister's safety, Mr. Jones," Veronica made herself say. "What are your plans for the day?"

"I'll be busy with the mining conference, but I expect we will return in the early evening."

"Very good," Veronica said. His return would mean they weren't in the house alone overnight. "As soon as you leave, Neza and I will be heading over to the police substation, the bank, and to speak with the neighbors. Will you be needing dinner?"

"No, I don't believe so."

Airik watched her twisting in her chair with agitation. Veronica, such a beautiful, melodic name made to be whispered in the dark, still looked anxious, and he wanted to reassure her again.

"I'm sure Shelby will be fine, and if she is not, I will do everything in my power to help you."

"Thank you, Mr. Jones," Veronica said. She let go of her beads, reached over the table and squeezed his hand, surprising both him and herself. "You are very kind."

They sat there, gazing at each other for a timeless, endless moment, and then both pulled away in confusion.

"We'd best be on our way. I have meetings," Airik said, trying not to sound flustered. His heart raced in the most unsettling manner, it was difficult to breathe, plus his body's other reaction was more extreme. He was happy again to be wearing a loose coverall concealing the evidence of how Veronica made him feel.

"Yes, I do too," Veronica said, wondering why her hand tingled, her heart pounded, and why she had been so uncharacteristically forward with a strange man. "I've got to return all the stemware, and warn everyone in the neighborhood and downtown about what happened. Enjoy your day."

She watched Mr. Jones leave the dining room, looking not quite as reserved as he usually did. She hoped she hadn't offended him. Her own emotions were in turmoil. She knew nothing about this man, other than he had been generous with his time. The question was why. And why did she care?

Veronica looked up to see Neza watching her.

"We'd better get started packing the stemware into the handcart," Veronica told her, hoping her great aunt would take the hint and not make pointed comments about being overly friendly with guests.

"Yes, we should," Neza replied but said nothing else. She wondered what she had just seen. Veronica had refused any introductions since her divorce from Dean, saying that she didn't have the energy or time to waste on men. Mr. Jones seemed nice enough, but she knew nothing about him and, since he wasn't from Panschin, there was no one in her extended circle of acquaintances whom she could ask. Still, it was a good sign her niece might be finally healing from Dean's betrayal.

Airik arrived back in Dome Six after a quiet trip on the transtube, ignored by everyone around them. Fortunately, Upton silently struggled with his hangover and had not asked questions about what transpired in the dining room of the White Elephant with Veronica. Airik knew Elliot and Carmine would not ask (it was not their place) nor would they, unlike Upton, gossip to anyone on the Shelleen staff.

He had no way of answering any questions on the subject as he didn't understand his own behavior. Instead Airik focused on the list of what he needed done, starting with careful instructions for Elliot. On their arrival, Carmine led the way down a series of alleys to a service entrance for the Twelve Happiness Luxury Hotel. As on the trip out the day before, they went unnoticed in their drab coveralls. Carmine's muttered comment about the hotel's poor security reminded him of the White Elephant and made him worry over what would happen to the Bradwells. He pushed those concerns away.

It was a relief to arrive at the Shelleen suite and focus on what Gaston had done the day before in his absence. The head of Shelleen's mining department had been waiting anxiously for his daimyo's return with a sheaf of annotated reports and a schedule for the day.

Airik reviewed the reports quickly, commenting as he went. When finished, he looked up at Gaston.

"Good work, Gaston."

"Thank you, sir."

To Gaston, it looked like wherever Airik went, it had been good for him. The daimyo had grasped everything he had highlighted and spotted a few things he had missed. Gaston resolved to question Upton since he knew neither the bodyguard or the valet would tell him anything. He might, however, be able to coax some gossip out of the secretary. *He* looked unwell enough to be indiscreet. Knowing how much of a killjoy Airik was, Gaston thought it unlikely Upton had gone out barhopping; Airik would never let his secretary get away with fun when he could be slaving over reports for the betterment of Shelleen. Panschin's spore-laden air had probably given Upton a sinus infection, similar to Gaston's own affliction. He blew his nose again, wishing once more he had never come to Panschin. It had been unsettling in a myriad of ways.

"I have the following modifications to the Jandinaire specifications. I'm pleased you did not sign anything," Airik said and handed over his heavily annotated report.

"No sir. It felt too good to be true," Gaston replied.

He had spent the previous evening (when not sneezing) fending off various members of the Jandinaire family who a) all wanted to know where Airik was; b) know why he, Gaston, wasn't agreeing to everything they were pushing since Airik wasn't around to say no; c) refused to answer any of Gaston's questions about references from satisfied customers; and d) asked probing questions of their own about which Jandinaire beauty Airik preferred as his bride and how soon could the wedding be scheduled.

It had been maddening, especially since his constant sneezing didn't keep the Jandinaire family, already aswarm with Panschin's germs, away from him. Any decent, right-thinking family should have recognized he was ill and given him some peace in which to recuperate. The Jandinaire family's behavior guaranteed Gaston would never look with favor on any of their recommendations.

"Good eyes, Gaston," Airik said, filling Gaston with pride. "You were correct in your evaluation." Now why, Airik thought, couldn't you have been this competent before I arrived in Panschin? He made a mental note that Gaston needed more supervision, rather than less, to perform at his best. One more burden to deal with.

Airik looked over the schedule, noting, among other things, a lengthy business lunch with Maerski in the conference dining facility. Having read their proposal the day before and thought about it since, he could guess what pressure and falsehoods were in store. And of course, he could expect to be pestered about which of Maerski's eligible young ladies he wished to wed right away for the good of both demesnes. He thought of Veronica and returning to her and the peace of the White Elephant at the end of the day. It made the prospect of the coming day easier to bear.

"Gaston?"

"Yes sir?"

"Elliot will be in and out, doing a research project for me. We'll be returning to the White Elephant at the end of the day. I plan on keeping this schedule until the end of the mining conference. Let's get started," Airik said.

Gaston looked pleased at knowing exactly what to do. Yes, Airik noted, Gaston required closer supervision.

He put Veronica Bradwell firmly out of his mind. She was not his concern. The Red Mercury lode was.

Veronica insisted Neza accompany her on her rounds. The thought of leaving her elderly aunt home alone and at risk was too upsetting. They loaded up the handcart with the borrowed, washed stemware and set out, starting with Mrs. Grisson. They worked their way down the list and with each set of glassware returned, Veronica showed her neighbor one of Shelby's sketches of the thug, told them what had happened, and received in return a promise to keep an eye out. The neighborhood would be abuzz with gossip. There was every chance that everyone who lived in their district would know of the Bradwell's situation by the evening, followed by the rest of Dome Two within a few days.

She did not bring up Mr. Burgess to any of the neighbors, other than Mrs. Grisson. That worthy lady wouldn't gossip when asked not to and, more importantly, she was an often-surprising fountain of information. She did not know Mr. Burgess but she would look into him via sources of her own.

The bank was next. The tellers were equally interested in the threat and the sketch, enough that Veronica was allowed to speak with the manager of the branch, Mr. Wong. He had, to Veronica's relief, already been told about the incident by Mr. Cobb. He was very interested in her own interpretation, saying it was best to have all the facts. Mr. Wong was also happy to be paid the current month and the next month's lease payments. It was a real pleasure for Veronica to count out the coins with confidence. She paid the upcoming month in advance, deciding it was an act of optimism, rather than keeping the coins from Mr. Jones in her little hoard for a darker, less pleasant future.

Veronica had debated with herself during the walk over about asking Mr. Wong about Burgess and his bullying. In the end, she decided to not bring it up, since Mr. Wong would feel obligated to follow the dictates of his superior. There was no point in reminding him. Even better, there was always the chance Burgess had drunk enough plonk to have forgotten what he wanted to do when morning came. Since Mr. Wong did not bring up Burgess or his threat to kick her out, Veronica decided she was correct. Burgess might not remember at all, and Mr. Wong couldn't remind him if he didn't know in the first place.

Instead, she asked to speak to Mr. Cobb. If he was here, it would confirm Mrs. Grisson's report about his employment. It also would give her a chance to demonstrate she and her aunt were not ignorant about his plans, nefarious or otherwise, for her sister.

When he appeared from his office, he said warmly, "Miss Bradwell. Miss Molony. I have good news. On my way over to the bank this morning, I walked down your street and saw nothing out of the ordinary."

Veronica was startled. This was above and beyond the call of duty. Perhaps he was enough of an ally to be concerned about the White Elephant, even if he did not care what happened to its current inhabitants.

"Thank you." She hemmed for a moment, then plunged in.

"My sister said you would be taking her and the other members of the PanU Collective to the Steelio warrens." She focused intently on his face. "You will take care of her and them, will you not?"

Malcolm Cobb smiled at her, oblivious to the surprised glance Mr. Wong darted at him. "Of course, Miss Bradwell."

Mr. Wong frowned and said, "Miss Bradwell, Miss Molony, if anything were to happen to your sister because of Cobb's actions, I assure you, Second National would be most displeased with him." He threw an open look of dislike at Malcolm who ignored his supervisor as though he weren't standing there.

"Very kind of you," Veronica said, suddenly aware of hip-deep undercurrents washing up against the furniture in the once-splendid lobby of the Second National Bank of Panschin. It did not look like the two men approved of each other.

"I'm going to the police next," she said, hoping to see if they were at least united on that subject.

They were.

"I spoke with them again this morning," Malcolm said, "after I briefed Mr. Wong."

"The bank will fully support you, Miss Molony, Miss Bradwell, in your dealings with the police," Mr. Wong said, nodding to each woman in turn. "I plan on visiting the substation myself to insist on beefed-up patrols for both your home and your block."

"Thank you. My sister drew the thug last night, so I have a picture for you and your staff," Veronica said. She handed the drawing first to Malcolm Cobb, adding, "does her drawing match what you remember?"

He took the drawing and studied it, noticing how in a few, quick lines, Shelby had managed to capture how the thug looked with his shaved head, the scar on his neck, and his oddly cut suit. She had even managed to show a bit of his swaggering menace. Why then, was her painting so dreadful if this was so good?

"Your sister did an excellent job," Malcolm said. "Mr. Wong, you'll know best the order in which to circulate Miss Bradwell's sketch. I am not as familiar with Dome Two or where such a person might be staying."

Mr. Wong took the sketch and looked it over, showing no signs of recognition. When he finished, he turned to Malcolm and said, "I doubt very much, Cobb, if someone like this would lodge in Dome Two. You would be more likely to find a person of this ilk in some dive under Dome Four. You are far more likely to know of such places than I, or anyone here."

Veronica and Neza exchanged glances as the two men scowled at each other. Why would Mr. Cobb know anything about the tunnels under Dome Four? No one with even the remotest degree of respectability went there. The inhabitants, according to Lulu, were hostile to outsiders and especially slumming members of the upper classes once all their money had run out.

Then she remembered.

"There was someone else with that thug last night," Veronica said. Both bankers returned their attention to her at once, their unspoken fight forgotten.

"You recall my guest, Mr. Jones?" she asked.

"I do," Malcolm answered. Mr. Wong raised an eyebrow.

"His cousin, Elliot, noticed the thug being spoken to by another man, also oddly dressed and with the same odd accent. They left together. Elliot deduced the second man was the boss and he was unhappy with the thug's behavior towards me and my sister."

"Because he threatened you in front of witnesses," Malcolm said at once.

"A reasonable analysis, Cobb," Mr. Wong said, looking surprised at having to admit such a thing. "You do not have a sketch of this second man?"

"No, I'm afraid we don't," Veronica answered.

"This guest, Mr. Jones," Mr. Wong said. "Who is he?"

"Um," Veronica said. Now was not the time or location to admit she rented out rooms in direct violation of the lease, even if it was only for a few days here and there.

"A very distant set of cousins of mine from Barsoom," Neza lied, leaping into the conversation to save Veronica the struggle of coming up with a plausible story. Her niece was not the skilled liar her father had been. "They're here for the mining conference."

"Ah," Mr. Wong said, as understanding and acceptance bloomed. "Of course. Far better to stay with relatives, however distant, than to struggle with an overpriced, overcrowded hotel."

"Exactly," Neza said, building on her story. "Dome Two is quiet and so convenient to every place they need to go to. And it's always nice to reconnect with distant relations. It's been many, many years."

"So you and your nieces will not be alone in your house at night, then?" Malcolm asked.

"Yes, Mr. Jones and his cousins will be back every night," Neza said, hoping she was right and they didn't change their minds. If Airik Jones came back every night, he would see Veronica and perhaps something might come of it.

"That's good to know," Malcolm said.

"Yes, it is," Mr. Wong agreed, looking surprised again at agreeing with Malcolm Cobb.

Veronica and Neza left the bank and headed to the police substation.

"That was strange," Veronica said, once they were outside and safely out of earshot. "Why would Mr. Wong behave that way? As though Mr. Cobb didn't belong in the bank."

"I have no idea," Neza replied. "I'll ask Mrs. Grisson. The junior bank teller boarding with her should know."

"She might, but will she tell us?" Veronica said. "I suppose it doesn't matter if they dislike each other. They both don't want someone forcing us out of the White Elephant. Other than that dreadful Burgess, I mean."

Neza thought about this. "Do you think Mr. Cobb said anything about Burgess at the bank? How did *they* seem to get along?"

Veronica said, after a long, evaluating pause, "I would have to say they despised each other."

"Interesting," her aunt replied. "Here we are at last. I'll be glad to sit down for a change."

"Is your hip bothering you again?" Veronica asked in alarm. "I've been pushing you to get all this done."

"Not to worry," Neza said and then stopped talking as she labored up the multiple sandstone steps leading to the local police substation. With every step, she leaned heavily on her pink cane and panted while Veronica hovered anxiously around her, distracted from worries about Burgess as Neza knew she would be.

Like the White Elephant, the police substation was immaculately clean of terraformers. The courthouse next to it was equally pristine, every carved representation of justice sharply defined. The standard punishment for misdemeanors in Dome Two was scrubbing and scraping municipal buildings clean of their ever-growing sweater of algae and moss. The local law, at every level, took full advantage of the free labor provided by litterers, indigents, rowdy teens, pickpockets, shoplifters, and occasional drunkards. More serious crimes earned the culprits more time laboring for the good of the community. The free-city of Panschin didn't believe in allowing public offenders to sit around and do nothing while eating and sleeping at the taxpayers' expense.

The desk sergeant, a grizzled veteran of long service as evidenced by the tiger stripes of rank marching up his sleeve from wrist to shoulder, studied Shelby's sketches intently.

"Never seen this man before," the sergeant said finally. "I'll keep this sketch for the station house."

"Mr. Cobb at the bank said he spoke to you about increased foot patrols on our street," Veronica said.

"That he did, Miss Bradwell," the desk sergeant replied. "Twice. And, as much as we can, we'll send a man around regularly to keep an eye on things. However, with the mining conference in town, we're short-handed."

Neza took a look around the lobby, noticing several patrolmen sitting around enjoying their tea-break and ignoring the crowd waiting on the benches to be dealt with. "And what are those fine gentlemen doing, pray tell?"

"Taking a break from their double shifts, Miss Molony," the desk sergeant answered wearily. "I'm working one myself. Every pickpocket and mugger in Panschin is out in force during the conference. There were five bar brawls last night, including one right here in Dome Two at the Broken Pickaxe. Those were separate incidents from last night's full-on riot in the Daimyo's Arse under Dome Four. Trying to break up that fiasco put two of my men into the hospital."

"I thought Dome Two patrolmen stayed in Dome Two," Veronica snapped. "You know, keeping the local residents safe?"

"Not during the mining conference," the sergeant answered. "We go where we're needed. Visitors sleeping in the parks and using the planters as urinals are the least of my problems. After the conference is over, you'll see the entire museum scrubbed down, including that huge set of steps, its rooftop terrace, and the undersides of all the banisters with all the free labor I'm acquiring from the local idiots. The city's expecting to get the train station scrubbed clean, like always."

"I didn't realize you were so busy," Neza said, somewhat mollified at the lack of services she paid for.

"It will only get worse," the sergeant said. "If the conference goes like usual, we'll get more fights in the bars, more pickpockets, more thefts perpetrated on outsiders who don't know enough to lock up their stuff, more complaints of every kind." He smiled at them broadly, displaying a broken tooth from an encounter with a hooligan. "The city will earn thousands in fines from out-of-towners. That might be enough to pay the overtime every police unit in Panschin is clocking."

"I had no idea," Veronica said, wide-eyed. She had never once considered what happened in the streets of Panschin when out-of-towners flooded it for several event-packed weeks. She'd always assumed visitors were like Mr. Jones; respectable businessmen who spent the day in conferences discussing improvements in mining techniques, followed by quiet evenings reviewing reports. That led to a new concern.

"Oh. Oh my. What about PanU? My sister, Lulu, Florence, they all walk back and forth every day. They could be in danger." She thought of the thug grabbing Shelby off the street and disappearing with her into one of the abandoned houses in Dome Two. Her hand went to her string of cloudy beads, feeling the reassuring coolness.

The sergeant was polite enough to not scoff. "The ladies will be fine, just like you ladies are fine, walking around. The tunnels under Dome Four? Some parts of Dome One? Back alleys in sector five in Dome Six? District seven in Dome Three? That'd be different. PanU, like PCC and every other school in Panschin, beefs up its own security for the conference. They keep an eye out for their commuting students as well as their campus."

Neza looked over at Veronica and guessed where her thoughts had gone from the frightened look in her eyes.

"But you'll do your best."

"Yes, Miss Molony, we will. Keep your doors and windows locked, especially at night. Keep your eyes open. You've talked to all your neighbors?"

"Yes, we have," Veronica replied.

"That was the best thing you could do," the desk sergeant said. "Next best is talking to all the rickshaw haulers and sedan chair men. They're on the streets all the time, and they see everyone."

"I spoke with them," Veronica said.

"Very good. After that, the business owners. They know who's not from around here and guys like that thug, they have to sleep somewhere and take their meals from someone."

"We think," Veronica said, "that the thug we saw had a companion, but we don't know what he looks like other than he's also not from Panschin."

"See if you can get a description," the sergeant said. "Maybe your sister could draw something up."

"Thank you," Veronica said. She felt shaky and more grateful than ever that Mr. Jones, despite knowing so little about him and his party, had turned up to rent rooms at the White Elephant. Her little family would not be alone in the house, at least until the end of the mining conference.

But after that, they would be. It was a chilling thought.

Outside, she turned to her great-aunt. "It feels like we're on our own."

"We're not," Neza said with a confidence she did not feel. "Our neighbors don't want any trouble, any more than we do. They'll all watch for any signs."

They walked along the sidewalk, towards the business district. Veronica fretted with every step over what she should have said at the bank. Better to say it, she decided at last. Before we get to the Dappled Yak and drop off the last of the stemware. While we still have some privacy.

"I keep thinking I should have asked about that dreadful Burgess at the bank," Veronica said. "I didn't want to bring him up, but at the same time, I don't want us to be surprised. I'm as worried about him as that awful thug. Neza, do you know anything about him or his family from, you know, before?"

Her aunt sighed deeply. "No, I do not. I didn't recognize him when he came to the house, and he didn't say anything to me. Mr. Burgess was just another gallery-goer. I did notice his ridiculous suit. I can't imagine why a man his size and age thinks he should follow the latest, most extreme fashions. Mr. Cobb was much better dressed as well as being in far better shape."

"Shelby certainly thought so," Veronica said. "She told me that last night when she did *not* tell me about running off with him to the Steelio warren this afternoon."

"Shelby is not 'running off' with Malcolm Cobb," her aunt replied tartly. "She's going on a field trip to visit reality. Residents of the warrens won't spout that drivel PanU stuffed into her."

"Reality! You mean the one where my little sister might get mauled by some man we barely know?"

"She won't be alone, Veronica," Neza said soothingly. "The rest of the Collective will be along for the ride. You couldn't ask for a more intrusive, noisy, nosy pack of chaperones getting in the way, asking silly questions, and being constantly underfoot. And, may I say, this is exactly why Shelby didn't say anything to you. You are not her mother."

Veronica's face fell and Neza quickly said, "I'm sorry. I miss your mother every day, just like the two of you do."

"I know. It's just that I worry about Shelby. None of this has been easy for her since the indictments started flying around dear old dad."

"I do know, and it hasn't been easy for you either. But getting back to that Burgess, I don't know anything about him. I wasn't out socially that much before and now," Neza sighed again. "Almost all my connections are gone. I'll find out what I can, but don't expect much."

"I wish I knew why he dislikes Mr. Cobb so much," Veronica said. "And Mr. Wong too. I thought bankers stuck together against mere mortals like us. Like they're all part of some secret cabal."

Her aunt stopped to laugh and lean on her pink cane. "How melodramatic. I'm sure it's much more mundane than that. A disagreement about interest rates, no doubt."

Veronica laughed too. "True. What else would bankers talk about?"

"What the hellation is wrong with you, Cobb? Taking PanU students into the warrens?" Desmond Wong hissed, once he and Malcolm were safely behind closed doors and away from the gossipy tellers.

Malcolm faced his boss calmly. "I went to the PanU Artists' Collective exhibit last night at the White Elephant. I won't say I admired it because every painting there was dreadful. Miss Shelby Bradwell was gracious enough to tell me the philosophy behind making art that looked like the contents of a cesspool."

Mr. Wong was momentarily distracted as Malcolm knew he would be. "A cesspool?"

"I'm afraid so. It's what passes for art with our betters."

"Your betters, Cobb. Not mine."

Malcolm chose to ignore his boss's dig. "Miss Bradwell was interested in seeing what actual working people like in art as opposed to the drivel she's been fed at PanU. She assured me everyone in the Collective would be interested as well."

"You aren't concerned that your cover will be blown?" Mr. Wong asked sweetly.

"Seeing as how people gossip, I'd say that already happened."

"But *Shelby Bradwell*? Do you not know who she is? Are you that incompetent?"

A warm smile of remembrance flashed across Malcolm's face, softening the harsh lines.

"I do know who she is." He glared at his boss. "She is not her father, nor, I dare say, is her sister, Veronica. Nor their aunt, Miss Molony. Not based on what I saw in their house."

"Simon Bradwell made enemies, ruined lives." Mr. Wong fanned his hands in agitation. "He's not the only one to do so. I was pressured to accept you, and I'm being pressured now, over you and the Bradwells."

"Burgess already got to you, didn't he," Malcolm said.

"Last night," Mr. Wong admitted. "I don't like you, Cobb. I don't like your attitude. Your background is appalling. You have no family connections whatsoever, no social standing of any kind. I don't need you digging up trouble for us here in the branch in Dome Two."

Malcolm took a more careful look at his manager. Something else was going on, and he wondered, for the first time, why Desmond Wong had been left to rot in Dome Two and why he hadn't done anything with the unrecognized plum he had been given. It wasn't just incompetence.

"Burgess has something on you, doesn't he."

"He does *not*."

"He *does*. You never wanted me here. You made that plain from day one. So why did you, the manager of the main branch in the dome, accept a jumped-up tunnel rat? You should have been able to say no. Burgess forced you. He dumped me here with the rest of the dross to hide me where I wouldn't have to offend his dainty sensibilities by showing how much more capable I am than his precious protégés are.”

Desmond Wong spun around to stare out the window, past the long-faded, sound-muffling velvet drapes and up at the dome, trapping them beneath its weight.

Malcolm waited silently, his arms crossed. It felt good to speak his mind to Wong, that incompetent hack. It was a risk but it felt right. He had control of the moment and not Wong. He knew things Wong didn’t know, including who Airik Jones really was.

His patience was rewarded.

“You don’t know what you’re risking. Burgess can ruin your life,” Mr. Wong said quietly. “All the senior people here at our branch ran afoul of him. Their careers were over.”

“He has weaknesses,” Malcolm said. “I’ve been doing some quiet research.”

Mr. Wong spun around. “It won’t be enough. And I will not allow you to drag me and my family down any further.”

“You won’t be involved,” Malcolm said. “Just don’t get in my way. Your careers are not over. Why haven’t you done anything with Dome Two? The real estate here is of astonishing size and quality. Dome Six has nothing to compare to it. They won’t be building another dome for decades even while Panschin is bursting at the seams. You let the bank’s investments rot.”

Mr. Wong smiled slowly for the first time, a slight baring of teeth. “I meet the minimum standards, and that’s all I will do. I don’t draw attention to myself, to my staff, or to our families. I’m not expected to make a profit here in Dome Two so I don’t.”

“This is how you fight back,” Malcolm said, understanding dawning.

“Yes, and I suggest you do the same.”

“Burgess is already trying to dig a shaft to shove me into,” Malcolm said. “I won’t let him succeed because if he does, he’ll throw the Bradwells down after me, and I won’t let that happen.”

“You may not have a choice.”

Malcolm took a step forward and quit trying to look non-threatening. He watched in pleasure as Wong blanched and stepped back, closer to the large window overlooking a view of one of Dome Two’s luxuriously green public parks.

“You were right,” Malcolm said. “I do know where a thug like the one who threatened the Bradwells would hide under Dome Four. I have choices because if I have to, I can disappear into the tunnels, and Burgess will never find me."

To Malcolm's surprise, Desmond Wong gave him a look of pity.

"You could disappear," he said. "Your family won't be bothered because Steelio doesn't bank with us and even if they did, Steelio won't be bullied and how would Burgess know what happens in their warrens anyway?" Mr. Wong paused. His eyes had lost their usual dull lifelessness. They had become startlingly intelligent.

"But I don't believe the lovely Miss Shelby Bradwell or her sister or her aunt would go underneath into the warrens with you. Unlike you, they are not tunnel rats."

Malcolm stiffened. "I won't fail. Just stay out of my way."

"Do you plan on doing something about that ruffian threatening the Bradwells as well?"

"I do."

"Good. But I cannot help you. I cannot risk further damage to my family's future, my children's future. I will do what I've always done in Dome Two. Nothing. I'm very good at it. Now get out of my office."

"Of course, Mr. Wong," Malcolm said and walked out of his supervisor's office, his mind whirling. He might have been wrong in his assessment of his boss. If he was wrong here, where else was he making a mistake?

shelby walked through the streets of Dome Two to the PanU campus just like she always had but this morning, everything felt different. The ground was unsteady under her feet, as though the tunnels bored into the rock below Dome Two were twisting themselves into knots. Every step reminded her there was no place in Panschin that didn't have another layer beneath it, hidden but no less real for her obliviousness to it. Or many layers, all of them previously invisible, but now suddenly forcing their way into her life.

Lulu and Florence had given up trying to tell her more about life in the warrens during the walk from the White Elephant since she kept saying "I have to see for myself." It was an easy answer, keeping her mind clear for something else she didn't want to talk about with them.

What she was really thinking about was Malcolm Cobb.

Shelby had not drawn just the thug who had threatened her and Veronica the evening before. She had drawn *him* and concealed her sketch from everyone in the household. As she sketched out his broad shoulders, rugged face, and confident manner, she'd remembered where she had seen him. He had been one man among many, out and about in Dome Two, but one who stood out because of the way he walked, assured and self-possessed. Unlike her, Malcolm Cobb knew who he was and where his place was in the world.

She kept the drawing with her, carefully folded and tucked into her breast pocket. She couldn't show it to anyone but she did not want to leave it behind, hidden in the room she shared with Veronica. What if her sister went looking for something else and found her careful, lovingly detailed sketch of Malcolm Cobb?

Had he seen her before, out and about in Dome Two? It was possible, but he had not said so. Another question eating at her was how he could get her and the rest of the Collective down underneath into the Steelio warren. Malcolm Cobb was a banker. Bankers, in Shelby's limited experience, did not have anything to do with the people who dug out and processed the wealth of Panschin. Bankers floated high above the dirty realities of work, especially the work of the mines.

Yet, she would see him this afternoon, and go underneath with him into the warrens. But why Steelio? Lulu insisted Steelio was well-regarded as taking decent care of its workers and their families. Their warren was considered to be pleasant; that could be the reason. But how pleasant could housing inside underground tunnels be? The thought of going underneath was frightening, but not as frightening as losing the White Elephant to Mr. Burgess.

Lulu and Florence said their goodbyes at the elaborate arched stone gateway to PanU's campus. The entry to PCC was much less grand, consisting of a wide tunnel sloping underground to its classrooms and labs. The far sides of the tunnel's opening were fenced off, so no one could fall in by accident. It didn't need a roof since it never rained inside the dome. A roof would only block light from falling down into the depths.

Shelby stood off to one side, out of the traffic, and stared down into the broad opening. It was well-lit, the walls whitewashed and plastered with posters like those she saw in the hallways of PanU, and filled with all kinds of people coming and going. If Auntie Neza persuaded the bursar of PanU to transfer over her already paid tuition, she'd be going underground with Florence and Lulu every day. Going underground into the Steelio warrens with Malcolm Cobb was a step in the right direction, a way of adjusting to something deeply uncomfortable.

Shelby shuddered and turned away, then headed through the gateway into PanU's green and beautiful campus, open to the dome high above. The planters were filled to bursting with flowers and the small trees cast their lacy, fringed shadows onto the grass lawns and the paved brick sidewalks. A bird was singing in one of the small trees and another answered from across the red brick walkway. She knew nothing lived underground except people and the cold, unforgiving rock. She took the long way around, to better enjoy being aboveground in the watery sunlight the dome permitted.

When she finally reached her classrooms, she discovered one improvement over yesterday's awfulness. She was no longer topic number one in PanU's art department. That subject was now Reyansh Philpott and his threatened lawsuit against both Professor Vitebskin and PanU. Some students still wanted to talk about her and her father's crimes, but they also wanted to talk with her.

Anyone who had not been present during Professor Vitebskin's screaming match with Reyansh Philpott wanted to hear every detail of the incident. Since Shelby had a front-row seat, she was suddenly in demand from people who never spoke to her unless forced by mundane necessities. It was even more fascinating to discuss what Reyansh had yelled back to the professor, leading to the most fascinating topic of all: the lawsuit that Reyansh's father had filed against both the professor and the university. Reyansh hadn't made an idle threat. He, however, was not present to answer avid questions. He was, so rumor had it, giving depositions at that very moment about how Professor Vitebskin was highhanded, rude, overbearing, lecherous, incompetent, wasted PanU resources on personal projects, and played favorites thus discriminating against anyone whom the Professor disapproved of no matter what their artistic merits were.

Most fascinating of all, rumor had it that Reyansh was planning on calling witnesses of his own who would back up every salacious and libelous allegation. Since Professor Vitebskin cut a wide swath through both the faculty and the student body, there were plenty of names being bandied about.

When Shelby arrived, Professor Vitebskin was presiding over the studio, grimly ripping apart the substandard work submitted the previous week. His critiques were merciless, leaving the offending students near tears. Shelby watched him for a few painful moments, steeled herself, interrupted him (to the intense relief of another student who vanished for a good cry in the janitor's closet) and told him about Malcolm Cobb's invitation to the PanU Artists' Collective.

Professor Vitebskin tried to stare her down for having the temerity to interrupt him. Shelby Bradwell really was as stupid as she was beautiful. To his surprise, she didn't turn tail and run. He would have to waste words and time on her talentless self to get rid of her.

"Shelby," the professor barked at her. "You are naïve. That idiot banker only wants one thing from you. Think! How could some low-level flunky at a bank take you or anyone else into the Steelio warrens? He's never been deeper down in Panschin than the transtubes."

"He said he would be here at two. Mr. Cobb will take everyone," —

Shelby waved at the surrounding students either pretending to work or honestly loitering — "with him underneath into Steelio. The Collective talks all the time about art speaking to and for the people. All the professors here at PanU talk all the time about how the university supports the downtrodden masses. Well, do we? This is our chance to prove it."

Professor Vitebskin groaned and rolled his eyes in disgust. "Fine, Shelby. You do that. *I* am not going because *I* have better, more important things to do." He took a moment to glare around the studio. No one met his piercing, angry gaze. "If any of *you* layabouts want to go underneath with Shelby and be disappointed, at least that's better than standing around here and wasting my time."

He paused, got no response, then pointed at the next painting on the critique pile. "Who painted this heap of dung?"

Two PM duly arrived. The moment the clock ticked over, Professor Vitebskin smirked at Shelby in triumph. "He's not here."

"Miss Bradwell," Malcolm announced, as he strode in through the door thirty seconds later. "Ready to see the real Panschin? Everyone in the Collective is welcome to visit the Steelio warren."

"Mr. Cobb. You were able to find us," Shelby said. Then her brain processed how he was dressed and emptied itself out.

Professor Vitebskin recovered faster.

"I didn't know bankers shopped at secondhand clothing stores. Trying to impress us with your fake bona-fides? It won't work."

Malcolm smiled evenly. "This is my coverall, the one Steelio issued me. I wear it whenever I'm in the deepdown."

Professor Vitebskin, whose day had already been trying beyond belief, marched up to him. A safe target for his wrath had finally arrived and he planned to take full advantage of the opportunity.

"Complete and utter dross" the professor snarled, jabbing his finger at Malcolm to make his point, although he was careful to avoid actual, physical contact with the younger, larger, much more physically fit banker. "You work for a bank. What the seven hells do you know about the working class?"

"More than you," Malcolm replied coldly. He did not yield a centimeter to Professor Vitebskin. "I'm a scholarship boy from the

Steelio warren. I grew up there. My family still lives there and when I'm not at the bank, I'm underneath in the deepdown, helping my father, my brother, and my uncle dig copper for Steelio."

Shelby stared at him. Malcolm Cobb had looked good in his suit. In his coverall, he looked better. It showed his broad shoulders owed nothing to the skill of a tailor and demonstrated how trim his waist really was. Moreover, it was clear the Steelio coverall issued to him was the real thing, unlike the upscale department store versions worn by most of the students in PanU's studio.

Steelio's coverall was slate gray canvas, to better hide dirt and stains. The company name was emblazoned on both sleeves, up both legs, and across the back in vivid, reflective orange, the better to be seen in the dark. On the front, Malcolm's name was embroidered in the same orange, last name first, followed by his first initial. On the other side of his chest was Steelio in a fancy flowing script and his company identification number. He also had his last name emblazoned across his back, underneath the Steelio name. Every wear spot and stain (and there were many) were real and right where you would expect on a working garment. There were no raw, sanded scrapes; any spots like those had been carefully patched. He wore heavy, thick-soled and scuffed boots, with extra leather sewn over the toes to reinforce them. This was a style Shelby rarely observed among the students of PanU but was common among the maintenance staff.

"A scholarship boy? You mean a jumped-up tunnel rat," Professor Vitebskin sneered. "No wonder you know nothing about the meaning of art."

"I've toured the Panschin Museum, so I've seen real art. Unlike the piles of tailings at the White Elephant, those paintings are beautiful, or at least interesting and educational."

"So you're an ignorant philistine too!" Professor Vitebskin said.

Shelby watched them in disbelief, recounting as she did every time Professor Vitebskin or the other professors at PanU talked about serving the downtrodden. What else did he say that he didn't mean or that wasn't true? She swallowed hard. She really didn't know anything. She really was naïve. The realization was painful. She took a look around. They had drawn the usual appreciative audience since nothing ever happened discreetly at PanU. It was like living in the middle of a theater. An audience always appeared, lured by the promise of a free show.

She thought of Mr. Burgess and losing her home. Professor

Vitebskin complained about students and faculty wasting his time. How much of her time had he wasted since the day she started classes? Now he was wasting even more, time she could be spending trying to keep the White Elephant safe.

"Stop this right now," Shelby made herself shout. All eyes turned to her, and for a mercy, Professor Vitebskin shut up in his shock.

"Mr. Cobb is kind enough to take the Collective underground to the warrens," she said loudly. "I am going. Who else is coming with us?"

The studio went dead silent. She stared up at Malcolm's dark, approving eyes, her heart racing. He smiled at her. It suddenly struck Shelby — flushing in embarrassment and tearing her eyes away from him and looking at the suddenly busy studio — the other reason why he stood out so much, and not just because of how he was dressed. He wasn't much older than the other students but he wasn't a teenager playing at being a grownup. He was an adult.

"Well?" she asked even louder. "Anyone?"

Dear Gods, she was going to have to go underground with Malcolm Cobb alone.

She waited tensely, wishing someone, anyone, would fill the silence.

"I will," Kip said reluctantly. "You shouldn't go alone, Shelby."

He came out of the corner where he had been hiding from Professor Vitebskin's critiques – well-deserved in his case — and faced her, Malcolm, and the goggling, open-mouthed professor. The rest of the students looked equally shocked. Kip McGrant never did anything out of the ordinary that would excite gossip. His main concern had always been his image and reputation, both of which were bland.

"I'll go with you," he repeated.

Shelby was floored. "Kip? Are you sure?"

"Well, yeah." Kip darted a look over at Malcolm Cobb, looking threateningly large and decidedly out of place in the PanU art studio.

Malcolm said, "Anyone else? We'll be using the large freight elevator so I can take a crowd into the deepdown. You'll be safe. You have my word."

"For what that's worth," Professor Vitebskin muttered.

"You too, Professor Vitebskin," Malcolm said coldly. "You should see what real mining looks like instead of the dross you smear across canvas."

"Unlike other people, I have work to do. Get out of my studio."

"Let's go," Shelby said, wanting desperately to get the afternoon over with. To Kip she whispered, "Thank you."

He smiled at her, the way she had always wanted him to, when other, more important people were around to see him show her approval. It was a pleasant feeling to know Kip cared enough about her to demonstrate it, when it really mattered. Although, the traitorous thought lingered, why didn't he when it didn't matter? He could have introduced her as a fellow student to his parents at the gallery showing, yet he had not.

Malcolm took the lead to the metro station. Inside, he headed at once down the stairs, lower down, to a level Shelby had never been on. With each step downward, into the bowels of Mars, the sense of being surrounded by implacable, hating rock increased.

The people around them changed as well. They looked tired, and dirtier, and their clothing was shabbier. Yet many of them still laughed and joked among themselves, ignoring the tourists from another world.

Shelby wanted desperately to hold Kip's hand but instead, she kept her free hand firmly in her pocket. She clutched her satchel in the other, containing her precious sketchpads and pencils. Kip didn't speak at all, and kept his own hands shoved into his shiny new coverall's pockets. She noticed he left his drawing materials behind, making her wonder again why Kip was studying art. He didn't work at it like she did.

The path leveled off into a wide concourse, lit by industrial lamps. This gave Shelby a chance to study Kip some more. He bypassed everyone else as if they didn't exist. He looked so out of place with his fashionable haircut and bandbox-fresh appearance. In her drab coverall, she looked more like many of the other women. The main difference was her clothing didn't have a company name on it, showing who she worked for. Even so, Shelby was not alone in lacking a company logo embroidered all over her garments. There were young men in the crowd, some younger than Kip, but they already had a harder edge about them. They carried themselves like they could feel the weight of the stone above them. It was fascinating to see a different range of humanity, so different from PanU's student body and the usual foot-traffic on Dome Two's streets, and she stored up impressions to sketch from later.

Malcolm scanned the directory of routes, selected a transtube, and bought the tickets. He led them to the right track and through the open doors on the metal cylinder. By this time, Shelby's fascination had faded. She numbly followed him onboard and Kip brought up the rear, looking sullen and unhappy.

Once seated, Mr. Cobb turned to her. "Miss Bradwell." His face was concerned. "You'll be safe. I swear it."

Shelby fought for control. No one here was concerned in the least about whizzing underground in a tube of badly lit metal. The tunnel walls could be seen through the dirty transtube windows, and they were uniformly the colors of the paintings Professor Vitebskin championed.

So this was where he got his ideas, Shelby thought. He sees Panschin from the transtube windows. She had always heard he traveled via the expensive, upper tram level from Dome Six, the one used by anyone who could afford better than the mass transit system. Based on his choice of artistic subjects, he must not have.

The crowded transtube jolted down the tracks and nothing bad happened. No rocks fell from the ceiling. There were no signs of crumbling tunnel walls leading to them being trapped. She sat wedged between Malcolm and Kip, wishing she could hold someone's hand for the reassurance of a human touch. She had to make do with sitting between them. No one else in the transtube seemed to feel the least discomfort. Only her. It was disconcerting when the transtube jerked and she was pushed closer to Malcolm. He didn't seem to mind when that happened. Oddly, when she was pushed into Kip, he pulled away from her as though her presence was unwanted. Then why had he volunteered to come?

The trip seemed to take forever, yet none of Shelby's fears came true. The roof didn't collapse, crushing them into piles of bloody gravel. The transtube's air remained breathable so they didn't suffocate. She was stared at but not in a hostile manner. Gangs of marauding hooligans didn't race through the transtube, robbing the passengers of what few valuables they possessed. She didn't think that was because of Malcolm's presence either. It was all very mundane.

She remembered Veronica telling her in irritation "Shelby, you like drama but the rest of us don't, so stop making things more dramatic than they are." Had she been overdramatizing going underground into the deepdown? It was possible her sister was right. It might also indicate she'd overdramatized the situation with that awful cave-troll, Burgess. He was a threat but that didn't mean he would murder them in their beds, followed by composting their bodies to get rid of the evidence. The thug who threatened her and her sister was a more likely candidate. He, however, had the police looking for him along with every neighbor, business owner, and rickshaw hauler in Dome Two.

As Shelby gradually relaxed, she noticed that Kip was becoming tenser.

"Kip?" she whispered. "Are you all right?"

"No, I'm not," Kip mumbled. "This transtube is awful. It's crowded, and it stinks. Don't any of these people take baths?"

Shelby decided to ignore his pettiness. "I'm really glad you came along with me, Kip. I was afraid I would have to go alone."

She smiled anxiously up at his tightly drawn face, thinking of all the times she had wanted him to notice her. He never had, unless no one who mattered was around. Then he paid attention, chatting about the day's events and joking. No one mattered here. No one they knew would be on this line. Yet he still didn't seem to notice her, focusing on something inward that desperately needed his complete attention.

Shelby frowned and wondered what other situations she was misreading. She looked around the transtube again, taking in the crowd, both seated and a few hardy souls hanging from the straps, and wondered for the first time where they were in relation to Dome Two.

The transtube rattled to a stop at the station and more people got on and got off. It struck her that she could get off at this station and have no idea how to get home. She was entirely dependent on Malcolm Cobb keeping his word.

She did not want to ask him their location and betray still further how ignorant and naïve she was. She rarely traveled on the transtubes since her exile to Dome Two. There had been no need and no money and no desire to explore the rest of Panschin.

"Kip?" she whispered. "Do you know where we are?"

He twisted in his seat to get a better look at her face.

"How the hellation should I know? I've never been this deep before," Kip said. He looked very unfriendly so she turned away and looked straight across the transtube, peering between the other passengers to stare out through the window at the drab wall of the tunnel racing by.

Mr. Cobb must have heard her question. He leaned over and quietly said, "We'll be getting off at the next stop. The Steelio warren won't be far. They're not under a dome, but in an open space between the domes. They're under the original grow-tunnels."

Shelby said, "Are those still used?" then wanted to bite her tongue for saying something so silly.

"Sure are," Malcolm replied. He reminded himself again how sheltered Shelby Bradwell really was. Yet here she was anyway, daring the unknown. It made him want even more to protect her and have her smile up at him instead of at that useless Kip McGrant. "It's good for Steelio, since it's not under a dome. We've got long, long light-shafts opening from the grow-tunnels down to the warrens. We get real sunlight," he said with pride.

Shelby knew how deep the light-shafts were that fed light into the two basement levels in the White Elephant. There were light-shafts performing the same function for PCC. Their tiny, polished domes were scattered all over the PanU campus, bringing light into the classrooms and labs belowground.

"So the Steelio warrens aren't very deep?"

"We're pretty deep. Fifty meters and more."

"Oh." That was more than deep enough to die in a cave-in.

"Do many people live in Steelio?" She should have listened more closely to Lulu and Florence's explanations. On the other hand, it gave her something distracting to talk about.

"Over a hundred families. Steelio isn't one of the bigger operations."

"Oh." Shelby thought of children growing up in dark, cramped tunnels, never seeing sunshine or having room to run in.

"Steelio does a good job with its housing," Malcolm said, sensing her discomfort. "They never have to struggle recruiting workers, since the miners know their families will be treated reasonably well."

"There are companies that have to, uh, beg for workers?"

Malcolm frowned awfully. "Oh yes. The worst companies have to recruit desperate men from outside the city who don't understand what they're signing up for. They come from all over, looking for a better life but they don't always find it. Panschin has a fully deserved reputation for chewing up and spitting out men."

"That's not true," Kip mumbled. "I've never heard of such a thing."

"And what do you know about anything outside of your own

experience?" Malcolm asked coldly. "Do you ever go outside of Dome Six other than to attend PanU?"

"I get around," Kip retorted and sank back in his seat, more sullen than before.

"Kip?" Shelby said hesitantly. "Florence told us what happened to her father. What Chung/Banerjee did to her family. She hates them."

"Chung/Banerjee is not like that," Kip said very firmly. He sat up straight again, revived by irritation. "You don't know what you're talking about, Shelby."

She did not want to argue with Kip. What if he left? She'd be alone with Malcolm Cobb, and she'd never find her way home again. Shelby thought of Florence, who even more so than Lulu rarely discussed her upbringing. Florence who was determinedly cheerful and optimistic as though her positive attitude would ward off anything bad happening to her. Florence who regularly said how grateful she was to be attending PCC on a scholarship that would earn her a better life than the one her mother suffered or the one her sister ended up in, on her back and servicing any one with the coin to pay her. Chung/Banerjee had used up her father, spat out what remained, and abandoned what was left of the family.

That made her angry, so she said, "I do know what I'm talking about, Kip. Florence doesn't lie."

"She's lying now."

"She is not."

Malcolm interrupted. "Who is Florence, Miss Bradwell?"

"She's my friend," Shelby said. Her expressive face suddenly lit up, realizing how true that was. "She's really nice. Her and Lulu both."

"Ah," Malcolm said. "That must be why I saw her at the gallery showing at the White Elephant, helping you serve the nibbles."

"You know her?" Shelby said, taken aback and worried all over again. Florence would have told her if she knew Mr. Cobb. Why hadn't she said something?

"No, but I've seen her with you, and I suppose Lulu, walking around Dome Two," Malcolm said.

"You've seen me before?" Shelby sputtered. Oh dear Gods below, he was targeting her. She'd never make it home in one piece.

"Oh yes. You're hard to miss. I've seen you sketching all the different planters of flowers. You were so intent on them. I like the little yellow and purple ones best. They look like they have faces."

"Those are pansies," Shelby said, not knowing what else to say.

"I didn't know that," Malcolm replied.

How could he not know the name of a flower? The Steelio warrens must be awful, Shelby thought. How much worse are the rest?

"Who cares about dumb old flowers," Kip said suddenly, breaking the silence.

"I care," Shelby snapped. "Flowers are beautiful. They make the world more colorful and fantastic. There're dozens of varieties and all of them are lovely. My sister and I maintain the planters on our street for the neighborhood association."

"They're a waste of money," Kip said.

"Being underground getting to you, Kip?" Malcolm asked. He had observed the fine sheen of sweat across Kip's face and the faint tremor in his hands. Shelby was nervous, even frightened at times, but she wasn't sweating. It was a good sign.

"No. I'm fine," Kip said. "Quit bugging me about it."

"Sure. Where does Florence live, Miss Bradwell?" Malcolm asked, digging about for a neutral topic. He didn't want to reveal more of his ignorance about the flowers Shelby drew. His very practical education kept showing huge gaps, gaps that regularly tripped him up. He was coming to believe the gaps were on purpose, ensuring he couldn't climb as high as he wanted to in Panschin's hierarchy. He'd always remain a scholarship boy, routinely betrayed by his lack of social polish and inborn cultural knowledge. "In Dome Two as well?"

"Yes, with us, actually," Shelby replied and wanted to bite her tongue off again.

"With you? In the White Elephant?" Malcolm asked.

"We're allowed," Shelby shot back. "We're allowed to have live-in help. We're not renting out rooms like Mrs. —, uh, I mean, like some people do. My sister would never do that."

"You're friends with the servants?" Kip asked in horror. "How could you?"

Shelby turned to stare at Kip, equally horrified. "Because Florence is really nice, that's why. How could you say such a thing?"

Malcolm, for his part, interpreted what Shelby said and then not said. So, Florence, and probably Lulu too, lived with the Bradwells, trading unending housekeeping and possibly coin for room and board. It was a common enough arrangement, one he had already observed in

Dome Two, and everyone who used it did so to skirt their lease obligations. His own landlady had told him that if the bank official from First National came by and questioned him, he was to say he was a gardener; this despite the fact she knew who he worked for and knew he couldn't tell one plant from the next. And the "Mrs." that Shelby started to mention was probably another resourceful landlady, making the most of her only asset: a big house with lots of empty rooms desperately needing continuous maintenance. Interesting. It could be Mrs. Grisson, she of the pet chickens and the unauthorized but enterprising farming enterprise in Dome Two supplying the Dappled Yak.

"Because she's lying about Chung/Banerjee, that's why," Kip said.

"No, she isn't, Kip, and I don't want to hear another nasty word from you about Florence," Shelby replied sharply.

"I know Chung/Banerjee's reputation," Malcolm said. "They aren't the worst mining operation in Panschin but they're definitely down near the bottom of the shaft."

Kip seized his opening. "So who is the worst, since you think you know all about it."

"That would be Jandinaire," Malcolm growled. "Hands down."

"Yeah, okay, I'll accept that, maybe, you might be right on that part," Kip said. He sat back, mollified. "My dad says the same thing and so do my uncles. Jandinaire is a pack of liars. They falsify their data. Chung/Banerjee would never do that."

Malcolm suppressed a snort and chose not to say anything.

The transtube jolted harshly and suddenly, throwing Shelby against Malcolm's body. She swallowed a scream and began to shake. The tunnel roof had caved in for sure. He saw her distress and wrapped a reassuring arm around her.

"Sorry, I should have warned you. The transtube always bounces right at this point. Maintenance can't seem to keep the rails straight. Think of it as a signal that we're almost at our stop," Malcolm said.

Shelby found herself struggling to breathe, and not just because of the jolting. The jolt had practically thrown her into Mr. Cobb's lap, he didn't seem to mind, and she didn't know what to think of it herself. She was intensely aware of his maleness, his scent, and the hard, muscular body she was pressed against. He was reassuring, she decided, in a way that Kip could not be. Kip was sweating and looking ill, like *he* needed reassuring.

"Can't they fix this?" Kip asked. "Too incompetent?" His voice sounded strained, with a jittery edge.

"Kip, we're heading for the deepdown. Things don't always work the same down here the way they do on the surface," Malcolm answered absently. Shelby felt *wonderful* snuggled up against him, setting his nerves aflame. Even better, she had defended her girlfriend. She might be naïve and inexperienced, but she wasn't a snob.

The transtube's rattling slowed and slowed until it jolted to a halt.

"This is our stop," Malcolm said. He reluctantly pulled his arm away from her and stood. Shelby rose and realized Kip was still sitting hunched over.

"Kip. It's our stop," Shelby said. "Is something wrong?"

Kip glared up at her, his forehead dewy with sweat. A bead rolled down his cheek, dripping onto his clothes. "Quit fussing over me, Shelby. Let's go." He heaved himself to his feet and lurched over to the exit doors, elbowing people aside in his effort to escape the confined transtube.

Shelby fretted over what to do, then noticed Malcolm moving to catch up to Kip, his face concerned. But he left him alone so she decided she was exaggerating again. Kip was stressed, but fine, and she followed them both out of the transtube and onto the platform. She had never gone so far down under the surface and she had to travel further down still, into the deepdown of the Steelio warrens.

Malcolm again led the way down the dim corridor, gently pushing his way through the throng of people scurrying to work or plodding home. Shelby noticed that he was recognized by several people who passed them. He was greeted with smiles and nods. He also wasn't the only man wearing a Steelio coverall. Everyone who wore one of those identifying uniforms knew who Malcolm Cobb was and they all seemed to approve of his existence.

He stopped at a wide staircase winding into the deepdown like a corkscrew. Shelby stopped to look over the railing. The stairs seemed to go down and down and down.

Kip peered over the railing, too. "We have to go all the way down?"

"No, we'll be taking the freight elevator. It might be easier for you," Malcolm replied.

"An elevator," Shelby said slowly. "I've never been on one."

"I have," Kip said importantly. "The Twelve Happiness Luxury

Hotel has one. I went to a party there, and we took turns riding the elevator up and down."

"The freight elevator here is used to move ore up and supplies down," Malcolm said. "But the warrens are allowed to use them too as long as we don't interfere with scheduled operations."

The freight elevator was terrifying. It was a simple platform surrounded by a loose framework of timber and the open gearing mechanisms and cables letting it move up and down. The railing on the platform looked rickety and the walls of the shaft were raw, angry rock close enough to touch. Shelby had thought the lighting in the corridors was dim, but compared to the shaft, it was like being in Dome Two in midafternoon on a sunny day. She peered up the shaft and far, far, far above, there were tiny cracks of light demonstrating the beautiful surface world still existed.

"Watch your step," Malcolm said. He stepped onto the platform and held out his hand for Shelby to take so she too, could step onto the platform and descend still further down.

She hesitated, wanting to turn around and run back to somewhere, anywhere that didn't take her still further from the surface, from light and sun and air and color. As she stood there, steeling herself to step over the wide gap plummeting down to oblivion, someone else came running up.

"Malcolm! On your way down?"

Malcolm smiled easily. "Jeffen. I'm taking some visitors down from PanU to see Steelio's warrens."

Shelby turned to see this newcomer, intensely grateful she wouldn't have to step onto the platform that very minute.

"PanU, huh. Why would anyone from PanU come here?" Jeffen asked. He gave Kip a long, curious stare and an equally long, but more appreciative one to Shelby. Like Malcolm Cobb, he was wearing a Steelio coverall; a much dirtier one. He was, Shelby guessed, older than Malcolm Cobb, but not by very much.

"They're artists," Malcolm said. "They want to see more of Panschin than just what's aboveground."

Jeffen chuckled. "You're in for a treat. There's no place that beats Steelio."

"Can we just get on with it?" Kip muttered. He'd been hanging back too, as reluctant as Shelby to step on the unstable-looking platform.

"Jeffen, this is Miss Shelby Bradwell and Kip McGrant," Malcolm said. "Jeffen is one of Steelio's finest."

"Like I care," Kip mumbled.

"Kip, don't be rude," Shelby said. "It's nice to meet you, Jeffen." She thought she might have seen a flash of distaste on Jeffen's face when Malcolm said Kip's name and decided she was being overdramatic again. Jeffen was much more positive about her presence, despite her unfortunate last name. Maybe he didn't know who she was.

"So you're an artist," Jeffen said to her, ignoring Kip completely. "I like cloud pictures, myself."

Shelby leaped at the opening he gave her, delaying having to get on the platform with Malcolm Cobb.

"Really? I love clouds." Where did someone like Jeffen ever get to see clouds? Shelby hadn't seen real clouds in years, not since before dear old dad's downfall and her last trip to Panschin's summer-only, outside of the domes park. She still had her sketches pinned up in the room she shared with Veronica. "May I ask why that and not, oh, uh, rock formations?"

"Rocks? I see them all damn day. Don't need to see no more of them," Jeffen said and spat noisily onto the ground near his feet, narrowly missing Kip's. "But I remember clouds. My dad, he brought us here to Panschin when I was a tyke, and I still remember how beautiful they were, floating above the world so fluffy and clean and white."

Jeffen gazed dreamily into the distance, his eyes far away. "Still remember every detail." He snapped back to the present. "I cut cloud pictures out of magazines now. My wife and I got our walls and ceilings almost covered now with cloud pictures."

"That sounds lovely," Shelby said warmly. "I've gotten to see clouds too. They're so gorgeous. Every shade of white and little tinges of pink around the edges. They dance across the sky and the wind blows them into little wisps." She was lost for a moment, forgetting her surroundings in the vivid memory of the immense world of the Martian sky, always changing and always new.

Malcolm watched her expressive face, wishing he too could see what Shelby saw. If she was willing, he'd pay their way outside the domes to the public summer park and they could watch clouds together.

Kip was less impressed. "They're just big puffs of water vapor." He pressed his hand against the wall. His complexion, normally a true upper-class emerald, had gone ashy. His hand shook, a tremor passed over his body, and, despite the noticeably cooler air, a fresh sheen of sweat coated his cheeks, droplets rolling down his neck.

"Kip," Malcolm said. "What's wrong?"

"Nothing's wrong with me," Kip snapped. He turned to Shelby.

"I can't do this. I just can't. I'm sorry, Shelby. You're on your own."

Kip took a step away from the elevator's platform, stumbled and collapsed to his knees.

"Surface sickness," Malcolm said. "I was afraid of that."

"I'd say you're right," Jeffen replied.

Neither man made a move towards Kip.

Shelby stared at them and then raced to Kip's side, knelt down, and put an arm around him. He shrugged it off.

"Leave me alone, Shelby," he muttered. "This wouldn't be happening if I hadn't come along."

"Mr. Cobb, what do we do?" Shelby asked. "We have to help Kip." She pulled away, hurt and confused again by how Kip couldn't seem to make up his mind about how he felt about her. "What's surface sickness?"

"Some people just can't stand going underneath into the deepdown," Malcolm said. "They sweat and get the shakes. The deeper they go, the worse it gets. I've been watching Kip, and it looks like he's one of them. He'll be fine as soon as he's on his way back up to the surface."

"Malcolm," Jeffen said. "I'll take Kippy here back up topside so you and Miss Bradwell can go on to Steelio's warren. I'll find you."

"An excellent idea, Jeffen," Malcolm said. "Miss Bradwell, do you want to continue?"

She met his eyes, her heart racing. She did not want to continue. She wanted to run back up topside with Kip and never come underneath the surface again. Malcolm watched her steadily. Shelby tried to guess what he was thinking and kept coming up with the same scenario: He chose to support Mr. Burgess and she, her aunt, and her sister would lose their home.

She swallowed audibly and lifted her head proudly. "Yes, I'd like to continue on downwards and visit the Steelio warren."

Malcolm felt his heart leap. He wanted to shout with joy. Shelby Bradwell, his Dome Two princess, was showing every sign of being the woman he hoped she was. She was so beautiful and so brave, and he wanted her. She might give him a chance to prove himself worthy of her. The thought was intoxicating.

He said none of that, other than his face lighting up. "I'd be honored."

Jeffen pulled Kip, not very gently, to his feet. "Back up to the surface, Kippy. Soon as you start going upwards, you'll start feeling better."

Kip roused himself enough to say to Jeffen, "It's Kip, you oaf. Clean the dross out of your ears." To Malcolm he slurred, "If Shelby doesn't come back, I'll press charges." He leaned against Jeffen, who looked resigned at the task he had been handed. "Get me out of here."

Irritation flooded Shelby. "Kip, you are being so rude. I'm sure Jeffen will take good care of you. I will be fine with Mr. Cobb. Finer, I think, than I would be with you. I'll see you tomorrow in the studio."

She stepped firmly onto the freight elevator's platform, feeling very proud of herself that she didn't shake all over. She clutched her satchel tightly and tried not to think of it falling forever d0wn the shaft, down, down, down to wherever it finally bottomed out.

"I'm ready, Mr. Cobb."

Jeffen mouthed something at Malcolm, who nodded.

"Call me Malcolm, please." He pressed the button, the freight elevator lurched into life, and they began to descend down the shaft into the deepdown.

se his first name? That felt disturbingly intimate. What else did Malcolm Cobb want from her? As if she couldn't guess. The freight elevator lurched downward and there was nothing safe to hold onto and nowhere to run.

It lurched again, and Shelby squealed in panic and clutched at the railing. It shifted under her grasp, making her squeal louder. She had visions of the platform plummeting to the bottom of the shaft. She could imagine the air roaring past her and the sheer terror she would feel before they crashed at the bottom of the shaft, leaving their bodies in a heap of mangled, bloody bits.

"The platform is safe, Miss Bradwell, even if it doesn't act like it," Malcolm said. "If it will make you feel better, take my hand. And please, do not scream."

The platform lurched for a third time, but the crash she feared didn't happen. Shelby stepped as close to Malcolm as she dared, and grabbed his big, warm, strong hand, interlacing her fingers between his.

"Thank you," she whispered as the platform descended into darkness. She wondered if she dared ask him to put an arm around her. It was an intriguing thought, a frightening one, and even more intimate than using his first name. He had put his arm around her on the transtube and the feel of his muscled arm against her body been surprisingly pleasant, even thrilling if she were being honest. But what if her request gave him ideas of what else she might be willing to do?

Malcolm. He wanted her to use his given name. It was another step towards something she was still unsure about doing, no matter how badly she wanted to save her home.

She knew she was being silly and dramatic. He already knew her name. Why was she hesitating? Mr. Cobb — no, Malcolm — had already treated her with more respect than most of the boys at PanU ever had. Reyansh Philpott in particular stood out from the pack, and those angry memories made her tighten her fingers around Malcolm's.

Malcolm hadn't said one lewd word to her, implying she was some chola from the tunnels who didn't deserve anything better than a quick shag behind a hedge. He certainly hadn't pawed at her, even when she was shoved up against him on the transtube.

To distract herself, she seized on his odd request. Who would care or hear her?

"Why don't you want me to scream?" As if there was anyone around to help her.

"Because if you do, any man in the area will come running to save you. You'll get an escort back up to the surface."

"And this would be … bad?" Shelby asked, diverted by the prospect of escape from a freight elevator sinking into darkness.

"I'll get beaten to a bloody pulp. I'd rather avoid that."

"Oh. Uh, what would they want from me?"

"A walk in the park would be nice, but it wouldn't be expected," Malcolm answered. "The Steelio warren doesn't tolerate disrespectful behavior. They'd assume I was at fault, particularly since you are a visitor from up above."

"Oh."

She thought about it some more, feeling his warm, strong hand in hers as the platform lurched lower. It might be true, what Malcolm said. He'd had every opportunity to paw at her and he hadn't. Lulu and Florence had both insisted she would be safe, as would the rest of the Collective. Even alone, she realized he was protecting her, and they were right.

"Please, call me Shelby," she said softly. The words echoed in her head but on the platform, they were almost drowned out by the sound of the mechanism lowering them into the depths. But still, he heard her.

"I would be honored, Shelby."

Malcolm could feel his heart racing. Her hand was so warm in his, and she smelled faintly of something floral he didn't know the name of. He did know he already liked it. He wanted to bury his nose in Shelby's fluffy, lustrous brunette hair and drink in her scent. He wanted to do so much more with her. He forced his unruly thoughts back under control. It had been a while, and Shelby Bradwell wasn't some chola selling her only asset. She was, because of her father, a princess exiled from Dome Six, and he was a scholarship boy. He had to prove himself to her. He would do his damnedest to keep her family safe from Burgess. The thug from the gallery showing was a different challenge, but he'd already thought of who to ask and where to go. The thug would also give him a reason to regularly stop by, to see how she was doing.

Shelby could still say no to him, Malcolm realized, but he couldn't walk away, even if she asked. She needed his protection, and he'd do his best to keep her safe. He could live without her, but he couldn't live with himself if he let her be hurt.

The platform's gears ratcheted down. They were slowing. Shelby glimpsed light from below.

"Is that our stop? It's brighter," she said hopefully.

"Yes, that's the Steelio warren stop. The freight elevator goes a lot further down, to the working tunnels. There are a lot of stops between here and the current end of the line."

Further down. What a terrifying thought. Shelby could feel her hand tightening around Malcolm's again. He would expect things from her, she just knew it. The thought was attractive and scary in equal measures. Maybe not equal anymore. He was rapidly becoming more attractive. He was so sure and self-confident. He was a scholarship boy with everything that implied, starting with his intellect. He must have worked very hard to get where he was. Nobody had handed him anything, unlike Reyansh Philpott.

She was so brave. Malcolm was impressed all over again. Every line of Shelby's expressive face showed how scared she was, yet she hadn't insisted on scurrying back to the surface with that mazhor, Kip McGrant. Shelby would never be able to lie successfully; she showed every mood and emotion. He didn't think she knew who Kip was related to, and she probably wouldn't care if she did. Her friend Florence mattered more. It had been worth the risk to show Shelby Bradwell who he really was. She might say yes to him, too. She might be brave enough to love a jumped-up tunnel rat.

They stood in silence, wrapped in thought, as the platform clattered to a stop. The sudden brightness made Shelby squint. It took a few minutes more for her brain to process what she was seeing.

"Shelby," Malcolm said, breaking her trance. "We have to get off the platform. Someone else needs it further down."

"Oh, yes, I'm sorry," Shelby mumbled and stepped forward, over the gap that fell into darkness. She was mesmerized.

The freight elevator shaft opened up to a vast cavern as large as a pocket park in Dome Two. It was carved into the bedrock, but not all of it by the hand of man. The ceiling glittered with stalactites, shiny with damp, and reflecting with jeweled fragments of color the steady light of the electric bulbs. The far walls were whitewashed down to where a wainscoting would be and below that line, the walls of the cavern were thick with green moss, undulating over the rock like a hedge carved from stone.

The walls of the cavern had openings that led elsewhere. This was a gathering space, with far more living space wrapped around it. There were people of all ages, going about their business. There were children, running and playing games, just like the kids she sketched in the parks in Dome Two. Many looked up to witness the new arrivals. From their expressions, Shelby knew that Malcolm was recognized and welcomed. Perhaps she would be too, since she was with him.

It was impossible to judge how large the Steelio warren was. There could even be more large areas like this one.

"Is this…?" her voice trailed off, not knowing quite what she wanted to ask and not wanting to sound even more naïve than she already had. She kept her fingers interlaced with Malcolm's. She didn't feel comfortable letting go just yet.

"This is the main entrance to Steelio," Malcolm said, interpreting her unspoken question. He pointed. "We'll be going down the second tunnel to the left. It's the one with the blue and yellow design painted around it."

"Are those terraformers?" Shelby asked, gazing at the vividly green pretend-wainscoting. Live plants, down here, deep below the surface. She had convinced herself that nothing lived below the surface other than humans.

"Yes, they grow everywhere there's light, even artificial light," Malcolm said. "We let them grow wherever possible. They freshen the air and make it look nicer. Let's go look."

He led her to the wall, weaving between the bystanders, all of whom he knew by name. They stopped next to the tunnel opening framed in blue and yellow. Shelby gently stroked the wall, and the thick moss was as soft as any she had ever felt. Up close, she could see it was covered with tiny stars of paler green. A flick of red moving through the moss startled her.

"What was that?"

"A cave salamander," Malcolm said. "They eat insects that live in the moss."

"They *live* down here?"

"Sure do. They're shy and don't like to be touched, otherwise the kids down here would make pets of them. They'll bite too."

"Wait. There are other things, insects down here?"

"Yes, not just people. We brought life with us down into the tunnels and the bedrock has accepted all of us."

Shelby stood back up, her confusion showing. "I thought rocks were dead."

"They're not dead," Malcolm replied. "Rock isn't alive like a human or a salamander or" — he quirked a smile at her — "a pet chicken. But it isn't dead, either. It's different. The time scale rock lives at is almost forever. It's hard to explain but you get a feel for it, living so close to the bones of Mars."

Shelby puzzled over this, finally seizing on a point she could argue.

"You say the rock is alive?"

Malcolm hemmed for a moment as he tried to explain what he had grasped from living so close to the bones of the world. "Not exactly. Rock changes. It grows over eons, and over eons, it can become something else. That's being alive, isn't it?" He stroked the rock wall. "There are hundreds of different kinds, and they lace among each other, like thread in cloth. Other times, you find only one kind of rock, laying on top of another with a clear line between them, like blankets on a bed. You get a feel for stone, living so close to it. I don't know if people who live on the surface and never come into the deepdown can understand that."

"It, I mean, the rocks, don't, um, mind?"

"Mind what?"

"You dig it out, you bore holes through it. You rip minerals out of it and haul them away to the surface where they go someplace else." Shelby chewed on her lip trying to express what she felt. "You use it, and it has no choice."

Malcolm watched Shelby's white teeth biting into her full lower lip. The only thought in his head was how it would feel to kiss her and feel those soft, ripe lips under his own. He wrenched his attention back to what she was saying.

"I don't know that rock minds, exactly," he began. "The time scales have nothing in common, the regular living world and the stone world. I believe — *we* believe — that stones are aware in a way we can't understand. And there are things that live here, in the deepdown, besides what we humans introduced."

"The salamanders?" Shelby asked, her eyebrows raised up into her fluffy nimbus of hair.

"It's complicated. Mars was alive before Olde Earthe began terraforming it. Since then, we've changed Mars as it has changed us. We've also, uh…," he stopped, then started again. "We've awakened things."

Shelby took that in. "That's scary."

"Not if you're respectful." He watched her think that over, discordant emotions flashing across her face, and changed the subject.

"Let's go meet my family. They're waiting on us in our quarters."

Shelby's mouth dropped open in disbelief.

"You want me to meet your family?"

Malcolm stiffened. She was going to say something vicious about having to associate with the people who slaved below, doing some of the dirtiest, hardest work in Panschin.

Her face bloomed in a huge smile. "I would be so pleased."

Shelby followed him into the tunnel opening, edged all around in blue and yellow lines, her mind whirling. His family. Mr. Cobb, no, Malcolm, wanted her to meet his family. That hadn't happened since her father's disgrace, when the steady stream of invitations vanished. He was a banker, but he was also a scholarship boy, up from the mines. That made his offer even more unusual, since he had more to lose by associating with the daughter of the notorious Simon Bradwell. Did he know whose daughter she was? She fretted on that and decided that if he didn't bring up the subject, she had to. To do otherwise was unfair to him. Her downfall was complete and she'd never be accepted again in Panschin's polite society. Any doubts on that score had been settled by the gallery-showing at the White Elephant.

But Malcolm, he had a career ahead of him, a career that had already taken him from the deepdown to the surface. He had to understand associating with her could stop his career in its tracks as thoroughly as anything Mr. Burgess could do.

Malcolm was floored. Shelby wanted to meet his family, and she meant it. His beautiful Dome Two princess wasn't just being polite. She was looking forward to meeting his family as though they mattered, as though he was giving her a precious gift. His mind whirled as they walked down the passageway, lit overhead by tiny electric lights, the light reflecting off the scrubbed and whitewashed upper walls and ceiling.

The memory of how she had been treated at the gallery showing reared itself up and he realized it was a gift. No one in that world considered Shelby Bradwell worth wasting consideration on. Even that mazhor, Kip McGrant, had been unpleasant to her, despite being the only student in the Collective who agreed to come down into the warren. The thought of Kip sparked an avalanche of contempt, startling in its intensity. That fool wouldn't invite Shelby to meet his family, ever.

Then he remembered that he had seen the name McGrant before. It was in the case study of Simon Bradwell. He racked his brain for more, but he couldn't remember with Shelby's hand so warm in his, the delicate scent of her hair filling his nostrils, and the rise and fall of her breast with her breathing.

Malcolm was so distracted he almost went past the curtained door opening to his family's quarters. He caught himself in time and said,

"Here we are." Then he sang out, "Knock, knock!"

Shelby puzzled for a moment and realized there was no door, just the heavy, patched curtain. Malcolm's greeting was an acknowledgment of reality while still allowing privacy. The curtain was jerked aside by someone who had obviously been waiting for them, and she forgot her speculations as she stepped into his family's home.

The room was small, with whitewashed walls and ceilings and a moss wainscoting. Bright rag rugs covered the floor, helping to warm and soften the otherwise cool space. There were two more curtained doorways opening off the small room. Low benches ran along one wall, pulled away from the terraformers behind it. Behind the benches, an assortment of what looked like pictures cut from magazines were tacked to the walls above the moss.

Shelby didn't have time to observe further. The room was full of people of all ages, all wearing Steelio coveralls, and they all wanted to welcome Malcolm with hugs and kisses before wanting to meet her.

Malcolm made the introductions. Shelby concentrated on the names, hoping to remember them all. She hadn't had a welcome like this since before her father had been arrested.

The noise settled down, and she found herself seated at the table, with Malcolm next to her. The questions came thick and fast. Did she really draw? Was she a real artist? Had she brought anything to show them? Would she like something to eat? What did people eat in the domes? What was it like to live in a big house inside a dome? Didn't that huge glassteel bubble over her head bother her? All that space instead of a cozy tunnel must be so frightening!

Malcolm watched Shelby handling herself with aplomb, friendly and open and happy to be there. Finally, a question arose that Shelby couldn't answer.

"Where is everyone else?" one of the kids piped up, asking the question the adults had been carefully avoiding. "Our Malcolm said he'd bring a lot of artists."

Shelby smiled uncomfortably. "No one else in the Collective was able to come down, except Kip, I mean, and he got, uh," she looked over to Malcolm for the phrase.

"Kip developed surface sickness," Malcolm said. "He got as far as the freight elevator. Fortunately, we ran into Jeffen. He took Kip back up topside."

"That's too bad," an older man said. Shelby was fairly sure he was Malcolm's father, based on the resemblance and the warmth between them. It reminded her of her own father, funny and caring, before he was revealed as a thieving scoundrel and conman. A sudden flash of intense envy rippled through her. He still had his parents while hers were gone. She had to blink back sudden tears. To her surprise, Malcolm noticed her flash of distress.

"This must be all so overwhelming for you, Shelby. Do you need to take a break?" he whispered to her.

She smiled up at him. "No, you're so blessed. You have your whole family still with you. I miss my parents so much sometimes, even my dad. Seeing your family all together reminded me."

"Yes, we've been very fortunate," he answered quietly. "No one lost to injury or death."

At last the question came that she had been dreading. "Did you bring your own drawings?" The woman speaking, an aunt perhaps? had been eying her satchel, tucked up against her legs and securely closed. "I'd really love to see them."

This was it.

She would have to show her own, inadequate drawings to Malcolm's family and they would recognize her for the fraud she was, as fraudulent as her father. Shelby grabbed for the memory of Mrs. Grisson's happiness with the drawings of her grandchildren, traded for eggs. *She* had been delighted and said so, over and over. These people, Malcolm's family, might be equally generous. They wouldn't rip her apart the way Professor Vitebskin or the other members of the Collective would if they saw what she really liked to draw.

Malcolm felt her stiffen against him. He had no idea what Shelby drew, or if she was good at drawing at all. He had seen her sketching flowers in Dome Two and her horrible painting at the gallery showing. There was also her drawing of the thug who had threatened her and her sister. Shelby had captured him with a few lines and some shading, bringing his menace to life with pencil on paper. If she could do that, then she must be able to draw like he had imagined real artists could and she wasn't just wasting paint like the rest of the PanU Artists' Collective so obviously did.

"Uh, of course," Shelby said after an agonized moment of hesitation. "I'm not very good though, not like the rest of the Collective." She opened her satchel and pulled out her most recent sketchbook and opened it to a full-page drawing of a planter of flowers.

Malcolm recognized them. They were the purple and yellow ones. Shelby had called them pansies. Even though she had drawn them with pencil in shades of gray, the idea of their colors still came through, their resemblance to odd smiling faces clear.

Shelby smiled weakly as the crowd in the small room gathered around to stare in confusion.

"Oh, they're flowers!" the aunt said. "I cut those pictures out from magazines."

The rest of the family chimed in:

"I've only ever seen pictures."

"Did you draw them from a magazine?"

"What color are they really?"

"Do you see real flowers in Dome Two? How blessed you are."

"I've seen flowers like that. Steelio has a planter in their infirmary, just like your picture."

"Do you draw people?"

"Do you draw animals?"

"Do you draw kittens?"

"Yes, I draw all of those things," Shelby answered.

"She draws clouds too," Malcolm added. "Shelby told Jeffen on the lift."

The demand was immediate. "Show us!"

Shelby paged through her sketchbook slowly so everyone could see, marveling at the pleased response. She knew every one of her subjects were considered to be venal hackwork, the sort used to sell products in adverts or to illustrate twee stories in magazines. She had quickly learned to never show any of her drawings at PanU as her representational style brought only sneers at her bourgeoisie mind, backwardness, and complete lack of imagination. Only the drawing instructor, residing at the bottom of the PanU Art Department hierarchy, had been encouraging.

Yet these people, Malcolm's family, didn't have the same reaction at all. Like Mrs. Grisson and her boarders, they approved of what she drew. They understood what she was trying to express. They said the same things Veronica, Neza, Florence, and Lulu said. Shelby had always discounted what her family said about her drawings. They were family and they were supposed to be supportive so their words didn't mean anything.

Malcolm's family, on the other hand, like Mrs. Grisson, weren't relatives. They could say what they wanted. She thought suddenly of Lulu who could always be counted on to speak the truth, no matter whose feelings she trampled. She liked the drawings. Florence, far more tactful, had said the same. Lulu and Florence weren't strictly family, but they had become part of the Bradwells.

Maybe, Shelby thought reluctantly, she should have listened to her sister more than she listened to the admonishments of the Collective. She suddenly thought of Clyde Monez. He was still PanU's most successful art graduate, the only one who earned a living from drawing and painting. All of Professor Vitebskin's much vaunted protégés lived off family money. Their art, no matter how lauded, didn't pay the bills.

"Could you draw me?" a little girl asked. She was wearing a very worn coverall, cut down from someone's else's, probably her mother's. Someone, probably the same woman, had painstakingly embroidered little rows of triangles and circles around all the closures and hems in bright orange. Shelby realized, based on the color, where the thread must have come from. Whoever remade this child's coverall had tediously picked apart the Steelio logos to retrieve and reuse the bright orange thread for her own embroidery.

She smiled down at the tot. "You bet I can. But you'll have to hold still for a few minutes. Can you do that?"

"Yeth! I can hold still better than anybody!" the child answered. From behind her, her mother laughed in amused disbelief.

"Turn around slowly, sweetie, so I can study you, and then when I tell you to, I want you to stop where you are. Ready?" Shelby said.

"Okay," the little girl answered and began to slowly spin, her arms outstretched.

Shelby watched her for two full turns, her favorite pencil in hand and her sketchpad open to the next blank page. There it was, the pose she wanted.

"Stop now," she commanded and began to fill the paper with rapid lines. Everything else vanished. The deepdown and its terrors, the White Elephant and its threats, even Malcolm sitting next to her. Only the eye and the hand remained, concentrating on capturing life, youth, and a vivid joy in being alive.

The room was dead silent for several minutes.

Next to her, Malcolm watched in fascination as his little niece slowly appeared on the page in sweeping lines and soft shadings. Shelby Bradwell really could draw.

The little girl began to wiggle. "Are you done? Can I see?"

"Not yet, sweetie," Shelby said. "Wriggle all over and then stand the same way you did before. Can you remember how you held your arms?"

"Course I can," the tot answered.

Shelby and Malcolm's niece took several more breaks and her drawing grew in complexity. As she drew, Shelby mentally thanked her sister for arranging for her to draw Mrs. Grisson's grandchildren in exchange for eggs. Mrs. Grisson's youngest grandchildren had been just as eager to run and jump, and it gave her practice in handling models who couldn't hold still.

She shaded in the last parts of the child's loose ponytail and said, "done."

Shelby flipped over the sketchpad for her fascinated audience. To her pleased amazement, everyone there was delighted and said so.

Malcolm wondered if he had seen magic. From nothing but a pencil and paper, Shelby created life. Why she was wasting all this skill at PanU, painting sludge that they called fine art? Why she was discounting her abilities? Was this another gap in his education, being unable to appreciate art that revealed nothing of the world around him?

Perhaps, a rational voice whispered in him, the high caste you aspire to join had gone soft in the head and their taste in art was proof. Maybe it was another example of why the free-city of Panschin needed to educate talented members of the working class.

"Could you draw me next?" a little boy asked. His mother stood behind him looking eager.

"Of course," Shelby replied and ripped out the finished drawing, handing it to the little girl's joyful mother.

The afternoon passed quickly as Shelby drew two more of the children in the room while the adults talked, talked, and talked some more about life in the Steelio warren, what they did, and how proud they were of our Malcolm. They also kept offering Shelby tea and little blocks of fried yeast, similar to what she ate at home every day. The conversation swirled around her, a low friendly buzz that wrapped around her like a cozy blanket.

A gong sounded from outside their quarters, startling Shelby from her trance. She had been working out just the right angle of a cousin's tilted head and how to shade her hair so the curls stood out.

"Ah," Malcolm said. "Shift change is coming up. Shelby, we'll need to get you home."

"I'm not finished," Shelby said with a tinge of annoyance. "I'm not even a quarter of the way done with Cindy."

"I know, but my family have to get ready to go to work, and I have to get you home before it gets much later."

Shelby surprised herself with a sudden, huge yawn and flushed with embarrassment. "Excuse me, please."

"Not a problem," one of Malcolm's relatives announced. "We've been working you too hard."

Shelby looked over her sketch of Cindy, the bare bones waiting to be fleshed out into vivid life. "I'll have to come back to finish." She looked up at Malcolm. "Would that be all right with you and your family?"

He smiled at her, his face alight with approval. "Yes, whenever it suits you."

Gods below but she was as beautiful on the inside as she was on the outside. He ignored the significant glances and speculative whispers his hyperalert relatives were trading back and forth. They had been after him for some time now to settle down and marry, not understanding the bind he was in. A girl from the tunnels would never be accepted in his new, aboveground life. A girl from the class he aspired to would never accept his background and past. Shelby Bradwell looked to be the answer to their prayers. And, perhaps, she would be. He could hope. He could also hope Shelby wouldn't notice his mother's eager expression.

Shelby beamed at him, then stretched and wiggled her fingers loose. She was suddenly very tired and swallowed another yawn. Malcolm stood and reached his hand to her, lifting her to her feet. She was struck again at how concerned he was about her in a way no one outside of her family had been for a long, long time. Maybe he did mean to help them escape the wrath of Mr. Burgess. Perhaps, she reflected, holding onto his hand longer than necessary, he would help them with that awful goon, too. It could happen.

"Knock, knock" a voice called from outside. "It's Jeffen."

"Come on in," Malcolm's father answered promptly and he got up to welcome Jeffen inside.

"Oh! I completely forgot about Kip," Shelby gasped. "Thank you so much, Jeffen, for helping him. How is he?"

Malcolm had to push back a tinge of jealousy over Kip's position in Shelby's life. He reminded himself that she was simply showing concern for another student, the only one brave enough to venture outside of his familiar world and into the deepdown. He had to stifle a smug laugh. Kip McGrant, despite his family's business needs, would never travel into the deepdown again. He was physically unable to do so and that made him instantly useless to the McGrant family and their controlling interest in Chung/Banerjee. Served him right for being so hateful to Shelby. The thought struck him. Then why had Kip agreed to come along when no one else did? He would have to find out.

Jeffen turned his body so Shelby couldn't see (although others could) and twisted his fingers at Malcolm. More than one relative reared back and clapped their hands over their younger children's eyes.

He said, "Kippy's all right, Miss Bradwell. I got him all the way back up to the surface and then on to Dome Six and the infirmary. He's probably got a nurse hovering around him right this minute, fluffing his pillows, bathing his forehead, and bringing him his medicinal tea."

Shelby looked appalled. "He was that ill with surface sickness?"

"I wouldn't say that," Jeffen replied dryly. "*He* might have thought he was, but anyone else would have gone back to work once the shakes wore off, which they did as soon as we hit surface, and he'd had a nice cup of tea and a bun."

"But you were gone for hours," Shelby said, suddenly realizing how long she had been enjoying being surrounded by Malcolm's family. She felt a rush of guilt over not thinking once about Kip.

"Yeah, about that," Jeffen said. He made a face. "The McGrant family is kind of important, Kippy knows it, and he insisted on my taking him all the way to the infirmary in Dome Six even though Dome Three was close and the nurse station in the metro was even closer. He refused to go back to Dome Two and PanU and their infirmary and be embarrassed over running out on you, and when we finally got to Dome Six, I got to visit the cop shop and explain all about his adventures underground because, well, a nice young man like Kip McGrant wasn't the type to go slumming with the likes of me."

Shelby's face hardened. "Kip complained about you helping him?"

"Him getting surface sickness had to be somebody's fault."

"I am so sorry, Jeffen," Shelby said. "I will talk to Kip tomorrow, first thing."

"Not to worry," Jeffen said easily. "I got it straightened out. Fortunately, one of the lads at the Dome Six substation has a relative working for Steelio. He'd heard about Malcolm inviting some PanU art students into the warren."

"Oh." Shelby wanted to cringe. Another set of people were gossiping about her. At least they weren't, she hoped, being vicious and bringing up past family crimes.

"I owe you, Jeffen," Malcolm said. It was fortunate Shelby hadn't seen Jeffen's stunningly rude hand gesture and even better that she probably wouldn't have understood it if she had. Kip must have whined every step of the way. Jeffen probably had to carry him up the stairs between levels in the metro station. He wondered what the favor would cost him. Jeffen was not the type to let anything slide, ever.

"Damn right you do."

"Jeffen. Malcolm doesn't owe you anything," Shelby said firmly. She frowned at Malcolm to make sure he understood she meant it and turned her attention back to Jeffen to be sure he understood as well. "You did this favor for *me*. Kip's my friend, or well, he used to be." She bit her lip again, thinking over what she could afford and Jeffen might accept. "Could I give you a cloud painting to say thank you?"

Jeffen's face lit up. "Me and my wife would love one."

Shelby said, "I have one that I've been working on." She glanced shyly over at Malcolm. "If Malcolm wouldn't mind escorting me again into the warren, I could bring it over to you and your wife so you could see if you like it."

Malcolm smiled at her warmly, an expression every member of his family old enough to walk recognized, leading to even more speculative glances and whispers. He ignored them. "A lovely idea, Shelby. I didn't know you painted clouds."

She flushed with embarrassed pleasure. "Yes, I've really learned a lot from Professor Vitebskin about layering color in translucent washes. I could never show this painting at PanU because, well, you saw the gallery showing. But his techniques work really well for other subjects. I've been able to make clouds that look so real, floating above the world. Like you could touch them."

"That sounds great," Jeffen said. "I'll talk to my wife and to Malcolm and we'll set a time."

"Time," Shelby said suddenly. "I've got to get home! Veronica will worry." She turned and said, "Thank you all so much for hosting me. You've been so generous."

"It was our pleasure to meet you, Shelby," Malcolm's mother answered warmly. "You're welcome to return any time."

"I have to," Shelby laughed. "I have to finish Cindy's portrait."

"So you do," Malcolm's mother returned. She looked very pleased with the idea, along with the rest of his family.

For his part, Malcolm knew on his next visit, he'd be quizzed extensively about his relationship with Shelby Bradwell, what he planned to do about moving it forward, and why was he hesitating in the first place? She was such a nice girl and he wasn't getting any younger and it was time, dammit, for him to do his duty to the family, despite the fact that he was no longer a daily part of it or the Steelio warren. He looked over at Shelby, packing her satchel and laughing with his family, and any concerns about their interrogation evaporated like condensation on the dome.

"She's a nice girl," Jeffen whispered to Malcolm. "Damn good-looking too. But isn't she Simon Bradwell's daughter?"

Malcolm whispered back, "And if she is?"

"I know you got ambitions. You're not coming back to slave in the deepdown with the rest of us, not if you can help it."

"I'm not concerned and how did you know about her family anyway?"

"You're not the only one around here with ambitions who can read a newspaper," Jeffen replied. "Simon Bradwell's daughter isn't going to make you fit in better with the banking crowd."

"I don't fit in with them now, and what business is it of yours?"

"Just reminding you of reality, Malcolm," Jeffen said. "Like I said, you're not the only one with ambitions." He held up his left hand, angling it so Malcolm could see the small blue circle tattooed on the underside of his wrist.

"I'd heard you joined," Malcolm said.

"Nobody offered me a scholarship. And I'll take Miss Bradwell's cloud painting in lieu of what you owe me for hauling that mazhor's ass up to the surface."

Malcolm filed away Jeffen's blue circle, thinking hard. He could use this information, but he'd have to be very careful. "I appreciate that. And what will little Kippy McGrant owe you?'

Jeffen smiled, showing every one of his sharp teeth. "He'll find out. When I need him to."

Going back up the freight elevator turned out to be much easier than coming down had been. Shelby still held Malcolm's warm, strong hand in her own, thinking how gracious he had been and how his family had welcomed her. Would it matter if they knew she was Simon Bradwell's daughter? She would have to tell Malcolm. It might matter very much to him. Her lineage would only hurt him in the banking industry. Despite his generosity, he might still back Mr. Burgess and throw them all out of the White Elephant.

She gave herself a mental shake. She was being overly dramatic again. Thinking logically, Malcolm might not be interested in her as a woman since he really did seem to want to know more about the art world — the thought was suddenly disheartening — but he did not like

Mr. Burgess at all and Burgess despised Malcolm. Maybe because he was a scholarship boy? Based on her own experiences at PanU, Shelby could see how much that would matter. Quite a few people, and it didn't matter what their social station was, never forgave and they never forgot when someone else tried to change their place in the hierarchy. But Malcolm might not care about her background. It was a pleasant thought. And she could help him understand the fine art world better, something that might be useful to him in his career.

When they reached the upper station level, Malcolm took a quick look at the schedule.

"We'll have to wait for our tube. Would you like some tea and a sandwich, Shelby? This café has very nice tea buns to go with. My treat, of course."

She took a look around the crowded, noisy, dirty concourse. She would have never felt safe in a place like this on her own, but Malcolm made her feel at home.

She gazed up at his dark eyes, wanting to fall into them, and said, "oh yes. That would be wonderful."

Veronica paced, using all the aboveground floors of the White Elephant and its tiny garden to work off her anxiety. Outside, she worked her way up and down each of the raked gravel paths, circling inside the low wall and then back into the house. Inside, she found herself peering out of all the windows in turn and listening for the shriek of the gate. She had walked the perimeter of the rooftop terrace several times, to get a better view of the surrounding streets, hoping to catch a glimpse of her sister coming home. All she saw were the scatterings of the usual residents coming and going, along with the usual people on their way to and from Dome Two's business district.

She did not see who she wanted to see.

Where was Shelby? She'd been gone for hours.

Veronica could feel her anxiety choking her. What if Malcolm Cobb had lied? They knew nothing about him, other than where he worked. It was all very well for Mr. Jones to say they could go to Mr. Cobb's boss if her sister didn't return but what good would that do if Shelby was lying dead at the bottom of some mineshaft?

"Veronica," Neza said sharply from her seat in the dining room. "You're going to wear a rut in the rug."

"Shelby should be home by now!"

"She'll be fine. She's got the Collective with her."

"Exactly my point," Veronica snapped, rounding onto her aunt. "The Collective should have driven Mr. Cobb and the entire Steelio warren insane by now, been thrown out by the residents, and Shelby would be home safely."

Neza laughed heartily. "Now who's letting her imagination run away with her? That sounds like something your sister would say."

Lulu came around from the kitchen carrying, unusually for her, a tray with cups of tea on it. She wore a longsuffering expression. "Shelby will be fine. Steelio is very respectable. It's not like Mr. Cobb took her and the Collective into the tunnel bars under Dome Four."

Veronica accepted the peace offering, took a calming sip, and said, "but we don't know he didn't!"

Lulu groaned and rolled her eyes. "Quit panicking, Veronica. That's something Shelby would say. Mr. Cobb is a banker. He's never gone lower down in Panschin than the upper level of the transtubes. He couldn't find Dome Four without a guide let alone the tunnel levels underneath it."

Florence appeared with another tray holding the last of the algae dumplings from the gallery showing. Mysteriously, Mr. Jones from Barsoom and his party hadn't touched this Panschin favorite although they had eaten everything else laid out for their breakfast.

"Eat something. You'll feel better. Veronica, I can go to the Steelio warren with Evan to look for Shelby and," Florence frowned at the tray in distaste, "the rest of the Collective."

"I'll go too," Lulu said. "I've never been to Steelio's warren before but it's not that big. Shelby will be easy to find."

"How do you know?" Neza asked.

"A good question," Veronica said, grasping for reassurance allowing her to stay at the White Elephant with Neza while still taking care of her little sister. "How do you know you could find Shelby?"

From the look on her niece's face, it was obvious to Neza that Veronica was thinking she should go along in case Lulu and Florence get lost underground. But if Veronica went, who would call the police? And would they come since they were undoubtedly trying to suppress bar fights when they weren't arresting muggers and pickpockets? And what if that thug came back? What then?

Veronica picked up a dumpling and nibbled on it carefully, grateful for the distraction. They tasted even better the second day when the flavors had time to meld.

Lulu snickered. "Outsiders from PanU coming into a warren? Every single person there will be talking about it for the next year, hashing over every last detail. It won't be hard."

Outside, the gate shrieked its warning and the women turned as one towards the front door.

Veronica swallowed the last bite, leaped to her feet, ran to the front door and threw both sides open to the gathering dusk.

Evening in the Dome was a protracted affair, taking hours and hours to work itself from the afternoon sun to full night. Every light burning inside Dome Two reflected off the underside of the dome so it never got completely dark until after everyone, including the various street denizens, had gone to bed. Dome Two went totally dark only during the endless nights during the deepest part of the winter and only after the bars closed down. It was the only dome that did, the other domes always enjoying residual light from businesses and homes. Dome Six, like Dome Four, never went dark at all. There was always plenty of ambient light to see your path clearly, read signs, and conduct your business.

It wasn't Shelby coming down the raked white gravel path towards her, casting soft-edged shadows in the early twilight.

It was Mr. Jones and his party.

Veronica wanted to tear her hair out in dismay. It was good he had returned to the White Elephant since it meant she, her aunt, Lulu, and Florence wouldn't be alone but that reminded her that Mr. Jones said that Shelby would be fine and she wasn't.

Airik strode up the walkway and noticed at once how Veronica was upset and agitated. "Miss Bradwell," he called out, quickening his pace. It had been a pleasure returning to Dome Two after the day he had endured, fending off suspect business arrangements and unwanted marriage proposals. "What seems to be the problem?"

"Shelby's not back yet, Mr. Jones. We don't have any idea where she is."

"Ah," Mr. Jones replied. "I understand this is upsetting. However, recall Mr. Cobb invited the entire PanU Artists' Collective. It may take him some time to get the flock rounded up and herded back to PanU."

Veronica caught his implication and was momentarily distracted. "The Collective being like sheep?"

"They are a Collective, after all," Airik replied. "They act in unison. I observed little individuality between them during the gallery show. Despite their protests of nonconformity, their clothing, conversation, and painting styles were remarkably uniform. Thus, sheep."

Despite her nervousness, she had to laugh. "With Mr. Cobb being their shepherd, I suppose?"

"A thankless task, I am sure," Airik said. "If Shelby does not return soon, I will go myself to Steelio and speak to the authorities." His heart sang. He had managed, somehow, to make Veronica Bradwell laugh again. She genuinely thought he had a sense of humor. Unlike the other young women he had been introduced to since becoming the daimyo, she alone had no financial or matrimonial reason to laugh, yet she still did.

Upton put down the heavy satchel full of reports and the heavier typewriter case. He had been waiting eagerly to get inside and stared at Airik in consternation. He had made such a fuss about his anonymity and here he was, volunteering to reveal himself? Carmine and Eliot, bringing up the rear, exchanged glances but, good servants that they were, said nothing.

"That's very kind of you, Mr. Jones," Veronica said in astonishment. "But how could you get into the warren?"

"I met a representative of Steelio yesterday during a business meeting. I'm sure I can arrange to visit their warrens."

"I, yes, I would very much appreciate it, Mr. Jones," Veronica said. "Please, come inside."

As they walked inside, she didn't reveal her worse fear. What if that thug had spotted and kidnapped her little sister sometime during the day? He was still out there and it didn't look like the police were going to be as helpful as she had expected. Nobody at PanU would notice or care if Shelby showed up or not. Mr. Cobb could have taken the Collective down under into the Steelio warren without Shelby, since his offer had been to the Collective as a whole and not to her, personally. Would he care enough about Shelby to check on her whereabouts if she were missing?

Behind them, Upton sneezed violently, then kept on sneezing. He had the presence of mind to clutch the typewriter case, but let his satchel of briefing papers drop to the ground. Paper wouldn't break and the bag was cheap. Fortunately, the satchel was tightly buckled, sparing him the embarrassment of having to pick strewn papers up and sort them back into order.

"Oh lordy," Veronica said, distracted again but this time because a paying guest came first. "Panschin is getting to you. Let's get you inside with a cup of tea to open up your sinuses. Luckily, Lulu has already got the water hot."

The Jones party were guided in to the dining room. Veronica got them seated, and as she was pouring fresh hot tea, she heard the gate shriek its alarm.

"Shelby at last! Excuse me, please," Veronica said and raced to the front door. Airik rose and followed her, choosing not to examine his motives and ignoring the looks from the rest of his party.

Veronica got the front door open again and there, strolling up the gravel path to the pink granite doorstep was her former husband.

He opened his mouth the moment he saw her.

"Ronnie, we have to talk. It's critical," Dean Kangjuon called out to her.

"What? Whatever it is, it is not critical. And don't call me Ronnie."

"Fine, sweetheart, I really need this. I need you." Dean reached the doorstep and reached for her hands, his expression imploring her to understand the depths of his need.

Veronica rolled her eyes, shoved her hands into her pockets, and stepped back and up against the doorframe.

"Dean, not now. I'm worried about Shelby and I don't have time for you. Go away, please."

Airik appeared behind her and took in the view of Veronica's former husband. Interestingly, Dean Kangjuon's handsomeness seemed off compared to the previous evening. There was a slight puffiness around his left eye and across the cheek, as though he had been bruised. But his suspiciously perfect, emerald complexion was bruise-free. Airik vividly remembered Dean grabbing Veronica's arm, frowned, and stepped around her to confront him.

"Leave."

Dean took in Airik Jones standing on his former doorstep, blocking the doorway to his former home, alongside his former wife who did not look unhappy over *his* proximity, and his own face darkened.

"Ronnie, who is this fool again? A guest? He's not acting like a guest."

"My name is not Ronnie!"

Airik put his hand on Veronica's shoulder, a move that generated a flash of smile and made Dean frown still more.

"Allow me, Miss Bradwell?"

She nodded her head in approval, a fact both Dean and Airik noted although with opposite emotions. As for Veronica, if Airik Jones wanted to get rid of her ex-husband, then she wouldn't have to cope with him when Shelby needed her energy more.

"Mr. Kangjuon, I believe? I am a guest, a distant relative visiting from Barsoom for the mining conferences. The family branches have not been in close touch which is why you don't know me. Do not cast aspersions upon Miss Bradwell's character or I shall be forced to throw you over the garden wall into the street."

This wasn't a lie. Airik had heard similar stories about distant relatives so it was easy to reuse the anecdote. If you went far out enough on a family tree, it was possible for total strangers to be 12th cousins many times removed. Plus, looking at Dean Kangjuon seething on the doorstep and refusing to pay even the least respect to Miss Bradwell made him want to not just throw Dean over the garden wall but do it with enough force to shatter Dean's nose and jaw, permanently marring his handsomeness.

"You wouldn't dare, and you couldn't do it anyway," Dean blustered to Airik.

"Actually, I could," Airik replied.

He looked Dean over coldly, noting all the usual points on a human body that could be used to incapacitate its owner along with an estimate of Dean's weight and general fighting prowess. Dean did not stand like a man who had learned how to defend himself. Airik diligently practiced self-defense since it was both expected and sensible to do so for a man in his position. Bodyguards could only do so much and they could not be with you one hundred percent of the time.

"That is enough from both of you," Veronica said, irritated anew by the gentlemen's bravado. "Dean, you are offending my guest and I can't help you. Ask your parents for help. They have money and connections, and as you know very well, I have neither."

Dean cast Veronica a pleading look. He peered more closely at Airik's expression and body language, read the clear intent and stepped back a few paces, further down the walkway, but still close enough to be heard.

"Look, Ronnie, sweetie, I need you to help me. It has to be you and only you."

"A problem, Airik? Miss Bradwell?" Carmine asked, looming behind Veronica and Airik in the doorway.

"No, we'll be fine, Carmine," Airik replied calmly. "Mr. Kangjuon was just leaving."

Dean stared up at Carmine filling the doorway and recognition struck. He had seen this man occupying more than his fair share of space during the gallery showing, watching him closely when he had spoken to Veronica and her supposed guest, Mr. Jones.

"Fine, have it your way, sweetie. But I really do need you to help me. I'll come back when you're not busy" — Dean paused and smirked salaciously — "'entertaining'." He winked at his former wife.

Veronica reared back as if he had slapped her. "How can you expect me to do anything for you with this attitude?" she snapped. "What is wrong with you?"

The gate, ignored behind them all, screeched again.

"Veronica, I'm home!" Shelby called out. "Dean, what are you doing here?"

"Yeah, Dean, what are you doing here?" Lulu asked from where she stood at the corner of the house. She had slipped out the kitchen's back door and circled the White Elephant when Veronica had gone to answer the front door. Although she wouldn't dream of admitting it to anyone in the house, the thug's visits had bothered her and she remained hyperalert to any change in the routine. She patted her hip pocket and showed her teeth to Dean. "Remember my little friend?"

Dean spread out his hands and said, as contritely as he could manage, "Veronica, my sincere and heartfelt apologies. I've been under a lot of stress. I really do need your help."

He bowed deeply and gracefully to her, ignoring everyone else as not worth his time. "Later on, perhaps, we can talk when you have more time," he added and spun on his heel and strolled out of the tiny yard, giving Shelby and Malcolm Cobb a good looking over along with a wide berth.

Veronica gave Dean one last puzzled look. What was wrong with her ex-husband? He stopped by on occasion to chat her up, but never two days in a row. He was also never this nasty, other than insisting on calling her 'Ronnie' despite everything she said to him on the subject. She shoved that minor concern aside to greet her sister, home safe at last.

She ran down the gravel walk and hugged her sister tightly.

"I was so worried! I thought for sure you'd have been back hours ago," Veronica said. "Were the Collective a problem, driving everyone crazy?"

Shelby beamed at her. "I'm fine. Everything was great. Malcolm ... I mean ... Mr. Cobb and his family were so welcoming. And no, nobody from the Collective came with us. Besides Kip, I mean, and he got sick and went home early."

Veronica went cold and stepped back. "What? His family? The Collective didn't show up?" She took a longer look at Malcolm Cobb and stared, becoming aware that so was everyone else.

"Mr. Cobb? What on Mars are you wearing?" Veronica asked.

He smiled easily at her. "My Steelio coverall, Miss Bradwell."

Lulu strode up, her hand automatically reaching for her hip pocket where she kept her sheathed dagger hidden. She never went anywhere without it and hadn't since she was a child. The familiar feel of the hilt was reassuring.

"You stole someone's coverall? But you're a banker!" Lulu said.

From the door, Neza said, "Secondhand stores do sell used coveralls, Lulu. But even so, Mr. Cobb, wearing a Steelio uniform when you don't merit one is concerning."

Mr. Jones said, "I understood you worked for the Second National Bank of Panschin, Mr. Cobb. Not Steelio and certainly not as a miner."

Florence, from the opened window to the right of the doorway, stared in slack-jawed disbelief. Like Lulu, she was more disturbed than she admitted by the thug's two visits to the White Elephant, and she wanted to be sure she knew what was going on.

Carmine, from his vantage point in the doorway, said nothing but felt vindicated. He had noticed Mr. Cobb's hands during the gallery showing and wondered how much money a banker had to count to earn calluses. He didn't think there was that much money in the world, and he was correct. There wasn't.

Malcolm's smile got broader. No one here had known. He couldn't believe it. He'd been afraid that wherever he went, whoever he met, they saw his background as if he wore a flashing sign. He understood, for the first time, that when someone learned his background, it was because they had heard the story from someone else. He didn't bear the mark of Cain inked on his face as he had always believed. Even Lulu and Florence, born and bred in the tunnels, had not instantly branded him as an escapee from a warren. Best of all, the daimyo of Shelleen, pretending to be plain Mr. Jones from Barsoom, had not recognized him as an interloper into a class he wasn't born in and would never belong to.

Although the White Elephant household and their guests didn't notice (being otherwise occupied), Dean was quietly watching from behind a planter spilling over with marigolds. He didn't recognize the miner with Shelby, and he couldn't figure out why Ronnie was so worked up over him. He hadn't seen the man before, either on the property or anywhere else, and he knew everyone who was a regular at the White Elephant.

More interestingly, where and when had prim little Shelby picked up some prole from the tunnels? She'd always acted like such a prude, and yet here she was, keeping company with some strange man whom she was, no doubt, servicing on a regular basis. The miner, who did not look like anyone ever told *him* no, was almost as big as that damned hulk standing in back of Jones. That was worrying.

When he was sure no one was looking his way, Dean faded into the twilight, fretting over what it meant. He'd have to be more careful when he next saw Ronnie. They needed to be alone.

"Let me explain," Malcolm said to Veronica. He ignored Airik deliberately. If the daimyo of Shelleen was pretending to be an ordinary citizen, he could learn that this was none of his business. He didn't get to have his own way whenever he felt like it. He could damn well wait his turn.

"Please do," Veronica said. She was trying to get her thoughts into some kind of order. Mr. Cobb was a banker *and* a miner? Impossible, yet he was wearing a Steelio coverall that not only fit him and showed signs of authentic, hard usage, but also had his name embroidered across his chest.

"I'd be interested too," Airik said coolly, ignoring the snub. He noted Mr. Cobb's embroidered name, something that would be stitched only for a company-supplied uniform or an elaborate masquerade, and Mr. Cobb didn't strike him as being the type to play dress-up. Moreover, his coverall showed he descended underneath regularly, working in tight spots and getting filthy. The knees had been patched more than once and costumes didn't get that kind of wear or care.

Shelby beamed up at Malcolm and then at her sister. "It's a fascinating story," she said. "We talked all during the transtube ride and during supper."

"I'm a scholarship boy," Malcolm said. "Steelio likes pulling likely lads from the warren for more challenging positions. My brain" — he tapped his forehead — "got me into banking, but I still go into the deepdown when my family needs help."

"You're a scholarship boy?" Lulu interjected, still in shock. "Nobody does that. That's just lies."

"No," Malcolm replied. "It's just that not every mine owner cooperates. Chung/Banerjee doesn't and neither does Jandinaire. There are others, but those two are the worst. They never let their workers participate in the Panschin-wide exams whereas some other companies do if they feel like it or they want to curry favor. Steelio always allows the testers in."

Florence spoke for the first time. "No surprise with Chung/Banerjee. They do nothing for their crews or the families, the rat-fucking bastards." Seeing everyone turn to her — Florence *never* swore —she flushed furiously but stood her ground.

Airik's mind raced. "So, you would not recommend either of those companies?"

Malcolm eyed him carefully. "It depends on what you want."

"I'm interested in reliable and effective safety equipment," Airik said.

Florence and Lulu both laughed harshly, joined after a moment by Malcolm.

"No, not them," Malcolm said. "Not ever." Florence and Lulu nodded in agreement, both wearing the same lividly angry expression.

Airik nodded, filing away the information. It went a long way toward explaining why he wasn't getting the answers he wanted from Jandinaire and why the data he had been provided with had such gaping holes and inconsistencies. Chung/Banerjee was on tomorrow's schedule. With this new information, he could better determine where they were exaggerating.

"This is all very fascinating," Veronica interrupted. "However, *I* want to know what you did with my sister and where the hellation is the Collective? Why didn't they come along?"

"I don't know," Shelby said earnestly. "I told Professor Vitebskin and everyone when I got to PanU in the morning. Then when Malcolm, I mean Mr. Cobb arrived, only Kip agreed to go. Everyone else pretended we weren't there even though Professor Vitebskin was ripping people apart with his critiques. You would have thought people would have been glad to escape. He was just *awful*."

Veronica eyed her little sister carefully during her explanation. Malcolm? Her baby sister was calling the banker who held their lease

Malcolm? What happened to Mr. Cobb? And Shelby didn't look the least bit unhappy over having spent hours with Mr. Cobb, either. Almost as though, Veronica's eyes narrowed, Shelby was starting to fancy him. And from the way the banker was standing closely and smiling at her, Mr. Cobb fancied her sister.

Better to not ask right now, Veronica decided. This was a conversation best held behind closed doors and away from the guests. Instead she asked, "So Kip McGrant came along? And he got sick?"

"McGrant?" Florence blurted out. "Those bastards?"

"Do you know them?" Shelby asked in astonishment. "I didn't know you knew Kip's family."

"I know McGrant. They own a big chunk of Chung/Banerjee," Florence said, her face very tense. "When McGrant bought in, things got worse. They wanted everything to be 'efficient.' They didn't care what it did to the crews as long as they made quota. I didn't know Kip was part of that pack. I would have warned you."

Shelby's eyes went very wide. "So that's why Kip got so nasty about what Malcolm said about Chung/Banerjee."

"Yes," Malcolm said. "I'd agree."

"As I said," Veronica retorted, "all very fascinating, but what happened? Kip got sick?"

"He developed surface sickness, Miss Bradwell," Malcolm replied. "I'd guess Kip had never been lower down than the upper level of the transtube system. He didn't know he was susceptible until he went deeper down."

"Couldn't happen to a nicer family," Florence spat. "He'll be useless to the McGrant family if he can't go into the deepdown to check up on how hard the crews are working. They don't trust their own foremen, the sods. They have to see it for themselves and gloat."

Veronica said, very patiently, "Where is Kip?"

"Oh, he's fine," Shelby said. "Jeffen took him up to the Dome Six infirmary."

"He was that sick? And who is Jeffen?" Veronica asked, letting her exasperation show.

"Kip thought he was sick, Miss Bradwell," Malcolm said. "In my experience, once a person with surface sickness goes back up topside, they make a full recovery. As long as Kip never goes below, he'll never have a problem. Jeffen is a member of Steelio and an acquaintance of mine. He's very reliable."

"I believe Miss Bradwell's concern might be her and your liability," Airik said. "You did, after all, invite the Collective along for the journey and Kip is a member of that flock."

Malcolm said, "No worries on that score, Mr. Jones. Surface sickness is well-known in Panschin. Everyone who has it learns the same way Kip did. They go underneath once and never go back. We won't be sued."

Veronica, who hadn't thought of that possibility at all, gasped and her hand went to the string of cool, cloudy beads around her neck. "Oh lordy. Are you sure?"

"Yes," Malcolm replied.

"Hah! Shows how little you know about Chung/Banerjee and the McGrant family," Florence said roughly. "They'll sue. Sorry, Veronica, but you need to know."

A lawsuit, Veronica thought. Not again, please, dear gods above and below.

"Perhaps not," Airik said calmly. "If such a thing comes to pass, I'm sure I can reason with them."

"That's very considerate of you," Veronica said. "But you're from Barsoom. You'll be leaving when the conference is over, and I doubt they'll care what you have to say."

"They won't," Florence said.

"Nonetheless," Airik said. "I will look into it."

Malcolm hid his smile. If the daimyo of Shelleen weighed in, then the McGrant family would be put firmly in its place. On the other hand, they could still make trouble for the Bradwell family. Hearing McGrant's name ticked his memory again, but it refused to surface. And why was Airik Shelleen so concerned anyway? Interesting. Peng McGrant would find himself at the bottom of a mineshaft alongside Burgess, that fat cave-troll, if he went after the Bradwells when the daimyo of a demesne was concerned about their wellbeing.

Veronica swallowed, shuddered, and shoved unpleasant memories of past lawsuits away to deal with the problem standing in front of her. The court system of Panschin had not been kind to the Bradwell family and now wasn't the time to rip open that wound.

Airik was watching her closely and sensed her distress. He had Elliot's report on the Bradwell family but he hadn't read it yet. He could guess it wasn't going to be pretty. He felt driven to do something about this potential problem, although he couldn't think of what, yet, that wouldn't involve revealing who he was. And why did he want to anyway? He shoved that question of his motives back into its little box.

"What did you do all afternoon then, since you didn't have the Collective with you to tour the Steelio warren?" Veronica asked, hoping for some information that would not make the situation worse.

"I met Malcolm's entire family," Shelby gushed. "I sketched several of their kids, I saw the main entryway, did you know that there's cave salamanders down there? They're so pretty, so shiny red against the green moss, and they eat bugs. The tunnel entrances are all painted with different colored designs. We talked about what kind of pictures everyone likes, including kittens, and I promised Jeffen my cloud painting in exchange for getting Kip back up to the surface, and I have to go back to finish my portrait of Cindy. Oh, Malcolm bought me supper in the metro café too. We had to wait for a transtube."

"You have a cloud painting?" Veronica asked, picking out the only detail she could process. "You never showed it to me."

"It's not acceptable for PanU, but I think it's really good. I didn't feel comfortable showing it to anyone. Not yet. But I think now I can," Shelby finished. She glanced over at Malcolm and suddenly looked happier. "I have others."

Neza had stood unmoving at the doorway, listening and observing intently. She shifted her weight, her stiff joints protested, and she couldn't stop herself from groaning.

"Oh lordy," Veronica said, hearing her aunt. "You've been standing all this time. Let's get everyone inside. You need a nice cup of tea. Florence can you get some of your joint salve for Neza? Lulu? Mr. Jones' cousin, Upton, probably needs more of your throat tea."

She made shooing motions and herded everyone inside the White Elephant. When they were safely moving in the direction of the dining room, she found herself was standing alone on the doorstep with Airik.

Another question rose in her mind. "Mr. Jones," Veronica asked, "Could you really throw Dean over the garden wall?"

"Yes, but it's a low wall," Airik said. He turned back to look at the wall and thought. "If it was higher, and depending on how he struggled, I would have to have Carmine's assistance." He swept his hand in an arc to illustrate his further thinking. "For a wall over two meters in height, I would have to construct a catapult or a trebuchet to get the job done. Which one would depend on the materials I had available. That would take some time, of course, so Dean might escape before I finished."

Behind him he heard a gentle tinkling of laughter. Puzzled, he turned back. Veronica was leaning against the doorframe, one hand before her mouth and an arm across her waist, and she was struggling to keep down her amusement.

"I meant every word," he said, as if that explained everything. He wasn't exaggerating his prowess like Dean would have. He was simply stating facts. But he was glad he amused her.

When she could talk — before the image of Airik launching her ex-husband over the wall on a catapult set her off again — she said, "It's nice to know I can count on you." She hoped he was equally sincere about shielding her from a potential lawsuit as well.

"Is there a difference between catapults and trebuchets, then?" she added, smiling.

"The method of propulsion differs," Airik offered her his elbow. "I'll explain on the way to the dining room." He had made her laugh again. How wonderful.

At the long dining room table, Shelby made sure to sit next to Malcolm. Her choice did not go unnoticed by Neza, Florence, or Lulu, who did their best to discuss it via glances, gestures, and facial expressions so as to not make her uncomfortable with pointed words.

When Veronica and Airik walked in, Malcolm was describing life in the Steelio warren, the details of their visit, and Steelio's participation in Panschin's scholarship programs. Veronica spotted at once how her sister was filling in any blank spots in Malcolm's conversation, how she leaned into him, how she gazed up at him. Yep, her baby sister definitely fancied Malcolm Cobb.

It shouldn't be a surprise, Veronica reflected. Mr. Cobb was a good-looking man, he had clearly taken good care of Shelby, and he was treating her sister with respect. None of the boys at PanU had ever been so considerate. When they fell into bed after the gallery showing, Shelby had finally revealed to her sister about how she was regarded at PanU.

Contrast that with Mr. Cobb, who had introduced her to his family, something that no one who was anyone would ever do. The memory rose up of how Kip during the show couldn't be bothered to introduce Shelby to his family, even as a fellow student. And Mr. Cobb had eaten supper with her at a metro station café. That was, according to Shelby, something no one at PanU had ever bothered to do either. No one would sit with her in public just to chat. Her little sister was persona non grata in every way at PanU because of dear old dad. To have someone pay positive attention to Shelby was like watering a wilting flower. Her joyous response was a given.

Malcolm Cobb. Lordy, Veronica thought. She could only hope that he would continue to see her sister in such a positive light. Maybe, and her thoughts brightened, if Mr. Cobb felt strongly about her sister, he would keep the family safe from Mr. Burgess. But could she trust an emotion? Veronica thought of Dean again. No, affections could and did wither when circumstances changed. Damn Dean.

She sat down at the table and resolved to help Shelby when Malcolm Cobb walked away and abandoned them to their fate. Not everyone walked away when it got difficult. Neza had not. But Dean had, his family had, their own Bradwell relatives had. All their words of love and affection and familial bonds had proven worthless. Would Mr. Cobb be the same?

Airik sat next to Veronica, noticing again how her face had saddened with some unpleasant thoughts and how her eyes kept darting towards her sister and the banker. A discrepancy struck him about Mr. Cobb's narrative. There was a question he could ask for Veronica's benefit and it would satisfy his own curiosity as well.

"Mr. Cobb," Airik asked. "Why have you chosen to reveal your background? No one here knew you came up from the lowest class of Panschin. This information, if widespread, could only harm you in your chosen career. In fact, I would guess it already has, given how Burgess threatened you at the gallery showing."

Malcolm gave Airik a penetrating look. "I decided to stop lying. Both to myself and to everyone else. I *am* a jumped-up tunnel rat. I *am* a scholarship boy. People will gossip, whatever I do. My actions, my worth, my value to Dome Two and to Panschin are all undercut by lying about my roots. If I lie about them, then why should anyone believe me about anything else?"

He smiled coolly at Airik. "Particularly when lies about who we are can so easily be found out, Mr. Jones."

Airik gave an equally cool look to Malcolm Cobb. "This is true."

Cobb might know his true identity, Airik realized. It was a chilling thought. He would not make the mistake of discounting Malcolm Cobb again. Anyone who was intelligent enough to be plucked from the teeming horde in a warren and educated by the free-city of Panschin had to be clever, hardworking, and ambitious. No matter how strong his intellect was, if Malcolm Cobb had been lazy, he would have been tossed back into the deepdown. Which led to the next unpleasant question: What did Cobb want from the daimyo of Shelleen?

"Nonetheless," Airik continued, "there are sometimes reasons to be less than forthcoming. Persons such as Burgess see only weakness and not strength. They see only a chance to exploit for their own gain and damn the consequences to everyone else." He glanced around the table, making sure to let his eyes rest on Veronica, Neza, and Shelby.

Malcolm pursed his lips, as he parsed out the message being given to him by the daimyo of Shelleen. "This is true."

Veronica, for her part, wondered what they were talking about. It felt like a code. The conversation between Mr. Cobb and Mr. Jones reminded her of the morning in the bank. She was talking about one thing while Mr. Cobb and Mr. Wong were clearly discussing something else.

She was hit with an inspiration. Mr. Wong knew Malcolm's background, and he didn't like it one bit. Damn people anyway. She thought of her father again. His crimes had permanently tainted her and her sister. Mr. Cobb was likewise permanently stained by his background. His merits, like hers and Shelby's, mattered not at all.

I t's getting late," Veronica announced and indeed it was. It took hours for Shelby and Malcolm Cobb to detail their adventures. Her sister — always sharp-eyed — kept remembering new incidents and observations ranging from Malcolm's reception at PanU, the levels of the metro and its variety of riders, the freight elevator, Kip's behavior, the Steelio warren, and with each one, Mr. Cobb chimed in to amplify what she said. As they did so, they beamed at each other as though no one else was in the room.

Lordy, Veronica thought. Young love in action. Was I ever that soppy with Dean? Shelby hardly knows him. We know almost nothing about Mr. Cobb.

Airik thought, Is he using Shelby and to what end? If so, it will upset Veronica. Why do I care? I shouldn't care. They're not my responsibility. But I do.

Hmm, Neza thought. Not the man I would have chosen for my niece but a banker's still a banker and he might be able to keep us in our house. Gads, I'm getting cynical in my old age.

She could do a lot worse, Lulu thought. I was sure she would, falling over the first man who paid her any attention at all.

She could do a lot worse, Florence thought. Hope he treats her nice and doesn't use her up and then throw her away like that Upton Jones would.

Are those two ever going to shut up so I can go to bed? Upton wondered. And what the hell is wrong with Airik?

He sneezed violently again and mopped his running nose and streaming eyes with a handkerchief. Lulu kept offering him steaming mugs of the vilest tea he had ever tasted. He drank them because she insisted and if he didn't (she made it plain) she'd tip his head back and pour them down his gullet. She'll make a good nurse, Upton thought gloomily as he stared into another cup of hot, muddy, oily liquid well-laced with floating bits of something he preferred not to identify. Lulu's patients would obey her orders so they could escape faster to the safety of their own homes.

Elliot and Carmine's thoughts ran along the same vein: they didn't care about Shelby Bradwell and Malcolm Cobb or what they got up to together. Lord Airik was the one who counted and, very strange indeed, he cared a lot about what happened to that pair.

"Yes, it is late," Malcolm agreed. "Miss Bradwell? I'll be back in the morning when your sister, Lulu, and Florence head over to PanU."

Veronica went still. "Oh? And why is that?"

"I've been asking around about that thug and his boss. I'm sure the police have, too. There's no sign of them anywhere. That's worrisome," Malcolm replied.

"Panschin is the second-largest city on Mars," Airik said. "I wouldn't expect instant results from a search."

"You don't know Panschin," Malcolm said. "The domes and the tunnels are like self-contained cities. Even in Dome Six, with all the hotels, outsiders are tracked if only so the hotel can extract more money for services. There's no hiding in a smaller dome like Three or Five. Besides, mugged visitors are bad for business."

"But the mining conference," Veronica said and the implication struck her. Hordes of strangers had descended on the city. How could anyone keep track of them all? It would be easy to hide in the mob.

"Yes, it's huge," Malcolm said. "But all those visitors have to stay somewhere. Every hotel in every dome in Panschin is full up. Even among the mining crowd, guys like that thug stand out in a hotel and, as outsiders, they won't be in any of the tunnel lodging. They'd stand out even more."

"There are hotels in the tunnels and the warrens?" Airik asked. He hadn't thought of the possibilities for persons who did not want to be noticed.

"Not exactly," Malcolm said. Lulu and Florence both nodded in agreement as he spoke. "What happens is a visitor might stay somewhere underneath but only if they know how to get there in the first place. That thug and his boss won't be sleeping in a mining company barracks unless they sign on and then they'll be working constantly, not running around like tourists. Warrens like Steelio only allow relatives of residents. No outsiders. Causes trouble. And they're not sleeping in any of the parks. That's an instant arrest if you get caught."

"So where would they be?" Veronica asked, her hand returning to her string of cloudy beads.

"I don't know," Malcolm said. "It's possible they're squatting in one of the abandoned houses here in Dome Two, but they have to come outside to get food and water and everyone in Dome Two is on the lookout. It's almost as though they're hiding in some private home. But squatting seems more likely."

He looked around the table of people. "I will come by in the morning and then go to the bank. I should be able to walk Shelby and her friends home in the afternoon as well."

"Then you'll get to meet Trevor and Evan," Lulu said. "They're coming over tomorrow morning too."

"Our boyfriends," Florence added pointedly, wanting to make it clear to Upton (in case he recovered) that she wasn't available. Better to be safe than sorry with him and his roving eyes. She was glad again that Malcolm Cobb showed up. Shelby was naïve enough to believe a cad like Upton Jones meant the lies he told to get her into bed.

"I have some work to do here in the morning," Airik said. "We won't be leaving for the conference until I'm finished. We'll be back in the early evening."

"Then it's settled," Veronica said and stood up. She was already forming plans to interrogate her sister once all the witnesses had vanished. With Mr. Cobb, Trevor, and Evan walking her sister to PanU, she didn't have to fret over any kidnappings. Squatting in Dome Two. She repressed a shudder. So, Mr. Cobb also believed that was a possibility and not just because he fancied Shelby and wanted to see more of her.

With everyone gone, the White Elephant locked up for the night, and all the guests tucked up into their rooms, Veronica was at last able to corner Shelby. They shared a bedroom so there was no escape. As soon as she closed the door, she couldn't stop herself.

"You have gone crazy," she snarled. "Mr. Cobb? He only wants one thing and once he's got it, we're out in the cold!"

Veronica wanted to bite her tongue off. She had planned on calm and rational reasoning with her sister, not ensuring Shelby would never listen to her again.

"He does not! Malcolm was a perfect gentleman, unlike plenty of men I could mention, including Dean!" Shelby snarled back. She gasped, flushed, and clamped her hands over her mouth.

Her sister started back and put her hand on the dresser they shared, clutching for something to support herself.

"I didn't mean to say that about you or Mr. Cobb," Veronica said carefully. "And what about Dean, pray tell?"

"Put the vase down first," Shelby said.

Veronica looked at the lumpy vase in her hand, a souvenir of some relative's pottery-making class from decades ago. It was both ugly and worthless but it held water, so they still owned it.

"We are both going crazy," Veronica said. She carefully set the vase down. It was heavy enough to work as a blunt object. "Things keep happening, and I can't seem to keep up. What did Dean do?"

"You'll get mad."

"Too late now, sis," Veronica said. "I've been in mad for a while, now I'm on the border of rage. Tell me."

Shelby looked across the small room at the portrait of Madame Fluff on the opposite wall, surrounded by a halo of cloud sketches. She still missed their cat, even though it had been years. She had painted the picture from memory but, although she would never admit it, the image owed more than a little to a magazine illustration of a similar cat painted by Clyde Monez. She couldn't quite remember their pet as well as she wished.

"You won't like it."

"I already don't so get to the point."

"You won't believe me."

"I will. I have a much lower opinion of my former husband than I used to." Veronica sighed deeply, sat on the bed by her sister, and put an arm around her. "Dean isn't who I thought he was. I guess I can't judge people's characters at all."

"Yes, you can," Shelby said. "You want to believe that other people are like you. You know, decent and caring and hardworking and someone who would never abandon anyone she loves."

"Sweet of you, sis. So, what did my ex do to you?"

Shelby frowned at the floor. "I guess it wasn't much really, but it was still gross and upsetting. I mean, he's your husband, or he was." She paused, thinking and chewing on her lower lip.

"Yep, I got that part."

"If you'd stop interrupting me," Shelby said, "I can tell you this story, we can finish our fight about Malcolm, and still get some sleep and we won't keep everybody else up."

Veronica giggled, surprising them both. "How right you are."

Shelby sighed. "It was after everything started coming out about Dad. You remember. Every day was worse than the day before. Dean's mom, that awful witch, was saying the meanest things to everybody, including Dean, about how she'd never wanted Dean to marry you because our family was tainted and you were a slutty gold-digger and I wouldn't turn out any better."

Veronica turned to her sister in horror. "She said that about you? Really? I don't remember that last part." Her former mother-in-law had had plenty to say to everyone about how fortunate the family was when they discarded *her* but she hadn't heard Mrs. Kangjuon say anything nasty about Shelby.

"Oh yeah," Shelby replied sourly. "A former friend of mine couldn't wait to tell me. Anyway, everything got sold and I moved here with mom into the White Elephant, after we had to leave Dome Six. Dean was still living here. He'd always been nice to me, like a little sister. You know he's an only and I guess he liked pretending. But that day, the day I'm telling you about, was the day he told you he was leaving. You had a big fight."

"I remember," Veronica replied. "I begged him to stay with me. I loved him and how could he leave me when he loved me and I needed him? What a spineless cave-worm he was."

I was a spineless cave-worm, Veronica thought. I would have done just about anything to keep Dean and I meant nothing to him.

"Spineless is right," Shelby said. "He was packing his stuff, but he still got servants from his family to do the heavy lifting. He wasn't going to carry his own luggage when someone else could do it for him. You remember."

"Shelby please, you're dragging this out. This is painful."

"Painful for me too, Veronica," her sister said testily. "Anyways, I came in the gate when Dean was on his way out. Dean told me that if I wanted to rot in Dome Two, I could, but I was old enough and pretty enough that he'd set me up in a place of my own, and he could visit me. For, you know," Shelby flushed and ducked her head with embarrassment. "Sex," she whispered.

"Charming," Veronica said. "Just charming." Her hands went into fists of their own accord. I will never speak to Dean again, she thought. I don't care what he wants or how critically important he thinks it is.

Shelby gritted her teeth and continued. "He didn't touch me if that's what you're worried about. What he said was that I didn't have any talent except my looks and with dear old dad ruining our lives I was only good for one thing and he'd arrange for friends of his to visit me, too. Like I was some tunnel chola."

"Oh, Shelby," Veronica said. She could not stop a few stinging tears from leaking out. "Dean is a worthless heap of shit and you have loads of talent and he was jealous and you are not a tunnel chola."

Shelby twisted to glare at her sister. "Dean jealous of me? And quit crying over your ex. He's not worth it."

Veronica wiped her eyes angrily. "No, he's not. He told me once that he always wanted to draw and he envied you."

"Maybe if he'd picked up a pencil and practiced, he'd have been able to," Shelby snapped. "I practice all the time. I never saw Dean so much as doodle on a shopping list."

"No, I never saw him draw either, so I don't know why he said that. Dean propositioned you." Veronica lifted her sister's face to her own. "Are you absolutely sure that's all he did? If he touched you, I'll have to crack his skull open with that vase and then I'll go to jail and we'll be out a vase."

"Would you really?" Shelby asked.

"Yep, sure would," Veronica said. "I hope you come and visit me. Damn him and his family. Everyone says to trust your instincts. I trusted mine and look what I got. A husband who ran out on me as soon as things got the least bit hard and then he tried to set you, my little sister, up as a prostitute so he could pimp you out!"

They sat in silence for a few minutes.

"Well," Shelby said, "to be fair, he didn't try very hard. He leered at me and I was already mad over everything that was happening and I slugged him as hard as I could. Dean never brought it up again and I suppose he could have. He's been here often enough."

"Well that's worth something," Veronica said. She put her head in her hands, bone-tired. "I'll tell Neza tomorrow, Florence and Lulu too. Dean's never setting foot in the White Elephant again."

Shelby snickered. "Lulu wouldn't mind telling him to leave. It would let her slice pieces off of him if he resisted even the tiniest bit."

"I'm sure that would be bad, although I can't think why just now," Veronica said.

"So, are we done?" Shelby asked hopefully.

"Not even partly," her sister said. "You don't think Mr. Cobb wants the same thing?"

"I'm sure he does," Shelby said carefully. "But I'm older than I was when Dean hit on me, and Malcolm's being a really nice gentleman about it, and he treats me like I'm a princess, and he talks to me like I have a brain, and he's happy to be seen in public with me and he even introduced me to his family."

"His family. Proles from the Steelio warren," Veronica said.

"They are not proles," Shelby shot back. "They are very nice, friendly people. They love my pictures. And you should have seen them watching me and Malcolm. His entire family approves of me. His mother was asking when he would bring me back so I could meet everyone else!"

"Even so—," her sister began.

"You sound like auntie Neza," Shelby said. "'A nice boy from a good family,'" she sing-songed. "No one from PanU will give me the time of day other than to proposition me. I like Malcolm, he has a nice family, and he has a real career ahead of him, unlike, say Dean, who's never done anything useful except live off his family's money."

"I suppose," Veronica said. Thinking of Dean made her wince but her little sister was right. Dean hadn't done much since their divorce and his graduation from PanU. She'd moved on with her life as best she could while he … drifted, as aimless as terraformer spores caught in the breeze. What did he do with his days? Veronica realized suddenly she hadn't cared in a long time and now, she cared even less.

"It's true and you know it. Malcolm's really smart, he's confident, and he works hard. I could do a lot worse and seeing how everyone from 'decent families' treats me, I *would* do worse," Shelby said. She smiled dreamily at Madame Fluff's portrait. "I like him. The more I see him, the more I like him. He makes me feel all warm inside. I liked holding his hand and sitting next to him and," — she flushed — "I would like to kiss him and let him kiss me back." She hugged herself tightly, wishing Malcolm's arms were wrapped around her as they had been during the transtube ride.

Veronica looked away, up to Madame Fluff's portrait as well. She pursed her lips in distaste at the cat as she contemplated what Shelby seemed to be ignoring. It had to be said.

"He's a banker, but he's also from the tunnels. He must have worked hard to get where he is. That awful cave-troll, Burgess, wants to make trouble for him like he's going to make trouble for us."

"I know all that," Shelby said impatiently.

"Do you? We're Simon Bradwell's daughters," Veronica said. "Remember dear old dad? Everyone in Panschin does and they will for the next hundred years. Marrying Simon Bradwell's daughter isn't a good career move for an ambitious banker who's already got a problem background to overcome."

"I don't care," Shelby said. "And you're kind of early to be talking about my marrying Malcolm Cobb."

"The way you looked at him in the dining room tonight? I was wondering if you were going to elope with him tomorrow," Veronica said hotly. "You'd come home from PanU with a ring on your finger, both of your names tattooed on your left arm, and a certificate from the justice of the peace with the ink still wet."

Shelby snorted. "Gleesh, Veronica. You're supposed to be the sensible one, not me. I like Malcolm a lot and I think he fancies me. And maybe, that's all that it will be. And ..." she let her voice trail away.

"And?" Veronica asked.

"And if Malcolm likes me, he won't be working hard for that awful Burgess, looking to throw us out for lease violations. Maybe he can help us." Shelby ran her fingers through her hair, fluffing it back into a face-framing nimbus.

"That's uh, very practical of you," Veronica said slowly. "I could also say mercenary and cynical."

"You're the one with the literature vocabulary. Try realistic," Shelby said. "I like Malcolm and I would like to get to know him better and if he wants to help us out, I don't think we should say no."

They both stared at Madame Fluff who stared back. Her painted expression said nothing useful, but her real-life expression never had either.

"All right then," Veronica said. "You've got my permission. You're old enough to know your own mind, and it's not like you'd listen to me anyway. I'll talk to auntie Neza and see if I can get her to agree."

"Do you think she'd be upset with me?" Shelby asked. "Over Malcolm, I mean?"

"She was really enthused about you meeting a nice young man from a good family at PanU," Veronica said. "I don't think a scholarship boy from the tunnels was what she had in mind, no matter how hardworking or good-looking he is."

Shelby grinned. "So you think Malcolm is good-looking?"

Her sister grinned, too. "I guess, if you like big and good-looking in a rough-hewn sort of way. And really, who doesn't?" Airik Jones flashed through her mind, and she shoved away the vision.

"I'd love to draw him some more," Shelby said dreamily.

"Some more?" Veronica asked, eyebrows raised to her hairline.

"I sketched Malcolm last night, after I drew that thug for the police," Shelby admitted. "I carried his picture all day, in my breast pocket."

"Right over your heart," Veronica groaned. "You do have it bad."

"It would get crumpled in any of my other pockets," Shelby said.

"Heavens above forbid such a thing," Veronica said dryly. "I mean, the horror." She looked over at Madame Fluff's portrait again. Shelby had done a nice job, almost as nice as the painter of the kitten calendar downstairs, although she didn't remember Madame Fluff as having quite that adoring an expression. "But I did mean it about dear old dad and Malcolm's career as a banker. He has to know."

Shelby breathed out heavily, emptying her lungs of aggravation and breathed in as deeply, postponing an answer.

"Well?"

"I already thought about it, Veronica," Shelby said. "Malcolm never brought it up so maybe he doesn't know."

"Don't be naïve, Shelby," Veronica said, making her sister flinch and hunch her shoulders. "He's not stupid and I'm positive that whatever business college he went to must have covered dear old dad as a case study in fraud and embezzlement. The story was in every paper in Panschin for months. It was a current event *and* involved half the banks in the city. He must know."

"I understand all that," Shelby said. "He didn't bring it up, maybe because he does like me and he didn't want to upset me and spoil the day." She sighed again, even more deeply. "I already decided I'm going to tell him tomorrow morning. When we walk to PanU.”

“Very good but why didn’t you say something today?” Veronica asked.

“Gleesh, Veronica.” Shelby twisted and glared at her sister. “Let me have a daydream for at least twenty-four hours, okay? If Malcolm doesn’t know and I tell him and he vanishes down a mineshaft rather than be seen with,” — she waved her hands angrily — “that worthless Bradwell girl, well at least I got a wonderful day with him and learned how a nice man should treat me.”

“I’m sorry,” Veronica said softly. “You’re right. You deserve a dream day, and you deserve a dream life, and if Malcolm Cobb is worth anything, he’ll give you them because you are worth it.” She sat up straighter and pulled her sister into a tight hug.

Shelby yawned ostentatiously. She was tired and more than ready to sleep and dream of Malcolm. She was also tired of listening to Veronica. Unfortunately, if she knew her sister, and she did, Veronica had more to say.

“Shelby,” Veronica said.

Shelby, to her credit, did not roll her eyes.

“Can’t we blow out the candle and sleep? What is it now?” she asked.

Veronica sighed gustily. “I don’t know if I can,” she admitted. “On top of everything else, do I have to worry over Kip suing us for getting surface-sickness? You know him. Would he do that?”

Shelby gnawed on her lower lip. “I don’t know. Kip likes me, or at least I think he does. But he doesn’t want to admit it to anyone, including, I guess, himself. I don’t know why.”

“Probably dear old dad again,” Veronica said dismally. “I don’t think there’s anyone in Panschin he didn’t cheat.”

“Malcolm’s family,” Shelby said and snickered. “They’re unimportant and they don’t have any money. There must be transtubes crammed full of people dear old dad didn’t waste his time on.”

Veronica sighed. “Focus, Shelby. Would Kip sue us? I don’t think I could live through another court case and the newspapers making sure everyone who breathes knows how terrible we are. And we don’t have any money to fight.”

“I just don’t know,” her sister admitted. “Kip came with me when no one else would and then he got mean. It must have been the surface sickness coming out. But he wouldn't introduce me to his parents at the gallery showing, even though I'm a member of the Collective like everyone else."

She paused while Veronica waited patiently.

"Maybe he wouldn't but his family might," Shelby concluded.

"Wonderful," Veronica said wearily. "One more darn thing. Well, I doubt a team of lawyers will show up tomorrow morning and lay siege to the White Elephant. Lawsuits take time and I'll think of something."

"Yes," Shelby said dreamily. "We could hide in the Steelio warren with Malcolm."

Veronica groaned. "In the tunnels? Us? Okay, maybe us, but how about auntie Neza? She's never been lower down than the upper transtube levels. I just can't see her as a tunnel rat."

"Quit worrying, Veronica, and get some sleep."

Shelby got up, pulled the drapes closed, and blew out the candle. "Tomorrow's another day. Remember what you always say."

"It will get better," Veronica repeated obediently. "It has to."

Veronica lay in the velvety gray darkness listening to Shelby's breathing. Her baby sister did fancy Malcolm Cobb and she didn't care about his family's background. That was a pleasant surprise. Shelby saw the Cobb family, at least for now, as people and not just as proles who should keep to their place in the deepdown, ensuring the better classes of Panschin could live comfortably.

She smiled at the ceiling. That was one good thing to come out of the debacle that dear old dad had visited on the family. Any snobbishness in the Bradwell sisters had been beaten out of them. They had friends and family who were ostentatiously proud of their charity; those people had shunned them. Dome Two neighbors, who came from every walk of life, had been friendlier. It didn't matter what people said since they could and did say anything using nice, cheap words. It mattered how they treated you. That cost effort.

Malcolm Cobb treated Shelby like a princess. Maybe he did see her as precious and valuable. Certainly, once Kip ran out on her sister and left her underground, he could have taken Shelby anywhere and used her however he chose. But he had not. He'd taken her to the Steelio warren and showed Shelby around and brought her home, safe, sound, and happy. He had behaved as he said he would.

Veronica thought then of Airik Jones. He had been very helpful, unusually so for a guest who owed her nothing. His behavior said he valued her or least a quiet stay at the White Elephant. She stretched and wiggled and wondered if Dean showed up again, would Mr. Jones really throw Dean over the garden wall as he had promised. It would serve Dean right, especially if he landed hard and broke his jaw so he couldn't talk anymore.

She still couldn't figure out Mr. Jones. He was so average; average in height, average in build or least she thought so since a baggy coverall hid a multitude of sins, and average in looks. But he wasn't average in brains, that was clear enough. And when he needed to be, he stopped being average and suddenly became someone who expected other people to snap to attention. How odd. Almost as though Mr. Jones was someone else entirely. Not surprising really, since "Jones" probably wasn't his real name. But few people moved through life expecting to be obeyed. As if Mr. Jones held supreme power over other people's lives.

She slipped off into a pleasant but exceedingly unlikely dream of Airik Jones defending the White Elephant from Mr. Burgess leading an army of McGrant family lawyers, all of whom looked like sheep.

Airik closed the door behind him, sweated through his nightly exercise routine, and settled in to read Elliot's initial report on the Bradwell family. He expected it to be unfavorable, based on Veronica's hints and his observations.

It was not.

It was appalling.

Her father, Simon Bradwell, never met *anyone* he didn't consider a sheep waiting to be sheared, a goose waiting to be plucked. Worse, since he came from a highly respected family of long standing in Panschin, no one could believe that someone with such a proper upbringing could be other than reputable in his business dealings. Still worse was the utter naiveté that enfolded Simon Bradwell in a cocoon of decency and probity. Since no one could believe he was a crook, he got away with financial malfeasance for years even as red flags fluttered and sirens sounded. He even used his wife and daughters as cover, parading them about as evidence of his upright behavior. When suspicion fell on him, he stated publicly he would never do anything to harm them.

Elliot had been adamant when he discreetly handed the report to Airik after they had all gone upstairs to retire to their respective rooms.

"It is grossly incomplete, sir," his valet and part-time researcher insisted. "I merely scraped the topmost level of sod from the soil below. I could spend months reading the newspaper reports. This wouldn't include the case studies that have come out since the aborted trial. In addition, I would need to interview witnesses and read the reams of legal dossiers that have been filed."

"I see," Airik had replied when he took the sheaf of papers. "Continue your researches tomorrow and for every day after until I say otherwise."

"I am surprised to find, sir," Elliot added, "that the Miss Bradwells did not themselves end up in jail on some kind of charges."

Airik had looked up sharply. "Do you believe that they participated?"

"As of this date in my preliminary research? No, I do not," Elliot said. "However, their father permanently destroyed the finances of many, many families, leaving them bankrupt and destitute. Those families will never forgive his daughters for existing. Someone must suffer and since Simon Bradwell conveniently slit his wrists prior to the first trial and their mother is dead, they are the most likely candidates."

Airik reread Elliot's damning report. It was all beautifully and concisely laid out, well-organized so no important point could be missed, and as legible as he could want due to his valet's precise handwriting. Elliot was clearly wasted as a valet, skilled as he was at that task.

As Elliot insisted, and the report made clear, there was no end to the depths of Simon Bradwell's criminal career. That led directly to the worst fact of them all. The business leaders and bankers of Panschin were grossly incompetent. How could they have missed any of these activities?

A disturbing memory surfaced, reminding Airik of how easy it was to believe what you wanted to believe. He had, like everyone else in the Shelleen family, been sure no one in the family would put the demesne at risk for personal gain. Yet Howard Shelleen had. As the daimyo, Airik didn't have to punish Howard. He could have hidden the truth and claimed it was for the good of the demesne. Howard would have been assigned a lesser post with a grander name.

Instead, he believed that the better course was to reveal the truth to everyone, so they could see that justice was done. He punished Howard in the most publicly humiliating and painful way possible. The reputation of Shelleen was damaged by Howard; it was up to Airik to restore it, and in a way that ensured no one else in the Shelleen clan would dare cheat the family again.

Airik could still hear every one of Howard's screams during his flogging in front of the entire population of Shelleen. It had been agonizing to sit through. Howard was a favored uncle that the child Airik looked up to. But he had to be seen, unmoving, as though he was a heartless man of stone as so many of his own family believed. Yet agonizing as it was, they knew Airik would order it done again to protect the wellbeing of the demesne.

That led to another disturbing aspect of Elliot's report. As much damage as Howard had done to Shelleen, his wife, son, daughter-in-law, and grandchildren had not been punished. Airik searched for any entanglement involving them and found nothing. He had demanded that the family follow his lead and not ostracize Howard's immediate family. Howard had chosen to go into exile, retreating to his wife's home demesne of Kamandango with her, rather than face the family he had betrayed. Their son, daughter-in-law, and grandchildren had remained in Shelleen. Jason, Howard's only child, had been fiercely insistent about staying and cleaning up the damage his father had done.

Panschin had not been so generous to the Bradwell sisters.

Howard, unlike Simon Bradwell, had chosen to live. He took his punishment rather than suiciding and thus avoiding having to face the grief and agony he had caused to so many. He saw his family continue untarnished, unlike the Bradwell sisters.

Simon Bradwell, concluded Airik, was a heartless man of stone, as well as a coward. What did that say of Veronica? She was his daughter. Was she like her father? Or did she share Jason's traits of refusing to behave as she pleased and lying about her actions rather than face the truth. Based on what he saw, Veronica was nothing like her father.

But her father was a consummate liar.

Still, there was the incontrovertible fact that the Bradwell family had no money. Simon Bradwell's ill-gotten gains had vanished and no one knew where. If Veronica had even the smallest amount of his loot hidden away, she could have used it to escape Panschin. Her father would have. Yet Veronica had remained with her aunt and her sister, scraping by, allowing their home to be used as an art gallery in exchange for pennies from the door receipts. She had chosen to stay and face, every day, her father's victims who would never forgive or forget.

Airik chewed over Elliot's report a third time, making notes on the connections he found. Where had all that money gone? It was as if Simon Bradwell had a partner in the Panschin business community, someone who remained undetected. This partner had helped him embezzle and defraud countless members of Panschin's upper and business classes, yet remained unidentified.

Simon Bradwell had not acted alone. He had help, or at the very least, a blind eye turned onto his business dealings. To say otherwise would indict the Panschin business community as completely and utterly incompetent. Based on his own research, Airik decided that was untrue and his daily dealings with members of the business community reinforced his conclusion.

Airik carefully concealed Elliot's report within his own papers. It wouldn't do for Upton to read this. He wasn't happy slumming at the White Elephant, blaming it for his hangover and his sinus issues. His secretary would be overjoyed to return to the Twelve Happiness Luxury Hotel with its amenities and lures and charming women who would be delighted to fall over for him if it meant a chance of getting closer to the daimyo of Shelleen.

s promised, Malcolm Cobb arrived promptly at the front door of the White Elephant the next morning. He was admitted into the dining room where everyone was eating breakfast, including Trevor and Evan. This morning, he was back in his persona as the assistant manager of the Second National Bank of Panschin.

The inhabitants of the White Elephant — permanent, temporary, and regular visitors — gave him a careful looking over to see if the jumped-up tunnel rat showed underneath the fine tailoring. It did not, other than to Carmine and Airik. They studied Malcolm's hands and this time, correctly placed him in the category of men who weren't above getting their hands dirty.

Elliot was chagrined. Despite his training and experience as a gentleman's gentleman, he had missed the obvious tell.

As for himself, Malcolm was pleased again at new evidence he did not bear the mark of Cain stamped upon his face as he had always believed.

Upton didn't care one way or the other because he was feeling much, much better; enough so he was considering flirting with Florence despite her boyfriend's hostile presence. It had to be Florence since Shelby was a lost cause having only eyes for Malcolm; Veronica was off-limits since every time he turned her way, Airik scowled at him; Neza dismissed him as an amusing but silly boy; and Lulu scared the pants off him but not in the fun way.

Lulu, however, did want his undivided attention.

She leaned over the table, a mug of steaming hot, vile-smelling tea in her hand, smacked him on the shoulder with her free hand to get his attention, and glared into his startled face. Upton sat back abruptly, the attractive company around him no longer his main concern.

"You're feeling better. Good. I knew you would be," Lulu hissed. "But you, Mr. Upton Jones, are not better. You are still sick. You'll be dizzy from time to time and you need to take it easy. When you come back to the White Elephant, I'll get you more medicinal tea. In the meantime, drink this mug down, every last drop, and no shirking."

"Yes, ma'am," Upton squeaked, all thoughts of attractive women banished. He manfully swallowed his tea, then cringed when Lulu smiled gleefully and presented a second mugful. She was thoroughly enjoying their moment together, which made one of them.

"Thank you, Lulu," Airik said. "Upton has plenty of work waiting for him."

He would have to discover the ingredients of Lulu's foul-smelling brew. It had worked miracles on Upton's constitution. It might work for the rest of the Shelleen contingent back at the Twelve Happiness Luxury Hotel who were complaining about sinus infections, and using them to shirk their own duties. Despite the exorbitant fees he was paying the hotel, the hotel doctor wasn't keeping his staff healthy.

"Just doing my job, Mr. Jones," she replied.

"In fact," Airik said. "Would you pack an extra container or two of your medicinal tea for Upton? In case his symptoms recur during the day." If this worked, he would pay Lulu to make up a vat for the Shelleen contingent lazing about at the Twelve Happiness. Based on Upton's response to Lulu, if he hired her to go along with the tea, he could be assured of one hundred percent compliance from his staff.

"Of course," Lulu said, looking very pleased.

Upton did not look pleased, but he resigned himself to his fate. He did, after all, feel better which meant he could eventually escape Lulu's eagle-eye and ruthless ministrations. She really would make a good nurse.

"Veronica? We'll be heading out," Shelby said, gazing up at Malcolm mistily and not bothering to make eye contact with her sister at all.

"Of course," Veronica said. "I know you're with the group, but be careful anyway, okay?"

"No worries, Miss Bradwell," Malcolm said. "Nothing will happen." He didn't bother making eye contact with Veronica either, having only eyes for Shelby.

Trevor and Evan, gentlemen friends of Lulu and Florence, nodded in agreement.

Veronica sniffed and said, "I certainly hope so. It would be a nice change from the last few days."

Once the PanU group had left, Airik said, "Upton and I will be working on some reports upstairs. Elliot has some errands I need him to do."

"And Carmine?" Neza asked. "What are your plans?"

"I was planning on walking around the neighborhood," Carmine replied. "Get a feel for the area while uh, Airik, is working."

"How useful," the old lady replied. "Would you mind, Mr. Jones, if I borrowed your cousin for the morning? I have some errands to run, and I would appreciate the escort."

"Not at all," Airik said. "Upton and I won't be finished for an hour or so. Will that be enough time?"

"More than sufficient," Neza said.

Veronica felt relieved. She could catch up on her gardening (the new cash crops were coming up and had to be weeded free of terraformers) while Carmine made sure her elderly great-aunt was safe and carried the packages. And even better, anyone suspicious watching from inside an abandoned house would see Carmine with her aunt. No one would willingly take on someone Carmine's size, meaning auntie Neza would be protected even when Carmine wasn't right by her side.

Shelby walked quietly, holding hands with Malcolm and wishing for the perfect opening to arise for her to tell Malcolm about her tainted family history. But Trevor, Evan, Lulu, and Florence were full of questions about the scholarship program he had triumphed in, how he balanced his family life in the tunnels with the demands of the banking industry, and did he really still go into the deepdown? He answered them all, leading to more questions, making for an informative walk for all concerned.

Shelby had never considered how much a program like this meant in the tunnels. If Lulu and Florence's reactions meant anything, a comprehensive scholarship offered a way up and out for anyone with serious ambitions. Their own scholarships to nursing school, while deeply appreciated, kept them firmly within the ranks of the working classes. She thought again of PanU's preachings about helping the underclasses with art. How could anyone say with a straight face that a painting on a wall would bring about the brave new millennium?

Paintings in museums or in the homes of collectors didn't put food on tables or provide jobs other than to the artist or the gallery owner who sold the work.

Paintings were, or at least they should be, beautiful and inspiring. Yet Professor Vitebskin's anointed style was ugly. Drawing kittens and clouds, despite being decidedly déclassé, did provide beauty and comfort based on the number of pictures she had seen in the Steelio warren, clipped from adverts and pinned to walls. If auntie Neza was successful in persuading PanU to allow Shelby and her prepaid tuition to transfer to PCC's commercial arts department, she, Shelby, could draw beautiful objects in adverts that someone whom she would never know would appreciate and enjoy. How much more beauty could Shelby add to the world with the very best magazine illustrations she could draw? Far more than she would with ugly paintings of cesspool contents.

She could also make money drawing adverts.

It was galling to discover she was agreeing with her sister about the futility of avant-garde art.

The group stopped at the gate to PanU. Florence and Lulu disappeared into PCC's underground entrance while Evan and Trevor went on their ways, after kisses and cuddles.

"Shelby?" Malcolm said. "You'll be safe on campus, and I have to go."

She tightened her grip on his hand, so warm and strong in her own, small hand.

"Not yet," Shelby said. "Sit with me for a minute. I have to tell you this."

She led him over to a bench and as soon as they were seated, she plunged in.

"I'm Simon Bradwell's younger daughter. I don't know if you've heard of him but if anyone at the Second National Bank of Panschin finds out you're seeing me, you'll be ruined." She swallowed hard and fought back a sudden burst of stinging tears. "You need to know."

Malcolm smiled. To her surprise, he leaned in and brushed his lips across her own.

She gazed up at him, starry-eyed, wanting him to touch her lips with his own again.

"I know. Your dad is a case study at Panschin School of Business. And I don't care. You're not your father," Malcolm said. "You are you, beautiful and talented and brave Shelby Bradwell.”

“Malcolm,” Shelby said. “I’m serious.” *Why am I saying this stuff when he could be kissing me again? Because I have to, for him, darn it.*

“I know what I’m doing.”

“Are you sure? I have no connections who can help you.” She turned away bitterly; the chance of kisses forgotten. “All our relatives, except for auntie Neza, turned on us. I’m surprised we didn’t go to jail, me and Veronica, even though we never stole a penny. We’re pariahs because of dear old dad and so is everyone who associates with us.”

He turned her face back to his own. “I understand, better I think than you realize, how that feels. I’m a scholarship boy and that means at the fancy prep school I went to and then Panschin School of Business, I was always there on sufferance. Too many people there were waiting for me to fall on my face. If I failed, it was because I was worthless. If I succeeded, then I must have cheated. If I didn’t work, I was lazy. If I did work, I was showing off and making everyone else look bad.”

“But Mr. Burgess—,” Shelby began.

“Screw him.”

“Eeeouw! That would be *disgusting*,” Shelby said and dissolved into horrified giggles imagining a naked and panting Mr. Burgess.

Malcolm laughed with her. “Yeah, it would be. I better rethink how I say that.”

Shelby giggled a few more minutes, then sobered up. “But Mr. Burgess, despite wearing the PanU cafeteria drapes, is a problem. He’s a problem for us and for you. You can’t work your way out of him.”

Malcolm looked puzzled. “The cafeteria drapes?”

Shelby giggled again. “His suit, the one he wore at the gallery showing, looks just like the floral cafeteria drapes at PanU. I’m sure he doesn’t know.”

“I’m sure he doesn’t,” Malcolm said, looking highly amused. “That is funny.” He chuckled, then got back to the point.

“Shelby, I am serious. Burgess is a problem, but not one I can’t handle. He can’t throw you or your family out of the White Elephant because he has no grounds. I’ve seen your records. You’ve never missed a payment, and your house is immaculately maintained.”

“He’ll think of something,” Shelby said. She groaned in remembrance. “People did all the time, after dear old dad. And there’s you. He could hurt you.”

Malcolm smiled very coldly. "He's not as dangerous as he thinks he is. I've been working my way through the records at Second National. There's gaps in the files but there's something there. I'm sure of it. Something damaging to him personally."

"That sounds like wishful thinking," Shelby said. She leaned into his big, muscular body. He felt good, so warm and strong. She stored away the memory in case she never got another chance to sit next to Malcolm.

"He is not a banker in a melodrama. He can't do whatever he pleases and get away with it while twirling his mustache." Malcolm paused, considering exactly how he wanted to hint what he knew and Shelby and her sister did not. "He's not the daimyo of a demesne with the power of life and death over his peasants. Burgess has to follow rules. And he's made enough enemies that if he screwed up, and I can prove it, he'll find out that his friends will shove him down the nearest mineshaft to save themselves."

Shelby felt so good, leaning up into him. So soft, so feminine, so talented and concerned. She was everything he wanted in a woman. He'd been right to take the risk of revealing himself to his Dome Two princess. Shelby Bradwell was turning out to be everything he had hoped she would be.

He shifted and leaned over to kiss her again, longer this time, feeling her open up to him, wanting him.

Shelby closed her eyes and leaned into his kiss. Malcolm felt wonderful and only the sound of the campus clock striking the time made her pull away.

"I have to go," she said. "I'll be late."

"I'll try to be here to walk you home," Malcolm said.

She beamed up at him. "I'd love that, Malcolm." And I might be falling in love with you, she thought. You make it so easy.

I could fall in love with you, my Shelby, Malcolm thought. You are a delight.

Neither of them noticed Kip, peering from behind a large planter holding a lacy tree casting dappled shadows over him. He turned abruptly and marched into the quad, lost in his own jealous thoughts and sullen regrets.

Veronica walked to the gate with auntie Neza and Carmine. It was so reassuring to watch him escort her elderly aunt into the street. The horde of foot-traffic magically parted to make way for them and it didn't take long for auntie Neza to be accosted by everyone who had even the slightest idea who she was to ensure she was in good hands. That was also reassuring. The neighborhood residents were, as promised, looking out for the residents of the White Elephant.

She watched them march up the street towards the business district and then, seeing how the other pedestrians automatically made plenty of space for Carmine and by extension Neza, Veronica finally worked out what kind of servant he was for Airik Jones.

Elliot had been easy. He was obviously a valet and general assistant who handled the dreary daily details, making life easier for his employer. He was routine, if expensive. She knew people, or she used to, who employed valets. Her impeccably dressed father used to employ one; managing his extensive wardrobe, running errands, and seeing to his personal needs. He had been let go when their world started falling apart.

Upton was a secretary, doing all the routine paperwork, making appointments and managing a calendar, taking dictation; everything a busy executive needed to improve his own efficiency. It was even likely, based on their similar facial features, that Upton was, as they claimed, Mr. Jones' cousin. Lots of families employed every possible relative to squeeze some work out of them while keeping the business money within the family.

Simon Bradwell had employed many secretaries, only allowing each one to see a tiny portion of his business so none of them could grasp his overall scheme. Veronica had met most of them, indeed had testified in court that she didn't believe they had helped her father swindle his clients. He wouldn't have been that careless. He had certainly discouraged her from working in his office, even though she had offered her skills more than once so she could learn the business.

While it wasn't unexpected to see someone in either position, it was a surprise that a man who could afford a secretary *and* a valet would have come to stay at the White Elephant. Last-minute trip to Panschin or not, Veronica would have assumed someone with that kind of money would be well-connected enough to be staying with distant relatives or with business acquaintances. Mr. Jones' other choice would have been the Twelve Happiness Luxury Hotel. Veronica had been there once, early in her marriage to Dean. It was the most luxurious hotel she had ever seen in her admittedly limited experience. It was hard to believe even the Biennial Mining Conference would fill that hotel's gaspingly expensive rooms. If Mr. Jones could afford a valet and a secretary, he could afford the Twelve Happiness.

And then there was Carmine. One of the biggest men Veronica had ever seen, he over-filled whatever space he was occupying. He was both taller and broader than either Malcolm or that awful thug. There was no question, looking at Carmine, that he was a mountain of muscle and bone. He carried suitcases like they were bales of feathers. But hauling luggage wasn't his function in life.

Carmine was Mr. Jones' bodyguard.

Why did Mr. Jones need a bodyguard? Why did anyone need a bodyguard? Normal people didn't. You had to be very, very important or in daily danger to need someone around you to bust heads. Someone like that would never stay at the White Elephant unless he was hiding. Veronica wondered again who she had rented rooms to because she desperately needed their money. Mr. Jones had been polite, unexpectedly helpful, and considerate, but he did not act very, very important nor did he look over his shoulder constantly.

She liked him. He made her laugh. He seemed to appreciate her intelligence. But she knew nothing about him, she couldn't trust her instincts, and Airik Jones had to be lying about who he was. In addition to a valet and a secretary which could be explained away, he employed a bodyguard, which could not. She had never met anyone who employed one.

Veronica sank down onto the low stone wall, staring up the street at the pedestrians. Would auntie Neza come back alive? She would, she decided. Mr. Jones wanted to hide or he'd be at the Twelve Happiness or some other similar place right now. Nothing would happen to Neza with Carmine around and that implied nothing would happen to the residents of the White Elephant as long as Mr. Jones was around.

He wanted quiet and he was going to get it. That might even be the reason Mr. Jones allowed Carmine to escort her aunt. She provided the perfect excuse for the bodyguard to walk around the neighborhood, making sure nothing happened to disturb Mr. Jones.

But if he wanted privacy, why had he come downstairs to the gallery showing? Wouldn't that have risked his exposure? Veronica frowned at the street, thinking hard. Perhaps the risk was small. The attendees at the gallery showing were members of the PanU Artists' Collective, students, Professor Vitebskin, members of the Panschin art establishment, and their bored relatives.

She laughed suddenly. Of course! Not one of them were connected in any way to mining, other than Kip McGrant's tentative connection to Chung/Banerjee. Not one of them read anything out of a newspaper or magazine other than the society pages and the arts sections. Mr. Jones must have decided he'd be safe enough, and he had been correct.

That led to another conclusion. Perhaps Mr. Jones could do something to keep both Mr. Burgess and the McGrant family away as he implied. As long as he was sleeping under her roof, Mr. Jones wanted quiet anonymity, and he might be powerful enough to make that happen.

Veronica felt suddenly relieved. She didn't know who or what Airik Jones was, but for now, she could use him to keep her family safe. She would be realistic, as Shelby was being with Malcolm Cobb. As long as he was around, Mr. Jones gave her breathing room to think of something.

She stood and turned around and around, looking over her tiny domain. Knowing that auntie Neza was in good hands, that Shelby was safely on PanU's campus, meant she could focus on her current crop of vegetables. Their sale to the Dappled Yak would earn money she might need when the McGrant family's lawyers came calling after Airik Jones disappeared back into whatever life he had that required a bodyguard. Or if Mr. Burgess showed up to kick them out. Extra money would let the Bradwell sisters disappear into the tunnels where he'd never find them.

It didn't take Carmine long to realize that Neza Molony knew a good percentage of the residents of Dome Two. They all cautiously approached them and demanded to know of Neza who he was and what he was doing out and about with her. She smiled and made conversation and told everyone he was a distant relative from Barsoom, here in Panschin for the Biennial Mining Conference. Since she was relaxed and at ease, the residents of Dome Two relaxed as well, although more than one person very quietly informed Carmine that they would stop by on occasion to "visit" Neza, leaving a strong implication that they expected to see her alive.

It had not occurred to him that a Dome in Panschin resembled a village in Shelleen. If his elderly aunt took in a visitor from outside, it would be the talk of the village within a day and the rest of Shelleen with a few days. Dome Two, despite its alien nature and oddly dressed and oddly speaking population, behaved in the same manner. He was becoming fond of the odd Bradwell family and didn't want them to suffer harm. The residents of Dome Two, like the residents of the villages of Shelleen, looked out for one another. It was reassuring.

As they neared the small business district, Mrs. Grisson appeared, demanded an introduction, and attached herself to them. She was loaded with questions and had, for Carmine, disquietingly sharp eyes. He didn't think she bought the story of distant relatives, but she didn't question it either. It was almost as though that kind of story was expected to be told even when both tellers and hearers knew the truth was something else altogether.

That was different from Shelleen. He would have to figure out the motivation to lie on a subject that could be so easily uncovered.

As they neared the police substation, Carmine said, "I'll need to stop here for a bit. Got a question for the desk sergeant."

"Do you now," Neza said with a raised eyebrow. "I've got to speak with the laundry service. I can be back in about twenty minutes. Will that be enough time?"

"Mrs. Grisson going to stay with you, Miss Molony? If so, I'd be obliged. Otherwise, I'll stay with you."

Mrs. Grisson exchanged glances with Neza. "Sure will, Mr. Carmine *Jones*," she answered, emphasizing his last name as if she didn't believe it was Jones and wanted to be sure he knew it without her having to ask rude questions about why he was lying. "You take your time and I'll get Neza back here safe and sound."

Carmine stopped at the base of the sandstone stairs leading up to the police substation and watched them walk off, heads together and speaking rapidly. Miss Molony was, if he was any judge of old ladies, telling Mrs. Grisson everything that had occurred since they had last spoken, along with her opinions on the subject, and extrapolating what would happen between now and their next meeting.

He took a considering look at the substation. Like the White Elephant, it was pristine. The white stone walls reflected every bit of the watery sunshine the dome allowed. In better light, the building would sparkle. The building next door was even grander, decorated with a host of beautifully carved, life-size statues. He wondered again why the Panschin train station had been so filthy, caked with terraformers wherever anyone didn't walk or put their hands. It was so strange how some public buildings would be carefully maintained whereas other public places were left to wrack and ruin. That would never happen in Shelleen. The family wouldn't stand for it.

He marched up the steps and entered the broad entryway, designed to overawe visitors and impress upon them the importance of law and order. Like the White Elephant's atrium, the vast lobby had no roof; it was open to the dome high above, ringed at every floor with balconies crowded with desks piled with paper. The once grand space no longer awed visitors since the needs of daily policing filled the lobby with overflow benches to hold an assortment of people, all of whom needed to be stashed while waiting to be seen. The noise of arguing and the odor of bodies, accompanied by the reek of Panschin's weird algae-based diet, filled the air.

As Carmine stood there, allowing his eyes to adjust to what he was seeing, quiet fell around him. This was a normal occurrence for Carmine so he ignored it. The desk sergeant did not.

"Hey! You there, big man. Whaddayawant?"

Carmine turned, and realized he was being called by a gentleman of the law, presiding behind a tall desk. The sergeant's dark-blue uniform was covered with golden stripes that gleamed in the light with his every movement. There were stripes for rank, stripes for longevity, stripes that seemed to indicate specialized skills, and stripes that filled no function that Carmine could decipher, other than they meant something in Panschin.

"Yes, sir," Carmine said and walked through the throng, parting before him like clouds driven apart by the wind, to the high, polished bamboo desk. "I'm Carmine Jones, and I'm staying at the White Elephant."

"Ah," the desk sergeant replied. "Distant relatives of Miss Molony and her nieces, or so I've been told."

"Yes, sir, that's true," Carmine lied. "We're here from Barsoom for the mining conference." Word had gotten around fast, just like it would have in Shelleen.

"I'm glad to hear the ladies won't be alone. Why are you here?"

Carmine correctly interpreted the question as asking why he wasn't back at the White Elephant. "I was wondering about the thug who came by the gallery showing," he said. Then he dropped his voice so only the sergeant could hear, "See, I got briefed on what I might see in Panschin. I was told about a group called 'Blue Sun.'"

The desk sergeant leaned forward, suddenly much more interested.

"What do you know about them?"

"They run a lot of criminal-type stuff in Panschin," Carmine said earnestly. "See, here's the thing I don't know. I was told that if a man belonged to Blue Sun, he'd have their mark on him, a blue circle. I was told it could be seen if you knew what to look for. I don't know what to look for and would like to find out."

"You think this man might have been with Blue Sun?" the desk sergeant asked, his face very intent.

"Sir, I do not know. I did not get a good look at him or his boss."

"And why not?"

Carmine grinned suddenly. "Maybe they was avoiding me. People do that sometimes."

The desk sergeant grinned back. "Yes, I suppose that could happen. I'm guessing you saw Miss Shelby's drawing. Good likeness?"

"Yes sir, very good from what little I saw of the thug."

"Blue Sun men always have a solid blue circle tattooed where it can be seen, even when the man is fully dressed. It doesn't have to be large and it doesn't have to be obvious," the desk sergeant said. "You won't see a blue circle in the middle of someone's forehead. But you will see one. Think hard about what you saw."

"It'd be helpful if I could see an example," Carmine said. "I'm not sure of what I saw. But that thug, he wanted Miss Bradwell's house in the worst way. Didn't make no sense to me, what with empty houses all around the White Elephant falling apart and open to squatters. Maybe he thought there was something valuable stashed there?"

The desk sergeant sat back and thought about Simon Bradwell. No one had ever discovered where all the money he had stolen went. Was it possible some of those ill-gotten gains were hidden somewhere in the house? If someone thought loot was stashed there, it might explain the sudden interest in the White Elephant. Knowing the household's poverty, he hadn't considered that possibility and he should have.

He slapped his hand on the desk bell, making it ring loudly. A moment later, one of his young runners came trotting up.

The uniformed lad saluted and said, "Reporting for duty, sir."

"Run down to the Broken Pickaxe and tell Hurkle, he'll be behind the bar, I want him and I want him five minutes ago," the desk sergeant said. "If he gives you any lip, tell him he earned himself a raid. Now scat."

"On it, sir," the lad replied and ran for the front door and into the watery sunlight of the Dome.

"The Broken Pickaxe, sir?" Carmine asked.

"One of our local bars, and you can call me sergeant. My parents were married."

Carmine grinned again. "Okay, sergeant. I'm Carmine and not Mr. Jones. That's my boss."

"Aha, he's working for Mr. Jones," the sergeant thought. "Carmine's not Neza Molony's relative then, but claiming to be to save trouble with the bank if they ever find out her niece Veronica's renting out rooms."

"Hurkle's one of Blue Sun, or he used to be," the desk sergeant said. "So he claims."

"Didn't think groups like that ever let anyone leave, not alive anyway," Carmine said.

"You're a bright lad," the sergeant said. "They don't. Have a seat. Hurkle won't be long if he knows what's good for him."

As promised, it didn't take long for Hurkle to show up. He was a wiry, older man with thinning hair, and despite his thickening waist, he moved like the middleweight prizefighter he had once been. Carmine guessed he was about Neza Molony's age.

He strutted up to the tall desk and peered up at the representative of Panschin presiding behind it.

"This better be important, sergeant. I got customers waiting."

"At this time of day?" the sergeant scoffed.

"I got my regulars and you know it. Shift workers, and it's the end of their day even if it's not the end of yourn."

"Miss Molony's got visitors from Barsoom, here for the Biennial Mining Conference. This here's Carmine. He's got a question for you."

Hurkle and Carmine gave each other a careful looking-over, filing away little details like stance, ability to move quickly, broken noses, and heavily scarred knuckles against a possible future meeting that was less friendly.

"Yeah? Whaddayawant."

"I need to know what Blue Sun's tattoo looks like, Mr. Hurkle," Carmine replied. "That man threatening Miss Bradwell got me worried."

"You think he's Blue Sun?" Hurkle asked, his face stony.

"I do not know one way or the other," Carmine said. "I did not get a good look at him, and in case he comes back, I'd like to know what I'm dealing with."

"Show him, Hurkle, and quit wasting my time and yours," the desk sergeant said wearily.

Hurkle sniffed audibly, then turned his head to the side and showed off the right side of his thick neck. There, just below his cauliflower ear, was a faded blue circle, about the size of a large thumbnail. It wasn't especially showy against his dull, olive green skin, looking more like a shadow if you didn't know what it was.

Carmine peered at it closely. "This little blue circle could be anywhere?"

"Anywhere it shows," the sergeant said. "But it has to show, even when the man is fully dressed. Doesn't have to be obvious, just there."

"Happy now? I'm not with them no more and you know it, sergeant," Hurkle said. "And why, sergeant, are you putting me out for some out-of-towner?"

Carmine answered swiftly, to forestall the desk sergeant. "Because the only reason I can see for someone wanting that house when other houses are going begging is because there's something valuable hidden in it, like big bags of money. That kind of thing draws crooks and Blue Sun, so I am told, are a gang of crooks."

Hurkle gave him a disdainful look. "We are a social organization."

"Sure you are," the sergeant said. "But this matter concerns me. I couldn't understand why anyone would want that house. But Carmine is right. Would any of your former associates be interested in the White Elephant if Simon Bradwell hid bags of money in it?"

"They'd be interested. Who wouldn't be interested in big bags of money? But those ladies are as poor as mine mice and everyone in Dome Two knows it. Blue Sun is a social organization, and we'd do our best to help out the ladies, like we would any needy household," Hurkle said piously. "You know we hand out charity and take care of our own. We don't rob old ladies and their nieces."

"You help out Miss Molony and Miss Bradwell?" Carmine asked.

"I buy Miss Veronica's radishes when the Dappled Yak don't," Hurkle said. "Just like I buy Helga Grisson's eggs for the bar. Pickles them nice, she does."

"Hurkle," the desk sergeant said. "If you hear anything, I need to know. And spread the word with your former associates. Someone from outside of Panschin might be causing trouble, and I'm sure they don't want to get blamed."

Hurkle's face hardened. "No worries on that score, sergeant. Now if you're done showing off my old tats, I got customers waiting."

"Thank you, Mr. Hurkle, for taking time out of your day to help me," Carmine said. "If I got time later on, I'll stop by for a pint and a chat. So's I know who not to worry over."

"Just Hurkle," the bartender replied. "I like Miss Veronica, and I like Miss Molony more. It's not Blue Sun threatening them, and if it is, I *will* know the reason why." He spun on his heel and stalked out the door.

As Hurkle made his way through the crowded lobby, Carmine watched carefully. As he had suspected they might, people nodded politely and got out of the old man's way as if he were something more than just another elderly bartender.

"Happy?" the sergeant asked.

"Yes, sergeant, I am. And just so you know, since I'm guessing everyone in the dome will stop by to tell you, when I'm not with my boss, I'll be walking around the neighborhood," Carmine said. "Seeing what I can see."

Carmine walked out through the lobby, the crowd once again parting before him, while the desk sergeant thought hard. Carmine Jones' suggestion could be the reason why the ladies were being harassed. But who was his boss that he needed an employee like that one? He was hired muscle, if the desk sergeant was any judge, and very few mining executives needed hired muscle.

Dean slipped out of his flat in Dome Six far too early that morning. It was becoming increasingly urgent he speak to Veronica and it was becoming equally urgent that he catch her alone. Unfortunately, the early hour filled the transtubes to Dome Two with hordes of both the unwashed and the uncouth. None of them made room as they should for a gentleman; indeed, they didn't acknowledge his superior presence at all. It was all very lowering but Dean could no longer afford to take the upper-level tram.

By the time he reached Oleander Lane in Dome Two, he was seething with resentment against his situation and against Veronica for being so difficult. What had happened to the sweet, pliant, and so very agreeable Dome Six princess he had married?

The dome was dimly lit at dawn and the street still empty of early-morning traffic. He crouched behind a planter spilling over with marigolds, trying hard to keep from sneezing from their pollen-laden closeness. He knew Veronica loved flowers and couldn't understand why she no longer grew them in the White Elephant's tiny garden. She had more than enough space. When they had first married and moved into the White Elephant, she had filled most of the beds with all kinds of flowers. Those beds now were a wilderness of random green plants that didn't fulfill any function. It was irritating how she no longer cared when she used to make such a fuss over those useless flowers. Would it be worth stealing some from the planter as a peace offering?

As the street filled with pedestrians, Dean retreated to the abandoned house across the street from the White Elephant. He sat behind the wall, partly concealed by a statue so overgrown with terraformers it could have been a tall, narrow shrub. He had carefully dressed for the occasion, choosing his oldest, drabbest clothes to avoid notice and so far, it seemed to be working. The thought struck him that this might be why he had not gotten any respect on the transtube, actually having to argue over receiving a seat he had paid for. It just went to show the lower classes couldn't recognize their betters, going with superficial cues such as clothing instead of noticing topnotch breeding and quality manners.

He waited, bored and irritated, and waited some more, on edge as people arrived at the White Elephant and then gratified when they finally left. Shelby, that supposed prude, left holding hands with a man but not the one she had arrived with the night before. Clearly, she wasn't the innocent young miss she claimed to be. Worryingly, today's man was as large as the brutish miner she'd brought home the night before although much better dressed. Florence had her boyfriend hanging about as did Lulu, that vicious bitch. Then another man left, that supposed distant relative from Barsoom although Dean couldn't get a clear look at him as too many people were blocking his view, and at last, Neza left with still another hulking brute. What exactly was his former wife doing in that house, now that he was no longer there to keep an eye on things?

She stood by the garden wall, pensively watching her aunt Neza leave with that brute and then, to Dean's immense relief, his former wife didn't go back inside. Instead she got to work in the garden beds, on her hands and knees like the peasant she had become. His time to persuade Veronica had come at last. She was alone and whoever her fool houseguest was, he was gone, along with everyone else.

ean took another careful look around to make sure Veronica was alone in the White Elephant's tiny side garden and then waited while she settled in, concentrating on getting her hands filthy. He stood, dusted himself clean of terraformers, then casually walked across the street like he belonged there and indeed he did. The few passersby who nodded to him recognized him as Veronica's former husband and a still frequent and accepted visitor into her home.

A rickshaw hauler went so far as to say, "Mr. Kangjuon, I know you're not married to Miss Veronica no more, but I want you to know, we're keeping an eye out for her safety. That goon won't show up around here again with everyone in the dome watching out for him."

Dean forced a gracious smile. "Thank you. I know Veronica appreciates your concern and so do I."

He opened the unoiled gate carefully, wincing as it screeched. Why didn't Veronica maintain it anymore? Why didn't Neza say something? He was afraid its shriek would alert her, so he quickstepped down the path to where she was working on a bed before she could react. It was disgusting how she dug her hands into the soil between those weeds, wrenching apart lumps of slime and working them into the dirt.

She used to stroke him all over with those hands.

Veronica looked up at the gate's scream, suddenly alert, and then Dean came striding around the path right towards her. His mouth was open, ready with new lies and she didn't want to hear any of them.

She leapt to her feet and said, "Dean, get off my property right now or I'll call the police."

Dean frowned and then pasted a smile on his face. "Ronnie, sweetheart, I know we got off on the wrong foot last night, but I really—"

"I mean it, Dean," Veronica snarled. "I will never speak to you again. I will never help you again. I will never do anything for you again, no matter what it is. You gave me one of the worst days of my life and then you tried to turn my little sister into your whore so you could pimp her out to your friends! Shelby told me everything *so get OUT!*" Her voice rose with every word until she was screaming.

Upstairs, Airik heard her through the open window. He looked up from dictating to Upton about Chung/Banerjee's patented respirators. He dropped the papers on the table, stopped dictating in mid-sentence to Upton, and stepped to the open window to see what was happening to Veronica Bradwell.

Malcolm arrived at the bank with a spring in his step and a heart filled with joy. She saw him. He was no longer an invisible man of glass. His beautiful Dome Two princess saw him and, better, she wanted to see more of him. Shelby didn't care he was a scholarship boy, and she didn't sneer at his family. She cared enough about his well-being to worry over what being seen with the daughter of Simon Bradwell would do to him. Shelby cared, and he was going to do his damnedest to save her from Burgess.

The thug's whereabouts was worrisome and while he was making discreet inquiries, the fact remained the police would do a better job of finding him. His insistence on them doing their job along with Mr. Wong's demands should spur them to greater efforts. But they could not do anything about Burgess and his threats to evict her. He could.

Malcolm had no doubt Burgess would falsify records to get the Bradwells thrown out. It was up to him to make sure Burgess couldn't. And there was his other project, the one he had been working on for months. He was convinced Burgess was dirty, or at least grossly incompetent. There was something there, revealed by the mysterious holes in the Second National Bank of Panschin's records. Documents lacking a page, with amended text, heavily redacted, stained into unreadability, or missing entirely, told him as much.

But why? Burgess had — if not the respect of his peers — power, connections and wealth. Yet there had been something in his expression when he found out who was living in the White Elephant during the gallery showing. He had looked, if just for a moment, afraid. Perhaps his success had not been enough for him. Perhaps, like Simon Bradwell, he wanted more.

Malcolm had a sudden flash of insight into Mr. Burgess's character. Like Malcolm, he wanted more than what he had been granted at birth.

The difference was *he* didn't destroy other people's lives to get what he wanted. Burgess, like Simon Bradwell, not only didn't care what he did to the lives of others; he also took pleasure in trampling them.

There was something there. He could feel it. The reason *why* Burgess had reacted so strongly to discovering Veronica Bradwell lived in the White Elephant niggled at him. Burgess had not known this fact. How could he have? The lease was held by Neza Molony. She had not, Malcolm was unsure on the point but he believed it to be true, gone out much in Panschin society. She had never married and apparently lived a quiet life in the formerly fashionable Dome Two. Her grandparents had signed that lease when Dome Two was new and *the* place to live in Panschin. Then Simon Bradwell's schemes had imploded, and she had taken in her great-nieces to live with her in her empty mansion.

Why did Burgess care so much? The Bradwell sisters had virtually nothing left to their names and Neza Molony didn't have much more. There was nothing Burgess could seize that had not already been stripped from them by their social ruin, the string of lawsuits, and the loss of every single asset, other than an obscure relative who had given them sanctuary after Simon Bradwell's schemes came crashing down on them all.

Malcolm stopped dead by the massive front door to the once-grand building housing the Second National Bank of Panschin, his hand still on the polished brass handle. He knew. He had to prove it, but he knew.

Sajag Burgess had known Simon Bradwell.

Everyone at that level either knew each other or had friends and business partners in common. Maybe, they had known each other better than that. Maybe, they had worked together to swindle the citizens of Panschin. Or, perhaps, Burgess had been so incompetent that he had not recognized Simon Bradwell's schemes for what they were. If he had not done his due diligence, by extension the Second National Bank of Panschin would still be at fault, even after the passage of time. The Bank would be sued and would punish Burgess for raining down trouble upon it. In addition, Burgess himself would be personally liable and a ripe target for prosecution from those families whose fury at Simon Bradwell would never fade. Burgess was a wealthy man from a wealthy family. The lawsuits wouldn't stop until he was as destitute as the Bradwell sisters, and perhaps not even then.

It was hard to say which option was true. Burgess was a slimy sack of shit. He treated everyone below him socially as dross under his shoes and toadied to everyone higher up. Was he a crook? Or was he incompetent? Either way, he was afraid of the daughters of Simon Bradwell and what they might reveal.

Malcolm walked through the shabby lobby of the Second National Bank of Panschin towards his office, deep in thought.

"Nice of you to finally show up at work, Cobb," Mr. Wong said. "My office, now."

He had been laying in wait instead of remaining in his own office, where, Malcolm was sure, he normally did nothing but rearrange his pencils.

Malcolm concealed a growl. He had a far more important task ahead of him than listening to a lecture about dragging Shelby and the crème of Panschin's youth into the Steelio warren, particularly when those students, despite all their protests of solidarity, wanted nothing to do with actually setting foot into the deepdown.

"Yes, sir."

Once inside Mr. Wong's faded office, with the door firmly shut against the curious eyes of the tellers, Malcolm said, "As promised, I took good care of Miss Bradwell."

"Oh, I knew that," Mr. Wong said dismissively. "One of our junior tellers, Doris, boards with Mrs. Grisson and she already told me."

"Oh."

"Cobb." Mr. Wong sat back in his big chair with a slight smile. "The filing cabinets in the second subbasement need scrubbing, and you're just the man for the job."

Malcolm sucked in his breath and clenched his fists, not caring that Mr. Wong could see them. Cabinets that hadn't been looked at in over a century, and he was to scrape them clean of terraformers?

"Oh? May I ask why when we have janitors for that job?" he asked through gritted teeth.

Mr. Wong took his time answering, picking up and putting down one pencil after another across the pristine blotting paper on his desk, until each had been properly aligned with its fellows and Malcolm was seething, fully aware of his place in the hierarchy.

"You like to think you know things, Cobb," Mr. Wong said at last. "Did you know that this branch of Second National used to be the premier branch in our bank?"

"I was aware of that." Damn you, Malcolm thought. A useless hack looking for make-work to remind me who's the boss. I know Burgess has it in for you but do you have to punish me too?

"Did you know that, to ensure the safety and completeness of Second National's recordkeeping, a copy of every document generated within Second National, no matter how minor, is required to be filed here in our branch? As you might imagine, we have multiple subbasements jammed with filing cabinets, all carefully arranged in order by date and subject. Most of the senior executives do not know that little fact, although their secretaries do."

Malcolm stared at Mr. Wong. He was at a complete loss for words.

"Nothing to say, Cobb? That's not like you."

"Every document, Mr. Wong?" Malcolm said, his heart racing. His fingers loosened themselves from fists and fanned of their own accord.

"Every. Document. Did it never occur to you to wonder why we have so large a staff? That's sloppy thinking on your part, Cobb. Those files are being continuously updated and all that filing has to be done by someone." Mr. Wong gazed steadily at Malcolm; his eyes bright with intelligence instead of their usual dull haze.

Malcolm suddenly realized Mr. Wong was giving him the keys to a treasure trove of data; data that would allow him to prove Burgess was either a crook or an incompetent sack of slime. Down there, forgotten by everyone, was the information he needed to rescue Shelby and her sister.

"Thank you, Mr. Wong," Malcolm said gratefully. "I'll get right on it."

"The filing cabinets are labeled, and you *could* start cleaning wherever you choose. However, *I* demand you begin with the following cabinets," Mr. Wong said. He handed a sheet of paper to Malcolm covered with neat columns of his immaculate handwriting. "They are, I must say, the filthiest."

Malcolm read the dates, then met Mr. Wong's eyes, filled with reasons his boss could not say aloud. "Yes, sir," he said respectfully and this time, he meant it.

"Hurry," Mr. Wong said and pointed to the door.

Airik leaned out the upstairs window, trying to spot Veronica. He didn't see her and realized she had to be in the smaller side garden. He wasn't sure he recognized Dean Kangjuon's voice, then decided he had and he needed to get downstairs right away.

"Upton," he called on his way to the door. "Keep working."

His secretary stared after him, mouth open and his fingers unmoving on the typewriter's keys. What on Mars was wrong with Airik? He rarely paid attention to his surroundings when he was dictating a report and he certainly never stopped in mid-sentence. Upton got up and ran to the window. Straining his ears, he clearly heard Veronica telling someone to go away and that person refusing. Not seeing anyone from the window, he left the room and headed to the window at the end of the hallway, figuring it would oversee the side garden and it did.

The daimyo of Shelleen tore down the hallway. He was furious. Miss Bradwell, his Miss Bradwell, was being harassed again. Her worthless former husband had returned, despite being told in no uncertain terms to stay the hell away.

He turned the corner at the landing and trotted down the stairs several at a time. At the bottom, he raced for the front door rather than try to find his way through the maze of rooms to that side of the house.

"Ronnie! Wait, please, you don't understand!" Dean said, backing away from his no longer sweet and compliant ex-wife. She had turned into an armed harridan, menacing him with some sort of gardening tool with long claws that he knew he did not want to get close to.

Veronica swung the clawed hand cultivator at Dean. A large bird of prey would have envied those metal talons. She'd never used it on anything but turning over soil in a garden bed, but at that moment, she wanted to rake it across her ex-husband's face and chest, tearing his flesh down to the bone.

Upton found the window, opened it, and stuck his head through out. Below, he saw Miss Bradwell with a man. Not big enough to be the thug. Probably her idiot former husband, although Upton hadn't paid much attention to him. She appeared to have a tool in her hand, and she was swinging it at him. It looked like she was trying to bury it in his chest.

This looked promising. Then he broke into a grin. From around the corner of the White Elephant, he saw Airik, who was striding purposefully toward them.

Upton crossed his arms on the window sill and made himself comfortable. This looked *very* promising.

"I do understand!" Veronica swung the cultivator again and missed. "Get the hellation out of my garden!"

"If you don't help me, I'll lose everything, Ronnie."

"So? Join the crowd!"

"This is your fault!" Dean roared. "I wouldn't be in this fix if it weren't for you. You have to help me, you worthless bitch! You ruined me!"

"*What*? Get out!" Veronica screamed back. Her ears rang and a red haze descended over her eyes. She slashed at him with the hand cultivator and he stepped back, right into Airik Jones who had come racing around the building.

Airik didn't hesitate.

He drove his fist into the back of Dean's neck, snapping his head back and then forward. Dean went limp from pain and shock and staggered towards Veronica, who scrambled away. Airik grabbed Dean roughly by his collar, reached between his legs and grabbed him by the loose cloth, and hoisted him like a sack of potatoes. He strode to the low side wall of the ruined mansion next door and tossed Veronica's former husband over the wall and into the thick carpet of terraformers blanketing the garden of the ruin next door. The terraformers burst upwards in a cloud of gray and brown and gold bits, showering the surrounding area with debris and filling the air with dusty spores.

Veronica watched in shock. "You really can throw someone over a wall," she sputtered.

"It's a low wall," Airik said. "Plus, Kangjuon stopped fighting once I sucker-punched him." He panted, fighting to get his breathing under control. Adrenaline coursed through his veins, and he was having some trouble getting his heart rate back down. He was furious with Dean, as well as startled at his own quick and vicious response. Hundreds of hours of tedious exercises and boring training had paid off. He hadn't thought at all over what to do. He had just done it.

He looked at his fist curiously, then stretched out his fingers. His knuckles hurt and probably would for some time. He hunted regularly in Shelleen, but he had never experienced this surge of adrenaline-soaked rage, just as he didn't experience the same fury when practicing his self-defense.

"That should be bad, sucker-punching someone," Veronica said slowly. She tried to muster sympathy for her former husband, but her fear and nausea prevented her. "But I don't think I care."

"You shouldn't, Miss Bradwell. Kangjuon would have hurt you." Airik thought again of how Kangjuon had gripped Veronica's arm at the gallery showing, not wanting to let her go. Her former husband kept coming back, wanting something from her. She had nothing of material value left other than herself, yet he returned. That thought filled him with jealous fury.

Veronica looked at her hand cultivator. Her heart was still racing, and she had to take a steadying breath. She could have ripped Dean open with it. She had wanted to hurt him, a very unsettling thought. She waved it at Airik. Her eyes were very wide and her breathing was unsteady. "Maybe not."

Airik studied her hand cultivator. Veronica's hand was shaking badly, making the talons flash in the sun. The metal claws were discolored by bits of terraformers clinging to them.

"You would have had to keep him from taking the cultivator from you and using it against you. Kangjuon would have been strong enough to do that, and I think, angry enough." As he said it, Airik knew he was correct. Dean would have plunged the cultivator into Veronica's body, tearing at her, ripping her open, injuring her severely, possibly even killing her. He would have killed Dean for that, despite being in Panschin where he did not enjoy the power he held in Shelleen.

He stopped and stared at Veronica, who was swaying slightly from the shocking violence.

"I am very glad I came down as fast as I did. He would have hurt you."

Veronica sat down suddenly onto the gravel path. Her legs no longer wanted to support her. "Yes, you're right. Dean would have," she said wonderingly. "I don't know what's wrong with him."

Airik knelt by her side and placed his hand on her back.

She looked over at the stacked stone wall, high enough to easily conceal Dean's body from her sitting position. Was he dead? Please no, Veronica thought and closed her eyes in pain. His family will destroy me.

To her immense relief, she heard Dean groan, followed by a series of hacking coughs.

Dean's head appeared over the top of the wall. His hair and face were caked with terraformers.

Airik stiffened and stood.

"Leave, Mr. Kangjuon," he called out, "and do not come back."

Dean braced himself against a statue so overgrown with terraformers it had turned into a pillar of moss. He was smeared from head to foot with green and brown moss. He groaned and swore with every movement as he struggled to stand. Green and gold and brown motes swirled around him. Blood ran from his nose, leaving scarlet trickles across his face, his body, and onto the terraformers at his feet.

"I was afraid he was dead," Veronica said to Airik. She turned away from Dean, so she would not ever have to look at him again.

"The terraformers were thick enough to break his fall," Airik said, taking refuge in analytical thought. "I would surmise none of his bones were broken, or he would be making far more noise. Possibly a cracked rib although I believe he would be breathing with more difficulty if that were true."

"You could have cracked my skull open," Dean snarled. Some of his fight returned since he had a wall between him and his former wife's supposed houseguest. He winced and clutched the back of his head. The goose egg was developing fast. He could see stars mixed in with the floating spores and his head rang. His body ached all over; the knee-high carpet of terraformers hadn't been deep enough to completely cushion his fall.

"I didn't hit you that hard," Airik said. "If you cannot leave under your own power, I will summon the police and have them remove you for trespassing."

"I am going," Dean said to the cloud of spores dancing around him. He then glared at Veronica's back. "You will be sorry for this."

"I am not in the least bit sorry, and I will never speak to you again, Dean," Veronica replied, her back still turned to her ex-husband. With Airik's assistance, she struggled to her feet. She did not so much as glance at Dean and walked slowly down the path, back inside the safety of the White Elephant.

Airik stayed behind, watching Dean stagger across the overgrown garden of the ruin next door to its own front gate. He leaned for a moment, panting, and then opened the gate, dusted himself cleaner, and stumbled down the street clutching his head.

Only when he was out of sight did Airik go inside the White Elephant to find Veronica.

Upton gaped in open-mouthed shock from his vantage point at the second-floor window at the end of the hallway. Airik, who normally killed things by analyzing them until they died of boredom, hadn't hesitated. Reserved, tedious, awkward Airik had behaved like a savage from the Wild Side. He watched Airik follow Miss Bradwell around the side of the White Elephant and realized he didn't want to be caught out of place and scurried back into the room they were using as an office.

As his heart rate returned to normal, Upton realized again why the senior family had chosen Airik to be the daimyo. It wasn't his inspiring leadership and charisma. It wasn't his intelligence or his work ethic. It wasn't even his comprehensive plan to keep the Martian government out of Shelleen while developing the Red Mercury lode. Somehow, they had recognized that Airik could be utterly ruthless when he needed to be, as a daimyo had to be to succeed.

The secretary thought again of Howard Shelleen and his agonized screams in the stone courtyard, the horrible shrieks reverberating against the manor house and searing themselves into everyone's memory forever. Airik had a senior and important member of the family flogged in front of the peasants for damaging the demesne. What would Airik do to someone who wasn't a relative?

Maybe it was time he got back to work.

Upton looked over the report Airik had abandoned to rescue Veronica Bradwell. What would Airik want done next? Was there something he could do to would remind Airik that his secretary was a valued and productive member of the family? He coughed, then coughed again and launched into a sneezing fit. Airik throwing that buffoon into the blanket of terraformers in the yard next door had released a huge cloud of spores. They were drifting into every open window and would take hours to resettle. There was no breeze in the dome to safely disperse them far away.

When he was able to stop sneezing and hacking, Upton eyed the containers of tea Lulu had packed for him at Airik's direction. He had been feeling much better, despite the occasional bout of dizziness, and had planned to discreetly pour that nasty brew down a drain. Then he felt another attack rising at the back of his throat and reached for the container. He tried hard not to taste it and ignored the unpleasant floating chunks of herbs tickling his gullet on their way down.

After he swallowed it all, Upton sat back down, picked up the report, and began typing Airik's scattered notes. The tedious detail work was welcome as it let him block out just how strong, how decisive, Airik had been. How ruthless. And all, Upton thought wonderingly, in the service of some destitute nobody from Panschin.

Veronica mechanically walked into the White Elephant, through the atrium, down the hallways, and into the kitchen where she made herself tea, one step after the other, one scoop of the precious leaves into the strainer, waiting for the water to boil while she stared at the kitten calendar, and then slowly poured the scalding water over the leaves and let the comforting smell of mint fill her nose and block out the smell of coppery blood and fear and rotten moss.

She sat at the table, breathing in the scent of the mint, letting it fill her, sooth her, and allowing her to think again.

What was wrong with Dean? He had gone insane. Mr. Jones was right. Dean would have hurt her. Something was very wrong with her former husband. She was very lucky Mr. Jones had been there and even more fortunate that Mr. Jones had been willing to help her.

Why had he helped her? He didn't seem to expect anything from her. Mr. Jones had never been less than respectful; he was the model of a gentleman. He didn't, she thought, grasp the full ramifications of her being Simon Bradwell's daughter. If word got out, his business dealings would suffer. If he had, he would have treated her like the pariah the rest of Panschin society thought her to be. He would have left by now. It had to be, Veronica decided, that Mr. Jones needed a quiet stay for reasons of his own and he aimed to get it. If he had to keep Dean outside the White Elephant so he could get work done, he would. Her little family would be safe, at least until Mr. Jones left Panschin and returned to Barsoom. Or until someone told him whose nest of cave-vipers he was sleeping in.

What work did he need to do that required such privacy and a bodyguard?

"Miss Bradwell?"

Veronica started and gasped. Her heart raced again. She hadn't known she had closed her eyes, letting Mr. Jones slip into the room unawares. He was a paying guest and in the shabby kitchen of the White Elephant, rather than the far more presentable dining room.

She found her voice. "Forgive me. Let me bring you some tea to the dining room where you can be comfortable."

"I am quite fine, Miss Bradwell," Mr. Jones said. "I am concerned about you."

How could she have ever believed him to be average in appearance? There was nothing average about Airik Jones.

"I—," she sighed. "I don't know what to say other than to thank you again for helping me." Veronica looked up at Mr. Jones, standing next to her, meeting his concerned eyes.

Airik stared down into Veronica's dark, luminous eyes, wanting to fall into them like into a pool of cool water on a sultry summer day.

"It needed to be done," he said and wanted to wince again. Whenever he was around Veronica — such a beautiful name — every word out of his mouth sounded banal. Upton would have known what to say. His secretary always knew what to say to a lovely woman.

"Yes, it did," she said. She broke away from his face and stared at her own reflection in the polished table. "I don't know what's wrong with Dean. He was never, ever this way when we were married. He hated arguing. But lately, I just don't know." She wiped her eyes suddenly, surprising them both with a spurt of unwanted tears.

"I'm glad you helped me and even gladder you didn't kill Dean. His family would destroy what was left of us."

Airik frowned. "But he attacked you. He had been making threats."

Veronica snorted at his incomprehension of the facts of life in Panschin. "None of that would matter to the Kangjuon family. Dean's their only child. There are no grandchildren and very few other relatives, other than the most distant of cousins. The line will die with him if he doesn't remarry and father sons."

"Ah. A sad and familiar story, but nonetheless," Airik said. "That does not give him license to harass you."

"It shouldn't," Veronica agreed. "Would you like some tea in the dining room?" Why did I ask him again, she wondered. What is wrong with me?

Airik thought quickly. Veronica wanted to give him tea. Her hands wrapped around her cup were still trembling, making the tea shiver and threaten to spill over the lip of the cup and scald her. She was quite likely still in shock from the experience. She needed to show her gratitude in a more tangible way than words. She needed to focus on something other than her former husband attacking her. He could let her do this for him. It would please her and settle her, and he could sit with her in the dining room as she grew calmer.

"Yes, some tea in the dining room would be fine," he replied and was rewarded with Veronica's nervous and relieved smile.

Upton laid the finished report on the table and began sorting through the rest of Airik's papers. Amid the documents bearing the names of mining companies he uncovered a sheaf of papers that made him pause. He recognized Elliot's painfully precise handwriting and he picked up the document to see what secret project the valet had been doing for Airik.

The name 'Simon Bradwell' leaped out at him. Simon Bradwell? Was he a relation to the Bradwell sisters?

Upton began reading and then couldn't stop. They were staying with the daughters of a man who had done his best to ensure his name would be a byword for avarice and embezzlement for generations. Why on Mars were they still here if Airik knew? Did he dare say anything to Airik?

The secretary very carefully slid the document back into its place in the stack of reports. Did he dare say anything to anyone? Airik had chosen, for reasons known only to him, to remain at the White Elephant. He had to have understood that no one in Panschin would do business with him if they learned he was connected to Simon Bradwell's daughters.

He didn't know what to do. What would the senior members of the family say to this? Airik's furious face rose before his eyes. He could pretend he knew nothing, that's what he could do. It would be safer, at least for now. The Biennial Mining Conference would end, they would leave Panschin and return home to Shelleen. Perhaps, Upton thought hopefully, once Airik left this contaminated city of domes and spores, his sanity would return. Airik had to be insane. It was the only reasonable explanation for his behavior.

Another sudden wave of dizziness hit him. He sneezed violently, scattering the stack of documents he had held. When he finished snuffling and wiping, Upton began hastily reassembling the scattered papers. Airik had been clear which reports he needed for the day's scheduled meetings. Upton knew he didn't want to make any mistakes after seeing how Airik punished Veronica Bradwell's ex-husband.

Airik sipped the tea Veronica poured for him. He was relieved to see her hands had stopped trembling and her breathing had steadied. His own hands were steadier.

She sat next to him at the table, nibbling on a green cracker that smelled of yeast and moss. Probably something else grown in the food tanks of Panschin and processed into quasi-edibility, Airik decided. He didn't want to leave her alone and return to his work. He searched for a neutral topic to discuss and he couldn't think of any other than the weather, and there was no weather in Panschin.

He had not expected to miss the weather, the daily change of the wind and clouds, how the sun traveled across the sky, and how the stars filled each night. He missed rain, he missed being outside, he missed being part of the natural world. The domes kept the far north's climate at bay, but the residents lost as much as they gained. He missed the sun's movements and warmth and light. The White Elephant was well-designed to allow as much light inside as possible from what was available in the dome. Yet the house inside was never sunny and cheerful as the meanest peasant's cottage in Shelleen. It always felt like a heavily overcast day, gray and dismal.

He could not talk about the weather.

He watched her discreetly, how her hand kept going to the beads at her throat. Veronica had worn the same necklace, with its matching earbobs, since he had arrived. He still hadn't figured out what kind of stone the beads were carved from. Each bead was irregular in shape, a shiny, cloudy gray with bits of white and darker gray laced through it. Not one bead precisely matched its fellows. It was very unlike the jewelry styles he was familiar with.

This was something he could talk about. In his experience, many women liked to discuss jewelry, although Veronica Bradwell might not belong to that cohort since she didn't seem to own any, other than these odd cloudy beads.

Airik had always been fascinated by minerals but his own interests in crystalline structure and industrial usage didn't coincide with those of jewelry wearers. The subject had become increasingly awkward. He wanted to talk about the geologic processes whereby gems were formed and the potential marriage partners being foisted on him wanted to talk about how many diamonds he was willing to pay for. The avarice those young women displayed was off-putting in the extreme. Airik wasn't particularly imaginative and he knew it. Yet, it always seemed that when he brought up the subject of gemology, the woman (or her eager relatives) had credit signs flashing in their eyes.

He plunged in anyway. At the very least, he would learn what exceedingly rare stone her beads were made from.

"Miss Bradwell?"

"Yes?" Veronica looked up.

"I keep noticing your beads. I know something about gems, yet I don't recognize the variety of stone."

She smiled at him suddenly and the sun came out again, lighting up the dining room.

"I'm not surprised." Veronica fingered her necklace again, remembering. Her eyes were far away.

"I love jewelry. I just love it. So beautiful. So many kinds and types, sparkling gems by themselves and all the colors that gold comes in. I love owning and wearing jewelry, choosing something special to wear every day to match what I'm wearing and doing. They're wearable miniature works of art that I can touch and carry with me all day."

Airik's heart sank.

"This is an unusual stone?" he asked, trying not to think "gold-digger." He'd met so many of them and they had all said very similar things.

Veronica laughed, a gurgle like a brook skipping over smooth river stones on a bright, sunny day.

"They're not any kind of stone." She gazed across the table at him curiously. He looked so serious, as though what she said was of critical importance to him. "I bought them from a street vendor, before everything happened. They were so pretty. I thought they looked like the moons." She smiled again at nothing in particular, as though she was seeing something only she could see.

Airik waited, disconcerted. He hadn't known you could buy expensive jewelry from street vendors. The thought struck him. If the beads were valuable, why did she still have them? The Bradwell family was openly and obviously poor. Did she love her jewelry that much? The notion was disheartening.

"They're slag glass, that's what the old man told me. He salvaged the slag from the glassworks in Dome Four and turned the broken bits into beads."

"Slag glass?" He stared at her and at her beads. No wonder he hadn't recognized them as a gemstone. Slag glass was industrial waste, a byproduct left over at the end of a run.

"I thought they looked like the moons," Veronica said in a dreamy, wistful voice. "I saw them once. We're too far north in Panschin for them to go much above the horizon and, of course, you can't see them inside the domes at all. I had gone to a party at someone's summerhouse just before Dean and I got married. Then I saw these beads and I remembered that night, standing on the terrace and watching the stars come out and the moons racing each other."

"Our moons are unique," Airik said. "They come out during the day, too. Their rotation periods are very short and so you see them often."

Veronica chuckled softly. "If you live outside the domes, further south. Here, well, you don't see them. It looked like they were going to crash into each other."

"Yes, Phobos rotates in under eight hours while Deimos takes slightly more than a day, thus their orbits appear to frequently intersect." Airik wanted to kick himself. He was reciting a child's astronomy textbook. "They're actually made of carbonaceous chondrite; a sort of rubble that comprises most asteroids." Gods, but he wanted to kick himself harder. Now he sounded like a geology textbook. Maybe he should take lessons from Upton, despite the embarrassment of asking him. Upton always had something smooth to say.

To his intense relief, Veronica did not get up and walk away from him, radiating scorn.

"I didn't know that, about what they're made of. It sounds very unromantic."

"Asteroids are made from what made our solar system. The stuff of stars," Airik said.

She smiled at him and touched her necklace again, running her fingertips over the beads. "But not slag glass?"

"No, I would say not," Airik said.

"So my beads are not made of star stuff."

"I would not say that either," Airik said thoughtfully. "In the end, all of us are made of star stuff. Suns and their solar systems are made from what forms the galaxies. Matter is not created. Everything we are has existed since time began when the universe was formed. The shapes change but the essential nature does not. Silica becomes glass, but it remains, at heart, silica."

"You must think me very shallow," Veronica said pensively. "Dean thought I was being silly. Thinking that slag glass is beautiful or that it can resemble the moons of Mars."

"He was wrong and I would never think that," Airik said, equally pensive. "All kinds of things have beauty, even if it is not commonly recognized as such." He had always thought the layers of sedimentary rock, crumpled and heaving, to be beautiful. They said so much about eons of time and the slow, endlessly patient hand of nature. They spoke to their observer, if that person was willing to listen.

"This is your favorite necklace then?" he asked, not wanting to walk away.

Veronica chuckled; a sound threaded with sadness. "It's my only necklace. I had to sell everything else to pay bills."

She caught his expression. "Please, do *not* feel sorry for me. I don't. These beads are completely worthless, even the pawnshop wouldn't take them, and so I can keep them." She smiled again, her eyes once more far away. "When I touch them, I think of the moons of Mars and how, someday, I'll be able to see them again."

The gate squealed, and Veronica gasped and leapt to her feet, her heart racing again. Dean had come back, this time with Kangjuon lawyers, or lawyers sent by the McGrant family, or Mr. Burgess with the sheriff, come to evict them all.

"I will check, Miss Bradwell," Airik said firmly. "You've had a trying morning."

He marched to the front door and opened it for auntie Neza and Carmine, back from their errands.

However, Carmine's return meant he would have to attend to his own business dealings and leave Veronica. Veronica who could discover beauty where most people wouldn't, Veronica who did not wallow in misery despite what had happened to her, Veronica who sold jewelry she loved when it had to be done to save her family, Veronica with her limpid eyes and joyous smile, Veronica who accepted him as he was.

Veronica, who he was lying to, with every word he didn't say about his own background.

Veronica waited until after Airik Jones left for Dome Six to tell Neza what Shelby had admitted the previous night and what Dean had tried to do.

Neza said, "Dreadful. Just dreadful. I do not know where to start. Poor Shelby. Dean must have gone mad. He blamed you? But why?"

"I don't know," Veronica answered. "But he's not allowed back, ever."

"You never did anything to harm Dean."

"I know."

Neza stood up, painfully. Her joints were hurting worse than usual, and she suspected each day's new anxiety was having something to do with it. "I'd better go tell Mrs. Grisson to spread the word about Dean."

"No, wait," Veronica said quickly. "Dean won't come back, I'm sure of it. Wait until Shelby comes home with Florence and Lulu. Then we'll go to Mrs. Grisson's house."

Neza watched her niece carefully. "You don't want to leave anyone alone, do you."

"No, I don't," Veronica replied, trying very hard not to shiver and worry her aunt still more. "Thinking about it, Dean must have waited until everyone left, and he thought I was alone. He was watching the house."

"How bizarre," Neza said. "Dean never liked confrontations. Look how he backed down to his family over you rather than fight them. And he said he's ruined?"

"Yep, sure did," Veronica said. "He's Dean Kangjuon! He's his family's golden boy. He can do no wrong in anyone's eyes. He's got money, family, connections, good looks, status, reputation, everything he could want. Dean couldn't be ruined. He became one of Panschin's most eligible bachelors again the day we got divorced. I can't understand it at all, except that he's gone crazy."

Neza thought while Veronica got up and paced restlessly about the kitchen. If Dean wasn't going to come back, then now was the perfect time to speak with Mrs. Grisson. What Veronica wasn't saying, her aunt decided, was that *she* didn't want to be left in the house alone. And Mr. Jones had come to her rescue. That was interesting, too.

In the bank's basement archives, Malcolm Cobb hit paydirt in the second file drawer in the first cabinet he opened. He smiled icily at the decades-old report in his hand. It detailed one of Simon Bradwell's earliest investment schemes and Burgess had signed off on it in his own handwriting as "perfect for our clients and a guaranteed return for them and us." He added that Second National should support Simon Bradwell's future endeavors.

Hmm. Burgess might not have been dirty back then. Simon Bradwell might not have been lying either. Even so, any lawyer in Panschin could use this report to file the first of an avalanche of lawsuits on behalf of Simon Bradwell's defrauded clients. Burgess's reputation would be tainted, even if all he did was demonstrate incompetence.

But if he were dirty and involved in Simon Bradwell's embezzlement schemes, his reputation would be destroyed, his family left ruined and destitute, and he would earn a one-way ticket to the Dirac mines.

Why had Mr. Wong not done anything with these reports? Malcolm sat back, thinking hard. Because he wouldn't have suspected a connection between Burgess and Simon Bradwell. He had no reason to do so until *after* Burgess complained to him about Simon Bradwell's daughter, Veronica. Wong also had too much to lose. He couldn't disappear into the tunnels with his family; as born and bred Dome Six dwellers, they wouldn't know where to go and would have no one to help them make the difficult adjustments as they struggled to fit in.

But he could allow Malcolm to take the risk, a risk that would benefit both of them. He could carefully direct his underling's search, all the while doing what he was known to do here in the branch office: nothing. Even everything he had said in the office, if overheard, could be read as a punishment for Malcolm Cobb being uppity. Mr. Wong was demonstrating a subtle mind. What else did he know?

Malcolm realized something else. The daimyo of Shelleen had been correct: like Miss Bradwell, he needed allies, and they were sometimes found where you didn't expect them. But allies had their own agenda.

Mr. Wong had a subtle mind. That particular thought niggled insistently at Malcolm. There was risk and he was allowing Malcolm to take this risk, while carefully avoiding risk himself. Was there a trap? Malcolm looked at the report, typed on the letterhead of the headquarters of The Second National Bank of Panschin in Dome Six.

There lay the true risk, a cave-viper laying in wait for the unwary.

He had to use this treasure trove of proof to destroy Burgess without doing equal damage to Second National. If Burgess were to be proved either dirty or incompetent, then their employer, Second National, would also be attacked with lawsuits. The statute of limitations didn't run out on this kind of fraud. The bank would spend vaults full of cash defending itself against the avalanche of lawsuits. Public opinion would do the rest. The bank would be destroyed.

Malcolm leaned against the filing cabinet, sweating suddenly despite the cool, still air. There had to have been other senior people at Second National who knew Burgess was recommending Simon Bradwell to their clients. Burgess may even have had discreet assistance in covering up his malfeasance since the higher-ups did not want the bank tarnished.

He would have to proceed very carefully. He could no longer count on disappearing into the tunnels below Panschin if he made a mistake. Second National would punish him severely for bringing this mess to light. The bank had a far greater reach than Burgess did.

Another thought surfaced that made him sweat more. Simon Bradwell had done business with other banks in Panschin. He hadn't missed a single one. It wasn't just possible the other banks had related secrets hidden in their own subbasements full of filing cabinets. It was a certainty.

The Dirac mines beckoned. His family would end up there, too, sucked in for some no doubt very good, rational, and publicly acceptable reason. Mr. Steelio would be put under immense Panschin-wide pressure to yield them up and he would, if it meant protecting the rest of his company and his miners. He would lose Shelby. She would be destroyed, and it would be his fault.

Malcolm leaned his head back, studying the motes of dust dancing over the filing cabinets in the shafts of sun the series of deck prisms filtered down from above. He would have to be very, very careful.

And just why had Mr. Wong told him to hurry? Because he needed to race ahead of the avalanche of events or so Malcolm would rush ahead blindly, slip, and fall down the hidden shaft?

Airik spent the rest of the morning in one meeting after another. They were slowly becoming more productive as he learned more and the firms he dealt with began to understand he meant what he said about refusing specious business deals and unwanted marriage arrangements. Every time he pointed out flaws in their presentations, their irritation and respect grew. He wasn't just another ignorant yokel from the hinterland; a sheep waiting to be sheared, a goose waiting to be plucked. The Shelleen family had chosen him to be their daimyo, the youngest one ever, and they had not been wrong.

He learned more about them too, beginning to see how desperate some were to make a deal with Shelleen. Many business owners and daimyos were eager to work with Shelleen, but they didn't display a driving need to access Shelleen's cash reserves. Not Jandinaire and Chung/Banerjee. He could see the anxiety underlying every word their senior representatives said.

Airik also had repeated opportunities to compare Veronica's grace under pressure with the horde of marriage prospects being paraded in front of him.

The day's main luncheon for the conference was hosted by the Twelve Happiness Luxury Hotel. Airik knew there was no avoiding this one since the daimyos of all the attending mining tier demesnes were present, along with the heads of every mining concern in Panschin. As he expected, their eligible female relatives were also in attendance. Many were surprisingly well-briefed in mining technology as well as having all the credentials required to become the future daimyah of Shelleen. That did not make them look any better in Airik's eyes, but for no logical reason he could come up with.

The crush of daimyos, their staffs, and the powerful mining concerns ensured the luncheon was closed to anyone not on the guest list. Airik was annoyed to see he was carefully placed at the center table, surrounded by rings of tables so everyone in the room could watch what he did. The circular tables were large, each seating twelve, which would make conversation difficult. The underlying struggle over who got to sit where must have been intense, a suspicion Upton confirmed in a low voice when they entered the over-decorated lobby to the even more ornate ballroom.

"I did the best I could, sir. However, we don't own any portion of the Twelve Happiness and Maerski, Atto, Fuziwara, and Davis do, along with half the mining interests in the city."

"Then why don't those daimyos stay here?" Airik whispered. "If they are all investors?"

Upton winced at the thought of admitting he had erred. Airik despised the Twelve Happiness and repeated encounters with its staff only increased his irritation. He would have to confess that if he had asked the right questions when they were planning the trip, they could have avoided the hotel. He knew *now*. The other secretaries and personal assistants had been eager to fill him in.

There was no help for it. The secretary sighed and said, "The mining tier demesnes cooperatively lease a tower complex in Dome Six. Each family has a floor or a section of floor, depending on their needs and how much money they kicked in. The complex has all the services a hotel would offer. They also offer guest suites for important visitors."

Airik thought about this. "You mean I would not have had to be subjected to the Twelve Happiness?"

"Yes, sir."

"I see," Airik said. He looked over to where Maerski was standing, waiting to be seated, surrounded by his staff, and at each of the other daimyos, surrounded by their staff. The mining tier daimyos had turned out in force for this luncheon. Their staff members were, of course, well-placed relatives. As if they sensed his presence, they turned as one to beam at him, credit signs and desires for intimate family connections dancing in their eyes. They had the same predatory look he had observed in the Twelve Happiness staff and hunting cats in Shelleen.

Airik knew full well that prior to the discovery of the Red Mercury lode, Shelleen was considered to be a third-rate demesne at best and so beneath their notice. It was amazing how things could change, like time and pressure turning sand into sandstone.

"On the other hand, I would be continuously surrounded by the mining tier members of the Four Hundred, would I not?"

"Yes, sir."

Airik thought of his escape to the White Elephant. Returning there to Miss Bradwell felt like coming home. "Perhaps it was for the best that you did not know."

"Yes, sir," the secretary said, not knowing what else to say. He decided not to tell Airik the Shelleen contingent would have been allowed to stay for free, versus paying huge sums to the Twelve Happiness Luxury Hotel. Although, thinking on it, Shelleen would have paid in some other fashion. Daimyos were known for their charitable natures.

"They'll be seating us soon," Upton whispered to Airik. "You'll be placed at the center table with the daimyos of Maerski, Atto, Davis, and Fuziwara along with a representative of the Panschin mine owners."

"That's five people. Who will the other six be?" Airik asked, dreading the answer.

"The daimyos are each bringing a young lady of their family, sir. According to the stories I heard, the young ladies are the ones their families deem as the front-runners most likely to please you. They are new to you. They replaced everyone you've already met."

"I see," Airik said. "What do you know about the occupants of seats 10, 11, and 12?" He expected a mine owner and his candidate for daimyah for seats 10 and 11. Maybe he'd get fabulously lucky and the dean of the Mining and Engineering College of Panschin would get that last seat and they could discuss new scientific discoveries. On the other hand, the dean might push for a huge, no-strings grant from Shelleen for research purposes.

"The Panschin mine owners performed a religious ritual to determine who got chosen. Steelio won. He's got his niece, Olwyn, whom you met before, and another young lady from one of the other mining families who won the second round, a Miss Qiao," Upton said.

"A religious ritual? To pull names out of a hat?" Airik asked, his eyebrows raised.

"My source refused to go into detail, sir, other than to say the mine owners of Panschin insisted that it be done this way."

"I see," Airik said, although he did not. "They all agreed and they're honoring this ritual?" These owners were, based on his limited observations, cutthroat in their dealings with each other. Spirituality and a sense of unity did not enter into the equation at all.

"Yes, sir."

"And they're agreeing to seat the second young lady despite their own candidates from their own households?"

"Yes, sir."

"Upton, find out as much as you can about this religious ritual. I've not heard of anything of this nature before."

"I'll try, sir."

"Oh? You'll try?"

Upton thought of Airik sucker-punching Dean Kangjuon, gritted his teeth and said, "I don't think Panschin residents want to discuss their rituals with outsiders. As it was, I only found out because I overheard Steelio's secretary talking about it with one of Qiao & Schopenhour's reps. All they would admit to me was it had to be done this way."

"Interesting. Do the best you can."

"Yes, sir."

"My lord Shelleen, I am so very happy to see you've joined us," the concierge said, having suddenly appeared as if from nowhere. The concierge enjoyed, as Airik had discovered to his cost, a genuine talent for not being seen when he didn't want to be despite his gaudy, gleaming hotel livery that should have made him visible in a dense fog at midnight.

"I've hired some new willing young ladies who are eager to make *you* happy." He smirked and waggled his eyebrows at his prey.

Airik had been hoping to avoid the concierge and his insinuations. "No, absolutely not. In fact," he added, with a burst of inspiration, "if you continue to harass me on the subject, I shall complain to Maerski, Atto, Fuziwara, and Davis. As they are investors in this establishment, I feel sure they'd be interested in how I am treated."

The concierge frowned, then his face lit up and he smiled winningly again at Airik. "Of course, my lord Shelleen! I understand perfectly. You're going to be examining all these worthy gentlemen's daughters and you don't want to embarrass any of the young ladies with extracurricular activities." To Airik's horror, he winked salaciously. "Mum's the word on my part. We want you to be *happy* here at the Twelve Happiness Luxury Hotel. I'll check in later when we have more privacy to discuss how to provide you with *your* happy ending. I will *make* you be happy." The concierge winked again and vanished as quickly as he had appeared.

Airik turned to Upton as the bowing and scraping maître d'

appeared to seat him. "We will never stay at this hotel again. Never."

"Yes, sir," Upton said and was led away to his own table in the outermost ring at the outer limits of the ballroom, where he was seated with other secretaries and personal assistants. He was also the only male at the table, which raised his spirits. At least the gossip here would be good and Chung/Banerjee's two secretaries who were sitting on either side of him were both remarkably pretty and remarkably friendly. He had done his best to spread the rest of the Shelleen delegation two to a table. This not only ensured they would never be without an ally, but also serve as a check on any loose talk. Upton planned on questioning them closely after the dinner.

He wondered if Gaston or the rest of the group would even realize the hoops he had jumped through to keep them from being isolated and ganged-up on by predacious Panschin mine owners and their staffs. Gaston certainly would owe him. He had gotten Gaston placed as far away in the ballroom from Jandinaire as he could without losing status.

Gradually everyone settled into their seats. As guest of honor, Airik felt like he had been placed at the center of the target. He felt hemmed in and on display. Maerski, Atto, Fuziwara, and Davis insisted on introducing their family's daughters at once, making Steelio wait with his niece, Olwyn, and the other young lady, Miss Qiao. The aristocratic young women had the same hard, assessing stares Airik had come to recognize and detest; a stare that was replaced with a sweet and pliant attitude if they thought he was observing them. They didn't like each other, that was plain enough from the veiled glares and sotto-voce comments to their daimyos. How did any of them think he didn't see this?

He also observed that Miss Steelio and Miss Qiao were ignored to the point of rudeness by the Four Hundred young women, and they returned the favor although not as rudely.

Airik also couldn't help noticing how the business attire he had expected, since this was a business luncheon in the middle of the business day, had transformed itself into low-cut cocktail wear for the women. All six young ladies were, in fact, giving the underdressed waitresses employed by the Twelve Happiness Luxury Hotel a run for their money in terms of baring all to better increase their chances of dazzling him.

Their lavish jewelry was also impressive, a dazzling display of every kind of gem as well as the money they expected to be spent upon them. He thought again of gold-diggers, although it was highly doubtful if any of the six young women had ever touched a pick or a shovel with their manicured hands. He thought of Veronica's beads made of slag glass, worthless to everyone but her. To her, they were worth the moons.

It was uncomfortable and disconcerting. Upton, he thought wearily, would have known what to say and do, charming all around him while avoiding promises he didn't intend to keep. The daimyos and Mr. Steelio were hostile to each other and not much politer to each other's candidates. That was awkward too.

Instead, Airik focused on the meal in front of him. He realized that the heavily sauced entrée he was eating was very similar to the moss and yeast cracker Veronica nibbled on. It was a larger slab than her cracker but the odor and color were the same. Whoever had arranged for the meal — celebrating the cuisine of Panschin — had decided upon the entrées. Was this what there was to choose from? His previous meals at the Twelve Happiness, which he had selected from the gaspingly overpriced regular menu, had been better. He held up the forkful of sludge, thinking hard. He must have been eating imported foodstuffs.

Shelleen had never been a powerhouse in exporting. The demesne was self-sufficient, but generally had little grain, animal products, or minerals left over to sell to the wider world. It had been difficult to compete with the agricultural demesnes to the south who enjoyed better climates and better soil, as well as shorter distances to Barsoom and the great markets of the equator cities. With the Red Mercury lode's wealth to draw on, Airik could see possibilities opening up before him.

The lode wouldn't last forever, but in the meantime, he could improve his storage facilities and upgrade his peasants' equipment. He was already upgrading the in-demesne transportation capabilities for the lode, but those improvements could serve for all of the demesne's needs. Then there was his deal with Kenyatta. It would take decades, but Shelleen's soil would improve continuously and his peasants would gain additional expertise with livestock. With those improvements, he could position Shelleen as the premier provider of agricultural products to Panschin and perhaps to Northernmost as well. Conveniently, Shelleen was on the direct rail-line to Panschin, shortening the travel distances and lowering his own costs.

The markets were here. The evidence was right in front of him on his plate. Any group of people who willingly ate dough pockets filled with pond scum and moss crackers would, no question, be eager to eat something better such as the rye, barley, roots, and pulses that Shelleen grew in quantity. He could even consider growing the hardier and more shippable vegetable and fruit crops. Or, better, grow those crops, preserve them in-house, and then ship the finished goods and reap a bigger profit than plain commodities would bring. This trip to Panschin, challenging as it had been for him personally, would be beneficial to the demesne.

"You stupid bint! That is not what I ordered."

Airik looked up, distracted from thoughts of increasing Shelleen's wealth for generations to come.

Kendra Atto, the current frontrunner from that demesne, had apparently been given the wrong glass. Her beautiful face twisted with fury as she swore at the waitress. That woman was apologizing profusely, but Miss Atto was having none of it.

"Is there a problem?" Airik asked coldly.

"You bet there is, my lord Airik," Miss Atto said sweetly. She batted her amazingly lush purple-tinted eyelashes at him, a shade he had never before observed on a human body. "This fool didn't get my order right. I was quite specific about how I wanted my tea sweetened and she couldn't get something so simple correct."

"I see," Airik said.

Since he did not instantly condemn her behavior, she took that as encouragement. "If you don't keep the lower classes in their places, well, they try instantly to take advantage of you by doing less work. It's a constant struggle, don't you agree?"

Miss Atto smiled charmingly at Airik, while her peers watched carefully to see which way the wind would blow. Atto kept a blank face as he, too, waited to see if the daimyo of Shelleen raced to the aid of a damsel in distress.

"Were you clear in your directions?" Airik asked. He thought suddenly of Veronica being gracious to drunks and her sister doing the same, despite the provocations. The waitress, not much older than Miss Atto, but with far more tired eyes, watched warily. She wore an anxious, placating smile, while behind her, the maître d' came marching up, blood in his eye.

"Uh, yes, of course I was. I have to be when working with ignorant clods. The hotel must be hiring lazy peasants."

"Clods are lumps of soil. Were you aware, Miss Atto, that Shelleen is an agricultural demesne? As such, my peasants, and I have many, are the hardworking backbone supporting the entire demesne. They are neither ignorant and lazy, nor are they clods."

Miss Atto paled. "I didn't mean," she began.

"So you say," Airik said.

"My lord Shelleen," the maître d' said. "Is there a problem with our staff?"

"Not on my part," Airik said. "Just as I am sure no one else here at the table has a problem either."

"No, of course not," Miss Atto added hastily. "I was mistaken and I do apologize for my rudeness."

"Of course, Miss Atto," the maître d' replied smoothly. He caught the waitress's eye, she moved over to him at once, they exchanged a few whispers, and she left the table looking relieved. "No harm done, then."

As soon as the maître d' departed, after checking personally on what everyone wanted to drink – a process Airik noted was decidedly unclear as each person wanted something both completely different along with being extremely detailed as to size of ice cubes and amount and type of sweetener – the table burst into strained conversation on how well each person there treated their staff and workers at every level.

It should have been amusing.

It became amusing when Mr. Steelio, his niece, and Miss Qiao were able to provide specifics about their employees as opposed to vague generalities. This spurred the Four Hundred debs to go into greater, yet less plausible detail about generous treatment of maids and other household servants. Their daimyos were not amused. Based on their expressions, Airik surmised they were each revising their candidate list of prospective brides to ones he would find more appealing.

It became more amusing when Airik asked Mr. Steelio for details about the scholarship program that the free-city of Panschin used to discover hidden talent. Steelio had no idea how Airik knew about the program and said so, but nonetheless, he seized his opportunity to talk, to have his niece talk, and to have Miss Qiao talk. Maerski, Atto, Fuziwara, and Davis sat in a fuming silence, as did the daughters of their respective households.

As they spoke, Airik observed carefully. Why had Steelio, his niece, and Miss Qiao and not someone else been chosen by a religious ritual to represent the mine-owners of Panschin? None of them had any outstanding or unusual attribute that he could ascertain. Miss Qiao in particular was an odd choice. She was reasonably attractive to be sure, yet he would have expected that for the twelfth seat, the mine-owners of Panschin would have selected a ravishing beauty queen — hastily briefed on geology — to ensnare him.

Eventually the luncheon ended, after the waitresses handed around some sort of highly seasoned, tooth-hurtingly sweet greenish pudding piled high in crystal goblets. Airik tasted it, repressed his dismayed expression, and thought, "Shelleen will make wagonloads of money shipping anything we grow to Panschin. They'll buy it all, even the mangelwurzels. They won't care that they're eating winter livestock fodder because it will still taste better than this muck."

At the far side of the ballroom, as the only man at his table, Upton enjoyed his own luncheon very much. The company was charming, eager, very friendly, and remarkably pretty, more than making up for the dismal food. He wondered if the secretaries and personal assistants were normally this cheerful and gossipy with outsiders or had they been required to behave this way to gain inside information on what the daimyo of Shelleen wanted in a business deal. He was still coping with random attacks of dizziness, making it harder to consider what that meant other than having to drink more of Lulu's tea. The best possibility was that he might finally, finally, finally, after all this time in Panschin, get lucky. Maybe more than once, based on the smiles he kept seeing directed at him. And here the concierge of the Twelve Happiness thought he had to purchase a lady's company. He sniffed in disdain; where was the skill or thrill in that for either party? Best of all, getting lucky wouldn't involve signing a contract he would have to explain to Airik or the senior family.

The luncheon finally over, a scheduled social period allowed everyone who had to sit at a different table access to Airik. He had been hoping to avoid it in favor of a lecture on deep mine shaft ventilation procedures, but Gaston insisted he remain.

"It's necessary, sir. You've skipped too many other social functions and you must attend this one."

Airik thought about this statement. Gaston had been noticeably reluctant to tell him he "must" do something so the fact that he was doing so now spoke volumes.

"Very well, Gaston. Lead the way."

"Yes, sir." Gaston was deeply relieved. His own luncheon, despite the dreadful muck the hotel insisted on serving, had been pleasant. Why did anyone in Panschin eat this rubbish? Someone should do something about the situation although he couldn't think of who that someone might be. He had been seated far, far away from Jandinaire. His table-mates, unlike Jandinaire's staffers, had been knowledgeable and properly courteous, allowing him to learn answers to Airik's questions. He had been steeling himself for an argument with his daimyo and to have Airik agree so easily was even more pleasant. Wherever Airik was hiding was making him much easier to work with.

"A senior member of Chung/Banerjee wanted to speak with you prior to their presentation this afternoon, sir."

"Of course."

The well-dressed older man who approached them looked vaguely familiar. He was wearing a floral suit, although not an ostentatious one, and Airik thought he had seen that pattern of flowers and vines before.

"I'm Peng McGrant, my lord Shelleen," he introduced himself, not giving Gaston a chance to do it for him. "I'm deeply honored to meet you."

"Likewise," Airik said, trying to place him.

Peng McGrant was also looking puzzled and then suddenly chuckled.

"This is so amusing, my lord Shelleen. You know how they say that everyone has a double somewhere in the world?"

"I've heard that," Airik said. Where had he seen this man? He had met so many people since arriving in Panschin. The floral suit nagged at him.

"I was at a gallery showing in Dome Two the other day. My son Kip is a budding painter at PanU, and there was a rickshaw hauler there who looks similar to you," Mr. McGrant said. "Not nearly as refined and distinguished as yourself of course, but the resemblance is there."

"Ah," Airik thought.

He said, "I suppose that could be possible," trusting in the unlimited capacity of people to ignore what was in standing front of them in favor of what they expected to see.

Mr. McGrant chuckled again. "It was so amusing. My dearest friend, Sajag Burgess, had a terrible run-in with the fellow and put him in his place quite firmly. I must introduce you to him. Sajag is a prominent banker, highly placed in the Second National Bank of Panschin's hierarchy. He's a very amusing fellow and has been eager to meet with you."

Airik stiffened. There couldn't be two Burgesses highly placed in Second National who had argued with uppity rickshaw haulers at an art gallery show in Dome Two. His safe haven might be discovered. He'd have to leave the White Elephant and return to the Twelve Happiness. He'd have to leave Veronica.

He sought a way out that wouldn't cause a problem later on. Burgess had spoken to him for several minutes and could make the connection between a rude rickshaw hauler in Dome Two and the daimyo of Shelleen. It was unlikely, but he couldn't count on Burgess being completely incompetent.

"Aaaaah!"

Airik stopped worrying about discovery.

Shelby floated through her morning at PanU, oblivious to stares and whispers, buoyed by the realization that Malcolm wanted to see her again, wanted to help her and her family, and that he and his family thought she had talent.

The glow finally wore off hours later in the studio.

Kip was waiting for her, sitting at the center table and managing to sit alone and isolated in the crowd gossiping around him. As soon as she entered the room, he stood and walked up to her.

"Shelby, I'm so glad you're okay," Kip said. "I was worried about you."

"I was fine. Malcolm and his family took great care of me. You look better," Shelby said. She took a surreptitious glance around. They had drawn an audience ostentatiously ignoring them while hanging on every word and, very unlike him, Kip didn't care.

"Yeah, I'm better," Kip said. He looked at the floor. "I suppose it was good I found out now I have surface sickness. Instead of later."

"You'll never have to go underground, Kip. You're smart and talented and your family is well-off." Shelby thought of what Florence had said, about how Kip would be useless to his family. What a terrible thing to say about anyone. "You'll be an artist," she added encouragingly.

"Yeah, I suppose," Kip said. He looked around, as if trying to decide what to say. "But you're really all right?"

One of the other students, a hanger-on of Reyansh Philpott, interrupted.

"Like you care, Kippy? You ran out on Shelby and abandoned her in the deepdown with that miner, that's what I heard," Bhupathi Middleton said with a smirk.

"Buzz off," Kip said angrily.

"Yes, please do," Shelby snapped, making more than one person sit up and pay closer attention since she didn't normally go out of her way to attract attention. "Kip got sick. It's not his fault."

"I'm sorry, Shelby. I really am." Kip finally looked up at Shelby, meeting her eyes instead of studying the floor tiles. "Would you like tea and a bun after class with me? My treat."

Shelby blinked at him trying to figure out who this stranger was. Kip was finally giving her the attention she'd dreamed of, and she no longer wanted it.

"I'm sorry, but I can't. Malcolm's coming by to meet me." Shelby beamed at Kip. "I'm drawing his family members and I've got his little cousin Cindy's portrait to finish."

"Portraits? Of tunnel rats?" Professor Vitebskin interjected. "I suppose persons of that ilk don't know art when they see it so you'll be good enough for them."

Shelby thought she'd been struck across the face. "I am not a talentless hack, Professor," she gritted out.

"That remains to be seen," he said. Professor Vitebskin twisted his mouth as if he'd eaten something sour. "I am happy, of course, to see that you returned alive."

"Of course I did," Shelby retorted. "Mr. Cobb was a perfect gentleman."

"He's a tunnel rat."

"And you, Professor, are a hypocrite. I don't need this dross and I'm going home," Shelby said and spun on her heel and marched back towards the door.

"Shelby—," Kip started after her, then stopped in his tracks. He stared after her, crestfallen.

"Quit wasting your time, Kip," Professor Vitebskin said. "We need to discuss how you've been wasting *my* time. What is this dreck?" and he held up Kip's latest dismal effort.

"Hey Shelby!" Bhupathi called out.

She half-turned and hesitated so Bhupathi added "since you're putting out for tunnel rats, why aren't you putting out for me too? It's not like you have any talent for anything else."

Shelby stopped dead in her tracks while the rest of the students in the studio either looked uncomfortable or sniggered. She spun on her heel and marched straight up to Bhupathi Middleton and slapped him across his face as hard as she could. It was almost as satisfying as slapping Reyansh Philpott would have been.

The sound echoed through the suddenly silent studio.

"One more word like that from you or anyone else, and I'll ask Malcolm to break every bone in your body and throw you down a mineshaft!" Shelby screamed. "And he *will*!"

She marched out the door without a backward glance.

"You deserved it, you miscreant," Professor Vitebskin said self-righteously to Bhupathi. The mark of Shelby's hand was imprinted across his face, and he sat there stunned, yet obviously expecting the professor to take his side.

Professor Vitebskin added, "Our co-eds here at PanU should be treated with respect. You need to remember that."

fter an extremely questionable dessert, the luncheon was finally over and it was time for Upton to get back to work, shadowing Airik in case he needed something.

Upton arose from the table gracefully and then assisted each of the other guests in turn. He had been expecting that the ladies would manage their chairs on their own, but they did not. They *waited* for him, smiling and batting their eyes and sending him smoldering glances. It was disconcerting.

Perhaps, he thought, this was standard behavior in Panschin, but no. A quick glance at the surrounding tables showed him that everyone else at their status level, no matter their sex or age, managed to exit a chair on their own. It was just his table.

As he assisted each of the secretaries and personal assistants in turn to their feet, he came to the unhappy conclusion that his earlier suspicion was correct. The ladies were not friendly and charming because he was friendly and charming. It was because they had been required to do so by their bosses. Access to Upton meant access to his boss, the daimyo of Shelleen.

Well. He wouldn't, he decided, let that stop him from showing anyone who wanted one a stellar time; one the woman would not just remember forever but use as the gold standard by which every future partner would be judged and found wanting. He had value, too, and not just as the secretary to the daimyo of Shelleen. And here, Upton smiled to himself, certain members of the Shelleen family believed he was incapable of thinking with the head on his shoulders.

Once his duty as a gentleman was finished, courtesies reciprocated, cards exchanged, and schedules synchronized to ensure future, more intimate meetings, Upton worked his way through the mob towards the center table where Airik held court or was held hostage, depending on one's viewpoint.

It took some time to get there since he kept getting buttonholed by other staffers desperate for their bosses to be slotted into a gap in Airik's schedule. There were no gaps, leading to some eye-opening invitations to ensure him making a gap. Yes, sadly, it was his position and not his charming self that made him so popular. Knowing this didn't stop Upton from making arrangements for private meetings to come but when he did so, he told the other person that seeing him in a personal way guaranteed absolutely nothing when it came to access to Airik. Some of the invitations were rescinded after Upton made his little speech, but gratifyingly, not all of them.

No one offered him a bribe in cash.

Upton wondered about that. If these Panschin bosses were so desperate, then why didn't they? There was always the risk he'd refuse and then report the incident to Airik so perhaps that was the reason. Or maybe, hmmm, his reputation had preceded him to Panschin. Everyone knew he never took bribes.

Upton had just reached the inner circle of tables when he saw her, a young woman standing near Airik. Their eyes met briefly and his heart stood still, and his world turned upside down. The physical reaction was so strong he thought for a moment he had been punched in the stomach.

"Dizziness," he thought shakily. "I'm dizzy again and I'll have to drink more of that gods-awful damn tea of Lulu's."

She turned away and the connection was broken. Upton took a few more steps towards Airik, and then she turned back and their eyes met once more.

His reaction was stronger. He had to meet this beautiful goddess at once. The intimate arrangements he had made during the luncheon faded away. Airik was forgotten. The needs of Shelleen became a petty waste of time.

You, Upton thought. You.

Everything else vanished. He had to make his way through the mob to meet her. The other guests would part before them and he could speak to her and hear her beautiful voice, a voice that would be as lovely as she was. She would welcome him and tell him her lovely name. She would wrap her arms around him and kiss him deeply. She would whisper the most tantalizing suggestions to him and he would take her up on every one of them, thrilling her like no one else ever could. He would blanket her with kisses, not missing a single centimeter of her delectable skin. They would be happy forever, floating in a sea of endless bliss.

The other guests didn't receive the message from the Shelleen family gods, forcing Upton to shove his way through the mob, blind to everything but his destination. His beautiful goddess smiled tentatively at him and his focus narrowed even more.

Another wave of dizziness swept over him, he stilled, and his goddess's smile vanished. The loss spurred Upton to ignore the dizziness threatening to overwhelm him. She was so close; only a few meters away. He could not lose her. He stepped forward cautiously, just as he did when wading through tall grass in the marshes of Shelleen while hunting, but not cautiously enough.

A Panschin favorite food was algae-filled dumplings. The Twelve Happiness Luxury Hotel prided itself on its larger than usual, juicier than usual dumplings and, since the luncheon's menu had been designed to showcase Panschin's indigenous cuisine, dumplings featured prominently. Not every guest appreciated the effort the chef had put into his feather-light dumplings, the careful seasoning, the way they burst so delightfully when bitten into, filling the mouth with a surge of carefully curated and properly aged algae from the most select tanks. The visitors from Shelleen certainly avoided them like the plague.

The Twelve Happiness Luxury Hotel had, as would be expected, generously overfilled the serving dishes with algae dumplings to ensure the guests could happily eat as many of them as they wanted. Since not everyone did, there were some left when the tables were cleared for dessert. A rushed waitress spilled some and then, in the hurry to get everyone served, forgot to have the cleaning staff take care of the issue.

Upton found the dumplings with his questing foot and, true to their nature, as soon as his foot pressed down on them, they burst and smeared their hot, juicy, slick innards over the parquet floor. He flailed wildly, screamed, and lost his balance, heading to the floor and unable to stop himself. He took a chair down with him while trying to regain his balance and, as he skittered down to the floor, hit the table in back of him, upending its contents on him as he fell. The table still held a large serving dish loaded with more dumplings, many of which obligingly burst when they cascaded down upon Upton and the floor. As a parting shot, the heavy ceramic serving dish hit him on the head and shattered.

Pain shot through him from a variety of sources: his twisted ankle, his ribs from when he landed on the chair, the back of his skull where he smacked against the table, burning skin from the bursting hot dumplings, his head ringing from the heavy serving dish that crashed into it and broke into shards, the assorted little cuts from the shards, his dislocated shoulder from flailing wildly for support and missing and landing badly, and most of all, the pain of knowing he'd made a complete and utter ass of himself in front of his goddess.

As Upton lay there gasping on the floor, struggling manfully not to scream from the pain and make himself look even more ridiculous, he realized he had lost her. He didn't know who she was and now, seeing what a clumsy oaf he was, she would walk away without a backward glance and he'd be left alone forever; laying on a ballroom floor in Panschin and festooned with blobs of algae and shattered pastry.

The dumpling caught in his hair freed itself to ooze down his forehead and burst, getting algae up his nose and smearing across his face. He sneezed violently and couldn't stop, ensuring his humiliation was complete and informing him that he had cracked more than one rib. The new waves of pain multiplied the stars he was seeing into a shimmering haze filling his vision. He was having trouble hearing anything over the ringing in his ears and the roar of the aghast and amused crowd gathering around him, none of whom were being particularly helpful.

"Out of the way! Out of the way!"

Upton heard the voice and, through the haze of pain and dizziness, was able to think "help at last."

He was breathing as shallowly as he could, every breath a new adventure in pain. The shrieks from his twisted ankle, his battered skull, and dislocated shoulder paled in comparison to the bitter, stabbing complaints from his ribcage.

Someone was wiping his face clean with a wet napkin and he was able to open his eyes again to a new sea of shimmering stars. The veil parted and it was her. His goddess from across the room was kneeling next to him, wiping algae from his face.

Upton's humiliation increased to a new level.

She said "the doctor is on his way. We've got a stretcher coming. I want you to breath slowly and carefully. You'll be fine."

She waited a moment, then frowned when he didn't respond.

"Can you speak? Tell me who you are?"

"Yes, I'm Upton," Upton managed to croak out.

"How many fingers am I holding up?"

Her fingers went in and out of focus. "A lot?" Upton guessed. The veil kept threatening to close and he wouldn't be able to see her again.

She frowned at him again.

"I want you wiggle your fingers for me without moving anything else. Can you do that?"

Upton stared up at her concerned, beautiful face. The sensation of being punched in the stomach was stronger than ever, now that he had the delicate scent of her perfume in his nostrils competing with the algae.

Her expression changed to a stern one. "Can you wiggle your fingers?"

"For you, anything," Upton said slowly and did as he was told.

"Good. Now wiggle your toes and tell me if you can do it."

One foot was easy. The other foot, attached to his twisted ankle, made him gag with pain but he did it to make her happy. "I can move them." He refused to admit how much it hurt.

Airik appeared on his other side, kneeling down as well.

"My lord Shelleen," Upton's goddess said. "I don't believe this man's back is broken. Definitely a concussion."

Airik said, "you have some medical training then, Miss Qiao?"

"Yes, I do." She smiled reassuringly at the daimyo of Shelleen and Upton felt a surge of jealousy wash over him, strong enough to block the pain in his extremities for a few precious, welcome seconds. Why wasn't she smiling at him? Because he was a ridiculous ass, his brain reminded him, incapable of walking across a ballroom without tripping over his own feet.

His goddess then began carefully and professionally checking his body for injuries. Her running her hands up and down his body should have been exciting. Under the circumstances, it was anything but.

Despite the embarrassment, he couldn't stop himself from squealing when she ran her hands across his ribs.

"Cracked rib, I think, based on how he's breathing," his goddess told his daimyo.

Talk to me, not to him, Upton wanted to say but he couldn't manage the words. Despite the pain, the veil was closing.

"Coming through!" and the hotel doctor arrived with a pair of uniformed nurses, a team of orderlies, and a stretcher.

The doctor took charge, checked over Upton, and he felt himself being very gently moved to the stretcher and removed from the ballroom.

He didn't know what to do. If he closed his eyes, he couldn't see his goddess walking along at his side. If he opened them, he couldn't help but see how every single person they passed gaped and leaned in for a better look, snickered, or burst into loud conversation recounting racy or derogatory Upton stories. He felt like he was hovering over his body, separate from the pain, while feeling every single jolt from being carried in the stretcher.

Unconsciousness came as a relief.

Airik walked alongside Upton's stretcher thinking hard over what he would do without a secretary. He needed someone to take dictation, type reports, manage his schedule, and run errands. Upton was invaluable. There were no good replacements among the Shelleen contingent. He didn't dare try to hire a short-term replacement in Panschin. Doing so would ensure his refuge with Veronica in the White Elephant would be compromised. He did not, he discovered to his bemusement, want to share her presence with anyone else. More rationally, there were loyalty and confidentiality issues, along with the certainty that, during the Biennial Mining Conference, everyone who was competent was already working for someone else.

Elliot was rapidly becoming more useful as a researcher than a valet, but he couldn't take dictation and it was doubtful he could type up a report. Carmine would be even more useless. What would he do?

The hotel doctor led them to a small infirmary, suitable for the minor illnesses of the Twelve Happiness guests, when they could not be treated in their rooms but weren't sick enough to be transferred to the hospital in Dome Six. He took over Upton's care, giving orders to his staff, and asking Airik to move away from the patient.

Airik stepped back, out of the way of the scurrying nurses, to observe. To his surprise, Miss Qiao remained at his side. Was she that desperate to become the next daimyah of Shelleen, oozing concern for his relative?

"Miss Qiao, it's not necessary for you to remain," Airik said coolly.

"Oh, I know that. The doctor seems more than capable," Miss Qiao replied absently. Her eyes were intent upon the action taking place on the gurney in front of them. "The Twelve Happiness Luxury Hotel would never hire anyone who wasn't the best in their field. I, I feel concerned about the patient. He said his name was Upton? Am I correct?"

"Yes, you are."

She chewed on her lip nervously, ignoring the daimyo of Shelleen to peer around the doctor and his staff working on Upton, getting him stripped, cleaned up, cuts and bruises salved, ribs bandaged, his shoulder relocated (which roused him from unconsciousness enough to make him scream like a banshee, permanently embarrassing him when he was told about it later), and taping his twisted ankle.

"He sounded so groggy. He was difficult to understand," she said.

"I am not surprised. He slipped on algae dumplings and then had a heavy serving dish hit him on the head, along with everything else," Airik said. "Your concern is appreciated. You may go now."

Miss Qiao fluttered her hands in agitation. "I don't like leaving a patient in a strange place. I know the hotel doctor will take the best care of Upton, but he's in a strange place. That's upsetting to anyone. He'll need to have people around him that he knows."

"You are not a familiar face to my secretary, Miss Qiao."

She turned to glare at him. "I am aware of that, just as I am aware that Upton is not my patient."

"Quite correct, miss," the doctor said, from his position by the gurney on which Upton reclined, unconscious again but struggling back to a groggy, painful, partially aware state. "I do know what I'm doing."

"I know that, too, doctor," Miss Qiao retorted. "I don't feel comfortable leaving Upton alone."

"As long as you stay out of the way," the doctor said, striving for patience. "Keep to the back of the room, please."

He'd been under contract to the Twelve Happiness for years and very little surprised him anymore in how guests managed to injure themselves. Normally, they didn't do it in such a public fashion unless they were drunk. In the doctor's professional opinion, the way this Miss Qiao was acting implied she and Upton knew each other far better than anyone around them grasped. He caught the eyes of his disapproving nurse and rolled his own in response. They'd seen this behavior before. The families didn't approve and it was only a matter of time before the relationship was revealed, causing pain and heartbreak all around.

"Miss Qiao," Airik began again, trying to figure out why she was being so obstinate. Usually, people who knew he was the daimyo of Shelleen (if they weren't trying to sell him something) couldn't acquiesce fast enough.

"Sir, my lord Shelleen, let me be the first to say how very sorry I am this happened to you," a new voice intruded.

Airik turned and there, filling the doorway to the infirmary room and then some, was Sajag Burgess. As before, he was wearing a luridly patterned floral suit, this one demonstrating his fondness for yellow cabbage roses. Unlike before, he also wore an oily, obsequious smile to accompany his glad-handing countenance.

"Very generous of you, particularly since I am not the person lying in agony on the bed," Airik said dryly.

"Who are you, pray tell? Interfering in a medical procedure in an infirmary?" Miss Qiao asked sharply.

"I'm Sajag Burgess as everyone who knows anyone in Panschin would know."

Mr. Burgess frowned mightily at Miss Qiao, taking in her plunging neckline, tightly corseted waist, bare arms, and floor-length skirt slit to her right hip, all in a vivid fuchsia with an overlay of black lace. The fuchsia contrasted beautifully with her grass-green skin while the extensive exposure of skin demonstrated how perfect her complexion was, all over. Then he turned his attention back to Airik, the frown replaced with his oily smile.

"Is this prostitute bothering you, my lord Shelleen? I'll have hotel security throw her out."

"I am not a prostitute!" Miss Qiao gasped in outrage. "I was informed I *had* to wear this dress, despite being invited to a business luncheon and not a cocktail party. Unlike you, who chose to wear a ridiculous suit suitable only as a bedspread."

Aha, Airik thought. So that's why the women at my table dressed as they did.

"How dare you impugn my sartorial choices, you tart," Mr. Burgess shot back. "I am a gentleman and I wear the latest fashions in gentlemen's wear. This suit is straight from Barsoom."

Your tailor lied and you didn't check, Airik thought. Another sign of your incompetence.

"If you are going to fight in my infirmary, I'll have hotel security throw all of you out," the doctor said firmly. "You are disturbing my patient."

Upton groaned from his infirmary bed.

Horrified, Miss Qiao put her hand to her mouth, once again completely focused on Upton. "My deepest apologies, doctor. How is Upton?"

"Do you know who I am?" Mr. Burgess threatened.

"An idiot who is interfering with a doctor's sworn duty to a patient," Airik said coldly. "Have you no understanding of the situation?"

"My lord Shelleen," Mr. Burgess said, openly and obviously hurt, with his plump hand to his breast, obscuring a cabbage rose, and tears welling in his eyes. "I am quite cognizant of the situation just as I am equally cognizant of the respect due to you. This tart, as well as this quack, are not properly respecting you."

"I am not a tart," Miss Qiao snapped, momentarily distracted from Upton's fluttering eyelids.

"Nor am I a quack," the doctor said, equally insulted. To his orderly he said, "Landis, get hotel security on the double."

"Yes, sir, doctor," the orderly replied with a grin and disappeared behind another door. Employment at the Twelve Happiness Luxury Hotel was never boring. Even better, fun events like this one frequently led to the discreet and lucrative practice of selling lurid stories to the gossip rags and broadsheet peddlers. The trade was so lucrative that, during his absence, he could count on the nurses and the orderlies to get the names and details correct, so they could split the proceeds.

"Mr. Burgess," Airik said coldly. "I will be the judge of who is respectful and who is not. You sir, are not. I will demand hotel security have you removed and furthermore, I will inform my fellow members of the Four Hundred along with the Panschin mine-owners association that you are not to be allowed anywhere in my presence again."

Mr. Burgess went ashen. "Sir, I did not mean to offend you," he groveled.

"Miss Qiao is my guest. You may start by apologizing to her," Airik said even more coldly.

Mr. Burgess's complexion took on a waxy hue as the blood drained from his face. "I had no idea."

Upton groaned again, distracting them again.

"Doctor! Upton needs you," Miss Qiao said, fluttering her hands again in her agitation. "He's suffering."

"You said you had some medical training, Miss Qiao," the doctor said calmly. "Do try to be dispassionate. It's better for the patient."

"May I ask, Miss Qiao, why you are so concerned over my secretary?" Airik asked.

Miss Qiao turned back to Airik, confused. "Upton is your secretary?"

"I did say so earlier."

She reran the conversation of the last five minutes back, discovering as she did so that she hadn't paid him much attention. "You did? Are you sure?"

"Positive," Airik replied coolly. "Why are you so concerned?"

"Yes, why are you?" Mr. Burgess interjected into the conversation.

Both Airik and Miss Qiao glared at Mr. Burgess.

"Stay out of this," Airik said, dismissing Mr. Burgess with a cold look.

Mr. Burgess stopped being obsequious.

"How dare you speak to me this way. You may be the daimyo of Shelleen, but I am a power in Panschin and I will make sure no one here does business with you."

"Who are you again?" Miss Qiao asked, then turned back to Upton who appeared to be slowly waking up and regretting his return to consciousness.

"Qiao. Would that mean you are part of Qiao & Schopenhour?" Mr. Burgess asked in a silky voice.

"Yes," she replied absently, not bothering to address Mr. Burgess to his face. "I'm a member of the family."

Mr. Burgess smiled evilly at her back; an expression Airik recognized at once from the gallery showing. "Second National holds your commercial paper. I think I'll call in those loans."

That got her undivided attention. She spun on her heel and strode up to him, jabbing her finger into a yielding cabbage rose. "You wouldn't dare! Qiao & Schopenhour have never defaulted on any loan and you have no reason to do such a thing."

"I can do what I want," Mr. Burgess replied happily. "I run the Second National Bank of Panschin."

"All of it?" Airik asked. "I was under the impression you were one of a pack of vice-presidents, carefully placed to be out of the way so you couldn't damage day-to-day business operations."

Mr. Burgess reared back, stung and furious. "You know nothing of the power structure in Panschin. You may be a daimyo, but you're still an ignorant yokel from the hinterlands." He stopped suddenly; finally getting a good look at Airik in the much better lighting in the infirmary, no longer surrounded by the distractions of a crowded ballroom.

"Haven't we met before?"

"No," Airik replied coldly. "We have not."

"There was this rickshaw hauler in Dome Two who tried to cheat me. You remind me of him. I'm ruining him, and I'll ruin you," Mr. Burgess said cheerfully.

"Hotel security," the uniformed man announced from his position at the door. "Still got your problem, doc?"

"I certainly do," the doctor replied. "See that morbidly obese, walking cardiac arrest in the floral suit? Get rid of him. He's disturbing my patient and his family."

Upton obligingly groaned again from his bed, making Miss Qiao gasp and push her way to his side, taking his hand gently in her own. The Twelve Happiness nurse recognized a concerned girlfriend when she saw one so she passed over the cooling cloth for Miss Qiao to use on Upton's fevered brow.

Airik watched her in puzzlement. She didn't claim to know Upton from some earlier assignation, didn't appear to know what Upton's position was in Shelleen, and Upton himself had said they had not met when he was explaining the seating arrangements. For someone who was angling to become the next daimyah of Shelleen, Miss Qiao was paying very little attention to *him* and paying all her attention to a stranger and a secretary at that.

The security guard took in Miss Qiao kneeling at the bedside, Airik hovering over her and dismissed them as family. He agreed with the doctor's assessment (something that didn't always happen) and said, "You with those curtains wrapped around you. Time to go."

He tapped his billy club against his hand and showed his teeth like a big hunting cat, making Mr. Burgess blanch.

"Try not to resist, sir. The hotel doesn't like it when we get the carpet bloody. The stains don't come out."

The rest of the security team wore the same uniform (a drab, dull stain-hiding red), enjoyed the same mountainous build, carried the same billy clubs, and sported the same predatory grins.

The decision was easy.

"I will have the lot of you fired," Mr. Burgess threatened and ambled to the door, glancing repeatedly over his shoulder at Airik and Miss Qiao as he went. He had never previously met the tart in fuchsia, but he knew her family and they would suffer. As for the daimyo of Shelleen, he looked mighty familiar. He and that damned rude, cheating rickshaw hauler could have been brothers. It was time to put more pressure on the rickshaw guild to find and punish the impertinent devil.

"Just doing our jobs," said the unconcerned security guard. He had heard *that* statement frequently in his career at the Twelve Happiness Luxury Hotel and it never came to anything, despite the status of the speaker. The threat of embarrassing stories, along with excruciating and detailed caricatures in the Panschin gossip columns ensured job security for him and his team and no legal actions against the hotel.

"Be happy. We are," the security guard added with a manic grin.

Mr. Burgess stopped dead in his tracks.

"I am not happy. None of this is making me happy. Do any of you know what will make me happy? Getting every last one of you fired and sent into the Dirac mines as slave labor," Mr. Burgess spat.

The security guard grinned even more broadly and his eyes lit up. "One more word out of you and I'm authorized to split your head open." He and his crew held up their billy clubs, all looking eager for a happy session with a difficult guest.

Mr. Burgess knew when he was beaten. "Fine," he said and began, very slowly, moving again towards the door while trying at the same time to figure out what was going on with the obviously drunken secretary, the tart, and the daimyo of Shelleen.

"No body fluids on my floors, please," the doctor called out. "I get enough as it is. Keep it out in the hallway."

"You got it, doc."

Upton groaned again from his bed.

"Very good," said the doctor approvingly. "He's coming around. We'll get some pain tea into him and keep him here overnight for observation for the concussion and his ribs. After that, we'll see. You there, Shelleen, what is your relationship to my patient?"

"I am Airik, the daimyo of Shelleen," Airik said. "Upton is both a cousin and my secretary. You'll be wanting his most recent medical history as it may have some bearing on what happened."

Airik plunged into Upton's sinus issues since their arrival in Panschin.

Miss Qiao listened carefully, while never letting go of Upton's hand. His sinus infection would have to be monitored since it, along with his cracked ribs, would affect his breathing and possibly lead to a more severe illness. Pneumonia and a wide variety of fungal infections were never far away in Panschin and the better ventilation in Dome Six did not change that fact. As she calmed down, she was able to think more dispassionately, just as the hotel doctor had advised.

"Doctor, could you give us a moment of privacy?" Airik said.

The doctor looked over Upton again, taking in his poor color and peeling back an eyelid to check his pupils and said, "Make it quick."

"Of course," Airik replied. Here was someone who didn't toady to him or try to sell him something. He wondered how long it would last.

As soon as the doctor stepped away, Airik said, "Miss Qiao. I insist on knowing why you are so concerned about my secretary. Has he, in some way, made you promises?"

"No, he has not." She chewed on her lip, thinking on exactly what she wanted to say. It was all so strange.

"Quickly please," Airik said. "The doctor will return and I have my own duties I must attend to."

"It's hard to explain," Miss Qiao began.

"Try. I recommend you start with when you met Upton."

"I've never seen him before today. I saw him walking towards me across the ballroom and, well, I…" she paused in her confusion. "I would like to stay with him but for no rational reason I can give you. I just need to."

Airik considered her, kneeling next to Upton and how she gazed at him in fascination, gently laving his brow of the sweat beading upon it. Qiao & Schopenhour had become another research project for Elliot, to determine if there was any kind of connection between them and Shelleen, or worse, if Upton had indeed made illicit promises to Miss Qiao and she was too ashamed to admit it. Servant's gossip, something Elliot could access, might provide the answer.

His decision made, Airik said, "Very well. Stay here. I will send someone by periodically to check on Upton."

Airik then spoke to the doctor and his staff, answering the new set of questions about contacts and room numbers. He knew Gaston awaited him in the ballroom, and it was time to return to do damage control, awkwardly socialize, and figure out how he was going to replace Upton.

He turned to take one last, puzzled look at Miss Qiao cooing over Upton. His secretary was gradually waking up and he couldn't stop staring open-mouthed at Miss Qiao. Something was going on, that was clear enough. How on Mars had Upton found the time? Airik was sure he had kept his secretary continuously busy since their arrival in Panschin and a quick mental tally of each day's schedule confirmed his belief. Who was lying to him about this relationship?

"Winifred! Get away from that lecherous cad this instant!"

The doctor turned to his nurse and whispered, "Discovered. And in less than half an hour too. You win the bet." She twinkled back, quietly triumphant.

Airik whipped around to see who this was and saw an elderly, richly but sedately dressed man, followed by a middle-aged man, equally well dressed at the infirmary door. Neither of them wore trendy floral brocade suits, reserving their floral trim to the lapels and cuffs. They appeared to be relatives, based on facial features. He didn't recognize either of them from any of his meetings to date in Panschin.

Miss Qiao did, based on her gasp and suddenly anxious expression.

"Zu fu, my apologies for ignoring you." She leapt to her feet and bowed to the elderly man, then bowed again to the younger man.

"Fuqin, is there a problem?" Miss Qiao asked anxiously, her hands nervously clasped.

"Allow me, Miss Qiao," Airik said calmly. She gaped at him in surprise, an expression he noted with interest. She didn't appear to expect him to come to her rescue, unlike, say, Kendra Atto had during the luncheon.

"Don't interfere with my granddaughter," the older man said sternly. "I know who you are, sir, and I most definitely know who that blackguard in the bed is."

"Then who are you?" Airik asked. "I've only recently met Miss Qiao but that does not mean I will allow anyone to badger her."

"Winifred, make the introductions," the older man said.

She ducked her head again, smiling nervously. "Yes, Zu fu. My lord Shelleen, this is my honored grandfather, Marmaduke Qiao. Zu fu, may I present Airik, the daimyo of Shelleen."

She bowed again to the younger man. "My lord Shelleen, this is my honored father, Bertram Qiao."

"Charmed," Airik said and got to the point. "To my knowledge, my secretary, Upton, has never spoken to Miss Qiao prior to their meeting in the ballroom after the business luncheon. Moreover, …"

"We do not…," the older Mr. Qiao tried to interrupt.

"You do, and you would be wise to listen so do not interrupt me again," Airik said icily. "Sajag Burgess, who left just before you arrived, threatened Miss Qiao and by extension you, by stating he would call in your commercial loans."

The older Mr. Qiao's eyes widened and his glance flicked over to his son. Their attention, Airik observed, was now intently focused on him and not on Winifred Qiao. She had become unimportant. Interesting.

"He threatened me with a loss of business arrangements in Panschin," Airik continued. "I believe Burgess to be a fool, and I also believe he is of no danger to me. There are plenty of firms that want to partner with Shelleen. You may not have the luxury of ignoring him."

"Winifred, did you have something to do with this?" the younger Mr. Qiao asked sternly.

She paled, so Airik answered for her. "She did not. Burgess attempted to bully her because he enjoys bullying young women."

"And how do you know this piece of gossip, my lord Shelleen?" the older Mr. Qiao asked silkily.

"Via prior observation." Airik paused while they processed this tidbit and then returned to the previous, unpleasant subject. "I am aware of my secretary's reputation. That said, Upton had never met Miss Qiao prior to his accident in the ballroom. I have no idea what connection they have, but I will find out. Do keep in mind she was chosen to sit at my table by your own religious rituals, something I, as an outsider, had nothing to do with."

He watched the Qiaos' expressions closely. It was readily apparent he, as an outsider, was not expected to know anything about how Miss Qiao's name was pulled from a hat. The fact he did raised him in the older Mr. Qiao's opinion, while flummoxing the younger Mr. Qiao with the fact that he knew at all.

Upton groaned again, but this time because he was attempting to lever himself into a sitting position.

"I've never met Miss Qiao," he slurred. He slumped back onto the bed, his face gray from the effort. Miss Qiao bent over him again and he managed a dreamy smile for her. "Beautiful," he whispered softly enough that only she could hear him.

"That roué made an assignation with every single woman from his table at the luncheon. He is a bounder and thus completely and totally unsuitable to even speak to my daughter," the younger Mr. Qiao said firmly.

"How could he manage such a feat without annoying every woman at the table?" Airik marveled. "They were all present and listening. This seems an unlikely story."

He thought, "Those secretaries and assistants were angling for access to me and Upton took advantage of the opportunity. That has to stop." He glanced over at the bed again. The doctor was checking Upton's vital signs while the nurse prepared an unpleasantly scented medicinal tea and Miss Qiao hovered, out of the way but obviously not wanting to leave his side despite her frowning father and grandfather.

The issue of Upton's assignations had taken care of itself. His secretary wasn't going anywhere and with the injuries he had sustained, he wouldn't be capable of much frolicking with any enterprising woman who came down to the infirmary looking for him. The doctor and his staff looked to be vigilant chaperones while he remained under their care, based on their quick call to hotel security. A request to the doctor should ensure continued vigilance. Once he was released to the Shelleen suite, Upton would be attended regularly while he healed and would remain unable to frolic as he chose. Airik decided he would insist on constant supervision rather than deal with such a messy issue again. Who knew what promises Upton might make?

He eyed the Qiaos, hovering near Miss Qiao and Upton. His secretary was mumbling something unintelligible to her, her head bent over his mouth and her face rapt. Airik wanted to sigh. Wonderful. Upton was probably making promises to Miss Qiao he didn't intend to keep, or more likely, since his speech was so slurred, what he was saying could be misconstrued into whatever the listener wanted to hear.

His decision made, Airik strode up to the elder Mr. Qiao. The younger Mr. Qiao, a dutiful son, was right behind his father and also stopped rather than walk past his elder.

"Mr. Qiao. As the daimyo of Shelleen, I will honor promises made by my secretary to your granddaughter. However," Airik frowned at their suddenly gleeful faces, "I insist on public verification along with written proof of any statements. People can say anything and often do."

The elder Mr. Qiao bowed. "You are gracious."

"I am a gentleman. I am also practical. I must leave and deal with Burgess making mischief to suit his own ego. What do you know of him?"

The elder Mr. Qiao exchanged glances with his son and gave him a nod, signaling that he was to speak on this matter.

"My lord Shelleen," the younger Mr. Qiao said, bowing as he spoke. "Burgess has been a problem for many people but not, until today, for us. We are unsure why he has retained the power he has at Second National since, if he were elsewhere, he would have been sent to sift through tailings long ago. Now that he has become a potential problem for Qiao & Schopenhour, we shall look into the issue along with investigating his background."

Airik thought of Burgess threatening Veronica Bradwell and he allowed himself a cool smile, making the younger Mr. Qiao blanch and the older Mr. Qiao nod approvingly. "Keep me posted. I have reasons of my own for wishing to see Burgess on his knees, sifting through tailings using his bare hands."

"Of course, my lord Shelleen," said the younger Mr. Qiao.

"We have heard of what happened to Howard Shelleen. Your great-uncle once-removed, I believe?" said the elder Mr. Qiao.

"Then you know the needs of my demesne come first and I do not tolerate lying or malfeasance from anyone," Airik replied.

"Indeed. It will be a pleasure working with Shelleen." He looked around the infirmary, and at Miss Qiao hovering over Upton. "Allies can be found in unexpected places, can they not?" said the elder Mr. Qiao.

"Yes, they can," said the daimyo of Shelleen.

Shelby was filled with a red haze of fury. She was so angry she couldn't think at all and then she couldn't think of anything else other than what Reyansh's friend, Bhupathi Middleton, had said to her. She stomped her way from the studio, out of the art department building and across the green and pleasant campus. This was how everyone at PanU thought of her. She'd never be anything but a tunnel chola to those worthless, wretched, entitled bastards. It didn't matter what she did or how hard she worked.

She didn't matter.

She stopped walking, shuddered in her relief upon reaching sanctuary, and slumped onto a bench near the edge of the PanU campus. It was her favorite bench and she had mindlessly gone to it. This bench was hidden behind a screen of small trees in planters and not readily visible from any of the walkways or buildings. She had never seen anyone else sitting here, tucked away from the hustle and bustle of the campus and facing the blank, back wall of a maintenance building. It was her bench and she had sat on it far too many times fighting back hurt and angry tears.

Shelby let herself cry, again, at last, where no one would hear her. Damn them all.

A bird called overhead, then another, breaking through her misery. She lifted her head to see if she could spot them. Veronica always liked hearing about the birds on the campus and always wanted to know when Shelby saw one and what it was doing and if it was one of the ubiquitous steppe sparrows or something more exotic. The bird fluttered down onto the gravel in front of her and chirped again at her.

It was a steppe sparrow, small and speckled brown and openly looking for a handout. The birds on the PanU campus knew the students were easy marks for crumbs and this one, almost too fat to fly, was no exception.

"I've got nothing for you," Shelby said softly. The bird hopped closer to her, eyeing her with anticipation. It had eyes like shiny jet beads, rimmed in white. Veronica had once owned strings of jet beads, but they hadn't been as vibrant as the sparrow's eyes.

"I've got nothing for anyone," she repeated. She wiped her eyes, stinging from her salty tears.

The sparrow jumped up and down and chirped eagerly.

"You aren't listening," she scolded the sparrow. "I've got nothing. I am nothing."

The bird hopped closer, almost close enough to touch. It chirped again, more demandingly.

"Fine. I'll show you," Shelby said and began rooting around in her pockets. The bird took it as a signal that food was coming and fluttered up to the far end of the bench. To her surprise, Shelby turned up a cracker, still wrapped in a twist of paper. She had forgotten it. Malcolm had bought her supper the evening before in the metro station and she hadn't eaten this last cracker with her soup. She hadn't wanted to throw it away and had wrapped it up in a bit of scrap paper salvaged from her pocket, afraid he would say something about her cheapness.

He had smiled instead and said, "I can't waste food either. I've been hungry more than once." He had gone on to tell her more about the Steelio warren and how different it was from the fancy private school he attended during the week. There, he had routinely seen the other students take what they then refused to eat; fancy treats he had never seen in the warren. When he could, he discreetly salvaged unwanted treats to bring home to his family in the warren. Mr. Steelio made sure his people ate, but sometimes, there wasn't quite enough to feed people who did hard, physical labor all day, every day. Some days, you wanted more and you went to bed hungry.

She looked at the cracker in her hand for a long moment and unwrapped it, the bird hopping up and down in its eagerness for a treat. Her eye caught her bag, holding her sketchbook and pencils, including the new pencils Veronica had bought her when she had made the deal to trade Shelby's sketches for Mrs. Grisson's eggs.

Malcolm Cobb had never given up. He wasn't giving up now. He hadn't let anyone else define him. He was, so he said, going to help them with Mr. Burgess and keep them from being thrown out. Why, Shelby wondered, was she giving up so easily? She had talent. Her family knew it and said so. Florence had Shelby's sketch of her boyfriend pinned to her wall where she could see it every morning when she woke up and every evening when she went to bed. Lulu, who could be relied on to tell you the truth — especially if it was unpleasant — had one of Shelby's flower drawings in a similar location. Mrs. Grisson loved her portraits of her grandchildren. Malcolm's family had loved her sketches of their kids.

Why was she listening to people who deliberately made ugly art? To Professor Vitebskin who couldn't draw at all and relied on a junior professor he openly disdained to teach the students the skill?

Why was she listening to anyone who belittled her? Yes, her father was Simon Bradwell. Yes, he had scammed anyone he could. But she wasn't him. If she could see the difference between herself and her father, then other people could too. They might not, because they were idiots or they were being cruel. It didn't matter. She wasn't her father. She didn't have to let his actions define her.

She wasn't a tunnel chola either. Anyone who knew her at all knew Shelby wasn't that kind of a girl. She didn't chase after boys, like half of her classmates did. She didn't put out. She'd barely been kissed and anyone who knew her knew that. People told lies but she didn't have to listen to them and act like what they said was the truth.

The sparrow chirped at her, rapid and sharp, demanding her attention. Shelby tilted her head and watched it while it watched her. The sparrow didn't care who she was. If she fed it the cracker, it would eat the crumbs gratefully. If she didn't, it would flutter off uncaring and look for someone else. It didn't define itself by what she did or said or who she was related to.

"You know who you are, don't you," she said thoughtfully. "Have a cracker."

She carefully unwrapped the now-broken cracker, finished crumbling it, and scattered the crumbs on the gravel in front of her. The bird hopped down, she got out her sketchpad and began drawing the sparrow, eating the crumbs left from her supper with Malcolm.

Focusing on the sparrow at her feet, joined within minutes by another sparrow, then a third, let Shelby calm down. She let the birds flow from her eyes, down her arm to her hand and out through her pencil and onto the page of blank paper. They looked so funny, squabbling with each other over a crumb when a larger one was ignored. The blank pages filled themselves with chattering sparrows, bright-eyed and eager, and joyful to be alive and eating crumbs from the metro café.

The crumbs gone, the sparrows hopped up and down, cheeping at her.

"I've got nothing left for you," Shelby said.

The sparrows waited expectantly and then, while she sat there unmoving, decided she really didn't have any more crackers and fluttered off.

She looked over her drawings of the sparrows. They looked alive on the pages, bright and inquisitive. Why didn't she trust what she saw on the page? Why did she listen to people who hated her? They didn't know her, and they didn't want to know her. All they could see was the daughter of Simon Bradwell, a talentless hack and a slut, a gold-digger who deserved everything she got until she erased her father's crimes with her blood and tears.

They didn't see her, anymore than they saw Malcolm. Professor Vitebskin saw Malcolm at the gallery showing and thought he was a banker but when he saw him again in his Steelio coverall, that image went away. He couldn't see the complexity of the man standing in front of him. He could only see the image in his own head. Malcolm did understand her, just as he said he did. He experienced the same incomprehension every day.

Shelby studied her sparrows again, filling the pages with lively movement. Veronica would like seeing them. She didn't often come to the PanU campus anymore to watch the sparrows. Veronica, Shelby suddenly realized, rarely left Dome Two and when she did, she only went to a few places; the places she had to go to where she knew how she would be treated. And she rarely went alone. When she was inside Dome Two, it wasn't just to have help dragging the wagon of produce to the Dappled Yak or the leftover radishes to the Broken Pickaxe. It wasn't just to have someone along to talk to. It was so she, Veronica, wouldn't be alone when facing down someone who saw Simon Bradwell's older daughter; a daughter who should have known her father was swindling the citizens of Panschin.

Her sister struggled every day too. But she didn't give up. She kept moving forward, slowly and painfully, but she kept moving.

"All right then" Shelby said to the air around her. "All right then. I won't give up either."

That left the problem of what she would do next. PanU wasn't working for her, and it didn't look like it ever would. Auntie Neza had an appointment with the bursar to see if she could transfer her paid tuition to PCC. If Neza was able to persuade the bursar, she wouldn't have to keep struggling in a place that despised her.

There was the scary concept of going underground into the PCC campus, but that wasn't as frightening as it had been. If Lulu and Florence and hundreds of other students went underground into the classrooms every day, she could too. She'd been underground with Malcolm and been safe. Nothing bad happened when you went underground, at least not if you didn't suffer from surface sickness and she didn't.

Shelby spared a thought for Kip. Poor Kip. He couldn't go underground ever again. Lucky for him he had a family wealthy enough that he wouldn't have to. It was hard to believe the McGrant family would, as Florence insisted, ostracize him for something he couldn't help. She recalled the rest of the Bradwell family, the relatives who had turned their backs on her and Veronica. Only Neza had stood up for them. Poor Kip. She could hope, for his sake, that the McGrant family wasn't like her Bradwell relatives.

She had people who loved her.

Shelby stood, stretched and packed away her drawing supplies. It was early, hours before Malcolm had said he would come by. She'd leave a note for him, pinned to the bulletin board where messages were traded back and forth among the student body, along with another note for Florence and Lulu so they didn't worry and could stay late to study. Then she'd go home to her sister and her aunt. They were her family, they accepted her, and they valued her. They saw her as she was and they loved her. She loved them too and it was time she told them that.

"You're home early," Veronica said suspiciously. "What happened?"

"I'm fine," Shelby said. "Really fine. Nothing bad, I promise."

Her sister studied her with some concern from where she crouched, working over another bed of tiny lettuces, breaking up the clumps of terraformers and working them under the soil.

"Uh huh," Veronica said. "I know how that place treats you."

Shelby sighed gustily. "The day was fine until the end. But I think I learned something anyway."

"And what would that be?" Veronica asked. She rocked back on her heels, watching her little sister. Shelby had dried tear tracks on her face but she didn't look as distraught as Veronica had come to expect after a crying jag.

"I want to attend PCC. I really do." Shelby stopped, dropped her bag, crouched down by her sister and hauled out her sketchbook.

"Look at my sparrows," she said, holding out a page full of chirping birds squabbling over crumbs. Aren't they good?"

Veronica stared at them and smiled, her face lighting up with joy. "It's like they're alive."

"I'm really good, Veronica. I can draw."

"Yep, just like we've been telling you."

"I think I know that now. I can draw people and animals and flowers and that means I can find work as a commercial artist once I've gotten some better training at PCC. PanU is just a waste of time and money. I'll never learn to be an artist *there*."

Veronica sat back. "That's new from you. So you've changed your opinion on fine art?"

Shelby laughed. "Not fine art, no. I think I can get there, someday, if I work hard. Avant-garde art, yes. Normal people don't like it and for good reason. It's ugly."

"Well," Veronica said. "I guess PanU was worth it after all."

"I wouldn't say that," Shelby retorted.

"I would," Veronica replied. "You had to learn for yourself and, I think, you would have always wondered what you would have gotten from PanU's Art Department. Now you know."

"Now I know." Shelby turned the page of her sketchbook to another drawing, this one of a fat squirrel she had sketched earlier in the week. "Isn't he cute? He'll sell a magazine."

Veronica smiled at the squirrel. "He sure is. He looks alive, grooming his tail. Look at those cunning little paws."

"I did learn a lot at PanU from Professor Vitebskin, though. I learned how to handle paint really well. I just won't use it the way he wants me to, to paint dirt." Shelby stopped and smiled hesitantly at her sister.

"I have some paintings, other paintings. You've never seen them. But I think they're good."

"You mean like the cloud painting you promised to Jeffen in the Steelio warren? The one you've never shown us?"

"Yes. I want to show you them today. When Florence and Lulu get home. I'll show you all of them."

Veronica could feel her heart lifting after her dreadful morning.

"We would love that. Neza's inside making tea. Shall we join her?"

"Oh, absolutely. I want to tell her how much I want to go to PCC. I'm going to be as good as Clyde Monez."

Veronica chuckled. "Better. You'll be better than Clyde Monez."

Shelby showed off her drawings of steppe sparrows to Auntie Neza and then began leafing through her sketchpad to show off other drawings, talking about them in a way she never had before.

Veronica marveled at her little sister. She was proud of her drawings. She was showing them off. She normally never wanted anyone to see what she had done. Maybe Malcolm Cobb was good for her. Shelby was willing to listen to him when she hadn't listened to her family. Her little sister fancied him. He seemed to feel the same way about her. Veronica thought of Dean and how wrong she had been trusting him. She said a little prayer that Malcolm be the man Shelby believed him to be and that he wasn't just using her sister.

The gate shrieked its warning, startling the three women.

"Would that be Mr. Jones coming back?" Shelby asked.

"I don't think so," Veronica said, worried and anxious all over again. Her hand went automatically to her beads. "You stay here while I check. It might be a lawyer for the McGrant family or something from Mr. Burgess at the bank."

"Don't go borrowing trouble, Veronica," Neza said, striving for calm. "It's probably nothing."

Veronica leaped to her feet with a determined expression. "You stay here, auntie Neza, with Shelby. If I don't come back in a few minutes, run out the back door to Mrs. Grisson's."

"Veronica," Shelby said. "What on Mars?"

"Go, Veronica," Neza said, her expression tight and controlled. She started massaging her hands. "I'll tell Shelby what happened."

"Something happened?" Shelby asked, suddenly aware that she might not have been the only member of the White Elephant household who had endured a difficult morning.

"Yep," Veronica called over her shoulder as she ran to the front door. "It sure did."

Veronica stopped at the heavy double door leading to the front garden. She didn't want to open it. She didn't even want to look through the pink glass panes. What if there was a team of lawyers from the McGrant family looking to sue them over Kip's surface sickness? She knew from bitter experience that it was unlikely but only because lawsuits took time and not enough time had passed for the initial filing. Court cases were cruelly drawn-out affairs, sanding off skin and then muscle, a layer at a time, until the bloody bones underneath were eventually exposed. She leaned her hands against the door, breathing hard. Whoever was on the other side of the door, coming up the gravel walkway, would just have to wait.

What she was really afraid of, and fretting over the McGrant family lawyers kept her from thinking about it, was Mr. Burgess. It probably wouldn't be him. It would be some lower-level bank employee — someone from Dome Six to ensure the local branch staff could not warn her — armed with a stack of documents and the sheriff at his side to evict them from the White Elephant.

She couldn't comply. She couldn't leave her home and go somewhere else in Panschin. The White Elephant was her sanctuary, her haven, where she kept her and her little family fed and safe.

She steeled herself, wanting to vomit. She forcing the bile down, and waited for the heavy knock on the door. But no knock came. She waited and waited and heard nothing. She could feel the sweat beading on her forehead and trickling down her back. Dean's visit, which would have become assault, had upset her even more than she'd realized.

More minutes ticked by until Veronica forced herself to unbolt the front door and swing it wide to whatever awaited on the other side.

The gravel pathway before her was empty. There was no one there. The front garden was empty. There was no package, no message, nothing. She was alone.

Veronica stared out, confused and upset and wondering if she had gone insane. Had she heard the gate shriek its warning? Yes, she had because so had auntie Neza.

The kitchen. Neza and Shelby were in the kitchen. Veronica pushed the door closed hurriedly, not bothering to bolt it or even shut it firmly in her rush, and ran headlong back to the kitchen. The kitchen had a back door. Maybe it was Mrs. Grisson come to visit, she told herself, wanting it to be true because who else could it be? Mrs. Grisson always used the back door and she kept an irregular schedule.

But as she neared the kitchen, she realized that the house was silent. Neza and Shelby must have, while she was agonizing over opening the front door, already left for Mrs. Grisson's house and she would have to chase after them. Yet, wouldn't she have heard cheerful voices if it was Mrs. Grisson come to call? Veronica pushed open the kitchen's swinging door and saw why the room was silent.

Dean was standing there, his face livid with bruises, old and new, and he was not alone. Next to him, grinning at her, was the thug with the shaved head who had come to the door previously wanting the White Elephant, the one who had then come to the gallery showing and told her again his boss wanted her home and she had to leave. He had dumped his jacket on the floor and the shirt he wore underneath, its sleeves rolled up, demonstrated he was made of heavy muscle. His biceps looked like boulders.

Worse, he had another man with him, also openly enjoying the reek of fear. Other than normal hair, this man could have been the thug's twin, equally large and brutal-looking; he was not the boss Shelby had sketched from Elliot's description. He was someone new.

Shelby sat hunched over at the table, openly terrified and with a fresh bruise beginning to bloom across her beautiful face where someone had hit her. Neza was slumped at the table in the chair next to her, unmoving except for her hands, rubbing each other over and over.

"Hey, Ronnie," Dean said. "You should have listened to me. It would have been better for both of us." His voice was raspy, like he had been screaming.

"That's not my name," Veronica said automatically. She stepped back towards the doorway, her mind blank except for one thing. Dean knew the thug who had come to the door. How could that be possible?

"Sound's like a good name to me," the first thug said. "I like it, specially since you don't, you uppity bitch."

"You run," the second thug said, "and I'll hit your luscious sister again. There's other things I'd like to do to your sister, and you too." He grinned suddenly, showing off front teeth that had been filed into points.

Veronica stopped dead in her tracks.

"I won't run," she said. She was having trouble breathing and her ears were full of the sound of her pounding pulse. Airik Jones wasn't here to save her from Dean this time. He wouldn't return with his bodyguard for hours.

"Good girl," the filed-teeth thug said. "Follow orders and you'll be okay." The first thug shot him a poisonous glare and he clamped his mouth shut.

"Ronnie, you have got to sign the papers for the house over to me," Dean said. He looked miserable. "Please, Ronnie, for all our sakes."

"Dean, I can't do that," Veronica said slowly. Her eyes were very wide.

"Ronnie! You're still arguing with me? What the hellation is wrong with you," Dean sputtered. "Do you have any understanding of what these two gentlemen and their boss will do to me if you don't sign?"

"Nothing good, I'm sure," Veronica said, swallowing fresh bile.

"It won't be," the first thug said and he grinned at her again, licking his lips. "I've been waiting for this."

"But Dean, I can't," Veronica said slowly. "The lease isn't in my name."

Dean paled, showing his bruises more strongly. His complexion had always been perfect, a rich upper-class emerald, and Veronica suddenly realized why his skin had been so even in his last visits compared to now. He had been covering bruises with cosmetics. Too many of the bruises she saw had mellowed and darkened; they weren't new.

"What?"

"Dean, this is auntie Neza's house. I thought you knew that."

"But I thought she signed it over to you when we got married," Dean protested. "For us and our children."

"No, Dean, she didn't. She was going to but she never got around to it. It wasn't like we were in a hurry. We had all the time in the world."

Veronica glanced sideways at the thugs who were watching her and Dean closely and listening carefully. If she could explain things, she might be able to save her sister and her aunt, or at least delay long enough for someone to show up. Right at that moment, she realized how grateful she would be if Mr. Burgess showed up with the sheriff, followed by a team of lawyers armed with lawsuits filed by the McGrant family. However distasteful, those people were rational and wouldn't physically harm her or her sister and aunt.

"That isn't what you told us, Dean boy," the first thug said. He was apparently the leader of the pair. "That isn't what you told my boss. Remember him?"

Dean cringed. He remembered.

Veronica spared a moment to wonder if the mysterious real boss was somewhere in the White Elephant measuring for new carpets and drapes and had to stifle terrified giggles at the thought.

"What happened, Dean, is …" Veronica said, trying for calm.

"Tell me," the first thug interrupted her. "Not that worthless, sodding little ponce."

"My apologies," Veronica said, trying for a placating smile. "My father, Simon Bradwell, got into trouble. He was a thief, a swindler, an embezzler."

"Got that part. Dean told us."

She couldn't think. She couldn't think at all, only answer mechanically.

"When everything started falling apart and my father's schemes were discovered, auntie Neza decided not to sign over the White Elephant to me."

"I didn't know that," Dean said.

"Shut up," the first thug said to Dean and punched him lightly in the ribs, making Dean suck in his breath and cringe back, as though he'd been hit there before.

"I was afraid we'd lose the White Elephant," Neza said hoarsely. "When the lawsuits started flying, I knew if I kept the house in my name, it would be safe. I wasn't involved in your father's schemes. My family name is different." She never once looked up from the table, keeping her eyes firmly on her reflection in the polished bamboo surface.

"It's true," Veronica said. Dean must have forgotten or maybe she never told him. Too many awful things had happened back then, piling on one on top of another, like an avalanche that never stopped spilling down rocks.

"Dean," Neza said. "I could sign the lease over to you right now, but you're not a relative anymore. The local branch will have questions. You know they will. So will the neighbors."

"You don't talk to that worthless ponce, either," the thug said sharply.

"My deepest apologies. I won't forget again," Neza said and returned her eyes to her hands, twisting around themselves on the shining table.

"Dean told us the local bank is run by some hack who spends all his time arranging his pencils. Nobody there cares," the thug said with a smirk. "We got Dean to cover for us if they do."

Veronica thought, Dean, you don't know about Malcolm Cobb. You don't know about Mr. Burgess threatening to evict us all. The bank hates surprises. No matter what you say, someone will show up and figure out what you did. You think Lulu won't ask questions when she gets home? *They'll* figure out you set them up to fail. Dean, you are an *idiot*.

"Dean, why did you do this?" The question burst out and she wanted to bite her tongue off when she saw the first thug's face darken with fury.

"Please, forgive my rudeness," Veronica added hastily to him. She didn't dare forget that *he* was in charge.

Dean looked down at the stone flags at his feet, refusing to meet her eyes.

"Cause he owes us money, that's why," the first thug said silkily. "Can't pay his gambling debts and so he offered us your fine, fine house."

Veronica stared at Dean in shocked horror.

"You *gambled*? You idiot!" she screamed. "After what my father did? He ruined us and you went gambling? Were you insane?" A dim part of her brain kept telling her to shut up but she couldn't stop.

"Your father was the one who introduced me to the casinos!" Dean yelled back. "It's his damn fault I'm in this fix. If I hadn't married you, I would never be in this fix! It's your fault!"

"It is not! You could have said no!"

"You said you'd never speak to me again! Yet here you are, screaming at me!"

"Screaming isn't speaking and I wouldn't be screaming at you now, except you *forced* me to, you idiot, by being such a *complete and utter FOOL*!"

"Enough!" the first thug roared and leaped to his feet. "Fun as it is to watch exes fight, I got business to attend to."

"Please, forgive me, sir," Veronica said. She struggled to breathe. "Gambling is a sore spot for me. My father—"

"I don't care."

"Of course, sir," Veronica said, trying hard for another apologetic smile. She spared a glance at Dean. He was sweating visibly and shaking. He knew these people. He had brought them to the White Elephant. The realization struck her like another blow. He must have been hiding this thug, his partner with the filed teeth, and their boss in his flat in Dome Six. Dean was the reason for the threats. Dean was why the thug and his partner and his boss hadn't been found. Dean, her former husband, had managed to betray her again.

It was like her father all over again. Dean only thought of himself, just as Simon Bradwell had. No one else mattered. And gambling! Dean of all people knew how her father's chronic gambling had collapsed his house of cards. He couldn't pay those debts and so he kept swindling his clients to pay his losses until he could no longer cover his tracks.

The shaven-headed thug stood up and swaggered to where Veronica stood, by the door that led to the rest of the house and escape. He towered over her, dominating the kitchen.

"You're being polite to me now," he said.

Veronica didn't know what to say so she said nothing, other than smiling weakly at him.

"Learned some manners at last, I guess."

He touched her face, gently running his fingers down her cheek.

"You're smarter than your ex. He never deserved you. Sold you out as soon as he could."

She wanted to scream and run. She couldn't do anything but stand there, his hand stroking her face, and pray he didn't hurt her as the filed-teeth goon had hurt Shelby. Her sister sat still as a statue, other than tears leaking down her cheeks and radiating fear. Neza didn't look any better and neither one could fight off two thugs. He was so close she could smell his sour breath and see the play of muscles in his thick, bare forearms. He could break her in half and not work up a sweat.

"I'm very sorry to hear that," Veronica said tightly. "We were happy, once." She couldn't stop a tear sliding down her cheek, where he had run his fingers across her face, the gesture of a lover. The skin on his fingers were rough with work and his nails were dirty, edged with something the color of dried blood. "Dean loved me."

"Not anymore. Dean is stupid and he don't learn. He didn't know when he was well off. But it looks like you might."

"Thank you," Veronica managed.

She had to think. She could never overpower these men. She didn't think she could take on Dean who, from the way he was moving so stiffly, was sporting more injuries than could be accounted for by Airik Jones throwing him over a low wall. These two thugs must have beaten

Dean. She didn't feel a particle of sympathy for his plight.

She realized something else. No matter what this thug or his partner said to her about cooperating and being safe, he was lying. She, her sister, and auntie Neza were witnesses. This man wouldn't take the risk of them talking to anyone.

"Would you like some tea? I could make you some tea for you and your companion," Veronica said, while thinking she had lost her mind from fear.

"You do learn. I like it when you're nice to me," the first thug said, moving closer to her, leaning over her, his face almost touching hers. "Your ex, he was never good enough for you."

He watched her face, enjoying her fear and knowing she knew who was in charge.

Veronica thought she would faint. She forced herself to remain upright through sheer will, and then he stepped back a pace, like a cat playing with a mouse, offering hope when there was none and there never would be.

"No. I don't want your tea. I want your house," the thug said coldly. His face had gone stony again.

That still didn't make any sense. Why would he want a house? The White Elephant was immaculate, that was true, but it was possible to bring any of the ruined mansions in Dome Two up to the same standards with hard work. Dean could sign a lease for them and no one would know who really controlled the building. The thug and his boss had to have a place already where gambling took place, since Dean found them and lost his money. Perhaps they needed a better place than what they occupied at the moment, but Dean Kangjuon had the social connections to arrange whatever they wanted in Dome Two. He could have arranged whatever they wanted in any of the domes.

What did they really want from her and Shelby?

She wanted to scream at the thought that sprang to mind and bit down on her tongue until blood came and filled her mouth with copper.

But if they wanted to rape her or Shelby, no one would be standing around in the kitchen of the White Elephant.

What could they want?

It felt like time was slowing down. She was being given a gift, a chance to think. Dean gambled with them. Dean owed them money. They wanted money. It made no sense they wanted the White Elephant. She had no money.

However, dear old dad had once had mountains of money. No one had ever discovered where all the money Simon Bradwell stole had gone. The gambling dens he frequented had been investigated and, according to their sketchy records, he hadn't lost all that money at their tables. There was plenty that was unaccounted for. Dean knew the story. Everyone in Panschin knew.

"I found dad's money, at least some of it," Veronica blurted out. Dear Gods below, let Dean not figure out she was lying.

"You found some of the money he stole?" Dean snarled. "You let me think you had nothing. You lying bitch!"

The first thug strode back across the kitchen and smacked Dean in his chest, and he crumpled to the flagstone floor. He made wet, sickening sounds.

The thug glared down at him. "Shut up."

Dean went silent, curled into a ball of agony on the floor.

The thug took the few steps back to Veronica, frozen by the door.

"Tell me. I heard all about your dad; he stole more money than an army of bank robbers could have done."

"You are quite correct," Veronica said. Her heart was pounding so hard she could barely hear him. "He did."

"Then why you living like this? Letting those ugly pictures in your house for money?"

"I just found it a few days ago. I had to decide what to do. The courts, the police, I wouldn't be able to keep it," she answered. "I wanted to keep it."

"Then where is it? Your ex, he said this place had nothing in it of value other than you and your luscious sister." The thug leaned over her again, his face so close to hers she could count the pores on his nose and see how close his mouth was to hers.

She stared at him; her eyes wide with terror. Would he believe her? "In the tunnels, underneath the second subbasement."

The thug straightened and watched her carefully for a few minutes, minutes that slowly, slowly ticked by, each instant ratcheting up her fear. He wouldn't believe her. He would hurt her. He would hurt Shelby. He would hurt Neza.

Then he marched back to Dean and roughly pulled him back to his feet.

"You were in those tunnels, Dean. You said there was nothing there. They were empty. Are you still lying to me?"

Dean stared up at him, his face contorted with fear and fury. How had she ever thought him the handsomest man she had ever met?

"There was nothing! You think I'd have been gambling in your place if I had found Simon Bradwell's stash? I'd still be welcome in the decent places."

"I found it by accident, Dean," Veronica said quickly to forestall the thug hitting Dean again and then hitting someone else in his rage. "I slipped and knocked into the wall and a piece of stone fell down and there was this little niche. That's where it is."

The thug studied her coolly. "How much?"

"I don't know. A bag of coin. It was heavy."

He marched back up to her, putting his face up against hers.

"And you left it there? You expect me to believe that?"

She stared up at his hard, icy blue eyes. "If I brought up the money, I'd have to share it with my sister and my aunt. I want out of Panschin more than anything. If I told anyone, the court might find out and seize it for restitutions."

He didn't say anything so she continued. "If I didn't tell anyone, I could disappear. Leave Panschin forever." There it was; a truth she had never admitted to anyone, and barely admitted to herself. She wanted to escape Panschin and go where no one knew her, or her past as Simon Bradwell's daughter.

He smiled abruptly. "That makes sense. This place is a hellhole."

"I know the tunnels," Dean said quickly. "I'll go down with Veronica and bring back the money."

The filed-teeth thug who had been sitting quietly, his hand rubbing on Shelby's thigh, snorted and said "You'd bash your ex's skull in and do a runner with the coin."

The first thug turned back to Dean; his face angry again. "If I want you to talk, I'll tell you to talk. You are not going down into those tunnels. You are going to stay here and get the old lady to sign those papers over to you. I am going down into the tunnel with my partner and your ex-wife." He stopped and looked over across at Shelby, making herself as small as she could. "And her. She's coming with us too."

Shelby sucked in her breath audibly and more tears trickled down her cheeks but she stayed silent. She pleaded with her sister with her eyes. She would, she knew, never fret over what someone said to her again. This was real. Words hurt, but not like fists. She knew that *now*. Worse, she had a very good idea *now* how much more the two goons could hurt her. They would enjoy it too. The goon with the filed teeth kept rubbing his hand on her thigh and across her breasts, sending her a message that couldn't be plainer.

"You. Old lady," the first thug said. "You don't sign those papers for this house over to Dean, your nieces don't stay healthy for long. Got me?"

Neza lifted her head to him and said clearly and precisely, "I understand perfectly." She did not look at Veronica or Shelby and then returned her eyes to her hands, twisting around themselves.

he thug put his hand under Veronica's chin and lifted her face up to him like a lover demanding a kiss. He leaned into her until his mouth was almost on hers and said, "Behave or you, your sister, and your aunt will suffer. Got me?"

Veronica stared up into his ice-blue eyes. They held all the warmth of chips of glass. She wanted to tear herself away from his touch, but she could see he wanted her to pull away, to scream, to shake, to give him the excuse to hurt her in front of her aunt and her sister to ensure they didn't fight back. In front of Dean to humiliate him further, making sure he didn't dare disobey.

"Yes, I understand," she choked out. She caught the flash of disappointment in his eyes and prayed he would do as he said.

"You are worth a dozen of that spineless worm you married," he said and smiled at her without humor.

"It was the right thing to do at the time," she replied, refusing to look away and repressing a shudder so he didn't know how frightened she was. "I loved Dean."

"You made a mistake."

"Yes, but not then," Veronica said. She audibly swallowed more bile, knowing she spoke the truth, just as this terrifying man was speaking truth to her.

"I always appreciate bravery and loyalty, even when it's wasted on worms like Dean," he answered.

He let go of her chin and she wanted to cringe back into the doorway, letting the wall support her. Instead she stood and waited, sweat trickling down her back. He watched her for a long, long moment before speaking.

"Take us down to the tunnel to your dad's money. No tricks or you'll never stop paying."

"No tricks," Veronica agreed.

He turned back to the table where Shelby sat shivering, her face tight with anguish, the filed-teeth goon stroking her hair and whispering something to her while she tried not to cringe, Neza rubbing her hands together but otherwise frozen, and Dean standing hunched over nearby, his arms wrapped around his chest and his face stricken and ashamed. Veronica caught his eye, and he looked away rather than face her.

Veronica swallowed hard as the filed-teeth thug ran his hand over Shelby's breasts, making her little sister cry harder, yet remaining as silent and unmoving as possible.

"However," she said, striving to sound even-tempered and calm, "I must insist you tell your partner to keep his hands off my sister."

The first thug spun around on his heel and marched back to Veronica. She stepped back, her back against the door jamb, and waited in agony for him to strike her.

He leaned over her again, closer than ever, almost touching her body with his own, brutally muscular one. "You insist?"

"I'm afraid I must." She wanted to faint and never wake up.

He stared at her and she could feel her knees weaken and she gave mental thanks to the door jamb for holding her up.

He grinned suddenly. "Fine."

He spun back around and stepped away from Veronica. She could feel herself sag in relief.

"Frankie, hands off. For now. Get the sister and let's go," the thug commanded. "Dean, you get that paper signed, or I'll beat you again. You think I hurt you? I haven't even got started."

Dean cringed again and Veronica again wondered what had happened to the man she had fallen in love with. Was she such a dreadful judge of character that she had not seen his underlying weakness? Or had he never been tested and found wanting?

It didn't matter. What mattered was keeping herself, her sister, and her aunt alive. Dean Kangjuon no longer mattered. Neither did the White Elephant. They could have the house if it meant safety.

Shelby stumbled to her feet and shambled to her, her shoulders hunched to avoid a blow or more unwanted hands from the thug with filed teeth. How long would that last? His name was Frankie. She'd have to remember so she could tell the police later on.

Veronica led the way, first thug close behind. She could feel his eyes boring into her back, and she expected him to say something vile, or worse, hit her. But he remained silent and kept his hands to himself. So did his partner. She could hear her sister gasping for air between swallowing frightened tears. She still didn't know the first thug's name. What would she tell the police when they asked? Veronica wondered if she should ask. It was unlikely they would escape, but she clung to the hope that they would and she would be able to tell the police everything they needed to find and arrest the thugs and Dean.

They walked, single file, from the kitchen and down the hallway, then down the center staircase descending from the atrium to the first subbasement and then the second. Her hand strayed to her necklace of cloudy, gray beads. Airik Jones had said they were ultimately made of star stuff, like everything in the solar system. What would he say when he returned to the White Elephant in the evening and discovered her former husband had betrayed her again and she was dead? She didn't believe he would walk away without a backward glance. Nor would Malcolm Cobb, when he didn't find Shelby and had to listen to whatever lies Dean told him. Dean was a fool to think he could get away with this insane scheme and even more of a fool to think that he wouldn't pay and pay and pay when the two thugs understood what he had done to them.

And they would. So would their boss, wherever he was. They weren't from Panschin so Dean fooled them about how things were done in the city, but they would learn fast. Not telling them about Airik Jones and Malcolm Cobb would be the only revenge she could have.

She wondered, too, if she would live long enough to learn why they wanted the White Elephant when houses in Dome Two went begging. It made no sense.

It felt like it took forever to descend the multiple stairs down to the second subbasement and lead the way to the hatch to the tunnels below. It was tucked into the far corner of the farthest room from the sunlit stairwell, a room that only had a single, dim light shaft to illuminate it. Just enough light to see by, but no more.

Still worse than realizing how she had misjudged Dean was realizing how she had misunderstood the gravity of the thug's first visit. She had believed Mr. Burgess was the real threat and had been unable to believe anyone would want the White Elephant so badly. She had been wrong and because she had been so wrong, she had imperiled her little family. Florence and Lulu would come home and find Dean and the thugs. Would they be able to escape? Or would their bodies join her, Shelby, and Neza in the tunnels below?

It didn't bear thinking about, yet Veronica could not stop herself. She still hadn't figured out what to do. They would reach the tunnels and the unnamed thug would discover she had lied to him about finding a cache of Simon Bradwell's money. He would hurt her worse than he was undoubtedly planning on.

The hatch lay in the floor before her and she stopped in front of it. The last time she had gone below was with Dean, long ago, when they had been happy, in love, and living in the White Elephant. They had explored every level and room and then explored the tunnels below. The thug wouldn't know how much time had passed. He wouldn't know the reason why the room didn't look abandoned. The floor was swept clean and the lanterns on the otherwise empty shelves dusted, because if they didn't dust thoroughly, and sweep walls, ceilings, and floors weekly, even this dim, second subbasement room would be carpeted with terraformers in short order. He would think she still used the hatch.

She and Dean had puzzled over what they had found. The maze had levels, one below the next, on down and down, connected by narrow shafts with bamboo ladders abandoned in place. The tunnels seemed to go on forever, empty of everything except darkness and time. Some sections were very narrow forcing them to squeeze through; others had ceilings so low, they had walked bent over. There was some ventilation, left over from long ago, but never enough to keep the tunnels from being both stifling and chilly. They had never discovered a lighting system like those found in the mining tunnels.

But apart from the White Elephant, the mansions in Dome Two didn't appear to be connected to the underlying network of tunnels that laced the bedrock. She and Dean had explored the empty, echoing dark maze many times and never found where the tunnels led, nor did they find hatches opening into the subbasements of the surrounding mansions. The maze of tunnels twisted like roots of plants, apparently following seams of some mineral or other, dug out when Panschin was newly founded and the earliest settlers were learning how to survive in the frozen northern wastelands of Mars.

Eventually, the novelty wore off, and they stopped exploring. She got bored with stumbling around in the endless dark night of the maze, seeing nothing but dead rock. It was more fun for her to explore every street and alley, every park and grotto and cul-de-sac in Dome Two with Dean. There had been very little to see underground other than dead rock. One passageway looked much like the other. Sometimes there were cryptic markings in chalk on the walls, but neither she nor Dean had been able to decipher the exact meaning of those markings.

Although, Veronica remembered, Dean had continued exploring underground without her. She never asked him, but now she wondered if he had been trying to decipher the markings and understand the maze.

"This is it," Veronica said. "We light the lanterns, open the hatch, and climb down the ladder into the tunnels."

The thug studied the hatch set into the floor. It was a square of scuffed bamboo, about a meter across, with a large iron ring set in at one end.

"Lift it up," he said.

She darted a glance at him. "I'll have to move around as I do so. It's heavy for me."

Veronica knelt and began tugging on the iron ring with both hands. It was heavier than she remembered, and she wrenched it upwards, enough to slide a waiting shim in place. With the shim in place, she repositioned herself to pull up the hatch from the other side. An idea flashed through her haze of panic. She could make the hatch look heavier than it really was and make the thug discount her as weak. It was something she *could* do, that wouldn't make things worse.

The thug silently watched her heaving it slowly up, then said, "Get out of the way. I'll do it."

He lifted the hatch as easily as Veronica lifted the lid on her jewelry box, long since sold along with all its beautiful, shining contents. The opening was black, the light from the flickering lanterns and the light shaft barely penetrating. The only thing that could be clearly seen was the top rungs of the ladder, set in the side of the tunnel, descending into darkness.

It had always been awkward for Veronica to swing over the side of the hatch and lower her body down into the depths. She steeled herself.

"This is how you have to go down the ladder. I'll climb down first, and then Shelby."

He grinned at her, his teeth flashing in the lantern light.

"Oh no. You will go down, then I will go down, and then Shelby will go down and then my partner will go down. So's you two can't run off in the tunnels."

"As you wish," Veronica said placatingly. "Although we wouldn't get far without lanterns. It's terrifying."

He moved right up against her. "Worse than me?"

She stared up at his eyes, colorless in the dim light, hearing her blood pound in her ears. "You and the tunnels are both terrifying," she said at last. She caught a flash of satisfaction in his eyes.

She turned to stare down into the depths. What was she going to do? Why had she so stupidly lied about finding a cache of dear old dad's money? There was nothing she could do now other than to swing herself down the ladder and climb down so she did, rung by rung, feeling her way down the ladder carefully into the darkness. Dean had always gone first, clutching a lantern, so when she climbed down, a lighted destination was waiting for her.

It took longer than she remembered to reach the bottom, but at last her questing foot found solid ground. She stepped back from the ladder with relief despite being surrounded by darkness like she never experienced in the Dome, even in the depths of winter. She wiped her hands clean on her coverall, trying not to shudder at the gritty sludge caking her skin. Clumps of dead terraformers had clung to the rungs all the way down.

"I made it," Veronica called into the lighted square far above her. She could make out the shadowy outline of the head of the thug looking down at her. For a panicked moment, she imagined him closing the hatch and leaving her to die below.

"Took you long enough," the thug called down. "I didn't know it was that far down."

"These are old, old mining tunnels," Veronica called, her voice echoing up the shaft. "They have to be dug much deeper so there's enough rock between them and the weight of the house. If tunnels are too close to a building, the building could collapse into the tunnels."

She waited. She could dimly see the thug swing his big body over the edge and feel for a rung downwards. Once he went down a few rungs, his partner leaned over and handed him a lit lantern. The light was startlingly bright, illuminating the rough walls of the shaft and the old, old bamboo ladder. The walls were patchy with discolored clumps of dead terraformers, slimy to touch when they weren't gritty and disgusting to rub up against. The thug had broad shoulders, ensuring he had a tighter fit going down the shaft than Dean ever had.

"I'm coming down," he called. "You better be waiting for me or your sister will suffer."

"I will not move from this spot," Veronica called up. "Shelby? It will be fine. I'm waiting for you."

"Okay," her sister called down. Her voice was shaky and rough.

The thug climbed down slowly. Veronica noticed that he seemed awkward on the ladder. A tiny spark of hope sprang up. He didn't seem comfortable squeezing himself down the shaft. Maybe she could use that.

As he descended, clutching the lantern awkwardly in one hand, she could see his hesitation. The lantern's movements threw wild, frightening shadows down the shaft and onto the ground below. He grunted in disgust more than once, and she thought he might have found a patch of dead terraformers when he bumped into an outcropping of rock or felt them ooze under his hands. The bamboo ladder creaked alarmingly under his weight. He didn't have much room to move around in the shaft, not nearly as much as she or Dean had.

"You're almost there," she called out. "Just a few more rungs and you'll be back on solid ground."

He stepped finally onto the ground, feeling for it cautiously first and then eagerly. The thug stepped away from the ladder and held his lantern up high. The flame in the lantern didn't do much to light up the small, natural cave, but it blinded Veronica. She had to turn away and blink to let her eyes readjust from the near-total darkness.

He turned around and around, very slowly, and examined the walls; trying to understand what he was seeing. The small, natural cavern had multiple openings in the walls, all of them black holes into oblivion. The cavern's ceiling was rough and irregular, spiked with stalactites. The floor was uneven bedrock, studded with toe-catching lumps. The walls were likewise uneven, but lacked the terraformers lining the shaft leading to the hatch. The cavern walls were silent, dead rock, the color of shadows and eons of time.

Veronica waited quietly, watching for how he reacted.

At last he spoke. "Where's the money?"

Veronica looked around, thinking hard, remembering the paths she and Dean had taken. She caught sight of one of the cryptic chalk markings and the clumsy one Dean had drawn next to it, long ago; a rough map indicating the territory they had explored. She knew what it meant and it looked similar to the older, stranger markings.

"We have to go down the left passageway and then take a turn down a side passageway. It's not far after that."

He stared into the black opening she pointed towards.

"Will there be light from the hatch?"

"No, not at all. We'll need the lanterns."

"Frankie," he called up. "Wait there. Hands off the sister. For now."

"You, Ronnie," he said to her.

"That's not my name," she answered automatically and flinched. "Forgive me." She thought fast. "What is your name, if I may? I would like to know what I may call you."

He stepped right up against her again, forcing her to retreat a few steps until the wall stopped her. It was cool and damp. The moisture seeped instantly into the back of her coverall and chilled her. She stepped forward enough to not feel it even though it meant standing closer to him.

"You can call me sweetheart."

"Um," Veronica said, not knowing what to say at all as she stared at his implacable face. He waited, and she could sense him wanting her to answer. She blurted out "That seems so informal, seeing as we barely know each other."

"That's gonna change," he replied and grinned at her again. "I been thinking. I don't know why I need Dean when I got you. Your aunt don't need to sign any papers. You want to keep her safe? Your sister safe? Then you do what I tell you. You tell those bank people what they want to hear. You tell the neighbors what they need to know. You tell that professor with the ugly pictures he's not coming back. We'll all be happy."

Despite his brutish appearance, he wasn't stupid, Veronica realized. She'd have to be cautious.

"I don't know that 'happy' is the word I would choose," she said carefully.

"You'll change your mind. I'll take better care of you than Dean ever did."

"I will keep your gracious offer in mind," Veronica said in her most noncommittal, bland voice; the one she used when dealing with process-servers, bill collectors, and when testifying in court.

"You do that." He watched her face in the shifting lantern light.

"Your sister is gorgeous, but you, Ronnie, you got backbone. You got fire and nerve."

"Thank you. You're very generous," Veronica managed to say. Her mouth was so dry it was hard to speak. She caught a flash in his eyes. He was enjoying himself. He was toying with her, playing with her, leading her on so she might hope. If she was forced to agree and work for him to keep her aunt and sister safe, she'd never stop paying.

He turned away from her and called up the shaft "Frankie. Send the sister down."

"Shelby, it will be fine," Veronica called up. "Go slow and you'll be safe. Feel for each rung, and you'll be fine. If you feel something under your hands, it's just dead terraformers. It's a long way down but I'm waiting right here for you."

"You weren't that careful with me, Ronnie," the thug said.

She would *not* call him sweetheart, but she could tell him the honest truth. "Shelby is afraid of the tunnels, and she never likes going underground, even into our own basements or the metro to use the transtubes. I do not believe you are afraid of anything."

He smirked, his teeth flashing in the lantern light. "You got that right."

Veronica chose not contradict him but he did not look comfortable, standing in the tiny pool of light surrounded by thick night. She had seen him now twice before today, spoken with him each time, but here at the bottom of the ladder shaft in the cavern, he looked afraid.

Then, to her horror, he draped his free arm around her, yanking her closer to his heavily muscled body. She went very still, not daring to pull away and noticed the faintest of tremors in his heavy arm, wrapped around her. He had not bothered to put on his jacket before coming down into the tunnels and she had not thought to say anything about how it would be noticeably colder. Was he cold? Or was he afraid? She wasn't going to run her hands over his arms to check for goose bumps.

She waited quietly, pressed against his bulk, and watched Shelby slowly descend the ladder, audibly gasping and panting for air. Her sister was terrified, even as she moved further away with each step from the filed-teeth thug who had hit her.

Shelby took each rung of the ladder downward, hesitating and sweating despite the cold. Going down meant darkness and the tunnels, with Malcolm nowhere near her to help. There was no one anywhere near to hear her scream and come running to rescue her. How long ago that visit to Steelio seemed. Going back up meant Frankie; leering at her, and, despite what his partner had ordered, touching her and whispering the vilest suggestions to her.

What was happening to Veronica, down there at the bottom of the shaft? When she looked, she saw shadows and then the thug pulling her sister against himself. He wasn't yelling and Veronica wasn't screaming or fighting, so that was something.

Shelby couldn't think of why Veronica didn't tell her at once about finding dear old dad's money hidden in the tunnels. When had she found the time to look? Her sister, Shelby concluded, must have gone crazy with the stress to do such a thing.

The rickety ladder creaked under her weight. Shelby clenched her fingers around the rungs. As she waited for the shuddering to stop, she remembered a reason why Veronica would have gone into the tunnels without Dean to explore. If dear old dad needed to hide a bag of coin where it would never be found but would still be accessible, under the White Elephant would be the place. Simon Bradwell had visited the house, before he was unmasked, but otherwise everyone in Panschin knew he thought Dome Two was a decaying ruin that needed to be torn down and rebuilt. He had said so often enough.

Did he say that to ensure no one would think to search here?

Shelby continued her descent. Each rung downward was a chore, the sensation of each cautious foot feeling for the next rung frightening. She tried to place her hands where Veronica had been, where the thug had been, so the rungs were clear of terraformers oozing between her fingers. Shelby prayed that Veronica knew what she was doing because she couldn't think of anything to do other than running and screaming in hysterical panic. It took all her focus to breathe and move quietly and do exactly as she was told.

Was the thug afraid? It was a possibility. Veronica let herself shiver against him. It was effortless to shake and release some fear.

"Afraid?" he breathed into her ear; his breath warm against her neck.

He asked an easy question and she had a truthful, disarming answer.

"It's dark, it's cold, you're warm, and yes, I'm afraid," she admitted.

She waited in the darkness, feeling him breathe against her. He must have been cold; it was surprising he wasn't shivering since he was wearing a thin shirt with rolled-up sleeves. His breathing was more rapid than she would have thought it would be from the exercise of climbing down the ladder.

"It is always this cold?"

"Yes, always. It gets colder for quite a ways down." Veronica stopped to think. "I've heard that in the true deepdown, the tunnels get warmer and warmer, until the miners are working almost naked in the heat."

He took that in.

"How the hell could that happen?"

"It never made sense to me but I believe it's the heat generated by the core of Mars. I would have thought the tunnels would have to go many hundreds of klicks further down and yet, apparently they don't have to."

"You're smart. I like that."

She had to keep him talking. She might learn something useful about him.

"Thank you. Dean didn't always like my being smarter than he was."

As soon as the words left her mouth, she winced again.

"You think I'm stupid?" he asked, his voice irritated. "Cause I don't know that shit?"

"No, no, of course not," Veronica replied as soothingly as she could. "But you're not from Panschin and because we're a mining city, even those of us who have nothing to do with the mines learn a few facts about how they operate."

She very deliberately pushed against him ever so slightly closer, enough to seem normal in the chilly air but not enough to seem suspicious. "If I left Panschin and went somewhere else, I wouldn't know anything about how things are done. For example, I've only seen the sky a few times. When I did, I stared and stared. There were clouds and they moved like they were alive."

He thought about that. "The domes."

"Yes, the domes. They alter everything."

"Veronica?" Shelby asked in a quavering voice. "Am I close?"

"Yes, Shelby, yes you are," Veronica said. "Almost there. Just a few more rungs."

Shelby descended the last few rungs, panting audibly, and when her feet touched the ground, she sagged against the ladder, whimpering in her fear.

"I would like to go to my sister and reassure her," Veronica said.

"Sure. Why not," the thug answered.

He let go of her. She trotted over to Shelby, saying, "Here I come. I'm going to put my arms around you while you get a hold of yourself. Can you do that?"

Shelby, Veronica noted, was frightened enough to not snap back at her for sounding like a mother managing a fretful toddler.

Shelby clung to her and shook. As she held her sister, with her hands concealed from the thug, Veronica slid the wires of her earbobs out of her ears and palmed them. She could use them to leave a trail for whoever came down the ladder, looking for their bodies.

"That's enough," the thug announced. "Get out of the way so my partner can come down. Frankie! Come down now. You two, over here right next to me."

"Of course," Veronica said. To Shelby she said, "Stay with me and do as we're told." She knew the thug heard her so she didn't dare say anything more.

She took Shelby's trembling hand and forced herself to walk closer to the thug, one step after the other. She thought about escaping down the tunnel, but they would be lost instantly inside the maze without lanterns. Shelby would panic and scream in the dark, and they'd be easily found.

Veronica stopped walking. They'd be easily found because the thug and his partner had lanterns and they did not.

"I'm waiting."

The idea fled into the darkness. "My apologies," Veronica said. "Shelby still has the shakes from climbing down the ladder." It was true.

"I don't care."

Another few steps and they were next to him. Veronica put her arm around Shelby and said, "We'll stop here."

"All right," her sister whispered.

The thug put his arm around her again, pulling her close to him, and Shelby went too. He was shaking, ever so slightly. Veronica realized he was cold, but he was also afraid. He was working hard to not show fear. He would never admit it, but standing beneath dozens of meters of cold, dead rock in almost total darkness and eerie silence was eating at him.

They waited in silence as Frankie slowly descended the ladder. It creaked and groaned under his weight, louder than it had under anyone else. The sound echoed up and down the shaft ominously. Veronica didn't know how old the ladder was; it had to date back to the days when the tunnel had been dug out and before the White Elephant had been built, perhaps before Dome Two was constructed.

Should she say something? It was better to sound helpful, she decided.

"I think the ladder will have to be replaced eventually," she said quietly.

The thug went still and his arm tightened across her chest.

"You think we can't get back up again? Dean didn't say nothing about that."

"Oh, no. I'm sure it will last for many more years," Veronica said hastily. "But it's like everything in Panschin. It has to be repaired or replaced eventually."

"But not yet."

"No, we'll be fine," she said soothingly.

"Frankie!" the thug called up. "Quit fooling around and get down here."

"I don't like this," Frankie called down.

"You'll like what I do to you even less if you don't quit wasting my time," the thug returned sharply.

So, Veronica thought. Frankie doesn't like the shaft. He won't like the tunnels either.

She felt her sister shift against her, staring around them at the rough walls of the small cavern and into the twisting, shifting shadows. The thug held his lantern steadily, but Frankie's lantern swung with each rung downward, making shadows dance and reveal, then conceal the uneven rock walls. The constantly shifting light made the floor of the cavern look rougher than it was. Veronica knew how uneven the ground was, with unexpected knobs of rock waiting for unwary toes and worse, sudden low spots that jarred the teeth when you found one. There was even in one of the passageways, not too far from where they stood, a shaft going down to another level. It would be easy to fall down the shaft, missing the ladder to one side, and land on the bedrock far below, a heap of broken bones and torn flesh.

She remembered during previous explorations with Dean that strange noises would echo up and down the tunnels and shafts. They had never discovered where they came from or if they were on some schedule. If they heard a noise, it would be frightening to the thug and his partner. She fretted over saying something because strange creaking sounds would also terrify Shelby.

"Veronica?" Shelby asked, her voice quavering. She pushed up harder against her sister, making the thug tighten his arm around Veronica.

"There's nothing to be afraid of, Shelby," Veronica said. "The tunnels are safe, as long as you're careful."

"I'm the one you should worry about," the thug growled. "Not the tunnels. Nothing alive down here, that's what Dean said."

"Veronica?" Shelby said again, her voice even more uncertain. "I think I see a cave-viper?" Her voice rose up and she began to whimper.

"What?" the thug said in alarm.

"Shelby," Veronica snapped. "There is no such thing as cave-vipers. I've spent plenty of time in these tunnels and never seen anything like that. They are not real."

"But Veronica," Shelby said and then squealed, pushing against the thug in her panic.

"Shelby! Get a hold of yourself," Veronica hissed.

"What the fuck are cave-vipers?" the thug said angrily. He was breathing harder. Up above, Frankie stopped on the ladder. He clung to it, holding his lantern more steadily and listening. He was breathing so loudly, he was almost panting.

"Cave-vipers are a story people in Panschin tell their kids to keep them out of the tunnels," Veronica said in her most soothing voice. "Shelby knows this. Don't you, Shelby?"

"I know it's supposed to be a story," Shelby squeaked, "but I saw something move."

"Shelby, you saw the shadows move. That's all it was. When Frankie gets to the ground, his lantern will stop swinging around and you'll see. I promise."

"What are cave-vipers supposed to be?" the thug asked. "Dean didn't say nothing about them." His breathing had quickened again, becoming irregular and loud in the moody shadows swirling around them.

"A kind of snake," Veronica said. "I've seen pictures of snakes but we don't have any in Panschin. They're long and thin, like stuffed stockings would be. They crawl on the ground but I'm not sure how they move since they don't have legs."

"I know what a snake is," the thug snarled.

"I don't," Veronica said matter-of-factly. "I've never seen a real one, only pictures in books. Nobody I know has ever seen one, except people who've been to Barsoom, I suppose. They might have. Are there snakes in Barsoom?"

"Why the hell do you think I'm from Barsoom?"

"I don't. Barsoom is the only free-city on Mars where there might be snakes. They certainly won't have them in Northernmost. It's even colder than Panschin, being up at the pole. I'm told they have everything in Barsoom so if there are snakes on Mars, that's where they would be. Do people keep them as pets?"

She could feel his puzzlement at her inane babbling.

"I don't know and I don't care," he answered finally. "Dean said there was nothing alive in the tunnels."

"Well," Veronica began slowly. "Dean wasn't quite correct about that."

"What. Do. You. Mean."

"There are terraformers. That dead moss you felt on the ladder and lining the shaft. When there's any regular light at all, it comes roaring back to life and grows as long as there's light. Then it goes dormant, and eventually dies if the light doesn't come back. The spores are everywhere in Panschin, even in the deepdown. When Dean and I came down to explore, we experimented with leaving lit lanterns to see how fast they would grow."

"Dean didn't say nothing about that."

"I'm sorry. They freshen the air. They're mostly harmless."

"Mostly harmless?"

"We have a lot of fungal diseases in Panschin," Veronica replied in her blandest voice. "You seem very healthy so I'm sure you won't have any problems. Most people don't."

"Our mother died of a fungal infection," Shelby added in a very small voice.

"Yes, sometimes people do," Veronica said. "Please, Shelby, now is not the time to discuss mama's death."

"I'm breathing these spores?"

"Since the moment the train pulled into the station, even before you got off it," Veronica said. "They are everywhere."

"This place is a hellhole, and I want the two of you to shut up about cave-vipers and terraformers," the thug said.

"Yes, of course," Veronica said. She gave her sister a warning squeeze. "Frankie, get down here now."

Frankie swore and cursed from his perch, then began climbing down faster than before. The ladder creaked with every step, making him swear under his breath. Veronica watched in silence, with Shelby shivering next to her. So, she thought. Frankie is more afraid of the thug than the tunnel and probably with very good reason.

Frankie finally neared the bottom of the ladder and whined, "How close am I?" He refused to look down.

"You're not helping him out," the thug said, his voice almost bored again.

"Because he doesn't matter to me, but you and my sister do," Veronica returned in her most expressionless voice.

"So I matter?"

"You know you do," Veronica said. She couldn't see his face but she thought, from the way he shifted his weight against her, that he was pleased.

Once Frankie had joined them, the thug said, "I want the money. Now."

"We go down this tunnel a ways and then turn," Veronica said. "It's past the light from the shaft" — she heard Frankie suck in his breath — "and the floor of the tunnel is uneven so be careful." She stopped and twisted inside his circling arm so she could see the thug's face, watching her.

"May I have the lantern?"

"No."

"You'll have to hold it high then, so I can see."

"You just lead the way to that money. I'll hold your hand so's you won't be scared."

You don't care if I'm scared. You think I might run, Veronica thought. She said, "How thoughtful of you. Thank you. I would like to hold Shelby's hand as well, so she doesn't get scared."

"No. Your sister gets to walk behind me. Frankie will bring up the rear."

"As long as he keeps his hands to himself," Veronica said testily. "If Frankie grabs at her, she'll panic and someone will fall. There is a downwards shaft nearby and I don't want her or you to fall into it."

He stared down at her for a long, long moment. He was, Veronica was beginning to understand, pleased when she stood up for herself but only when it benefited him. The moment he didn't derive some gain, or she was too assertive to amuse him, he would punish her. He wanted her to push back, so he'd feel fully justified when he beat her.

Cave-vipers would be less dangerous.

"Let's get started down the tunnel, then. Shall we?" She smiled as graciously as she could and when he nodded his assent, Veronica started toward the inky tunnel leading down into the endless night and hoped, with every step, she could think of something she could do to save herself and her sister. Mr. Burgess would be easy to manage after this, assuming she survived to speak with him.

As she stepped into the opening, she palmed her earbobs and let them fall to the ground, hoping they wouldn't be noticed in the shifting lantern light. They landed on the stone underfoot, one after the other, with tiny, echoing pings.

Shelby, as Veronica prayed she would, squealed and cried "What was that?"

"Yeah, what was that noise?" the thug snarled. His hand tightened on Veronica's, squeezing her fingers painfully.

"It's nothing," Veronica said calmly. "The tunnels make noises sometimes. Sound carries a long, long way. Dean and I would hear odd sounds but we never, ever saw anything."

"Then let's go. I want my money," the thug said.

She turned and smiled at him reassuringly. "Of course."

irik grimly made his way back to the ballroom at the Twelve Happiness Luxury Hotel. He had to find a substitute for Upton right away; he needed Elliot to research Qiao & Schopenhour and to figure out, via servants' gossip, the connection between his secretary and Miss Qiao; he had to anticipate what arrangements Qiao & Schopenhour would claim Upton agreed to; and, worst of all, he still had to socialize in the ballroom with a pack of greedy, grasping strangers. Every one of those guests had witnessed Upton's accident and would be gossiping about it. His fall was probably spectacular enough to make the social columns all the way to Barsoom, complete with wild speculation about Upton's drunken habits, a detailed rehash of his skirt-chasing lifestyle (including naming names), and speculation that exposure to Red Mercury was causing insanity in the Shelleen family.

It was going to be a challenge to steer conversations back to safety equipment.

There was also Mr. Burgess. The younger Mr. Qiao had made a fascinating statement, demanding careful thought. How did Burgess retain his power? He appeared to be a badly dressed buffoon, yet buffoons did not stay employed in positions of authority no matter how powerful their families were.

He could add Burgess to Elliot's list of research tasks.

He should, Airik knew, have someone else from the Shelleen delegation doing this work, but he didn't dare reveal a connection to the White Elephant. It had become a refuge in Panschin, a free-city he was rapidly coming to dislike. He did not want to examine why it felt like going home when he saw Veronica Bradwell.

There lay another, bigger reason for hiding his connection. The Shelleen family would have plenty to say to him about associating with the daughter of such a notorious embezzler and scoundrel. Gaston would insist he sever all ties rather than risk damaging Shelleen's business dealings, and he would be correct to do so. The senior members of the family would back Gaston on that point. Despite any questions or concerns Elliot might harbor on the subject, he would not reveal them. His valet knew his place.

Airik steeled himself and plunged into the whirl of people in the Twelve Happiness ballroom.

Malcolm Cobb read document after document in the second subbasement under the branch office of the Second National Bank of Panschin. The evidence was damning when examined en masse and in order as opposed to how the documents had been processed, each separate and unrelated from its fellows. Burgess was either the most incompetent buffoon the bank had on staff — unlikely but possible — or he was utterly corrupt; a far more likely possibility.

Yet Malcolm couldn't reveal what he found. Burgess had taken great care to implicate his fellow senior officers. If he fell from power, he'd take his peers along with him to the Dirac mines.

Anything Malcolm revealed would have to be done with the utmost care so he did not end up being punished for airing the bank's dirty laundry. And worse, the reports indicated Burgess and Simon Bradwell had worked with other banks whose senior executives also would not want their dirty laundry aired out for the free-city residents to see. And sue over.

It was galling. Every name he read in the myriad of documents belonged to an executive or family who were already wealthy and powerful, yet what they had wasn't enough. They wanted more. If he brought this situation to public attention, *he* would suffer, along with his family and Shelby and her little family. It was grotesquely unfair.

Seeing the record of corruption made Malcolm want, more than ever, to rise to the top of the ladder at Second National. He wanted to become bank president, along with chairman of the board. With each step up the corporate ladder, he could better clean house. He might not be able to prosecute anyone within Second National's corporate structure, but he could make sure there was closer and more rigorous oversight in the future.

But he couldn't do that if he didn't solve this problem first.

There had to be a way, besides sending copies of files anonymously to the newspapers and the Martian government. Both those options would take far too long and could be ignored by the recipients. Plenty of open and obvious malfeasance already had been. Malcolm had to wonder how much money had changed hands as sumptuous gifts, luxurious travel junkets, lavish entertainments, and well-paid sinecures for friends and relatives. There wouldn't have been anything so clumsy as an out-and out-bribe.

He thought of Mr. Wong, no doubt rearranging his pencils three floors above him in his once-grand office with the huge windows overlooking the park. Mr. Wong had detailed knowledge of what was hidden in these filing cabinets; he knew exactly where to guide Malcolm's explorations.

Yet he had done nothing with the information. Why was that? The answer was obvious. He knew exactly how risky it was and he did not choose to risk himself or his family.

But he would let Malcolm Cobb lay his neck on the line. Yes, indeed he would.

Malcolm could see that Desmond Wong had a subtle mind. He couldn't fail, no matter what happened. If Malcolm was prosecuted for the temerity of revealing all this corruption, then his own, well-detached hands remained clean. Malcolm Cobb was just another uppity scholarship boy who didn't know how things were done; a tunnel rat who deserved everything he got.

If Malcolm succeeded, then Mr. Wong could enjoy watching his enemy, Mr. Burgess, be punished while his own hands remained clean. In addition, Mr. Wong might have other enemies in Second National who would be put on notice.

Hmm. Now that was an interesting line of speculation. Why *had* Mr. Wong been sent to rot in Dome Two? What was his family background? Malcolm leaned against another filing cabinet, thinking hard. He knew nothing about Desmond Wong.

That had to change.

He straightened and stretched to work out the kinks in his shoulders. Desmond Wong would become another research project, but one that had to wait until after he had rescued Shelby from Burgess.

Malcolm sighed gustily. He had no idea where to start.

Another thought struck him. He turned around slowly, taking in the ranks and ranks of filing cabinets filling this room in the second subbasement under the main branch office. There were other rooms in the basement catacombs, each filled with row upon row of filing cabinets. What else was buried here, forgotten by all? What else did Mr. Wong know, yet chose not to reveal?

Malcolm could feel himself smile. If he dethroned Burgess, Desmond Wong had provided him with all the information he needed to fuel his rise to the top of Second National. With this treasure trove, there would be no skeleton in Second National's closets that Malcolm wouldn't know about. Some of the confidential memos he had already come across on personnel issues were jaw-dropping.

And all the while, he would owe Desmond Wong.

Mr. Wong, Malcolm suddenly realized, *was* taking a risk. He was betting on a lizard in the lizard races but not one favored by the odds makers. He was betting Malcolm wouldn't ruin him, too. He was betting that Malcolm Cobb, scholarship boy and jumped-up tunnel rat, had more integrity than his better-bred peers.

He would reward that faith, as long as Desmond Wong didn't play him false. Whatever he had done in the past to ensure his exile might be found in a filing cabinet. Or would Desmond Wong have carefully removed the evidence? Possibly. He had access and no oversight to stop him.

His stomach growled suddenly, reminding him it was getting on towards lunch. He didn't have time to eat at the Dappled Yak, and he didn't want to join the rest of the branch office's staff. Socializing with them over lunch was still very awkward. Malcolm sighed again. It would be faster and maybe, while he listened to the bank staff gossip about people he didn't know, he'd think of something he could do about Mr. Burgess to save Shelby.

Airik left the ballroom with a strong sense of relief. Mr. Burgess had carefully avoided him; it was easy enough to do for both of them since Mr. Burgess, draped in yellow cabbage roses, could not hide in the crowd. He had learned one thing during his strained conversations. Nobody liked Sajag Burgess and nobody could explain to Airik's satisfaction why he held the power he did. That was interesting and led directly to speculation as to what kind of hold Mr. Burgess had over some of the businessmen of Panschin along with his peers at Second National.

Even more interesting was that Maerski, Atto, Davis, and Fuziwara didn't know either, despite their extensive dealings and subsidiary holdings in Panschin. He expected better of them. Airik had quite a bit of background information on the political and business leaders in his own free-city of Purnell, despite Shelleen never having been rich enough to influence their policies. That situation was changing, thanks to the Red Mercury lode. Similarly, he knew far more about the demesnes surrounding Shelleen than he had in the past and for the same reason.

Yet the daimyos of the demesnes encircling Panschin didn't know what was happening in their own backyard.

That was interesting too, as it implied that the leading demesnes in the Northern Mining Tier weren't nearly as capable in their business dealings as their public relations claimed they were. This could leave more room for Shelleen's expansion into the mining business. His demesne had substantial mineral deposits, mostly unexploited.

Airik allowed himself a smile. He would make Shelleen rich and do it in such a way that the wealth would benefit his demesne for generations. Shelleen would become a powerhouse in the quadrant. They'd no longer be an ignored and scorned backwater, always last on the list for political alliances, business deals, and advantageous marriages.

"Sir?"

"Yes, Gaston," Airik said, storing away thoughts of which deposit to exploit first and whether or not he should go to the trouble of doing his own in-house refining, thus possibly earning a better profit.

"I've been sorting through the reports you had been working on with Upton, getting ready for the next round of meetings. Where is the report on Chung/Banerjee? I can't find it."

"It's not in Upton's case?"

"No, sir. The contents were wildly disarrayed, so I had to check each piece of paper." Gaston stopped and sneezed violently. After mopping his face clean, he said, "I've seen Upton sneezing. Has Panschin been getting to him? He's normally fastidious about his paperwork for you."

"Yes, it has," Airik said. On his way out of the infirmary, the hotel doctor uttered the dread word "pneumonia" as something he was watching out for. "Unfortunately, he's barely conscious in the infirmary so I doubt we'll get an answer from him."

"We have to have that report, sir, for the meeting. It contains all the data from Chung/Banerjee along with my estimates."

"Is that the only one missing?"

"I believe so, but I was only searching for this report."

"Damnation," Airik said.

He knew where the report was. It was undoubtedly sitting in the stack of papers in the room he was using as an office at the White Elephant. No one here knew where the White Elephant was, and he didn't want them to know. Elliot was most likely ensconced at the main library in Dome Six and wouldn't be back for hours. Or he could be someplace else, tracking down a lead. Carmine couldn't read well enough to be sent to get it and come back with the correct report. If he brought back the entire stack of documents, he'd bring back the report on Simon Bradwell and Gaston might see it.

There was no help for it. On the other hand, he'd get to see Veronica Bradwell again and, perhaps, have her smile at him before he returned to Dome Six and the meeting with Chung/Banerjee. The thought was energizing.

"I have to retrieve it," Airik said.

"Can't someone else?" Gaston asked. Maybe he'd find out where Airik was hiding, and he could hide there too, away from the increasingly maddening Twelve Happiness Luxury Hotel. The concierge, aware of Gaston's tastes in excruciating and embarrassing detail, would not leave him alone. That person — Gaston refused to use the term "gentleman" — having spotted a lucrative stream of income for the hotel, wanted to keep it free-flowing. Gaston desperately wished again he had never come to Panschin. It had brought back terrible memories; memories he had tried to bury since his arrival in ways he would have never dreamed he would do.

"No. It won't take long. I'll return in well under an hour. I'll take Carmine along. I trust you can handle the Chung/Banerjee delegation effectively."

Gaston looked uncomfortable, frowning at him; then his face brightened as he realized what Airik had said. He knew what Shelleen required of Chung/Banerjee and by taking care of things in Airik's absence, he could prove his continued worth to the daimyo of Shelleen. He, Gaston, was the senior head of Shelleen's tiny mining division, after all. It was his duty and his privilege to represent the daimyo.

"Yes, sir," Gaston said, much happier. "I'll have them primed for your return."

Ah, Airik thought. With the right push, I can get something useful out of Gaston.

Malcolm sat at the end of the large lunch table in the branch office, cautiously eating his carefully selected sandwich. Whoever had chosen the menu, once they knew he was eating in, had gone to great pains to choose the messiest sandwiches. He felt paranoid thinking such a thing, but he didn't let that stop him from selecting the sandwich that seemed least likely to spurt its juicy innards all over his best everyday suit when he bit into it.

This particular sandwich wasn't his favorite by any means. Sadly, what he preferred was messy to eat, even if delicious. He wondered, with an inward sigh, when he'd be able to eat something he liked without fretting over his table manners being dissected for flaws.

As he ate, he listened to the conversation swirling around him. Despite the widely different levels in status, the branch staffers knew each other well. Some even socialized outside of work. He wouldn't have believed that Mr. Wong would know anything about his junior tellers' lives or the names of his loan officers' children. Nonetheless, the idle chatter filling the air showed he did.

Mr. Wong had told him the senior members of the local branch had been exiled here by Burgess, so they had that in common. Yet Mr. Wong also knew what his junior tellers' lives were like enough to comment on what they were sharing. It was eye-opening, seeing how a friendly social life could co-exist with a business life. With enough time, he might be invited into the conversation, as the staffers got to know him better and came to understand he wasn't a threat.

One thing Malcolm had learned from his scholarship experiences was how much business was done outside the office. It wasn't that different really from the Steelio warren. You learned who you could rely on and who you couldn't based on what a person did at home as well as in the tunnels. Friendships could and did cross status lines inside Steelio. There were a leagues and groups to join, bringing together people with common interests.

Then it hit him. There was his answer.

If he could prove Burgess knew Simon Bradwell on a social level, outside of the office, he could demonstrate a connection that couldn't be ignored and shield the bank executives that Burgess had implicated in Bradwell's schemes. From what he had discovered in the filing cabinets, Malcolm knew which executive at Second National to approach first: a man who made no secret of his rivalry with and open distaste for Burgess. Some of the confidential, high-level memos he had scanned had been most enlightening. This executive would become an eager ally if it meant seeing Sajag Burgess thrown out on his knees onto a pile of tailings.

Malcolm finished his sandwich hurriedly. Shelby had told him she had never heard of Burgess. It had been clear that neither Burgess nor Veronica knew each other. But there was their elderly aunt, Neza Molony. Her niece had married Simon Bradwell. She belonged to the correct social strata. She might know which social organizations or clubs that Simon Bradwell and Burgess had in common. Neza Molony also had compelling reasons to revisit the past, seeking a connection between the nephew by marriage who had ruined her great-nieces and the man threatening her and them with homelessness and further ruin.

"Mr. Wong," he said.

"Yes, Cobb?" Mr. Wong answered, taking his time about it. "Eager to get back to those filing cabinets?"

Malcolm caught a gleam in Mr. Wong's eye. He was unsure of what Mr. Wong was implying. That was the problem with being too subtle of mind. It was far too easy for the recipient to miss the clue being sent. He would have to go with what he knew he had to do next and Mr. Wong would have to live with it.

"I am, sir. They certainly did need a thorough scrubbing and I'll be returning to them frequently. However, I need to check in at the White Elephant and reassure the residents that the bank is doing everything possible to assist them," Malcolm said. He very carefully did not mention Mr. Burgess's name.

"A good choice, Cobb," Mr. Wong replied. "You'll clear your lungs out from the dust in the second subbasement and reassure our clients that they come first with us here at the local branch, no matter what outside pressures are brought to bear."

So, he had interpreted Mr. Wong correctly. "Thank you, sir," Malcolm said.

On his way to the White Elephant, Malcolm worked out how to follow the lode seam, starting with Neza Molony. She had to know *something* about the social milieu Simon Bradwell and Sajag Burgess lived and worked in. She was born into it and people at that level absorbed the rules and structures through osmosis. She might also be able to supply names to him for further research, names of people who might be willing to speak to him.

The difficulty was that it would take so much time. He suspected that Burgess wouldn't give him much time. Burgess had his own agenda, one that involved keeping his nefarious activities safely undercover. Otherwise, he wouldn't have cared so much about Veronica Bradwell. Was it possible that Burgess was worried about discovery?

Well, sure he was worried. He had to be. Burgess, like Simon Bradwell, knew damn well he was dirty and couldn't bear public exposure. Yet there was something else. Malcolm could almost see the thought waving at him. He had a sudden intuition that Burgess knew he was standing on scree, shifting and sliding beneath his feet. There was no reason to think such a thing. Burgess had covered his tracks for years. Yet he had reacted very strongly to Veronica Bradwell, threatening to evict her at his earliest opportunity.

It had been an overreaction, Malcolm decided. The most sensible response would have been to stalk off in a huff, ignoring Miss Bradwell as dross beneath his notice. Evicting her would resurrect old scandals. Rehashing those old scandals might lead to questions or speculation connecting Mr. Burgess with Simon Bradwell, since all the previous case studies and news coverage had never linked their names.

Hmm. Perhaps Mr. Burgess was under pressure from someone else.

Malcolm frowned at his unruly thoughts. Speculating about other pressures on Burgess didn't help him dig out his own seam of ore. Since he knew nothing about those pressures, he could do nothing with the idea.

There was an alternative route he could follow, but it was dangerous and put him in the position of self-corruption and becoming beholden to a group he wanted nothing to do with.

He could ask Jeffen what Blue Sun knew about Sajag Burgess.

Jeffen was low-ranking in Blue Sun's hierarchy. Jeffen wouldn't know anything but someone higher up might know of some activity Burgess needed to conceal from his business and social connections.

Unfortunately, merely asking the question would put him in debt to both Jeffen and Blue Sun. They would both expect repayment of their choosing, on their schedule. Malcolm would lose before he even got started in his plans for eventually running Second National. Worse, if Blue Sun had no actionable information, he would have put himself in debt for nothing.

Another thought: What if Burgess was already working with Blue Sun? Merely asking Jeffen the question would ensure Malcolm's ruin along with his family and Shelby's. Shelby giving a cloud painting to Jeffen would not protect her. Jeffen didn't have enough clout to protect anyone from his masters.

There was also the thug. Was that thug connected with Blue Sun? Malcolm hadn't spotted the telltale blue circle but they were never obvious. If the goon was a free-lancer, Blue Sun might be interested but not to help the Bradwells. They'd want someone so enterprising to join their organization. In fact, they would insist. Or, the thug might be a member, in which case Blue Sun would be even less inclined to help him or the Bradwells. It was better to leave the thug to the police.

No, approaching Jeffen and asking Blue Sun for help was deeply problematic.

Then the scattered passersby approaching him spread out to make room for someone else hurrying through. The Malcolm's surprise, they automatically provided elbowroom for the daimyo of Shelleen and his hulking bodyguard.

Airik expected the crowds to part before him whenever he walked out and about with Carmine. It happened effortlessly. It was a pleasant side-effect of having a bodyguard of unusual size. Street crowds had never made room for him when he was plain Airik Shelleen. They weren't making room for him now. They were making room for Carmine; he was just along for the ride.

What Airik did not expect was recognizing someone on the street in Dome Two in Panschin, particularly during the business day.

Malcolm Cobb spotted Airik and veered over towards him. Here was a potential ally. The pretend Mr. Jones had shown a definite interest in keeping Veronica Bradwell safe from the thug, and he had shown an even stronger distaste for Burgess. It was possible he might have, during his days at the Biennial Mining Conference, learned something about Burgess. He routinely spoke to high-status people who would never speak to a former tunnel-rat.

It was not time to inform Mr. Jones that his identity wasn't a secret to Malcolm Cobb. It also wasn't the right moment to remind Mr. Jones that if he wanted his identity to remain a secret, he should have changed his obviously non-Panschin clothes (expensive and well-cut as they were) back to the drab standard-issue coverall he had worn before. The bodyguard, Carmine, was wearing a coverall, but he never blended in no matter what he wore.

"Mr. Jones," Malcolm said. "I was on my way to the White Elephant. May I presume you are going there also?"

"I am," Airik replied.

So, Mr. Jones wasn't going to volunteer information about his activities. Malcolm decided to get to the point in hopes of spurring a response.

"You recall Mr. Burgess's threats to Miss Bradwell?" Malcolm said.

He watched with interest as Airik Jones' face darkened with a well-controlled fury. The daimyo of Shelleen had a connection to Veronica Bradwell and not just because he wanted to hide in Dome Two for some mysterious reason. Good. He could work with that.

"I do." Airik Malcolm Cobb. The banker was still behaving as though he didn't recognize Airik's identity. Good. That gave him time to plan what to do when Cobb asked him to invest in some ridiculous business scheme.

"I've been asking questions about Sajag Burgess at the Biennial Mining Conference. How does he retain any power?" Airik asked. "He seems a buffoon, yet no one could provide me with reasons why he isn't on his knees sifting tailings."

Malcolm smiled inwardly. So, the daimyo of Shelleen cared very much. It might be time to lay some of his cards on the table.

"Are you familiar with the name Simon Bradwell?" Malcolm said.

To Malcolm's great interest, the daimyo of Shelleen stopped walking. His bodyguard also stopped walking and watched Malcolm carefully while openly listening.

"I am," Airik replied. What should he reveal? Veronica Bradwell should have meant nothing to him, yet she was becoming very important indeed. He had been looking forward to seeing her again, from the moment he left the Twelve Happiness Luxury Hotel and descended into Panschin's metro system and during his walk from the transit station. The thought of seeing her, of amusing her, of hearing her liquid laugh and warming himself in her smile had put a spring in his step. He could reassure himself she had recovered from Dean Kangjuon's attack.

What did he want to admit to some assistant manager of the Second National Bank of Panschin about her background or more importantly, his own? However, during each of their previous meetings, Malcolm Cobb had not seemed like a buffoon. He stepped in when the thug had accosted Veronica. He was most decidedly interested in Shelby Bradwell, enough to reveal a checkered background that would have gotten him thrown out of any household concerned with keeping up appearances. He had even revealed his background to the PanU Artists' Collective, guaranteeing that he could not conceal it in the future. Malcolm Cobb demonstrated integrity, unlike himself.

His mind made up, Airik said, "Walk with me."

They resumed their path to the White Elephant, with Carmine leading the way.

Airik said, "I am fully aware of Miss Bradwell's relationship to Simon Bradwell. I have only a beginning understanding of her father's criminal behavior towards his clients, since the case is so complex. I believe, based on what I have learned within the last few days, that Simon Bradwell had extensive assistance from someone very highly placed. He must have, in order to conceal his embezzlement for so long. What I do not understand is why no one else seems to have noticed those discrepancies."

Malcolm smiled coldly. "No one noticed because Sajag Burgess worked very closely with Simon Bradwell, covering their tracks. No one noticed because Burgess was very careful to implicate all of his peers at Second National. If they noticed, they would also have been sentenced to the Dirac mines, along with Burgess and Simon Bradwell."

"Ah," Airik said. "You know this to be true?"

"I've gained access to a treasure trove of files, complete in every detail."

"Which also implicate the hierarchy of Second National?"

"Oh, yes," Malcolm said. "I have to be very careful or I, my entire family, and the Bradwells will end up in the Dirac mines instead. I can't air Second National's dirty laundry without punishment."

"I see. May I assume Simon Bradwell enjoyed similar relationships with the other banks of Panschin?" Airik asked.

"I believe so," Malcolm said. "It's logical and explains so much. However, I don't have access to any other institution's files, so I am basing my assumptions on the evidence I have along with the case studies I've read."

Airik thought hard as they walked. He could offer refuge in Shelleen to Veronica, her sister, her aunt, and, he sighed inwardly, Malcolm Cobb and quite probably Lulu and Florence as well. Then there was Malcolm Cobb's family. He'd have to take in everyone who was threatened. His family would have plenty to say to him about harboring fugitives, even if they were fugitives from the justice of a free-city outside of the day-to-day purview of Shelleen. No Four Hundred family cared what a free-city got up to as long as they didn't interfere with the aristocracy. Four Hundred families were above the law within the government corridors and made their own law on their demesnes. At least Cobb's family were miners and could be put to work at once in Shelleen's mines. They might even become an asset with their expert mining knowledge.

He would see Veronica every day, while his family scrutinized their every interaction with the single-minded intensity of cats stalking mice.

He wasn't ready for that step. Instead, Airik said, "I watched Burgess threaten to call in Qiao & Schopenhour's commercial paper."

Malcolm stopped walking and turned to Airik in shock, making him stop as well. "Burgess actually said that? Publicly? To Marmaduke Qiao?"

"No. He threatened Miss Winifred Qiao, but by extension the entire firm and both families. He wanted to bully her. I informed Marmaduke and Bertram Qiao upon their arrival after Burgess left."

"Well," Malcolm said, utterly astonished. "Burgess is dancing on the edge of a bottomless pit. I can't imagine why he'd do something so asinine. He must have thought she'd stay quiet."

"She might have, but I wasn't going to."

"You've put Qiao & Schopenhour in your debt."

Airik allowed himself a cool smile. "Good. How are they regarded in Panschin?"

Malcolm thought, Still not going to admit who you are to me. But since you'll be in *my* debt, I can live with it.

Aloud, he said, "Qiao & Schopenhour are a top-notch mining firm in Panschin, along with plenty of other interests. However, get every last detail in your contract spelled out in full and in writing. Don't sign anything without a careful review. Do not make any assumptions, no matter how minor. Marmaduke follows contracts to the letter, but if you miss a detail, he'll take full advantage, feeling he shouldn't have to take care of your firm. That's your job. He's not a social climber either and so never toadies to a demesne, like Maerski, say, in order to do business."

"I see," Airik said. "Are there Schopenhours still with the firm?"

"Plenty, along with plenty of Qiaos, but the person who counts is Marmaduke. He makes the decisions. As long as you're thinking of doing business with Qiao & Schopenhour, keep this in mind. Marmaduke won't live forever and it's expected in some quarters that the firm will tear itself apart in a bloodbath as soon as the families are positive he's dead."

"You said in some quarters," Airik said. "Do you believe this?"

Malcolm wanted to leap with joy. The daimyo of Shelleen was listening to him carefully and asking him, a scholarship boy and former tunnel-rat, for his opinion.

"*I* don't because I don't believe Marmaduke would ever leave the firm in the lurch. He spent his whole life building it with his partner, Kantu Schopenhour, dead these last few years. Marmaduke wants to see it thrive for ten generations. I'm sure he's got a succession plan in place and his successor, most likely Bertram, primed to step in. He allows rumors about a bloodbath since then, when he's gone, the firm will be underestimated."

"And now Sajag Burgess has gotten his attention," Airik said. He remembered how the elder Mr. Qiao had signaled the younger Mr. Qiao to speak. Yes, it was quite likely Malcolm Cobb was correct in his analysis.

"Yes. Unfortunately, it won't be fast enough for me to help Shelby," Malcolm replied. "Or Veronica," he added, watching Airik's face closely. "Marmaduke prefers a slow, drawn-out process, sanding off the skin one layer at a time down to the bone. He's never hasty. The people who run afoul of him never forget it, nor do they recover."

"Interesting," Airik said. He was coming to the understanding that Malcolm Cobb was very intelligent and observant; so much so that it was becoming impossible to believe Cobb didn't know who he was. Instead, Malcolm Cobb was choosing to pretend he didn't recognize the daimyo of Shelleen for reasons of his own.

Malcolm broke the silence since the daimyo of Shelleen wasn't leaping to rescue Veronica or Shelby, damn him. He said, "I'm a scholarship boy. I don't have the background or resources to figure out how and where Burgess and Bradwell interacted on a social basis, but I'm sure they did. If I can prove they knew each other well and did business together outside the formal institution of the bank, I might be able to force the issue. I know you're not from Panschin, but it's obvious you're not just another middle manager. Do you have any suggestions?"

Airik gave him a cool look. "Why would you say that?"

Malcolm laughed heartily. "I'm not an idiot. You have a valet, a secretary, and a bodyguard. That's not the norm for midlevel businessmen."

"Carmine—," Airik began.

"—Is a bodyguard," Malcolm said harshly. "It's obvious. I saw Carmine in action at the gallery showing. I saw how the street crowd couldn't get out of his way fast enough. I'm not going to ask why you need a bodyguard since it's not my business. I need a suggestion about where to go after I speak with Neza Molony."

As Malcolm turned back to check the street sign, he caught a gleam of amusement in Carmine's eyes.

Airik chewed over Malcolm's words. Damnation. Did he want to continue pretending he was plain Mr. Jones from Barsoom to the banker? He tabled that concern and moved on to helping Veronica without revealing his true identity.

"I would suggest starting with Steelio, Mr. Cobb. You're from their warren, so I assume Mr. Steelio knows you, your family, and your abilities and reputation."

"I hadn't thought of him," Malcolm admitted. "I try not to use Mr. Steelio. He's done so much for me and because I'm trying to get ahead on my own merits without reminding everyone I'm a tunnel rat."

"In this case," Airik said, "I believe you should. I've spoken with Steelio twice and he seems competent and honest."

"He is that," Malcolm agreed fervently. "Steelio warrens are the best by far. I'm not the only scholarship boy that Steelio has promoted, either."

They reached Oleander Lane and turned down it towards the White Elephant. As they walked past the ruined mansions encased in cocoons of terraformers, Airik thought of a change of subject, one that would keep Malcolm Cobb from selling him some get-rich-quick scheme.

"How do the domes stay clean of terraformers?"

"They're electrified," Malcolm said. "A small charge pulses through the glassteel at regular intervals, just enough to keep the terraformers at bay."

"I see," Airik said. "I had wondered. Dome Six, unlike every other place in Panschin I've observed, does not seem overrun with terraformers. How does that Dome manage?"

"Same way," Malcolm answered. "All the buildings have a regular pulse of electricity passed through their structure. Only Dome Six was built to stay self-cleaning. Everywhere else in Panschin, the terraformers have to be scrubbed clean off every single structure and everywhere light reaches inside them."

"How much power does that draw?"

"A lot. Enough that the city could have provided streetlights in all the domes and cut the price of electricity by two-thirds for everyone in Panschin," Malcolm said bitterly. "Hey." He stopped at the gate to the White Elephant and stared at the house. "The front door is ajar."

"I don't see Miss Bradwell in the garden," Airik said. He thought of Dean Kangjuon and his attempted assault on Veronica. "Something is wrong."

Airik opened the gate, hearing the now-familiar shriek, and started down the pathway to the partially opened front door. It had never been left open without the door being attended to by someone.

"Burgess," said Malcolm and strode after him, followed by Carmine.

Sir," Carmine called, trying to get in front of Airik.

"Not now," Airik snapped and ran into the house. He stopped in the atrium to listen, Malcolm behind him. The house was dead quiet. They looked around and saw nobody.

From upstairs, they heard a crash, followed by a shrill scream and someone cursing.

"That doesn't sound like Burgess," Malcolm said. The men turned as one and ran up the atrium stairs, Malcolm found himself chasing up the left staircase with Airik while Carmine pounded up the farther away, right-hand staircase, trying to get ahead of his boss.

They followed the sounds of cursing and screaming, punctuated with loud thwacks of wood on flesh, down the family's hallway. There was a softer, angry voice as well, soft enough that they couldn't hear it clearly.

The doors to the hallway were open and they looked in each. Veronica and Shelby's room was empty.

Neza's bedroom was not empty.

Dean lay writhing on the floor, clutching his knee and cursing while Neza whacked him wherever she could reach with her shiny pink cane. She wasn't doing much damage, not being strong enough, but at some point she had managed to get the best of him.

"You bastard," she scolded. "You did this to us. You heartless, worthless bastard."

"I had to," Dean sobbed as he tried to roll away, trying to protect his knees and ribs from her cane. He made no attempt to fight her.

"No, you did not. You are weak, Dean," Neza said coldly. "Weak."

"Miss Molony," Airik and Malcolm spoke at the same time.

Neza gasped and looked up, her face a sudden study in terror, but when she recognized them, she relaxed. Dean did not. He recognized Airik and moaned, pulling himself tighter into a ball and turning his face towards the wall.

"What is going on?" Airik asked. "Where is Veronica?"

"And Shelby?" Malcolm asked. "And who's that?" He pointed at Dean.

"Miss Bradwell's worthless former husband," Airik answered.

"Betraying former husband," Neza said wearily. She stopped hitting Dean and leaned on her cane. She was shaking with exhaustion and fear. "You have to save my nieces. They're in the tunnels under the White Elephant with that thug and his partner."

"What?" Malcolm said. "That goon came back? He has a partner?"

"There are tunnels under the building?" Airik asked. "Wait. Is there a connection between Dean and the thug who threatened Miss Brad-well?"

"I'll explain on the way downstairs," Neza said. "They haven't been gone long, just long enough for me to limp upstairs with Dean to retrieve the lease paperwork."

"She tripped me and hit my knee with her cane," Dean whined. "I think she broke it."

Airik thought quickly. A connection between Dean and the thug might be why Veronica's former husband had been so persistent. He needed facts.

"Carmine," Airik said. "You keep an eye on Dean. Neza, explain now. Not on the way."

"Neza," Malcolm said, "I agree. Now."

"No," Neza spat out. "On the way. We have to hurry." She limped towards the open doorway, heading determinedly towards the hallway and the landing. She did not look to see if they followed and started talking as if they were. Malcolm and Airik had no choice but to follow.

All three men listened in horror as Neza explained what had happened as she hobbled down the hallway, supported by Malcolm on one side and Airik on the other. Carmine followed behind, carrying a weeping Dean.

By the time they reached the stairwell landing leading to the first floor, Airik had reached his conclusions.

"Mr. Cobb," Airik said.

"Call me Malcolm," Malcolm said.

"You still go into the tunnels on a regular basis. What is below us here?"

"Old, old tunnels," Malcolm said. "This region was dug out generations ago."

"Do these tunnels lead anywhere or are they blind alleys?"

"I doubt anyone knows anymore. I need to go down now, to rescue Shelby and Veronica. You can go for help, Mr. Jones," Malcolm said.

"No. I'm going with you."

"I'm still a miner, Mr. Jones." Malcolm gave Airik a long, searching look over Neza's head. "I know tunnels, I know mine sign, I know what to expect. How much time have *you* spent in the deepdown?"

"Enough to know what I'm doing," Airik replied.

"You certainly aren't dressed for it."

"Neither are you."

"Sir," Carmine said. "You can't go down there."

On the atrium floor, Airik let go of Neza, helped her to a chair, and turned back to Carmine, stony faced, who was still coming down the stairs carrying Dean.

"Are you telling me I can't?"

"Yes sir, I am. You can't. It's my job to keep you safe."

"No, it is not. Your job is to do what I tell you to do. You stay with Neza. Extract any information out of Dean you can about the thug and his partner and their boss, I don't care how. The thug's boss is out there, and he may come here looking for them. You'll need to ready for that risk. Do not allow anyone else inside other than the police."

"What the hell am I doing here in Panschin if I'm not protecting you?" Carmine protested.

"Following my orders," Airik replied.

"I wouldn't take you into the deepdown anyway," Malcolm interjected. "I know how to wiggle through tight spaces in the dark. I've left plenty of skin behind to prove it. You're bigger than I am, and I can't help Shelby and Veronica if I'm trying to shepherd two newbies through a squeeze.

"As for you, *Mr. Jones*," he added. "What kind of real experience does the daimyo of Shelleen have in the deepdown?"

"I thought you recognized me," Airik said, not bothering to deny reality.

"Stop this foolish posturing this instant," Neza snapped, her patience completely gone. She smacked her cane on the floor for emphasis, making Dean cringe back against Carmine's chest. "My nieces are in danger. Quit this yammering and either go down and rescue them or go get help."

"Neza, give me directions to the correct room in your second subbasement," Airik said. "I expect detailed information from Dean and yourself about the situation upon my return. Carmine. Guard the house. Malcolm, shall we go?"

"Yes, my lord Shelleen."

"Call me Airik," Airik replied. He headed down the stairwell to the lowest level of the White Elephant, Malcolm close behind.

The very short trip, made faster by fear and dread, didn't leave much time for Airik to brief Malcolm on his earlier life as just another member of the Shelleen family, working in and eventually slated to run its small mining operations, until the discovery of the Red Mercury lode.

In the second subbasement room, Malcolm lit the remaining pair of lanterns.

As he did so, they heard a scream, broken and wavering, echoing up the shaft through the open hatch.

Malcolm flung himself at the hatch and scrambled down the ladder, lantern in hand. If the daimyo of Shelleen wanted to follow, he was welcome to do so. Malcolm could only hope he wasn't too late. He also hoped he wouldn't have to rescue Airik Shelleen from the perils of the deepdown. He'd leave the man behind if it meant saving Shelby and Veronica, despite the host of problems that would arise from doing so.

He knew he was heading towards a fight in the tunnels, always a dicey proposition, especially since he'd probably have to do it in the dark. It wasn't like the thugs — two of them according to Neza — would politely move to a larger cavern where there would be room to maneuver and hang up lanterns for better lighting. This fight would be up-close, in the shadows, and vicious; knives and fists, knees and elbows and feet, surrounded by unyielding, uncaring rock that did its own damage to flesh slammed against it.

The deepdown always craved a blood meal. It did not discriminate based on motives.

Veronica took a cautious step forward, feeling the thug's eyes boring into her back. Then another. She couldn't see what lay before her very well. The thug held up the lantern but she blocked most of it, and what was left of the pool of light didn't extend far enough for her to move quickly. The shadows capered across the ceiling, walls and floor of the small cavern behind her as well as the much narrower passageway before her, revealing and concealing. The light reflected spots of glitter here and there from water drips which helped to conceal the earbobs she had thrown down at the mouth of the tunnel.

"You're not moving fast enough," the thug said.

"I'm afraid of tripping," Veronica replied as calmly as she could manage. "It's uneven so you should watch your feet."

They worked their way slowly down the tunnel, Veronica keeping her hand on the wall so she wouldn't miss the turn. There were two right-hand side openings, and she decided, on the spur of the moment, to take the second, farther away one. This particular tunnel's width varied wildly, from the narrow opening near the hatch to considerably wider farther along when they reached a long-ago vestige of some ancient cavern. The wider section held the two side tunnels. After that, this particular tunnel tightened to a squeeze just wide enough to walk through without brushing the sides with her shoulders, and she had to duck her head. The thug and his partner wouldn't make it through that section easily. Her measured, painstaking progress gave her more time to think what she could do to salvage the situation. She wished desperately she had never made up such a stupid lie about finding dear old dad's stash of coin.

No one was coming to save her and her sister. She had to do it, but how? Shelby wouldn't be any help. Her sister, Veronica knew, was too terrified to think rationally. At least she was capable of following directions, rather than panicking, and running blindly down a tunnel, screaming all the way.

She herself was able to think again, but what to do? She couldn't fight off the thug or his partner. They were probably armed, knives at the very least, and they had no inhibitions about hurting anyone with their fists. Dean's injuries were livid and painful proof. She had nothing in her pockets, not even a gardening tool. She wanted to stroke and rub her bead necklace again but the thug held one hand and she was keeping her other hand on the wall.

In fact, why was he clutching her hand? She wouldn't escape and leave him to take out his fury on Shelby. His hand was sweaty in hers and he was breathing harder than he should have for such minor exertion.

Then Veronica realized something: He wasn't grasping her hand to keep her from running off. The thug was afraid. He was afraid of being dozens of meters below the surface in a narrow tunnel. It was dark, cold, alien, and unwelcome to life. He didn't know where he was. As the ceiling of the tunnel got lower and closer, he had to lower his arm holding the lantern and duck his head more. Pebbles moved and shifted under their feet, making a whispery, rattling sound, and his fingers squeezed painfully around hers every time they did.

He was afraid. And if the thug was afraid, it was a good bet his partner, Frankie, was terrified. Shelby was trapped between them. She could, Veronica realized with a start, tear her hand free and run down the tunnel and escape. But she wouldn't escape without her sister.

He was afraid. He was afraid of the tunnel maze. He was afraid of the millions of tons of rock overhead waiting to crush him into jelly. He was afraid of the dark. He was afraid of getting lost and dying of thirst in the endless labyrinth of night.

She did have an advantage over him; several in fact. She wasn't afraid of the dark, total as it was. She knew nothing lived down here. She knew the tunnels wouldn't collapse. She knew something about the maze they formed. There were dead ends, shafts leading farther downwards, and crisscrossing passageways that had fooled her and Dean into walking in circles. It was possible to hide but only if it was dark. The tunnels would help when they got narrow and low, too narrow and too low for the thug and his partner to wiggle through. She had to get to Shelby and pull her away and then they could hide, invisible in the dark. They wouldn't even have to go very far, if they remained silent.

They could hide in the dark, but only if it was dark for everyone. She had to break the lanterns, leaving them all on an even footing. These tunnels had no bioluminescence. One time, she and Dean had experimented with blowing out the lantern. The darkness was complete, total, all encompassing, thick and smothering in its intensity. Nothing was visible, only solid blackness. Closing her eyes during deep winter nights was the palest imitation of the endless midnight living underneath Panschin in the deepdown. She supposed it was like being blind, but with the added pressure of suffocation. Eventually, if you waited long enough in the dark, as she and Dean had discovered, your brain decided that you could see; black shapes moving against a black background, but it was a trick, a deceiving hallucination designed to make you stumble into stone and hurt yourself.

When she and Dean had experimented, sound and touch became all-important ways to navigate; one hand on the tunnel wall, stepping as cautiously as possible on the uneven floor, keeping the other hand overhead to avoid the rocky outcroppings hanging down from the tunnel ceiling. They had to listen intently, hoping to hear something, anything to indicate where they were. Sometimes there were strange sounds, but not the ones they made themselves. Sometimes they could be right next to each other, yet hear almost nothing, whereas in other places in the tunnels, sound bounced around like rubber balls, echoing and ricocheting until they didn't know where it came from. Sometimes the sounds knocked against the tunnel walls like someone at the door and other times they dragged and wavered, changing pitch and volume randomly.

She and Shelby could hide in the dark.

The turn into the side passageway came at last, and she led the group down the new tunnel, darker and narrower than before, with a much rougher floor. The light seeping down the hatch had long since vanished as if it had never existed. This tunnel would widen suddenly, becoming wide enough for her to walk with her arms outstretched and not brush the walls. The natural cavity would then suddenly get narrow, leaving far less room to maneuver. The rock overhead was lower, rough and uneven, and it wouldn't be long before the thug following her would slam his head into a rock outcropping. He'd have to stoop. Time was running out for her to figure out how to get away with Shelby and hide in the dark.

It was cold and she couldn't stop herself from shivering. The thug must have been even colder, with only his thin shirt to protect him. Shelby's teeth chattered, but she couldn't tell whether from cold or fear or both. The ceiling of the tunnel had damp spots and droplets of icy water fell at random, making Veronica and Shelby both gasp when one landed.

Frankie snarled and swore suddenly, stumbling against Shelby who squealed and pushed up against the thug in her panic, pushing him into Veronica and stopping her in her tracks. His lantern swung with the impact, making the shadows writhe.

"What the fuck is wrong with you, Frankie," the thug growled, correctly interpreting Shelby's frightened shove into him and her whimpered pleas as her attempt to escape Frankie rather than attack him.

"If you can't keep your damn hands to yourself, I'll cut them off."

"It's not my fault," Frankie whined. "I tripped on something."

"Cause you ain't paying attention, you coglione."

"Please be careful, Shelby," Veronica said.

"What about me?" the thug demanded. He tightened his fingers around her hand again. He was standing so close to her, he could pull her against him effortlessly. She wouldn't be able to move.

She had to say something supportive.

"I do want you to be careful. It's just that I don't believe a man like you needs constant reassurance and handholding the way Shelby does, or Frankie for that matter," she replied. Veronica carefully did not say one word about the thug's hand wrapped around her own or how his breathing had quickened.

"I don't need handholding," Frankie spat.

"Then why are you grabbing at me?" Shelby whimpered. "You keep putting your hands on me." She pushed closer to the thug, desperate to get away from Frankie. Veronica could hear her sister's panting breath and chattering teeth and knew Shelby was close to her breaking point.

"I did not, you lying bitch," Frankie muttered.

"Shut up, both of you," the thug said. "Keep moving."

He held the lantern up higher, but it swung as he did, making the shadows leap and the slow water seeps catch the light and flash. They were in the widest part of this tunnel, with space to turn and move. The tunnel walls were mottled dark browns and roughly cut, worn away by time and ancient water. One wall had strange chalk markings on it, blurred into the rock by time and moisture. Each uneven spot formed a pool of blackness that shifted and moved as his lantern swung from his hand. The ceiling was markedly uneven, with lumps of rock hanging down, dripping onto the floor. He couldn't hold the lantern as high as he had before. A stalactite would knock it out of his hand if he wasn't careful.

The thug pointed at the blurry chalk scrawl. "What's that mark?"

"I don't know," Veronica answered. "Dean and I never worked out what they meant. They're kind of random."

Actually, they weren't. She didn't know what the symbols meant but nearly always, there was a chalk drawing near a junction of tunnels or near a downshaft.

Then a sound rolled down through the tunnel, gaining in volume, whooshing and echoing from somewhere else, and dying away slowly, causing the thug and Frankie to gasp. Veronica heard Shelby squeal again, more frightened than before.

Veronica snatched her hand from the tunnel wall and seized her necklace. She wrenched it off, scattering beads onto the ground. Each bead landed with a ping, the multiple sounds rattling and echoing in the tunnel, echoing the earlier sound. She caught the broken strand, with its handful of remaining beads and thrust them into her pocket. The dropped beads skittering across the tunnel floor caught the light, like tiny eyes, and set tiny pebbles moving when they knocked into them.

As she had hoped, the thug stopped at once, and even better, Shelby shrieked, "Cave-vipers!" and lunged against the thug, throwing him off balance. He stepped on a patch of wet slick stone and his foot slipped, making him curse, as he stumbled and banged painfully into the tunnel wall.

He let go of Veronica's hand.

She whipped around and slapped his lantern, knocking it from his hand and smashing it into the tunnel wall.

The flame vanished.

That left Frankie's lantern. He was yelling about cave-vipers and turning, swinging his lantern wildly trying to see where they lay in wait to bite him. How could she reach it and break it, without getting too close? He'd grab her, or worse, the thug would. The thug scrabbled madly, reaching for her in the tunnel while she stumbled away from his grasping hands. He wouldn't let go of her a second time. With one lantern gone, the cavern got that much darker, the moving shadows blacker.

Another creaking noise rolled down the tunnel terrifying Shelby anew.

She screamed as loudly as only Shelby could, finishing with "It's caving in! The tunnel's caving in! We're going to die!"

Frankie screamed louder than Shelby, deafening in the tunnel, and swung his lantern to avoid falling rock and hit a stalactite.

The tunnel plunged into darkness.

Trying to reach Shelby, screaming in terror, Veronica stumbled against the thug who grabbed at her in the inky blackness. He tried to pull her to him, forcing her against the tunnel wall. She yanked free, and she could hear her coverall tear, and shoved him blindly. She heard him collide against the damp, rough wall and the sound of someone smacking his head against the rock. Shelby's screams echoed up and down the tunnel, deafening and covering any sound she made. She stumbled over the thug in the darkness again, then caught her sister's arm.

Shelby screamed louder and tried to pull away from her sister's grip.

"Shelby, grab my hand," Veronica hissed. To her intense relief, her sister heard her and stopped fighting. Her screams subsided to whimpers and pants. She found Shelby's hand and yanked her down the tunnel and away from the thug and Frankie, both cursing and swatting at the darkness. She felt one of their hands on her, but she pulled away, bruised but free. She was willing to scrape up against the slimy, chilly tunnel walls and use them to guide her away, whereas he was afraid of getting too close to them. He was tall enough to slam his head on the stalactites and she was short enough to miss them.

The darkness was complete; suffocating and immobilizing. It pressed down against all of them, a heavy physical force of its own. A few halting steps were all that were needed to put Veronica and Shelby out of his reach, steps that scraped her skin against the tunnel wall and smashed her feet against the rough floor.

The tunnel narrowed without warning and the ceiling got lower, working to her advantage. She could maneuver without hitting her head on a rock outcrop and, based on his louder curses, the thug could not.

Then Shelby started screaming again. She screamed and screamed and screamed, her screams echoing and reverberating against the tunnel walls. It was earsplitting and completely concealed the sounds of Veronica's breathing and movements.

Words finally became clear in Shelby's hysterics: "It touched me! Something touched me!"

Veronica tugged Shelby closer to her, trying to drag her a few steps farther away up the constricting tunnel. Had the thug and Frankie gotten closer? Close enough to reach them, and that was what Shelby felt? She yanked and tugged and dragged her screaming sister farther down the increasingly narrow passageway, the smothering darkness blocking every sense other than touch and sound and the smell of sweaty fear. Then she slipped, taking her sister down onto the tunnel floor with her as she stumbled to her knees. Her sister struggled against her, wanting to run and run and run away but there was no safe place to run to.

She squirmed, wrapping herself around Shelby to trap her in place, and finally worked a hand free to clamp over Shelby's mouth. Silencing Shelby didn't silence the tunnel; her screams reverberated back and forth, slowly dying. As the noise ebbed away, Veronica's hearing struggled to return. Her ears rang. But Veronica could hear the thug and Frankie yelling at each other, and at her. The thug's rage was incandescent, almost visible in the total and smothering blackness.

If they caught her now, they would beat her and Shelby to death, after raping them both. The thug and Frankie would then be lost forever in the deepdown, dying slowly of thirst and the insanity brought on by the all-encompassing weight of darkness. Their bodies might be found eventually, along with her and her sister's.

Veronica pushed the frightening images aside. Thinking that way led to madness and freezing in fear and not to escape. They were still alive, the thug didn't have his hands on her, and that meant she still had a chance.

She whispered to Shelby, "Shut up! Shut up! Stop fighting me."

Her sister wriggled and squirmed, trying to climb closer to her, but she kept quiet when Veronica removed her hand. She could feel Shelby's face, wet with tears and snot, her hair in strings. She could feel her violent shivering.

"Shh," Veronica soothed in a whisper. "Shh. We have to be absolutely quiet." She held her sister tightly, sharing welcome body heat and reassuring touch.

Shelby gulped, the sound clearly audible, and Veronica heard the thug inhale sharply from somewhere not too far away.

"That bitch! She's not far." The thug's voice was harsher, revealing how vicious he really was.

"I can't see a damn thing," Frankie whined.

"Neither can I. Shut up and listen."

"Can't we go back?"

"We need them. We need *her*," the thug growled. "You think that useless Dean's gonna be able to lie to those bank guys? They'll believe *her*."

"You just want the money," Frankie spat.

"Oh, I want that money. More than ever. And I want Ronnie. She'll regret trying to cheat me every single day of the rest of her life." He paused, taking a deep, shuddering breath. "I'm gonna enjoy what I do to her. I'm gonna take my time. I won't leave a mark where it will show, but she will never forget what she did to me for one second. She'll never cheat me again. She won't dare."

Veronica couldn't stop herself from shaking. It would be better to die in the tunnels with Shelby than go near him.

"What if we can't get back?" Frankie asked. He hiccupped, sounding as if he was near to tears, and she could hear his teeth chattering.

"We just go back the way we came, you poncy little sod. Try and think. Don't know why the boss said you had to come to Panschin along with me. Manuel would have been better for this job. You are useless."

"I wish I'd stayed in Barsoom," Frankie whimpered.

"I wish you'd stayed in Barsoom, too," the thug growled. "This was a plum assignment. It would get me rank. I'd run this hellhole of a town eventually. You screwed this up for me, panicking and breaking the lantern and letting Ronnie get away."

There was a bit of quiet, then Frankie said, very slowly, "The big boss won't like this."

"No. He won't. That's why we are gonna find Ronnie, we are gonna find that money, we are gonna control that house, and I am gonna take over Panschin. I am not gonna fail. I know what happens to guys who fail."

"I wish I'd never come here," Frankie whined.

"So do I. Shut your gob and let me think."

Veronica thought, So. Just like I thought, they're not from Panschin. They don't know anything about being underground.

She shifted around Shelby so they could whisper close to each other's ears, feeling her way in the dark. She didn't dare let go of her sister in their shared blindness. Hugging her kept them both from shivering as much from cold and fear.

"Shelby," Veronica whispered. "There are no cave-vipers. I want you to remember that."

"But I heard them," Shelby whispered back. "Something touched me."

"That was Frankie. You heard pebbles underfoot, and my breaking my necklace, and you let your imagination run away with you, just like you always do."

"That was *not* him, and I do not let ...." Shelby stopped, distracted. "You broke your necklace?"

"And I dropped my earbobs. To leave a trail."

"Why are you wasting time telling me this?" Shelby whispered. "We have to get away."

Thank the gods above and below, Veronica thought. If she gets mad at me, my sister might be able to think again and that means she can help me. I hope. "Because I'm going to throw the rest of my beads at the thug and Frankie and I'm going to yell 'cave-vipers.' I don't want you to panic."

"You will? What should I do?"

"I want you to hold my hand while we work our way along the tunnel wall away from them. Do not let go of my hand, no matter what. And Shelby?"

"Yeah?"

"I want you to scream like you've never screamed before about cave-vipers and cave-ins and cave-trolls and anything else scary you can think of. If those goons panic, they'll hurt themselves trying to get away. There's a mine shaft downwards in a side tunnel not too far from here. Maybe they'll run into it in the dark, fall in, and break every bone in their bodies."

"What if we run into it?" Shelby hissed.

"We're going to be careful. They don't know, and they won't be. Do not let go of my hand."

"You better be right," Shelby muttered, a vestige of her normal self peeking through her distraught nervousness.

"Me or them, Shelby. You choose," Veronica whispered back harshly.

"You. Throw the beads."

Veronica carefully felt down her body, reaching the pocket where she had stashed the remains of her cloudy bead necklace made from slag glass, her last piece of jewelry. It was the jewelry she had been able to keep because it was completely worthless to anyone but her. It wasn't worthless now. Just like all her other jewelry, long since sold to save her little family, this last string of beads, like its matching earbobs, would save her little family.

She palmed the string, letting the beads slide off into her hand; crouched and twisted around back the way they had come. She needed to toss her loose beads so they made noise, pings and tinkles, and maybe even shake the scree they landed in, making it hiss like something slithering in the dark.

"Stand up, Shelby," Veronica whispered. "Up against the tunnel wall. Real slow so you don't hit your head on hanging rock."

Shelby shuddered all over and whispered, "It's freezing and wet."

Veronica had her arms wrapped around her sister. She could feel her sister's shivers and how hard she was trying to keep her teeth from chattering so the noise would not betray them.

"I know. Try and be brave and then scream after I yell 'cave-vipers' and toss my beads. Then we'll walk away as quiet as mine mice."

"Got it."

Veronica slowly stood, and freed her arms, letting go of Shelby's shivering body. She kept one hand gripping Shelby's and other holding her beads. She gritted her teeth. Would the thug and his partner panic? He was afraid, furiously angry, but still thinking. Frankie, though. Frankie was near panic from the sound of his voice, and his noisy, stumbling, toe-stubbing walk, and the sound of his arms hitting into the tunnel walls, and his whining every time he did so.

She flung the beads wide. She could hear them hitting the ceiling, the walls, and the tunnel floor in the loose scree. The sounds reverberated, and then she heard something else, from farther away, something that sounded like movement.

"Cave-vipers!"

Shelby screamed and screamed and screamed, releasing all her fear and terror. She screamed about cave-vipers and cave-ins and cave-trolls. Veronica screamed too, increasing the noise level and pulled her sister's hand. She edged them down the tunnel, nearer the shaft, keeping her back to the cold, damp wall. Shelby followed closely, screaming herself into hoarseness, but keeping up with her sister, step by step into the claustrophobic blackness weighing down on them and on everything else in the tunnels under Panschin.

Malcolm scrambled down the ladder faster than he had ever descended a shaft before. On the way down, he automatically processed the dead terraformers, the bare rungs on the ladder where someone's hands had recently been, the way it creaked under his weight showing its age, the natural stone of the shaft and tool marks showing where men had widened and shaped it, the depth of the shaft, much deeper than he had expected. Why was this shaft here? It had also been narrower than he expected, with little room to maneuver.

It would be damn near impossible to haul someone injured up this ladder without specialized gear and a crew working both ends.

All the while down, he heard someone screaming, the words lost in the sound, coming from somewhere farther down and farther away. It was impossible to tell in the tunnels where sounds came from; sometimes, they just appeared and no one knew why or from where. Other times, there were knockings. Knockings were a warning from what lived in the deepdown, a warning to get out.

He jumped the last few rungs, trusting to his experience and what his eyes told him about the cavern floor. He hit a sheet of uneven but relatively flat rock and moved quickly to the center of the small, natural cavern. He could stand upright here and raise his arm high, allowing the lantern to fill the space with dim light. Malcolm turned slowly, counting the tunnel mouths opening off the cavern. The bare rock left no sign of footsteps. He could still hear screaming and voices but he couldn't tell where they came from. Shelby and Veronica could be trapped in any of them. They might not even be together anymore.

He knew nothing of the thug or his partner. Did they have experience underground? If they did, they could be anywhere. They would have lanterns to light the way. There wasn't a hint of light seeping from any of the tunnel mouths, indicating tunnel bends and the lanterns being far away. If they were members of Blue Sun, they were likely to be seasoned old hands and fully comfortable in the deepdown.

As Malcolm turned slowly back to the ladder, he watched Airik climb down rapidly, and then also leap confidently over the last few rungs.

As soon as Airik's feet touched the ground, he lifted his lantern and spun around, taking in the tunnel mouths, and then strode over to Malcolm.

"There's mine sign," Malcolm said, pointing to the pair of chalk markings on the wall. "This place is at the center of a maze of natural caverns and passages along with man-carved tunnels. There's nothing heading back to the surface anywhere near here, but there's a lot of downshafts. There's another natural cave down the tunnel left from the ladder and across the way. Someone else drew the other chalk marking, a map of some sort, I believe, but the person who drew it didn't know how to indicate mine features."

"Do you see any sign of where Veronica and Shelby were taken?" Airik asked.

"No. And the sound won't tell us."

Airik frowned. "No, it won't." He lifted his lantern high, memorizing the mine sign Malcolm indicated. He stepped back and turned more slowly, studying the openings, and stopped suddenly.

"There." He pointed at a tunnel mouth that looked just like the others. "Veronica went down that tunnel. I assume she's with her sister."

Malcolm gave him a look. "How can you know? The ground by the tunnel mouths is too smooth to take tracks."

Airik smiled at the tunnel's mouth, feeling a surge of hope wash over him.

"Veronica left me a sign." He walked over and picked up first one earbob and then the other and held them up for Malcolm to see. "She knew I would recognize them. She knew I would come for her."

Malcolm studied the earbobs, cloudy gray lumps of glass hanging from fine wires, flashing in the lantern light.

"You're right. They don't belong down here. We'll take this tunnel to start with. There's a downshaft a few hundred meters down this tunnel along with some side corridors. The real question is are those two thugs with the girls?"

Airik considered this rapidly.

"I'd say yes. Veronica kept her earbobs together. I don't believe the thugs are familiar with the tunnels below Panschin because if they were, they wouldn't have needed Veronica to show them how to get down below nor would they have needed her to lead them to Simon Bradwell's stash. They could have found it at their leisure. Bags of money do not get up and walk away on their own, particularly if they are hidden in a tunnel.

Malcolm's eyes widened. "They're not from Panschin. The thug I saw wasn't dressed right, like your clothes aren't from Panschin." His face lit up with relief. "They're not Blue Sun. They probably won't know what they're doing underground."

"What is Blue Sun?" Airik asked.

"I'll fill you in as we go. Quiet and fast. You know how sound can travel."

"I heard knocking while on the ladder," Airik admitted reluctantly.

"Yeah. We've got to move," Malcolm replied. If Airik knows what knocking means, he's not a complete amateur, he thought with some relief. And he handled himself well on the shaft ladder.

He moved quietly towards the tunnel mouth, Airik at his side.

"Can these lanterns be dimmed?" Airik asked. "I don't want them to see us before we see them. I don't believe in handicapping myself in a fight."

"Have you ever been in a fight? A real one, like a bar brawl?"

Airik thought of hitting Dean from behind. His knuckles still hurt from the punch. "Only once, but I have trained extensively. I can defend myself."

"But can you take a punch?"

"Yes. I've done it often enough in practice." Some of those punches had hurt like hell too, leaving bruises that sometimes lasted for days. It would, Airik understood, hurt far more when his opponent wasn't concerned about inflicting permanent injury or killing him.

"Don't expect these guys to play nice or fair."

Airik smiled coldly. "I'm not a fool. I don't plan on giving them the chance. We'll ambush them."

He paused for a moment. "The ideal conclusion is getting Veronica, Shelby, and us back aboveground safe and unharmed. If possible, I'd like to keep the thugs alive and in good enough condition to be questioned thoroughly."

Malcolm thought, Yeesh. Bet you've got someone on tap who can do questioning back in Shelleen or you know someone who does. "And if we can't?" he asked.

"They can die underground from their injuries," Airik replied coldly. "As long as we rescue Veronica and Shelby."

Veronica grimly led the way, clutching Shelby's hand with a death grip. The tunnel got narrower and she had to feel her way, keeping her free hand in front of her, looking via touch for head-height obstacles, while keeping her side and shoulder pressed up against the cold rock wall. The stone was rough, abrading her hand and scraping her coverall into ribbons, and she knew she had bleeding cuts.

Every one of them stung. She hurt all over from being slammed into the rock. It was cold, so cold, but she didn't dare stop. She could hear angry shouts behind her but they kept wavering in and out of focus. Were they still real? Or was her own exhaustion and fear making her hear things that weren't there?

She couldn't ask Shelby. Her sister shook and trembled, her feet unsteady, and she kept bumping into her in the dark. Shelby was near to exhaustion as well.

They would have to stop and rest, Veronica decided. She was so tired. Lunch seemed a long, long time ago and she was thirsty, but not thirsty enough to lick the rivulets of water seeping down the rock walls.

A rock shifted, her sister squealed, and then clamped her mouth shut, panting. Veronica stopped moving.

After a very long moment, Shelby whispered. "Veronica?"

"Yes, sweetie?" Veronica whispered back.

"I tripped on a rock and caught my foot on my shoelace. We have to stop so I can retie it."

"Do you have to?" Veronica asked, fretting about how close they still were to the thug and his partner. She had no idea how far apart they were anymore. It was impossible to tell without light to guide her. The thug and his partner were noisy enough, but sound carried so strangely underground. She and Shelby hadn't traveled very far at all; having to creep forward blindly, slow careful footstep by footstep, one hand on the wall, the other hand grasping her sister's, starting at every sound of a shifting pebble.

"I'll trip again and hurt my foot. I think I can tie my shoe in the dark. My hands are so cold." Shelby's voice was hoarse from screaming, much worse than Veronica's.

Veronica fretted about the narrow passageway coming up. They had to be almost there but she couldn't remember anymore and without light, there was no way to tell until they crashed into it. Once they squirmed through the natural crevice, they'd be safe enough. The tall thug, with his broad shoulders, wouldn't fit without being willing to leave plenty of skin on the tunnel walls. He wouldn't know about the other side of the crevice and he wouldn't seeing it coming in the dark.

This was as good a place as any to stop, rest, and warn Shelby about the approaching squeeze.

"All right. I'll hold you so we can warm up a bit, let your hands warm up so you can work your fingers. Do you have anything to eat in your pockets?"

"No. I gave my last cracker to the sparrows I drew."

Veronica thought of the fat PanU sparrows, fluttering around in the open air, safe and free, and envied them their crumbs. She swallowed a sigh.

"Well, they were the cutest sparrows I've ever seen. We'll sit here."

She sat down, pulling Shelby down with her and arranged themselves so Shelby was sitting in her lap and they were huddled as close as possible, conserving precious body heat. She edged away from the cold rock wall, trusting she could find it again easily and hoping she'd arranged herself and her sister so when they got moving again, they went forwards toward the narrow crevice instead of back toward the thug and Frankie. She felt for the rock wall, trying to memorize the uneven feel of the stone so she could choose the correct direction when they were able to move again. The ground beneath them was clean, bare rock so she couldn't make any kind of mark she'd find again with her fingers. Veronica did not tell her sister what she was doing. There was no reason to upset her still further.

"They really were cute," her sister said, once they had settled themselves. "An advert with those sparrows would sell birdseed." Shelby stopped and thought. "Do people really buy seeds just for birds? I mean besides in Barsoom?" Her voice shook, raspy and afraid.

Talking about sparrows would make a good distraction for Shelby, helping her to calm down before blindly crawling through the crevice into the pitch-black unknown that lay beyond it.

"They do in the private parks in Dome Six," Veronica whispered back. "I bought some once from a little kiosk back when Dean and I were married and I was still allowed in. Those sparrows were even fatter than the ones at PanU."

"Dean did this to you, to us," Shelby whispered. "What a bastard."

Veronica compressed her lips together. "I know. I trusted him. I trusted my own instincts and I was wrong. I can't trust myself and I can't trust what people say."

"I think you can, if it's the right person," her sister replied, thinking of Malcolm Cobb revealing his background publicly and irrevocably at PanU. She would have never known he was a scholarship boy. He had chosen to trust her with something important.

"Don't be naïve," Veronica said harshly. "Think of Dean."

"You're being naïve this time," Shelby growled back. "Dean was a golden boy for his family and everyone else in Panschin. He couldn't lose. Everyone trusted him. *He* never risked a thing."

"Until he did," Veronica muttered. "He was weak. Just like dear old dad."

"He sure was. You trusted him but he never earned your trust because he couldn't lose no matter what he did. Other people aren't like that. Malcolm's not like that."

"I hope Malcolm figures out what happened. He's a miner as well as our banker. He might come down after us," Veronica said.

"I know he will," Shelby replied confidently. "Do you think Mr. Jones might come down too?"

Veronica stared off into the darkness. It was already starting to form shapes of black shifting against black. Shelby, warm against her, was real and she clung to her sister's reality. "I don't know. He didn't expect to return to the White Elephant until evening. Everything will be over by then."

She wanted to cry and blinked her salty tears away. She'd never see him again. Airik Jones had said her beads were made of star stuff. She'd never see a star again and now her beads were gone, in a vain hope of escape. However, Mr. Jones would not stand idly by when he returned to the White Elephant and found Dean in place, with the thug and his partner. Mr. Jones wanted privacy and quiet, he had paid for privacy and quiet, and he aimed to get them. He did not like Dean and wouldn't believe anything Dean said. The thought was warming and welcome. Mr. Jones wouldn't arrive alone either. He'd have his companions, especially his bodyguard, Carmine. Mr. Jones would be safe enough and if he wasn't, well, someone who had an entourage was guaranteed to have people who would come looking for him.

Who was Airik Jones? Veronica wondered. She still didn't know. But at a minimum, she knew he was someone who would give Dean Kangjuon a world of trouble. Could she trust a man she knew nothing about? Unfortunately, he had no reason to come down into the tunnels under the White Elephant, unlike Mr. Cobb who openly fancied Shelby, who was responsible for their lease, and who was also familiar with Panschin's underground ways.

"Veronica," Shelby whispered. "I think I see something. Down from where we came."

"Black shapes on a black background?" Veronica asked. "That's your eyes playing tricks on you. Don't trust them." She was so tired, so very tired. Shelby, she knew, couldn't be in better shape. They had to stay awake, until after they forced themselves through the crevice. They could rest, even sleep then safely. Hypothermia from the cold would become their main enemy, but there was nothing she could do about that other than huddle with Shelby.

"It's like sitting at the bottom of a bottle of ink," Shelby whispered back. "Even the air is thick. I thought I knew what black was, from all my painting."

"Nothing is like the night underground," Veronica replied. "Nothing. Ready to re-tie your shoe so we can keep moving?"

Shelby stretched against her sister and wiggled her fingers free. She had kept them clamped in her armpits to warm them while her sister held her tightly.

"Yes, I think so. Will the tunnel get narrower after this?"

"Yes, but I'm not sure when. It'll get very low and tight, we'll have to stoop, even crawl for a while, before we have to squirm through the crevice, but then the passage opens up and we can stand up straight. We'll be safe."

Veronica suddenly realized she wasn't hearing yelling and cursing anymore. She heard her whispered conversation with Shelby. There was a sound, soft as if something was moving. What had happened to the thug and Frankie? Were they dead? Had they given up and gone back?

"Hey, Ronnie," the thug said, his voice clear and close in the dark and a hand grabbed at her ankle. "Miss me?"

Veronica screamed in abject terror as did Shelby and they both started kicking madly at the hands clutching at their ankles and feet. He had found them.

Malcolm and Airik moved swiftly down the passageway. There were patches of scree and sand here and there, showing signs of footsteps. The difficulty, as always, was it was impossible to tell how old the footmarks were. Change in the deepdown came with geologic slowness. Malcolm couldn't help but notice how at his ease the daimyo of Shelleen was in maneuvering through the tunnel, stepping confidently and always avoiding the stalactites and other obstacles with a minimum of fuss. He hadn't been lying about being comfortable in the deepdown.

They stopped regularly to listen. The yelling and screaming would start and stop, encouraging them to move faster, but not too fast. Moving too fast in the deepdown led to tripping and injuries.

The tunnel they were in widened, as Malcolm expected from the mine sign. As per someone's long-ago chalk sketch, there were the two side passages, first one and then the second, farther away one, around the bend and out of sight.

Both men paced anxiously back and forth in the passageway between the tunnel openings, studying the ground, hoping to see some indication of where Veronica and Shelby had gone. Straight ahead? Or had they taken one of the side passageways? It was impossible to tell. The floor of the tunnel had returned to smooth rock, showing no signs of any one ever having been there before.

Malcolm frowned over his three choices. He thought over the mine sign indications of what lay ahead. All three corridors quickly became problematic for amateurs. Was Veronica leading the way? According to Neza, she did know something about the tunnels below the White Elephant, having explored them with Dean. But it had been some years since she had been down below and how much would she remember? How thoroughly had she and Dean explored? Neza had said Shelby rarely went below the first subbasement of the White Elephant. Shelby herself had admitted her trip to the Steelio warren was the first time she'd been lower down than the transtubes. Shelby wouldn't know the first thing.

If Airik was correct in his assessment, the thug and his partner knew next to nothing about handling themselves underground. They would know even less about what lived below Panschin. Did Veronica know? She wasn't part of the deepdown community so no one would tell her.

Veronica had to be in the lead, as the only person who had ever been below. Which passage would she choose? And what had Simon Bradwell been doing underground in the first place? That was puzzling in the extreme. There were easier ways to conceal bags of coin, particularly for an upper-class man with zero mining background.

"I've been considering if we should split up to search more quickly," Airik said calmly. "That said, if we do, neither of us will be able to assist the other."

Malcolm pondered how Veronica had managed to leave a sign for Airik to follow. He could not remember, but Airik would know. He'd obviously paid plenty of attention to Veronica Bradwell if he recognized her earbobs.

"Did Veronica wear other jewelry?"

Airik stilled, remembering his first conversation with her in the atrium of the White Elephant and how her sleek, dark hair lay against her neck and how beautiful her voice was. She had been bathed in the sunlight falling down through the roof opening, her prettiness completely at odds with the horrible paintings desecrating the atrium. He would rescue Veronica or die trying.

"Yes. She did. A string of cloudy gray beads to match her earbobs. She may have used them to mark her trail."

He knew he was correct as he spoke. Veronica Bradwell had sold every piece of jewelry she owned to make ends meet and she would willingly discard her last remaining piece if it meant a chance of saving her sister, just as she had discarded her earbobs. She knew he would understand the message she left for him. She knew him. She was trusting him, despite his lies to her about who he really was.

"Like breadcrumbs," Malcolm said, hoping he'd recognize the beads against the rock as beads and not ignore them as damp pebbles. If Veronica dropped a bead here and a bead there, they'd be easy to miss.

"Yes. Let's go down each passageway a short way and see if we spot them. The beads will stand out in the lantern light."

The sound of whooshing came rolling down the tunnel like running water, filling it and then receding, leaving only echoes behind.

"Any idea what that sound was?" Airik asked as soon as it passed.

"No. I've never heard anything like that in Steelio's tunnels."

Then the screaming started again, more frightened and angrier, as though it came from multiple voices.

Airik immediately said, "First passageway. Look for her beads." He set off down the tunnel, lantern high to check for glitter. Malcolm followed, moving quickly.

The screams died almost instantly as they worked their way down the first passageway.

"Wrong one," Malcolm said. "We could hear them in the main tunnel and if they were in this one, we'd hear them clearly."

"Agreed."

Airik turned around and darted back up the passageway to where it had branched off, Malcolm right behind him.

Once back in the original tunnel, the sound of cries and screams resumed and then died away. Malcolm set a quicker pace to the second tunnel opening and within minutes, Airik spotted Veronica's beads scattered about, along with a large patch of scree and sand, churned up by footsteps.

"Wait," Airik said, holding up his hand. "Listen."

"Doesn't sound like the girls."

"No. Someone's very angry. Must be the thug and his partner."

Malcolm's mind raced. "The girls must have gotten away. If those two were still with Veronica and Shelby, they wouldn't be cursing like that."

"I agree. Was the mine sign clear enough that we could follow in the dark so they don't know we're coming?"

Malcolm thought carefully, reviewing the information he had memorized from the initial chalk drawing and the ones he had observed since then, tying the data in with what he'd actually experienced since climbing down the ladder in the shaft. "No, not at all. We'd be almost as bad off as them."

"Damnation," Airik said. "We can't ambush them if they can see us coming. Wait." He stopped and studied the tunnel ahead of them.

"Shouldn't we be seeing some light seepage from their lanterns? They can't be that far ahead of us."

Malcolm stared past the edge of their lanterns' pool of light into the solidly black tunnel.

"Yes, we should. If we're this close, there should be at least a glimmer."

Airik thought of Veronica and Shelby, trapped in the endless, terrifying night of the deepdown. Nothing, absolutely nothing in his experience was as suffocating as being underground without a light source.

"If their lanterns are broken," he took refuge in analytical thought, "then the thugs will be disoriented. Our lanterns will betray us, but they'll also be blinding to them. Can you get us back if we lose our lanterns?"

"Oh sure," Malcolm replied confidently. "We go back the way we came. I've been keeping track of steps and turns. I wouldn't like doing it in the dark, but I can." He tapped his head. He'd been having to duck frequently to avoid stalactites.

"And they probably can't," Airik said. "They won't know to track side passages and count steps like I have." He caught Malcolm's raised eyebrows. "Yes, I can get Veronica and Shelby back by myself if I have to. I've also been looking for signs of struggle and this is the first indication of trouble I've seen. Nothing on the tunnel walls other than what you'd expect, plus Panschin mine sign."

"Let's go," Malcolm said and led the way further down the tunnel, the endless night in front of them retreating from their lanterns with every step while crawling up behind them. "If we're quiet, they won't hear us and they won't be expecting us."

They traveled down the tunnel, following its bends, hearing the sounds vanish as the tunnel widened, and then, thirty-six steps more (by Airik's count) they clearly heard Veronica's agonized scream followed by her sister's. At the same time, he spotted the rest of Veronica's beads, scattered everywhere as though they had been thrown wildly about. Each bead caught the lantern light; glittering eyes in the dark watching his every move.

Beyond the pool of lantern light lay the endless night under Panschin and not very far away up the tunnel lay the squeeze; where the passageway narrowed and the ceiling drew close and craggy, forcing anyone wanting to pass beyond to crawl and squirm through via the unyielding, uncaring rocky crevice.

By silent agreement, Airik and Malcolm stopped for a moment of planning.

"We'll have to be careful," Airik whispered. "I don't want to harm either of the girls by accident."

"We won't have that much room and these guys won't be afraid of hurting us," Malcolm said. "Best bet is to take the thugs by surprise and smash their heads into the nearest rock surface until they stop moving."

"You've done this before?"

"Not in the deepdown, but I know the stories. Bar fights have way more room then we've got here and much better lighting. Got any weapons besides a pocket knife? We should have thought of this earlier."

"No. I think a rock might be better here, in these close quarters anyway. I'd rather not slash Veronica or Shelby open by accident, or have my knife taken from me by one of them." That was a distinct possibility. Airik regularly used a knife as a tool, but never as a weapon.

"Agreed," Malcolm said. "Those guys are probably experienced street fighters. We're not."

"No. Fast, ruthless, and hard is our only option. We'll attack their joints. No one fights on two broken knees."

They moved slowly forward, keeping the lanterns lower so as to not betray their progress by the light spilling ahead of them. Then they saw the legs of a man, crouching, the front half of his body partially concealed by the sudden tightening of the rock walls and the bend in the tunnel. The light from the lanterns barely penetrated the opening of the squeeze, blocked as it was by the goon stooping as he worked his way through it.

"There," Malcolm said. "They're heading for the squeeze. It'll get tighter for them fast."

Airik allowed himself a wintry smile. "Easy."

Veronica screamed and screamed, kicking madly at the hands grabbing at her ankles in the dark. She knew she hit his clutching hands at least once, hearing the thug scream in pain and rage. She hoped she broke at least a finger or two, but his fury propelled him forward.

She broke free and sidled back into the suddenly tighter, lower passageway, roughly shoving Shelby behind her. Veronica had to hope she didn't slam Shelby into the rock surrounding them, injuring her or breaking a bone.

Shelby kicked and kicked, hoping she wasn't kicking her sister in the dark. She couldn't tell from Veronica's screams. She was afraid to use her own hands to push the thug's unwanted ones away, afraid he would grab hold and never let go and she couldn't tell if a hand was Veronica's. She had no room to move around in; the rock walls encased her and Veronica. She scrabbled backwards, tearing her hands on the coarse rock under her body, trying hard not to hit her head on the stone surrounding her.

Despite their care, they both smacked into each other and into the rock, trying to back up into the lower, tighter passageway. Veronica's head rang when she caught her head on a rock outcropping. It tore open her scalp, letting blood trickle into her eyes and blinding her as much as the dark did. Only fear and adrenaline kept the pain from stopping her.

"*You bitch*," the thug roared, his voice reverberating inside the tunnel. "You did this to me. I trusted you."

Veronica screamed again — "get *away* from me" — wanting to cover his booming voice with her own, deafening him since she couldn't fight him. She was getting so tired. Only adrenaline and fear kept her moving.

"Light!" Shelby yelled. "I see light!" She screamed again, this time in terror as something grabbed at her legs.

Veronica's hands were raw from scrabbling along the floor. She couldn't clear her vision. Worse, Shelby was hallucinating. There was no light. There was no one down here besides her, her sister, Frankie, and the thug. He had a hand clamped around her shin, and he was slowly, slowly dragging her back towards him, despite her panicked attempts to escape. His hand was so strong, his fingers biting into her flesh. She kicked blindly with her free foot, praying she wasn't kicking her sister. She couldn't tell from Shelby's voice whether she was screaming because she was being hurt or because she was terrified.

Then she heard Frankie's deeper, horrified shriek. It cut through the clamor, echoing and filling the tunnel like a physical force.

"Something's grabbed me! It's biting into me!" He screamed in mortal terror, the sound abruptly cut short into gurgles and whimpers.

"Frankie!" the thug called out in alarm. He let go of Veronica's leg, allowing her to squirm backwards, shoving Shelby up the tunnel wall and farther away from him. The tunnel abruptly narrowed again and she slammed her shoulder into the rock, jarring her entire body into agony. She could see again. Stars of pain filled her vision. The blackness inside the deepdown was better, crawling shapes of black on black.

Frankie screamed again in panic, making Shelby scream even louder, her voice hoarse with terror. Then, suddenly, sharply, his voice cut off as though something *had* eaten him and finished swallowing.

Airik and Malcolm, working together, grabbed the goon's legs, yanking him back from the rapidly narrowing passageway. They had both picked up loose rocks and they used them, battering the thug's body, not giving him a chance to speak, or fight back, or realize what was happening to him. They slammed rocks again and again into his knees, his hips, his ribs, his shoulders and elbows, and finally, his head, shutting off his screams like blowing out a candle. Only the echo remained, reverberating in the tunnel.

One down, but from his appearance not the one Airik remembered from the gallery showing. This must be the partner Neza mentioned.

Airik, in the rational portion of his mind, marveled over how savagely violent he could become, using his own hands rather than ordering someone else to perform such a dehumanizing task. Slicing the throat of a deer he had hunted, bleeding it out, and then gutting it was nothing like this. But it had to be done and so he had. Malcolm Cobb had been no different.

He saw the other man lunging toward them in the narrow space, despite being blinded by the sudden lantern light. He wasn't terrified of the deepdown. This man — Airik recognized the thug from the gallery showing at the White Elephant — was a professional. He had twisted around to come back to them, and his free hand showed a long knife, its razor-sharp blade gleaming in the lantern light. This man would fight to the death.

Airik didn't want that death to be his, nor Malcolm's. He especially didn't want Veronica or Shelby to suffer because of his hesitation. No, this thug was the one who needed to stop breathing.

Airik grasped the rock, selected because it was well-shaped to fit his hand, lunged and slammed it into the thug's shoulder, Malcolm attacked from the other side, hitting with his carefully chosen stone. The knife slash across his thigh burned. When had that happened? He staggered, stepped back, and remembered he had feet and habitually wore boots with heavily reinforced toes. So, he used them, kicking at the thug's legs, trying to knock him over.

Airik was avoiding that vivid, gleaming knife blade slashing through the air. He had lost his rock, but he feinted several times, hoping to catch hold of an arm or at least distract the thug from Malcolm's attack. The thug turned and stabbed at Malcolm, who backed away. Somewhere, Veronica was screaming, and he thought, Shelby too. Good. They were still alive. One of the lanterns got smashed, cutting the light in half.

The thug pressed his advantage, jabbing at Malcolm, who stayed just out of range. Airik put his hand to his burning chest, the knife slash across it feeling like a line of fire, and felt his rock hammer still tucked into its custom-made pocket in his fine wool suit, now ripped open across the front. He had forgotten it. It would work as a weapon. He wrenched it out and caught Malcolm's attention with it.

Malcolm gave a swift nod and held his ground. "C'mon … c'mon … take a shot," and he spat at the thug's face.

The thug lunged. Malcolm brushed the thrust aside, grabbed the thug's arm, and fell toward the unyielding, uncaring stone, pulling the man behind him.

Airik swung the hammer, slamming it as hard as he could on the thug's spine. He kneeled and took a precious second to aim before swinging again, trying for the base of the skull and the brain stem. The thug's shaved head caught the light, making it an easy target. His rock hammer connected again, not the point where it would do the most damage, but smashing where the neck joined the shoulder blades. His trusty rock hammer had not been designed to punch a neat hole through bone; it had been designed to shatter rock so it performed this minor task admirably. The blow sent reverberations shooting up his own arm.

The thug screamed, a wild, shaking, primal sound and rolled off Malcolm, who wrenched himself free and slammed the thug into the wall. He palmed the man's head and bashed it against the wall, smearing blood across the greedy rock, blood that shone almost black in the yellow light of the lantern.

The smell of blood was like copper and iron, and there were other, more dreadful odors filled the tight confines of the tunnel. The thug made wet, whining noises, and stopped resisting. Malcolm held him against the wall and let him slump to the floor. His body twitched.

Airik spared him a dispassionate glance. The thug wasn't dead, but he would be soon enough without medical intervention. His partner wasn't much better off. Other people, on the other hand, needed his attention far more. Veronica. Shelby. Malcolm. And, he supposed, he would benefit as well. The knife slashes burned. His suit was in ruins, but the layers of fine wool had given him some protection. He didn't know what protection Veronica had had, if this thug had used his knife on her.

Veronica didn't hesitate. As soon as the thug let go of her leg, she scrabbled back, smacking into her sister on one side and the rock wall on her other. The narrow crevice was coming up fast and only one of them could crawl through at a time. She had to get Shelby through first. She pushed and squirmed, forcing her sister to retreat, praying that Shelby wouldn't hit her head on the rock wall.

"Veronica!" Shelby hissed. "Stop it. Stop it now." She stopped dead, forcing her sister to stop as well or crawl over top of her in the dark.

"No! Get moving while they're distracted," Veronica snarled back. "Stop being difficult. They can't get through the crevice and we can. Turn over and crawl through on your hands and knees. I'm right behind you."

"No, Veronica," Shelby snapped. "I see light!"

"You're hallucinating, Shelby."

"I am *not*. I think it's Malcolm. Are your eyes even open?"

Veronica stopped moving and rested against her sister's body, shaking with exhaustion. Were her eyes open? No, she had closed them to stop seeing black shapes squirming against the black surrounding them, and to keep the blood from the cut on her forehead from irritating her eyes. She heard sounds of a fight, but probably not between the thug and Frankie. The thug had more than enough sense to wait until he was back aboveground to discipline his partner.

"Shelby?" Veronica asked in a very small voice. "Do you really see light?"

"Yes," Shelby hissed. "Open your eyes and look!"

"But Shelby,"

"Trust me."

Veronica could feel Shelby twisting around behind her and then her sister wrapped her arms around her, holding her warm and snug, her breath a welcome summer breeze compared to the cold air surrounding them.

"I've got you," Shelby murmured. "Trust me and open your eyes."

Veronica let herself slump into her sister's arms. She was so tired.

"All right," she whispered and opened her eyes slowly. The blood that seeped down from her forehead cut stung and blurred her vision, but Shelby was correct. There was light, blinding light after being trapped in the darkness for so long. She could still see. There was light. She couldn't see clearly, but there was light.

Then she heard a voice call out, a voice she recognized and had been afraid she would never hear again.

"Miss Bradwell? It's Airik Jones. Mr. Cobb and I are here."

"Shelby? It's Malcolm. Are you all right? I came for you as soon as I could."

Veronica was overwhelmed with emotion and this time, she let the salty tears leak out. She wasn't surprised Malcolm had climbed down into the tunnels for Shelby, but Airik Jones had come for her. He had no reason to at all, and an infinite number of reasons not to, but he had come down into the deepdown anyway. For her.

She let Airik help her wiggle back from the crevice, back into the wider passageway, lit by a single lantern. She got to her knees, and saw the thug and Frankie, sprawled out on the tunnel floor, roughly shoved out of the way and up against each other so she and Shelby could stumble around them. They were still breathing, groaning really, and her only thought was they had earned every minute of the pain.

Veronica struggled to stand. Every muscle protested, and she ached all over. She started to shiver, then shuddered all over and couldn't stop, her teeth chattering until her jaws hurt. Airik stripped off his ruined suit jacket and draped it over her shoulders. It was warm with his body heat and still smelled of him.

She noticed that Malcolm did the same for her sister, and wrapped his arms around her.

"Miss Bradwell?"

Airik was speaking to her. She had to focus. She looked up at his concerned face, so welcome a sight. How could she have ever thought he was average looking?

"Yes?"

"Can you walk? We need to get you and your sister aboveground and get some medical care."

Veronica smiled up at him. "Yes, of course." There was a dark, seeping line across his chest where his fine, ivory shirt had been slashed and hung open. "You need a doctor too, I think."

"Yes, but it can wait. You and your sister first."

"How did you find us?"

Airik smiled warmly at her. "I found your earbobs and then the beads from your necklace. The ones made of star stuff. You left signs for me to follow. You knew I would come for you."

He wrapped his arms around Veronica and helped her up. She fit perfectly against his body, as if she had been made for him. She shivered in Airik's arms; deeply grateful he had chosen to take his chances in the deepdown for a near stranger. He believed she had discarded her beads for him, but thinking about it, who else would have noticed but Airik Jones? She had left a sign for him, even though she hadn't realized it at the time.

"Ronnie," the thug hissed up from the ground. She gasped and Airik tightened his arms around her.

"Ronnie," the thug said, louder this time. His voice was thick and gurgling. "You're leaving me. Give me a kiss before you go."

Airik said, "I will not allow you to further harass Miss Bradwell."

Veronica stared at the thug, laying on his side, staring up at her. His eyes glinted in the lantern light; the rest of his face hidden in the shadows.

"It's all right, Mr. Jones," she said. "I do have something I'd like to say to him."

Airik let go and she forced herself to step closer to the thug, his eyes gleaming in the lantern light, a dark mirror of blood already forming beneath his head. She crouched down, keeping at arm's length so he couldn't reach her despite his injuries. One arm lay at an unnatural angle, as did both his legs.

"You were correct," Veronica said. "Dean did not deserve me."

He grinned up at her, his sharp teeth catching the light. His battered face was already swollen.

"You also do not deserve me. You do not deserve my kiss. And sweetheart," she smiled sweetly at him. "I lied about finding my dad's coin."

He chuckled thickly, a sound like blood gurgling in his lungs.

"You got backbone, Ronnie. You're made of nerve and fire."

Airik stomped his foot down hard. Veronica was startled by the sudden motion, and she saw that the thug's hand had been groping towards his dropped knife.

"That's quite enough," Airik said. He ground his foot down harder, onto the thug's hand.

"You," the thug said, twisting his head with a grimace of pain to look Airik in the eye. "You don't deserve her either." He twisted away from Airik and stared back at Veronica, his face unreadable again, his eyes like chips of glass.

"I'll let Miss Bradwell be the judge of that. Shall we go?"

She stood up clumsily, letting Airik help her and leaned against him as they walked back up the tunnel, towards light and freedom and safety.

"You lied about finding dear old dad's money?" Shelby rasped behind her. "You lied? That was stupid!" Veronica couldn't see, but she had no doubt Shelby was glaring daggers at her sister.

"I had wondered," Malcolm said. "It didn't make any sense to me. That said, I agree with Airik. It's time to go."

Veronica giggled, near hysteria. "It was stupid and I don't know what I was thinking." She had to force herself to stop.

She did not look back at the thug, slowly, slowly feeding the stone below him with his life's blood. She did not know how he watched her until Malcolm's lantern disappeared around the bend, the light fading slowly as they walked away, returning endless night back to the deepdown of Panschin.

She did hear him call out to her.

"Ronnie, Ronnie. No forgiveness."

His voice faded until there was nothing, and she focused on Airik Jones' arm warm and protective around her.

he trip back through the tunnels was much faster for Veronica and Shelby, considerably slower for Airik and Malcolm. Veronica wanted desperately to escape back aboveground and never again enter the deepdown. She had to lean on Airik to keep from stumbling. He was more surefooted, despite the wounds in his thigh and across his chest. In the lantern light, she could see that both slashes seeped blood through the linen shirt Malcolm used as a bandage, the thigh wound more so. He favored that leg as he walked. Malcolm had sacrificed his linen shirt to tie up the leg wound, even while Shelby still wore his jacket.

Veronica fretted over using Airik as a crutch, although he didn't seem to mind. She was cut, scraped, bruised, and hurting all over, but she hadn't been slashed open the way he had been.

"Fortunately, the wounds are not that deep," Airik replied to her concerns. "I didn't get out of the way fast enough, and I was saved by my tailoring. I admit they hurt like hell, and I will be very happy to see a doctor."

"We were lucky," Malcolm added. "All of us." He had his own share of bruises, scrapes, and cuts, but none as serious as Airik's wounds. He'd be hurting for days as it was. They all would.

"Very lucky," Airik said dryly. "He was aiming for my abdomen and missed." The thug intended to gut him like a deer.

"I still can't understand why you lied about finding a stash of dear old dad's," Shelby muttered.

"I guess I was hoping Dean would go down underneath with the thug and Frankie," Veronica said. "Then we could escape. Or maybe, we'd go down, you and me, and we'd escape."

Shelby glared at her sister. "Leaving auntie Neza behind with them?"

"I wasn't thinking clearly," Veronica retorted.

"I'll say."

"We are still not finished," Airik said firmly, cutting off Veronica and Shelby's incipient squabble. It reminded him of his cousins arguing over trivia, and he thought it a good sign; they were recovering, at least a little. "The thug and Frankie have a boss in Panschin. Did the thug tell you his name?"

Veronica shuddered all over, pushing up into him. Airik savored her warmth next to him. He was understanding Veronica better, and he guessed she had to tell him something unpleasant.

"I asked him, when we were at the bottom of the shaft and waiting for Shelby to climb down," she said. "He told me to call him 'Sweetheart.'"

"Yeek," Shelby gasped, wide-eyed. She made a gagging sound. "That's awfully personal." She snuggled closer to Malcolm, a very personal gesture considering his bare chest and one he found most agreeable, and not just because he was cold.

"I know," Veronica replied. "He was planning on getting rid of Dean and forcing me to lie to the bank and the neighbors." She shivered again, glad all over that Airik had come down the shaft into the tunnels with Malcolm.

Airik took that in; understanding how the thug — he would not call him "sweetheart" — would use Veronica, ways she obviously didn't want to discuss with her sister. It forcibly reminded him of the bride trade with Dairapaska, a trauma imposed by his predecessor on the peasants of two demesnes. Despite the passage of years, cleaning up the repercussions from that transaction still occupied too much of his time.

"That is concerning," he said, wanting to shift the conversation. "Not the getting rid of Dean part. I fully understand the urge. I'm concerned about the plans of the thug and his mystery boss. The boss is still out there. He may come back. Did either Frankie or the thug reveal anything to you that may clarify why they wanted the White Elephant?"

"Airik is correct," Malcolm said. "We're not done. None of this will make any sense until we figure out why they wanted the house so badly."

"He wanted to run Panschin," Veronica said slowly, "although I can't imagine how someone like that could do so." She repeated what the thug had told her and what she had overheard him say to Frankie.

When Veronica finished, Airik said, "So they are from Barsoom. They're under a lot of pressure to succeed. That's a start."

"But why would anyone from Barsoom want a house in Panschin so badly?" Veronica asked, struggling to form the words. Her throat was raw from screaming, and Shelby sounded worse. "There are plenty of them in Dome Two. Dean could have signed a lease for any of them, and no one would have suspected a thing."

"There's something we're not seeing," Malcolm said. "Dean might know."

"This is also why we have to get back up quickly," Airik added. "We all require medical attention but so do the thug and Frankie. They know why they needed the White Elephant, but we still don't. I am sure they can be persuaded to confess, but they have to be alive to do so."

"Is that why you and Malcolm didn't kill them?" Shelby asked.

Airik exchanged glances with Malcolm. "Yes."

The light from the shaft spilling into the natural cavern provided a welcome beacon. At the base of the ladder, Airik insisted Malcolm go up first, to ensure no threat lay waiting for them, then Veronica, then Shelby, and lastly himself to help them on their way.

"But your injuries," Veronica protested. "We need to get you to a doctor."

"I'll be fine." The wounds seared him like lines of fire. His chest wound was starting to clot but fresh blood still seeped through the deeper slash on his leg, despite Malcolm's shirt. He would carry the scars to his dying day. Since the thug had missed disemboweling him, that day was still far in the future.

The trip back up through the basement levels was uneventful. Anxiously waiting in the atrium were Neza, Carmine, and Dean. Neza and Dean were sitting in chairs brought from the dining room. Dean was tied to his chair.

Neza levered herself up as soon as she spotted her nieces coming up the staircase from the lower level.

At the same time, the gate creaked loudly and everyone froze. Carmine took charge of the door, throwing it wide after checking to see who was pounding up the front walkway.

It was Mrs. Grisson, excited and upset, closely trailed by her younger, fitter relatives, who were all struggling to get her to pay attention to her own safety and failing.

They stopped in the doorway and gaped, and Veronica realized they must look quite a sight: filthy, bloody and their clothes in shambles.

Helga Grisson didn't hesitate. "Neza! What happened? My grandson finally got around to telling me he saw that goon our Shelby drew the picture of, and he was with Dean! And another goon! The police are already on their way," she poured out breathlessly. At that point, Mrs. Grisson finally noticed Dean tied to the chair and stopped to stare at him.

"So that worthless wretch *was* involved." She marched up to Dean and boxed him in the ear, rattling his head.

Neza smirked conspiratorially at Mrs. Grisson.

"How could you? Your mother will be so ashamed," Mrs. Grisson said sternly, wagging her finger right in Dean's face. She turned and waved her oldest son towards the stairwell. "Go search the house, top to bottom."

Her oldest son frowned but dutifully went off on his errand, taking a brother-in-law with him. Like most of the neighbors, he had been inside the White Elephant frequently and was familiar with the layout.

"I don't need to talk to you," Dean said firmly. He shook his head to clear it, then shook it again, blinking repeatedly all the while.

"You do need to talk to *me*," Veronica said even more firmly. "Why did you do this?"

"While they're talking, sir, I've got to get you to a doctor," Carmine said quietly to Airik. Despite his words, he wore the expression of someone doing his job, while knowing he was going to be ignored.

"It can wait, Carmine," Airik replied. "This is more important."

"Be sure to tell the family, when they ask, that you said so," Carmine answered.

"Dean," Veronica said. She crouched down next to him, forcing him to meet her eyes. "Who are those people? How did you meet them? And why do they need the White Elephant so badly? Houses go begging in Dome Two. You know that. Everyone knows that."

"Where's Tallon and Frankie?"

"If you mean the thug and his partner, they're still in the tunnels," Veronica said.

"They'll need medical attention and quickly," Airik said. He noted Dean's flinch. "They'll die of hypothermia if we don't get them out. That is, if their injuries don't kill them first."

"Let them die," Dean said wearily.

"No. We need to know who they are, and what they're doing," Airik replied. "Dead men don't answer questions."

"Dean," Veronica said again. "What happened."

Dean groaned and shifted his weight in the chair. "I'm sorry, Ronnie. I am so sorry."

He caught her irritated expression. "You'll always be Ronnie to me, my own special nickname for you. I should have never left you. I should have never listened to my family. I should have never gone gambling with your father. I should have quit when I was ahead. I am so, so sorry."

"I got that part, Dean," Veronica said. "Do go on."

"Your dad took me gambling. It was fun and I won. I won a lot. Then my luck changed. Everything fell down the shaft when I left you. I kept gambling but I ran out of money and no decent casino would let me in. I couldn't pay my debts, you see," Dean said.

She rolled her eyes. "Get to the point, Dean."

"Then I met Tallon and his boss. I was looking for a place that would let me in and win back what I'd lost. They run games out of hotel rooms in Dome Six. They move around a lot. I lost a lot of money to them and they said they'd kill me if I didn't pay up."

"Dean, you could have asked your parents," Veronica said. "I'm sure they would have helped you."

"Not anymore," Dean said. "They cut me off a while back." He looked away, ashamed, then sighed and continued. "They threatened to kill my parents. They would have too."

"Anyway, I would overhear Tallon and the boss talking. They made me hide them in my flat so I couldn't avoid them. They wanted a house as a basis for operations and I thought of the White Elephant."

"That was stupid," Malcolm said. "Houses in Dome Two go begging. You could have avoided all of this."

"I know that, idiot," Dean shot back. "I told them I could get them a house. They didn't want any of them. What they wanted was a house that let them come and go unseen. They're part of some group called Knights of Mars. They wanted to avoid some group in Panschin called Blue Sun. I don't know who any of those people are but they thought it was important."

"Is it important?" Airik asked. There had only been enough time in the tunnel for Malcolm to give him the most cursory information on Blue Sun.

Veronica shrugged, as did Shelby and Neza.

But Malcolm did not shrug, Airik noticed. Neither did Carmine, nor did Mrs. Grisson, her sons or her boarders.

"I don't know who Knights of Mars are," Malcolm said. "Blue Sun is a criminal syndicate that runs gambling, protection rackets, drugs, prostitution, you name it, here in Panschin. They don't like rivals."

"All true, sir," Carmine offered. "Don't know about Knights of Mars but they might be similar. Also, Dean's sticking to what he confessed to me and Miss Molony."

"This is all fascinating," Airik said. "But why this particular house?"

"Yes, Dean," Veronica said. "You used to love me, once. Why did you offer my house to those horrible people?"

"Because of the tunnels," Dean said. He smiled wistfully at Veronica. His handsomeness was obscured by bruises and swelling but some of his old charm still showed. "Remember when we explored them, you and me?"

"Yes, they never went anywhere and so we stopped."

"You stopped because you got bored. I didn't get bored. I love exploring, especially underground. I kept exploring the tunnels. There's a narrow passageway you didn't go through. If you wiggle through it, it connects to another set of tunnels and those tunnels have an exit inside an unused storage closet in the Panschin train station. We kept hearing that whooshing noise when we explored. Remember? I wanted to find its source and I did."

"Was that the train?" Malcolm asked, as understanding dawned. "The underground tracks are that close?"

"Yes," Dean replied. "The White Elephant has a direct connection to the train station."

"So?" Veronica said. "So? The train station is open to everyone! So are the transtubes. Why would anyone want to crawl through the tunnels to get from there to here?"

"The train station and the transtubes are not open to smugglers," Malcolm said thoughtfully.

Airik shot him a look. "You believe a group like Blue Sun doesn't smuggle contraband?"

"I'm sure they do," Malcolm replied. "But I'm equally sure they won't tolerate sharing turf with some gang from Barsoom."

Airik considered this. "A tunnel connection would allow Knights of Mars, whoever they are, concealed access. They would arrive at the train station and disappear into Panschin."

"That was the idea," Dean said tiredly. "I never found another upshaft like the one connected to the White Elephant and I looked. I'm so sorry, Ronnie."

"You should be," Veronica said. "That thug. He was awful." She shuddered, moving closer to Airik. Some portion of her brain noticed how easy that had become and how it didn't bother Airik Jones at all.

Dean noticed too, briefly closing his eyes in pain over what he had thrown away.

"The way you stood up to Tallon fascinated him. He couldn't stop talking about you after the gallery show. What he wanted from you. What he would do to you. I couldn't warn you. I didn't dare. All I could do," Dean stopped, looking more ashamed than ever. "All I could do was make you angry so you would say no."

Veronica gaped at him. "That was stupid!"

It was easier to focus on what a fool Dean had been than to think about the plans the thug had for her. Tallon was a good name for him. She hadn't been wrong to fear him.

"I know." Dean roused himself. "You're smarter than I am. I hoped you would think of something because I couldn't. I was in so far over my head I couldn't do anything right."

"You just made it worse!"

"Yeah." Dean looked away again, staring at one of Professor Vitebskin's more dreadful paintings rather than see her face or Airik Jones hovering protectively behind her. "Tallon enjoyed beating me up. He was furious about seeing me at the gallery showing."

"That's why you ran like a rabbit," Carmine said. "I wondered what set you off."

"I saw him and the boss. I had to get out of there."

"Does this boss have a name?" Airik asked.

"Not that I ever heard. They always called him 'boss.'"

Dean slumped in his chair. "I screwed up. Ronnie, I am so sorry." Tears leaked from his eyes, leaving tracks in the dirt smudging his face. "We were happy once. Tallon was right, the bastard. I didn't deserve you."

"The police will be here soon," Veronica said. "They'll want to know everything."

"I'll tell them. I've already lost everything that matters, Ronnie, starting with you." Dean chuckled weakly. "I'll go underground again, but it will be in the Dirac mines."

Malcolm had been thinking hard. This new information about Knights of Mars, whoever they were, was critical. He knew who would appreciate it enough to hunt down the missing boss without wasting any time on debates. They wouldn't be concerned about legal niceties either.

"Veronica, Shelby, I don't want to, but I have to leave you here. The boss is still a threat, but I can do something about him now," he said. "I'll check back periodically to make sure you're safe."

"Everyone will be staying with me," Mrs. Grisson announced. "With me and my sons and sons-in-law and boarders. Over to my place, where no one knows."

"You have to go?" Shelby rasped, clinging to his arm and looking up at him, wide-eyed. She looked suddenly puzzled and added, "But why did you come over at this time of day, Malcolm? I'm so grateful, but I didn't expect to see you until the end of the day at PanU." She shuddered, thinking of what could have happened.

"I needed to talk to your aunt Neza about Simon Bradwell and Mr. Burgess," Malcolm answered, gently combing his fingers through her tangled hair.

"What?" Neza said, startled. She had been listening carefully as well, when not whispering to Mrs. Grisson, confirming what Dean had confessed earlier.

"Did they socialize? Were they ever together outside of a business setting? I'm following a seam of information. If I can prove a connection, I can keep Burgess from evicting you," Malcolm said.

"I have no idea, particularly since I never met the man before," Neza said. "Simon didn't often come to Dome Two. He thought it was beneath him and we didn't get along. Burgess strikes me as the same sort."

Veronica nodded in agreement, as did Shelby.

"Sajag Burgess wants to evict you?" Dean asked curiously.

Veronica laughed weakly. "Yes, he does. It seems so unimportant now after nearly dying in the tunnels."

Dean smiled wistfully again at Veronica. "I can help you, Ronnie. I told you your dad took me gambling. Posh, high-end casinos in Dome Six. Classy places. Only the best people go there."

"Yes, you did, but I don't see why that matters," Veronica said.

"His favorite gambling partner was Sajag Burgess."

All eyes turned back to Dean.

"What?" said Veronica and Shelby in one voice.

"Are you sure?" Airik said.

"The connection I need," Malcolm said, his face lighting up.

"Nothing surprises me about your worthless father anymore," Neza said, tight-lipped with disapproval.

Mrs. Grisson tsked loudly and repeatedly.

"He was so lucky at the tables," Dean said. "That's why Sajag wears those exaggerated fashions. He thinks it makes him luckier and I suppose it does. He never lost when I gambled with them." Dean frowned and added, more softly, "He pretends he doesn't know me anymore."

Malcolm stared at Dean. His mind raced, recalling details from the case studies that had never been explained. Among other things, the casino where Simon Bradwell gambled away his clients' money insisted that the initials SB in their records always meant him and no one else.

"Was there anyone else Simon Bradwell gambled with regularly?" Malcolm asked carefully. He would have to find corroborative evidence and one of those people might be willing to talk to him.

"Peng McGrant," Dean replied promptly. "He was a lucky gambler too. He bragged all the time about how he'd won enough at the tables to let his family buy into Chung/Banerjee. He never scored as big again, but he still did alright. He won't talk to me anymore either."

"Anyone else?" Malcolm said. "I'll need a list."

"I would be interested as well," Airik said. "I don't … I mean, my firm doesn't like doing business with gamblers. They are not reliable."

"Dean. Why didn't you tell me any of this before?" Veronica asked. Peng McGrant! Maybe they wouldn't be sued by the McGrant family over Kip's surface sickness. The McGrant family wouldn't want to admit the senior member of the family went gambling with the notorious Simon Bradwell.

He sighed again. "I knew how you felt about gambling and it didn't seem important. What did it matter who your father met over the tables? He's been dead for years."

The gate shrieked again, followed by a herd of footsteps on the gravel walkway.

"That'll be the police," Mrs. Grisson said importantly. "And about time, too. I sent my grandson begging for help when I headed over here."

She had been listening avidly to Dean's story, storing every detail to rehash later on with Neza and everyone else living in Dome Two. She'd dine out for months … no, *years* … on this story.

"It matters now," Veronica said. "Please, Dean."

"Anything for you, Ronnie. I owe it to you."

Someone pounded on the door.

"Open up! This is the police."

"I'll get it," Carmine said. "Might as well do something useful around here."

It took some time for Malcolm to extricate himself from the police squadron that invaded the White Elephant. Mrs. Grisson had gotten action from them in a way that neither he nor Mr. Wong had managed. He would have to figure out how much power she wielded in the neighborhood, since it was apparently quite a lot. She might be willing to discuss her small-scale farming business as a way of jumpstarting more economic activity in Dome Two, if he approached her properly. But that task would have to wait.

Interviewed and patched up by the police surgeon's team of medics and wearing a shirt borrowed from Carmine, he ran back to the Dome Two branch of Second National. He had had time to think while the medic dressed his wounds (Veronica had insisted Airik be treated by the police surgeon himself who concurred with her assessment) while Dean ratted out the thug and Frankie to the police. He worked out his order of approach carefully; when not listening to Dean's confessions and while doing his damnedest not to flinch in front of Shelby when his wounds were being dressed.

Mr. Wong came first. If he judged Mr. Wong correctly, he was a valuable ally who despised Burgess and deemed the concerns of the branch's clients to be more important than what headquarters wanted them to be. If he was wrong, he could beg the daimyo of Shelleen to let him, the Bradwells, and his own family go into exile in Shelleen. Swearing fealty to a demesne, distasteful as that would be, would be far better than seeing everyone he loved end up in the Dirac mines alongside Dean Kangjuon.

That included Shelby. He was falling in love with her. Having to go into the deepdown to save her and her sister crystallized his emotions.

She might not feel the same way, although he had hopes she did, but that didn't matter. She was safe, and he wanted to keep her safe. He still felt her goodbye kisses on his lips.

Malcolm darted into the lobby, getting the attention of not just the customers but the goggling staff. He looked rough; bruised, filthy, and wearing Carmine's oddly cut shirt rather than the tailored suit the staff was used to seeing. He didn't hesitate at Mr. Wong's office door and barged right in.

"Mr. Wong."

Mr. Wong cut him off. "Don't barge into my office, Cobb. That's why I have a door."

"Mr. Wong? Listen." Malcolm dove into what had happened and what he needed. As he had hoped, once he got started, Mr. Wong sat back down, waved away the security guard who had arrived at his door, and his eyes lit up.

"So. Burgess indulges in high-stakes gambling and he did it with Simon Bradwell," Mr. Wong said after a long, thoughtful silence spent focusing on what mattered to him the most. "I'm sure he cheats."

"I hadn't thought of that," Malcolm said.

Mr. Wong gave him a pitying look. "No one wins long-term in a casino without cheating. The odds favor the house by immense margins. What is your next move?"

"I'll need to use the branch's skynet connection. I must speak with the following people in a hurry, to forestall Burgess's next move." Malcolm rattled off a list of names, starting with the head of Steelio.

As he did, he watched Mr. Wong, nodding approval when he named the various executives at Second National (all of whom Mr. Wong knew) and looking thoughtful at Steelio.

"Good thinking, Cobb. You're taking full advantage of our filing cabinets of data. I assume you'll be out of the office for the rest of the day?"

"Yes, Mr. Wong. I'm not sure about tomorrow."

"Keep me posted and do not slam my door on the way out. When you return, be properly dressed. Do the same for any meetings you manage to arrange with the Second National executives."

Malcolm restrained himself from rolling his eyes. Mr. Wong was correct. He could not give them a reason to ignore him, a jumped-up tunnel rat.

"Yes, Mr. Wong."

He was halfway to the door when Mr. Wong said, "Cobb? I have a few contacts at First National and at Mercantile and Commerce. I'll have a name or two for you when you return."

Malcolm turned and said, "Thank you, Mr. Wong."

Mr. Wong smiled icily. "I want to see Burgess sifting tailings on his knees to his dying day."

"He will, sir. In the Dirac mines."

"Oh, and Cobb?"

"Yes, Mr. Wong?" Malcolm said, clamping his mouth shut so he didn't tell Mr. Wong to stop wasting his time by dragging out the conversation.

"Miss Molony and the Bradwell sisters will be safe?"

"Yes, Mr. Wong. The police are there now and this time, they won't be too busy to ignore the situation."

"Very good. Our clients come first. I shall commend Mrs. Grisson when I see her next."

"Do you know her?"

Mr. Wong gave Malcolm another pitying look. "I know everyone important in Dome Two."

During *his* interview, Airik summarized the events to the desk sergeant rapidly, completely, and in perfect order. He then demanded that the police go down into the tunnels to find Tallon and Frankie, a demand echoed by Malcolm, before he left on errands of his own.

The desk sergeant (Mrs. Grisson had insisted via her grandson he come in person, and she got her way), even as he listened and took notes, kept wondering who this man was who needed a bodyguard. This visitor to Panschin *ordered* him about as though he regularly expected and got prompt obedience and all while having the bloody slash across his chest and the other one on his leg cleaned and stitched closed by the police surgeon. It had to hurt like hell, yet this man didn't seem to notice, other than to hold Veronica Bradwell's hand, squeezing her fingers with each stab of the needle through his flesh and exhaling after each stitch.

Arrangements were made for a crew to descend into the tunnels under the White Elephant and render first aid to Tallon and Frankie. They would wait in the cavern for the rescue and recovery team to bring the more specialized gear needed to haul someone strapped into a spinal board up a long, narrow shaft.

Airik waited impatiently for news while the police surgeon did his work, cleaning his wounds and then securing them, stitch by careful stitch. He was grateful that Veronica did not flee so as to avoid the unpleasantness of field surgery. She had insisted that he be treated first and the police surgeon concurred, over his own objections that she and her sister be attended to by the surgeon and not the medics.

He would have preferred that Shelby vanish but she had grabbed a sketchbook, placed herself where she could observe without being in the way, and was drawing the procedure, whispering all the while (her throat was raw from screaming) about verisimilitude and how the anatomy textbooks she used at PanU didn't show how bloody it all was. It was nice to know she was recovering from her ordeal but he could have done without her monologue on his musculature. It was a shame Malcolm had left so promptly after his interview and medical treatment; he would have kept Shelby occupied sketching his bare chest.

To his chagrin, Veronica was disinterested in his appearance. At any rate, she didn't stare the way her sister did.

Dean kept talking and talking and talking, keeping his eyes carefully averted from his own medical care. He chose to focus on one of Professor Vitebskin's paintings, probably as added punishment. The police stenographer took rapid notes, barely keeping up with the questions and answers.

Veronica held Airik's hand throughout his stitching up. He squeezed her fingers tighter than the thug ever had, down underneath the White Elephant, but she didn't mind. Airik Jones had come for her. She was still having trouble processing the fact that he did, rather than fetching the police and avoiding all the trouble. Working out his rationale gave her something to think about rather than Airik's nearly nude body stretched out before her on her dining room table.

The police surgeon had cut away the remains of Airik's pants and shirt, revealing something other than what Veronica expected from the baggy coveralls she had seen him wearing. The coverall had not covered up a multitude of sins as they usually did. Airik Jones once again wasn't average. He was very fit, well-muscled and well-proportioned, and very distracting.

"You could have thrown Dean over a higher wall, Mr. Jones," she said to him quietly and was rewarded with a tight smile.

"I like to give myself maneuvering room in case of error." Damnation, Airik thought. He'd become "Mr. Jones" again after the pleasure of hearing Veronica say his name.

"You gave yourself a huge margin, I think," Veronica said and squeezed his hand. "Thank you." With her free hand, she brushed a lock of hair from his forehead.

"Well, I did have to allow for Dean fighting back. He was an unknown quantity."

"True." She gazed down at him, keeping her eyes carefully on his face, above his broad shoulders and off the crisp curls of hair on his chest, and he relaxed into the warmth of her smile. The pain was suddenly easier to bear.

The police surgeon was putting in the last few stitches when his medic came racing back up the stairs from the second subbasement hatch.

"Sergeant," the medic said, coming to a panting halt in front of the desk sergeant. "They're dead."

"Damnation," Airik said. "I wanted them brought up alive for questioning."

"Oh, you did?" the sergeant said. "That's not your decision to make." Who the hell did this guy think he was?

"Nonetheless," Airik retorted. "The rescue team should have been sent down faster."

"It wouldn't have mattered," the medic said, eying Airik. Who the hell was this guy? "They've been dead for a while. I'd estimate since well before we climbed down the shaft and found them. They'll have to be hauled into the morgue so the surgeon can get a more accurate time of death."

"Exposure?" asked the desk sergeant. "Or their injuries?"

"Hypothermia?" Airik asked at the same time. "Or their injuries?"

The medic shot him a look, exchanged glances with the surgeon, and focused on their boss, the desk sergeant.

"Neither. The bald one cut the other thug's throat and then cut his own."

"In the pitch-black dark of the deepdown?" the police sergeant asked, appalled. "He did it by feeling his way around?"

"Judging by the blood trails. He did a messy job. They bled out. Blood everywhere."

Dean had been listening, hunched over with pain and renewed fear.

"That sounds like Tallon," he muttered. "I don't think his boss tolerates failure. Frankie wouldn't have had the guts."

"Indeed," Airik said. He thought of what Veronica had repeated to him from overhearing Tallon and Frankie in the tunnels.

Veronica squeezed his hand, looking ill. "Lordy. Murdering his partner and dying by his own hand was better than failing. Lordy."

"I'd agree. His doing so ensured neither of those two could be questioned," Airik said. He glanced over at Dean, who was looking nauseous.

"Sergeant?"

"Yes, Mr. Jones?" the desk sergeant replied warily.

"Keep Mr. Kangjuon under guard. He's our only source of information unless and until you are able to find and arrest their mystery boss."

"Who the hell are you to tell me how to do my job?" the desk sergeant asked in annoyance.

Airik watched him steadily while the surgeon bandaged up his stitches. "Are you going to? If not, I will make the arrangements myself."

"I'll be taking care of Kangjuon personally," the desk sergeant said icily. "Since this potentially involves Blue Sun, I don't want any mistakes. And who the hell are you again, anyway?"

"I told you yesterday, Sergeant," Carmine said, answering for the daimyo of Shelleen. "He's Airik Jones of Barsoom. Distant relative of Miss Molony and Miss Bradwell."

"So you said. And why weren't *you* down there, rescuing Miss Bradwell and her sister?" the desk sergeant snapped. "You put your employer at risk."

Airik waded back in. "I needed Carmine to take charge of the house, watch Dean, keep everyone else out, and make sure Miss Molony was kept safe. I had no way of knowing if the boss would come to the White Elephant or if he would have brought more armed men. Nor did I have time to waste."

"Lordy," Veronica snapped. "You two arguing is a waste of time. Sergeant, I know you'll make sure Dean is guarded. Have you sent anyone to Dean's flat to see if the boss is still hiding there?"

"Already done, Miss Bradwell."

Competence at last, Airik thought but chose not to say so aloud. He also did not say "Where the hell were the police earlier?"

"He might not be there," Dean fretted. "He moved around a lot, exploring Panschin. He said he was looking for hotel rooms to use temporarily."

"We'll find him," the desk sergeant said confidently.

"I certainly hope so," Neza said tartly. "That man will murder us in our beds if you don't. He knows where we live."

Mrs. Grisson patted Neza's hand reassuringly and whispered to her.

Veronica bit her lip, thinking, and unconsciously squeezed Airik's hand. She didn't want to let go. Mr. Jones would leave at the end of the conference. He'd go back to Barsoom. Who would be here if Tallon's boss showed up? If Tallon was afraid of failing his boss, then she needed to be as well. She let her eyes range around the White Elephant's dining room and fell upon Shelby, busily capturing the members of the police squadron, Airik stretched out on the dining room table undergoing field surgery, Dean tied to a chair.

Dean. Shelby had sketched Dean while he was cleaned up and treated. Dean knew what Tallon's boss looked like. So far, all they had was the image Shelby had drawn from Elliot's description. Dean could fill in the details and then the police would have a better chance of spotting Tallon's boss in the crowd.

"Sergeant? Shelby? Dean?" Veronica got their attention and got them started. It was something she could do to keep her little family safe and, if she was lucky, the police would find Tallon's boss before Airik Jones left Panschin and left her.

Carmine quietly watched the proceedings from his post against the wall. The family wouldn't believe what Airik had done. Despite selecting him as the daimyo, they underestimated him every day. What would they say to this? Airik wouldn't brag to them, but he wouldn't be able to hide the scars.

It was especially interesting watching Airik with Miss Bradwell. It was clear she liked him, but she didn't know who he was, so she liked him because she liked him. His position in life didn't color her view.

Carmine had been assigned to Airik since he had been chosen as the daimyo. He'd gotten to know his boss better, he believed, than most of the family. He'd never seen Airik act this way with any woman. Airik fancied Veronica Bradwell; enough to go underground and rescue her at great risk to his life.

His daimyo had to marry for the good of the demesne. It was a pity he could not marry Veronica Bradwell. She'd be good for him. Instead, Airik Shelleen would have to make a political match. Whoever the family chose, and they had infinitely more options than they had had in the past, the young lady wouldn't make him laugh the way Miss Bradwell did.

Carmine sighed. Too bad the family would never accept her. Elliot had filled him in about the research project he was doing on Simon Bradwell. Miss Bradwell was a pariah.

Carmine thought of his own wife and little daughter, waiting for him at home in Shelleen. He'd have a happy homecoming. Airik wouldn't. Airik would slave for the good of the demesne for his entire life yet never have a chance at the joy he, Carmine, got every day with his own wife and daughter. All those ladies of the Four Hundred saw a gold mine and a stepping stone to power and not a man.

The police surgeon had finished his work — very neat stitching too in Carmine's professional opinion — yet Airik didn't show any eagerness to leap up and get back to the round of meetings waiting for him. He wanted to remain in the dining room of the White Elephant and hold Miss Bradwell's hand. Time to be reminded of his duty.

"My lord? I mean, sir? Airik?"

The desk sergeant shot a glance at Carmine and then at the police surgeon. My lord. Who the hell was this guy?

"Yes, Carmine?"

"We need to get back. You got that conference with Chung/ Banerjee and we're already late."

Airik frowned. Carmine was correct. The needs of Shelleen rose up before him. He would have to leave Veronica. He would come back that evening and for the next few evenings and then leave for Shelleen when the conference was over.

What would happen to her? He didn't want to leave her, Airik realized. But Veronica Bradwell would never leave her home and her family in Panschin while he could never walk away from his responsibility to Shelleen. Honor and duty made their own demands.

She was watching him steadily. He could not decipher her expression.

"Carmine is correct. I must go."

"Will you be back this evening?"

"Yes." Airik smiled up at her, memorizing her face. "I'll need Mrs. Grisson's address in case you aren't here." She smiled at him again as he spoke.

"Of course."

He thought of his hurried conversation with Malcolm Cobb. If Malcolm came through on his promise, at least he could leave her that small gift.

"I'll be back every evening, until the conference ends."

"I would like that."

He wished she would kiss him like Shelby had kissed Malcolm when he left. But she wouldn't; he was a virtual stranger to Veronica Bradwell and soon he would leave Panschin and leave her. As a gentleman, he certainly couldn't embrace her. What if she didn't want him to?

From their vantage point, Neza and Mrs. Grisson watched intently and sadly. The conclusion was foregone and there was nothing they or anyone could do about it.

Malcolm resented every minute he had to spend in his boarding house room getting cleaned up and dressed to meet his carefully selected senior executives. But it did give him time to think over his approach to them in his quest for allies against Mr. Burgess.

If the information he had read in the filing cabinets still held true, this small group despised Sajag Burgess. None of them had openly moved against their enemy but that could change with the information Malcolm had unearthed, along with knowing that Burgess openly consorted in casinos with Simon Bradwell.

Mr. Steelio had also made time for him, later in the day, after he had met with the daimyo of Shelleen. As soon as Mr. Steelio's secretary proudly told him of the potentially lucrative meeting, Malcolm made the snap decision. He would not reveal he knew Airik. He would not use the daimyo of Shelleen to better himself. That also meant he couldn't say there was a distinct possibility the daimyo of Shelleen would be late for his meeting.

Mr. Steelio also agreed to send a message along to Jeffen. He, however, would not be available until the end of his shift. Malcolm had thought carefully over whether to reveal *why* he needed to speak to Jeffen so badly. In the end, Malcolm decided not to. Jeffen was a low-level member of Blue Sun, and he wouldn't be doing Jeffen any favors by revealing to Steelio his employee's divided loyalty.

It was frustrating to have to wait. He needed to speak with Jeffen *first*, before anyone else, since Tallon's boss could get wind of what was happening and flee Panschin. The police were searching for him, but Blue Sun had a long reach into areas where the police rarely went. They were just as likely to succeed and wouldn't fret over legalities such as jurisdiction.

The operation against Burgess would take far more time, but Burgess couldn't move quickly to evict the Bradwells. Legal proceedings took time and had to be done according to the bank's procedures. Burgess could try, but he wasn't the mustache-twirling villain in a melodrama. There were rules.

He now understood why Burgess had reacted so strongly when he met Veronica Bradwell at the gallery showing. Even so, it was extreme. There might be other pressures forcing his hand, causing Burgess to be less cautious. Perhaps, Malcolm thought, Burgess was not as secure in his position within Second National's hierarchy as he believed. If so, his potential allies had the fuse already in hand, but needed the match to set it alight. He had a pack of them in the bank's filing cabinets.

He smiled at his reflection in the cracked mirror, his image split in two like always. These executives would owe a jumped-up tunnel rat even if they wouldn't admit it.

The meetings with the Second National executives went very well, putting Malcolm into a better frame of mind over leaving Shelby behind at the White Elephant. He had guessed correctly. They had been waiting for the right moment, the right information, to force the issue with the board, and he gave them what they had been waiting for.

Burgess would end up on his knees in short order.

They would not, of course, keep a lowly assistant manager and scholarship boy in the decision-making loop. Oh no. Malcolm had to smile at that piece of foolishness. Did none of them truly understand how he had discovered the files?

They would document their actions and copies would be duly filed in the basement catacombs of his branch office in Dome Two, where he could read them at his leisure. This foolishness also indicated that, despite their supposedly better breeding, education, and upbringing, he could out-think them.

Sitting in the transtube, heading to Steelio's office, Malcolm allowed himself one of his favorite daydreams: the one where he became the President and Chairman of the Board of the Second National Bank of Panschin. He could dig rings around this kind of competition.

His background as a scholarship boy would get in the way. There was nothing he could do to fix the situation, other than demonstrate impeccable competence. Hellation, even normal competence might be enough, considering the poor quality of his competition.

There was also Shelby Bradwell. He was falling in love with her. He thought she might feel the same way about him, based on what she said and did. Her kisses were so sweet. She had whispered to him, as he said his goodbyes, that she wanted to see him again. She was his dream girl and better, she, despite her worthless, embezzling father, belonged to the class he aspired to join. But would Shelby's background handicap him in his rise to the top of the Panschin banking hierarchy?

She was so beautiful, so talented, so caring, so special. She saw him as a man and she understood the pressure he was under. She accepted his family. Yet, the people who didn't despise him because of his own background would despise him because of her father, Simon Bradwell.

Shelby was a liability. She knew it herself. She had told him so, rather than see his reputation damaged. She trusted him enough to be honest, as he had been honest with her about his background.

She had been worth the risk, then.

He considered her carefully, as the transtube rolled through the tunnel, connecting the domes above with the tunnel world below. She inflamed his senses. He couldn't think logically around her. He wanted her. He could only think clearly when she was at the other end of Panschin, not sitting next to him, warm and sweet and touchable, the scent of her hair filling his nostrils, the heat from her body stimulating his own body.

She was a liability.

However, he was a liability to her. She might be able to rise above what her father did to her, but not with a scholarship boy. She needed a man from the upper classes whose family could paper over her status as a pariah.

Together though, did their liabilities cancel each other out? Or did they magnify them? Was Shelby worth the risk to his career? Was he worth the risk to hers? She had talent, real talent, of a kind he had never observed in his life. He vividly recalled the paintings at the Panschin Museum of Art, as well as the best magazine illustrations, and compared them to what he had seen at the gallery showing of the PanU Artists' Collective. Her work could, with time and effort, easily sell to magazines and advertisers. They needed art that would make them money, so they were a more discriminating market than art collectors. Her work could even, possibly, rise to the level of the art museum, unlike the dross desecrating the White Elephant.

He could not help her in that world the way a scion of an upper-class family could; a scion like Kip McGrant.

Shelby worked at her drawings. They *mattered* to her. He thought of how traumatized Shelby had been, dragged underneath the White Elephant by Tallon and Frankie. She had wept and shook when he held her after the fight in the deepdown, after he and Airik had defeated those goons.

As upset as she was, she had pulled herself together for the long journey back. And when they had made it through the tunnels, climbed back up the narrow shaft, and arrived in the atrium of White Elephant, she picked up her sketchbook and began drawing what she saw.

She was so brave, so talented, so focused.

Would she be better off with that mazhor, Kip? The McGrant family was rich and well-connected.

The thought of Shelby with some other man (especially one like Kip) made him nauseous, jealous, resentful, but most of all, bereft and ungrateful for the gift he had been offered by what lived below in the deepdown.

Malcolm leaned against the backrest, oblivious to the other passengers, all with lives and fears and hopes of their own. He let the decision come to him of its own accord.

She was his Dome Two princess, and he would fight for her. He would risk his career for her. She had to make her choice, but he could stack the deck in his favor by being the best choice she could make.

He had already started the process whereby Sajag Burgess would no longer be a threat. Speaking to Mr. Steelio would help it along as well as lead him to a better social standing. After that, he would do a favor for Blue Sun by telling them about a threat they knew nothing about. As long as he was discreet and kept his hands clean, he could avoid blowback from dealing with Blue Sun.

He didn't want to become the President and Chairman of the Board of the Second National Bank of Panschin if he had to do it without her. His victory would be worthless if he couldn't share it with Shelby Bradwell.

The meeting with Mr. Steelio was brief and positive. Malcolm left with a list of suggestions and letters of introduction to other possible sources of information, all leading to Burgess's destruction. He also came out of the meeting knowing he should have spoken with Mr. Steelio earlier. There was, it turned out, a network of scholarship boys who helped each other navigate the rituals of upper-class Panschin society. He had to ask to be invited because they would not come to him. Jeffen came next. There was always the risk that Blue Sun would want more from him, but it was a risk Malcolm had to take to keep Shelby and her sister safe. He'd have to keep his hands scrupulously clean. He wondered if he should ask about Sajag Burgess or should he let his new allies in the executive suite in Second National take care of that task for him. He couldn't decide and, in the end, decided to see where the conversation with Jeffen led him.

After Jeffen, he would speak to the shaman. Malcolm carefully stored away his concerns so they would not distract him when dealing with a representative of Blue Sun, even one as low in the hierarchy as Jeffen. Blood in the tunnels was one thing. Everyone spilled a little, with cuts and scrapes. They were an unavoidable hazard of working in the deepdown. This lake of blood, violently spilled and ending in death, was something else altogether.

He frowned to himself. He would have to tell Jeffen about this matter too, so he could pass it along to his own, second set of masters. They would understand the seriousness.

Veronica watched Airik Jones leave for his meeting with Chung/Banerjee with a heavy heart. He had seemed so distant and formal, a startling contrast to their closeness in the tunnels. His wounds had to be painful, so perhaps that was why.

She couldn't do anything for him, other than persuade auntie Neza and Mrs. Grisson that she would be safe for the evening back at the White Elephant when Mr. Jones returned for the night. He had paid for his rooms, and he would be expecting them.

She wondered if she should have kissed him before he left. He had saved her and her sister at great risk to his life. But she didn't know him. She still didn't know anything about his family or even if "Jones" was his last name. She didn't know why he needed a bodyguard. She didn't know how he felt about her. There was so much she didn't know.

It was paralyzing.

She wished she had kissed him. It had felt so good to have his arm around her, leaning on him, knowing he had come for her. She put her hand into her pocket, feeling her earbobs that she had dropped to mark the way. He had returned them to her before he left, while apologizing for not rescuing the remains of her bead necklace.

Veronica spared a glance at Shelby, hard at work capturing on paper Dean's description of the mysterious boss from Barsoom. Shelby knew where she stood with Malcolm. The two of them had made it plain enough to everyone in the room. She had no idea her sister would be so willing to kiss and cuddle a man in front of their great-aunt, along with the goggling and whispering neighbors, particularly a man she and the family had only recently met.

Neza did not seem to disapprove. She smiled fondly on them when she wasn't whispering to Mrs. Grisson. Malcolm Cobb was not from a family that her great-aunt would have ever considered worthwhile in the past. He certainly wasn't what auntie Neza had been hoping for since the day Shelby started classes at PanU.

Yet there they were, and Neza openly approved. Well, he was a banker, and he said he would keep the family from being evicted, so that might be the reason. Veronica tsked at herself for being so cynical. Malcolm Cobb had trusted them enough to reveal who he was, and he was proving himself still more.

Airik Jones owed her nothing, even as she owed him her life. What if he hadn't come down with Malcolm? Malcolm had grown up in the Steelio warrens, but he would have been one man against two. Why had Mr. Jones gone down below? She should have asked him.

She would ask him tonight, when he returned from his meetings. She might find out more about the mysterious Mr. Jones.

Veronica wished again that she had kissed him when he left. He would leave for good for Barsoom soon enough, and she would never have the chance again.

Shelby concentrated on refining her sketch of Tallon and Frankie's boss. Dean hadn't been as observant as Elliot had been, and she didn't know the right questions to elicit telling details.

"Sergeant?"

"Yes, Miss Bradwell?" the desk sergeant replied, looking up from his plan to search the neighboring streets and houses. Neza and Mrs. Grisson were assisting him; helpful and irritating by turns. Between the two of them, they knew virtually everyone living in the dome. He knew he would have to put their immense social network to good use in the future to maintain order in Dome Two.

"Does Dome Six have a police artist?"

"Yes, they do, Miss Bradwell." The desk sergeant came over to study her latest sketch, the one Dean was most pleased with. He frowned at it.

"Doesn't look much like the one you drew before."

"I know," Shelby said, frustrated. "Dean's not been very helpful."

"I'm trying," Dean said wearily. "I'll see that man in my nightmares forever."

"Yes, but *I* can't see him. Sergeant? If you could get the police artist to come to Dome Two to work with Elliot and Dean, I think you'd get a much better picture. You'd know who to look for."

"I'll see what I can do, Miss Bradwell," the sergeant replied. "Dome Six keeps him busy."

"With what? Littering complaints?" Neza inserted herself into the conversation. She leaned over to study Shelby's drawings.

The sergeant laughed harshly. "Dome Six gets plenty of muggings, pickpockets, and purse-snatching. More than we do, truthfully."

"Really?" Shelby said. She'd always believed Dome Two was more dangerous, yet thinking it over, she realized she'd never been harassed other than at PanU by other students. Nor had she heard of one of the neighbors complaining about a recent robbery.

"That's where the population and the money is," the sergeant replied dryly. He studied her sketch again. "You thought about becoming a police artist yourself, Miss Bradwell? You've got the knack of making a picture look like a real person."

Shelby felt herself glow with pleasure. Here was proof again, from someone with nothing to gain by saying so. She could draw. She had talent. She'd already started thinking about her future away from PanU before she'd come home. But when Dean had come in through the kitchen door of the White Elephant with Tallon and Frankie, she had stopped thinking.

Then Malcolm and Mr. Jones had finally showed up. She hadn't thought much when she'd walked back through the tunnels with

Malcolm's arm around her. She'd been so glad to be alive, to be next to him. His very male presence filled her brain completely with thoughts that made her blush at the time. Recalling them made her blush harder.

They'd made it back up the ladder safely, to auntie Neza, and she'd done what she always did. She started sketching. Yet all the while, on some hidden level in her mind, Shelby realized, she'd been thinking about her future and the desk sergeant's off-hand remark brought it back.

She wanted to spend her future with Malcolm Cobb. She wanted to be an artist. She wanted to earn a living with her talent. Beauty mattered to her, and she wanted to share that beauty with Panschin. Like Malcolm, she wasn't going to lie about who and what she was. She could be as good an artist as Clyde Monez. But she wouldn't do what Clyde Monez did. She wouldn't lie.

She would talk to Professor Vitebskin in the morning. It wouldn't matter what he said in response, but he would know the truth. They both would.

Airik sat awkwardly in the transtube, his bruises, stitches, and the heavy bandaging bothering him with every breath and movement. The police surgeon had been adamant about him seeing a doctor as soon as possible to check for infection. Every time he shifted his weight, trying to get more comfortable, Carmine looked concerned. After the tenth readjustment, Carmine asked if he wanted to move up to the first-class tube to stretch out on a lounge.

"No, I'm fine," he replied.

"Make sure you tell the family you said so," Carmine said dryly. "They won't believe me."

No one else paid them much attention other than to glance over and look puzzled. Airik had earlier silently blessed Elliot for packing several changes of clothes for the White Elephant, insisting that, as a gentleman, he should be ready to dress for dinner. Airik hadn't needed to, and now, he was decidedly overdressed for the afternoon transtube. But this suit was clean and undamaged. It was also too tight because of the bandages around his chest and leg.

The message his body was sending was clear: He'd have to check in with the Twelve Happiness doctor in the infirmary. That would also allow him to check on Upton's condition.

He would be even later returning to the Chung/Banerjee meeting. Airik could only hope that Gaston had not signed any contracts ensnaring Shelleen in a business deal he would come to regret. The prospectus had looked bad from the start, and the additional information he had gotten at the White Elephant had inclined him to refuse any partnerships. The final straw was discovering from Dean Kangjuon, of all people, that Peng McGrant had bought his stake in the company via his gambling wins.

It was all too much.

Dean had said the McGrant family had no mining background; they were merely looking for a company they could milk of cash until it folded, thus recouping all their spent money via a tax-dodging effort and earning a profit at the expense of the original company. That explanation, Airik reflected, went a long way towards explaining his impressions. He patted the report he had just finished reading again, the one Upton had left behind.

Upton's carelessness had been providential. He would have returned to the White Elephant in the evening, as always, and discovered the bodies. Tallon would have murdered Veronica for lying about finding some of Simon Bradwell's coin, Shelby and Neza as witnesses, possibly Lulu and Florence, and most of all, Dean, for being such a fool. Having watched Mrs. Grisson in action with the local police, Airik realized she knew everyone in Dome Two, and she would have never accepted anything Dean said about the new owners of the White Elephant.

He would have lost Veronica Bradwell.

It was unlikely Malcolm would have succeeded on his own. It had taken both of them, fighting together, to injure Tallon and Frankie enough to stop them. The sound of crunching bones and snapping joints would visit him in his nightmares, joining Howard Shelleen's screams. Airik also understood he would do it again, despite the cost, just as he would punish Howard again for betraying the demesne. Scars were the price you paid for doing what needed to be done.

He would have lost Veronica.

The thought ate at him, more painful than the itching, burning lines seared across his chest and thigh, hurting more than the bruises and aches he felt everywhere. Beautiful, clever, strong, considerate Veronica would have died in the tunnels in terror and agony.

She should have meant nothing to him other than a struggling bed and breakfast owner. Yet she did. Tallon had been correct; she was made of fire and nerve, with a spine of the finest steel.

"Our stop is next, sir," Carmine murmured.

Airik hadn't realized he had closed his eyes. He was more tired than he imagined. He stretched them open and stifled a yawn. "So it is."

"You gonna see the hotel doc on your own or am I gonna have to drag you into their infirmary?"

"I'll walk under my own power, thank you," Airik said. "I need to check on Upton's condition anyway."

"What happened to him? I got the craziest story from one of the waitresses."

"I'll fill you in on the way."

"And when we get there, you'll see the doc. First thing, before you do anything else. Sir."

"It wouldn't be sensible to do otherwise," Airik said.

Carmine, good servant that he was, managed to bite back his thoughts on that subject.

"Hmmm," the hotel doctor said, examining Airik's fresh stitches on chest and thigh, along with his collection of bruises. "What were you doing in Dome Two to earn this?"

From his prone position on the padded table, Airik eyed him suspiciously.

"Why do you ask about Dome Two?"

"That's Dr. Coben's stitching and knots. He does very neat work. Gets a lot of practice in the tunnel bars under Dome Four." The hotel doctor smiled brightly at Airik. "We're on the same team in the footie league."

"I thought he was the police surgeon for Dome Two."

"Dr. Coben is, but Dome Four is right next to Dome Two so the police department covers both sections. Dome Four doesn't rate a substation of its own since there's not much trouble aboveground and the city won't put a substation in their tunnels."

"Then why do you assume I was in Dome Two?"

The hotel doctor gave Airik a pitying look.

"I cannot imagine how the daimyo of Shelleen would manage to find his way into the tunnel bars under Dome Four. Dome Two you could find. The museums are there so the city provides plenty of signs."

Airik thought about this as the doctor smeared stinging, antiseptic jelly over his stitches, adding to their irritation. Panschin was a more closely-knit city than he had assumed. In many ways, it resembled the villages of Shelleen, running on gossip and personal connections.

"How is Upton doing?"

The hotel doctor frowned. "He has to stay overnight and all day tomorrow. He isn't breathing well. I'm getting more worried about his sinuses and lungs than his other ailments. Pneumonia, you know."

"Damnation," Airik said. Where was he going to find another secretary?

"Doctor?" Winifred Qiao opened the door and trotted in on silent, bare feet. "Upton's breathing is changing for the worse. He needs you right away."

"I am with a patient, Miss Qiao. I will be there shortly," the doctor answered testily. "Where's my head nurse?"

"With Upton. *She* sent me." Winifred stopped and realized who the doctor was treating. "My lord Shelleen. I, uh, didn't recognize you."

She blinked at Airik's bare chest, adorned with a stitched-together slash, then ran her eyes down his nearly nude body to his thigh wound. He was sporting a constellation of bruises, blooming brown and purple against his grassy green skin.

"What on Mars were you getting up to in Dome Two?" she asked.

Waiting quietly in the background, Carmine did his best to hide a grin.

Airik said, "You know Dr. Coben as well?" Miss Qiao must not have left the infirmary. She was still wearing her fuchsia cocktail dress but she had removed her very impractical, high-heeled sandals.

"Oh, yes," Winifred replied. "He has a very distinctive stitching style. He gets a lot of practice from tunnel bar fights. A broken whiskey bottle does terrible damage."

"Do not speak about my injuries to anyone, Miss Qiao," Airik said firmly.

She reared back, deeply offended. "Patient confidentiality comes first, my lord Shelleen. I know my duty." She frowned and added, "Upton's been worried about what you're going to do about a secretary. He won't be able to work with you for days, maybe a few weeks."

"No diagnoses, Miss Qiao," the doctor said. "We don't know for sure, not yet."

"Of course, Doctor," Winifred Qiao said.

"There," the hotel doctor wiped his hands and replaced the lid on the salve. "All done. Get dressed. Stop by every morning and every evening for a check-up. I want to make sure that doesn't get infected. Make sure to tell Dr. Coben, if you see him, that you're seeing me as well. I'll have my dispensary compound a pain-relieving tea for you. It will be sent to your suite when it's ready."

"My thanks," Airik replied as the doctor was leaving. Along with a sizable bill, I'm sure, he thought. He'd have to ask Lulu at the White Elephant if she had a brew of her own. Her other tea had worked so well for his secretary.

He eased himself to a sitting position and said, "Miss Qiao? I need to speak with you."

"Upton needs me," she protested. She had reached the door, intent on following the doctor to Upton's bedside.

Airik held up a hand. "This is a business matter. Wait."

He was gratified to see Miss Qiao pause and turn to him.

With Carmine's assistance, he slowly eased himself into his shirt. "I was told Marmaduke Qiao follows contracts to the letter. Is that correct?"

"My esteemed grandfather wouldn't renege on a contract," Miss Qiao said firmly. "It would be dishonorable."

"Do you feel the same way about patient confidentiality?"

"Of course," she said, offended again. "I am a member of Qiao & Schopenhour as well as being in training for medicine.

"So you don't plan on discussing, say, Upton's medical issues with your family, despite the obvious advantage to do so?" Airik asked.

"Never."

"Very good. I will remember what you said. I'll need to speak with Marmaduke and Bertram as quickly as possible. I'll be meeting with Chung/Banerjee" — Airik noticed with interest the look of distaste that crossed Winifred Qiao's face — "and they may interrupt that meeting."

"May I tell them what this meeting is in reference to?" Miss Qiao said.

"Among other things, I require a replacement secretary," Airik said. "Reliable, competent, loyal to me, and totally discreet as I do not need Shelleen's business dealings discussed with Qiao & Schopenhour now or ever or with anyone else."

"Qiao & Schopenhour will honor your contract to the letter," Miss

Qiao said. "Make sure you're complete and detailed with your requirements."

Next, the pants. One of us should be embarrassed, he thought, but I'm too sore and Miss Qiao is too professional. He eased them on and said, "And if Marmaduke were to die tomorrow? Would that remain true?"

"Yes, it would," Miss Qiao replied icily. "Everyone in our family, unlike some other companies in Panschin, knows how to honor a contract. My esteemed grandfather's death will not change that fact."

Airik allowed himself a smile. So, Malcolm Cobb had been correct.

"You implied you have other needs, my lord Shelleen?" she added.

"I do, but I will not discuss them with you."

"Very good. I'll make the arrangements and then I must return to Upton."

Airik eyed her carefully. Her once tastefully arranged hair was coming out of its elaborate crown and, judging on her fuchsia dress spattered with body fluids, she had not left the infirmary.

"You never saw my secretary before today's luncheon?"

"Never." She smiled suddenly, her face lighting up. "I will always treasure the memory of today, when we first met."

"Wiping algae dumplings off Upton's face after he slipped and cracked his skull and two ribs?" Airik asked dryly.

She giggled suddenly. "Yes, even though it was ridiculous as well as painful for my poor Upton."

"I see. You may go," Airik said. He finished dressing for his meeting with Chung/Banerjee. Fortunately, it took place upstairs in the suite so he wouldn't have to leave the hotel.

As he walked to the suite, he thought over how he would word his other request to Qiao & Schopenhour.

The memory unsettled him and had since they left the thugs dying in the tunnel. Tallon had called out, as they were leaving him and Frankie behind in the unending darkness under Panschin, "Ronnie, Ronnie. No forgiveness."

Did the thug mean that his boss wouldn't forgive him for failing? Did the thug mean he didn't forgive Veronica? Or worse, was it a warning that his mysterious boss would harm Veronica Bradwell for foiling his plan to take over the White Elephant and run Panschin?

Malcolm Cobb had seemed sure he could do something about finding this boss from Knights of Mars. The police were looking as well.

But what if they failed?

Every day since arriving in Panschin, Airik was reminded anew how little he understood the free-city. His research was proving to be wildly inadequate and inaccurate. He could do very little to protect Veronica, her sister, and her aunt, other than insist that they relocate to Shelleen. But he might be able to persuade Qiao & Schopenhour to look for the mysterious boss. It wouldn't hurt to have a third set of allies. The prospect of having Shelleen in their debt would encourage them to say yes to his request.

As he worked his painful way from the infirmary, through the lobby, and up the four flights of marble stairs to the suite, Airik parsed out the exact wording he wanted for the contract with Qiao & Schopenhour. Carmine, at his side, noticed his abstracted silence and remained silent himself.

Carmine opened the door to the suite for Airik, and he strode into the room.

Everyone looked up and stared.

"Airik, what happened to you?" Gaston cried out, after staring in horror at the bruise stealing across Airik's jaw and cheek.

Gaston turned and said to Carmine, "And what the hell were you doing that you let this happen to the daimyo?"

"Carmine was following my orders," Airik said coldly.

"I was, my lord Gaston," Carmine said. "The daimyo did what was needed and very necessary it was, in my opinion." He inclined his head to Gaston and retired back to his usual position, holding up the wall where he could watch everyone.

"Then what happened?" Gaston asked again, noticing that Airik was dressed for a formal dinner rather than wearing the business suit he had worn only a few hours ago.

"It can wait," Airik said even more coldly. "I have the report on Chung/Banerjee along with additional information. Mr. McGrant, explain why, as a financier with Mercantile and Commerce, you bought into a failing mining firm with gambling winnings. You have zero mining background."

Peng McGrant leaped to his feet. "How dare you make such an accusation."

Airik noted with interest how none of the Chung/Banerjee staffers sprang to their boss's defense; instead they maintained blank faces or silently stared at briefing papers.

"Dean Kangjuon told me. His information reinforced the issues I observed in your prospectus." Airik watched Peng McGrant's face pale, then turned on Gaston. "Did you sign anything?"

Gaston looked offended. "No sir, I did not. I did not like what I saw, nor did I like the answers I was getting from McGrant. I do not believe that Chung/Banerjee is any better run than Jandinaire. I recommend we avoid both companies."

Airik allowed himself a cool smile.

"I concur. Now let's discuss what Chung/Banerjee can do for Shelleen." The thought occurred to him that Qiao & Schopenhour might not have the information he did; unlikely but possible. They might be open to swallowing up a rival and doing business with Shelleen afterwards. Then they would be back in Shelleen's debt.

For Peng McGrant, the meeting tumbled down the shaft very quickly, and he greeted the knock on the suite door with relief.

Carmine ushered in Marmaduke and Bertram Qiao, followed by their staff.

Marmaduke's eyes widened on seeing the bruises on Airik's face, as did the rest of his staff.

"My dearest granddaughter, Winifred, said you had a contract you wished to discuss?"

"I do," Airik said. "Before we start, were you aware of how Peng McGrant bought into Chung/Banerjee?"

Marmaduke Qiao inclined his head, indicating that his son would speak.

"We are not," Bertram Qiao said. "We have heard disturbing rumors and had wondered, but we have no facts. We do not, by the way, recommend dealing with Chung/Banerjee. There are better companies in Panschin, ones that are not being driven into the ground, their employees ruined, and their assets strip-mined for frivolities and riotous living."

Peng McGrant scowled and made a move to leave.

"Stay," Airik commanded. "This concerns your company." He plunged in, revealing everything Dean Kangjuon had told him about the deals and connections between Peng McGrant, Sajag Burgess, and Simon Bradwell, all made over the tables in Panschin's casinos.

When he finished, Peng McGrant had sunk into his chair and refused to meet anyone's eyes. Members of his staff whispered among themselves, glaring hostilely at their boss.

"Fascinating," Bertram Qiao said. "Your information fits so well with what we have observed."

"Next," Airik said, "I need a secretary while Upton is convalescing. Here are my requirements. In addition, I have another request but I must speak about that one privately."

"Of course, my lord Shelleen," Bertram Qiao murmured. "It will be a pleasure to do business with Shelleen." He bowed deeply and his eyes gleamed as he watched Peng McGrant sink deeper into his chair.

Airik thought long and hard over what he wanted to say to Qiao & Schopenhour about Knights of Mars and the threat to Veronica Bradwell and her family. In the end, he decided to be truthful. It was rewarding to watch their eyes widen and their respect for him grow.

When he finished, Bertram Qiao said, "We will be happy to assist in looking for this man. Blue Sun, while a constant problem, can be managed. They are a known quantity. They understand how things are done in Panschin. On occasion, they are useful. There are, shall we say, certain requirements when dealing with what lives below, in the deepdown. Outsiders from Barsoom will not understand. We will not take that risk."

"My thanks," Airik said, while wondering exactly what lived in the deepdown under Panschin and how it was different from the mines of Shelleen. Perhaps it was linked to the mysterious religious ritual that had gotten Steelio, his niece, and Winifred Qiao a seat at his table for the luncheon.

Bertram Qiao exchanged worried glances with his father.

"Have you, my lord Airik," he asked delicately, "made arrangements to deal with the bloodshed that occurred underneath Dome Two? This concerns us."

"I have not," Airik said slowly. "Isn't that a police matter?"

"It is." Bertram and Marmaduke exchanged glances again. "We will deal with them and make sure the proprieties are observed."

"What proprieties are those?" Airik asked suspiciously.

"Oh, no need to worry yourself. Merely a Panschin superstition," Marmaduke said easily, taking the lead. "We'll take care of it." His son nodded in agreement.

"I see," Airik said, although he did not.

He would have to expand Elliot's researches. Perhaps he could persuade Malcolm Cobb to tell him. The banker, having been raised in the Steelio warren would be sure to know all about what lived in the deepdown. He remembered watching Malcolm's face when the medic had come back up from discovering the bodies of Tallon and Frankie. The banker had looked terrified, as did many in the crowd of policemen and Mrs. Grisson's relatives and boarders. He had refused to speak about it to Airik, other than saying he would "take care of it."

Airik wondered if that concern had made Malcolm Cobb leave sooner than he otherwise would have, abandoning Shelby and her sister because something much more critical had gotten his attention.

J effen was waiting for Malcolm in the small pub that served the residents of the Steelio Warren. On his way to Jeffen's table tucked in the corner, Malcolm nodded to the people he recognized.

Jeffen was not alone. He had a friend with him, a man Malcolm vaguely recognized from working in the deepdown.

"You needed to talk to me?" Jeffen asked, even before Malcolm sat down with his beer. "This better be good. I don't like getting Mr. Steelio's personal attention unless I earn it."

"It is," Malcolm replied. He leaned over and whispered, "It's in regards to Blue Sun."

Jeffen sat back and raised an eyebrow at Malcolm.

"Back room. Follow me." To the other man, Jeffen said, "wait here."

He picked up his mug of beer, Malcolm did the same, and led the way to the side door partially hidden by a large cabinet at the end of the bar. The door, made of bamboo rather than a wool curtain, could not be seen from the entrance to the pub. Malcolm had noticed it before and never given it a second thought.

The door opened up into a small meeting room with a table, a selection of mis-matched chairs, and shelves crowded with a huge collection of empty bottles waiting to be washed and refilled. One wall was lined with locked cabinets. The exposed rock had been whitewashed, to help the skimpy lighting. There was also a second bamboo door, but not one leading back to the pub. Malcolm had to wonder where this door went, since it couldn't lead back to the main passageway.

"Have a seat. You looking to join?" Jeffen asked. "A straight arrow like you?"

"Never," Malcolm replied. "But I have information that Blue Sun needs. I hope you can pass it on to someone higher up who can act on it."

"Higher up, huh," Jeffen said. "What, you think I'm some low-level foot soldier? A few rungs down the ladder from an assistant manager?"

Malcolm studied him for a moment. Jeffen was only a few years older than he was.

"Aren't you?"

Jeffen leaned forward on his elbows. "No. I am not. I am here because I got a message from Steelio himself. You're one of his fair-haired boys. Tell me why I got to listen to you."

"Give me a minute, while I rearrange everything I thought I knew," Malcolm admitted.

"I'm counting the seconds." Jeffen's eyes wandered around the small room. His attitude was clearly, openly, bored and hostile.

"What do you know about Knights of Mars?" Malcolm asked. The reason for Jeffen's friend, waiting patiently outside, was becoming clear. He'd seen Carmine do the same for Airik, patiently waiting and watching. Jeffen's friend and Carmine were of a similar size too.

Jeffen took a long, long pull on his beer before answering.

"They're an organization similar to Blue Sun, based out of Barsoom. I don't know much more, except that we don't want them in Panschin. Thirty seconds."

"They're trying to infiltrate Panschin and seize control, unseen by anyone, including Blue Sun."

"That changes things," Jeffen replied. He set his mug down on the table, making it ring. "Take as much time as you need. Start at the beginning."

"You recall Shelby Bradwell?"

"Yeah? What's she got to do with Knights of Mars. Something else her sodding bastard of a father did?"

"No, it's because of the house Shelby, her sister, and her aunt live in Dome Two. It's called the White Elephant."

Malcolm dove into the story, carefully omitting the fact that Airik Jones, visiting businessman from Barsoom, was the daimyo of Shelleen.

As he spoke, Jeffen interrupted to ask probing questions. Some of them sought more detailed information, but some led to unexpected connections and insights. With each question, Malcolm realized anew that Jeffen should have been picked for the scholarship program just as he had been. He was far, far more intelligent than he let on.

After Malcolm had finished talking, Jeffen called in his muscle and sent him for another round and a plate of algae dumplings. "Let me think on this," he said.

When the food and beer was served, Jeffen broke his silence.

"Hellation. He took a swallow. "A house in Dome Two connected directly to the train station via abandoned tunnels. It would work. They'd move people, goods, and weapons in and out, and we'd never know. Where's that Dean Kangjuon now?"

"In police custody, under armed guard, or so they implied. He'll be on his way to trial and will probably end up in the Dirac mines in short order for that stunt."

"I'll give you a list of Blue Sun-controlled Dirac mines. He needs to get sent to one of them, if you want to keep him alive."

"They have that kind of reach?" Malcolm asked, disconcerted.

"Yeah, but so does Knights of Mars. If your informant ends up in a Dirac mine they control, and they find out, he'll be beaten to death in short order."

"I'll pass it along," Malcolm said. "Carefully. I assume you don't need this list made public?"

Jeffen grinned. "You are a smart one. I don't. How's Shelby handling this? She wasn't real comfortable being underground when you brought her down."

Malcolm sighed gustily. "I don't know if I'll get her back into the warren any time soon. That cloud painting she promised you?"

Jeffen's face turned cold. "I do."

"Shelby wants to know if you and your wife can come to the White Elephant to pick it up."

Jeffen grinned widely, friendly again. "In her house? We're allowed in her house? That house?"

Malcolm grinned back. "They let me in. We'll make a day of it. We'll show you around Dome Two and take you to lunch at the Dappled Yak."

He paused and eyed Jeffen. Handling Jeffen was becoming like handling explosives. Powerful, valuable, and touchy, but very, very useful as long as he was exquisitely cautious. "Do you want to see the hatch and the tunnel access while you're at the White Elephant? We can climb down and trace the tunnel route to the train station."

Jeffen looked away, suddenly uncomfortable. "I dunno. I need to. But that area's got to be cleansed and purified first. You should know that, even though you don't earn your living in the deepdown anymore."

"I'm seeing the shaman next."

Jeffen was visibly relieved. "Good. Murdering your partner and then cutting your own throat in the pitch-black deepdown sounds like something ignorant that Knights of Mars would do. They don't understand what lives beneath. We can't allow them in Panschin," Jeffen said. "It's not even a matter of competition."

"No, I didn't think so."

They sat in silence for a few minutes, nibbling on algae dumplings.

Jeffen broke the quiet. "Blue Sun owes no one. What do you want in exchange?"

Malcolm sat back. "Finding this mystery boss. I don't care what you do to him, so long as word doesn't get back to his bosses in Barsoom and put my Shelby and her family in danger."

"That was a given the moment you told me," Jeffen replied. "What do *you* want from Blue Sun? So's we're square."

"Give me a minute." Did he want to ask about Burgess and his gambling habits? Malcolm thought, then decided not to. The Second National executives would take care of Burgess for him so there was no reason to muddy the issue. He still didn't know if Burgess had his dealings with Blue Sun. Now that he had a better idea about Jeffen, it would be much safer to steer clear because it was possible that Jeffen did know and had reasons of his own to keep Burgess safe.

But there was something else.

"All right. This is what I want," Malcolm said. "You know I got ambitions. I plan on becoming the President of Second National and Chairman of the Board."

Jeffen stared at him, his turn to be disconcerted. "You want Blue Sun's help?"

"No, never," Malcolm said. "I can do this on my own just fine. The place is loaded with idiots and mazhors. I'm gonna clean house. I want Second National to be the best bank in Panschin, the most honest bank. I want it to be a bank people can rely on, not one that will cheat its clients with bad investments like Simon Bradwell was peddling."

"Okay, still with you," Jeffen said. "But what's that got to do with us?"

"I want Blue Sun to stay away from Second National. If I find Blue Sun money in my bank, I'll prosecute. No money laundering, no embezzling, no scams, no extortion cash, no drug and whore money, nothing. Stay away from my bank."

Jeffen smiled slowly. "That makes two things Blue Sun owes you."

"What?" Malcolm said. "I just told you I'd investigate and prosecute. How do you owe me?"

"And here I thought you was smart," Jeffen sniffed. "Who do you recommend we use, who won't care like you do?" His eyes gleamed.

"First National," Malcolm replied promptly. "They got poor oversight. Then there's…." He stopped suddenly and smirked. "You can figure it out on your own, I'm sure."

"So what do you want from us?"

"Jeffen, I'll be honest," Malcolm said thoughtfully. "I don't know. I guess for Blue Sun to stay out of my business and away from my family. I'll do the same for you. That enough?"

"It'll do. For now," Jeffen said. "Shelby coming along for your ride to the top?"

Malcolm beamed. "If she'll have me."

"She's a nice girl," Jeffen said. "Too bad about her old man. Maybe your liabilities will cancel hers out."

Malcolm scowled. Jeffen saw all too well the bind he was in with Shelby. "That's my plan. In the meantime, talk to your wife and set up a time to visit the White Elephant. If you come in the next two weeks, you'll get to see just how good an artist Shelby really is. The place is hosting the PanU Artists' Collective art show."

"They any good?" Jeffen asked curiously.

"They're *awful*," Malcolm replied with a grimace. "Shit smeared on canvases. I was floored when I walked in. Just could not believe what I was seeing. Yet this avant-garde art is approved by our betters. It has to be a scam to fool the moneyed people. No one with any sense would hang this dross on their walls. You'll have a laugh."

"You really want to join the upper-classes if they like that kind of dross?"

"Damn right I do," Malcolm said. "They've gone soft in the head if those heaps of tailings are any indication. Panschin needs people like me to keep the city moving forward."

He stopped and gave Jeffen a considering look. "They need people like you, too. We counter-balance idiots like Kip McGrant."

"That mazhor." Jeffen spat onto the floor.

"Yeah."

Jeffen ate the last algae dumpling, then stood up. "If we're done, I got work to do, and you got to go see the shaman."

"We're done," Malcolm said. "And Jeffen? Thank you."

Jeffen showed his teeth. "Keep an eye on the papers. You'll know when we succeed."

"A body dumped in a Dome Six park?"

"These things happen when strangers come to Panschin."

"So they do," Malcolm said. "So they do."

Veronica fretted and stewed the rest of the afternoon at Mrs. Grisson's house. She should have said something, she should have done something, she should have kissed Airik Jones when the opportunity presented itself. The Biennial Mining Conference would be over in another week and he would be gone for good, gone back to Barsoom.

She'd never see him again.

She owed him everything. He'd rescued her and her sister. Auntie Neza was alive and unhurt. They knew why the thug had wanted the White Elephant.

Airik Jones had come to mean something to her, even though she probably meant not that much to him. He'd leave. Why wouldn't he? He had a family in Barsoom waiting for him. He might, the thought stabbed her heart, already be married to someone else, someone who appreciated his intelligence and sly, dry wit. Someone who loved how very un-average he was.

She couldn't kiss him now. The crisis had passed, and it wouldn't be seemly. She should have thrown her arms around him then and kissed him soundly, lingeringly, letting him know how much she appreciated his valor. She could have passed it off as being overcome by the moment. Now, with him back at the Biennial Mining Conference and her swept off to Mrs. Grisson's house, her chance was gone.

Veronica sighed. Here she was, mooning over a man about whom she knew almost nothing, other than she fancied him. If Airik Jones were to discover the depths of what her father had done, he wouldn't give her the time of day, at least not publicly. It reminded her of how Shelby was treated, and her sister should have been young enough to remain untainted. Shelby had not had to defend herself in court against charges that she had helped dear old dad defraud everyone who trusted him.

What could she do? She could mope about and stay right where she was. Or she could make sure Mr. Jones was properly taken care of, just as he had paid for. That meant — she eyed Neza and Mrs. Grisson rehashing the dreadful experience over tea and biscuits for the benefit of the remaining members of Mrs. Grisson's household, along with a selection of agog neighbors — persuading her aunt to let her stay at the White Elephant when he returned from his meetings.

With Mr. Jones back in the house, along with his servants, she wouldn't be alone. Lulu and Florence would be home by then. She observed Shelby, sketching variants of her drawings of the mystery boss, trying to combine Elliot's and Dean's descriptions into an accurate composite. Shelby never paid much attention to her surroundings when she was drawing; she would remain completely focused on her subject. Her little sister could remain with Mrs. Grisson or go back home. Either one would work for her if she was kept distracted.

The White Elephant was waiting for her. Dean had been hauled off to the police substation for interrogation. Mrs. Grisson's oldest son was staying at the house, overseeing the police team as they investigated the second subbasement and the hatch to the tunnels. The rescue and recovery team should have hauled up the thugs' bodies by now and delivered to the morgue. They were no longer a threat to her or to the house. Veronica couldn't bring herself to feel any sympathy for Frankie, having Tallon slash his throat open in the pitch-black deepdown, multiple times if the medic's initial report was accurate. He'd earned it for hurting Shelby. And then Tallon had shoved his knife into his own throat, stabbing up into his brain to ensure he died quickly.

It didn't bear thinking what Tallon would have done to her when he discovered she had lied about finding a stash of dear old dad's coin. Veronica was glad he was dead. He'd never hurt anyone again. Even so, grateful as she was that he was dead, the image would haunt her. She pushed it firmly away, hoping it would fade with time.

She wondered how much damage the police were doing to her garden, her main source of income, as they checked every aspect of her house and garden. Maybe she could talk Neza into letting her go back to keep the police from trampling the greens. With all those beat patrolmen scurrying around, Tallon's mystery boss wouldn't dare come near the house. She'd be perfectly safe, and she could get back to work.

The time to be worried about safety would be after the Biennial

Mining Conference ended and Mr. Jones left for Barsoom and the police moved on to other problems.

The threat of Mr. Burgess evicting them paled by comparison. Mrs. Grisson would take them in, temporarily to be sure, but she'd help them find new lodgings. She, her sister, and her aunt would still be alive.

Alive to starve.

Veronica paced nervously around the perimeter of Mrs. Grisson's dining room. It was larger than the White Elephant's, a good thing because Mrs. Grisson had converted her ballroom into a warren of rooms for boarders. She kept staring out the windows at the vegetable beds filling the yard. Mrs. Grisson grew a different selection of vegetables than she did; that way, they could split the market.

What would she do to earn coin if she couldn't grow vegetables for market? Veronica closed her eyes in pain. Writing gardening articles wasn't working. She'd be on her knees scrubbing terraformers in short order, but luckily, she'd gotten good at that task in the last few years.

She kept staring out at Mrs. Grisson's garden beds as she paced. Her own needed her attention if she was to get the Dappled Yak's order ready tomorrow morning.

Hmm. Two reasons to go home might be enough to get auntie Neza to agree, along with the fact that she wouldn't be alone. Her aunt could stay with Mrs. Grisson if she wanted to. The two of them would discuss the thugs' home invasion for the next year.

"Veronica," Neza said, interrupting her thoughts.

"Yes?" Veronica answered. She'd thought Neza hadn't been paying any attention, being intent on filling in the avid listeners with every detail of the past few days.

"You're going to wear ruts in the rug. Would you like to sit down and have some more tea?"

Veronica looked at her empty cup. When had she finished drinking it?

"No, I don't think so. I've been thinking that I should go back home. I've got work to do in the gardens to get ready for the Dappled Yak's order and Mr. Jones will be back this evening. I need to clean up from the police before he returns."

Neza gave her a long, considering look, as did Mrs. Grisson. The two old ladies exchanged glances, fraught with meaning, while Veronica waited patiently.

"You know, Veronica," her aunt said thoughtfully. "You're probably correct. The house will be a mess and Mr. Jones did pay for rooms through the end of the mining conference."

"Uh," Veronica said. She'd been braced for an argument. She rallied with "Right. Yes, he did. It wouldn't do to not deliver on the contract. What if he were to ask for his money back?"

"Yes, what if," Neza said dryly.

"And I won't be alone. Lulu and Florence will be home soon and, of course, Mr. Jones has his servants with him," Veronica added, just in case Neza changed her mind. "Shelby could come home too." Inspiration struck. "Lulu and Florence could invite Trevor and Evan over."

Veronica smiled brightly at her great-aunt who nodded agreeably.

"Yes, I think that could work," Neza said.

"I think Neza's right, dearie," Mrs. Grisson added firmly. "Mr. Jones did pay for those rooms and an agreement's an agreement. I'll have one of my boys take one of your spare rooms and another of my boys can bunk down in your ballroom. Just to be sure you're okay."

"How thoughtful of you," Veronica gushed. Lordy, but auntie Neza was giving up easily. Having Mrs. Grisson, her bosom companion, agree meant it was a sure thing.

"Huh? Did I hear my name?" Shelby asked, finally noticing the conversation going on around her. Her voice was still hoarse and would be for days. She coughed, reached for her own tea, and took a sip.

"Yes, dear girl," Neza said. "Veronica needs to move back to the White Elephant. She wanted to know if you wanted to come along. Mr. Jones will be expecting a clean house to sleep in tonight."

Shelby gaped, her teacup shaking in her hand. "But we were attacked! Those thugs' boss is still roaming around Panschin. He'll murder us in our beds."

Neza frowned at her.

Mrs. Grisson said, "I'll inform the desk sergeant I expect regular foot patrols. He won't ignore *me*, not after what happened. Besides, Shelby, didn't that nice young man of yours say he was going to do something about hunting down the thugs' boss?"

Shelby opened her mouth to protest, then closed it again before answering.

"Um, yes?" She set down her teacup and thought. Maybe she could persuade Malcolm to doss down in the White Elephant as well. There were plenty of empty bedrooms. He'd be sleeping in the same house, maybe even on the same floor, possibly the same wing! He'd be so near to her. The thought was exciting. He could have breakfast with her. He might be willing to walk with her to PanU in the morning again. She could tell him about her decision to confront Professor Vitebskin. She could spend more time with him, just like he was a real boyfriend. He fancied her; she was sure of it. She'd see more of him, a lot more. If they spent more time together, he might decide he liked her enough to ignore what dear old dad had done despite the damage her background would do to his career prospects. She had to seize this golden chance.

Everyone was watching her, waiting for what she would say.

"Yes, yes, he did," Shelby affirmed eagerly.

Neza smiled fondly at her, and then at Veronica. "How nice. Then it's settled. We'll get you back home in plenty of time for Mr. Jones."

"Thank you," Veronica said, thinking furiously. That had been far too easy, almost as though auntie Neza had ulterior motives. Veronica sniffed. She did want to see Mr. Jones again, but it meant nothing, not to her, not to him, and not to anyone else. Nothing would come of it. He'd go back to Barsoom and leave her alone in Panschin. The pain stabbed through her heart again.

He would go home to someone else.

Her little sister, at least, would see more of Malcolm Cobb. That had to count for something, Veronica decided. One of them would be happy.

Malcolm had a long discussion with the Steelio warren shaman about what happened in the tunnels beneath the White Elephant. As with his conversation with Jeffen, he carefully avoided identifying who Airik Jones really was.

When they finished, the shaman said, "this will be a big job. Murder and suicide! That area won't be safe for anyone for decades if it is not cleansed and purified. The stones themselves have drunk too deep of blood. I will make the arrangements."

"My deepest thanks, mùshī," Malcolm replied, his head bowed.

The shaman gave him a long, considering look. "You can find this Mr. Jones?"

"Yes, mùshī. He is staying at the White Elephant."

"Good," the shaman said. "You and he will need to be purified as well."

"Uh," Malcolm said. "I'll do my best. What about the Bradwell sisters?"

The shaman thought about this carefully as he stood in the small chapel carved from the living rock. His feet were bare, and he had both hands resting on the rock slab, forming the altar. He closed his eyes and let what lives beneath speak to him.

Malcolm waited patiently. His own bare feet were freezing from standing on the living rock, but he ignored his discomfort, like he shut down the discomfort from his bruised and aching body.

The shaman opened his eyes. "They should be all right. They did no harm to anyone. The only blood they shed was their own in the normal manner of scrapes. You and Mr. Jones, however, must undergo the ritual if either of you ever plan to enter the deepdown again."

"Yes, mùshī," Malcolm said. Airik had shown he was comfortable in the deepdown but it was doubtful that anyone from Shelleen truly understood what lived in the bones of Mars. He would have to be persuaded.

The shaman caught his hesitation. "You said Mr. Jones is from Barsoom. Nonetheless, he must do this for his own safety."

"Yes, of course, mùshī," Malcolm said. "There is something Mr. Jones wants done. Miss Bradwell broke her necklace of glass beads to leave a trail. He would like the beads collected and returned to him so he can have them restrung for her."

The shaman remained expressionless. "That will take some time. No one can be allowed in that section of the tunnels until after I and my brothers have finished cleansing the area."

"Yes, mùshī, so I told him," Malcolm said.

"Does Mr. Jones understand that few miners of Panschin will willingly go into that area even after we have finished?"

Malcolm smiled coolly. "Money talks. He's ready to pay. There will be someone who will do this for him. After the tunnel has been cleansed and is safe again."

He thought of something else suddenly, another potential problem. "It's a crime scene. Will that be an issue?"

"No. The police of Panschin have their own shaman who will ensure their safety during their investigation. When they are complete, they will let me and my brothers know. Then we will begin."

"My deepest thanks, honored mùshī," Malcolm said. "As soon as I can persuade Mr. Jones, I will tell you."

The shaman said, "Do not delay, Malcolm. What lives beneath will crave more blood after a feast like that one. Much more. Do not delay."

It felt like leading a parade, Veronica reflected, as she marched back to the White Elephant followed by her sister, her aunt, Mrs. Grisson, and a host of the available boarders, relatives, and neighbors. The walk back let her see again how foolish Dean had been, thinking he could have persuaded all these people that nothing was amiss.

Tallon had been much, much smarter. He had realized how important she was in getting the neighbors and the bank to accept his presence in the White Elephant. He probably wouldn't have murdered her when he found out she had lied. What he would have done to her, though, day after endless, torturous, punishing day, was make her wish he had murdered her.

Veronica shuddered again. Mr. Jones coming to get the missing report and Malcolm coming to speak with Neza had saved her and Shelby and Neza. According to Neza, they hadn't hesitated. They had both decided to descend into the tunnels at once to rescue her and her sister.

Tallon might still have murdered her and Shelby. If Mr. Jones and Malcolm had gone for the police, he would have been desperate enough and steel-nerved enough to make sure the police found nothing but bodies.

No witnesses. He wouldn't have left anyone alive, including himself.

What a narrow escape. She should have flung her arms around Mr. Jones and kissed him all over. She should have given more of herself than her kisses to him. Her mouth on his, her body against his, flesh to flesh becoming one. Her wayward thoughts made her flush with heat. He had become so very un-average, so very appealing.

Yet the fact remained, she didn't know anything about him.

She couldn't trust her instincts. She kept being wrong, with Dean as a prime example. He had said Tallon had threatened his parents. They were, quite naturally, more important to him than her, his ex-wife. Her, he would sacrifice and he had. She had still believed he cared about her. How wrong she had been.

"Penny for your thoughts," Neza said.

"Oh, it's nothing," Veronica said. She knew suddenly that Dean was nothing. He wasn't worth stewing over, any more than being haunted by Tallon was worth fretting about. Dean was in police custody because of his stupidity, and his parents — who had stopped being fond of *her* the moment dear old dad's crimes began surfacing — would get to enjoy public humiliation and ridicule.

That was worth a smile, so she told Neza.

Neza laughed and laughed, warming Veronica's heart. "I suppose they'll visit Dean in the Dirac mines," she finally said.

"No," Veronica said thoughtfully. "I don't think they will." She chuckled too. "What would their friends say about them going to such a place?"

"After everything they said about you, I don't feel the least bit sorry for them," Neza said firmly.

She suddenly felt much lighter and freer. It would be petty, Veronica knew, to enjoy watching the Kangjuons suffer a bit of what she and her sister had endured, but she would enjoy it anyway. She was alive. She hadn't died in the tunnels. The sun was shining somewhere on the other side of the dome. Mr. Burgess might still evict her, but she, her sister, and her aunt were alive. They had friends. They had neighbors. They had allies.

She wasn't alone. Even when Mr. Jones left her behind in Panschin, she wouldn't be alone.

Veronica's heart skipped a beat when they arrived at the White Elephant. The gate was wide open and the police were carrying out the bodies of Tallon and Frankie on stretchers to the waiting Black Maria. The bodies were draped in sheets for more discreet transport.

She made herself walk up to the supervising patrolman, fear suddenly attacking her.

"They are dead?" she demanded. Her hand went to her throat, bare of beads.

"Yes, Miss Bradwell," the patrolman answered. He answered her unspoken question. "It took longer than expected to haul them up the upshaft. There's things that had to be done underneath."

"What things?"

He tugged at his collar. "You're not from a mining family, is that correct, Miss Bradwell?"

"No, I'm not," Veronica said. "What does that have to do with anything?"

"I'll let the shaman explain."

He led her, followed by Neza and Shelby and the rest of the entourage into the White Elephant, carefully skirting the bodies as they were carried past. In the atrium he introduced her to an impressively bearded man wearing long robes. Every shade of gray and brown swirled around in them, but handsomely; not discordant like the painting looming above him. The gold police badge pinned to his chest stood out, an incongruous note. His feet were bare.

The patrolman ducked his head in respect.

"Honored mùshī, this is Miss Bradwell."

"Miss Bradwell," the shaman smiled at her. "You are not familiar with the ways of the deepdown?"

"No, I am not," Veronica answered. "Obviously, not nearly as much as I should be."

"Blood was spilled under your home, feeding what lives beneath. I am overseeing the safety of the police as they work in the tunnels underneath us. My brothers will arrive soon, to continue our rituals where those two thugs died. Your house will be purified as will be the tunnel network below it."

"Uh," Veronica said, at a loss. He smiled at her encouragingly. The patrolmen standing around all seemed to think the presence of the shaman was normal and expected. Then she remembered the many strange stories about what lived in the tunnels. Cave vipers were just the most common example.

"We won't be haunted or disturbed?"

"No, Miss Bradwell, you shouldn't be."

"How long will this take? I have visitors from out of town for the Biennial Mining Conference. I don't want them disturbed."

"Miss Bradwell, this takes precedence. I'll also need to speak with Mr. Jones since he, like Mr. Cobb, fought with those two in the deepdown. Their lives and their souls are at risk."

"Oh. Well, we don't want that," Veronica said, not knowing what else to say.

"No, Miss Bradwell. We do not."

She took a look around, seeing dirt and terraformers tracked in everywhere. Fortunately, her vegetable beds outside remained pristine, just as she had left them. The police of Dome Two were more considerate of her gardening than the PanU Artists' Collective had been.

She glanced back at Neza and Shelby, who looked equally puzzled. Mrs. Grisson, right behind them, looked pleased as though things were being handled properly. Well. If Mrs. Grisson approved, then she needed to approve.

"Please, do what you need to do," Veronica said. "In the meantime, I need to clean up for my out of town guests. Will that be all right?"

"Of course, Miss Bradwell. And may I say that I am impressed by your gardens."

"Thank you," she said. "I supply the Dappled Yak with produce."

"I have eaten your vegetables," he said, smiling. "Delicious. If you will excuse me, now that the bodies have been removed, I must return to the tunnel beneath us and await my brothers."

"Of course," Veronica said, resolving to ask Mrs. Grisson later exactly what was going on under her feet.

The rest of the afternoon went by swiftly. Getting back to work in the garden beds let Veronica focus on something alive, growing, and earning her money as opposed to rape and murder in the tunnels. The police finished up and left, allowing Neza and Shelby to begin cleaning up, with Mrs. Grisson and the other neighbors pitching in. The gardens gave Veronica her excuse to escape outside, under the dome, rather than inside the White Elephant. The cleanup had to take place but her vegetable beds would earn more much-needed coin in the morning.

The afternoon's high point was the arrival of a trio of shamans, all wearing similar robes, all impressively bearded, and all sporting bare feet. They marched up the gravel pathways without a twinge or flinch. Veronica led them through the atrium, noticing as she did how each man cast a look around at Professor Vitebskin's most prized art selections and flinched, grimaced, then turned away.

They wanted her to take them below, to the waiting hatch.

She had to force herself to walk down both flights of the curved staircase, down the shadowy passageway, and then into the dim room in the second subbasement that held the hatch. The shamans followed her silently, and she was grateful they didn't expect her to talk.

"Uh," Veronica said, when they reached the hatch. It had been left open, a square mouth filled with black, with only the faintest glimmer of light shifting and twisting at its bottom.

She had to repress a shudder. She wouldn't climb back down the ladder to explore the tunnel maze under the White Elephant ever again; not voluntarily. Still, she asked, "Do you need me to lead the way?"

"No, Miss Bradwell," the leader of the group said. His robe had flecks of sparkle woven into the coarse cloth, like mica shining in the low granite walls encircling the White Elephant. "That won't be necessary." He studied her open discomfort for a moment. "We'll be able to find our way back upstairs when we're finished. You won't have to wait for us."

"Thank you," Veronica said, deeply relieved. She kept feeling as though the thug was watching her, resenting her, hating her for living and escaping him. She couldn't stop a shudder this time, thinking of Tallon and what he had said as she walked away from him.

She blurted out "the thug said 'no forgiveness' when I left him to die in the dark." She could still hear his rasping voice, thick with unswallowed blood and see the dark, mirrored pool forming under his head.

"Miss Bradwell?" the lead shaman said, watching her distraught face. "Part of our ritual cleanses ghosts and other evil spirits. The souls of those two men will be sent on their journey. They will not return, not to the tunnels below, and not to your house. They will not speak to you again."

"But he said…," she couldn't repeat it.

"There is always forgiveness, even for one such as he. He, however, along with his companion, will have to earn his forgiveness over many, many lives to come." The shaman smiled reassuringly. "He earned his fate as did his companion. You, Miss Bradwell, are forgiven. Rest easy."

"Thank you," Veronica said. She prayed their ritual would work. She looked for something else to say and settled on "it's very cold down there. I can provide wool socks or slippers."

"Not necessary, Miss Bradwell. The living stone speaks to us via our flesh."

"Oh." She really didn't know what to say to that.

"You may go."

"Thank you," Veronica said and fled upstairs to light and sun and air and green, growing things that she knew were actually alive.

Once his private business was concluded with Qiao & Schopenhour, Airik allowed himself to enjoy eviscerating Peng McGrant in the meeting that followed. He vividly remembered what Florence had said; that the McGrant family would sue the Bradwells over Kip's surface sickness, despite Veronica and Shelby having nothing to do with it.

His new secretary, Inigo Schopenhour, seemed competent. He swiftly wrote down everything said by the participants. His stenography skills looked faster than Upton's had been, a good sign.

The next test, Airik knew, would be discretion. Could he trust any member of Qiao & Schopenhour as he made notes on the events of the day? He eyed Bertram who was twisting the knife into Peng McGrant by demanding new concessions be granted to Qiao & Schopenhour, in exchange for keeping Chung/Banerjee afloat. Apparently, although rumors abounded in the Panschin business community about the health of Chung/Banerjee, firms like Qiao & Schopenhour did not have the facts at hand. Now, they did, and they could use those facts to their own advantage. They would owe Shelleen.

Airik had to wonder if, despite the regular presence of powerhouse demesnes like Maerski, Davis, Atto, and Fuziwara in the business world of Panschin, Qiao & Schopenhour understood how much power a demesne wielded. If they lied about the discretion of his new secretary, a member of their own family, he would destroy them. In his experience, business people in the free-cities liked to think they were untouchable by the Four Hundred.

They were wrong. Whatever struggles one Four Hundred family had with another, they formed a united front when dealing with citizens of the government corridors.

The meeting over, Airik's new secretary whispered to him about the next item on his schedule: a joint conference with those four demesnes, Maerski, Davis, Atto, and Fuziwara. Airik wanted to groan. Despite the claims of "wanting to work closely together" what those daimyos really wanted was control over his land, his Red Mercury lode, and entrée into his family to retain that control for generations to come.

They still treated him like he was an ignorant yokel from a third-tier agricultural demesne, someone who didn't understand anything about how the mining and extraction industry worked. He took a look around the suite's conference room. Qiao & Schopenhour no longer believed that, nor did Chung/Banerjee, and Airik supposed, based on what Gaston had said, neither did Jandinaire. He would teach this group of aristocrats the same lesson. Shelleen was no longer third-tier.

The walk with Gaston and Inigo and some of the Shelleen staff from the Twelve Happiness Luxury Hotel to the tower complex owned by the Four Hundred mining families was interesting. Every step confirmed to Airik that he had done the right thing for him in relocating to the White Elephant. Dome Six was noisy, surprisingly dirty up-close, and crowded. It had all the disadvantages of Barsoom along with the dome keeping out the rain that would have washed it clean regularly.

He brushed his fingers on the buildings and signs as he walked by. Could he feel the tingle of electrical current keeping Dome Six free of terraformers? He couldn't, but it was obviously enough to deter them. That led to another conclusion: since Dome Six was self-cleaning of terraformers, the residents seemed to think this meant it was self-cleaning for everything else. It wasn't. Airik caught the glint of beady eyes staring from a fetid, dim alley, reminding him unpleasantly of how Veronica's beads strewn in the tunnel had shone like eyes in the dark.

He hoped Malcolm could arrange for their recovery. She would smile at him when he returned them, restrung, so she could wear her beads of star stuff again. He searched for a distraction from the memory of how her smile warmed him, how her laugh reminded him of a brook sparkling in the sun.

He was in Panschin on business. That should be his focus.

"Inigo," Airik asked. "I see what appears to be eyes down that alley. What is it?"

"Rats, my lord Shelleen," Inigo replied. "Dome Six is infested with them."

"Are the other domes as well?" This was the distraction he needed.

"It varies, my lord. They all have some. Rats eat terraformers in the other domes, but then they die of fungal infections which keeps the population down. In Dome Four, there's plenty to eat but it's all toxic so they don't live long. There are weird mutations too. Here in Dome Six, there's no terraformers to eat so they eat garbage instead."

"I see," Airik said. "Since they are eating a healthier diet, they live longer and breed more readily?"

"Yes, my lord, you have the right of it."

"Why are there no cats?"

"Cats don't tolerate terraformers well, my lord. The spores cause breathing issues. They're expensive pets because of their medical bills."

"I see," Airik said, thinking of the hordes of barn cats in Shelleen, happily producing litter after litter of kittens to be eaten by hawks and foxes, when they weren't busily devouring rats and mice. No one wasted medical care on cats.

"The terraformers affect every aspect of the ecosystem of Panschin," he observed.

"Yes sir, they do." Inigo discreetly coughed and then blew his nose. "I have traveled some, and I've never seen anything like Panschin."

"I must agree," Airik replied. "Upton told me about the Four Hundred tower complex. Have you been there?"

"No sir." Inigo frowned. "The Four Hundred owners don't normally allow anyone inside but other members of their class. Previous meetings with Qiao & Schopenhour have taken place in our headquarters or neutral ground. I don't know why."

"Interesting," Airik said.

"Here we are, sir," Inigo said, stopping at an imposing doorway set into the gleaming, creamy yellow stone wall. Several uniformed guards stood idly by the door, watching the crowds go by. Airik suddenly realized the wall they had been walking past filled the block, from cross street to cross street, with no windows or other openings other than this arched doorway. The huge pair of doors filled the space, with a smaller side entrance next to it, with no window to allow a peek inside. The doorway was framed in elaborately carved stone with a shield mounted at the top, containing the sigils of Maerski, Atto, Davis, and Fuziwara. Other participating demesnes had smaller insignia circling the large shield, moons orbiting the gas giants. Airik recalled Veronica and her joke about Professor Vitebskin. It was obvious here who held sway.

The head guard, evidenced by his collection of shiny brass buttons, rows of gold stripes, and colored ribbons on his black uniform, bowed.

"Greetings, my lord Shelleen." His eyes widened slightly at the sight of the bruise smeared across Airik's jaw and cheek. The guard turned off his welcoming smile and pointed at Inigo, smartly dressed in current but conservative Panschin fashions. "Is this" — he hesitated — "*person* part of your entourage?"

"Yes, he is," Airik said coldly, nettled by the guard's tone. "My replacement secretary, Inigo Schopenhour, on loan from Qiao & Schopenhour. I expect full access for him. If you do not allow him to accompany me every step of the way, this meeting is canceled. I can find other demesnes to do business with."

"My deepest apologies, my lord Shelleen," the guard murmured. "Wait here please, while I confirm your request." He slipped back inside, via a much smaller, side entrance tucked into the side of the arched opening. The wall was thicker than it appeared from the street, probably to better support its three-meter height. Airik had to wonder what else the wall contained. It wasn't insulation, not inside a dome. It seemed equally unlikely that the walls were meant to repel invaders since Panschin was riddled with underground tunnels. Sappers could dig upwards from anywhere.

Interesting, Airik thought. Upton's illness may prove beneficial. Why won't they let in residents of Panschin? He tapped his new secretary on the shoulder and whispered, "Watch everything and report back to me afterwards."

"Yes, sir," Inigo whispered.

"Do you know anything about this, Gaston?" Airik asked, low voiced.

"No sir," Gaston replied. "It seems strange. We've never stopped anyone from Purnell from coming inside our buildings. They're guests! They have guest rights."

"Yes, very strange."

The guard returned within minutes, apologizing profusely for the delay.

"If you would follow me, sir, the daimyos are waiting for you in the main conference room." The guard threw open both sides of the heavy, ornately carved doors, giving a glimpse to the street of what was normally concealed.

Airik paid careful attention as he followed the guard; Gaston, Inigo, and some other Shelleen staff following him, Carmine bringing up the rear. The creamy yellow wall enclosed what looked like an entire block of Dome Six. Inside the courtyard were closely spaced five-story towers, mostly made of glass windows and balconies, with creamy yellow stone acting as the support work. The courtyard's paths were made of the same stone, separating wide beds of grass and flowers framing the towers. The enclosure was clean, green, spacious compared to the rest of Dome Six, and delicately scented by flowers.

In every way, it was greener, more tasteful, and quieter than the Twelve Happiness Luxury Hotel. He could have stayed here, instead of the hotel. But if he'd stayed here, he wouldn't have met Veronica. He wished she was here now. She'd be fascinated by the expansive — for Panschin — lawns edged by flower beds. The grass, real grass, was dotted with tiny blue flowers.

Airik felt a sudden pang of homesickness seeing grass again, along with dwarf flowering trees scattered artistically across the small lawns. There were birds in the trees, steppes sparrows by their song. A squirrel on the grass eyed him curiously. Inigo, he noted with interest, was struggling to balance discretion with staring openly in amazement. This, then, was unusual.

The residents of the towers were also in the courtyard, going about their business, although they all stopped to watch the procession. So, strangers inside were also unusual. One of them, a young woman, beamed and ran up the path to meet him.

"My lord Shelleen," she gushed. "I'm so happy to see you again. How is dear Upton?"

It took Airik a moment to recognize her, since she no longer had fluffy purple eyelashes and was wearing a prim business suit instead of a painted-on cocktail dress with a plunging neckline.

"Miss Atto," he said and bowed gracefully. She was too well-placed and timed on the path. She had been waiting for his arrival.

"And us too! Don't forget us!" Airik found himself surrounded by the other three young women of the demesne he had met at the luncheon. In addition, they had brought along their sisters and cousins, their heavy perfumes overpowering the delicacy of flowers, and chattering eagerly about nothing in particular.

Airik stopped dead on the pathway and motioned for them to be quiet. "I understood there was to be a discussion of how Maerski, Atto, Fuziwara, and Davis could provide assistance in better developing Shelleen's resources?"

"Yes, of course, my lord Airik," Miss Atto burbled. "Right this way." She turned and pranced down the pathway to the nearest tower. Airik caught flashes of distaste on the faces of the competing demesne hopefuls aimed at Kendra Atto, flashes that turned instantly sweet when the maiden in question noticed him noticing.

He didn't move, instead whispering to Inigo, "Tell me what you know of Kendra Atto."

His new secretary looked uncomfortable. "I can't breach a confidence, sir."

Airik eyed him. "Your personal impression of Miss Atto will do. Swiftly."

"Yes, sir," Inigo replied. "Intelligent, focused, driven, supremely well connected, scrawny for my tastes but otherwise attractive, and hugely ambitious."

"I see," Airik said. It was about what he expected; both of Miss Atto and of what Inigo Schopenhour would be willing to admit, other than the carefully buried scrawny remark. Veronica flashed before him, and he found himself agreeing with the secretary. He forced her image away.

"My lord Airik! Please, we've got so much to talk about," Kendra Atto called back, her voice and expression sharper, when she realized that the daimyo of Shelleen wasn't following her like a puppy on a leash.

"She's also got a mean streak and a temper like a cave troll," Inigo added in a barely audible, rushed whisper. "Don't get anywhere near her."

Airik had a sudden flash of Kendra's treatment of the waitress at the luncheon over her drink order being incorrect. If she behaved that way in front of witnesses, how would she behave behind closed doors? Veronica carrying her tray of mismatched wineglasses rose before him, smiling and pleasant. Veronica who laughed because she liked him as a man and not as the daimyo of Shelleen.

"My thanks," Airik whispered back. "Notice everything, write everything down. We'll debrief afterwards."

"Yes, my lord," Inigo said as they went into the tower to the conference room.

The conference room filled, based on the evidence provided by the extensive glass windows, most of the first floor of the tower. It allowed a superb view of the green courtyard, a private oasis concealed from the rest of Dome Six.

The young women of the four demesnes fluttered around Airik, competing to ask questions about "poor, dear Upton" and exclaiming over the bruise marring his face and wanting to know if he had gotten it because of Upton's accident. The daimyos of Maerski, Atto, Fuziwara, and Davis watched, eagle-eyed, to see if any of their candidates caught his attention.

After a few minutes spent waiting for those aristocratic gentlemen to take the lead, Airik announced, "I'm here on business. Nothing else."

"I suppose we should start then," Maerski said, taking charge. "Airik, please have a seat." He snapped his fingers for refreshments, provided by hovering, liveried servants carrying silver trays. Airik was forcibly reminded of watching Veronica respond to finger-snapping guests at the gallery showing at the White Elephant.

He shoved the memory away and sat as indicated next to Maerski. A smiling Kendra swiftly slid into the seat next to him, the one where his secretary normally would sit. One of the other young women, Maerski's main candidate, shot daggers at her rival, as did everyone from Fuziwara and Davis.

"No," Airik said. "I need my secretary close by to take notes."

"He is not one of us," Maerski said slowly. "A member of Qiao & Schopenhour, you said?"

"I did," Airik replied.

"He'll have to leave," Maerski said. "Here's our joint proposal." He bared his teeth and slid a contract across the table to Airik. He held out a pen, to make it easier for Airik to sign.

Airik ignored the order, picked up the proposal, and scanned the executive summary. He quickly leafed through the rest of the proposal, noticing all the while the complacent smiles of the four daimyos. They had expected him to knuckle under to their demand. Inigo, looking resentful, was being directed by a member of security toward a door.

Airik stood.

"No. Shelleen will not work with any of you. I am not a sheep waiting to be shorn as this proposal indicates you believe me to be. I do not work without a secretary, taking notes of every word said."

He looked around the room, meeting the eyes of each of the daimyos, then dismissed them with a flick of his head.

"Gaston, Inigo, we are done here. Inigo, lead the way to Steelio."

"But Airik," Maerski protested. "We have the resources Shelleen needs." The other three daimyos nodded in agreement.

Airik smiled, lowering the temperature of the room several degrees.

"I can easily find similar resources. There are other mining demesnes in the Northern Mining Tier. There are even, if further away, daimyos from the Southern Mining Tier eager to partner with Shelleen. There are many extraction businesses here in Panschin, as well as in Northernmost and Giloon. When you have rewritten your proposal, you may present it to me at the Twelve Happiness for my consideration. Good day, gentlemen. Ladies."

He strode to the door, Carmine already waiting to open it for him.

Airik fumed silently during the short walk back to the wall separating the Four Hundred tower complex from the rest of Dome Six.

Once he was back on the street and out of earshot of the Four Hundred tower complex, he said to Gaston, "This is what they think of us, that we're yokels. I will not stand for it. Shelleen is not third-rate. We are not ignorant. We are not geese waiting to be plucked."

"You are correct, Airik," Gaston growled. He held up the proposal with a wink. "I snatched your copy from the table and read the executive summary as we were walking out. Appalling. You would think they were trying to cheat ignorant sidewalk vendors."

Airik smiled in surprise. Gaston had shown initiative, and on something he hadn't thought of doing himself.

"Very good thinking, Gaston. Inigo, make copies of the proposal as soon as possible. That way, Gaston and I can both read it separately and compare our reactions."

"Yes, sir, my lord," Inigo murmured. He would get to read every word himself, while typing up copies. If Airik allowed him, he could pass on the information to Qiao & Schopenhour. Marmaduke would be pleased with this insight into the minds of the four mining demesnes surrounding Panschin. They were a constant thorn in the side of every business in the free-city.

Another block passed as Airik figured out the other thing that bothered him about the abortive meeting.

"Inigo, Gaston, you saw Kendra Atto shove her way to sit next to me but she wasn't Maerski's candidate. I would have expected a daughter of his own house. Do you know why she was allowed? The other women don't like her from my observations."

Gaston shrugged.

Inigo said, "Kendra Atto is supremely well-connected. She's the granddaughter of both Atto and Maerski."

"Ah," Airik said. "But even so."

"Maerski is an only. His direct line has been declining in vitality, generation over generation. His only son didn't survive infancy. His only daughter married Atto's son, also an only. Their only child is Kendra. She is his only direct grandchild just as she is Atto's only direct grandchild. There are many other young women in both families but Kendra is the favored one on both sides," Inigo said.

"Even so," Gaston protested. "They should not ignore other members of the family."

"I agree," Airik said. "This is foolish behavior on both daimyos' parts. It does not show them as capable of seeing to the best interests of their demesne. I predict neither one will last much longer as daimyo."

Inigo glanced at Airik in surprise. "Very astute of you, my lord. That's the gossip in Panschin. It's also believed that if Kendra had been male, she'd already be in the running as the next daimyo of Atto despite her age, temper, and lack of seasoning."

"Her ambition," Airik said.

"Gods below, yes," Inigo replied. "She'll crush everyone like a tunnel cave-in. No survivors."

Airik arrived early for his meeting with Steelio. It went well, reinforcing his decision that he did not have to work with the Northern Mining Tier demesnes if he did not choose to. There were other businesses that would be thrilled to work with Shelleen and not expect to gain control over his demesne in exchange.

Interestingly, Steelio's niece appeared to know Inigo Schopenhour quite well, based on the shy smiles and quick touches they exchanged when the pair thought no one was looking. He'd have to remind his new secretary that confidentiality applied to everyone he dealt with, not just Qiao & Schopenhour.

Steelio's niece laughed at something his new secretary said as they left her uncle's offices. Veronica rose again, unbidden. Airik had to force himself to push her away, yet again. He could not stop thinking about her. He worried over how she was coping with the aftermath of trauma. He didn't know when she would laugh again so easily, so freely. He would have to find something amusing to say in order to hear her liquid, heart-melting trill again.

"Sir? My lord Shelleen?" Inigo asked.

"Yes, what is it," Airik said sharply.

"We're ahead of schedule. Do you wish to return to the hotel and review the proposal from Maerski, Atto, Davis, and Fuziwara more closely while preparing for the evening's dinner?" Inigo asked.

He had forgotten completely. He wouldn't be able to go back to the White Elephant and spend the evening quietly reviewing papers in the dining room, with Veronica bringing him tea and moss crackers if he wanted them. He wouldn't see her until late. Instead he'd have to socialize with the upper classes of Panschin and the Four Hundred. He'd be swarmed by hopeful young women, all of them angling to become the daimyah of Shelleen. He felt increasing pressure from the family for him to select a bride and produce children. He had to set the example. Shelleen was an agricultural demesne. The fertility of the daimyo shouldn't matter, compared to the land, yet it did. To many in Shelleen, the two were connected.

The image of Kendra Atto rose before him, credit signs dancing in her eyes, draped in costly jewelry that meant nothing to her, other than a sign of her power over him. The young women would all be like her, women who had ignored him until he became Shelleen's daimyo. After that, he had been noticed, evaluated, and dismissed as still not quite worthwhile, as third-tier.

Then he announced the Red Mercury lode. On that day, he stopped being invisible. Every day since, he become a magnet. He had not changed. Those young women and their avaricious families did not see him. They never saw him. They saw a means to reach wealth and power.

If the Red Mercury lode were to disappear overnight, those gold-diggers would disappear as well, proving he had never been the lure.

Veronica saw him. He had made her laugh. Amazingly, she thought he had a sense of humor. She had no reason to smile at him, yet she did.

Those young women would have little interest in what the Shelleen family needed. He doubted if they would care even the slightest about his peasants.

Veronica would care. Her every action demonstrated how she cared for her family. She knew her neighbors well, people of lower castes in Panschin based on the crowd Mrs. Grisson had brought with her and the police from the substation. She had not sneered at them or thought them clods as Kendra Atto would.

"Sir?" Inigo asked again, looking concerned.

"Yes," Airik made himself say. "An excellent idea."

His new secretary had more freedom than he did in matters of the heart.

Veronica would accept his family but they would not accept her. She brought nothing to them that they valued; no connections, no wealth, no spectacular beauty, no aristocratic breeding. His family would welcome Kendra Atto, never knowing until it was too late they had welcomed a woman who would never consider them as her equals. The daimyos of the demesnes surrounding Panschin still considered Shelleen to be third-rate, and she would share their attitude.

As they walked back towards the Twelve Happiness Luxury Hotel, the dome overhead began to dim, as the sun on the other side sank into the west. It was a signal many of the other pedestrians around them had been waiting for. The nightly serenade of party horns began to shred the atmosphere. Airik wanted to cringe and flee to the calm of Dome Two.

He gritted his teeth and walked faster to reach the relative safety of the Twelve Happiness. There was no other choice. The demands of Shelleen came first.

Veronica paced nervously from floor to floor, and room to room. It was very late, yet Mr. Jones had not returned to the White Elephant. As she had when waiting for Shelby the previous evening, she made a circuit around the rooftop terrace to scan the streets, then walked to the atrium to look out the front door into the twilight. She even made a cautious foray into the garden, circling within the low stone wall that anyone could easily climb over, the wall that Mr. Jones had effortlessly thrown Dean over.

She did not make her trip alone. As promised, Mrs. Grisson had sent over several of her boarders and her oldest son. They walked around the White Elephant as well. Veronica was unsure if their nervous checking and rechecking of the windows was reassuring or designed to make her even jumpier. Tallon's mysterious boss was still out there. Despite the presence of the beat patrolman, nonchalantly working his way down the street, he could be easily hiding in one of the ruined mansions across the way.

What if Mr. Jones' injuries were more serious? Would he demand his money back? She'd already spent a good chunk of it, paying the lease for the next two months. Worse, what if he sued her? She knew it was foolish. She was borrowing trouble, she knew it, yet she couldn't stop fretting. He was here in Panschin on business and businessmen routinely worked out deals over dinner. Dear old dad had done it all the time. It was the logical explanation for his tardiness.

Malcolm Cobb had returned from his day and stopped to see how everyone was doing. Shelby had welcomed him effusively and asked him if he wouldn't mind spending the night. He had been delighted at the prospect of sleeping on the floor of an empty bedroom at the end of their wing. Veronica had exchanged glances with auntie Neza and Mrs. Grisson; hers was disapproving and theirs not nearly so much so. Veronica wondered if she'd have to remind Malcolm and Shelby that the White Elephant wasn't a country villa in a melodrama. They couldn't sneak around from room to room, indulging themselves in clandestine meetings. The residents were on edge and liable to raise a club first and ask questions later.

The house was full to bursting for the first time in decades. Trevor and Evan, Lulu and Florence's boyfriends were cheerfully sharing another empty bedroom at the end of the family wing. Mrs. Grisson's son and helpful boarders were downstairs, dividing themselves up between the dining room and the ballroom.

The only people missing were Mr. Jones and his party. They were late, very late.

Malcolm had reminded her that business dinners could run very late during the Biennial Mining Conference. He was also surprisingly sanguine about the whereabouts of the thug's mystery boss.

"I don't think he'll be much of a problem," Malcolm had said, but he refused to go into details.

Veronica paced the yard again, circling the house and peering at the dim light filling the dome. What if Mr. Jones didn't come back? She hadn't thanked him properly. She should have kissed him when she had the chance.

A few circuits later, Veronica made her way back up both flights of stairs to the rooftop terrace to better observe the streets. She saw him at last, accompanied by Carmine, unmistakable because of his size, and Elliot, but she couldn't decide if she was seeing Upton. The dim light made it harder to make out his face. Then she knew. The fourth man in Mr. Jones' party was a stranger.

She swallowed a scream. It was the thug's boss. He had come back to seek his revenge. She clung to the wrought-iron railing surrounding the rooftop terrace, shaking and nauseous. Mr. Jones and his entourage walked closer, in the dim light of the dome, and sanity forced panic back into its box.

Whoever the stranger was, he couldn't be the thug's boss. Carmine, Mr. Jones' bodyguard wouldn't look so relaxed and neither would Mr. Jones. Veronica sagged against the terrace knee-wall in relief. It was someone else. Airik was safe. This time she would kiss him. She wouldn't hold herself back.

Veronica ran down both flights of stairs and out of the White Elephant, down the gravel path, and towards the shrieking gate as he approached from the street.

"Mr. Jones," Veronica cried out. "You're back safe. I was getting concerned."

"I'm fine," Airik called back. Veronica had thought of him. The thought warmed him like fire.

They both walked swiftly, but not quite a run, towards the gate separating them, and at that in-between point, no longer on the public street and not yet in the private garden surrounding the White Elephant, Veronica Bradwell reached up and hugged Airik Jones and kissed him and he kissed her back. Lost in each other's arms, they ignored the fascinated audience.

S he fell into his kiss. This was what she wanted, had been wanting since she met Airik Jones. The feel of his strong arms wrapped around her, the taste of his lips, the sensation of everything being right in the world.

He shifted his weight against her, and she remembered where she was, standing at the gate of the White Elephant. She was kissing a guest — a stranger from Barsoom — as though he was her lover returned home from weeks away.

She tore her mouth away from his and pulled back, her mind a jumble of shame and bafflement at her own behavior.

"I'm so, so sorry," Veronica babbled. "Please forgive me for being so forward. It's just that after this morning …" Her voice trailed off. "I'm so sorry." She blinked back tears.

She retreated into the garden of the White Elephant, away from the street, away from him. Mr. Jones, normally so reserved, looked distraught. He took a step forward, favoring his hurt leg.

"I hurt you. Your stitches. I'm so sorry. Please, come inside. It won't happen again," she said, trying to make amends. "I won't impose."

"You didn't," he replied quickly. "You never hurt me."

"Veronica? Veronica Bradwell?"

She turned at a man's voice, one she hadn't heard since dear old dad had brought the domes crashing down. A man who had watched her behave shamelessly with a stranger.

"Inigo?"

"Yes, it's me," Inigo Schopenhour said. He was staring at her as though they had never met although they had once been good friends.

"Lordy, it's been a long time," Veronica said, startled and confused. "Wait. How do you know Mr. Jones? And where is Upton?"

"Mr. Jones?" Inigo asked, as muddled as she was. He looked around as though trying to place himself within the alien confines of Dome Two.

"She means me," Airik said and glanced meaningfully at Inigo.

"Mr. Jones, right, my new employer," he added hastily. "I'm his replacement secretary. Upton took ill."

"How dreadful. Please, come inside," Veronica said. "Mr. Jones, I'm so sorry for upsetting you."

"You could never do that," Airik replied. She had kissed him, and it was everything he had wanted. Her warmth, her scent, the feel of her lush body pressed against his. He couldn't think straight. He could only watch as his new secretary clasped both of Veronica's hands and fight down the flare of white-hot jealousy that surged through him. He should have been holding her hands. It was a relief when his new secretary let go of her hands, still looking bewildered.

"We should get inside, sir, I mean Airik," Carmine said. "Off the street."

"Yes, absolutely," Veronica said, seizing the lifeline Carmine had thrown her. "I'll make tea for you." She eyed Inigo and smiled hesitantly. He had been a good friend, before. He had clasped her hands in greeting, as he had done so often before. Perhaps he wouldn't slander her in front of Mr. Jones. He never had in the past. But he had vanished from her life, after dear old dad's crimes had been laid bare for all to see. Many other old friends had, but he had never been cruel. He hadn't spread vicious gossip. He hadn't told everyone she should have known. He hadn't come to ogle her sobbing in a courtroom while she defended herself and her sister. He hadn't made her situation worse.

He hadn't done anything at all, one way or the other.

She could do better than that, and, perhaps, remind Inigo why they had once been friends.

"You should be pleased, Mr. Jones," Veronica said warmly. "I don't know if Inigo told you, but he's part of Qiao & Schopenhour. They're a very well-regarded family company here in Panschin. He's very capable."

"Yes, he has been," Airik said, feeling numb. She knew his replacement secretary, his secretary who knew who he really was. He felt like he was on a knife's-edge, unsure of how to handle this new development.

For his part, Inigo Schopenhour couldn't think either. Veronica Bradwell! He hadn't seen her since Simon Bradwell's embezzlement scheme had collapsed so publicly, destroying his family along with the finances of all his clients. She had disappeared, only appearing in public when she had a court date, and he hadn't known where she'd gone. To his shame, he knew he hadn't looked hard. It hadn't occurred to him that she would still be living in the same house he had visited in the past; the one she had shared with Dean Kangjuon, her former husband.

He had done nothing to help her, even though she had helped him enormously. Veronica had been instrumental in helping him meet Olwyn Steelio without either family knowing they were courting. It had been far harder to arrange discreet meetings without Veronica to run interference. The shame at how he had abandoned her burned harder. He hadn't treated her any better than that worthless cad, Dean. Inigo wondered what had happened to Dean Kangjuon. He had run into Dean a few times since his divorce from Veronica and each time Dean looked worse. Dean looked like he was falling apart, as though he hadn't been able to manage without Veronica.

Veronica led them into the White Elephant. Airik watched her retreating hips for a moment, then tapped Inigo Schopenhour's shoulder.

"Yes, sir?"

His new secretary's face was a complex mix of emotions, none of which Airik could decipher without close study. He ignored them.

"Miss Bradwell does not know who I am. Do not tell her. Do not tell anyone. I sleep here because it's the only place in Panschin I've found that lets me sleep and think in peace," Airik said softly.

"Yes, sir."

"I will not have my refuge damaged. If you reveal me, I will destroy you and Qiao & Schopenhour."

Nausea roiled through Inigo. "Yes, sir." He had heard the stories about run-ins with the demesnes surrounding Panschin. Even with Shelleen as far away as it was, Airik, as daimyo, enjoyed that kind of power. The Four Hundred stuck together. Maerski, Atto, Davis, and Fuziwara, despite Airik's snub earlier, would back him to the hilt if it meant crushing an annoying free-city company and picking over the bones.

Airik turned away and marched up the gravel pathway to the welcoming door of the White Elephant, his face set in stone. Veronica waited for him, and he would have to lie to her again, only this time, he'd have to force someone she knew to lie to her as well.

Veronica silently blessed Lulu. She had kept the water hot and ready for tea. She poured a cup of mint tea for Mr. Jones in the dining room, the soothing scent of mint curling around them.

It didn't sooth her as it usually did. Mr. Jones seemed so distant and uncomfortable. She shouldn't have kissed him. She had upset him. She had offended him with her brazen forwardness. She recalled how he had asked her when he had first arrived about "intimate introductions" and how adamant she had been about not providing such services and wanted to cringe in humiliation.

Inigo Schopenhour had been equally stiff, which shouldn't have been a surprise. He knew she was a pariah in Panschin. She had to hope he didn't say anything to Mr. Jones. He would lose business, and it would be her fault for not warning him.

It was a relief when Malcolm Cobb entered the dining room, or she thought it would be.

"Airik," he said as he sat down. "We have to talk right away."

"Cobb?" Inigo gasped. This had been a day of surprises for him and here was one more.

"Inigo Schopenhour?" Malcolm asked. "What are you doing here?"

"I'm, um, Mr. Jones' replacement secretary." Inigo's eyes darted over towards Airik. "I could ask the same of you."

"I'm the assistant manager of the local branch of Second National. Miss Bradwell and her aunt lease from us."

"You two know each other?" Airik asked. This kept getting more complicated.

"Yes," Malcolm said. "We shared some classes at Panschin School of Business."

"Cobb's a scholarship boy from the Steelio warren," Inigo added, wanting to ensure the daimyo of Shelleen knew who was sharing his airspace. He'd always believed Malcolm Cobb to be very bright, considering his severely disadvantaged background. Was it possible he didn't know who he was speaking to so abruptly?

"An excellent program," Airik said coolly. "I never believed in wasting talent just because the person in question has less than aristocratic breeding. I was impressed that Steelio felt the same."

"You know about it?" Inigo asked, disconcerted. "We at Qiao &

Schopenhour, um, sometimes, …"

Malcolm interrupted him. "Qiao & Schopenhour sometimes participates, when it suits them. They don't regularly look for talent like Steelio does. I always thought Marmaduke was missing a good bet. It's surprising really, seeing how quick-witted he is on every other subject."

"Bertram feels differently," Inigo said sharply. "Expect the policy to change."

"It should," Malcolm snapped. "Qiao & Schopenhour loses loyal and hardworking talent every year they don't participate."

"Tea, anyone?" Veronica said, trying to prevent the impending tunnel collapse. "Sweet biscuits?" She desperately wished she had opened a few extra bottles of Professor Vitebskin's plonk at the end of the gallery showing, storing them for an occasion like this one. They had been retrieved so she couldn't do it now. Mint tea wasn't going to be strong enough.

"Thank you, Veronica," Malcolm said graciously.

"Of course, Veronica," Inigo said as well.

"You take good care of everyone, Miss Bradwell," Airik said. He wished he could say her melodious first name but she had become formal and distant again. He'd eat what appeared to be another variety of compressed moss cracker for her, inedible as they were guaranteed to be for anyone not from Panschin. He selected the smallest one from her proffered tray and bit into it, proving both statements. He was counting on the mint tea to kill the taste and thankfully, it did. Strong mint tea was reliable that way.

"You needed to speak with me, Malcolm?" Airik asked, once the mint washed his tongue free of gritty moss. He was interested to see Inigo startle at his familiarity with a scholarship boy.

"Yes, about our little adventure this afternoon. I spoke with the shaman. You must, if you ever want to enter the deepdown again, anywhere on Mars, undergo a purification ritual."

"Oh," Veronica gasped. Her hand went automatically to her throat, were her cool, cloudy gray beads should have been. "The shamans who came to the White Elephant said the same thing."

"A purification ritual?" Airik asked. He'd be able to learn more about Panschin's religious traditions, the ones that no one was willing to talk about with outsiders. Veronica's hand was at her throat, in a gesture he now recognized as anxiety. He'd have to get her beads back to her, and, perhaps, something else if she was willing to accept a personal gift from him. She was wearing the matching earbobs again, the ones he had rescued for her from the cavern floor that she had dropped as a clue for him.

"Were you involved in some sort of incident in the tunnels, my, um, I mean Mr. Jones?" Inigo said. A flash of fear streaked across his face.

"Winifred said nothing to you? Marmaduke?"

"No sir. That would be a breach of confidentiality."

"Very good," Airik replied. "Yes, as it happens, I was."

"Mr. Jones and Mr. Cobb were extremely brave," Veronica said. She smiled at Airik shyly, wishing she could hold his hand. She should have kissed him in the tunnels when it would have been welcome and understood in the excitement. "My sister and I might have died."

Inigo goggled at her. "You and Shelby? Almost died in the deepdown?" He turned his attention back to the daimyo of Shelleen.

"You must perform the ritual as soon as possible, my lord," he said.

"I'll make the arrangements for tomorrow," Malcolm said.

"I have meetings all day," Airik protested.

"Doesn't matter," Inigo said.

"Everyone from Panschin will understand," Malcolm added.

"Even the mining tier daimyos won't argue," Inigo said. "Not for this."

"You don't know what happened in the tunnel," Airik said, puzzled.

"If the shamans say you have to be purified, then you have to be purified," Inigo replied stoutly.

"We both must do this," Malcolm said.

"I see," Airik said.

Veronica reached out and grasped Airik's hand, twining her fingers through his, enjoying the feel of his warm skin against her own. He tightened his fingers around hers, not letting her free her hand and she didn't pull away.

"You have to go, Mr. Jones," she said, gazing into his eyes. "The shamans insisted. They said you wouldn't be safe underneath ever again if you did not. I promised I would speak to you." Her dark eyes were like shadowed pools of water in the summer, deep and clear and welcomingly cool. He wanted to linger there, lost in their depths.

Airik blinked, trying to return to reality. "But what about you and your sister?"

"I asked," Veronica said, falling into his hazel eyes. They were a complex mix of green shading to brown and she could gaze into them forever. "We didn't shed blood the wrong way. We've been already blessed, and the White Elephant has been as well."

Airik smiled at Veronica, his heart leaping. She had touched him again. He mattered to her, at least a little. Her hand in his set his body aflame.

"Well then, if I must," he said to Veronica. "Safety underground can't be taken for granted." He didn't add, I want to be safe for you, so I can return to you, but he thought it.

"No, no it can't," Veronica replied to him. She wanted to add, I want you to be safe always. Safe with me.

Back upstairs in his room, Airik finished the last of his notes for the day.

"Anything else, my lord?" Inigo asked. He was exhausted, his hands hurt, and he was hoping to hear a 'no'. The daimyo of Shelleen was a more demanding boss than he had expected. He also needed time to process the events of the day.

"Be here at the White Elephant first thing in the morning. We'll proceed from here to Dome Six for seminars and meetings, until Malcolm says the shamans are ready for me."

"Very good, sir," Inigo replied. Another long day lay ahead of him. Airik obviously believed in working from dawn until almost midnight.

He got up to leave, then hesitated by the door to the shadowy hallway. There was barely enough light to make the transom window glow from the reflected light inside the dome falling through the skylight and the deck prisms. Dome Six never got this dark. He'd forgotten how spooky dark and eerily quiet Dome Two could become.

"My lord Shelleen. I know it's not my place to say this," Inigo ventured.

Airik observed him coolly.

Inigo thought of all he had not done for Veronica when she needed his support and forced himself to open his mouth.

"Don't lie to Veronica, my lord. Too many people lied to her starting with her worthless father. Did you know she was married? Her husband, Dean Kangjuon, walked out on her when she needed him the most. She doesn't need more trauma in her life and neither does Shelby."

"I have no intention of harming Miss Bradwell," Airik replied. "I will see you in the morning, first thing."

"Yes, sir," Inigo said, and fled for the familiar lights and sounds of Dome Six.

Soon thereafter, Elliot approached Airik.

"If I may be so bold, sir?"

"Yes, what is it," Airik said wearily. His stitches were hurting and his body ached all over. The pain tea Lulu insisted would help had yet to kick in. His evening exercise routine was going to be a challenge, enough that he was thinking seriously about skipping it.

"You are not my lord Upton. You do not trifle with the affections of ladies, young or old. Miss Bradwell, while a charming young lady, will never be accepted by the family."

"Thank you for your input, Elliot. You may go," Airik said. He knew his valet was correct.

Right after that, Carmine said, "I've got to make a circuit around the house. See that everything's locked up tight."

"Malcolm implied that the thug's boss wouldn't be an issue," Airik said.

"Yeah, he did, but that don't mean he's right. I'll check anyways."

"Very good," Airik said.

Carmine made no move to leave.

"What is it?"

"I like Miss Bradwell. I know what everyone else will tell you, but I like her, and I think she's good for you."

"Thank you for your input, Carmine. You may go," Airik said. Unfortunately, his bodyguard was also correct. The needs of Shelleen weighed on him and sleep came as a welcome relief.

Breakfast was a noisy affair with the extra guests. Veronica set up a buffet in the dining room to better accommodate everyone. As she was refilling cups with hot tea, she heard the gate shriek its warning.

Her hands went numb and the teapot shook, spattering drops of tea on the tablecloth, little dark pools like thinned down blood. Airik rose promptly and gently took the teapot from her nerveless hands.

"I'll get the door, Miss Bradwell. You sit down."

"No, sir, Airik," Carmine said. "*I'll* get the door." He was already up and moving, followed by Malcolm Cobb who had to leave Shelby's side. Shelby looked as frightened as her sister and auntie Neza. Everyone in the dining room was alert, waiting to hear something or moving to windows to see who was coming up the gravel pathway.

Carmine and Malcolm returned a few minutes later, smiling, and accompanied by a yawning Inigo Schopenhour and surprisingly, Hurkle, the bartender from the Broken Pickaxe.

Hurkle held up the *Panschin Gazette*, opened to an inside page to better display the headline:

Dome Six Park Horror!

Victim Beaten to Death
First Murder of the Biennial Mining Conference
We're Doing Better Than Last Time!

"Hello, Hurkle," auntie Neza said in surprise. "It's nice of you to drop by and bring us a newspaper, but why?"

Hurkle winked at auntie Neza. "I heard about what happened from the desk sergeant over to the substation. By the way, nice work, Mr. Jones, Malcolm, and you too, Neza. Then I saw the early edition of the paper and thought I'd share the good news right away."

"And you are?" Airik asked.

"The bartender over to the Broken Pickaxe here in Dome Two," Carmine answered for Hurkle. "We met at the police substation."

"A stalwart member of our local community, Airik," Malcolm said. "I'll take you there and buy you a pint, if you've a mind." He got a flabbergasted look from Inigo, which he ignored.

"A friend of mine," auntie Neza said.

"Hurkle buys some of my vegetables," Veronica added. "Especially the radishes."

"You grow vegetables?" Malcolm asked curiously. "I thought that was Mrs. Grisson?"

"We both do, so we can split the market," Veronica said promptly. She winced. "I mean, it's a hobby. Not a lease-breaking violation. No money changes hands." Lordy did that sound like a lie, probably because it was one. On the other hand, after yesterday, why fret over a little violation like market gardening? They were all alive to argue over the finer points of the lease.

"You need to get up to speed on who does what here in Dome Two, my boy," Hurkle said. "We're not like the other domes."

"I'm working on it," Malcolm said. "Don't fret over your agricultural efforts, Veronica. I intend to rewrite some of the leases here in Dome Two to encourage that sort of entrepreneurship."

"Ahem. Why isn't a dead body in the park not on the front page of the newspaper?" Airik asked in exasperation. "And what does that have to do with us?"

"It's the Biennial Mining Conference, sir," Inigo answered. "There's always a body or two that turns up in a park."

"We're really doing well this conference season," Malcolm said. "Usually by now, there's been two or three murders of out-of-towners as opposed to the residents killing each other. That happens all year round."

"Besides," Inigo added. "Front page news about murders discourages out-of-towners coming to Panschin on business."

"Can't have that," Malcolm agreed. "The chamber of commerce works hard to make Panschin look safe."

Airik wanted to roll his eyes, an uncharacteristic gesture for him. Panschin kept getting weirder. It had to be the ever-present fug of terraformers. There was no other explanation.

"All true, Mr. Jones. You're seeing the shamans today, I hope?" Hurkle said.

"If I can make the time," Airik replied, thinking of the crushing load of seminars he was facing. The importance of meeting a pack of shamans to learn more about Panschin's religious system had vanished overnight, unlike his aches and bruises.

He was answered with a dozen variations of "You must do this or someone will drag you underground to get it done."

"Not to worry. I've already penciled it into your schedule, Mr. Jones," Inigo said. "I'll readjust as needed when Cobb gets me the time slot."

"Fine, fine" Airik said testily, "but again, what does a dead body in the park have to do with us?"

"Desk sergeant told me that, based on our Shelby's sketches, this particular body was identified as the boss of those two thugs who tried to murder our Veronica and our Shelby," Hurkle announced. "Confirmed by Mr. Kangjuon at the morgue."

Airik stopped cold. "But he was murdered. By whom?"

"Oh, these things happen," Malcolm said calmly. "He's from Barsoom, remember, so this boss-type must have gone exploring where he's not supposed to. Probably did something stupid in the tunnel bars under Dome Four."

"Then wouldn't his body have been dumped in a tunnel down there?" Airik asked.

He was answered with gasps of horror and shock and a wide variety of "never, far too dangerous, bodies are always left in the park."

"I see," Airik said at last. "Which is why I have to undergo a ritual purification despite not having actually killed anyone?"

The answer this time was a chorus of yeses.

"Everyone in Panschin will understand your absence, Mr. Jones," Inigo reassured him. "There won't be any questions."

"Not even from all the other businessmen from outside of Panschin?" Airik asked.

"It will be explained, sir," Inigo replied.

Airik wondered how he was going to explain it to the Shelleen contingent. If nothing else, Gaston would get to prove his abilities again, during yet another absence of the daimyo of Shelleen.

An inconsistency leaped out at him.

"Why do I have to be ritually purified when apparently the tunnel bars under Dome Four are soaked in blood and mayhem?" Airik asked testily.

"Dome Four is so toxic, what with the refineries and manufacturing and all, that what lives beneath doesn't live there," Malcolm answered. "Too poisonous."

"But humans can go there?" Airik asked, his eyebrows raised as high as they could go.

"This is Panschin, Mr. Jones," Inigo said. "It's not like we have plenty of open, safe real estate for activities of the type that go on under Dome Four."

"Besides, the shamans do go through Dome Four's tunnels on a regular basis," Malcolm added. "Just in case."

"I see," Airik said, although he did not. It had to be the terraformers. Despite his extensive travels, he'd never run into any place like

Panschin.

Skimming the *Panschin Gazette* story, Veronica felt a weight she didn't know she was carrying lift off her shoulders. The mysterious boss was dead and horribly so, based on the lurid newspaper article. The reporter hadn't spared the bloody adjectives to describe the condition of the victim. He had been beaten to death, sustained many broken bones, and the fingers of both hands were hacked off. The fingers had been dumped next to the body. They were, according to the coroner, amputated while the victim was still alive. Other things had been done too, making her stomach roil. His face had been left relatively undamaged, a thoughtful touch as it made identification easier.

It was a horrible way to die and Veronica couldn't muster one drop of sympathy. She thought of Tallon, dying in the tunnel in the dark after murdering Frankie. They were inhuman, the pack of them. The death of the mystery boss meant that Tallon's threat of "no forgiveness" had been empty.

She could feel the tightness in her chest ease. No one would come from Barsoom looking for her or Shelby or Neza. They could fade into safe, quiet anonymity.

She caught Mr. Jones protesting having to meet the shamans and reached across the table to grasp his hand.

He turned at once to gaze into her face.

"You have to do this, Mr. Jones. Please. For your safety."

Mr. Jones smiled at her, and she could feel herself smiling back.

"I will, Miss Bradwell. I will," he answered. For you, he thought.

On the way out of the dining room, Hurkle tapped Malcolm on the shoulder.

"A moment in private, my boy," he said.

"Yes, Hurkle? What is it," Malcolm asked. Shelby was packing for her classes at PanU, and she had asked if he would walk with her. She seemed distracted, nervous and jumpy, even though the thugs' boss was, according to the frequently reliable *Panschin Gazette*, dead.

Hurkle whispered, "Jeffen sent me a message. He says, 'Thanks for the tip, we got an ore-car load of info out of him, and the job's done.'"

Malcolm stared at the elderly bartender. "You know Jeffen?"

"An up and coming go-getter, our Jeffen is. Course I know him." Hurkle winked at Malcolm. "You got to get up to speed on Dome Two, Malcolm."

"Yes, I certainly do," Malcolm said slowly. He could only hope he would remain free of Blue Sun while he did so. He hadn't realized Hurkle was a member.

"Very nice work in the tunnels under the White Elephant. You didn't hesitate. I like that," Hurkle added. "Now that I know what to be on the lookout for, it won't happen again to Neza or her girls."

"Thank you, Hurkle," Malcolm said.

"Oh, and Malcolm? Let Mr. Wong know that I'll be paying attention from here on out to what goes on at the White Elephant, seeing as how it's got that hidden connection to the train station."

Malcolm's eyes went wider. He didn't know what to say, other than nod in agreement.

Shelby clutched Malcolm's hand all the way to PanU. She hadn't told him much about her plans for the day, other than she was going to change her situation at PanU. She nervously rehearsed what she wanted to say to Professor Vitebskin while they walked. She had to tear herself away from Malcolm at the stone archway, wanting to stay and kiss him rather than face the professor and any members of the PanU Artists' Collective who might be standing around. Malcolm was very easy to kiss, and he obviously enjoyed kissing her.

Malcolm had carried her bulging portfolio, but it was her burden now.

She wished she could ask him to accompany her, but she wasn't a child. She wasn't naïve. She was an adult and needed to behave like one. Shelby had to remind herself that her sister had been married at this age. She could do this. She had talent. She had worth, even if no one at PanU was capable of recognizing it.

If she didn't believe in herself, then it was a sure bet no one else would.

If she could live through what Tallon and Frankie had done, Professor Vitebskin should be easy to manage. He was an egotistical lecher but he wasn't a rapist and a murderer.

She fretted through her morning, oblivious to the other students milling around. They didn't know what had happened. It was a reprieve of sorts since then she would have had to discuss her home being invaded and what she, as Simon Bradwell's daughter, must have done to deserve it.

Shelby made herself walk through the doors of the studio. She was onstage and would provide a show for the rest of the PanU Artists' Collective. They'd gossip still more, but it was the right thing to do for her. She wouldn't lie. She'd always heard that the truth would set her free, but she didn't feel free. She felt nauseated.

"Professor? I need to speak with you," Shelby announced to the studio at large. Professor Vitebskin was in the middle of gleefully dissecting Bhupathi Middleton's latest effort.

"Later," he replied absently and returned to his evisceration of the painting in front of him.

Bhupathi shot Shelby a pleading look. She eyed him for a moment, quivering in his anxiety over what Professor Vitebskin was loudly saying about his total lack of effort and talent. Bhupathi had upset her with silly words the previous day. They were hurtful and he was rude, but he would never be the kind of threat that Tallon or Frankie were. They'd eat him up for a snack and go looking for their next victim. She said a little prayer of thanks again to the gods above and below that Tallon and Frankie were dead, along with their boss.

"Now," Shelby said firmly and loudly. "It's important."

Professor Vitebskin turned and scowled at Shelby.

"Don't be naïve. Important for you does not mean important for me, Shelby."

She didn't flinch, even though the usual audience was already gathering to see what was happening.

"This is important for both of us, Professor," Shelby retorted.

"Fine, fine, let's get this over with then. Bhupathi, do not move from that spot."

"Yes, sir," Bhupathi muttered. He gave Shelby a look of thanks and tried hard to blend into the furniture while watching what she did so he could tell all his friends later.

Shelby stood there, all eyes on her, and wondered where her carefully planned speech had gone.

"Well?" Professor Vitebskin demanded, his hands on his hips. "I'm on a time schedule here." He was, too. It was nearing the end of the term, he had dozens of works to evaluate and grade, and Reyansh Philpott's lawsuit was looming over him like a tunnel waiting to collapse and crush everything living beneath it into a bloody smear. Beautiful, zero talent, and dim-witted; that was Shelby Bradwell in a nutshell.

"You are correct, Professor Vitebskin," Shelby made herself say. "I don't belong here."

He smirked at her. Not completely dim-witted, then.

"But not because I don't have talent. I do have talent, but it's not the right kind for your studio. My auntie Neza has an appointment with the bursar. She's going to see if they can transfer my tuition over to PCC and their school of commercial art."

"What?" Professor Vitebskin asked. "You're leaving?"

"Yes, Professor. I'm trying to and I'm not going to lie to you like Clyde Monez did." Shelby smiled tightly. Here came the difficult part. "I hope you will persuade the bursar to transfer over my tuition money. Your studio isn't the right place for me but I'm still glad I was here."

Shelby stopped and lifted her heavy portfolio onto the table. "I wanted to show you what I've been working on. I learned so much from you about handling paint in gossamer layers. I couldn't have learned these techniques from anyone else. Only you, Professor Vitebskin."

She opened her portfolio and pulled out the painting of marigolds she had been working on first. Shelby had shown off her secret efforts to the family, Malcolm, and guests the previous evening, trying to distract her sister from fretting over Airik Jones' late arrival. It had worked too, for a while. She could still hear their astonished praise and appreciation.

The oversized marigolds blazed in the studio, layer upon layer of delicate hazes of paint in every shade of fire from the deepest red of embers to the white-hot heat produced by a blast furnace. The flowers were framed by lacy green leaves, carefully shaded from green so dark it was almost black to the gold of new leaves in early spring.

She next laid out the pansies, smiling floral faces in violet and purple and sunny yellow laid upon milky white. These blooms were larger, hand-size to show their intricate detail. Her greens were more varied here, dappled with freckles of dancing sunlight.

She brought out her cloud painting last, the one she had promised to Jeffen. The clouds floated on the canvas, diaphanous layers of white upon white, pure and clean, round and fat like the real clouds she remembered from a long-ago trip to the summer park of Panschin. Her sky was ethereal, the azure deepening imperceptibly across the canvas just as the sky changed its color from horizon to zenith, and tinged with salmon pink from Martian dust.

Professor Vitebskin stared at the blazing, glorious canvases that lit up the studio while Shelby waited anxiously for a verdict.

"Shelby?" Kip pushed his way forward through the gaping, whispering mob of students and smiled hesitantly at her, then let his eyes fall onto her paintings.

"Those are really good," Kip said, sounding as if he couldn't quite believe what he was saying.

"I wouldn't say *that*, but they are different from your usual efforts," Professor Vitebskin said, blinking at the storm of colors never permitted in his studio.

"You really are a genius with paint, Professor," Shelby said. "I don't use your techniques like you do, but I could never have painted my flowers and clouds if I hadn't studied with you, here at PanU."

"You talked about clouds with Jeffen when we went into the warren," Kip said. "I didn't know you painted them."

"Yes," Shelby said, beaming with pride. "I remembered every minute of watching them when I went to the outdoors summer park. I could never figure out how to paint clouds that looked right until I learned how to manipulate paint layers from Professor Vitebskin."

Professor Vitebskin picked up the marigolds painting and carried it to the window, turning it this way and that as he examined Shelby's technique. He said, after some moments, "You did learn something then, Shelby."

"Yes, professor. I did. I want to take what I learned to PCC. I may end up drawing ladies' shoes for department store adverts but they'll be the best ladies' shoes in Panschin," Shelby replied. "I'll finish out this term, of course, but I won't return next term. I hope you will talk to the bursar about transferring my tuition since I won't be here."

Professor Vitebskin laid the marigolds down and picked up the clouds, letting himself fall emotionally into the painting. "These don't get you a better grade, by the way," he said absently, studying the sheer layers of paint building into the illusion of round, lush curves of air made solid.

"No, I didn't think they would," Shelby said.

"No extra-credit, either," Professor Vitebskin added.

"I don't expect it," Shelby said.

Professor Vitebskin continued to study Shelby's clouds as a cover for his thoughts. He was actually considering the White Elephant's value as a gallery space. Its ballroom and atrium were the finest venue he had come across for displaying works of art of all sizes. If he lost access to that beautiful, virtually free mansion, so convenient and exciting for Dome Six visitors, he'd have to resort to PanU's lackluster facilities. Losing Shelby as a student meant losing access to that glorious building.

However, if he played his cards correctly, he'd still have access to the White Elephant. He could share display space with the drivel that PCC students and instructors would produce. Their pitiful attempts would make his own protégés' paintings shine all the brighter. He could lead the entire art establishment in Panschin, including — he suppressed a shudder — commercial and instructional "art". Those hacks would be thrilled to associate with the PanU Artists' Collective. He'd suggest a group showing to the commercial art department at PCC the day after Shelby transferred, to be held, naturally, at the White Elephant. It was a given none of those mediocre dabblers would think of it themselves, and he couldn't count on dim-witted Shelby to do it for him.

"I will talk to the bursar as soon as possible, Shelby. I'm sure I can get them to consider your aunt's request favorably," Professor Vitebskin said with an encouraging smile.

Her relieved smile was as bright as her marigolds painting.

"Thank you so much, Professor Vitebskin," Shelby gushed. "It means the world to me."

"Well," Professor Vitebskin replied. "We always want what's best for our students at PanU and you, Shelby, are no exception."

"Shelby?" Kip said. "Are you busy?"

Shelby turned and said, "Well, yes, of course. I've got to finish up all my work here at PanU, since I won't be back after the term ends."

"I meant tonight," Kip said. "Maybe we could go out? Get tea and a bun?"

Everyone in the studio turned to stare at Kip in open disbelief, including Professor Vitebskin.

It took a moment for Shelby to understand Kip, since his words were so unexpected.

"Oh, that is so sweet of you, Kip," she said warmly. "But I can't. Malcolm's taking me to dinner at the Dappled Yak and then the theater afterwards. I've never even been inside the Dappled Yak." She beamed at him, along with the rest of the crowded studio. "I'm sure we can still be friends, though."

Kip's face fell. "Friends. Sure." He turned away and Shelby transferred her attention to carefully repacking her paintings. He did not watch her leave the studio, head held high and radiantly happy, accepting whispered congratulations on her flower and cloud paintings and her upcoming date.

As soon as Shelby left, Professor Vitebskin said "Bhupathi, I'll get back to you and this piece of insipid dross in a minute so don't run off and hide like you're trying to do. Kip? Over here."

"Yes, professor?" Kip said wearily.

Professor Vitebskin gave Kip a careful looking over, making him wait for long minutes until he was seething with resentment.

"I could never figure out," the professor said, "why a talentless poseur like you was wasting my time and your parents' money in my studio. It was Shelby, wasn't it. You wanted to be close to her but you didn't have the spine to say or do something about it."

"You don't know what you're talking about, Professor Vitebskin," Kip answered, his voice rough.

"I most certainly do. You are feckless, Kip. You lost Shelby to that jumped-up tunnel rat because you were so worried about what people would say about you caring about Simon Bradwell's daughter. Or did her father defraud the McGrant family? Was that it?"

"You're wrong," Kip retorted but he could not meet the professor's eyes or the eyes of the avid crowd around them.

"I am not. You don't deserve her. You fail the term. Get out of my studio and find some other PanU department and waste their time and your parents' money," Professor Vitebskin said cheerfully. "And Kip? I want to thank you for finally, *finally* contributing something worthwhile to my day. Bhupathi, you're next."

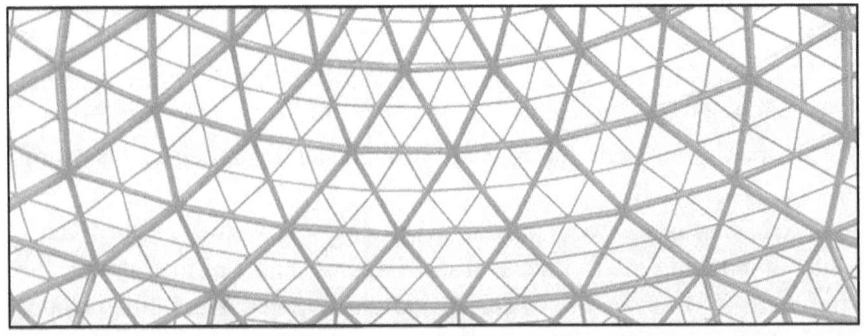

urkle's word was better than the *Panschin Gazette's*. If he said the thug's boss was dead, then it was most likely true. Mrs. Grisson's son and helpful boarders left to get back to their own lives, armed with fresh, exciting gossip that would buy their drinks for weeks to come. Lulu and Florence left as well, accompanied by Trevor and Evan, heading towards their day at PCC.

Veronica saw Shelby off to PanU, clutching Malcolm Cobb's hand while he carried her portfolio.

Veronica felt very proud watching Shelby march off to confront Professor Vitebskin. Her little sister was growing up. Her paintings — the paintings she had concealed for so long — had been beautiful with their vivid, glowing colors and meticulous details. Neza had insisted on having Malcolm hold them up, one at a time in the atrium, to bathe in the sunshine pouring down. They outshone all of Professor Vitebskin's choices, radiant with joyous life.

With each set of departures for the day, the White Elephant became quieter and emptier.

Then came Airik Jones' turn, with Inigo, Elliot, and Carmine.

Veronica met him at the doorway to the garden, wanting to reassure him and be reassured.

"Mr. Jones, take care, please. You're still injured." Why was she babbling about the obvious?

"So I am, Miss Bradwell," Airik replied. Gads but he sounded like a fool.

She took a deep breath. "Please, do make time to see the shamans. I know it may seem silly to an outsider. I hardly understand it myself. But you must do the purification ritual to stay safe."

He watched her bosom rise and fall, mesmerized.

"Yes, I will. It should be interesting." Airik wanted to cringe. He tore his eyes away. He couldn't think of anything clever or reassuring to say to Veronica. He could hardly talk about the weather as a fallback position, since there wasn't any inside the dome.

She laughed suddenly, a gurgling that reminded him again of rippling brooks catching and reflecting sunlight at their observer. "Yes, it will be that. I'm sure they don't have anything like it in Barsoom."

"No, they don't," Airik said. He was still lying to her. Would he ever stop?

"Sir? Mr. Jones?" Inigo interrupted reluctantly. "We'll be late for your first seminar of the day if we don't get moving." He could not figure out what was going on with the daimyo of Shelleen and Veronica Bradwell. One would almost think they fancied each other but were too shy and awkward to say so. He had to laugh at such a ridiculous notion. Veronica had once been a good friend, capable and talented, but she remained Simon Bradwell's daughter. The daimyo of Shelleen could and would look far higher for a wife.

Airik gritted his teeth. He did not want to leave Veronica. He examined the thought. He didn't want to leave her ever again. He wanted to come home to her. He was falling in love with Veronica Bradwell. The realization of his own emotions was intense. He had to accept his feelings for her were true. He could no longer ignore them. They crowded into his every waking moment and invaded his dreams.

Acknowledging them, however, did not mean acting on them.

But Inigo was correct. He had work to do, his duties to Shelleen to execute. He could not stay with Veronica.

"I must go. I will be back this evening again." He sounded like a fool.

She smiled at him. "I'll be waiting." Lordy, but she sounded inane, especially since she was talking to a paying guest who would leave for Barsoom at the end of the Biennial Mining Conference. She wasn't talking to her lover, much as she wished he could be. His kiss had been wonderful.

She watched Airik Jones and his entourage walk down the street, towards the transtube station and Dome Six until he was swallowed by the morning crowds.

"He's a fine young man," Neza said softly. She'd been watching her niece and wishing she could do something to help.

"Yes, he is," Veronica said and bit her lip hard to keep her emotions throttled down.

"We're very, very fortunate that he was late in coming to Panschin for the conference and decided to stay with us at the White Elephant." Veronica paused, facing dreary reality. "But he'll return home to Barsoom and nothing will come of it. I have to get the order ready for the Dappled Yak. Please excuse me, auntie Neza."

She wished she could leave Panschin for Barsoom with Airik Jones. No one in Barsoom knew who she was, and if they did, they wouldn't care. She would be able to see the sky and the moons of Mars racing in front of the stars anytime she wanted. She would have the chance of a new life, free of the constrictions of Panschin.

She would be with him.

The chef/owner at the Dappled Yak was, as always, pleased with Veronica's produce and bought everything, not always a guarantee. They gossiped about doings in the neighborhood while he sorted through her greens, tasting and deciding what he would cook for the next few days. She was able to reassure him and the rest of the staff that the thugs would not be coming back, but she didn't go into detail, not wanting to relive the struggle with Tallon and Frankie in the endless night underneath Panschin.

She was ready to leave, anticipating a pocket jingling with coin to go with the empty wagon, when one of the waitresses interrupted their conversation.

Veronica waited impatiently while the two conferred in whispers, glancing over at her periodically. She needed her coin and knew better than to leave without it. The chef/owner had already admitted he had the money available today. If she came back later, some other creditor would get paid and she'd go to the end of the line. Cash flow was always an issue with small businesses like this one.

"Veronica?" the chef/owner asked, with a big, unnerving smile on his face. "Important clients are having lunch today."

She eyed him warily. "I'm glad you have important clients but what does that have to do with me?"

"It's the PanU board of trustees. They recently started meeting here for their monthly luncheon, in large part because of your wonderful home-grown, perfectly fresh greens."

"How nice. I'm glad they like them." Veronica tensed, guessing what was coming.

"They're meeting today, and they want to meet you. Find out how you grow such wonderful salad greens and other vegetables." The chef/owner grinned wider, showing every one of his sharp white teeth.

She felt her stomach drop. He needed her to do this, keeping these lucrative customers happy, but meeting strangers was difficult. They'd ask her name. Not enough time had passed for Simon Bradwell to be forgotten in Panschin; she didn't think enough time would ever pass.

"You know about my father," Veronica said slowly. "What if they ask my name? They may not come back, knowing that you do business with me."

"I'm sure they won't bother, and if they do, don't tell them your real name. They want to feel good about themselves, and, to be blunt, I want them to feel good too, so they come back and tell all their friends. I need their business," the owner replied. He showed his teeth again in an imitation of a cheery smile. "You need my business. One big circle, Veronica."

His implication was clear.

"Of course," she said, forcing a tight smile. Maybe they wouldn't recognize her. It had been a long time since she'd last been in court and seen a sketch of herself testifying in the newspaper. Those drawings were never very accurate. Shelby did a better job than whoever the *Panschin Gazette* was employing. These important clients might never have met her father.

Veronica steeled herself and followed the chef/owner through the bustling kitchen and past the swinging doors. She hadn't been inside the restaurant proper since her divorce from Dean. Afterwards, as Simon Bradwell's empire collapsed with one blaring headline after another to ensure anyone who could read a newspaper knew what was happening, she had neither the money nor the inclination to go out in public.

It looked as she remembered it; murals of fanciful landscapes adorned the walls, a parquet floor dotted with circles of light from the deck prisms overhead, and many small round tables, each with a yellow gingham tablecloth and a small vase holding a flower. Today, they were red zinnias, just starting to fade. Perhaps, Veronica thought, looking for a distraction, she should consider growing flowers for sale. She deeply missed growing quantities of flowers and filling the White Elephant with them. But she couldn't. Her family could eat ugly, unsellable vegetables, but they couldn't eat zinnias, easy as they were to grow. Unsold flowers fed the soul, but did nothing to feed the belly.

There were many people enjoying their lunch so the Dappled Yak owner must be earning *some* money. He'd make more tonight when Malcolm brought Shelby here for dinner. Perhaps she could charge a few pennies more for her produce. She glanced at him. It was worth asking, particularly since he knew how much she disliked going out in public.

The chef/owner led the way to the large side alcove, reserved for larger groups. She had enjoyed a wonderful luncheon there, helping a friend celebrate her engagement. That friend no longer spoke to her, not after dear old dad was revealed as a swindler and a crook.

The group sitting around the long table were laughing over something and didn't pay any attention to her arrival. It gave Veronica a moment to see if she recognized anyone.

She did. Oh lordy. She did.

"Ladies, gentlemen," the owner announced with a flourish, before she could escape. "This is our very own supplier, Veronica B."

"Hello," Veronica said brightly. Damn him. He had implied he wouldn't say her name. He'd just made it impossible to claim she wasn't related to Simon Bradwell.

The conversation stopped and all eyes turned to her, silhouetted in a pool of light spilling through the deck prism overhead.

"*You!*" Sajag Burgess spat out. "You grew this rubbish? I knew I was becoming nauseous from eating it."

"Yes, Mr. Burgess," Veronica ground out. "I did. I raise the finest salad greens in Panschin which is why the Dappled Yak serves them."

"A likely story. Ladies, gentlemen, this *person* is the daughter of the notorious Simon Bradwell," Mr. Burgess said loudly, drawing the attention of his fellow PanU board members as well as the other diners in the restaurant. "She should be in jail."

The owner of the Dappled Yak looked appalled and stepped back, leaving Veronica alone. Fury roared through her. Mr. Burgess was an obese nothing compared to Tallon, now on ice in the Panschin morgue.

"In jail along with *you*, Mr. Burgess," Veronica snapped back. "Have you ever told your fellow board members that you used to gamble regularly in the casinos of Panschin with my father? Exactly where did all that money go that my father embezzled? Into *your* pockets? I've always wondered. They never found most of it, yet you, gambling with my father, always seemed so wealthy, even when he lost. Maybe you were in cahoots with Simon Bradwell!"

"I was *not*!" Mr. Burgess yelled, aghast. "I never associated with Simon Bradwell."

"You *did*! Dean Kangjuon gambled with the both of you on a regular basis, and he'll testify in court. You never lost money, so he said. You must have cheated because no one can win at the tables forever, not without cheating!"

"How dare you," Mr. Burgess began.

"How dare *I*?" Veronica yelled back, cutting him off. "You work for the Second National Bank of Panschin! You referred clients to my father so he could rob them! He gave you a cut, didn't he? It's either that or you are the most incompetent banker in Panschin! Nothing else makes sense."

"Veronica?" the owner said placatingly.

"You wanted to show me off like a museum exhibit," Veronica snarled at him. "I warned you someone would recognize me."

The Dappled Yak owner retreated from her fury.

"You grow these greens, young woman?" one of the board members asked. She was an older woman, older than Neza, Veronica thought.

"Yes, ma'am, I do," Veronica said. "It's how I pay the bills. Mr. Burgess and dear old dad ensured that my sister, my great-aunt, and I are bankrupt. And now Mr. Burgess is trying to evict us from our home! My auntie Neza has lived there her entire life and this *person* wants to throw us out. It has to be because he feels guilty over gambling with my father and defrauding the citizens of Panschin with my father."

"You gambled with Simon Bradwell?" one of the other board members asked Mr. Burgess. "You claimed you didn't know him at all."

"I did not socialize with that crook," Mr. Burgess said righteously. "I had barely any contact with him."

"Yes, you *did*," Veronica shouted. "I've seen your signature on documents my father handed out, documents that encouraged people to invest with my father. Are you trying to say you let your signature be *forged*? Are you that incompetent or are you lying?"

"I do not lie!" Mr. Burgess growled, lumbering to his feet and looming over the table like a mountain upholstered in floral drapery.

"I think you do," the older woman on the board said slowly. "My sister, gods above and below rest her soul, told me once that you recommended Simon Bradwell to her. I didn't think anything of it at the time since so many people did, but now, hearing Miss Bradwell, I have to wonder."

"Mrs. Smythe, many people were taken in by Simon Bradwell," Mr. Burgess began.

"Because you helped him *lie* to Second National clients," Veronica shouted over him. "Why else would you recommend a thief and a fraud and a conman? Because he paid you off! Because you two were working together all along! Because you gambled besides him in the casinos of Panschin, wearing your lucky suits!"

"Lucky suit?" one of the other board members asked.

"He wears those ridiculous, exaggerated floral suits because he believes it makes him lucky at the tables," Veronica replied. "Why else would anyone wear clothing that could be sewn from the PanU cafeteria drapes?"

More than one person, both at the PanU board table and out in the larger restaurant laughed, making Mr. Burgess's face grow darker with fury and embarrassment.

"These are strong accusations," another board member offered.

Veronica peered at him, sitting in a more shadowy portion of the alcove and then remembered why he looked familiar. He had been with Kip McGrant at the gallery showing. Shelby had told her he was Peng McGrant. Florence had said Peng McGrant would sue the Bradwell family because of Kip's surface sickness. Peng McGrant also indulged in high-stakes gambling with Simon Bradwell.

"Mr. McGrant," she said sweetly. "I didn't know you were on PanU's board."

He blanched. He hadn't, she understood looking at his face, realized she knew who he was, and he was suddenly afraid of what she might say to the rest of the PanU board. She could give him a reason to support her cause.

"I don't know if you were told, Mr. McGrant, but your son, Kip, was the only member of the PanU Artists' Collective who was brave and responsible enough to go into the Steelio warren with my sister Shelby."

"My Kip did that?" Mr. McGrant asked, shocked and relieved at the change of subject.

"Yes, he did. You should be very proud of your son, Mr. McGrant," Veronica replied smoothly. "I know he unexpectedly developed surface sickness, but he's a conscientious and talented young man nonetheless.

Kip is an asset to your family." She decided to stop there rather than lay on more praise, particularly since there wasn't anything else positive she could say about Kip.

"The Steelio warren?" Mrs. Smythe asked curiously.

"Yes, ma'am," Veronica said. "My sister, Shelby, was invited to the warren along with the rest of the PanU Artists' Collective to get a better understanding of how art affects the working classes. Kip was the only other student who agreed to go."

"Very nice behavior on your son's part, Peng," Mrs. Smythe said to Mr. McGrant. "Kip clearly takes after his father."

Veronica smiled even more sweetly while biting back saying that Peng McGrant was another of dear old dad's gambling partners.

"Why are we even listening to this deranged woman?" Mr. Burgess said. "She's trying to poison us with her salad!"

"The salad isn't poisonous," Mrs. Smythe retorted. "I've enjoyed it many times at the Dappled Yak. You, Mr. Burgess, on the other hand, *are* poisonous. I think you lied to my sister. Your favorable advice about Simon Bradwell ruined my sister. My sister committed suicide because of *you*, Mr. Burgess." She was shaking with fury and near tears.

"I am so sorry to hear about your sister, Mrs. Smythe," Veronica said gently. "My father destroyed lives wherever he went. He didn't care about anyone but himself. Please accept my condolences on your loss."

"You take after your mother, I think, Miss Bradwell," Mrs. Smythe said, regaining some of her composure. She wiped her eyes with a napkin.

"Thank you, ma'am. That's very generous of you. My sister, my auntie Neza, and I miss her every day, just as you miss your sister," Veronica said. "Death is final and awful."

"Veronica?" the chef/owner said carefully, seizing his opening. "Didn't you say you had other appointments before I asked you over here?"

"Why yes, I did. But I want my money first for my vegetables," Veronica snapped. "I need it to pay my lease. You of all people know how close to the bone we are."

"Absolutely," the owner replied, trying hard to sound helpful and caring while wishing he had lied to the board about the presence of his salad supplier. "We'll get that taken care of back in the kitchen."

"Thank you for your time," Veronica said smoothly to the PanU board members. "I loved PanU when I went there. It's a wonderful university and I wish I had been able to complete my studies. I would recommend, however, that you examine Mr. Burgess's financial dealings with the board. He's either the most incompetent banker in Panschin or he's just as big a fraud and embezzler as my father, Simon Bradwell, was. Please don't let harm come to PanU."

Another diner at the table said to the group, "I think you should do just that. I don't wish to join a board that has a member operating under such a cloud of suspicion and incompetence."

"Mr. Qiao, Bertram," Mr. Burgess sputtered. "I never—"

"I've heard many unpleasant rumors about you, Burgess," Mr. Qiao said. "My firm has wondered how you retained power despite your obvious malfeasances. Perhaps this is an explanation."

"I would agree," Mrs. Smythe said, her lips compressed into a tight, unhappy line.

"Miss Bradwell obviously operates a market gardening scheme, in direct violation of the lease," Mr. Burgess said coldly. "She is trying to hide her own sins by accusing me. I am merely doing my duty to Second National."

"By evicting people working to pay their bills like a banker in some tawdry melodrama?" Mrs. Smythe said even more coldly. "Yet you could not manage due diligence to your clients, such as my dear, lost sister."

"I have heard some rumors as well," Peng McGrant said cautiously, glancing nervously at Bertram Qiao as he did so.

"Peng!" Mr. Burgess cried, his hand clutching his heart, and his face distraught. Mr. McGrant turned away and studied the remains of his salad.

Veronica smiled coolly. "Please excuse me. I know you are all busy people. Do enjoy the salad."

She marched back to the Dappled Yak kitchen, head held high, and followed by a gale of chatter and stares. Mr. Burgess would have plenty of work on his hands, trying to cover up what he had done with Simon Bradwell. She'd have to thank Dean for telling her. She'd have to ask Inigo which member of Qiao & Schopenhour was joining the PanU board of trustees since she didn't recognize him.

She winced inwardly.

She'd also have to talk to Airik Jones when he returned this evening. She couldn't lie by omission to him any longer. He had to know who she really was and how it would affect him. This incident proved it.

Airik couldn't sit comfortably on the transtube, twisting and turning in his seat.

"Sir?" Inigo said carefully. "I'm sure there's space in the first-class compartment." He took another wary look around again at the third-class compartment. He'd never sat in one before. It was crowded with the kind of people he did not normally associate with.

Airik glared at him. "Will the first-class compartment of this particular transtube arrive faster in Dome Six?"

"No, sir," Inigo replied.

"Sir," Carmine said. "When we get to the hotel, you're seeing the doc again. You said you'd see him every morning and evening."

"I've got a full day ahead of me," Airik snapped. "Squeezing in a meeting with the shamans will eat too much time as it is."

"You're in pain, sir," Elliot interposed from his seat. He'd helped Airik undress the previous night and tsked over the stitches and bruises. "Your functioning will be impaired."

"Got to agree with Elliot, sir," Carmine said. "It's hard to concentrate when everything hurts."

Inigo wanted desperately to ask why the daimyo of Shelleen was in such pain but didn't dare, particularly not in the third-class compartment on the transtube. And why had Airik insisted on the third-class compartment?

Then he got it. Airik was wearing a plebian coverall and was hoping to go unnoticed. It might even be working since, he, Inigo, was getting the hostile stares, and it must be because of his expensive, well-tailored business suit. Everyone around them was ignoring Airik, Carmine, and Elliot, all wearing anonymous standard-issue Panschin coveralls.

Carmine frowned. "Sir, you got to see the doc. You got to see how my lord Upton's doing anyways."

"Good time management, sir," Elliot added.

"And if you don't go on your own, I'll carry you there," Carmine said with great finality.

"Fine," Airik said. He should, he knew, be gratified by how much his people were concerned about his health, but it was annoying. He also knew that Carmine would do as he threatened. His bodyguard was still angry because he was ordered to stay aboveground instead of keeping his daimyo from injury.

Inside the hotel, Airik sent Elliot upstairs with a message to Gaston about the change in schedule. His valet wouldn't return afterwards. He had his own assigned researches to attend to.

At the infirmary, the hotel doctor was waiting anxiously. So was Winifred Qiao, dressed in a neat medical coverall with the Qiao & Schopenhour logo on it and her name embroidered over her heart. She must have sent out for clothes overnight. She was pacing back and forth in her agitation.

"Good to see you again, my lord Shelleen," the doctor said. "Strip and while I'm examining you, we'll talk about Upton."

"His condition has declined?" Airik asked. He had thought Upton was holding his own, based on his visit the previous evening.

"Yes."

"Winifred?" Inigo asked. "What are you doing here?"

"I'm with Upton," she replied absently. "We'll talk later."

Airik wriggled out of his clothes revealing his constellation of bruises and stitches. The bruises were darkening and spreading, showing every time his body had been slammed by a fist, a boot, or was shoved into the unyielding stone in the tunnels under the White Elephant.

"What happened?" Inigo gasped in horror. No wonder Airik had to see the shamans. He'd insist again, even though it meant agreeing with Malcolm Cobb, something he had thought he'd never do. The questions suddenly arose: Cobb was involved, but how? Had he been injured too? Had he let the daimyo of Shelleen take the brunt of whatever occurred?

"Patient confidentiality, Inigo," Winifred snapped at him before Airik could speak.

"Itchy? Pain? Aches?" the hotel doctor asked as he inspected Airik's wounds.

"All of the above," Airik admitted.

"Good, good, just as I expected. Your bruises will get worse before they get better. Let's put some salve on while we chat about Upton."

"He's not doing well?" Airik asked.

"No. He might have avoided pneumonia, but the cracked ribs aren't letting him breathe properly. I want to transfer him to the Dome Six hospital for a few days. They'll tent him to make it easier to breathe. I need your approval."

"I'll be going along, my lord Shelleen," Winifred said. "I'll make sure my Upton gets properly taken care of."

The door to the infirmary was thrown open and Gaston stomped in.

"Airik, we need to talk right now—," he stopped and stared. "Good Gods above and below and of the harvest! What were you doing?" Gaston was visibly shocked at Airik's constellation of bruises and the black lines of catgut stitching his wounds closed.

Gaston whipped around and snarled at Carmine, "Where in seven hells were you?"

"Doing what my lord Shelleen told me to, as I told you yesterday," Carmine said. "You think I liked sitting on my hands? I didn't!"

"Enough!" Airik shouted. "Doctor, send Upton to the hospital and keep me informed as to his progress. Miss Qiao, my thanks. Inigo, take notes of the conversation. Gaston, what is the problem now?"

Gaston shut his mouth and reordered his thoughts while Airik fumed as the doctor smeared more stinging salve across his injuries.

"Atto contacted Auntie Zilpah back in Shelleen," Gaston said. "He informed her and, by extension, the family, that you have been ignoring the potential brides being presented to you by the daimyos of the Northern Mining Tier, starting with Kendra. Then, immediately afterwards, Maerski did the same. Zilpah then contacted me, breathing fire, and informed *me* in no uncertain terms to inform *you* that this trip to Panschin had multiple aims. The family expects you to marry and soon."

Airik wanted to rant and swear. Instead he said, very coldly, "Inform Zilpah, the family, Atto and Maerski, that I will never marry Kendra Atto. Nor will I marry any member of the Atto family or the Maerski family after that stunt. I will choose a bride in my own time and of my own choice. In addition, inform Atto and Maerski that I will look at any business deal they propose with even less favor than I do now."

"Yes, Airik, but..." Gaston's voice trailed off, seeing Airik's expression. He thought of Howard Shelleen again. He wondered what had happened to whoever Airik had tangled with and where their body was. There had been a gruesome story in the morning newspapers about a body discovered in a Dome Six park.

"Was there anything else?"

"Yes, yes there was. Some fool named Cobb insisted that you meet him in front of the hotel within the hour for a purification ritual," Gaston said, back on safer ground.

"Ah. That was fast," Airik said. "I will be there. You will take charge in my absence. Inigo, attend my scheduled seminars and take detailed notes. I will review them upon my return."

"What? You can't miss this morning's sessions!" Gaston protested.

Meanwhile, the hotel doctor looked at Airik's injuries again and blanched as did Winifred Qiao. "You acquired your contusions and wounds in the deepdown under Dome Two, didn't you," the doctor said.

"I did," Airik said.

The hotel doctor turned to Gaston. "Doctor's orders. My lord Shelleen must do this. Everyone in Panschin will understand. I've got to get Upton prepped for his trip to the hospital's pneumonia wing." He got up and headed out of the room, followed by Winifred Qiao, visibly uneasy.

"Sir?" Inigo said to Gaston. "Permit me to make the explanations. Everyone in Panschin, including the Northern Mining Tier demesnes will understand."

"But I don't understand!" Gaston pleaded.

"I'll explain on the way," Inigo said as if he was soothing a fractious child. "You head Shelleen's mining department. I assume you are familiar with the deepdown and what lives beneath?"

"Well, yes, I suppose I am, in a way, but," Gaston said uneasily. "I don't see…" He stopped suddenly; his face ashen. He fell into a chair. "Oh, gods, Airik. What did you do?"

Back in the suite, Airik refused to enlighten Gaston on more than the basics. He insisted on focusing on what work he could get finished before meeting Malcolm Cobb in the Twelve Happiness lobby. When word was carried upstairs, by the concierge himself, Airik said, "Gaston, I will return as quickly as possible. Inigo, make the explanations as needed. Carmine, you will accompany me."

The concierge, uncharacteristically subdued and waiting anxiously for his response, looked relieved.

Airik then made his painful way back down the four flights of marble stairs, silently cursing the architect for mis-designing them with every step. Carmine followed silently, wishing he had been able to persuade the daimyo to take the elevator instead. Airik had also refused to be carried.

Malcolm Cobb was waiting in the lobby.

"Airik," he said, "I'll lead the way." He gave the bodyguard a considering look. "It won't be necessary for Carmine to go underneath with us."

"Yes, it is," Carmine replied, beating Airik to the punch. "It's how my lord got Gaston to agree."

"He would have still agreed," Airik said. "Gaston told me when we got back to the suite that what lives beneath spoke to him once in Shelleen."

"Really?" Malcolm asked, shocked to his core. "Really? Why isn't he a shaman?"

"Gaston is a member of the Shelleen family," Airik replied stiffly. "Shelleen is primarily agricultural. Although we have mining operations, they do not enjoy the prestige they should. What lives beneath does not receive the respect that the harvest deities do."

"That's appalling," Malcolm said.

"Shelleen is a different world. Lead the way. I don't have time to waste."

At the metro station, Malcolm led them to a staircase plunging further down under Panschin. Then another. Then a much dirtier, more crowded metro station, with dingier transtubes.

Airik observed this section of Panschin carefully, one that the chamber of commerce had not touted. He was happy that Gaston and Carmine both had insisted he take along the bodyguard. No one, to his relief, paid any attention. A short ride later, Malcolm changed transtubes again, leaving Airik hopelessly lost.

"You do know where we are going?" Airik asked quietly.

"I do. The chamber is sacred. None of the transtubes or mining operations go near it so we have to work our way around the city to get there. There's no direct route."

"Not even above ground?" Airik said. "Through the upper levels connecting the domes?"

"No. We'll be at the passageway soon."

"I am underground. Won't that be a problem?" Airik asked dryly. "I understood that I could never go underground again."

Malcolm grinned. "We'll be fine. I have the talisman and its protection, by extension, covers you." He pulled a fist-sized chunk of azure crystal from his pocket.

Airik was caught by the crystal's flashing beauty. "May I see? I'm not familiar with this mineral."

"Don't drop it," Malcolm said.

"Never."

Airik held the crystal carefully, turning it this way and that, admiring how it caught the light from its many, natural facets. Even on closer inspection, he couldn't identify the mineral. He thought suddenly of Veronica. She would love the stone's beauty, leading to thoughts of how a crystal like this could be cut into gems that would enhance her own beauty. The blue reminded him of a summer day in Shelleen; with a sky that Veronica had never seen. She would be entranced by that sky, vast and open and always changing, unlike the dome.

"Other people are looking at us now, because of that pretty rock," Carmine said. "That gonna be a problem, Mr. Cobb?"

"No."

Carmine watched the other riders each glance carefully at the crystal in Airik's hands, then sidle away, leaving an island of space surrounding them in an otherwise crowded metal tube.

Guess not, he thought and relaxed into his seat.

taring into the heart of the azure crystal was mesmerizing and oddly soothing. Airik could feel the pain from his injuries subside. He stopped himself. It must be the pain tea the doctor had supplied. It was finally working. To think otherwise was foolish.

On the other hand, the azure crystal, cool and surprisingly heavy for its size in his hand, reminded him strongly of bluekaps. He had never seen one, but he knew miners who claimed they had. Bluekaps were minor sprites, dancing bits of azure fire, and they could be helpful when they chose to be. They were on par with knockers, which were mostly sound.

Bluekaps and knockers were a part of what lived in most underground areas. He couldn't deny their existence, but they made him uneasy since it led to thoughts of what else haunted the bones of Mars.

Until he heard Gaston's confession, Airik had never known anyone who admitted that what lived beneath had spoken to them. He'd have to find out more from Gaston, and he wished that he asked him to come along. Back in the suite, when Airik pressed him for details, Gaston became agitated and refused to go into detail. Just as Airik himself had refused to detail his experiences in the deepdown under the White Elephant. Was it the same?

No, Airik reasoned. He said nothing because he didn't want to lose the peace he found with Veronica. Gaston would insist he leave the White Elephant, leave her. Gaston did not have a business-related concern for his refusal to speak.

Airik stared deeper into the heart of the azure crystal and thought about Gaston. They belonged to the Shelleen family, and they worked in Shelleen's tiny mining department. Yet he knew very little about Gaston. That had to change. He could not get the best performance from the older man if he didn't know what drove him. Perhaps, Airik mused, he could ask the shaman he was about to meet.

Airik glanced over at Malcolm Cobb. Based on Malcolm's reaction to Gaston's confession, having what lived beneath speak to a person was unusual and highly prized in Panschin. If anyone understood what lived beneath, it had to be the residents of a city devoted to the extraction industries.

Yes, he would do that. It would be good for Gaston, and by extension, good for Shelleen. He thought of the Red Mercury lode: intensely valuable, dangerous to work with, and virulently toxic in a way that Shelleen's other mining operations were not. Yes, he would speak to the shaman.

The transtube rattled and shook and slowed to a halt.

"Our stop," Malcolm announced and stood up, wincing. He caught Airik's glance.

"Yeah, I hurt all over. I got a hell of a knock on the head like you did, but my hair covers the lump. You got the worst of it. I don't know why."

"It will be difficult to ask Tallon," Airik said, permitting himself a smile and then wishing he hadn't. Veronica might have laughed but Malcolm did not.

Airik looked around the metro station. It looked like the others; dirty, tired, and caked with terraformers where they weren't scraped away by foot-traffic or chars. He thought of his schedule.

"Is it much further?"

"Yeah. This way."

Malcolm led them down the metro station platform to a door at the far end. This door, the first that Airik had seen like it, was painted the same azure as the crystal tucked into his pocket.

Behind the door was a long, meandering tunnel, just like so many other tunnels under Panschin. It was poorly lit, carved from the living rock, and had a bend, concealing what lay at its end. The ventilation was better than Airik expected, probably because the walls and ceiling of the tunnel were thick with terraformers. Someone, however, kept the lights scrubbed clean.

The tunnel sloped down noticeably. As they walked along, turning down new tunnels regularly, Airik asked "where in Panschin are we? Are we under a particular dome?"

Malcolm frowned. "I'm not sure. And if I was, I don't know if I would tell you."

"It must be on a map somewhere," Airik said. "Otherwise, wouldn't this chamber get damaged by mining operations or manufacturing around it?" He was thinking over the toxicity under Dome Four. This chamber couldn't be there. That left five domes along with the connecting areas between them.

"It is mapped, and all mining and other operations, no matter how valuable the seam is, are diverted around the chamber," Malcolm said.

"Even gold?" Airik said. He would have said Dirac, so critical to the terraforming process, but the nearest Dirac mine to Panschin lay over one hundred klicks to the west.

"Yes. A number of years back, some rich newcomer bought out one of the mining companies in Panschin and insisted on following a seam into the chamber. Everyone who worked in the deepdown went on a work stoppage, along with almost everyone aboveground. The newcomer got hauled in for personal interviews with every single other mine owner in Panschin, followed by personal interviews with Maerski, Atto, Fuziwara, and Davis."

"And did that work?" Airik asked.

Malcolm chuckled without any humor. "Eventually. His dead body, badly beaten, was found in a park in Dome Six. After that discovery, his heirs became easy to work with."

"I imagine they would be," Airik said dryly. "I have to say that sounds similar to what happened to Tallon's boss."

"Yes, it does," Malcolm said with finality.

They walked in silence for another klick (Airik counted breaths, steps, and turns) when Malcolm stopped at another door, incongruous with its azure paint gleaming against the living stone encrusted with terraformers in every shade of green and brown.

Malcolm knocked, and the door was opened by an impressively gray-bearded shaman, his feet bare and wearing a floor-length robe of shades of brown and gray, swirled together. The hem of his robe was encrusted with bits of mica, glinting with every movement and there were more bits of mica woven throughout the coarse cloth.

"Honored mùshī," Malcolm said. "This is Airik and Carmine."

The shaman bowed deeply. "Welcome, Airik. Welcome, Carmine. Airik, you shed blood in the deepdown, but Carmine did not."

"This is true," Airik said. "I would like Carmine to accompany me, if that is permitted."

"He may, but to observe only." The shaman gave Carmine a good looking-over. "He does not go normally into the deepdown. It is not part of his life."

"No, sir," Carmine answered. "It is not. I appreciate being allowed to stay with my boss." He was secretly relieved that whatever they would do to Airik wouldn't involve him. He had been fine on the transtubes and the metro stations, even as the group descended lower and lower under the surface of Mars. The tunnel made him feel itchy, and this strange priest made him even more uncomfortable. Besides, if he wasn't being ritually cleansed, he might be able to rescue Airik if necessary. Carmine prayed it wouldn't be. He didn't like the idea of hauling Airik back up that maze of tunnels at a dead run and then finding his way back to the surface.

The shaman led the way into a small chamber, glinting with bits of blue and gold mica. It was natural in most respects, Airik noticed. Only here and there were the tool marks of men, carefully removing impediments to moving around. There was also a heavy wool curtain, dyed azure, mounted on the far wall.

"Before we proceed farther," the shaman said, "you must remove your boots. The living stone speaks to us through our flesh."

Airik glanced at Malcolm, already squatting to untie his bootlaces. He had neglected to mention this part. What else had Malcolm not bothered telling him? It was too late now. He sat down awkwardly in the small, empty cavern and unlaced his boots. He glanced over at Carmine. His bodyguard looked resigned as he stripped off his own heavy boots and wool socks.

When Airik stood again, the stone was icy-cold under his feet, making him think of hypothermia as well as magnifying his other aches and pains. It did make sense, sort of. He'd always believed stone was alive, although on a radically different timescale than humans used. How else could stone communicate, other than via touch?

The shaman observed him quietly, offering no hint as to what was to come.

"What next?" Airik asked, wanting to get this over with so he could return to the world above, a world that despite its confusions, he understood far better than this one.

"We wait," the shaman said. "When the moment is right, we will enter the chamber."

"The stone will tell you?" Airik asked.

"Yes, but so will my brother. There are other participants and we must wait for them to arrive."

Airik pointedly glanced around at the otherwise empty chamber.

More of his time was going to be wasted. "I see."

The shaman smiled briefly. "There is another antechamber to the main hall of crystal. The other participants will convene there. They are uncontaminated and must remain so."

"I see," Airik said. Well. He had wanted to know more about the religious system of Panschin, and he was getting what he wanted.

His feet were on the verge of going numb when the curtain was pushed aside and another, much older shaman, dressed similarly but with a snowy white beard and hair, said, "We are ready, my brother."

"Go inside," the first shaman said. "I will wait here. Carmine, you will go last. Stand just inside the curtain but go no farther."

Carmine bowed his head respectfully. Priests, no matter how strange, were priests, and it was never safe to be rude to one. He didn't fancy taking a curse home with him to Shelleen.

"Thank you, sir," the bodyguard said and followed Airik and Malcolm through the curtain.

Airik took a few steps inside and then stopped, sucking in his breath in audible wonder. This cavern was much larger, roughly circular, lined with crystals, and it glittered in the candlelight. Azure predominated but every color of the rainbow was present. The ceiling was lofty, dotted with slim, gleaming stalactites hanging down like icicles. The stalactites were of the same azure crystal that Malcolm had handed to him on the transtube. That crystal still resided in his pocket. The floor of the cavern was surprisingly free of stalagmites. He surmised, based on tool marks, the others had been removed to make it easier to move around. The ones that remained were of the same azure crystal that Malcolm had handed to him on the transtube. That crystal still resided in his pocket.

Then his eye was drawn to the stalagmite in the center. Next to it, a gash tore the ground open. Its edges were rough and uneven, natural and not shaped by the hand of man. The cavern was surprisingly well lit with candles and everything glittered, magnifying the light, yet the gash into the bones of Mars swallowed the light. It was filled with darkness, as though full of black water, and darkness moved inside the gash. He could not see into it, despite the presence of the lights; not so much as a fingertip deep. Not a single reflection lay upon its surface.

The blackness within shifted as if alive. It felt alien, but not wrong or evil. Just strange and different and, yes, Airik examined the odd sensation, it was curious. It was curious about him. It did not know him, but it wanted to.

He opened his mouth to speak, and the snowy-bearded shaman held up his hand to stop him. Airik complied, sensing that something else didn't want him to speak either. He waited, sensed a wisp of communication, and then he reached into his pocket and dug out the azure crystal and held it up for the shaman to see. He felt a sense of rightness. He had heard correctly.

Was this what Gaston meant by having what lived beneath speak to him? Airik examined his emotions and decided it was not. The sensation was strange, but not terrifying or overwhelming.

The shaman looked pleased. He took the talisman from Airik and placed it carefully on the top of the beautifully carved stalagmite by the gash in the ground. The talisman caught the light, a piece of sky in the deepdown.

Malcolm looked pleased as well, and Airik felt again that he had reacted correctly. There was no sense of hurry. Stone never rushed. It had all the time in the world. Unfortunately, he did not. But there was no way to hurry up these events to suit his schedule.

He stepped closer to the gash, as did Malcolm, and that felt right too. Airik waited, letting himself hear the sounds of the bones of Mars, watch the play of light from the flickering candles, feel the cold stone beneath his feet and the movement of air across his face, and smell the living rock.

As he waited, more of his surroundings began to make sense. Next to the stalagmite holding the talisman stood a wide low table also carved from the rock. On it rested a large blue crystal pitcher and a collection of blue crystal goblets. Like Veronica's stemware at the gallery showing, each goblet was shaped differently. The table was clear of terraformers as was the entire chamber, including the stone ceiling far overhead. That seemed very unusual, based on what he had been told and had observed.

There was a rustle and Airik noticed another azure curtain on the far side of the crystal cavern. It parted and a group of miners entered, one by one, wearing coveralls indicating they were employed by the mining firms of Panschin. They all had bare feet. The first man in was, Airik realized suddenly, not a man but a boy, just on the cusp of adolescence. The miners entered in rough order of age. A very old man brought up the rear, his hair gray and his face wrinkled and aged with time. They made a dozen in all.

They arranged themselves in a circle around Airik, Malcolm, and the shaman, standing near the gash in the ground. Only Carmine remained at his position by the first azure wool curtain, standing alertly, ready to snatch Airik and bolt back up the tunnel at a second's warning. He watched tensely.

The shaman began to sing; long, low, sonorous, a song without words. His tones filled the hall of crystal, echoing back and forth. His voice died away and a heartbeat after the chamber fell silent, the youngest boy began to sing, his voice high and clear. He was young enough that his voice had not broken. One by one, in order of age, the other miners joined in with the same wordless song, filling the hall with the music of the human voice. The song built and built, while Airik stood there, trying not to shiver in the chilly air, without the least idea of what to do.

He waited and waited, hoping for a signal from someone or something, but nothing came. Then Malcolm began to sing as well, with the same wordless rise and fall of notes. At that point, Airik sensed something wanted him to sing as well.

Airik opened his mouth and did his best to add a wordless song to the other voices, suddenly thinking as he did of the endless fields of barley and rye that Shelleen grew and how much he missed the warmth of the sun and the wind teasing his hair, the slow progression of the day from first light to the vast panoply of stars filling the sky at night. He missed the changing weather; the small changes from day to day and the much greater changes from season to season. He missed the marshes, the rise and fall of the endless seas of grass, the unexpected pockets of forest tucked into low dells between the hills where the streams lay, the orchards in bloom in the spring, their blossoms perfuming the air. He missed the singing birds, knowing which bird was singing by its call. He missed the array of beasts from the field mice to the hawks wheeling overhead in the sky hunting them. He missed the animals being raised, the sheep and the chickens and all the other creatures. He missed his extended family, squabbling and fractious and very dear. He missed his peasants, laboring for the betterment of Shelleen; peasants who depended on the rightness of his decisions for their own wellbeing.

He missed Shelleen desperately and only sheer force of will kept him from falling to his knees from homesickness.

As Airik sang, he realized something else. He wanted to share all of

Shelleen with Veronica Bradwell. His voice shifted as he thought of Veronica, how she would delight in the sky overhead, the sensation of rain on her face, and the stately progression of the seasons. She knew virtually nothing of the world outside the domes of Panschin other than through the filter of paper. There was so much he could show her, share with her, a world of wonder and amazement. He understood, for the first time, his own mind and what was best for him. He loved her.

But would it be best for her? He could only ask.

He became suddenly aware that the voices around him were stilling. He waited for the signal, continuing on with his own wordless song, and he was the last person to finish singing. It felt correct, pouring out himself; his memories, his wishes, his innermost thoughts. Something he was unable to even comprehend was pleased.

The shaman seemed pleased as well, based on his expression. He did not speak and Airik remained silent. Another unspoken signal passed and this time, the oldest miner in the hall of crystal began to sing again. As he did so, the shaman lifted the blue crystal pitcher and poured water into a goblet. As the shaman slowly, ceremoniously filled each goblet, one by one, each miner began to sing. Then, with the penultimate goblet, Malcolm added his own voice. The shaman poured more water from the inexhaustible pitcher into the last goblet and as he did so, Airik felt the urge to sing again, this time of the struggle in the tunnel under the White Elephant.

This song was darker, lower, threaded with pain and terror and an overwhelming sense of loss. Airik learned he would have lost Veronica, had he not acted without hesitation. This song went on and on, filling the hall of crystal with reverberating echoes as he relived every terrifying moment.

Once again, the voices died away with his being the last.

When the last echo fell silent, the youngest boy began again to sing and as his voice soared up to the peak of the hall of crystal, the shaman carefully poured the first goblet of water he had filled into the gash filled with swirling darkness. The water sank without a splash, without a trace, swallowed by what lived beneath.

As the shaman lifted and poured each of the remaining goblets of water into the gash, each of the dozen miners began his own song, culminating in Malcolm's and Airik's.

Again, wordless, the songs died away. When the last echo vanished, the youngest boy genuflected before the gash and backed out of the hall of crystal. When everyone else departed, only Malcolm, Airik, the shaman, and a wide-eyed Carmine remained, still waiting by the azure wool curtain and as far away from the gash as he could get without actually pressing up against the wall of the cavern.

Airik waited. He was, he thought, the focus of what lived beneath's attention. Unlike Malcolm, it did not know him, but it was learning. He was a stranger from a strange land, alien in every way to what swirled and shifted in the gash that reached into the bones of Mars. The sense of what to do next rose again, and he walked to the low table, an altar he now realized, lifted the pitcher, and poured the remaining water into the gash. As he did so, Airik felt compelled to sing again, this time to ask for forgiveness for spilling blood, despite the necessity of doing so. Behind him, Malcolm's voice joined in.

It felt right. It felt correct. He was known, accepted, and forgiven.

When the last of the water was swallowed by the gash, a process that took far longer than it should have for the size of the pitcher, Airik set the pitcher back down as softly as he could. He sang on, as did Malcolm and the shaman, and waited for the sensation that what lived beneath was satisfied. The signal came, and he stopped as did Malcolm. The shaman sang on, filling the hall of crystal with his voice alone. He stopped and when the last echo of the shaman's voice disappeared, Airik felt, not compelled exactly, but needing again to do what was right and correct.

He genuflected deeply before the gash and, just as the other miners had done, backed away slowly and silently towards the azure curtain. Airik caught Carmine's eye, indicating that Carmine pass through the curtain first.

When Carmine — openly relieved — had done so, Malcolm went next, then Airik, and the shaman last of all, returning to the everyday world of Panschin.

Airik wanted to speak with the shaman, but found he couldn't. He silently pulled on his wool socks and boots, then followed an equally silent Malcolm, Carmine, and the shaman out of the antechamber and into the tunnel they had come from.

He remained unable to speak until they neared the tunnel door that led to the transtube station. Then and only then, did Airik feel the grip on his tongue loosen.

The shaman, silently waiting by the azure door, seemed to know he wanted to speak.

What honorific had Malcolm used? Ah, there it was.

"Honored mùshī," Airik pronounced carefully. "I have questions."

"No doubt," the shaman replied.

It was vividly apparent the shaman wasn't going to make it easy. Nor, Airik cast a quick glance at Malcolm, was he going to help.

What would be most likely to get a positive response?

"My second here in Panschin, Gaston, once experienced what lives beneath speak to him. The memory still distresses him. Shelleen has small mining operations, yet we do not have the rituals you do. Would you speak with him?"

To Airik's surprise, the shaman looked as though he had been expecting his question.

"I will do so. I will arrive at your hotel this evening."

"My deepest thanks," Airik said. He felt, again, he needed to say something else, but he couldn't sense the elusive wisp that had guided him before nor could he find words to express the thought. The words would not take shape, as though something was preventing it.

"Airik?" the shaman said, breaking the silence. "Your homeland is very beautiful. Do not lie to the young woman."

Airik started, then glared at Malcolm.

"I said nothing, other than what was necessary," Malcolm said swiftly, answering Airik's unspoken question.

"What lives beneath told me," the shaman said with the calm of ancient stone, unmoving, unchanging, unaffected by time or the needs of mortals. "It knows you."

"I see," Airik replied, utterly flummoxed. "I will inform Gaston of your arrival this evening. My deepest thanks once again. Malcolm, lead the way."

He did not speak again until they were safely on the transtube, returning to the surface and the living world.

"Malcolm," Airik demanded. "What did you tell these shamans?"

Malcolm took his time answering. "I explained what we had done, where and why, and what Tallon did to Frankie and himself. I did not, at any time, say you were other than Airik Jones of Barsoom." He heaved a gusty sigh. "The shaman knew I lied by omission, that I knew who you really were."

"What lives beneath told him?" Airik asked, his eyebrows up as high as they would go.

"Oh yes. You can't lie to a shaman, especially if you're barefoot. I told him you had to have privacy to better take care of your own people. I assume that's the reason for your charade?"

"Yes, it is."

"I thought so. I couldn't see any other reason for you staying in the White Elephant when you had the Twelve Happiness Luxury Hotel or the tower complex belonging to the mining demesnes available to you."

"The Twelve Happiness is maddening," Airik admitted. "Upton, my secretary, didn't know about the mining demesne tower complex. If he had, I would have stayed there."

"It's for the best he didn't," Malcolm said. "I don't think I could have managed Tallon and Frankie as well on my own in the deepdown. Because you were there, I made it safely to the surface and did what had to be done."

Airik gave him a long, considering look. He recalled what Bertram Qiao had said about Blue Sun, Malcolm's confidence that mysterious boss had been taken care of and what he had said about the recalcitrant newcomer and his drive to mine out a seam that intersected with the hall of crystal, and what the *Panschin Gazette* had to say about the body in the park in Dome Six.

He looked around the crowded, noisy transtube and leaned over to whisper into Malcolm's ear.

"Did you ask Blue Sun to find Tallon's boss?"

Malcolm's face went stony but he whispered back, "Yes. I knew they wouldn't tolerate Knights of Mars infiltrating Panschin and that meant Shelby and her family would be safe."

"Are you affiliated with them?"

"No. Never." Malcolm's face hardened still further. "Blue Sun understands the needs of the deepdown. They can even be useful on occasion, but they're violent and dangerous. Tallon would have fit in, if he'd been Panschin born and bred."

Airik thought of Veronica's bubbling laugh, grace under pressure, and determination, Shelby's talent, Neza's dry wit, Lulu's sharpness, and Florence's sweetness; a house of women with no way of defending themselves.

"Keep it that way," he ordered. "And thank you for not lying to me."

This time it was Malcolm's turn to give Airik a long, considering look.

"I could not lie. Not after what we did in the deepdown and the purification ritual afterwards."

Malcolm paused, waiting to see what Airik would say.

"You should not either," he added.

Veronica spent the remainder of the day working out what she wanted to say to Airik Jones upon his return as she scrubbed every surface clean from terraformers trying to attach themselves. It was painful, more painful that she would have believed, having to revisit the past. But he needed to know. He had done so much for her and her family, at great risk to himself. It would not be fair, to him or to his company, to not know the risk he was running if he was discovered to be staying with her in the White Elephant.

She was not her father. She was not Simon Bradwell. She wouldn't cheat or lie, nor harm Airik Jones by omission.

Fortunately, Shelby was keeping busy with finishing her schoolwork when she wasn't trying on every piece of clothing the household still owned in anticipation of her date with Malcolm that evening. Neza had her duties to occupy herself. No one paid much attention to Veronica as she worked throughout the day, sweeping down colonizing terraformers from the White Elephant while she rehearsed her speech and swallowed her tears.

He would leave. It was the sensible thing to do. She wouldn't see him again. He would go someplace else in Panschin, most likely the Twelve Happiness Luxury Hotel. It was impossible to think Airik Jones couldn't afford to stay there since he could afford a staff, just as it was impossible to believe that the hotel didn't have a few of their stunningly expensive rooms free.

And when the conference was over, Airik Jones would leave for Barsoom and his life there. It was equally hard for Veronica to believe that he wasn't a sought-after man within his social circle. He was so very un-average; decisive, well-mannered, intelligent, and with a sly, dry wit all his own. He looked good, too. She kept seeing his bared muscular body, stretched out on her dining room table as the police surgeon attended his wounds. His self-control, as his knife wounds were stitched closed, was admirable.

There was nothing average about Airik Jones. He deserved the best. If he wasn't already married, Veronica mused, it was only because his family hadn't yet found someone of his caliber. The thought was deeply painful.

She wished again she could run away from Panschin with Airik, despite barely knowing him, and go where no one would look at her and see her father's crimes weighing her down, while judging her every move and statement. It would mean leaving Shelby and Neza, but now that Shelby had met Malcolm Cobb, she was no longer so worried about what would happen to her sister. And for Shelby to work up the nerve to speak to Professor Vitebskin about transferring to PCC! Veronica was so proud of how much her little sister had grown up in the last few days. Shelby would make it; Veronica was sure of it now.

But would she, Veronica, make it? Airik filled her thoughts and invaded her dreams. She barely knew him, but she knew his courage, his intelligence, his refusal to pretend that nothing was happening despite how uncomfortable it was.

She was falling in love with him but nothing would come of it. He would go home to Barsoom and leave her alone in Panschin. She could give him only one gift and that was the gift of honesty. After that, it was up to him what he did with it.

Malcolm left Airik and Carmine as soon as they reached the Dome Six metro station. It was a relief to Airik to walk back to the Twelve Happiness hotel, outside and aboveground in the busy, cheerful streets of Dome Six. The dome did not feel as confining as it once had, compared to the tunnels below. Carmine remained silent, as he had on the transtube, until they reached the front of the building with its tiny green lawn. It was a child's imitation of the endless seas of grass in Shelleen.

"That was weird," the bodyguard said, as if staring at grass permitted him to speak again. "I watched it move."

"Did what lives beneath speak to you?" Airik asked.

"I'm not sure. I couldn't move, couldn't speak, like I had turned into a tree. Or stone. It was weird. How did you know what to do?"

"I believe," Airik said slowly, "that what lives beneath knew what it wanted from me, and it encouraged me to give it what it wanted."

"Panschin just keeps getting weirder and weirder," Carmine said. "If you don't mind my saying so, sir, I want to go home."

"So do I." Airik made a move towards the hotel's front doors.

"Sir. Wait please. One other thing," Carmine said with great reluctance. "I got to agree with that shaman. Stop lying to Miss Bradwell. I don't know how he knew, if Malcolm Cobb didn't tell him, but he did. It's not a good idea to be disrespectful of strange priests and those priests were the strangest I've ever heard of."

Airik raised an eyebrow.

Carmine paled, while looking more determined, almost as though he was being prodded. "It's not my place…"

"No, it is not. But do continue."

Carmine grimly plowed on. "I got a cousin who signed on to working the Red Mercury lode, sir. He writes us regular. He wrote it is spooky-weird down there, not like the tin mine he's used to. Does whatever lives beneath Panschin live under Shelleen? Do they talk? I don't want nothing bad to happen to my cousin or any of his crew."

"I will take your concerns under advisement," Airik said, feeling troubled. His bodyguard never complained nor did he use his position to benefit any of his relatives. This was new.

"Thank you, sir." Carmine frowned. "Did my lord Gaston really have that whatever it is speak to him?"

"So he said," Airik replied.

Carmine looked even more uneasy. "Then Shelleen and Panschin might be connected somehow. You got to make this better, sir. I don't know what you got to do, but you got to."

"I shall, Carmine," Airik said calmly. His mind raced. He had not heard of these concerns from his supervisor at the Red Mercury lode. Was simple competence too much to ask for? He would have to investigate when he returned to Shelleen. However, Carmine raised an interesting point and one he had not thought of. Could there be a direct connection between whatever haunted the mines of Shelleen and what lived beneath in Panschin? If so, he needed to speak with the shaman again, for the benefit of Shelleen and not just for Gaston's peace of mind.

"What else did your cousin say?" Airik asked.

Airik found both Gaston and Inigo immersed in seminars. His new secretary, to his relief, did demonstrate simple competence. Inigo's notes on the meetings and presentations Airik had missed were complete and concise. He had fully expected Airik to return.

Gaston, on the other hand, had apparently been a nervous wreck during Airik's absence and was openly relieved to discover that the daimyo of Shelleen was both alive and sane.

"Thank all the gods of the harvest, Airik," Gaston kept saying. "You're alive. You've come back."

Airik studied him coolly.

"Did you believe I wouldn't?"

"I didn't know what to think." Gaston cast his eyes around the crowded conference center. They were the discreet focus of everyone in the room. "Those idiots were no help. I will admit Inigo was correct. No one batted an eye over your need to speak with, with, I won't say it."

"What lives beneath?" Airik said carefully, wanting to see how Gaston reacted.

His second in command paled visibly and swallowed.

"Yes, that," Gaston whispered.

"Apparently, you were honored above most men by being spoken to," Airik said.

"I could have lived my entire life without that honor," Gaston said, keeping his eyes carefully on the floor. "I thought I was insane. That alien … being … pouring through me, inspecting me on a cellular level. My every thought and action laid bare. Coming to Panschin brought it all back." He shuddered visibly.

"You were not insane. I made arrangements for the shaman who purified me to speak with you this evening."

Gaston forgot himself enough to clutch the front of Airik's coverall.

"You did what?" he gasped, wide-eyed.

"It seems to be necessary." Airik pointedly peeled Gaston's clutching fingers, one by one, away from the front of his garment. "There may be a connection between what lives beneath in Panschin and in our mines in Shelleen. Moreover, Carmine told me that his cousin, an experienced miner of ours working in the Red Mercury lode, has seen and felt strange things. Things that made him afraid in a way that he never has been before in any of Shelleen's own mines."

Gaston looked at his hands — hanging in the air where Airik had left them — as though he did not recognize them. "That mine is toxic."

"And vital to the terraforming project, Gaston. Vital to the wellbeing of everyone on Mars. It is also vital to my plans for Shelleen. I will make it as safe as possible for everyone concerned, and if that means you have to speak to a shaman of Panschin, then you will do so. This evening."

Gaston stared at Airik's implacable face and remembered Howard Shelleen screaming in the plaza.

"And if I refuse?" Gaston asked very quietly. The skin on his back twitched.

"You are not allowed to refuse, Gaston. The wellbeing of all of Shelleen may depend upon you. All of Mars, in fact."

"Yes, sir," Gaston replied. This was why the family had chosen Airik to be the daimyo. He used people ruthlessly and made them accept why they were being used.

"You spoke to Maerski and Atto?" Airik said, after giving Gaston a moment to reflect on his lack of options.

"Yes, sir," Gaston replied, deeply grateful to be on safer, less strange and shifting scree. "They were angry and unhappy."

"Good. Have they presented a new set of proposals?"

"Yes, sir. They are not much better than the previous set."

"I will rely on your judgment," Airik said. "Tell them to try again."

"Thank you, sir," Gaston said. "Fuziwara and Davis also submitted new proposals, independent of the previous set and of the other two demesnes. They are much better for Shelleen."

Airik smiled coolly. "So. Those daimyos do not see the need to follow Maerski and Atto like puppies on leashes. I suspect it will not be long before those demesnes find themselves looking through the families for new daimyos to lead them."

Gaston gave a look around the crowded conference room. "You are correct, Airik. Based on what I have heard this morning, Maerski and Atto overreached. When they return to their homes, they may face votes of no confidence." He paused. "Have you considered what you will do about *our* family's demand on you?"

Airik got a faraway look on his face. "I have. I will let you know in the morning. After you tell me about your conversation with the shaman this evening."

"Yes, sir," Gaston said, while wondering at Airik's expression. If he didn't know better, he would have sworn that cold, sensible, unemotional Airik looked wistful.

The rest of the day passed in a haze of seminars and meetings, one blending into the next. Airik had to force himself to concentrate because he saw Veronica's face when he didn't. What would she say to him when he revealed himself to her? When he admitted how he had deceived her?

There was also the haze of gossip swirling about him: over what he had done to merit the attention of the shamans of Panschin and what lived beneath; how he had faced down Maerski and Atto; and how he had made Chung/Banerjee come to heel while putting Qiao & Schopenhour into his debt. Gossip, at least, he could easily ignore in favor of business.

One point in gossip's favor was that no one attending the Biennial Mining Conference treated him or Shelleen as third-tier anymore. Airik had forced them to respect him.

But none of that respect, grudging or otherwise, would mean much when he returned to the White Elephant in the evening and spoke to Veronica.

What would she say? He had to ask. The need to do so was overwhelming and could no longer be ignored or set aside.

He would ask and then the decision would be hers.

Veronica flinched when she heard the gate open. She would do that for some time to come, even when she had a good idea of who it was setting foot on the property.

And indeed, when she answered the door, Malcolm Cobb was standing on the other side, looking happy and eager to see Shelby. He was impeccably dressed as always, in another suit to replace the one he had ruined underneath the White Elephant. He had a small, beautifully wrapped box in his hand.

Veronica met him with a smile and said, "I'll call Shelby, Malcolm."

"No, not yet," Malcolm said. "I'd like to speak privately with you and Neza for a few minutes first."

"Sure," said Veronica. "My aunt is in the kitchen."

Malcolm followed Veronica through the atrium, marveling again at how dreadful Professor Vitebskin's paintings looked, even against the beautiful, creamy walls bathed in the last of the day's light. Shelby's paintings had glowed in this same setting. Her talent was astonishing and he could not understand why Professor Vitebskin and the PanU Artists' Collective didn't see it. Soft in the head was the only explanation.

Neza was sitting in the kitchen, darning socks and drinking tea. Lulu and Florence were there as well, finishing up their own school work for the term. From the look of the counter, Veronica had been preparing supper. Malcolm set the gift-wrapped box on the table. Its red ribbon echoed the ribbon on the kitten calendar hanging on the wall.

"Malcolm, how nice to see you again," Neza said warmly. She looked over at Veronica. "Where is Shelby?"

"Most likely still fussing over her hair," Lulu interrupted, rolling her eyes as she spoke.

"Malcolm wants to speak with us privately, auntie Neza," Veronica said. She made no move to ask Lulu or Florence to leave. Malcolm knew why and the knowledge warmed him. They were family, despite their wildly differing statuses. He was accepted, too. He had been invited into the private, family kitchen instead of the more formal dining room.

"I want you all to know," he began. "I'm very serious about my intentions toward Shelby. She is wonderful, and if she'll have me, I want to spend my life with her."

The women exchanged glances.

"Shelby's got a temper," Veronica said.

"She can be overly dramatic," Neza said.

"She's flighty," Florence said.

"She's naïve," Lulu said.

"She's Simon Bradwell's daughter," Veronica said. "And so am I."

"So?" Malcolm said. "We all have our faults. Shelby's also talented and brave and beautiful and my family likes her and she likes them. She's the girl of my dreams. As for me, I'm a jumped-up tunnel rat and a scholarship boy, but I'm not letting my past define me, and I won't do that to Shelby."

"Brave words," Veronica said.

"My liabilities more than cancel out Shelby's," Malcolm said roughly. "I am going to become the president of the Second National Bank of Panschin, and I am going to become the chairman of its board, and I want Shelby by my side. Those victories would be worthless without Shelby to share them with."

"Really?" Shelby asked from the doorway. Her eyes were brilliant.

Malcolm turned and walked over to her.

"Really." He leaned over and very gently brushed his lips against hers.

Shelby stood up on tiptoe and flung her arms around him, holding him as though she would never let go, throwing herself into his kiss. Malcolm wrapped his arms around her, reveling in the sensation of her body pressed up against his.

They were oblivious to everyone else in the kitchen watching them.

"Well," Neza said. "I can guess Shelby's answer when he gets around to formally proposing."

"Is Shelby wearing your best dress, Florence?" Veronica asked.

"Yes, and it looks better on her than it does on me, darn it," Florence said.

"She could do a lot worse," Lulu said and actually smiled. "I can approve of him."

The other women turned as one to study Lulu.

"Well, I can," Lulu insisted. "I was positive she'd run off with the first low-life who showed any attention to her at all. You know, someone like that cad, Upton Jones, or that drippy Kippy." She made gagging motions.

"Oh, come now," Veronica giggled. "Shelby's not that naïve."

"Hah!" said Lulu.

Shelby broke off her kiss with Malcolm and glared at the women sitting around the table.

"I can hear you, you know. I would never be that silly."

"No, you never would be," Malcolm agreed, beaming at her.

Young love, Veronica thought, feeling old and jaded, and then thought of Airik Jones and how magical it felt when she kissed him. She pushed the memory away.

"Did you have a dinner reservation at the Dappled Yak?" she asked.

"We do," Malcolm said. "Oh, almost forgot." He let go of Shelby and picked up the box from the table. "I got this for you."

"Oooh," Shelby said, her eyes lighting up. "A present for me? Really?"

"Really."

Shelby carefully untied the red ribbon and handed it to Veronica. It would be perfect to tie up her hair with later; a memory of this wonderful night she would save as a keepsake. Then she opened up the pretty box, which she would also keep, and gasped.

"Oh, Malcolm, they're gorgeous." Shelby was overjoyed. She lifted a cluster of silk pansies, purple and white and yellow with delicately hand-painted faces. She showed it to everyone for them to admire.

"I watched you sketch flowers before I knew who you were," Malcolm explained. "When I saw these flowers like the ones you drew, I bought them, hoping that someday, I would be able to give them to you when we met."

"Oh, Malcolm," Shelby said, her eyes misty.

"May I pin them on your dress?"

"Oh, Malcolm, of course."

The silk pansies blazed against Florence's pale-green dress, beautifully setting off Shelby's complexion and hair. She spun and turned, showing off the flowers, vivid in her own happiness. No matter what the future brought, she would treasure the silk pansies forever.

Malcolm turned to the women sitting at the table. "Shelby and I will go out to the theater after dinner, but we won't be back too late."

"I should hope not," Neza said. "I'm an old lady and I need my rest. I won't get any until I know our Shelby's safe and sound back home."

"We'll all be up, I'm sure," Veronica added.

"Yep," Florence said. "We have to study."

"Don't forget," Lulu said. "I know where you work." She patted her hip pocket thoughtfully, the one where she kept her knife.

"You don't have to wait up," Shelby said, annoyed at how everyone was treating her like a naïve little girl.

"Yes, I do," said auntie Neza.

"I can't lock up the house without you inside," said Veronica.

"What if I want to know all about the show you're seeing so I can see if I want to go with Evan?" said Florence.

"I might make a mistake in the dark with my target," said Lulu.

"All good points," chuckled Malcolm while Shelby made faces over her family's shenanigans. He took Shelby's arm and steered her towards the door.

From the window, Veronica watched her little sister leave the White Elephant's garden clinging to Malcolm Cobb's arm. Shelby was glowing, she was so happy.

I hope, Veronica thought, that you will always be happy, Shelby. You deserve it. Her face was wistful.

"You deserve that happiness, too," Neza said quietly, watching the play of emotions on Veronica's face.

"Everyone does," Veronica said.

The day was finally over, culminating in another business dinner featuring more of Panschin's inedible cuisine. This one seemed to be focused on varieties of moss enlivened with fermented yeast. Grimly eating what was set before him reminded Airik that he would earn trainloads of money for Shelleen by providing Panschin with agricultural products. As he was considering which crops would sell best and be fastest to market, Airik caught sight of Gaston rising from the table. He headed for the exit, probably to disappear upstairs into the Shelleen suite. He shelved his plans and strode after Gaston and cornered him by the door.

"No," Airik said. "You must meet the shaman."

Gaston looked mulish and terrified and nauseated, a mass of conflicting emotions and all of them negative.

"Airik," he hissed. "You don't have any idea what it's like, to have *something* you can't even begin to understand strip you bare, flay your nerves, and slice your brain into sheets of tissue and examine them one by one with a magnifying glass." He had his hand braced against the wall for support and was breathing hard. Sweat beaded his brow.

"You are correct. I do not," Airik replied. "I do know that the greater good of Shelleen demands you speak with the shaman." He watched Gaston's face twist. "The greater good of Mars. We both know how toxic the Red Mercury lode is. It may be worse than we thought. Did you know the peasants believe the area to be plagued by witches? I must offer incentives to keep the lode going and the area farmed to keep control in my hands. We still risk the Martian government seizing our land."

"Witches?" Gaston did not look surprised, which did come as a surprise to Airik.

"Yes. I had discounted their fears as peasant superstition, but I am no longer certain."

"Why do you offer incentives to peasants?"

"Because they are the hardworking backbone of Shelleen. Managed correctly, they are productive. Managed incorrectly, they riot. You know this, Gaston. You do recall the turmoil in Dairapaska as well as how close Shelleen came to open revolt?"

"Yes, I do," Gaston replied sullenly.

"Then stop changing the subject. If you cannot be persuaded—," Airik began, his face like stone.

"Enough," Gaston interrupted his daimyo. "I will do my duty. I will not cheat the demesne as Howard did. But understand me, Airik. You talk of duty. What about your duty to the demesne? You must take care of my wife and my daughter, if harm comes to me because of what lives beneath."

"I will," Airik said. "You have my word on it."

Gaston gave Airik a long, long look. "My daughter has no dowry, not anymore. Will you see that she marries well no matter what happens to me?"

"You do not have the reputation of a gambler or a spendthrift, nor does your wife. May I assume the Twelve Happiness Luxury Hotel's 'special amenities' swallowed up her dowry?" Airik asked coldly.

Gaston blanched. Airik was the daimyo for many reasons, his penetrating intellect being one of them.

He stiffened his spine. "Yes, it did. I will pay for them myself, of course." He had enough self-respect to not admit he'd been using those amenities to keep mind and body fully occupied when he wasn't working. When he didn't shield himself, he could feel something examining him from the inside out. Sleep had been another agonizing challenge.

"You are correct."

"But my daughter—" Gaston began.

"Will be provided for, as is right and customary for every daughter of our house. Shelleen is first-tier now, whereas before we were third-tier at best. She will not lack for suitors in the coming years," Airik said.

"In fact," he added thoughtfully, "having a father who speaks with what lives beneath may be an enormous factor in her favor with the sons of the mining tier demesnes."

Gaston went still, a glimmer of hope on his face. "I had not thought of that.”

“No, I didn’t think you had.” Airik, seeing Gaston cringe at another example of his incompetence being laid bare. He decided to soften the blow. “Your experience was beyond anything we in Shelleen are familiar with. I do not believe that any of us could process such a … a happening.”

He thought of his encounter in the cavern of crystal. “My own experience was strange enough. What lives beneath only nudged me towards a path of its choosing. It did not speak to me.”

“You were blessed,” Gaston said.

“Yes,” Airik replied, seeing Gaston’s haunted expression, “perhaps I was. But you were as well. The shaman is waiting for you.” Airik frowned suddenly. “In fact, I need to ask him something myself, something that I was not allowed to do earlier.”

According to the clocks, evening was coming on, yet Dome Six was brilliantly lit. The lights from the buildings reflected off every surface, including the one overhead. The nightly cacophony of party horns had begun, along with the usual crowds and revelry. Airik stared at the underside of the glassteel bowl and realized that there were detectable changes inside a dome, if one knew what to look for. Dome Two, at this time, would not just be darker and far quieter. Its dome had a dirtier, yet more serene aspect, one that seemed to better reflect what was happening in the world on the other side. Dome Six was supposedly clearer, yet its appearance didn’t change as much when the sun moved overhead. Dome Two did.

Only the tiny lawn in front of the Twelve Happiness Luxury Hotel was an oasis of quiet and relative darkness. No one went near it. That stemmed, Airik decided, from the shaman standing in the middle of the lawn, eyes closed, hands lifted up to the dome overhead, and openly lost in the sensation of live grass under his bare feet. Even more interesting was the fact that the hotel bellmen, normally aggressive protectors of the lawn, were carefully pretending to see nothing. If anything, they were keeping a watch for gawkers, shooing them away so the shaman remained undisturbed.

“Is that him?” Gaston asked. “The shaman who performed the ritual for you?”

“Yes,” Airik said. “Interesting. Something has changed. I no longer feel constrained in what I can say to him."

"Something stopped you from speaking?" Gaston asked and shuddered. "Yes, it did."

"What did we awaken on Mars?" Gaston mused. His complexion had gone gray and sweat beaded his forehead.

"Changing the subject again? Something or somethings very old and powerful, I suspect," Airik replied quietly. "We and they are alien, but these beings, for lack of a better word, do not seem malevolent."

"*These* beings, Airik," Gaston snapped, some color returning with anger. "There are others. I was told such while you were undergoing your ritual. That's why you had to do it. Some of what lives beneath don't care about us, some are curious, and some are hostile."

"I see," Airik said. "I was not told, but I can't say I'm surprised."

"You see why I don't want to speak to that man?" Gaston said. "What if he serves something evil? What if what spoke to me was malevolent?"

Airik gave Gaston a long, cool look. "You are sane, Gaston. If what spoke to you was evil, you would not have survived the experience."

"How comforting," Gaston said dryly. He sat down on the steps leading up to the hotel and stripped off his shoes and socks. "Remember, you promised to take care of my wife and daughter. Also remember you have other duties to Shelleen, ones *you* have been avoiding." When he finished, he marched down to the sidewalk and then stopped as soon as his feet touched the grass, remaining on the outer edge of the lawn. His face was set and unhappy, and his body remained poised to flee.

Airik watched. The shaman had been oblivious to their presence on the steps of the hotel, yet the moment Gaston set foot onto the lawn, he shook himself and seemed to awaken.

"Come closer," the shaman said, waving Gaston to him with both hands. He ignored Airik, Inigo and Carmine.

Gaston shrugged, muttered something, and took another, reluctant step forward.

Airik moved closer himself, stopping on the ornate tiled border surrounding the lawn, and said, "I have questions of my own. Will you come into the hotel so we may speak privately?"

"No. I will not enter that building," the shaman replied. "Here will do."

"I see," Airik said, pushing away annoyance over having to speak in front of an audience. "My concern is Miss Bradwell and her sister. She was also in the deepdown with us. She also fought off Tallon and Frankie, as did her sister. Are they safe? What must be done for them?"

Gaston turned to watch Airik and listen closely, while carefully keeping his feet motionless in the soft grass. The daimyo had refused to name who had been involved during their earlier conversation.

So did Inigo.

For his part, Carmine watched the shaman warily. He wasn't hearing anything new.

"Miss Bradwell is known to what lives beneath," the shaman said. "She and her husband," — he paused, as if listening — "often went into the deepdown to explore. What lives beneath knows them both intimately although they themselves remained unaware."

"Former husband," Airik spat out, feeling a surge of jealousy at the thought of Dean Kangjuon being Veronica's lover and even more rage at how cavalierly Dean had treated such a precious gift. His outburst earned him more searching looks from Gaston and Inigo, both of whom noticed Airik's clenched fists.

"That is not a concern of what lives beneath," the shaman said serenely. "However, to answer your question, Miss Bradwell made her own sacrifice to save herself and her sister, a sacrifice that meant the moons to her. Her sacrifice was accepted. Her home and the tunnels beneath it were cleansed, and she and her sister and her aunt were purified as needed."

Airik thought his heart would stop. "I made arrangements with Malcolm Cobb to retrieve Miss Bradwell's beads. Will that compromise her safety?"

"No. Her sacrifice was made and accepted. What happens to the beads afterwards is immaterial."

"Who is Miss Bradwell?" Gaston asked, struggling to add things up from the scraps he knew.

"My hostess at the bed and breakfast I am sleeping at in Dome Two," Airik replied. He watched Gaston stare at him in confusion as he worked out had happened.

"You, the daimyo of Shelleen, risked your life and the needs of our demesne for some fourth-rate *innkeeper*?" Gaston sputtered.

"Yes, I did, Gaston," Airik said. "I am returning to her now, and I will ask her for her hand. In the morning, when I see you next, I will tell you her answer."

Airik said to Inigo behind him, "You are dismissed. Be at the White Elephant first thing in the morning."

"Yes, sir," Inigo replied while trying desperately to maintain the correct blank face of a good secretary. Veronica Bradwell! Did the daimyo of Shelleen have any idea who her father was?

Airik walked away, Carmine following behind, leaving Gaston open-mouthed upon the tiny lawn in front of the Twelve Happiness Luxury Hotel and Inigo, equally dumbfounded, on the steps. As Airik strode towards the Dome Six hospital to check on Upton, he had to wonder if this was why he had not been able to speak about Veronica's safety earlier. Something was forcing him to reveal more than he wanted to Gaston.

Gaston thought in wonder, I work with this man on a near-daily basis, yet I do not know him at all. The grass was cool and welcome beneath his feet and some of his anxiety vanished, as though it bled away into the soil and the underlaying stone.

Inigo thought, I should tell Marmaduke at once. Damn the confidentiality agreement I signed.

"Come, Gaston," the shaman said. "We have much to discuss. Inigo, remember your vows. All of them."

Inigo gasped, and gasped again when he caught Gaston's furious, knowing glare. Both the shaman and Gaston had grasped his intentions, the information provided to them by what lives beneath. Then he thought of his vow to Olwyn Steelio and sank to his knees on the steps of the hotel, oblivious to the gaping audience of hotel bellmen.

Veronica heard the gate shriek its warning and forced herself to get up calmly. The most likely person, based on the time, was Mr. Jones. Shelby and Malcolm wouldn't be back for a few more hours, assuming their evening went well, with no angry recriminations from the other patrons about dear old dad. No one else was due to come by this late. Dean was in police custody, Tallon and Frankie were dead, and so was their boss.

It had to be Mr. Jones.

It was past time to tell him the truth of what he was facing by staying with her.

"I've been thinking about just this subject," Shelby said slowly. Her voice was still rough.

"Being harassed by idiots because of your worthless father?" Malcolm asked.

They were walking hand in hand through the park in the center of the business district on their way to the theater; the same park where Malcolm had so often watched Shelby sketch the planters of flowers and wondered who this Dome Two princess was and if she would ever give the time of day to someone like him.

"No, my darling," Shelby replied, smiling lovingly up at Malcolm. "That's nothing new. I told Bhupathi you'd throw him down a mine shaft for harassing me, but you wouldn't do that, would you?"

"He did that? Who is he again?" Malcolm asked, feeling the surge of protectiveness wash over him again.

"Another student at PanU. He was rude and lewd, and he upset me but that was before Tallon and Frankie showed me what viciousness really is. Bhupathi's a little boy and not worth your time. What I mean," Shelby said, "is that you wouldn't throw some rude jerk down a mineshaft because of what lives beneath. You stay aboveground if you have to fight."

"Yeah, I do, if I have a choice" Malcolm admitted. "That's what the parks are for. Except Dome Four. Pretty much anything goes there, but even so, usually nobody gets killed. Killing is saved for aboveground."

The man behind them sitting on the ground groaned and rubbed his jaw carefully.

Shelby spared him a contemptuous glance, then let her eyes linger on the planter he slumped next to, overflowing with pansies. Even when Malcolm hadn't known who she was, he'd understood how much she loved flowers. The beautiful silk pansy pin proved it. She glanced down at it admiringly, then turned her attention back to Malcolm.

"That man won't bother me again."

"That was the point," Malcolm said. "Now about this Bhupathi guy."

Shelby laughed, sparkling music to Malcolm's ears. She openly appreciated him defending her. "Leave him be. I'm not going back to PanU, and I won't see him again. Do people bother you like this?"

"Generally not to my face, unless they're a lot higher up the social scale, and they can afford the risk," Malcolm said. "Like Burgess."

"Is he going to throw us out?" Shelby asked cautiously. She couldn't stop herself from clutching at Malcolm's strong arm, leaning into his body.

"No. I made sure he's got troubles of his own at the bank and after what you told me Veronica said this morning in the Dappled Yak to the PanU board, he's got even more." Malcolm smiled complacently. "I think he'll be resigning from Second National soon, to avoid public shame and maybe even prosecution."

"I hope they do prosecute," Shelby said vehemently. "He must have been in cahoots with dear old dad. Like Veronica said, it makes sense."

"It does," Malcolm agreed. "Things are looking up, for all of us."

He turned and leaned over to kiss Shelby, reveling in the feel of her wrapping her arms around him and kissing him back with unpracticed but eager enthusiasm.

Eventually, Shelby broke off the kiss and said, "You really believe things will get better?"

"Absolutely," Malcolm said. "Allies are found in unexpected places and Veronica found a set in the PanU board. Bertram Qiao wasn't a huge surprise, but Peng McGrant of all people! Amazing. I'm choosing to take that as an omen. Our future will be very good."

He did not add — although he had been wondering about it since Shelby had told him about Veronica and the PanU board — how much the daimyo of Shelleen had been involved. Airik had warned Qiao & Schopenhour about Burgess pulling their commercial paper. He'd gotten more access to them, based on Inigo becoming his substitute secretary. He had to have worked with Bertram Qiao and most likely Marmaduke himself, since Bertram didn't go against his father's wishes, ever, even when his father wasn't around. Sajag Burgess's destruction would come soon and be complete and terrible. Marmaduke Qiao would see to that and the daimyo of Shelleen wouldn't have to lift another finger.

The question now, Malcolm thought, was how long Airik would continue concealing his true self from Veronica Bradwell. He wished he could tell Shelby everything, reassuring her but his own promise to Airik stopped him.

He kissed Shelby again and whispered, "I'm falling in love with you."

Shelby clutched Malcolm closer to her, thrilled, and whispered back, "I am too."

Airik opened the gate, hearing its now familiar shriek. It had come to mean he was home. How strange. He was at home in the White Elephant; a run-down mansion inside a dome that kept out the frigid northern weather located in the bizarre free-city of Panschin; a place utterly unlike Shelleen. Veronica made it home. With every step closer to the White Elephant and then stepping through the gate, he could feel the tensions of the day loosen their hold.

He was home where Veronica was waiting.

But a new source of tensions returned. What would she say to him when he told her who he was? Would she accept his reasons for lying to her and to everyone else? Would she still accept him?

He stopped where he was, no longer on the street yet not within the garden of the White Elephant. He was caught in the in-between place, where the gate was.

He couldn't move.

He could only ask.

Only she could free him.

Veronica had been waiting for the gate's call while trying to conceal her anxiety from Neza, Florence, and Lulu. As soon as she heard the gate, she leaped to her feet and ran to the atrium, threw open the door and ran down the path. Airik Jones stood there at the gate, no longer on the street but not yet entering the White Elephant's garden, as though he was waiting for her.

When she reached him, she did not throw her arms about him to kiss him as she had the evening before, although she desperately wanted to. He was home.

Instead, she stopped, just shy of the gate. What would Airik say when she told him who she was and how, if anyone in Panschin knew, they would turn away from him and his company?

Airik stared at Veronica in the dim, soft light the dome allowed and finally found his voice.

"Miss Bradwell."

Veronica unfroze and spoke at the same moment. "Mr. Jones."

"I," they both spoke again.

Veronica laughed suddenly, at the absurdity.

"Mr. Jones, I must speak with you. In private."

Airik managed to say, "Yes, I must as well."

Neither of them moved.

Carmine, behind Airik and still on the street threw a meaningful glance at Elliot. The valet had rejoined them in the Dome Two metro station. During the journey, he reported that Upton had not enjoyed any prior connection to Winifred Qiao, at least according to the servant's gossip.

"If you don't mind sir, I'd like to go down to the Broken Pickaxe for a pint," Carmine asked. "I need one after today."

"As you wish," Airik said, relief evident in his voice. One witness to his upcoming humiliation gone.

"Sir?" Elliot said, having caught Carmine's meaning. "I have extensive notes to write up from today's research. If you don't need me, I'd like to work on them in my room, if I may."

"Of course," Airik said, relieved again.

Veronica watched the bodyguard depart down the street while the valet waited patiently for his turn through the gate that Airik Jones was blocking. Good. Two less people to see her be humiliated by admitting what her father had done. An idea struck her.

Airik stepped aside, back into the street, and Elliot bolted through the gate, sidestepping around Veronica with a nod and disappeared into the White Elephant.

"Miss Bradwell," Airik began.

"Not here," Veronica said quietly. "What I have to say can't be said in the street." She looked back over her shoulder, at the White Elephant. "We'll have privacy on the terrace, up on the roof."

She was going to ask him to leave. He knew it was a ridiculous notion, but what else could it be? It was what he was most afraid of. Airik made himself say, "Of course, Miss Bradwell. I have things to say as well."

He followed her up the gravel path. It was late in the dome and quiet; the only sound was the crunch of gravel beneath their feet, a barely audible hum of insects, and the low murmur of voices far away. Nearby, a cricket chirped, shockingly loud.

He forced himself to pay attention to the staircase leading up to the rooftop terrace. These stairs had been designed to be comfortable for the user, unlike the Twelve Happiness Luxury Hotel's grand staircase. His leg pained him and would for days to come; this staircase didn't aggravate the injury still further. He had never been above the second floor in the White Elephant. Airik welcomed the distraction of walking upwards into a great hole in the roof, the dome far above. There should have been stars overhead. He had no idea what the weather was doing on the other side of the dome. Thinking about the weather provided a distraction from following Veronica up the stairs. He was close enough to touch her, and oh, he wanted to.

Veronica could hear Airik's footsteps behind her, echoing in the empty stairwell. He was so reserved, so formal. She could be assured of one thing. He was enough of a gentleman to be polite to her, after she told him the full truth about Simon Bradwell. He had gone into the tunnels to rescue her and Shelby. Would he have done such a thing if he knew how evil their father had been? How many lives he had ruined?

She emerged onto the rooftop terrace, stepped away from the stairs and walked to the chairs at the far end. The view, as always, was lovely and familiar and constrained by the dome. She stared at the rooftops in the business district and the glimpse between the buildings of the small park at its center. People were wandering up and down the streets, most of them in the business district. It was late and no one in Dome Two approved of carousing in the streets the way they did in Dome Six. That was one activity Veronica didn't miss.

Airik followed Veronica and emerged above the floor, step by step, until he stood on the multi-colored tile that formed the rooftop terrace. The tile formed a mosaic of grasses and flowers underfoot, like a tapestry or a poor imitation of the meadows of Shelleen. He followed Veronica towards the far end.

All around him he could see the dome, concealing the sky and forming a horizon that never moved, never changed, caging the buildings within itself. The world was huge but the dome hid that vastness from its residents. The air was calmer than the calmest day within Shelleen, but it carried the scents of what lived in the dome along with the hum of voices far away.

"Please, do sit down," Veronica said, indicating the best of the chairs.

She wished, seeing the bare tabletop, that she had thought ahead to provide mint tea and moss crackers to Mr. Jones. Tea would wet her throat, helping her to force out the words.

"After you," Airik said, waving at a chair.

"No."

"Please sit. I must speak with you," Airik said firmly.

"No," Veronica replied equally firmly. "What I have to say will affect every one of your business dealings in Panschin during the mining conference. Your supervisors in Barsoom would not be pleased if they knew you shortchanged your company."

Airik wanted to smile. Whatever Veronica had to say, she still thought of what it would do to him. Perhaps she wasn't going to throw him out immediately. He had been borrowing trouble to even think she would do such a thing.

He sat down and said, "P lease, proceed, Miss Bradwell." He could listen to her beautiful voice one more time, before he told her the truth.

Veronica turned away from Airik, to keep from seeing the disdain appear on his face. "My father is Simon Bradwell. He was a crook."

"Yes, you did imply that during the gallery showing," Airik said.

"You only know the barest minimum," Veronica said, her voice catching. "Let me fill you in. If anyone in Panschin realizes that you've been staying here with me, they will refuse to do business with you."

She began to pace back and forth, just out of arm's reach, and told Airik what Simon Bradwell had done to his clients, his business partners, his community, his friends, and his family. Then she went into the repercussions, ones that still echoed and reverberated under the domes of Panschin, repercussions that routinely punished her and Shelby, and even auntie Neza.

Airik listened carefully and courteously, while comparing what Veronica said to what Elliot had discovered. They matched. In fact, she went beyond what Elliot learned. She was being completely honest, hiding nothing. He wanted to interrupt, seeing how distraught her face was and hearing how her voice shook, to tell her he already knew. But he realized that she needed to unburden herself, as she had needed to speak the previous day; the morning he had sucker-punched Dean and thrown him over the wall.

Knowing what he knew now, he should have punched Dean harder.

Veronica finished with, "Now you know. No one will do business with you if you stay with me and they find out." She turned to face him and in the dim light from the street her tears were golden rivulets running down her cheeks. "I don't want to ask you to leave, I don't. You've done more for me than anyone has in forever. You saved me and my sister, with Malcolm. My aunt is safe. So are Lulu and Florence. But Mr. Jones, you have to understand. Being here harms you, and I would never want to do that."

She stopped, swallowed, and said, "I want you to stay, but you can't." She wished she dared to add *I want you to stay forever*.

From over the rooftops a rooster crowed, startling them both.

"Mrs. Grisson's chickens, I presume?" Airik asked, casting about for something to say that would not add to her anguish.

"Yes, she keeps them on her rooftop terrace. She says they lay eggs better up there than when she keeps them hidden in her subbasement," Veronica said. Gods, but she sounded like a fool, talking about Mrs. Grisson's chickens when her heart was breaking.

"Improved lighting is most likely the reason she is successful," Airik said. She must think he was an idiot, maundering on about poultry and their need for sunlight to encourage egg production. He wanted to hold her and kiss away her tears.

"I suppose so," Veronica said, wishing he would say something, anything, about her father instead of avoiding the elephant on the terrace in favor of chickens on the rooftop.

Airik stood and walked to where Veronica stood and took her hands in his. "Miss Bradwell. I have many things to say to you, but I will start by saying how much I appreciate your honesty."

She made no effort to pull her hands away from his. This would be the last time he ever touched her, and she wanted to remember how his fingers felt entwined with hers.

"Thank you."

"However, I already knew all about Simon Bradwell. Elliot has done an excellent job researching your father and his embezzlement."

Veronica tightened her fingers around his. "He has? But you're still here. Your company."

Airik's heart leaped. She still thought of his wellbeing first, as distressed as she was over her father.

"I am my company. There is no one in Panschin or anywhere else on Mars who will refuse to work with me and it will not matter to them in the least where I stay." Airik paused, watching Veronica's expressive face as she processed what he told her.

"But I have been lying to you since the day I arrived."

eronica tore her hands free and stepped back. "You lied to me?"

"Since the moment I arrived."

Another liar. Nothing new here, yet the pain was worse because it was Airik. She was beginning to trust him because of his actions. She *wanted* to trust him, to care for him, to run away with him to Barsoom and escape Panschin. She wanted him.

"I already figured out that Carmine and Elliot aren't your relatives, and they probably aren't related to each other," Veronica said, her voice rough. Her eyes starting to sting. Lordy, did she sound like an idiot, stating an obvious and unimportant point.

He had lied. But why? It made no sense.

"You are correct on both points," Airik said. His carefully prepared speech had vaporized when he saw her again at the gate and refused to return when he needed it.

I know what you are, Veronica thought suddenly, her heart racing. Why you lied. She stepped back again, well out of his reach. Her eyes went very wide.

Airik saw the flash of terror on Veronica's face and wanted desperately to reassure her. What made her afraid of him? He was nothing like the thugs lying on ice in the Panschin morgue, even though he hadn't hesitated to beat them senseless.

"Please don't be afraid," he said.

"I should be afraid! You're some sort of gangster, aren't you?" Veronica cried. "Why else do you need a bodyguard? Normal people don't! Why else would a man as obviously wealthy as you are need to hide in the White Elephant? This is why you needed privacy."

She stepped back again, closer to the stairwell opening and escape. "You're like Tallon." She wished desperately to recall those words but it was too late now. "Or Tallon's boss."

She should have never said anything. By admitting the complete truth about Simon Bradwell, she'd given him a weapon to use against her and her family. She paused. He already knew and didn't seem to care. She was missing something.

Airik's mind raced. If he stepped forward, Veronica would run for the stairwell screaming and rouse the neighborhood. Based on his observations, everyone — despite Tallon along with his partner and his boss being on ice at the Panschin morgue — was still on edge. The situation would not end well, not for him.

"I am nothing like Tallon or his boss." Not quite true. He did have life and death power over everyone and everything in Shelleen. He didn't hesitate to use that power as needed, even within his family, as he proved with Howard. It was best not to bring up those points in a free-city, not yet.

"If I were like Tallon and his boss, I would not have gone underneath into the tunnels with Malcolm Cobb. I wouldn't have cared what happened to you or your sister or your aunt or your friends," Airik said carefully.

Veronica stopped, just at the edge of the staircase leading down to safety. She set her hand on the lacy iron railing to steady herself.

"That's probably true."

The more Airik Jones talked, the more she would be able to tell the police. They'd listen now, after what happened with Tallon. And Airik Jones had never threatened her, like Tallon had. He'd come to her rescue when he had no reason to do so, during the gallery show.

Veronica's hand went to her throat, to where her beads had once been. She could feel the cool weight of her earbobs against her neck, the earbobs she'd sacrificed, hoping that they would leave a clue for whoever came down into the tunnels below afterwards. Airik had not only seen them, he'd understood her desperate message and picked them up to return to her.

He had thought of her and did something completely unnecessary in the heat of the moment.

She'd seen the documents Airik had worked on, when she'd cleaned his rooms of incipient terraformer spores. They were all related to mining and safety equipment. Everything she'd overheard when he was dictating to Upton and then to Inigo said the same thing. Moreover, Qiao & Schopenhour would never allow a member of their own family to work for anyone whose background they didn't know, in complete detail.

"It is true," Airik said.

"Airik Jones isn't your name either."

"Airik is, but Jones is not."

"But you are a businessman in the mining industry."

"Yes, I am, but I have many other business interests as well, particularly in agricultural products." At least that was absolutely true, Airik thought, as well as being innocuous to admit to.

That seemed true, she reflected. He knew far more about chickens than a mining industrialist should. He'd commented knowledgeably about her gardening efforts during one of their morning breakfasts. Very few people in Panschin knew anything about plants or growing them.

Airik Jones wasn't threatening her, as Tallon had. She knew now, oh how she knew, what a thug would say and do. Airik had never been dangerous. Except to Dean. And to Tallon and Frankie. And that had been necessary for her own safety. He hadn't backed down before Professor Vitebskin, either. Even Mrs. Wangmo had learned he wasn't to be trifled with. Airik had interceded for her. He could be dangerous, but only when he chose to be.

He had chosen to, when he could have turned his back on her as so many other people had. Friends who knew her from childhood, relatives who claimed they would always be there. Dean, who had sworn he would love her forever. They had all turned their backs when Simon Bradwell's embezzlement schemes had been revealed. She had trusted them, and they'd betrayed her.

He was waiting for her, allowing her time and space to think. As always, Airik was considerate.

"Why would you lie?" she asked cautiously. "No one in Panschin would care who you are."

"They would care," Airik said, suddenly seeing a way to make Veronica understand his position. "Just as everyone in Panschin cares about your father. They do not see you. They only see your father. They make their judgments of you and your sister and your aunt based on your father's behavior, not yours."

Veronica swallowed; her mouth dry. That was true enough. She'd seen it again this very morning at the Dappled Yak. She dragged dear old dad's crimes behind her like a millstone. She'd have to leave Panschin to escape them and maybe not even then.

"Even so, you didn't have to lie to *me*. I have no importance to the mining industry."

"I didn't know you then. I do now. I came here to the White

Elephant because I needed peace and quiet to think and to sleep. The Twelve Happiness is maddening."

Veronica laughed suddenly. "Here has been quieter and more peaceful than the Twelve Happiness? Here? Really?"

Airik smiled as his heart leaped. He had made her laugh again. He wanted to always make her laugh.

"Even with all the excitement, it has been quieter in every way compared to that hellhole. To start with, there are no nightly revels filling the streets with noise and party horns," Airik said.

Veronica laughed again, a burble like a stream skipping over rocks and its water catching the sunshine, shattering into rainbows. "That's true enough. I never did like that nonstop party every single night."

She stopped, let go of the railing, and stepped closer.

"But you still didn't have to lie."

"I did, Veronica." Airik met her eyes and stepped closer, then closer again to catch her hands in his own.

"I didn't know that you would see me and only me. No one else sees me."

Veronica thought about pulling away; Airik was standing so close to her. Yet nothing about him reminded her of how Tallon had stood so close, threatening her, making it clear he would hurt her and enjoy it. Airik was nothing like Tallon. She *wanted* to feel her fingers entwined with his, his flesh against hers.

He never wanted to let go of her hands.

"I am the daimyo of Shelleen," Airik said. "My position is all anyone sees."

She gaped at him, hurt and disappointed all over again.

"That is impossible. You're making that up. Daimyos and other members of the aristocracy stay in Dome Six in the Four Hundred complex. Everyone knows that," Veronica said flatly.

She went to pull her hands away and Airik tightened his fingers around hers just enough to say "don't go" but not enough to hold her if she tore free. He wanted to pull her closer still, up against his body, savoring her warmth and kissing her and never letting go. He restrained himself and stood unmoving, separate, apart, other than his hands clasping hers.

"I am the daimyo of Shelleen. Malcolm Cobb recognized me when he met me at the gallery showing. Confirm the truth with him."

Veronica stopped tugging half-heartedly at his hands, wanting to force him to be the one to let her go. "He never said anything."

"When he revealed he knew who I was, just before we went into the tunnels under the White Elephant to rescue you and Shelby, I requested that he remain silent. The same is true of Inigo Schopenhour when I hired him."

"I … I, that is just not possible. How could you think people wouldn't recognize you?" she asked sharply.

She still treated him as she always had; as Airik and no one else. She had not let go of his hands. He drew strength from the delicious feel of her hands in his own, smiled wryly, and said "I was counting on people seeing what they expect to see. No one expects to see the richest daimyo in the quadrant in Dome Two, wearing a coverall like a common laborer, and so they didn't. Even Burgess, who should have known better, thought I was a rickshaw hauler. In addition, the newspaper images of me were of poor quality. I don't look nearly as heroic as those drawings imply."

"Yes, Shelby does a better job of capturing likenesses."

Lordy. Why was she talking about Shelby's drawing talent? She couldn't think around him. None of this could be happening.

"Based on my observations, she does. Your sister is very skilled."

Airik struggled to recall one word of his carefully rehearsed speech to get the conversation back on track, and nothing came. It had been wiped from his mind. That had to be why he was babbling about Shelby and not Veronica; so close he could feel the warmth radiating from her body, smell the violet scent of her hair. Her fingers tingled in his.

She couldn't form coherent thoughts. He was standing so close she could hear him breath, see the rise and fall of his broad chest, and remember how delicious he looked, sprawled nearly naked on her dining room table, stoically enduring the police surgeon stitching him up. Everything she had observed said there was nothing average about Airik Jones.

He stumbled on. "Since I discovered the lode and became the daimyo, I've been besieged by idiots eager to sell me get-rich-quick schemes."

"Like my father would have," Veronica said, waiting to see the familiar disdain on Airik's face that she saw on so many other faces.

"Yes. Simon Bradwell would have seen me as a rare and lucrative prize."

It was the simple truth he spoke, but he didn't sneer at her, only gazed at her eyes as though he wanted to fall into them.

"You, Veronica, you are not your father," Airik said. "I didn't know you when I arrived at the White Elephant. I could not take the risk and so I lied to you. Forgive me, please."

She stared up at his face. He was so close; a single step would bring her lips to his. Her body felt on fire and she had to force herself to think and to answer him. She didn't dare move, not even to let go of his hands as she didn't think she could control what her body did. His touch was electric.

"There is nothing to forgive."

Airik Jones was the daimyo of Shelleen.

It all fit. She'd read of the Red Mercury lode and the immense wealth it would generate. Its discovery would ensure the vast terraforming project transforming Mars from a ball of arid red sand into a living world could continue, even without Olde Earthe's input. He would be harassed wherever he went. It was natural he had an entourage that included a bodyguard. It wouldn't matter who he associated with; everyone on Mars would eagerly do business with him. It wasn't a surprise she didn't recognize him. As he said, the newspaper sketches didn't much resemble him and moreover, who would ever believe a man in a coverall standing on the doorstep of a struggling bed and breakfast in Dome Two could be anyone important.

He was the unmarried daimyo of Shelleen; making him a prize beyond measure.

Airik would be courted and wooed by all the beauties of the Four Hundred along with the daughters of the richest merchants on Mars. They would be wealthy, well-dowered, and well-connected, perfect matches for him. Every one of them would be ecstatic to become his bride and the daimyah of his demesne. No wonder he was unmarried; his family had yet to find someone worthy enough for him and they had the entire planet to choose from. Each realization was another stab through her heart.

And all the while, she had treated him like he was just another man, renting a room for the night.

Shame filled her for not recognizing him, and she was able to let go of his hands and step back.

"I must ask your pardon, sir—"

"Airik, or Mr. Jones if you insist on formality," he replied at once, interrupting her. "Never sir, not from you." He reached for her hands again.

"Even so …" She couldn't speak, only stare into his cool, intelligent hazel eyes. She had at least gotten one thing correct. There was nothing average about Airik Jones. His hands wrapped around hers burned.

"You have done nothing I need to forgive," Airik said. "You gave me the greatest gift you could. You saw me as human. You accepted me."

Veronica laughed, a liquid trill like a bird song to his ears. "Mr. Jones, Airik, you are being absurd. People must accept you everywhere you go."

He smiled at her, his face lighting up. "You see me as a man, just as you did now. Not a sheep to be shorn, a stepping stone to power, or a fountain of wealth. You see *me*, the same as I see you."

"I suppose that means," Veronica said hopefully, "that you will continue to stay with us at the White Elephant until the end of the Biennial Mining Conference? I can't refund your money. It's already spent or earmarked for my bills."

Gods above and below but she sounded mercenary, exactly like everyone else scrambling for a piece of his wealth. Say yes, please. I can keep seeing you and store up memories for when you've left me behind in Panschin, she thought.

"I do not plan on leaving."

Her heart leaped. She would have a few more days with Airik, before he left for Shelleen, wherever that was. It fell just as swiftly. He would be gone, gone to a marriage his family brokered, one that would provide more wealth and connections to his demesne, gone from Panschin, gone from her life.

Airik watched the expressions fly across Veronica's face; elation when he said he wouldn't leave followed by intense sadness that she strove to control.

"I see *you*, Veronica. Your charm, your grace under pressure, your strength, your courage."

"You're very kind."

His fingers tightened around hers. "I am not being kind. I am being accurate. Veronica, I will say this badly. I have to force myself to not think of you, to focus on my work and my duties to Shelleen. You fill my mind. I am falling in love with you."

Those were words she wanted to hear, but they brought up memories of someone else.

"Dean said that to me. He swore he would love me forever and look what he did."

"I am *nothing* like Dean," Airik said vehemently and stepped closer. "Duty and honor matter to me immensely. Shelleen comes first with me, always, until the day I met you."

They were almost touching.

"Those are brave words, Airik," Veronica said gently. "They mean the world to me. You're a brave man. You saved me and my sister in the tunnels. You spoke up for us. I will remember you forever, when you leave Panschin."

"I don't want you to remember me. I want you to marry me." Airik blurted out. "I want you to come home with me to Shelleen, if you can find it in your heart to leave your home in Panschin."

The blood pounded in her ears and her throat felt thick. His hands holding hers were the only thing keeping her steady. She had to save him from himself, despite the cost to her.

"Your family will never accept me. I am a pariah."

"I do have some control over my family," Airik replied. "I am the daimyo. I have a plaque saying so in the Four Hundred headquarters in Barsoom."

"Speaking of which, neither will the Four Hundred."

"I don't care."

They stood there, on the dim terrace for a long, long moment. Veronica's throat had closed up, choking off rational words while her heart thought it would break. Airik was offering her everything she could want: a life with him, the most extraordinary man she had ever met, a man she wanted to spend her life with, a man she loved with all her heart.

Airik watched her face and knew what he was asking. His heart sank. Panschin was her home, and he was asking her to leave everything she knew, to come to an alien world.

He broke the silence. "Veronica. It is my duty and my honor to serve Shelleen. My family chose me to be the daimyo. It is my responsibility to lead my family, to safeguard my demesne, and to ensure the wellbeing of my peasants. I swore oaths to the gods of Shelleen that I would do everything in my power to rule wisely. I know I'm asking something enormous, that you leave your home, your family. I understand your reluctance."

"Airik," she began. "You can't know…" and stopped, words failing her again. Tears filled her eyes.

"Because of you, Veronica, I will fail in one of my paramount duties as daimyo. I cannot in good faith marry anyone else, knowing I left my heart in Panschin with you."

She could not stop her tears.

"I love you, Airik. But your family won't accept me, and I can't bring anything to you."

Airik let go of Veronica's hands and pulled her close to him so he could wrap his arms around her and kiss her. She sank against him, reveling in the feel of his lips against hers, her arms around him. Her senses sang, and she wanted to kiss him forever.

He broke the kiss and gazed into her velvety, light brown eyes. They reminded him of pools of water, catching the light on their surface and with hidden and unexpected depths to explore.

She spoke first, holding a finger across his mouth so he would remain silent.

"Your family will insist on someone of your caliber, Airik, and it won't be me."

He very gently moved her finger from his mouth, kissing it as he did so.

"My beautiful Veronica," Airik said. "The daimyah of Shelleen must care for every person in the demesne, from the highest to the lowest. I've seen your caring, how you treat your neighbors and family and how highly they regard you. You are grace under pressure. You don't whine or complain about your past. You work hard to take care of your family. I have seen your courage. You can speak with anyone and not think less of them because their status is lower than yours. I have never met anyone who is better qualified than you."

Veronica smiled up at Airik, then laughed again. "What a job description!"

"It *is* a job and a difficult one. You're the most logical and sensible choice," Airik said. He kissed her again suddenly, more demanding, and she could feel the strength of his body and how much he desired her.

"You set my senses on fire," he whispered to her between kisses. "Will you come to Shelleen with me? Marry me there?"

Veronica pulled back with extreme reluctance. "I want to, more than you can ever know. But your family—."

"Will welcome you when they get to know you. Trust me."

She gazed up at him, her expression stony. "Dean's family welcomed me with open arms. Then, afterwards, I wasn't welcome. I sobbed over both my miscarriages, but then dear old dad happened, and for the first time ever, I was glad I'd miscarried. A child would have tied me to that family forever, and they would have despised me forever."

Airik's face went cold. "My family does not turn its back on its members. My uncle, Howard, cheated the demesne but his family was not punished for his own sins. He chose to leave, to go to his wife's home demesne, but their son chose to remain in Shelleen. Jason was and is a valued member of the family."

Veronica felt herself relax. He meant it. Airik had not promised anything he hadn't delivered. Whether his relatives meant it was another matter. He asked her to trust him. She turned the request over and over in her mind. Could she? Everything Airik had said and done since she had met him said she could. True, he had lied about his true name, but she could understand his reasoning. Nothing else he had done had been a lie.

"Come with me to Shelleen, Veronica. If you like what you see, we'll marry in front of my family and my peasants."

An expression of intense pain spread across his face, worrying her, and he forced himself to continue. "If you do not like Shelleen, I will accept and understand your choice. It is nothing like Panschin and as the daimyah, you must live there. With me. You will have to leave Panschin."

Veronica thought of leaving behind the White Elephant, every room filled with memories both happy and agonized, her garden, the neighborhood full of people she knew so well. She'd leave behind a familiar, constricting world; one that was, despite its pleasures, soaked with grief and pain. Everywhere she went in Panschin, she remained Veronica Bradwell, the daughter of Simon Bradwell, the daughter who should have known what he was doing. In Shelleen, she would be Veronica, Airik's wife, and she would be with him.

She would be with him, a man she loved and respected and admired; a man who had proved that he could be trusted.

"I can do that if it means being with you, Airik," Veronica whispered and kissed him. "I will trust you."

He kissed her back, wanting more than kisses, and swept her up in his arms and carried her over to the low couch by the table.

"You are beautiful, my beautiful Veronica, inside and out," and he kissed her more, reveling in how eagerly she responded.

She kissed him thoroughly, enjoying every moment of how very unaverage Airik was.

Back in the kitchen, Lulu looked up from her studying across the table to Neza. She was sitting at the other side, still patiently darning socks. Enough time had passed that her once full workbasket was almost empty.

"Veronica and Mr. Jones have been up on the terrace for a long time now. Should I check?" Lulu patted her pocket.

Neza considered. The windows were open, letting in what passed for a breeze inside Dome Two along with the low hum of people going about their business and the buzz of insects.

"No," she said thoughtfully. "I don't think so. Veronica would either be screaming for help or already downstairs. Let's give them their privacy."

Lulu smirked. "Gonna get both girls married off then? A banker *and* a mining executive from Barsoom. Not bad."

"I like him," Florence said from behind her pile of books. "He's always been polite, and he must be rich to afford servants."

"Yep," Lulu nodded. "There's no comparison between that worthless Dean and Mr. Jones."

"No," Neza agreed and beamed. "Barsoom's a long ways away, but there are letters. Besides, a rich mining executive will need to visit Panschin regularly."

"True. Every Biennial Mining Conference at a minimum," Florence said.

The women smiled at each other.

"Even better, between a banker and a rich mining executive, you'd be able to keep the house," Lulu said. "Malcolm can move right in. He'll keep that idiot Burgess out."

Neza gave a long look to Lulu and Florence in turn. She said, "I want you both to stay for as long as you like, and I know Shelby and Veronica will agree. You two are part of the family. Trevor and Evan are welcome as well. The White Elephant is home for all of us."

he end of the Biennial Mining Conference had arrived at last. So much had changed. Veronica stretched luxuriously as she snuggled up on the low sofa on the rooftop terrace next to Airik in the late afternoon light. The final ball was scheduled for that evening at the Twelve Happiness Luxury Hotel, and she'd be attending with Airik making her first formal appearance as his fiancée. Shelby and Malcolm Cobb had been invited as well, as guests of the daimyo of Shelleen.

The next morning, she would leave with Airik on the early morning train bound south towards the great cities of the Equator. They'd get off at the train station in Purnell, and then make the several days journey to Shelleen.

It was all so exciting, as well as teary. Airik had already informed Neza that they would be visiting Panschin regularly to keep up with the business arrangements he was making with Qiao & Schopenhour as well as Steelio. Airik had also hammered out deals with two of the quad demesnes, Fuziwara and Davis. Everyone from Shelleen would be going back home except Upton and Gaston. Upton was slowly recovering from his bout with pneumonia and his other ailments but was not well enough to travel.

Upton was another reason for Shelleen to maintain close ties with Panschin. Winifred Qiao stubbornly remained at his side during his hospital stay. It was apparent to everyone they would marry. The question was where would they live: in Panschin as her family was pushing for and where Upton could supervise Shelleen's new ventures? Or in Shelleen as his family expected and demanded.

Gaston had spent most of his time with the shamans and was slowly adjusting to a new reality.

There had been much to talk about. Shelleen was another world and not just because it wasn't enclosed under domes. Veronica was looking forward to it, despite the sadness in leaving Shelby, Neza, Florence,

Lulu, and now Malcolm Cobb. His family had been surprisingly accepting, as Airik had said they would be.

The gate shrieked its warning and she bolted upright. It still bothered her as it did everyone else in the household. Her hand went automatically to her throat, no longer bare. Airik had given her the glassy gray beads he had been able to retrieve, her beads made of star stuff. Not enough of them had been found to remake her necklace so he had purchased hammered silver stars to string between each of the polished lumps of slag glass.

"Let Carmine get it," Airik said lazily and kissed Veronica again.

A few moments later, Carmine climbed to the rooftop terrace.

"Got a message for Miss Veronica, sir," he said and held out an envelope.

"The mail already came this morning," Veronica said, taking the envelope from Carmine.

"Hand-delivered by a boy in a police uniform," Carmine said.

"How strange."

She ripped out the envelope and pulled out a short note.

Her eyes widened and she frowned. "It's from Dean!"

"Read it aloud please, Veronica," Airik said. Damn Dean. Wasn't he supposed to be cooling his heels in the Panschin city jail awaiting trial? He pushed down a surge of jealousy and anger. Those emotions were no longer warranted. Dean couldn't harm Veronica any more. He would never be in her presence again.

Veronica started reading:

Dear Ronnie,

I am so, so sorry. That bastard Tallon was right. I didn't deserve you then and I deserve you even less now.

I've been catching up on my reading here in the jail, when I'm not scrubbing off terraformers down at the main courthouse in Dome One. I never paid any attention to current events, but I do now. The jail provides copies of all Panschin's newspapers, even if they are a few days late, so I'm all caught up. It's been something to do. I had no idea how much I missed.

My parents cut me off completely and I needed the money for my legal fees .Forgive me, Ronnie.

Dean

"How bizarre," Veronica said when she finished reading Dean's note. "Why would he think I care anymore?"

"I believe Dean might be regretting his actions with you, my dearest," Airik replied. "Although I can't understand what this incoherent note has to do with his legal bills. I'm certainly not paying them."

"Absolutely not," Veronica said firmly. "Dean can work it out for himself after what he did to us."

As they waited in the first-class seating area at the train station, Airik marveled over how much had changed for him and for Shelleen. Gaston had found a new calling and would be working closely with the shamans of Panschin to investigate what was happening inside the Red Mercury lode. Upton, of all people, would be marrying; something no one in the family believed he would ever willingly do. He had made new business deals, not just related to the Red Mercury lode, but in a host of new areas. Shelleen would be enriched for generations to come. Shelleen would become a powerhouse in the quadrant, economically and politically. From Northernmost to Southernmost, from Easternmost to Westernmost, Shelleen was no longer third-tier in anyone's eyes.

And he had met Veronica, his soon-to-be bride and the daimyah of Shelleen. The thought thrilled him. He loved her deeply and expected that each day, he would love her more. He hugged her again. He would never tire of hugging Veronica.

Even the train station was changing. Teams of men, and quite a few women, were scrubbing every part of the train station clean of its heavy sweater of terraformers. The Biennial Mining Conference had generated its usual crowd of community service providers.

"My lord Shelleen!" a voice called out from the station. "Wait! I must speak with you at once!"

"Lordy," Veronica said. "I see now why you lied to me. Do these fortune hunters ever let you alone?" This had been their third interruption since they'd arrived.

"I have hopes that when the novelty wears off, they will," Airik replied calmly.

"It's quite likely," Malcolm said. "Something new and exciting will come along, and you'll turn into yesterday's news." He, Shelby, Neza,

Florence, and Lulu had come to the train station to see Airik and Veronica off.

"Sir?" Carmine asked, upon his return from checking the caller's identity.

"Yes?"

"It's the concierge from the Twelve Happiness Luxury Hotel. He insists that he speak with you."

"All those bills were paid," Airik said indignantly. "To the penny. I audited them myself."

"Yes, my lord Shelleen, they were," the concierge said, forcing his way past the barriers to where they were seated. He was huffing and puffing from his gallop through the train station. He cut a dazzling figure in his Twelve Happiness silver and acid green livery. The early morning sun spilling through the newly cleaned skylights made him sparkle, catching the eye of the other passengers. It attracted fresh attention to Airik and Veronica, making onlookers move closer to hear what was being said.

"*This* is what I must speak to you about. You know, if you had just *told* me you wanted to enjoy a heroic fantasy about rescuing damsels, I could have *arranged* it," the concierge sputtered. He was more indignant than Airik was.

"What are you talking about?" Airik asked.

"*This!*"

The concierge displayed the morning edition of the *Panschin Gazette*.

The rows of headlines filled the entire top quarter of the newspaper:

Daimyo Rescues Bradwell Daughters!

Murder, Mayhem Under Dome Two!

Violent Blood Spilled in the Deepdown!

Shelleen Hero Knows Whereabouts of Stolen Loot!

Bradwell Ex-Hubby Reveals Scandalous Details!

Set alongside the blaring headline was a small, inset sketch of Veronica and Dean, taken from their wedding day. Dean looked even handsomer than he had in real life while Veronica wasn't as pretty and gazed in pathetic adoration and gratitude at her new husband. The much larger, lurid image filling the rest of the front page purported to be of the events described in the story, starting on page two.

The group studied the picture, open-mouthed.

"Why am I half-dressed? I'd die of hypothermia," Airik sputtered. "And am I waving a sword around?"

"At least you're wearing pants! Shelby and I are virtually naked!" Veronica gasped in horror.

"Why isn't Malcolm in that picture?" Shelby asked, her hand across her face to cover her embarrassment over being on the front page of a newspaper wearing a scrap of gauze and a string of beads.

"I am!" Malcolm said indignantly. "See? I'm cowering behind that boulder!"

"Gracious. You need to get a job at that newspaper, Shelby," Neza said, blinking. "The artist doesn't seem to understand female anatomy. No woman could possibly be that, ahem, bosomy."

"I thought there were only two goons, Tallon and Frankie?" Florence said. "You're fighting a small army."

"You're standing ankle-deep in blood in that picture," Lulu said. "Even with all those bodies laying around, there aren't enough to spill a lake of blood *that* big."

"Sir?" Carmine said. "Next time you throw that Dean over a wall, make sure you break his neck."

"Do you think Dean sold this … *fairy tale* … to the *Gazette*?" Veronica said.

"Yes, I think we have discovered how Dean expects to pay his legal bills," Airik said. He gave mental thanks the ridiculous story and even more ridiculous illustration would remain in Panschin.

"You didn't need to indulge in any of that risky business!" the concierge said stoutly. "I have willing young ladies on staff for just such purposes. The Twelve Happiness Luxury Hotel happily fulfills every fantasy, even ones like *this*."

Airik smiled at Veronica, his own true love. "I prefer reality."

She laughed, making the daimyo of Shelleen's heart leap with joy.

The editor of the *Panschin Gazette* gazed in deep admiration at the elaborate drawing his staff artist handed in, and on deadline no less.

"Damn, but this illo will sell newspapers," the editor said triumphantly.

The artist, a long-time newspaper illustrator, looked complacent.

"You said you wanted lurid and racy to go with a lurid and racy story, boss. Well, you got it. Good thing we had mugs on file for most of the principals."

"That's why that Cobb guy is hiding behind a boulder?"

"Sure is."

"Kind of racy for a family publication," the city desk chief said thoughtfully, studying the drawing. "This will sell out in minutes. We'll have to run multiple editions. Simon Bradwell, his beautiful daughters, the daimyo of Shelleen, and murder in the deepdown. It can't miss."

"An award-winner for sure," the editor said, beaming as he thought of finally snagging a trophy for the empty shelf behind his desk. "What a find that idiot Kangjuon was and cheap too! The *Dispatch* would have paid twice as much for an exclusive on this story."

"Story's ready. Illo's ready. Let's go to press and print money," the city desk chief said cheerfully.

"I think we should do more," the editor said, beaming with joy as the idea swelled. "This is a big story, one that might put us on the map. I recommend we forward it not just to Barsoom, but Northernmost, Southernmost, Easternmost, and Westernmost. Let everyone on Mars know that the *Panschin Gazette* gets the scoop."

"Your newspaper, sir," the butler said. He held out a silver tray bearing a carefully folded morning edition of the *Panschin Gazette* to Sajag Burgess.

Mr. Burgess ignored the proffered newspaper. All the news in it would be bad, and he already had enough troubles. At least with the Biennial Mining Conference over, he would no longer risk running into the irritating daimyo of Shelleen. That purblind fool refused to admit the importance of Sajag Burgess.

"You should at least read the frontpage story, sir," the butler said coolly.

"Mr. Burgess glared at his butler, then caught sight of the masthead of the paper.

"Do you not understand 'no', you useless fool? You've been serving me long enough to know I would never read that worthless birdcage liner. *The Dispatch* and the *Times* are both more reliable, at least as reliable as a newspaper can be."

The butler remained imperturbable, but it took some effort to control his smirk. He had been waiting for this glorious moment for a long, long time. He set the tray down and unfolded the *Panschin Gazette*, displaying the lurid illustration in all its lewd glory.

"You are mentioned prominently in the story, sir. You may wish to know what is being said about you prior to arriving in your office."

Mr. Burgess stared at the headline, then said in growing horror, "The daimyo of Shelleen and Simon Bradwell's *daughters*?"

"Yes, sir."

"Give me that, you oaf." Mr. Burgess snatched the *Gazette* and studied the illustration, then turned to page two, skimming the utterly ridiculous story until he came across his name near the end.

"I did not gamble with Simon Bradwell!" he snarled. He threw the newspaper across the room, suddenly nauseous. The breakfast he had been eating with such enjoyment was ruined.

"Of course, sir," the butler replied and eased his way out of the dining room. He subscribed to the *Gazette* and had read every word of the story before bringing it to his employer. So, the fat fool had gambled with Simon Bradwell. He had always thought so and now, thanks to the ex-husband, everyone else in Panschin would think so, too. It served him right.

As soon as his butler disappeared, Mr. Burgess lunged for the *Gazette* pages scattered across the carpet and read the entire story, twice over. His breakfast roiled within him. That damn Kangjuon had revealed his hitherto concealed connection with Simon Bradwell for everyone in

Panschin to read about. The PanU board of trustees was already asking uncomfortable questions because of that bitch, Veronica Bradwell. Worse, the president of Second National had insisted on a meeting today. The bank's president had refused to say what the purpose of the meeting was or who else was attending.

Sajag Burgess sat back in his oversized chair, sweating and struggling to breathe. What did the bank know? He had other secrets and could only pray those wouldn't be revealed as well. This story would ensure those other participants would race to tell all, if only to protect themselves. He'd be the laughingstock of Panschin. A sudden chill wafted over his body, revealing the dreadful future bearing down on him. He'd end up, after a sensational trial, on his knees in the Dirac mines for the rest of his life.

He was ruined, and it was the fault of that damned Veronica Bradwell. He could feel his heart's erratic beating, and it hurt even more to breathe, like an elephant was sitting on his chest. He braced his hands on the table, fighting for another breath. It might be that his luck had finally run out.

His chest spasmed. Or maybe not.

Peng McGrant's hands shook as he bought a copy of the *Panschin Gazette* from the newsstand while on his way to his office.

"Racy story, Mr. McGrant," the newsstand operator said cheerfully. "It's been selling like mad all morning."

"Have you read it?" Peng asked carefully, after taking in the lurid headlines and even more eye-popping illustration.

"Not yet, Mr. McGrant. Haven't had a chance. Been too busy selling them. The *Gazette* rep already said they'll be reprinting this edition, it's been selling so well," the newsstand operation replied.

As the two men spoke, another customer ran up to the newsstand, snatched a copy of the *Gazette*, paid, and walked away, eyes glazed as he gaped at the Bradwell sisters' astounding cleavage and long, bare legs on display.

"Thank you," Peng said, forcing a calm he didn't feel. The daimyo of Shelleen involved with Simon Bradwell's daughters. It couldn't be. They were ruined pariahs. Yet Veronica Bradwell knew his son, as did her sister, Shelby. He hadn't known that fact until the dreadful PanU board of trustees' luncheon. He'd questioned Kip as soon as he saw his son about his relationship with Shelby Bradwell. Kip had been uncharacteristically sullen, refusing to say anything other than confirm the bare facts Veronica Bradwell told the PanU board of trustees.

His Kip, his only son and presumed heir, had surface sickness, because of that damned Shelby Bradwell.

Peng made his way into his office, past whispering co-workers who had apparently read the *Gazette* story based on how the chatter rose and fell as he neared a group. Whatever lies the *Panschin Gazette* printed included allegations about him. There was no other reason for his staff to refuse to meet his eyes and comment sotto voce as soon as he was out of hearing range.

How much did Veronica Bradwell know about his relationship with her father, Simon Bradwell? Apparently not much or she would have informed the board, along with everyone else present that dreadful day in the Dappled Yak. She hadn't hesitated to rat out Sajag.

He sat down, behind a closed door, and read the story carefully. When he finished, he folded the newspaper and set it aside to think. Dean Kangjuon, that sodding little ponce, had spilled an entire ore-car of information about him, Sajag, and Simon Bradwell. Yet that relationship, explosive as it was, wasn't the headline story it should have been.

The dramatic actions of the daimyo of Shelleen in the deepdown took precedence.

However, the collusion story was on its way, like the walls of a tunnel shivering and cracking in anticipation of its impending collapse. Peng was sure of it. Nothing would stop this cave-in. Simon Bradwell was still a major topic of discussion and a lawsuit magnet in Panschin, whereas daimyos from the provinces were not. The question, now, was damage control so he could protect his own family. He had already started cutting ties with Sajag after that dreadful luncheon. Chung/Banerjee's business needs required it. Those concessions he had been forced into by Shelleen and Qiao & Schopenhour made him shudder.

What could he do? Peng started a mental list. To defend himself and keep his own family safe, he'd visit the courthouse right away and speak with the Financial Oversight Commission. If he turned state's evidence against Sajag, he might survive. He'd be destroyed financially. He'd lose his position with Mercantile and Commerce. He'd be fighting lawsuits for decades to come.

But he wouldn't be sifting tailings on his knees in the Dirac mines alongside Sajag. He'd be free. His family would be safe. He'd lose control of Chung/Banerjee but he'd already drained that company of most of its assets. Qiao & Schopenhour could pick over the bones. He could flee Panschin and never return.

He caught sight of the initial report from his lawyer and picked it up. This was the first thing to jettison, even more important than visiting the Financial Oversight Commission. He had intended to file a lawsuit against Veronica and Shelby Bradwell for dragging Kip into the deepdown and his subsequent development of surface sickness. Kip was useless as far as the future management of Chung/Banerjee was concerned. He had to have recompense for losing the services of his heir.

But if the daimyo of Shelleen was interested enough in the wellbeing of the Bradwell sisters to rescue them from the deepdown, then they had powerful friends. This lawsuit's opportunity had passed. More importantly, money he would have spent on the lawsuit now had a more compelling use: keeping him out of the Dirac mines.

Damn Sajag. He had been amazingly stupid, threatening the Bradwell sisters with eviction. If he'd kept his foolish, fat mouth shut at the gallery showing and ignored Veronica Bradwell as beneath his notice, no one would have ever connected him to them. Shelleen might still have rescued the Bradwell sisters, but Dean Kangjuon's eyewitness evidence about the gambling relationship between him, Sajag, and Simon Bradwell might not have come to light.

Peng drafted a letter to his lawyer, instructing them to drop the lawsuit with the Bradwell sisters over exposing Kip to surface sickness at once. He carried it to his secretary. Based on her expression, she had already read the *Panschin Gazette*. With that matter taken care of, he returned to his office, shutting the door firmly on the rising gossip flooding the hallways and offices of his building.

He then began listing every illegality he knew of that Sajag had been involved in, carefully considering as he did so how he could minimize his exposure. He and Sajag had been friends for years, but his own safety came first.

It was time to cut his losses, starting with shoving Sajag Burgess down the mineshaft. The remaining question was how many other people he could incriminate in order to secure his freedom. Simon Bradwell had worked with more bankers than just Sajag Burgess. Peng knew some names and could guess who the others were. He wondered how many other members of Panschin's elite Dean Kangjuon had observed gambling with Simon Bradwell and had yet to mention. This round of troubles centering on Simon Bradwell was just beginning and would shake Panschin to its foundations.

"Professor Vitebskin! Look at this!" Bhupathi Middleton yelled as he ran into the Art Department studio at PanU. "You won't believe what happened to Shelby!"

Professor Vitebskin groaned. Yesterday had been the last day of the term and finals started tomorrow. This was supposed to be a quiet day for him as he gathered his forces to fight Reyansh Philpott's lawsuit.

"I am not changing your grade, Bhupathi," the professor spat out.

"I'm not talking about that, Professor," Bhupathi said. "I'm talking about this!" He smirked and spread out the *Panschin Gazette* so Professor Vitebskin could better admire the amazingly lurid illustration that filled the page and the astonishing headlines above it.

Professor Vitebskin gaped at the illustration. Neither Shelby nor her sister had ever enjoyed a figure with that degree of voluptuousness. If Shelby had, he would have pursued her as a bed partner the moment she arrived at PanU. He gave himself a mental shake. No, he wouldn't have. Using the White Elephant as a gallery space was more important than any co-ed, no matter how luscious. He was still arguing with the bursar's office about transferring Shelby Bradwell's tuition payments to PCC so he could retain access to that marvelous gallery space.

The headline penetrated. The daimyo of Shelleen? Who in seven hells was that?

He snatched the paper from Bhupathi, read the headlines again, sniffed at the scandalous main picture with its ridiculous and unlikely anatomy, sneered at the poorly drawn expressions on the small wedding picture of Veronica and Dean Kangjuon, turned the page and began to read.

While Professor Vitebskin read, he became gradually aware of Bhupathi anxiously bouncing from foot to foot, instead of leaving him in peace.

"What do you want?" he barked.

"Uh," Bhupathi hemmed. "I did bring you the newspaper. I thought you should see it." He smiled brightly at Professor Vitebskin.

The professor glared at Bhupathi, reminding him who was still in charge. When he felt Bhupathi was sufficiently reminded and properly wilted, he said, "Five points extra credit."

"Thank you, sir!" Bhupathi sang out. Five points extra credit would let him maintain his gentleman's C. His family would be placated for another term. He'd be able to remain at PanU and not have to work for his family's sanitation business, lucrative though it was.

"Don't slam the door on your way out, Bhupathi," Professor Vitebskin growled from behind the newspaper.

"Yes, sir, and thank you, sir," Bhupathi replied as he skipped to the door and out of the studio and towards another few glorious weeks of freedom. Exams were still coming, but he no longer had a flunking grade from Professor Vitebskin.

Professor Vitebskin read and reread the newspaper article, making notes as he went along. He studied the main drawing carefully. Hellation. That idiot yokel from the hinterlands who had disparaged the wonderful art he had presented in the White Elephant was the daimyo of Shelleen. The rich daimyo of Shelleen. The well-connected daimyo of Shelleen. Double hellation.

A thought struck. Then another one.

Professor Vitebskin bared his teeth to the empty studio.

If the daimyo of Shelleen was interested enough in Shelby Bradwell to rescue her and her sister from certain death in the deepdown, then he was interested enough to say something to PanU if her tuition didn't get transferred. This newspaper article would convince the bursar's office they needed to transfer Shelby's tuition to PCC and do it right away. Getting the bursar's office to transfer Shelby's tuition, as he had promised, would suddenly become easy instead of the slog it had turned into. He'd maintain access to the White Elephant for future gallery showings of the PanU Artists' Collective.

Beautiful, naïve Shelby Bradwell would be grateful to him. The daimyo of Shelleen might be grateful, too; grateful enough to consider sponsoring one of his protégées.

Even better, that obese bastard, Sajag Burgess, was ruined. If he'd been gambling with Simon Bradwell, what other criminal shenanigans had he been indulging in? Maybe, Professor Vitebskin allowed himself to hope, when Burgess collapsed under the hail of lawsuits sure to come, followed by his trial and sentencing to the Dirac mines, he'd drag down all his cronies as he tried to save himself. Cronies like Reyansh Philpott's father. Burgess was already, according to gossip racing across the PanU campus, on his way off the PanU board of trustees and facing an investigation.

His own troubles might clear away, all of their own accord. There was real hope, Professor Vitebskin thought for the first time in days, that the light he was seeing at the end of the tunnel was freedom and not an oncoming train roaring on its way to squash him into jelly.

"Hey Kip! Look what your would-be girlfriend got up to," Bhupathi proclaimed, slamming down a fresh copy of the *Panschin Gazette* onto the table. He hadn't expected to find Kip here, sulking in the PanU cafeteria, but he'd gotten lucky.

"Huh?" Kip said. "I don't have a girlfriend."

"But you could have," Bhupathi sing-songed. "Shelby was more than willing. Everybody knew, from watching her waste smiles on you. You just didn't have the stones to ask Simon Bradwell's daughter out. And now I know why, and I'll tell everyone!"

Kip glared at Bhupathi. "What are you talking about?"

"Don't keep up with current events, Kippy? That is so sad. I do. Look at this."

Bhupathi unrolled the *Gazette*, displaying the lurid illustration and its accompanying blaring headlines.

Kip stared, taken aback by Shelby and Veronica Bradwell's scanty outfits. Shelby looked like that under her clothes? Really?

He didn't realize he'd said it aloud until Bhupathi said, "That's artistic license, dummy. You know Shelby doesn't have a figure like that. Neither does her sister. A coverall won't cover up tits like *those*. She wouldn't be able to button it."

"Artistic license?" Kip was having trouble concentrating. The picture of Shelby looked even better than his most lewd fantasies. He felt light-headed.

"To sell newspapers. That's why they print pictures like this, moron. Remember Clyde Monez? 'The only art that sells better than cute animals is porn.' I heard that story about his after-dinner speech at the PanU alumni banquet. You missed it?" Bhupathi rolled his eyes in contempt. "Gleesh, Kip. Try and keep up."

"Gimme that paper," Kip said and snatched it up. He spent several minutes (after tearing his eyes away from the front-page illustration) reading the story while Bhupathi read it again over his shoulder.

"The daimyo of Shelleen, Kip," Bhupathi taunted. "With our Shelby. Your Shelby or she could have been."

Kip gave him a contemptuous look. "Not my Shelby, not anymore, and she's not with the daimyo of Shelleen. That'd be her sister. I saw him talking to Veronica at the White Elephant gallery showing. I didn't know who that poindexter was; hellation, nobody did. Shelby's keeping company with Malcolm Cobb."

"It doesn't say that in the article," Bhupathi replied.

"Newspapers get it wrong all the time, dummy, and they're wrong this time too," Kip said wearily. "I went underneath to the Steelio warren with her and that pretend banker, Cobb. You should have seen how he looked at her."

Bhupathi grinned. "I remember what happened. You bailed on her, leaving her to die in the deepdown with the proles and the trogs."

"I did not abandon Shelby," Kip shot back, revived. "I got sick. It wasn't my fault. Anyways, I saw Shelby on campus afterwards with that pretend banker. They walk around Dome Two holding hands." He stopped talking and stared off into space. "She's with him," he added morosely. She kisses him, he thought, but would not say aloud in front of that sneering jerk, Bhupathi.

"Because you wouldn't ask her out in the first place," Bhupathi smirked. "Afraid of what your family would say? Your dad who gambled with Shelby's old man, the notorious Simon Bradwell? What's your dad going to say now? Huh? Huh?"

"I don't know and I don't care."

"You better care. If he gambled with Simon Bradwell, your family's gonna get sued. The McGrant family has deep pockets."

"Yeah. We sure are. See you around."

Kip got up and marched out of the cafeteria without a backward glance, taking the *Panschin Gazette* with him. Maybe my dad won't sue Shelby anymore because I got surface sickness, Kip thought as he walked towards the upper-level tramline that would take him home to Dome Six. He could no longer tolerate even the upper transtubes without getting the shakes. The lower lines were out of the question. Kip consoled himself with the thought that his father wouldn't want to piss off the daimyo of Shelleen with a lawsuit. Not now, with this avalanche heading towards them.

"Edith, didn't you say you were at some ridiculous avant-garde art show in Dome Two? The building had a strange name?"

Edith Wangmo looked over the breakfast table at her husband. They normally ignored each other.

"Yes, dear, I did." The man never listened. Fortunately, she didn't have to listen to him either. "The White Elephant. Poor Lucretia Bradwell." Mrs. Wangmo shook her head. "She would be crushed at what's become of her daughters." She clucked her tongue over their sad, yet completely merited fate.

"How come you didn't tell me the daimyo of Shelleen was there? I could have arranged a meeting." Her husband set down the rag he read on a daily basis and glared at her.

"What are you talking about?"

"This! The daimyo of Shelleen knows the Bradwell girls. He's been staying with them in that house of Neza Molony's. He rescued them from certain death in the deepdown." Her husband tossed the newspaper at her. "Read it for yourself."

Edith Wangmo took the paper, glanced at the headline and full-front page illustration, then stared.

"Good gods above and below," she said.

"My point exactly. If the Bradwell girls know the daimyo, I want an introduction. You were their mother's best friend. What a business opportunity." Her husband's eyes were glazed, but not with lust inspired by Veronica and Shelby Bradwell spilling all over the front page. "Shelleen's as rich as any Olde Earthe mogul with that Red Mercury lode of his. I have the best idea ever. We'll be *rich*. All you have to do is get Veronica to arrange a meeting."

Mrs. Wangmo didn't know what to say, then rallied in the face of a golden opportunity. "You're quite right, dear. I'm sure dear Veronica will be happy to help out an old family friend. Such dear girls, her and her sister."

She closed her eyes in pain. Damnation and hellation. Veronica Bradwell and the daimyo of Shelleen. It didn't bear thinking about. Yet because of a bizarre turn in fortune, she'd have to grovel to that woman to keep the peace in her own household.

She studied the picture again. The half-naked man waving the sword did somewhat resemble the man who had spoken to her so rudely at the White Elephant gallery show, although she wouldn't have believed he was so aggressively fit. Coveralls covered up plenty. She glanced at her husband. *He* had never sported a chiseled torso like the daimyo of Shelleen enjoyed, nor had any of her lovers. It had to be an exaggeration intended to sell newspapers.

"Well?" her husband demanded. "Why are you sitting here? Get over to that White Elephant and get me a meeting ASAP."

"Yes, dear," Mrs. Wangmo said.

Mrs. Grisson read the *Panschin Gazette* with great interest, her eyebrows rising with each revelation.

When she was finished, she passed the newspaper to her oldest son, seated beside her at their huge dining room table. The boarders were sharing their copies, so there were plenty to go around.

"Neza's never going to hear the end of this," she said thoughtfully. "Neither will our Veronica or our Shelby. Those ridiculous outfits. Gracious."

"Might not be all bad," her son said and grinned. "It's not a bad thing to be good friends with a daimyo, even one from some ag demesne a long, long way away."

"True enough," Mrs. Grisson replied. "Now, about that broken step you'd said you'd fix."

"It's on the list, ma." Her son rolled his eyes. "Soon as I come home from work."

"A pint and a moment of your time, if you don't mind," Jeffen said when he entered the Broken Pickaxe.

"Jeffen, my lad," Hurkle replied in surprise. "It's early for business. I hadn't sent for you. What's up?"

"Not seen this morning's *Panschin Gazette*, then?" Jeffen asked. The old man was slipping. Another rung on the ladder was opening up for him.

Hurkle gave Jeffen a cold look. The lad was an up-and-comer, no doubt, but he was sometimes hasty. He didn't always think.

"I have and what of it?"

"How could you miss this?" Jeffen demanded, waving the *Panschin Gazette* at the bartender. "Malcolm Cobb and the daimyo of Shelleen! He never said one word to me about who he was with in the deepdown. Just some public-spirited businessman from Barsoom, here for the Biennial Mining Conference, was what he said. Blue Sun needs to take advantage of this. Shelleen's rolling in money. We got to get our share. That Red Mercury lode of his is a mint."

"I suppose you have some plan for what you want from Malcolm?"

"He needs to be in our pockets, being friends with a daimyo what holds the terraforming of Mars in his own pockets," Jeffen said. "But he is *not.*"

"Our Malcolm is right where he needs to be," Hurkle replied calmly.

"I told Malcolm that him and Blue Sun were square. If I'd known he was working with the daimyo of Shelleen, you think I'd let a golden opportunity like that go? Malcolm would be beholden to us forever."

"Jeffen, you did fine."

"I did not! I want Malcolm Cobb in my pocket, not prancing around like he don't owe a single care to Blue Sun," Jeffen snapped back.

Hurkle slammed the heavy mug he'd been polishing onto the shiny stone slab forming the bar, making it ring.

"Shut up, Jeffen and *think*!" Hurkle roared.

"I am thinking!" Jeffen grabbed at Hurkle's arm.

To his everlasting shock, the old man flung himself over the bar, kicked him in the face as he cleared it, and knocked him flat on the floor. Hurkle punched him again, rattling his brains and ensuring he stayed down.

"You are *not* thinking, Jeffen," Hurkle said coldly. He straddled Jeffen, pinning him to the sticky floor, demonstrating to the other early morning bar patrons why he was still a force to be reckoned with. "Or rather, you're thinking how jealous you are and always have been of Malcolm Cobb. Now think on this. You'da hated that fancy-dancy school he slogged his way through."

Hurkle slapped Jeffen again.

"You listening to me?"

"Yes," Jeffen slurred. His head rang from the blows.

"Yes, *sir,* and don't you forget it. I know you're hating me right now for disciplining you like this. You forgot I didn't get to be where I am today by being a fool or doing fool things, like you're heading to do. You *will* get over this and, someday, you'll thank me for this lesson."

"If you say so," Jeffen forced the word out, "*sir.*" His left eye was already starting to swell shut.

"Our Malcolm is right where we want him to be. He's on Blue Sun's side, while staying as shiny-clean as fresh-cut quartz. No taint on him. He's told us to not do business with Second National, and so we won't."

Hurkle grinned down at Jeffen. His sharp white teeth glinted.

"And all the while, our Malcolm's gonna be wondering when we'll come calling. He'll be careful. He won't want to cause us no trouble. We won't cause him no trouble. But he'll always be wondering when the hammer will drop. Let him wonder, Jeffen."

Jeffen stared up at Hurkle. A small portion of his mind marveled at how *fast* the old man had been. And how strong. Hurkle had earned his collection of middleweight boxing championship belts, displayed in glass cases around the bar. Hurkle hadn't gone soft after he retired from the ring and took up bartending. He wouldn't forget again.

The rest of his mind worked rapidly, following the line of logic that Hurkle had laid out.

"I'm gonna be friends with Malcolm, aren't I."

"Yes, you are, Jeffen."

"My wife really likes that cloud painting Shelby gave us."

"Good. Good. Your wife likes Shelby? Tell her to keep playing nice."

"She's not playing. She does like Shelby."

"Even better, Jeffen. It's good when men's wives get along. And after a while, our Malcolm won't see Blue Sun as a threat; as something he has to do something about. Blue Sun needs clean, respectable businessmen to do business with, but they got to stay clean and respectable for the game to work. We don't want Panschin to get more worked up than it already is over us, and we sure as hell don't want the Martian government involved and we really don't want those damn daimyos sticking their noses into our business."

"No, we sure don't," Jeffen agreed.

"Malcolm did us a huge favor, him and that Airik Shelleen. We wouldn't have knowed about Knights of Mars moving in. Malcolm and that Airik took care of Tallon and Frankie and let us take care of that boss. I looked up that Tallon and his boss, did you know that, Jeffen?"

"No, sir, I did not," Jeffen admitted. "I didn't know we had that kind of reach." His head still rang, and his shoulders were screaming about being slammed into the barroom floor. His entire back would be one big bruise.

"We do, Jeffen, but you're not high enough up to have access to Barsoom. Keep playing the reckless fool, and you won't ever get that high up. Frankie was just another foot-soldier. That boss from Knights of Mars? Bad news. And Tallon? Miss Veronica said he was planning on running Panschin. You want to know something that should scare you enough to shrivel your stones? Tallon was so good *that he could have.* And we wouldn't have knowed he was inside our domes until it was too late, if it hadn't been for our Malcolm and Airik Shelleen."

Jeffen made himself relax, a challenge with Hurkle's strong hands so near his own throat. He had heard the stories and been fool enough to discount them because of Hurkle's age. He wouldn't make that mistake a second time. "There gonna be blowback from Barsoom?"

"No, not so far," Hurkle said. "Maybe never. Barsoom's a long, long way away, accidents happen all the time in Panschin, and we'll be on our guard against Knights of Mars from now on. Because of our Malcolm."

The old bartender smiled down at him, unsettling and with all the warmth of a lizard. "You got to be subtle with our Malcolm. No threats. Nice and easy and friendly. That will keep our Malcolm right where we need him to be. On our side and just a wee bit nervous about Blue Sun, but not enough to cause trouble."

Jeffen held still, letting his thoughts dig their own path instead of the one he had been trying to squeeze them into. Hurkle watched his face intently, his hands ready.

"My deepest apologies, Hurkle, sir," Jeffen said sincerely. "I didn't think."

"No, you didn't. But you will now. You'll go far, Jeffen. Maybe to second in command, here in Panschin. That's what I foresee, if you can stay subtle-like, keep thinking long-term and not go off half-cocked like this tomfoolery again."

"But not in charge?"

Hurkle's face twisted with fury. "No. Blue Sun won't never let Panschin go to one of us locals, even a lad as promising as you. Not right now. Got to be one of the family from Barsoom, even though they don't know Panschin as they should. You though. You're more. You got something extra. I'll introduce you to the big boss. See what happens."

Jeffen breathed deeply, stunned at the honor. Someone from his level, despite how high he was, was never allowed near the head of Blue Sun in Panschin. "I would be most appreciative of that, sir."

"As you should be. We've been waiting a long time for a lad like you." Hurkle relaxed and shifted his weight back, off of Jeffen's abdomen, but he kept his hands near the younger man's neck. "You might be the one who seizes Panschin from those bastards. So keep those knives away from my back."

"Yes, sir, Hurkle."

Malcolm left Shelby, Neza, Florence, and Lulu at the White Elephant. The journey from the train station to Dome Two was repeatedly interrupted by acquaintances who had read the morning edition of the Panschin Gazette. He could guess what was waiting for him at Second National's headquarters in Dome Two.

"Cobb?" Mr. Wong called out as soon as he stepped over the threshold into the lobby.

"Yes, Mr. Wong?"

"My office. Now."

Once they were behind closed doors, Mr. Wong whipped out the *Panschin Gazette*.

"I've already seen it, Mr. Wong."

"So, I believe, has everyone else, despite it being the *Panschin Gazette* and not the *Dispatch* or the *Times*, far more reputable newspapers than this birdcage liner."

"I had nothing to do with getting that article into the newspaper, Mr. Wong," Malcolm said.

"But it's all true?"

"The illustration certainly isn't and Dean Kangjuon was far more of a sodding little ponce than he admits to in the story, but otherwise, yes, it's fairly accurate."

"Interesting," Mr. Wong said. He reclined back in his chair and steepled his fingers. "I noted with great interest Mr. Kangjuon admitting to the newspaper that he was an eyewitness to Simon Bradwell, Burgess, and McGrant gambling together in the casinos. He had not said anything in the past about their collusion during the run-up to Bradwell's trial."

"Many, many other people noticed as well, based on what was said to me during my walk from the train station," Malcolm said.

"Burgess is finished. He has a meeting this morning with the board of Second National. He won't remain an employee of our bank afterwards. I expect he'll be arrested the moment he's fired. Knowing Peng McGrant, he's probably deciding right now what to confess to the Financial Oversight Commission to avoid arrest."

"That was my assumption, Mr. Wong," Malcolm said. "I think McGrant may be considering tossing other people down the shaft as well to protect himself. Based on the reports I read in school and what's in our filing cabinets in the subbasements, we may be headed towards a major shakeup of Panschin's financial institutions. I cannot believe that Simon Bradwell's reach extended only to Burgess and McGrant."

Mr. Wong let an icy smile drift across his face. His eyes were startlingly bright and intelligent.

"I concur. The question, now, is who else did Dean Kangjuon witness gambling alongside Simon Bradwell, Burgess, and McGrant?" he asked.

"A very good question," Malcolm said. "I saw some interesting indications in the filing cabinets. I've been putting together a file of my own. I'd like to have your opinion as to whether or not I'm on the right track."

"You trust my judgment, then, Cobb?" Mr. Wong asked, letting his surprise and curiosity show.

"I do, Mr. Wong. You have a subtle mind. I want your help." Malcolm let himself smile at his boss, then decided to reveal more of himself. "My long-term goal has been to become the president of Second National as well as chairman of its board of trustees. I want Second National to be the best, cleanest, most reliable bank in Panschin."

"Do you now. You've been handed a golden opportunity to climb the ladder, with the shakeup to come. Will you, however, continue to see Miss Shelby Bradwell? Since she is tainted by association with her father?"

Malcolm leaned over the desk, putting his face closer to Mr. Wong. "I won't just see Miss Shelby Bradwell. I'm going to marry her. I figure my liabilities will more than cancel out hers."

"Your loyalty is commendable. Moreover, you may be correct, particularly since you will also become the brother-in-law of the daimyo of Shelleen," Mr. Wong said.

Malcolm's eyes widened. "You are guessing."

"I never guess. Mrs. Grisson told me. Good work, Cobb. While you're down in the second subbasement, researching, I'll write out my own guesses as to who will end up in the Dirac mines and why. We'll compare notes after lunch."

"I look forward to your insight. Thank you, Mr. Wong, for all your help." Malcolm bowed deeply, the first time he had ever willingly done so for Desmond Wong.

"You are quite welcome, Mr. Cobb."

In the early morning watery sunshine of Dome Six, Inigo Schopenhour knocked on the front door of the building he used to call home and waited for admittance. He did not wait long.

"Master Inigo," Prasanna said coldly from behind the ajar door. "You are no longer welcome in this house."

"I understand, Prasanna," Inigo said cheerfully. "However, I'm here on business. The firm must know what hit the newspapers so we can prepare for the coming avalanche." He patted the bulging satchel he was carrying.

"I see. Should I have the staff set a place for you at the breakfast table?" Prasanna asked.

"I am not sure," Inigo said. "I may not stay long. The family needs to know but they're still furious about my eloping with Olwyn Steelio."

"Yes, they are, Master Inigo," Prasanna said. "This way, please."

Inigo followed Prasanna to the familiar dining room. Much of the family, both Qiaos and Schopenhours, routinely met each morning for breakfast, where they discussed the day's plans. Until he had become the daimyo of Shelleen's temporary secretary, Inigo had always been a part of the daily business breakfast, learning the ways of Qiao & Schopenhour. Airik Shelleen expected the services of a secretary from dawn until midnight. Inigo had not participated in the family ritual since taking the job. With the daimyo on his way home, today was the first morning he was free yet he was uninvited. The fallout from his elopement made him wonder if he would ever be invited again.

Prasanna announced him to the room as though he were a stranger. The response was about what Inigo expected.

"That person is no longer welcome in this house," Marmaduke Qiao said from his seat at the head of the table. The room had gone dead silent, filled with hostility and subtle signs of infighting.

Inigo glanced toward his parents. Neither their anger nor their grief seemed to have faded. He wanted to sigh, but focused on business.

"I understand, honored zu fu," he said to Marmaduke and bowed. "I will leave after I pass these around. I realize the story is in the *Panschin Gazette* and the illustration is unsuitable, but nonetheless, the *Gazette* scooped every other newspaper in the city." He began passing around copies of the *Panschin Gazette*, closing his ears to horrified gasps at both the presence of a newspaper suitable only as a birdcage liner and at the lurid illustration.

"Panschin's financial institutions are about to be shaken to their foundations," he said to the roomful of appalled relatives. "Dean Kangjuon has gone public in the most newsworthy way possible with his witnessing of Sajag Burgess, Peng McGrant, and Simon Bradwell consorting together in gambling casinos."

Marmaduke took his own copy, sniffed at the illustration, and began to read, as did Bertram, and every other member of the family.

Inigo returned to the dining room doorway, where he waited patiently for Marmaduke's verdict. The old man hadn't ordered him tossed into the street so there was hope. Winifred had told him that family infighting over his elopement had been fierce. He no longer worked for Qiao & Schopenhour, and with Airik Shelleen on his way home, Inigo had expected to spend the day seeking new employment. He could have gone to work for Steelio but doing so would have ensured he would be ostracized forever by his family. Olwyn had agreed with his decision to not work for her family. They had been discussing requesting asylum in Shelleen, despite having to leave Panschin forever if they did.

After long, nerve-wracking minutes, Marmaduke Qiao folded the *Panschin Gazette* and laid it by his plate on the table.

"We had wondered when the news would break. This is not unexpected. What is the point of you being here?"

Even better, Inigo thought. Marmaduke was talking to him. He had to be under intense family pressure. Not everyone in the Qiao & Schopenhour families agreed with every last one of Marmaduke's decisions. Bertram looked to be more willing to listen to advice.

"The article is reasonably accurate, as these things go, honored zu fu. You notice that a man named Malcolm Cobb went into the deepdown to rescue the Bradwell sisters along with Airik Shelleen?"

"We had," Bertram said, answering for his father. "It was heroic, but Cobb is a mere assistant branch manager. What of it?"

"I know Malcolm Cobb, sir. We shared classes at PSB. He's very, very bright, focused, and ambitious. He's becoming friends with Airik Shelleen. He's going to be the brother-in-law of the daimyo of Shelleen when they each marry one of the Bradwell sisters. He said in my hearing that his goal is to become the president of Second National as well as its chairman of the board, and I believe he could do it. Since signing on with Airik Shelleen, I have seen a great deal of Malcolm Cobb, and he impresses me. His drive reminds me of both of my honored grandfathers."

"Interesting," Bertram said, after glancing at his father. "A personal connection is always worth cultivating with promising up-and-comers."

"What is this Cobb's background?" Marmaduke asked. "I have not heard of that family."

"Honored zu fu," Inigo said and bowed again. "Malcolm Cobb is a scholarship boy from the Steelio warren. He still labors in the deepdown when his family needs his help. My bride knows him, as does the Steelio family, and they fully support him in his goals."

The room went silent again and stayed that way as the Qiao and Schopenhour families waited to see what Marmaduke, head of the joint family, would say. He loathed Steelio. He had been deeply unhappy when the shaman had insisted on Steelio representing the mining interests of the free-city of Panschin at the luncheon hosted by the Twelve Happiness Luxury Hotel. Only the fact the shaman had insisted, with equal vehemence, that Winifred Qiao was to take the twelfth seat at the table had allowed Marmaduke Qiao to accept the choice of what lived beneath with some grace.

As a result of the shaman's choice, Winifred Qiao met the secretary of the daimyo of Shelleen. It was becoming readily apparent that Qiao & Schopenhour would benefit in many, many ways from that connection to the Four Hundred.

"I see," Marmaduke Qiao said. "Prasanna, have a place set for Master Inigo."

"Thank you, honored zu fu," Inigo said.

"We will have to make arrangements to meet your bride," Marmaduke added. "Olwyn, I believe?"

"Yes, honored zu fu," Inigo said. He dared glance over again at his parents and, as Winifred had implied, they both looked overjoyed at Marmaduke's decision. He was back in the fold as they had been begging.

"We shall have to include your bride's family," Bertram said and glanced at his father. "It would be unseemly to pretend she arose from nowhere."

"True," his father said, through tight lips. "After all, business is business but without our family, we have nothing worth working for."

Upton sprawled on his bed inside the pneumonia tent inside his private room in the pneumonia wing in the Dome Six hospital. He had never been so bored in his life. He stared at the ceiling, counting the dimples in the tiles through the sheer, tightly woven mesh surrounding him. He'd always thought a few weeks spent in bed would be heaven. It wasn't, not even with Winifred Qiao by his side, tirelessly seeing to his care.

They did not talk or otherwise entertain each other for hours on end. She was kept busy.

Most of Winifred's time was spent mercilessly making him drink vile concoctions, spoon-feeding him broth, massaging his chest to loosen the phlegm without aggravating his cracked ribs, getting him up to walk back and forth (but never outside the mesh tent), assisting to his personal needs (a humiliating process for him), bathing him when he sweated and warming him when he shivered, and in general, keeping him alive.

When Winifred needed a break, the other nurses were equally merciless. The nursing students trotting through on their training visits were clumsy but not any gentler.

Most embarrassing of all was when the junior class of nursing students came to visit from PCC. Upton was the star patient in the pneumonia wing in Dome Six so he was seen by everybody to ensure they were trained for all occasions. He was a complex patient completely unused to Panschin's array of fungal ailments, had a sinus infection, several cracked ribs making treatment more complicated, and had suffered a concussion along with a host of bumps, burns, cuts, and bruises. His now re-relocated shoulder still ached too.

He had been told that with his range of ailments he was worth six months at the medical school. He was not amused.

Sadly, Lulu and Florence had been part of that last crowd of nursing students.

Lulu had spotted him and called out "A-*ha*! I knew you hadn't been drinking your tea like I told you to."

Upton had dislocated his shoulder again scrambling under the bed when he sighted her, bearing down on him with vengeance in her eyes.

This was his new life: being bored to tears inside a pneumonia tent in the Dome Six hospital with the goddess of his dreams working phlegm out of his lungs instead of frolicking with him in the bed. It was a narrow bed, but they would have had fun making it work. Thinking about rolling with Winifred in the bed with him was his only respite from boredom, other than counting all the blemishes in the ceiling tiles and reading the day's newspapers from front to back. Upton knew a lot more about Panschin than he ever had before and it all reinforced his initial opinion. This place was weird.

"Upton!" Winifred called out from the door. She was out of breath, agog, and holding a presumably fresh newspaper since it was time for the morning editions. "Wait until you see this!" She parted the tent doors and slid inside its steamy atmosphere.

He beamed at her, all his aches and pains forgotten in the warmth of Winifred Qiao's presence.

"More news on that lizard racing betting scandal?" he asked. Upton had not known that lizards were bred and trained to race, although it had not surprised him that people bet on the outcomes of lizard races.

"Not at all. Wait till you see the front page." She giggled and held out the front page of the *Panschin Gazette* so he could goggle at the dueling headlines and the lurid illustration.

Upton stared. Blinked. Stared again. "Is that supposed to be Airik?" he asked at last. "Half-naked in a cavern waving a sword around? And Shelby and Veronica Bradwell?" He blinked again and decided not to comment on their near-nudity. His wayward brain painted a picture of how Winifred would look wearing nothing but a similar scrap of gauze and a string of beads: *delicious*. Despite his health issues, the blood rushed from his brain, leaving him lightheaded and sweating.

"Yes, it is," Winifred confirmed the story. "I'll read it to you."

When she finished, Upton asked to see the illustration again.

Then he smiled joyously at Winifred.

"Winifred, my darling," he said. "I want you to get that artist from the *Panschin Gazette* to visit me. I want to buy the original art."

"I can arrange it, but why? You can't hide this. Everyone in Panschin has already seen this paper. The newsstand operator told me they've printed multiple editions with more to come."

Upton's grin got wider and more gleeful. "Nobody in *Shelleen* has seen this newspaper. They won't *believe* it's Airik rescuing kidnapped damsels like some hero. I'm going to have that drawing framed, along with the story, as a solstice gift for Airik for his office. The family will never talk about me again, not with a story like this one about sensible, boring, rational, intellectual, do-the-right-thing, why-aren't-you-working Airik. In fact, I'll have copies made so every daimyo in our nine-square can have one. Every daimyo in our region!"

He laughed until he stopped because his cracked ribs reminded him not to, and then laughed anyway. He couldn't help himself. Then Winifred Qiao giggled, held his hands, and Upton Shelleen's day got even better.

About the Author

Odessa Moon has at various times painted, sewed, served in the Navy, worked as a sales clerk and cashier, taken care of her family, and gardened with enthusiasm. Her house and garden are a piece of performance art; a meditation on time, change, and entropy. She reads extensively, particularly on subjects like medieval history, the class struggle, colonization, and resource depletion. While growing up, she read plenty of science-fiction and fantasy and wondered what the authors hand-waved away about how difficult it really would be to terraform another planet. She read plenty of romance and wondered where the characters' relatives were and how they paid the bills. The series *The Steppes of Mars* is her attempt to combine all those interests.

When Ms. Moon is not writing, she improves the soil in her own garden and plants trees in her municipality. She recommends you do the same.

Visit Odessa at Peschel Press (www.peschelpress.com) or her website at www.odessamoon.com. She can be reached at odessa@peschelpress.com or written to at Peschel Press, P.O. Box 132, Hershey, PA 17033.

If you want to learn more about her books, sign up for the Peschel Press newsletter. Visit peschelpress.com or odessamoon.com and look for the signup box.

If you like this book — or even if you don't — could you leave a word or two at the online book retailer of your choice? Reviews sell books and she would appreciate it.

Acknowledgements

I want to thank everyone who helped make The White Elephant of Panschin possible. My beta readers Anne Simmons and Angel Raser pointed out flaws, holes, and inconsistencies in the story leading to the book you hold in your hands. Their careful, thoughtful reading and extensive notes made this a much better book than it would have been otherwise.

My cover artist, Jake Caleb (www.jcalebdesign.com), gave me a fabulous cover showing Veronica, Airik, Shelby, and Malcolm in front of the White Elephant and under Dome Two; looming, protecting, enclosing, and trapping them.

Our Dear Daughter, who sketched the terraformers which escaped to colonize the book in your hands.

Denise, the interlibrary loan librarian at the Hershey Public Library, got me all the books I could ever need to flesh out the background.

And of course, my dearest Bill. He believed in me when I didn't and didn't complain too much about editing 260,000 words into the book you're holding now.

The Bride from Dairapaska

*On a terraformed Mars, an abused wife
risks all to save her family and change the world*

By Odessa Moon

On a terraformed Mars, young Debbie Miller was sent far from her rural village as part of a marriage compact between the rulers of two demesnes. A peasant who knew only obedience, she accepted her duty to bear her husband's children and work alongside him. But when they were sent to build a village in a barren patch of nowhere, her abusive husband forces her to take action. She flees with her children and their dog into the vast open steppes where dying was preferable to life with him.

Debbie only wanted to escape, but her encounter with the Steppes Riders, and especially Yannick of Kenyatta, unwittingly ignites changes that attract the attention of Mars' ruling families. Left to her own resources, Debbie must adapt to her new life and figure out how to defend her adopted people.

The Steppes of Mars series imagines a transformed world where a disaster on Earth decades ago cut off all contact with its wealth and resources. Experience a Mars where its genetically modified inhabitants have developed their own cultures, beliefs, and religions. A semi-feudal world where ruling families control vast demesnes under a central government at Barsoom. A world of limited resources where train travel is possible but cars and planes are not. A world of free-cities — open and domed — villages, vast fields and steppes, and people banding together to survive and thrive in this harsh new world.

COMING IN 2021: The Vanished Pearls of Orlov

www.ingramcontent.com/pod-product-compliance
Lightning Source LLC
Chambersburg PA
CBHW032152180726

48284CB00001B/14